CHILDREN OF THEIR TIME

Also by Jenny Glanfield

THE HOTEL QUADRIGA
VIKTORIA

CHILDREN OF THEIR TIME

Jenny Glanfield

LITTLE, BROWN AND COMPANY

A *Little, Brown* Book

First published in Great Britain in 1994
by Little, Brown and Company

A CIP catalogue record for this book
is available from the British Library.

ISBN 0 316 90795 2

Typeset by Hewer Text Composition Services, Edinburgh
Printed and bound in Great Britain by
Clays Ltd, St Ives plc

Little, Brown and Company (UK) Limited
Brettenham House
Lancaster Place
London WC2E 7EN

For Ilse and Manfred Kricke
and their children
Sophie-Luise and Ernst-Albert

Contents

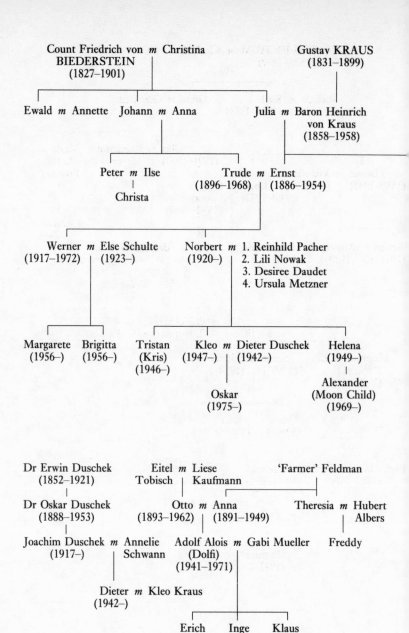

Count Friedrich von *m* Christina
BIEDERSTEIN
(1827–1901)

Gustav KRAUS
(1831–1899)

Ewald *m* Annette   Johann *m* Anna

Julia *m* Baron Heinrich
von Kraus
(1858–1958)

Peter *m* Ilse
|
Christa

Trude *m* Ernst
(1896–1968) | (1886–1954)

Werner *m* Else Schulte
(1917–1972) | (1923–)

Norbert *m* 1. Reinhild Pacher
(1920–) | 2. Lili Nowak
          3. Desiree Daudet
          4. Ursula Metzner

Margarete   Brigitta
(1956–)   (1956–)

Tristan
(Kris)
(1946–)

Kleo *m* Dieter Duschek
(1947–) | (1942–)

Helena
(1949–)
|
Alexander
(Moon Child)
(1969–)

Oskar
(1975–)

Dr Erwin Duschek
(1852–1921)

Eitel *m* Liese
Tobisch | Kaufmann

'Farmer' Feldman

Dr Oskar Duschek
(1888–1953)

Otto *m* Anna
(1893–1962) | (1891–1949)

Theresia *m* Hubert
           | Albers

Joachim Duschek *m* Annelie
(1917–) | Schwann

Adolf Alois *m* Gabi Mueller
(Dolfi)
(1941–1971)

Freddy

Dieter *m* Kleo Kraus
(1942–)

Erich   Inge   Klaus
(1963–)   (1966–)   (1970–)

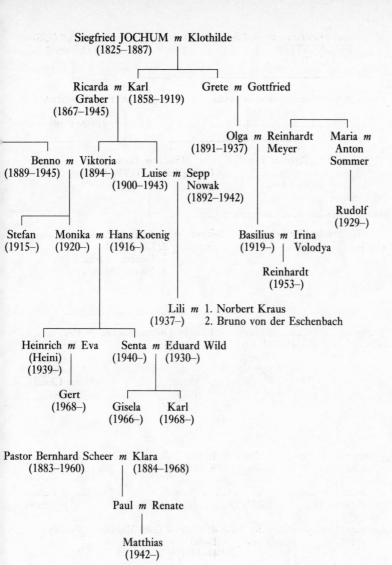

Siegfried JOCHUM *m* Klothilde
(1825–1887)

Ricarda *m* Karl
Graber (1858–1919)
(1867–1945)

Grete *m* Gottfried

Olga *m* Reinhardt
(1891–1937) Meyer

Maria *m*
Anton
Sommer

Benno *m* Viktoria
(1889–1945) (1894–)

Luise *m* Sepp
(1900–1943) Nowak
(1892–1942)

Rudolf
(1929–)

Stefan
(1915–)

Monika *m* Hans Koenig
(1920–) (1916–)

Basilius *m* Irina
(1919–) Volodya

Reinhardt
(1953–)

Lili *m* 1. Norbert Kraus
(1937–) 2. Bruno von der Eschenbach

Heinrich *m* Eva
(Heini)
(1939–)

Senta *m* Eduard Wild
(1940–) (1930–)

Gert
(1968–)

Gisela
(1966–)

Karl
(1968–)

Pastor Bernhard Scheer *m* Klara
(1883–1960) (1884–1968)

Paul *m* Renate

Matthias
(1942–)

PART ONE

1945–1950

Die Krähen schrein
und ziehen schwirren Flugs zur Stadt:
Bald wird es schnein . . .
Weh dem, der keine Heimat hat!

> Friedrich Nietzsche

(The crows cry
and fly off townwards, with a beat of wings:
Soon it will snow . . .
Woe to him, who has no home!)

Chapter 1

The American military jeep jolted over bomb-cratered streets between the blackened ruins of burnt-out buildings, that gaped bleakly, roofless, windowless and often wall-less to the sky. Major thoroughfares had been partially cleared by bulldozers, but everywhere else people – mostly women – were moving rubble. Makeshift dwellings had been constructed from planks, piles of bricks and tarpaulins. Mothers were cooking meals on the pavement over improvised stoves. Long queues waited outside shops and at free-standing water pumps. Dotted among the ruins were little crosses, marking the spots where air-raid victims had died – their corpses still buried under the debris. From time to time, the jeep overtook a hand-drawn death cart.

Caught in the grip of that awful fascination which seized every newcomer to Berlin, Mortimer Allen held fast to the windscreen as Hiram Malone steered the jeep expertly along its precarious route towards the city centre. Fifty-two years old, with grey eyes and a lock of greying hair which flopped waywardly over his high forehead, Mortimer was a tall, well-built American of German extraction, married to an Englishwoman. Until 1940, he had been the Berlin correspondent for the *New York News*. For the next five years, he had covered the war from London. Now, he was back in Berlin again.

He pulled a pack of Camels from his pocket, took one for himself, gave one to Hiram, then turned and offered them to Stefan Jochum, perched in the back of the jeep.

His face pale under his peaked British Army cap, his brown eyes troubled behind his sunglasses, Stefan accepted the cigarette gratefully, trying to control the trembling in his fingers and ignore the churning in his stomach. He had known, of course, about the thousand-bomber raids and the firestorms which had swept Berlin, and of the final battle that April, when Russian troops had fought their way foot by foot towards the Chancellery and Hitler's bunker. But still he was unprepared for this terrible city wasteland.

It was six years since he had left Berlin, despising his mother, hating the Nazis and dreading the thought of war between Britain and Germany, never dreaming that when war came it would be so long and quite so cataclysmic. Six years, during which he had steeled himself against sentiment, thinking only of Germany as the enemy, and of Berlin, not as the city of his birth, but as the heartland of Hitlerism.

Yet for all that, it was his home. His family still lived here – if they had survived the devastation. The last news Stefan had received of his family had been from Mortimer in 1940. Not even through the Red Cross had he been able to discover anything. With millions of prisoners of war, refugees and displaced persons on the move throughout Europe, the Red Cross did not have the time or manpower to try to locate the relatives of a young German who had spent the war years in England.

A man dressed in the tattered remains of German army uniform, his boots bound together with rags, shuffled across the road, looking to neither right nor left. Hiram hooted, braked hard, swerved and missed him by inches. The ex-soldier continued on his way, seemingly unaware of how near he had been to death. 'That's what's left of Hitler's army,' the driver said derisively.

They passed the shell of the Potsdamer Station and entered the Potsdamer Platz, the historical heart of Berlin, now littered with wrecked tanks and burnt-out army lorries. A military vehicle hooted impatiently and Hiram picked up speed. On their left was the Tiergarten, barely recognizable now as the lush park with duckponds and rose gardens that Stefan and Mortimer remembered. Instead, littered with the detritus of war, it resembled the battlefield it had so recently been, its scorched grass scarred by trenches and machine gun emplacements, its broken trees overshadowed by the monstrous fortress of a flak tower, still standing despite the bombardments it had received.

Hiram drove round the Brandenburg Gate, its base littered

with more remains of trucks, tanks, armoured cars and guns. Atop the twelve doric columns stood the battered bronze statue of the Quadriga, the four-wheeled chariot drawn by four prancing horses and driven by Viktoria, goddess of victory, created to commemorate peace between France and Prussia in 1795. Fluttering from the Gate was a big red flag bearing the hammer and sickle.

Ahead of them stretched Unter den Linden, once Berlin's most prestigious thoroughfare, but the lime trees which had given the broad avenue its name were gone and the buildings that had lined its either side were gutted. The central promenade was dominated by a massive poster of Stalin.

'This is where the Soviet sector starts,' Hiram said.

Nothing was further from Stefan's mind at that moment than the political divisions of Berlin. Panic gripping his heart, he was peering at the ruins, trying to identify the site of the Hotel Quadriga. He gave a sudden shout and Hiram slewed to a halt, turning questioningly in his seat.

'This was Captain Jochum's home,' Mortimer explained.

While Hiram let out a low whistle, Stefan got slowly out of the jeep, shaking his head in stunned disbelief, remembering the hotel as he had last seen it: its imposing granite portico; white marble steps leading up to glass revolving doors, guarded by two commissionaires in cobalt blue; the balcony; the elegantly appointed suites and public rooms, restaurants and bars . . .

The hotel had been built by his grandparents, Karl and Ricarda Jochum, and opened on the very day his mother, Viktoria, had been born in June 1894. Stefan himself had been born there, just over thirty years ago, on 28 April 1915. He had always believed the hotel to be indestructible, that no matter what else changed in the world it would remain.

But now there were only hunks of granite and blocks of shattered bricks, charred remains of blackened beams, remnants of baths and marble floors, and over all hung a pall of soot and ash. More than anything Stefan had seen so far, the Hotel Quadriga represented a monument to total war.

Some children emerged from the ruins, scruffy street urchins with dirty faces and ragged clothes. One of them approached Mortimer and whined pleadingly, '*Schokolade, Schokolade.*'

5

Among the first things Mortimer had learned upon his arrival in Germany was the power chocolate and cigarettes held over the hungry population. Jumping out of the jeep, he reached in his pocket for a candy bar. 'Here you are, kid.' As the boy grabbed it, he asked in German, 'What happened to this place?'

'The Russians burned it down.'

'And the owners? What happened to them?'

Stefan spun round, but the boy, frightened by Mortimer's inquisitorial tone, took to his heels. Stefan chased after him, but the boy was too quick. Like rats, he and the others slunk away into the shadowy ruins.

Mortimer placed an avuncular hand on Stefan's shoulder. 'He wouldn't know anything, anyway. Your parents probably weren't even here. Your father, Benno, undoubtedly decided they should all go to your country house at Heiligensee . . .'

'Possibly.' But Stefan did not believe it. The Quadriga had always been the most important thing in his mother's life. No matter what dangers had faced their family in the past, Viktoria had put the hotel first. She would never have left the Quadriga, even on his father's orders. She might have sent the rest of the family to their cottage on the outskirts of Berlin, but she would have remained at the hotel.

'Or maybe they went to Café Jochum . . .' Mortimer said. It was a slim hope but all he could suggest. They returned to the jeep and he asked Hiram, 'Can you find your way to the Kurfuerstendamm?'

It had not taken Hiram long to come to grips with the layout of Berlin, despite the devastation. However, the pro-nunciation of street names was another matter. 'You mean the Ku'damm?'

Mortimer gave a wry smile. 'Yeah, I guess I do.'

Hiram drove them across the city into the British sector. Although not as severely damaged as Unter den Linden, hardly an entire building was standing on the Kurfuerstendamm, Berlin's equivalent to New York's Fifth Avenue, London's Oxford Street or Paris's Champs-Elysées. The beer halls, pavement cafés, night clubs, department stores and cinemas: all were now gaunt shells.

6

Suddenly, Stefan shouted incredulously, 'Look!' Before them lurched the blackened skeleton of Café Jochum. Twisted steel girders hung suspended in mid-air. Remains of a staircase described incredible contortions against stark, windowless, concrete walls gaping up towards the sky, all that remained of one of Berlin's most controversial buildings, the vast, avant-garde edifice designed by the Bauhaus architect Erich Mendelsohn and originally managed by Stefan's Aunt Luise. But set beside a path cleared through the rubble was a hand-painted sign, reading: CAFE JOCHUM – FIVE O'CLOCK TEA IS NOW BEING SERVED.

Alongside it was another notice, saying, 'Entry strictly forbidden to civilians'. But Stefan hardly noticed this. He was out of the jeep almost before it had pulled to a halt and, followed more slowly by Mortimer, he descended a flight of steps and entered a room thick with cigarette smoke, full of American and British soldiers. In the corner, a man was playing a violin, badly in need of tuning. Three shabbily dressed, elderly waiters balanced trays high above their heads.

A middle-aged woman emerged from the back of the room and stopped for a moment to survey the scene. Her pallid face was devoid of make-up, telltale lines of suffering were etched round her blue eyes, her body was thin and her hair snowy-white. 'Mortimer,' Stefan breathed, 'she's alive!'

Mortimer watched her make her way through the crowded tables towards the entrance. Once, in what now seemed another world, when Viktoria Jochum-Kraus's hair had been golden and she had moved regally through the marbled halls of the Hotel Quadriga, he had thought himself in love with her. But their affair had never taken place: personal circumstances and politics had created an ever-widening rift between them, until the war had caused a very final separation. So it was better to leave Viktoria and Stefan to have their reunion in private.

Stefan stepped forward into the room and Viktoria, not recognizing him, tall and distinguished in his sunglasses and peaked cap, said in English, 'Welcome to Café Jochum.'

Stefan removed his glasses and a smile lit up his face, as he stretched out his hands. 'Mama, I'm home.'

7

For a moment, Viktoria stood speechless and disbelieving, then she put her arms round him and buried her face in the rough material of his uniform. 'Stefan, oh Stefan . . .'

Viktoria led Stefan through the café to the cramped stockroom, which now also served as her bedroom and office, furnished with a camp bed, an old kitchen table and a wooden chair, and illuminated by an oil lamp, which she lit with shaking fingers. 'Stefan, I can't believe it's really you. Not a day has passed when I haven't thought of you and prayed you were safe . . .'

'I came as soon as I could. If you hadn't been in Berlin, it would have been easier. In the end, Mortimer got permission for me to travel with him.'

'Mortimer?' Viktoria spoke his name with a sense of unreality. Once the American journalist had been so important to her. Now he was just an incident from an almost forgotten past.

'We went to the Quadriga. A boy told us the Russians burned it down. What happened?'

Viktoria gave no further thought to Mortimer but gazed at Stefan, the son whom she had loved so dearly and hurt so badly that he had fled to England in the dark days just before the outbreak of war in August 1939. And now he was back, she must hurt him again with news almost too dreadful to tell. 'First, tell me about yourself,' she prevaricated. 'What did you . . . ?'

But Stefan brushed her questions aside impatiently. 'Where's Papa?' he asked. 'And Aunt Luise and Grandmama? Monika – and Christa . . . ?'

Sitting down on the bed, Viktoria patted the space beside her, took his hand in hers and falteringly started on her story. Sometimes she got things out of sequence. Sometimes her voice choked with emotion and she had to clear her throat before she could continue. But for the most part, she spoke dispassionately, as if the events she was describing had happened, not to her, but to someone else. It was the only way she had discovered of living with her grief.

Stefan listened numbly. His sister Monika and her two children had spent the war with Monika's parents-in-law in Fuerstenmark, a small village some hundred miles north-east of Berlin in Lower Pomerania. 'Monika's husband, Hans, was

8

taken prisoner of war in 1942,' Viktoria said. 'The last time I heard from Monika was in March. Now Fuerstenmark is under Russian occupation I have no idea how she is. The Russians did such terrible things . . .'

Apart from that, it was like a roll-call of the dead. Viktoria's sister, Luise, had been killed in an air raid, although her little daughter, Lili, had survived. Luise's husband, the Luftwaffe pilot Sepp Nowak, had died in Russia.

The von Biederstein family was all dead. Count Peter von Biederstein had been shot on 20 July 1944, for his part in the assassination plot against Hitler. Peter's wife, Ilse, had been taken to Ravensbrueck concentration camp and never heard of again. And – Viktoria paused for a moment, then bravely continued – Christa herself was also dead. She had been raped by Russian soldiers and found drowned in the lake at Heiligensee.

Stefan gave a rasping sob. Christa was the reason he had left Berlin in such haste. He had hated the Nazis. But above all, he could not bear to remain near the girl he loved and whom he had suddenly discovered was his half-sister.

But worse was to come. Viktoria's husband Benno was gone, burned to death in the fire which had destroyed the Hotel Quadriga during the very last days of the war, when Russian soldiers had run amok in the building. Viktoria ran her fingers through her white hair, the physical legacy of the shocks she had suffered. 'I would have died, too,' she said, 'if it hadn't been for our bar-keeper, Hasso Annuschek. You remember him? He pulled me from the flames and took me to his sister's home in Wedding.'

Her voice wavered, then she pulled herself together. 'I stayed with Hasso until it was possible for me to get out to Heiligensee, where your grandmother and Lili were. I had only been at Heiligensee a few days when Russian troops commandeered the cottage. So your Grandmother and I left Lili with the caretakers, Fritz and Hilde Weber, and came here. We made a shelter from tarpaulins to sleep under at night and during the day we cleared a path through the rubble to the cellar doors.' She glanced absently at her hands, red and calloused, the nails short and broken. 'It took about six weeks. The day

9

we broke through into the cellar, Mama died. She had a heart attack . . .'

Tears welled in Stefan's eyes. Sepp and Luise Nowak, his favourite uncle and aunt . . . Ricarda Jochum, his adored grandmother . . . Christa, whom he had loved so deeply . . . Benno Kraus, who had brought him up as his son . . .

Viktoria took him in her arms, stroking his hair as if he were a child. For six years, the thought of seeing Stefan again had sustained her through even the worst adversities. But although their reunion should have been one of the most emotional moments of her life, it left her curiously emotionless.

What had she hoped of their meeting? Not that Stefan should pity her, no. But she had imagined that he would show compassion and understanding for all that she had undergone, that their past differences would be forgotten and they would be brought together by their common sorrow.

Now she was forced to recognize that in this, her last remaining dream, as in all the others, she was doomed to be disappointed. Her son was back, but he came too late.

When she had most needed him, he had not been there. He had not experienced the horrors of the war. He had not helped drag Luise's body from the ruins. He had not been present when the Russians arrived. He had not seen the Quadriga consumed by fire. He had not shared the agonizing weeks that had followed Benno's death – Benno, the man she had deceived, the only man who had ever truly loved her, who had stayed at her side through all their misfortunes, right to the bitter end.

Stefan had not spent back-breaking hours moving rubble. He had not been with her when her mother Ricarda had died. He had not known the utter aloneness and despair she had endured after Ricarda's body had been taken away to be burned on a communal pyre. He did not know how it felt to be too exhausted, too bereft, too full of grief to weep . . .

For over sixty years, there had been a Café Jochum in Berlin. Karl Jochum had built the first in 1883 on the Potsdamer Platz, the city centre in those far-off days, when Berlin was the new capital of a new German empire. Forty years later, in 1923, the original café had been sold and another opened on the

10

Kurfuerstendamm, which had become a fashionable meeting place for the artists, actors and writers who had made Berlin famous in the 1920s.

Then, in 1929, Wall Street had crashed and the ensuing Depression had hit a Germany whose new and fragile prosperity was based on American loans, which were suddenly withdrawn. Banks collapsed. Unemployment soared. Three successive chancellors plunged the country deeper towards economic collapse. On 30 January 1933, Adolf Hitler, leader of the National Socialist Party, was appointed the new German Chancellor. The Propaganda Minister, Dr Goebbels, gave vent to vituperative outbursts against the decadent influences of the intelligentsia, Communists and Jews. The clientèle of Café Jochum disappeared.

Now, twelve years later, all that remained was its cellar. What the Nazis had started, British bombs had finished.

Mortimer Allen sat at a small table in a gloomy recess of the cellar, sipping a glass of beer. 'There are several stories from Berlin which interest me right now,' Anthony Rutherford had said during Mortimer's briefing with the news agency chief before he left London. 'First, there's the Occupation. I'd like information on the French, American and Russian as well as the British armies. See if you can't get some unusual angle on them.'

At a series of wartime summit conferences, the last of which had been held at Potsdam that July, the future of postwar Germany had been decided. Eventually, it was agreed that, although Germany should cease to exist as a nation, it should not be dismembered and annexed by the conquerors, but permitted to remain as a single economic unit. It would be divided into four zones, each occupied and administered by one of the Four Powers – England, America, Russia and France – with supreme authority held by an Allied Control Council with headquarters in Berlin.

Berlin itself, an island in the middle of the Soviet zone, was divided into four sectors. At the beginning of July, American and British troops had moved into their respective sectors, which had, until then, been occupied solely by the Russians. A month later, the French had taken over theirs.

11

'Secondly, of course, war criminals,' Anthony had said. 'So far as I can see, we're dealing with three types here: the politicians and generals who gave the orders; the men who carried them out; and the civilians who financed Hitler and profited from Nazi policies. The rest of the world press is going to concentrate on the first two categories, Mortimer. But you have contacts they don't. You knew Baron Heinrich von Kraus . . .'

Yes, Mortimer had known the Baron. He was Viktoria's father-in-law and Stefan's grandfather. He had also been head of the world-famous Kraus Industries, whose massive fortunes had been founded in railways, arms manufacturing, chemicals and ship-building. Mortimer knew that contributions made to Nazi Party funds by Kraus Industries had helped Hitler to seize power and exercise a reign of terror over Europe for the past twelve years. He knew how greatly Kraus Industries had profited from Nazi legislation and from the war. Nothing would give him greater pleasure than to help bring the Baron to justice.

'And thirdly, how do Germans now view Hitler's Third Reich?' Anthony had asked. 'What do they think of the Occupying Powers? How does the German man in the street view the past, the present – and the future? And what about the Germans who opposed Hitler? Pastor Scheer, for example. You knew him, too, didn't you? He has been found in the Tyrol. Might be a nice idea to write a piece on him.'

The German resistance movement – such a small band. Stefan had been one of its members, until he had fled to England in 1939. Bernhard Scheer, the Lutheran pastor of the Berlin suburb of Schmargendorf, was another. In 1937, he had denounced Nazism from the pulpit, as a result of which he had been arrested by the Gestapo and spent the next eight years in concentration camps. Pastor Scheer had indeed survived. Most people who had tried to resist Hitler, however, had not . . .

A waiter materialized at Mortimer's side, interrupting his thoughts. 'Would you like another drink, sir? Or some light refreshment?'

Mortimer cast his eye down the simple bill of fare. *Boulette* . . . a traditional Berlin dish of meat balls in a rich sauce. What were the meat balls made of now – horse meat, dog meat? *Bratwurst* – undoubtedly more cereal, or sawdust, than pork. Goulash –

unlikely to contain much beef. Spam fritters – safe, maybe, but unappetizing. He glanced up at the waiter, an elderly, balding man with a broad, lined face. 'Just another beer.'

'Certainly, sir.' But the waiter did not go, continuing to study Mortimer with a quizzical expression, until he finally said, 'Excuse me, but aren't you Herr Allen?'

Only then did Mortimer recognize Hasso Annuschek, considerably changed from those distant prewar days at the Hotel Quadriga when Mortimer had sat on one side of the bar, while Hasso, a convinced Social Democrat, dispensed whiskys from the other, cheering him up with ironic jokes against Hitler. 'Hasso! It's been a long time . . .' But he did not hold out his hand to his former friend. He did not trust any German who had survived the Third Reich.

Trying to conceal his disappointment at this frigid reception, Hasso let fall his hand. So Mortimer Allen had become like all the other Americans he encountered, who assumed all Germans to be Nazis and treated them like dirt. 'Yes, Herr Allen, a dark and terrible time . . .'

Mortimer did not allow his personal feelings to get in the way of his job. 'Can you spare a few moments to tell me about it?'

Hasso looked round the café. 'A few moments, Herr Allen, but this is not the Quadriga bar . . .' He remained standing, the cuffs peeking out from under his shiny frock coat frayed and greyish, matching the pallid grey of his face, telling the story of his and Viktoria's war.

Mortimer looked at his watch. Already an hour had passed. He started to make his way towards the door through which Viktoria and Stefan had disappeared.

'Herr Allen, where are you going?'

'To find Stefan.'

An incredulous smile lit up Hasso's lined features. 'The English captain with Frau Viktoria is Herr Stefan?'

From the bar counter, an American voice shouted, 'Waddabout some service, you goddam Kraut?'

Hasso flinched, but ignoring his customers, he propelled Mortimer into the dark nether regions of the cellar.

Mortimer could not ignore Viktoria's outstretched hand. However he made the handshake brief and his voice was

13

devoid of feeling as he said, 'Hasso has briefly told me about your experiences. Allow me to offer my condolences.'

'Thank you, Mortimer. And thank you for bringing my son back to me.'

Hasso stepped forward from the shadows. 'Herr Stefan, I am glad you are back.'

Stefan seized his hand. 'Hasso! Thank you for everything you have done for my mother. She tells me that you saved her life.'

'I only wish I could have saved your father, too . . .'

Mortimer broke in on them. 'Hasso, any chance of a bottle of whisky?'

'Naturally, Herr Allen.' He went to a cupboard at the back of the room, unlocked it and said, 'We even have your favourite Jack Daniels.'

But Mortimer was unimpressed by this feat of memory. As Hasso filled their glasses, then hurried back into the café, he was thinking sardonically, remembering the muted luxury of the past, 'No, this is not the Quadriga bar.'

The whisky did little to cheer them. Stefan was still reeling under the shock of his mother's revelations, while Mortimer and Viktoria met again as strangers. Like Hasso, Viktoria recognized in Mortimer's expression the same repugnance towards her – a German – that she encountered daily among other Americans and the British. Both armies had issued strict orders to their troops not to fraternize with the enemy, telling them, 'In heart, body and spirit, every German is Hitler. Don't make friends with Hitler.'

'So you've re-opened Café Jochum, Viktoria,' Mortimer said. 'Quite a feat, considering how badly damaged the building is.'

Forcing her voice to remain steady, Viktoria explained, 'After it was bombed in 1943, Benno stored everything he could salvage here in the cellars – furniture, cooking utensils, wine, coffee, cans of food. He even had one of the cooking ranges brought down.'

'Most of your belongings must have gone up in flames with the Quadriga. How do you manage for money?'

Automatically, her hand slid to her waist, to the belt she always

14

wore next to her skin, containing the family jewellery: rings, necklaces, earrings, brooches and bracelets – rubies, sapphires, gold and diamonds – one or two of which she had already sold to buy essentials on the black market for the café. But she merely said, 'Benno took our personal valuables and papers to Heiligensee before the war ended. I have enough to get by on for the moment.'

'When did you open for business?'

'About six weeks ago, just after the first American and British troops arrived. Mortimer, I can't tell you how thankful we were to see them. Until the beginning of July we had feared Berlin was going to be left under Russian control. Then the first American soldiers drove into the city and the Russians gradually retreated to their own sector . . .'

But Mortimer chose to misinterpret what was intended as genuine gratitude towards the Western Allies as fear for her own well-being. 'Yes,' he cut in, 'I gather the Russians weren't exactly kindly disposed to you people, when they arrived in Berlin. And who can blame them? They knew about the atrocities committed by you. They knew about the extermination camps, about Majdanek, Treblinka, Auschwitz, Schlachtenhausen. On my way here, I visited Bergen-Belsen . . .'

Viktoria looked down at her glass. Although the newspapers were full of harrowing photographs and heart-rending reports from the concentration camps, these were something Berliners seldom discussed. The horrors which had taken place in such places were simply too terrible to comprehend, the feeling of guilt too great to be borne.

She had known about the detention camps. Most people had, even if they now denied it. Oranienburg, for example, just outside Berlin, had been built long before the war, in 1933, just after Hitler had seized power. But it had been a prison, not an extermination camp.

Not until the war was nearing its end, however, had she learned about the death camps set up by the SS in Poland, and then only by chance, from a Dutchman recently returned to Berlin from Cracow, whose train had come to an unscheduled halt at Schlachtenhausen station. For the rest of her life, she would remember his horrifyingly vivid description of Jews being forced out of a stationary freight train, of the stench of burning human flesh belching out from crematoria chimneys.

She had known, but she had been powerless to do anything, except give what little help she could to that small group of people who were conspiring to topple Hitler from power – or preferably kill him – and who so tragically failed in their valiant attempt, when Hitler survived the attack on his life on 20 July 1944.

So often, since the war had ended and the dreadful truth emerged of the full extent of the atrocities perpetrated by the SS, she had wondered whether she could have done more. But everyone had been helpless against the regime. Their mistake had been ever to allow the Nazis to come to power. Yet, at the time, Hitler had seemed to be the best solution to all the chronic ills from which Germany was suffering: the economic Depression, mass unemployment and growing internal unrest. Now they had to live with the consequences.

Unaware of the reason for her silence, Mortimer went on, harshly, 'The Third Reich is not something you Germans can sweep under the carpet and forget. You were the inflictors of a far more massive suffering than anything the Russians did to you.'

Stefan shifted uneasily on his chair and, for a moment, Viktoria hoped that he might rise to her defence. But he said nothing.

'You must be wondering why Stefan is wearing a British Army uniform?' Mortimer said.

She had been too preoccupied even to think about it.

'I'm working for CCG, the Control Commission for Germany,' Stefan explained. 'I'm based at Westerstedt, near Hamburg, in the British zone.'

Viktoria's feeling of disappointment and hurt intensified. So, although he was back, he was not going to stay with her. 'What are you doing there?' she asked.

'Interrogating refugees and displaced persons, and helping to identify possible war criminals.'

With a feeling of despair, she sipped her whisky. There was a lot she had omitted from her description of what had happened to the family. She had spoken of those who had died, but she had said little about those who still lived. Taking a deep breath, she

16

asked, 'Are you something to do with the International Military Tribunal being held in Nuremberg this autumn?'

'Not exactly, although it is possible that some of the men I uncover may appear in other trials,' Stefan replied.

'Benno's brother, your Uncle Ernst Kraus, has been arrested in the Ruhr. I understand from the papers that he may have to appear before the Nuremberg Tribunal.'

This news came as no surprise to Stefan. 'I knew that before I left England. Personally, I hold industrialists like him and my grandfather very largely responsible for Hitler coming to power and Germany starting the war. To show how strongly I feel, I no longer call myself Kraus, but Stefan Jochum.'

This was the opportunity Mortimer had been waiting for. 'The papers all describe Ernst Kraus as the "Steel King",' he said, 'but I thought that title was reserved for his father, Baron Heinrich. Does that mean the old man is dead?'

Viktoria had never liked any of the Kraus family except Benno and his nephew Norbert, and of all her husband's family she liked her father-in-law the least, always referring to him as the Baron, never as Father. Under different circumstances, she would have been fully prepared to give Mortimer any information he wanted about the Baron. But such closeness as there had once been between them had gone and Mortimer had now become like all the other Americans with whom she came in contact: filled with hatred and intent on revenge. So she merely said, 'So far as I know, he's still alive.'

'Then why hasn't he been arrested? Why only Ernst?'

'Because of ill health, possibly. Two years ago, he had a stroke.'

'So he finally handed over the reins to Ernst . . .'

Viktoria did not contradict him, although she knew the Baron had never relinquished control over his company to his eldest son.

'Where's the Baron now?'

'He left Berlin in January. He has a castle in Austria, near Innsbruck. I think he went there.'

Mortimer's eyes narrowed. The Baron might have retired, but he had still kept firm hold on his spoils, his rewards for helping Hitler. 'Of course. He acquired the castle after the annexation of Austria. Property of a Jewish banker, I believe. He profited very nicely from the persecution of the Jews, didn't he?'

Viktoria said nothing. She had no desire to defend the Baron but neither did she feel inclined to help Mortimer.

'If he was so ill, how did the Baron travel all the way to Austria? Surely he didn't go on his own?'

'His household servants and Werner were with him.'

'Werner?'

'His grandson – Ernst's son. Werner came to work with the Baron after the Baron had his stroke.' Viktoria felt no compunction about imparting this piece of information. She had no love lost for Werner.

'Yes, I remember.' Mortimer had met Werner Kraus at the Quadriga. A real chip off the old block, as he recalled. 'Didn't Ernst have two sons? What did the other one do to help the Fuehrer?'

It was beginning to feel like an inquisition. 'Norbert,' Viktoria said, struggling to control a rising anger. Norbert was another matter, as different from his brother Werner as Benno had been from his brother Ernst. 'He had nothing to do with Kraus Industries, but trained as an architect and worked for the Todt Organization, building fortifications. During the war, he fell in love with one of our reception clerks. They went to Luebeck, I believe.'

Mortimer squirrelled up another branch. 'You mentioned your personal papers earlier. Do you know if Benno's share certificates were among them? Have you inherited his shares in Kraus Industries?'

Viktoria felt a new sense of shock. She had given no thought to this aspect of Benno's death. In a country where all bank accounts were closed, where industry had ground to a halt, where all that mattered was survival from one day to the next, wills and share certificates were merely pieces of paper that held no meaning. 'I suppose so,' she said slowly.

At that moment, the door burst open and a hubbub of conversation intruded, a cacophony of English and American tongues – the confident voices of victors, laughing and singing. A dishevelled soldier stared at three of them. 'Gee,

18

I thought someone said there were some broads out the back.'

Mortimer looked sharply at Viktoria and she knew what he was thinking. Allied soldiers were a long way from home and, despite the non-fraternization rules, they did not see attractive young German frauleins as Hitlers: they saw them as girls. Already a black market in love had developed and the soldiers called their German girlfriends 'frats'. But, unlike several other establishments on the Kurfuerstendamm, Café Jochum did not double as a brothel. With quiet dignity, she told the GI, 'No, you are mistaken.'

Then the soldier noticed Mortimer's and Stefan's uniforms and hurriedly shut the door again.

Mortimer shrugged, emptied the last of the bottle into his glass and looked at his watch. 'You have to be up early in the morning, Stefan. We should be going.'

Stefan nodded unhappily, rose to his feet and took his mother's hand in his. 'Mama, I'm sorry . . .'

There was an aching emptiness in her, but it did not show on her face. 'Look after yourself, Stefan.'

Stefan kissed her, then he and Mortimer made their way through the crowded cellar café, up the stairs and back into the stark, black ruins of the Kurfuerstendamm, where Hiram was waiting.

They were both silent during the drive back to Mortimer's billet in the suburb of Dahlem. Mortimer was thinking over the information he had gleaned from Viktoria and preparing in his mind his next article for Anthony Rutherford. Stefan was trying to come to terms with the knowledge that everything and everyone he had ever known and loved was either dead or changed beyond recognition.

He had thought when he returned to Berlin that he was coming home, but the home and family he remembered no longer existed. Quite how he had imagined the reunion between himself and his mother, he was no longer sure, but he had expected an emotional reconciliation and certainly that she would beg him to stay with her in Berlin. Instead of which, she had been apparently unaware of his feelings, uncaring of the pain she was causing him with her dreadful news and indifferent to his whereabouts.

19

Suddenly, he was thankful he was returning to Westerfeld the next day. It seemed that he had more in common with the homeless people thronging the camp than he had realized.

Chapter 2

The cottage in the old fishing village of Alt-Heiligensee on the furthest north-western tip of Berlin, had been in Ricarda Jochum's family for many generations. Originally, it had been a farm, but over the years the agricultural land had been sold to neighbouring farmers and by the time Viktoria was born all that had remained was the house itself and about three acres of garden reaching down to the Nieder-Neuendorfer See, one of several lakes formed by the River Havel.

As children, Viktoria and her sister Luise had spent all their holidays at the cottage and, later, when they were married, they had continued the family tradition with their own children. Fritz and Hilde Weber, who lived on the main street, near the church, kept house for the Jochums when they were in residence and looked after the cottage when they were away.

The war had left Alt-Heiligensee virtually unscathed. After Luise had died in an air raid, Ricarda had taken Lili to the cottage for safety and, shortly afterwards, Christa von Biederstein had joined them.

Then the Russians had reached that quiet backwater. Mongol soldiers had plundered, looted and raped. A Russian colonel and his staff had requisitioned the Jochum cottage. When Viktoria and her mother had returned to Café Jochum, Lili had gone to stay with the Webers.

The weekend following Stefan's return, Viktoria went back to Heiligensee for the first time since she and Ricarda had left. Although the underground and overhead railways, trams and buses were operating again, parts of the lines and many streets were still blocked, and much public transport had been so badly damaged as to be beyond repair. What remained functioned largely without windows and was very overcrowded. The passengers were crammed together, an ill-humoured, malodorous

21

mass of humanity, growing ever more bad-tempered with the free-for-all which ensued at every station, as people tried to get on or off the train. It was after several changes of transport and many frustrating waits that Viktoria finally arrived at the Webers' house.

Fritz and Hilde Weber greeted her joyfully, then immediately became concerned in case there was not enough food. Viktoria had already anticipated this. Fritz had been drafted into the People's Army in the last months of the war and returned with only one leg, meaning he could not work. The unemployed and children received the lowest categories of rations, a scant thousand calories a day. She handed Hilde an envelope containing some foreign currency and a bag of canned foods she had bought on the black market.

Her housekeeper thanked her profusely. 'I manage to get quite a lot from local farmers,' she said, 'but every little extra is welcome. What with the prices the farmers are charging and the difficulties in bringing food back from the Soviet zone . . .' She explained how, at the end of July, the Russians had been forced to move back to their own eastern sector and relinquish Heiligensee to the French, in whose sector the village properly lay. However, the Russian presence remained ominously near.

'Lili's in the garden,' Fritz said. 'I'll go and fetch her.' He lurched off on a crude crutch, his empty trouser leg pinned out of the way.

A few moments later, Lili ran into the room and threw herself into Viktoria's arms. 'Aunt Vicki! I thought you'd forgotten all about me.'

'Of course I haven't, darling.' Viktoria kissed her 7-year-old niece, so thin, so vital, so very much like her sister Luise at the same age, with auburn curls and huge, dark-lashed green eyes in a pale, heart-shaped face.

Hilde prepared her spoils, while Viktoria listened to Lili's chatter. How adaptable children were, she reflected. Lili could have few memories dating before the air raids. She had spent her childhood against a background of destruction and death, yet she showed no outward scars.

Over the meal, after telling the Webers about Stefan's return, Viktoria asked about the cottage. 'It's occupied by the French military now,' Hilde said. 'But I still go there to clean and Fritz does some work in the garden.'

'I have papers there. Mama and I buried them in the cellar at the end of the war. I need them.'

'I suppose you can always ask,' Fritz said. 'The French colonel doesn't seem a bad sort. He did a lot of business here before the war.'

After lunch, Viktoria and Lili went to the cottage. From the top of the drive, it looked very tranquil against a backdrop of tall trees, a horseshoe-shaped building with a gravelled courtyard, now full of French military vehicles, and a southern-facing verandah looking out over the lake.

An armed sentry peremptorily demanded to know their business and Viktoria explained, in fluent French, why she was there. The guard accompanied them to the main entrance, where they were eventually taken into the presence of a senior officer, whose office was in what had been the dining room. Of the elegant furniture and pictures which had once embellished the room there was no sign. Dully, Viktoria assumed that the Russians had taken them.

The officer scrutinized her papers, fired a number of questions at her and finally agreed that she might have her documents. Two soldiers accompanied her down into the cellar, where she indicated the flagstone under which she and Ricarda had buried the strongbox. While they were jemmying up the stone, she gazed around her. The cellar was unchanged from how she had last seen it. It still contained a couple of folded camp beds, some blankets, an oil lamp, a pile of old books, a chemical toilet – the means of survival during an air raid. Bad, sad memories . . . She shivered.

The soldiers uncovered the strongbox and carried it back upstairs to the officer. Viktoria handed him a key and he unlocked it. Swiftly, he leafed through the documents inside, then shrugged expressively.

She knew what he meant. Those papers – the deeds to the cottage, the hotel and Café Jochum; various insurance policies; Benno's share certificates; Ricarda's, Luise's, Benno's and her own wills – they were nothing but a paper legacy. In Occupied Berlin, papers indicated no entitlement to possession. She might

23

be the rightful owner of the cottage: but the French had commandeered it and they would stay as long as they chose.

She signed a receipt, then, the small strongbox under her arm and Lili's hand in hers, she left the cottage again.

Lili was very quiet during the walk back to the Webers' house. Her visit to the cottage had revived terrifying memories, of Russian soldiers rampaging through the property, of Christa's body lying face down in the lake, her clothes torn, her golden hair spread out around her. Christa, her friend, whom she had loved so much . . .

Just before they reached the Webers', she asked, 'Aunt Vicki, can I come home with you this evening?'

For a brief moment, Viktoria considered the idea, then rejected it. She would love to have Lili's company, but it would be unfair on the child. Here at least Hilde could get out to the country and occasionally obtain fresh produce. The air was clean and there was proper sanitation.

She could not subject Lili to the privations, hardships and constant threat of disease in the city centre; and, most of all, to the gangs of children who roamed the streets, living in cellars, begging, stealing or helping the black marketeers – children old beyond their years, who had never known a normal, settled world. 'Darling, don't you like it with the Webers?'

Lili bit her lip in a characteristic Jochum gesture. 'Yes, but . . .'

Viktoria squatted down and put her hands on her shoulders. 'Lili, try to understand. One day, when I have rebuilt Café Jochum, you can come and live with me, but now I'm living in a cellar. You wouldn't like it at all. There's nowhere to play, except in the ruins, and you wouldn't have a nice school and all your friends, like you do here.'

'You're my auntie. I want to be with you.'

Viktoria hardened her heart. 'No, darling, it's impossible.'

After Viktoria left that afternoon, Lili went into the garden and crawled into her secret place, a tumbledown shed, covered in ivy. There, she curled herself into a little ball and cried and cried and cried.

Next day, Viktoria made another arduous journey – to Wannsee, where the family lawyer, Dr Oskar Duschek, lived. She found him encamped in his garage, his house occupied by American soldiers. He had made himself as comfortable as possible, with a camp bed, planks spread across trestles to form a table, an antique cast iron stove and primitive toilet facilities.

He was no longer permitted to practise, he told Viktoria. Upon discovering that he had once acted for Baron Heinrich von Kraus, the denazification court had debarred him from his profession, ruling that he must work as a manual labourer. Although he had severed his association with the Baron in 1943, the court had refused to take that into account. 'Had the Kraus business gone to another firm,' Oskar said ruefully, 'I might have succeeded in convincing them of my integrity, but the Baron merely transferred his affairs from Berlin to Munich, from myself to my son Joachim. Disappointed though I am in Joachim, I could not bring myself to denounce him, even to save my own career.'

When Viktoria told him about Stefan, Dr Duschek listened sympathetically, noting the undertone of resentment in her voice, understanding the ambivalence of her feelings. But he could not help wishing that his own son possessed more of Stefan's moral rectitude.

When Viktoria went on to talk about Mortimer Allen, however, he felt a burst of anger. 'Mortimer asked some very searching questions,' she said, 'particularly about Kraus Industries. When I said that Ernst had been arrested, he wanted to know if the Baron had retired. He also asked if I had inherited Benno's shares.'

'Surely no business of his,' Dr Duschek commented sharply.

'No, but he reminded me of the papers I had left at Heiligensee. I've just retrieved them from the French.' She handed over a bulky envelope.

'That was wise of you.' Dr Duschek placed the documents on the table and went through them slowly. 'Yes, here is Benno's will. You do indeed inherit his ten per cent shareholding.'

'I don't want anything to do with Kraus Industries. I couldn't bring myself to say anything in front of Mortimer Allen, but I know some of the terrible activities the company was involved

25

in. I'd like to destroy the share certificates and put that part of my life behind me.'

Dr Duschek took off his glasses and cleaned them carefully, to give himself time to think. Finally, he said, 'I advise you not to over-react. Put the certificates in a safe place and don't worry about them.'

Viktoria bit her lip. Dr Duschek saw things from a legal angle. She saw them from an emotional one. 'I should also like to change my name. I am fifty-one. I shall never marry again. I should like to spend the rest of my life under the name I started with: Viktoria Jochum.'

'Such things can be arranged. I'll recommend you to one of my colleagues.' Dr Duschek started leafing through the other documents. 'Hmm, your mother's will is here, too. I remember drawing it up for her after Luise died. Yes, that's very straightforward. Her entire estate is divided between you and Lili, with you and myself as trustees of Lili's share until she is twenty-one. However,' – he peered at Viktoria over the top of his spectacles – 'the problem facing you now is what that estate consists of. Your cottage at Heiligensee is occupied by the French. The site of the Hotel Quadriga is in the Soviet sector . . .'

'When the Occupation ends, they must revert to me.'

'If the Occupation ends . . .' Dr Duschek shook his head gloomily and bundled the papers back into their envelope. 'In any case, you should take the deeds to the Military Government authorities in the respective sectors and register your entitlement.'

She took Oskar Duschek's advice and spent much of the next few weeks queuing at one military administration office after another, trying to obtain an interview with the right official and stake her claim to her properties. Neither the French nor the Soviet Military Administrations gave any indication as to when, if ever, she might be allowed to repossess her property, but each, eventually, noted her interests and gave her a piece of paper as proof.

Ernst Kraus was in an American camp, at Castle Kransberg high in the Taunus mountains, north of Frankfurt-am-Main.

26

For as long as he lived, Ernst would remember the occasion of his arrest in March 1945 and the black American military police lieutenant sticking a gun into his podgy stomach and pointing towards the ruins of Essen, saying, 'Those chimneys will never smoke again, Kraus. You may be president of a solitary prison cell, but you'll never run a business again. Your days are over. You're finished – kaput.'

Ernst had stammered, 'You've made a dreadful mistake. It isn't me you want – it's my father, Baron Heinrich von Kraus.'

'Come off it,' the black lieutenant had scoffed. 'You lived in the "Fortress". You ran the gunshops of Essen. You're the "Steel King"!'

But Ernst wasn't. He might be nearly sixty; he might have devoted his life to Kraus Industries; but he had never never ruled over the massive industrial empire. In fact, his own sons – Werner and Norbert – had more power than he did, for they each owned 35 per cent of the shares in the company, while he himself held only 10 per cent. And Werner certainly knew far more about Kraus Industries than his father, for ever since the Baron had suffered that slight stroke in 1943, Werner had worked at his grandfather's side at the Berlin head office, while Ernst, in the Ruhr, had been left in ignorance of everything that was taking place in the rest of Germany and the Occupied territories.

At Castle Kransberg, Ernst found himself in the company of his country's most prominent wartime civilians, the great technical brains of Germany, including Professor Albert Speer, Professor Ferdinand Porsche, Wernher von Braun and Dr Hjalmar Schacht. Unlike the other camps in which he had been incarcerated since his arrest, there were no bars at the windows of his spartan room. He and the other inmates were permitted to talk together, stroll through the castle grounds, read newspapers and occasionally listen to the radio. They were fed the same rations as their American gaolers and even allowed to stage their own entertainments: a weekly cabaret, poetry readings and scientific lectures. In a country where millions were homeless and facing starvation, Ernst had an almost luxurious existence.

But still the Americans did not release him. On the contrary, with his constant protestations of innocence, he became

27

something of a joke at Castle Kransberg, to the extent that one of his warders, another black American, sardonically christened him 'Snow White – purer than the goddam driven snow'.

For years, Ernst – a huge, gluttonous man – had suffered from pains in his chest, which he was certain heralded incipient heart failure, although his physician in Essen, Dr Eugen Dietrich, had always insisted that he was merely suffering from chronic indigestion. As autumn approached, these pains grew more acute.

One morning at the end of August, Ernst had just awoken, clutching his heart and pouring with perspiration, when a guard burst into his room and ordered him to accompany him to an interrogation room. He staggered out of bed, pulled on his clothes and followed the soldier down the stone corridors of the castle.

His interrogator was a middle-aged American, who introduced himself as Major David Wunsche. He asked about Ernst's role in Kraus Industries and listened carefully to his explanations of the production problems he had encountered due to the inefficiencies of the government system, and the personal disappointments he had faced because of his father's attitude towards him. Ernst had been talking for a good hour and feeling increasingly confident, when the Major asked, 'You did hold sole responsibility for the Ruhr operations?'

'Yes,' Ernst replied. It was not really true. Even in the Ruhr, he had held no executive power.

Major Wunsche glanced swiftly at the stenographer sitting in the far corner of the room, taking down every word Ernst said, then flicked open a file on the desk before him. 'Yesterday I interviewed a certain Dr Eugen Dietrich, who kept diary memoranda of his meetings with you, particularly those regarding the workforce. Let me read from his deposition. "... Polish slave labourers arrived at Essen by the trainload, many already suffering from malnutrition and contagious diseases. I did what I could to ameliorate their condition, but Herr Kraus refused me a sanatorium or even the most basic medicaments. For days on end, the water supply did not function. Rations were totally inadequate, often little more than watered-down soup and mouldy bread ..."

'On another occasion, a bomb landed in the slave labour camp and hundreds of Poles were killed and seriously wounded. When Dr Dietrich appealed to you for help, you —'

'You can hardly blame me for British bombs!' Ernst expostulated.

'You apparently said, "Damn the Poles!"'

'My mind must have been on other matters. My factories had received a direct hit.'

Major Wunsche's eyes turned a cold, hard, icy grey. 'Don't be misled by my name, Kraus. My family came from Poland. I am a Polish Jew.'

The pain in Ernst's chest returned, worse than ever before. He floundered, 'Dr Dietrich did not tell you the whole story. Such a decision could only be made by my father. I promised to speak to him . . .'

'Just now, you stated that you held sole responsibility for Kraus Industries in the Ruhr. Now you are saying that decisions regarding the slave labour force could only be made by your father.'

Too late, Ernst realized that he had been trapped. He slumped in his chair, burying his face in his hands. Major Wunsche pressed a bell for the guard and, with a dismissive flick of the wrist, ordered Ernst to be taken away.

When he wasn't attending press conferences and military briefings, Mortimer resumed his acquaintance with Berlin, often in the company of Gordon Cunningham, a young photographer from the British Army Film and Photographic Unit, who had come to Germany at the time of the Normandy landings, followed the Allied forces to Berlin and stayed on ever since. Together with Hiram, who had formed a liking for Mortimer, they made a fine team.

On one occasion, Hiram took them to the Platz der Republik, with the burnt-out shell of the old parliament building, the Reichstag, at one end, and the Kroll Opera House at the other. The square was crowded with people, handing over items from one bag that were hurriedly concealed in another. 'This is where the black market operates,' Hiram grinned. 'Here and at the Alexander Platz.'

'Where do the goods come from?' Mortimer asked.

'Some are smuggled in. Some come from stores Berliners have hidden away. But most come from us Americans. It's a good racket. Anyone can double his take-home pay just by selling his allowances of cigarettes, spirits and candy, and some guys have already developed a lucrative business, transferring the profits home and asking their folks to send more goods.'

'It's not legal?'

'Of course not. But everyone does it. Look at it this way: if it wasn't for us, Berliners would be starving.'

Gordon grinned. 'Where do you think I got my cameras? You can't find a Rolleiflex and a Leica IIIC for love nor money in England. I got these in exchange for two weeks' supply of cigarettes from the NAAFI.'

'Well, where next?' Mortimer asked Hiram.

'What about the Stettiner Station? You'll see something there to make you think.'

They did indeed and Gordon's Leica was put hard to work taking pictures which, with Mortimer's graphic prose, would be syndicated throughout the world. A railway service was now operating again, albeit to an erratic schedule. When they entered the station concourse, it was to find themselves in the midst of a vast crowd of people, surrounded by bundles, standing, sitting and lying in the last stages of despair, disease and exhaustion. Their clothes were old and dirty. Many wore no shoes. From all emanated a stench of putrefaction, starvation and ordure.

A woman in a ragged frock, with a baby in her arms, reached out feebly towards him, her eyes dull in hollow sockets, her voice little more than a whisper. 'My baby is ill. He has had nothing to eat for three days.' The child was wearing only a soiled napkin. Its stomach was distended, its face sunken and encrusted with sores.

Mortimer tried to conceal his revulsion. 'Where do you come from?'

'East Prussia. My baby had just been born and my mother was ill, so we could not flee with the others. Now the Russians have expelled us. We were given half an hour to pack our things. My mother died on the journey. Please, help us . . .'

Around her, others began to speak. 'I am from Breslau . . .'

30

'We come from the Sudetenland . . .' 'What shall we do? They will not allow us to leave the station . . .'

A Red Cross helper appeared in their vicinity. A hundred arms stretched towards her. A hundred voices repeated their clamouring questions. Mortimer flashed his press card at her. 'What on earth is going on?'

She gave a tired shrug of the shoulders. 'They are supposed to go from the station to transit camps before travelling on to the west, but half the camps are closed because of typhus. So, until a place can be found for them, they remain here. But we have no facilities, no food, no medicaments . . .'

'And the authorities?'

'The Russians care nothing for them. The Western Allies say the deportees are a German problem. The Department of Social Affairs issues permits which allow them to travel on to camps outside Berlin, but to get a permit takes a long while. Then they have to get another pass to leave the Russian sector. By that time, many are already dead. A hundred thousand deportees a week arrive in Berlin, perhaps more. And all over Germany, it is the same. Millions are homeless. Send this story to your newspaper. Tell America what is happening in Germany. We don't want sympathy but we do need help.'

Leaving the Red Cross worker to her hopeless task, Mortimer and Gordon got back into the jeep and drove down the Friedrich Strasse, following the route of the deportees dragging themselves towards the town hall, where permits were issued. Hiram turned along Unter den Linden, beside the almost unrecognizable University and into the Opera House Square, where once the Nazis had burned books in joyous fanaticism. There he drew to a halt. 'It's on foot now.'

Picking their way over rubble and round burnt-out tanks, they headed through the Lustgarten, past the wreck of the former Imperial Palace and the Cathedral towards the Alexander Platz. They were now well and truly into the Soviet sector. Street names were signposted in German and Cyrillic script. Everywhere were pictures of Stalin and posters bearing Communist slogans. There were a lot of Russian soldiers about, all seemingly armed to the teeth, their uniforms shabby and dirty compared

31

to those of American and British troops. Rather incongruously, many were carrying civilian suitcases.

When Mortimer remarked on this, Hiram explained, 'Black market again. The Russian troops have just received several years' back pay in Occupation Marks which they have to spend here. In case you don't know, there are two kind of marks in circulation – the old Reichsmarks and Occupation Marks – both about as worthless as each other. A GI can get ten thousand Occupation Marks for a Mickey Mouse watch. Ten thousand Marks is a thousand dollars.'

On the walls, between posters and official announcements, were a mass of little cards. Stepping closer, Mortimer saw they were notices. 'Exchange: silver brooch for women's shoes.' 'Elderly couple seek domestic situation. Own house destroyed.' 'Sought: my daughter, Liese Braun, twelve years old . . .'

'You see those notices everywhere,' Hiram said. 'Everyone in Berlin is looking for something or someone.' He threw the butt of his cigarette to the ground and immediately a small boy swooped on it. Clutching his bounty triumphantly, he slunk back into the ruins.

On another occasion, Mortimer went to Schmargendorf, but he did not take Gordon Cunningham with him. This was a very personal visit to a dear friend.

Pastor Scheer himself opened the door to the parsonage, looking much altered from the last time Mortimer had seen him, thin, stooped and considerably older than his sixty-two years. He studied Mortimer in perplexity for a moment, then exclaimed, 'Herr Allen! What an unexpected surprise! Klara will be pleased to see you.'

At that moment, Klara Scheer appeared from the kitchen. She too had changed. No longer the jolly, rosy-cheeked, buxom woman she had once been, she had lost several teeth and grown very scrawny.

'It is almost like the old days,' the pastor said, as they sat down at the once so familiar scrubbed pine kitchen table. 'Again we are together. We have survived and we have returned to our city. The Lord is indeed merciful.'

Klara put some cups on the table and sat down close

to her husband. From another room came the sound of a child's laughter, an almost uncanny sound. 'Our grandson,' she explained. 'Our son's house was bombed. When Bernhard returned and we were allowed to move back here, he and his wife and little boy came too. It is good for us to have young people around.'

'Yes, we are fortunate that so many of our family have survived,' the pastor said. 'But what will these children think when they are old enough to realize the stupidity and blindness of their parents and grandparents? Will we ever be able to explain convincingly the reasons why we permitted such evils to take place? We are leaving them a fearful legacy, my friend, for they must bear the brunt of our shame. We all bear a terrible burden of guilt, a guilt that will take generations to absolve.'

'Yet you fought the Nazis,' Mortimer argued. 'And many more died in the attempt.'

'We did not do enough and, therefore, we are still guilty.' The pastor lifted his coffee cup in a bony hand, crossed with the scars of deep weals.

'Have you seen Viktoria?' Klara asked.

Mortimer nodded.

'I think she's so courageous in re-opening her café.'

'Really?'

Pastor Scheer gave him a searching look. 'I was under the impression that you and Viktoria were once good friends?'

'She has changed. She's become cold and heartless . . .'

'Berlin is a city that has lost its heart, Herr Allen,' the pastor stated simply. 'I know what you are thinking. You believe she does not care. But you are mistaken. She is attempting, like many Berliners, to conceal her despair behind a mask of dignity. You must be less hasty to judge others. It is easy to think that every German who is alive today did nothing to resist Hitler, just as it is to assume they do not regret the past. That is the mistake your compatriots are making when they say the only good German is a dead German. It is my prayer that the world will one day understand that it is not race or politics which make men good or bad but the quality of their souls.'

At that moment, a skinny little boy with white-blond hair and big blue eyes wandered into the room. Pastor Scheer picked him

33

up and sat him on his lap. 'This is my grandson, Matthias. He is two, innocent of any crime. When you write your impressions of Germany, think of Matthias – and the thousands of children like him. His future lies in our hands . . .'

On 7 September 1945, the Allies staged a Victory Parade through Berlin. Mortimer chose not to watch the parade from the Press Stand but to mingle with the crowds, and there he suddenly came upon another figure from the past – Dr Oskar Duschek. The former laywer was shabbily dressed and the hand he extended to Mortimer was rough from manual labour.

At that moment, a unit of American soldiers marched past, singing, 'Yankee-Doodle's come to town . . .' Dr Duschek winced. 'I have witnessed many victory parades and although this one should gladden me because it represents the triumph of good over evil, still I find it disconcerting. Why must victors always demonstrate their military might? And don't the Western Allies realize that we Berliners did all we could to resist Hitler, just as now we shall do all we can to resist Stalin?'

'No, they don't,' Mortimer said, shortly.

Oskar Duschek continued imperturbably, 'I find it worrying that, once again, foreign powers are deciding Germany's future. If we are not careful, we may find ourselves in similar circumstances to those which followed the Treaty of Versailles in 1919.' He stared pensively across the Tiergarten. 'Then there is the Nuremberg Tribunal. Can justice possibly be dispensed in a court where the vanquished are tried by the victors? And just as important, who is to ensure that the right men are brought to trial?'

Mortimer's interest quickened. 'You have a particular man in mind?'

'Ernst Kraus,' Dr Duschek replied succinctly.

'You're not suggesting that Kraus Industries has no crimes to answer for?'

'Indeed not. But if anyone is to be tried, it should be the head of the company and by that, I mean Baron von Kraus.'

'I thought he'd had a stroke and retired.'

'It was a very mild stroke. To the best of my knowledge, he

34

did not retire, although he did transfer most of his shares to his grandsons.'

Mortimer's eyes narrowed. 'To his grandsons?'

'Yes, Werner, in particular, was always his blue-eyed boy.'

'So Werner holds more shares in the company than his father?'

'Exactly.'

'Do you have any proof?'

'None. Most of my records were destroyed when my office was bombed. Nevertheless, I believe the Baron deliberately made it appear that Ernst had taken over control of Kraus Industries so that he would avoid arrest, while simultaneously ensuring Ernst had no power by deeding his shares to young Werner and Norbert.'

Mortimer shrugged. Baron Heinrich had always been a cunning old bastard, quite capable of shopping his son to save his own hide. 'Even so, aren't you carrying legal niceties a little too far? What is the point of trying a sick old man? Why shouldn't Ernst stand trial in his place?'

'That is tantamount to saying that one of Goering's adjutants could appear in court in Goering's stead.'

Mortimer conceded the point. 'I suppose you haven't had any contact with the Baron since he left?'

'No, in recent years, my son Joachim handled his affairs.'

Mortimer glanced at him curiously. It sounded as if the Baron was not the only one to have little love lost for his son. 'And where is Joachim?'

'Inter-zonal communication is forbidden, but I assume he is still in Munich.' Oskar paused, then went on, 'Unlike us Germans, you are free to travel wherever you like. You could visit Joachim and speak to him yourself. If you discover what I say to be true, you could inform the American authorities.'

'Why should I bother?'

'Because, like me, you know it is vitally important that Nuremberg is seen to be a court of justice.'

The Victory Parade was still going on. Now it was the turn of the Russian heavy artillery. Mortimer gazed at the huge, lumbering guns and the Red Army soldiers marching beside them, but his mind was already ranging further afield. Earlier

35

that year in a London bar, he had met a major in American Military Intelligence, a third generation Polish-Jewish emigré called David Wunsche, who might be interested in Dr Duschek's story. Slowly, he said, 'OK, I may go to Munich.'

Two days later, as Mortimer's plane lifted off from Tempelhof airfield, he gazed down at the sprawling city wilderness. Fleetingly, he reflected that there was no such easy escape for the people of Berlin.

David Wunsche's face was grim as he absorbed the information Mortimer had just given him. 'This case is symptomatic of the problems facing us Americans. Joachim Duschek was interrogated and obligingly handed over a number of files relating to clients who were Nazis. Since he was so cooperative, he was allowed to retain his practice.'

'Did he admit to having acted for the Baron?'

'On that subject, he does seem to have suffered a convenient lapse of memory.' David Wunsche accepted one of Mortimer's cigarettes and inhaled deeply. 'I interviewed Ernst Kraus a few weeks ago. There is no doubt in my mind that he is guilty of war crimes. As for the Baron, a couple of Military Policemen saw him at Castle Waldesruh in June. The old man was in bad shape. His right side was completely paralysed.'

'Completely paralysed? Sounds like more than a mild stroke.'

Major Wunsche nodded. 'The MPs said there wasn't any danger of him going anywhere – other than to meet his maker.'

'I wouldn't bet on that,' Mortimer commented cynically. 'In any case, whatever his state of health, I still find it galling that he should be living in luxury in a castle that rightfully belongs to a Jewish banker.'

'A Jewish banker? The records said nothing about that.'

'I can assure you that the Baron acquired Schloss Waldesruh after the Austrian *Anschluss*.'

David Wunsche drew in his breath. 'Let's find Duschek.'

Dr Joachim Duschek's office was furnished in a traditional Bavarian fashion, with carved wooden tables and chairs and a large desk behind which the lawyer was sitting. He was a featureless man in his late twenties and Mortimer noticed that he held his right arm at a curious angle. 'What can I do for you, Major?' he asked in English.

Although Mortimer knew David Wunsche spoke German, the Major replied in English. 'I should like some information about yourself and your clients.'

'I have already been submitted to a thorough interrogation.'

'Not thorough enough, it would appear,' Major Wunsche said drily. 'Now, if we can start at the beginning. You were born in Berlin?'

With a certain amount of prompting, Joachim Duschek gave his life history. He had left university with an excellent law degree, joined the family firm of Duschek and Duschek, and looked set for a fine career until the war had intervened and he had been called up. In 1942, at the age of twenty-five, he had returned from the Western Front with a badly fractured right arm. Gradually, he had picked up the pieces of his life and married Annelie Schwann, the daughter of one of his father's Bavarian colleagues. Their son, Dieter, had been born ten months later.

Those ten months had witnessed the turning points of the war – the battles of Stalingrad and El Alamein. Allied air raids had intensified. The Berlin offices of Duschek and Duschek had been reduced to rubble. He and Annelie had moved to Munich.

'And you brought the business of Baron Heinrich von Kraus with you,' David Wunsche stated.

What could have been surprise or fear flickered briefly in Joachim's eyes. 'I handled a few personal matters for the Herr Baron,' he admitted cautiously.

'I want to see his files.'

'I have no files here relating to the Herr Baron.'

'Duschek, I'm a busy man with very limited patience, so let's cut the crap. Either you do what I say or I place you under arrest for obstructing the course of justice.'

Joachim decided to cooperate. 'I had nothing to do with Kraus Industries' affairs, but I do know that most of the Baron's papers are held in a Zurich bank.'

David Wunsche grimaced. Any hope of getting the Swiss to open their vaults was zero. 'When did you last see the Baron?'

'Last December.'

'You haven't heard from him since?'

'How could I? As you know, the Occupying Powers have decided that Austria is no longer a province of Germany but a country in its own right. The Americans have forbidden all communication between us and the Austrians.' There was an aggrieved note in Joachim's voice.

'How do you know the Baron is in Austria?'

'He was far from well when I saw him. He told me he was handing over the running of his company to his son, Ernst, and retiring to Schloss Waldesruh.'

'Why should the Baron hand over the running of Kraus Industries to his son, when he had already transferred his shareholding to his grandsons?'

Joachim squirmed. 'It was not a transfer of power. After his stroke, the Herr Baron gifted his shares to his grandsons. That way, his heirs would not have to pay death duties or inheritance tax.'

'So the Baron retained control of Kraus Industries throughout the war?'

Joachim shifted his right arm awkwardly. The old injury always made itself felt in moments of stress. 'I don't know. He didn't confide in me.'

Major Wunsche turned to Mortimer. 'It seems we have no choice but to pay a visit to Schloss Waldesruh.'

'But the Tyrol is in the French Occupation zone,' Joachim objected.

David Wunsche gave a grim smile. 'The French have as little love lost for the Krauses as we do. They're more than happy to cooperate with us.'

Joachim looked at him with unconcealed hatred. Right to the end of the war, he had persisted in a blind belief in the Fuehrer's invincibility. He would never be able to come to terms with the fact that Germany had lost the war and that the Allies now ruled Germany.

Chapter 3

Castle Waldesruh was a smallish, turreted building, situated among the snow-capped Alps. Above it, cattle grazed in pastures bright with wild flowers. Below were forests and lush meadowlands through which meandered a rutted track leading to the main road from Innsbruck to the Brenner Pass.

A man of medium height, with bespectacled, small grey eyes and a small mouth concealed under a clipped moustache, a bull neck and grossly overweight body, Werner Kraus stood at the library window and watched two French trucks, followed by an American military car, emerge from the woods and drive up this track. He rang the bell for Gottlieb Linke and, when the manservant arrived, pointed towards the valley. 'We have visitors.'

Gottlieb frowned. 'I shall go and prepare the Herr Baron.'

However, when Gottlieb reached his ground-floor bedroom, the Baron was sitting by the window in his wheelchair, his clothes in disarray, banging his stick on the floor.

'Don't you get so excited, sir,' Gottlieb said, retrieving a blanket and tucking it round his employer's knees. 'It's only a routine visit, I expect.' He spoke in that silly voice some adults use when talking to very young children or senile old people.

The Baron grimaced. He detested being fussed around as though he were a baby. He might be nearly eighty-seven years old and over twenty stone in weight; his right side might be partially paralysed, his florid face lopsided and his speech slurred from the two strokes he had suffered; but his mental faculties were still very much intact. Neither Gottlieb nor his wife Martha, who looked after the Baron's most intimate needs, realized that. They both assumed his death was imminent.

So, too, did the Baron's daughter-in-law Trude, a frumpy, indolent woman in her late forties, who had left her husband

39

Ernst in Essen while she scuttled to the safety of Austria in the terminal weeks of the war.

Only Werner knew the truth. He alone was aware that, although the Baron's body had failed him and his mind had lost much of its old agility, the old man still had a lot of life left in him. Just as he had in his heyday, the Baron still spent his every waking minute thinking about Kraus Industries, the empire he had built from virtually nothing until it had comprised some 600 subsidiaries throughout Europe in its heyday under Hitler.

Outside the castle, the trucks had drawn to a halt and were disgorging soldiers armed with sub-machine guns. The car doors opened and four men got out and marched purposefully towards the castle. The Baron's eyes narrowed. The two majors in American and French uniforms he had never seen before, but the journalist was very familiar to him. So, too, was the figure of Joachim Duschek. No, this was no routine visit . . .

A few moments later there was a peremptory hammering on the front door. The Baron slumped back in his chair and Gottlieb looked at him sympathetically, before hurrying away to open the door.

The household assembled in the hall. The American major, whose name appeared to be Wunsche, demanded their identities, while his French counterpart ticked off each name on a list. Only the Baron was silent, his eyes shut, his jaw drooping open, a dribble of spit running down his chin.

Major Wunsche turned to Werner. 'When we arrested him, we believed your father to be the head of Kraus Industries. Now we know that your shareholding is larger than his. Since you worked very closely with Baron Kraus, and on the assumption that you therefore exercised as much, if not more power than your father over the company's affairs, I am placing you under arrest.'

'Under arrest?' Werner echoed hollowly. 'What for?'

'Crimes against peace, war crimes and crimes against humanity . . .'

Panic-stricken, Werner exclaimed, 'You're mistaken. I didn't hold any power. I was no different from any other employee.'

'You mean you simply obeyed your father's orders?'

Werner managed to catch Joachim's eye. The lawyer gave an imperceptible nod towards the Baron and, suddenly, Werner saw his way out of the situation. As his grandfather had shifted the blame to Ernst, so Werner would now move it back to the Baron and thus save his own skin. 'My grandfather's orders.'

'The Baron made all policy decisions?'

'Yes, my grandfather gave me some of his shares for tax reasons, but he remained in sole control of Kraus Industries.'

David Wunsche stared at the Baron in his wheelchair. 'He can't have run the company in his state.'

'He had a second stroke in May, when the war was over. Before that he was in very good health for his age.'

'Would you swear to this on oath?'

Werner looked him straight in the eye. 'It is the truth.'

There it was: the Baron was responsible for all Kraus Industries' activities during the Third Reich. But as David Wunsche looked at the Baron's immobile figure, he could feel no satisfaction. With a heavy heart, he handed the bill of indictment to Dr Duschek.

The lawyer took the paper and solemnly read aloud a long list of charges. Funds from Kraus Industries had been used to bring the Nazis to power and to keep them there . . . Kraus Industries had profited from the Aryanization Programme by acquiring Jewish companies . . . Kraus Industries had taken part in military and industrial plans and preparations for a war of aggression . . . Kraus Industries had committed crimes against humanity in the exploitation and misuse of slave labour . . . As head of the company, Baron Kraus held ultimate responsibility for Kraus Industries' activities . . .

There was no flicker of understanding on the Baron's face. When he had finished reading, Joachim said angrily, 'You can see, he hasn't the slightest idea what's going on. If he goes to prison, it will kill him.'

For a long time, David Wunsche was silent. The thought of the Baron's death worried him not at all but the circumstances of it could prove vitally important. Finally, he said, 'In view of his health, the Baron will be placed under house arrest. Not, however, at Castle Waldesruh. For the time being, he will stay in the gardener's cabin. Then a medical examination will decide whether or not he is fit to stand trial.' He turned to Werner. 'And *you* are going to prison.'

41

'I protest!' Joachim exclaimed furiously. 'Herr von Kraus has committed no crime.'

David Wunsche stared icily at him. 'You don't seem to understand. The mere fact that he is a Kraus is a crime. The longer all members of the Kraus family are out of action, the less chance there is of Kraus Industries ever being in business again.'

Despite all Joachim's protests, the Major remained adamant. Werner was shoved into one of the trucks and, after concise instructions by Major Wunsche to the driver, driven away.

The rest of the occupants vacated the castle and were installed in a damp cottage deep in the grounds. It was a dismal, two-roomed shack, with an outside water supply and no cooking facilities. They were allowed to take a spirit stove, a few basic supplies, the bare modicum of clothing and bedding, and such necessaries as the Baron required.

Later that same afternoon, two French Military Policemen arrived at the cottage and Trude was forced to translate as they questioned herself, Gottlieb and Martha on every aspect of their lives, from their family background, education, military service, career and income, through to their political affiliations. Gottlieb, even though he protested that he had done nothing except wear a badge and pay his dues, was arrested for being a Nazi Party member. Indignantly, Martha protested, 'My Gottlieb never did anything wrong.'

One of the policemen laughed mockingly. 'You're coming with him. You're just as bad – a member of the Nazi Women's League!'

Stunned, Trude stood by as they too were driven away into the valley. Only when they had disappeared from sight, did the full implications of their arrest dawn on her. Her entire life had been spent in sheltered affluence. Nannies and governesses had taken care of her children and domestics had looked after her house. She had never made a decision beyond what to wear or what to order for dinner. Yet, suddenly, her husband, her son and her servants were in prison and she was left alone in a miserable hovel with her sick old father-in-law to look after.

A tear trickled down her plump cheek and her full lips quivered in petulant self-pity. 'Oh my God,' she cried, as she went back into the hut and closed the door, 'what am I going to do?'

42

The Baron opened one eye and launched his surprise. Squinnying at Trude with malicious pleasure, he said quite succinctly, 'Help me to the commode.'

Werner was taken to Nattenberg internment camp in Bavaria.

His first day there set a pattern for all that followed. Reveille was at dawn. After washing in cold water and gulping down an insipid breakfast of watery coffee and bread thinly spread with ersatz margarine, he was given the job of peeling sacks of potatoes, supervised by an armed gaoler. The weeks went by but nobody came to interrogate him and he began to wonder whether the Americans had devised a special punishment for him. Interrogation and even beating would at least mean that someone in authority was aware of his existence. Being ignored was torture of the worst kind.

His fellow inmates were a mixed bunch. Like himself, few were convinced National Socialists. Nearly all had been Nazis because their jobs had depended upon their joining the Party. They ranged from postmen, teachers and doctors, to district leaders, high-up civil servants, police officials and members of the SS, including a few officers from the SS Death's Head Unit.

Not long after his own arrival, this latter, rather élite group was joined by an old acquaintance of Werner's – a stocky man, with thinning grey-blond hair and blue eyes, framed by lashes so pale as to appear almost white, and a faint scar running down his forehead. Werner immediately recognized him as SS-Oberfuehrer Otto Tobisch.

Otto Tobisch had been born in 1893, the son of the Hotel Quadriga's first General Manager. Otto himself had worked as a page boy at the Quadriga but only ever nursed one ambition: to be a soldier. In 1910, he had been conscripted and had served throughout the 1914–18 war, finding himself on the Eastern Front when the Armistice was declared. Faced with demobilization, he had formed one of the notorious Free Corps brigades, which had helped put down the 1919 Communist Revolution in Germany and which had later been the basis for Hitler's stormtroopers.

In 1923, he had taken part in Hitler's abortive Munich

putsch and been forced to flee for sanctuary in Austria. But, in 1930, he had returned to Berlin as an officer in Heinrich Himmler's SS.

Werner had met him in 1940, after Otto's promotion to Commandant of Schlachtenhausen concentration camp outside Cracow, alongside which a new Kraus steel factory had been built. Already in charge of the company's Silesian and Polish operations, responsibility for the new works had devolved onto Werner's shoulders, although all his meetings with Otto had taken place in Breslau and he had never personally visited the camp, such visits being strictly forbidden by the SS.

Otto Tobisch told Werner that he had fled from Poland at the end of January and driven to safety at his wife's farm at Traunkirchen in the Austrian Salzkammergut, where he had pretended to be a deserter from the Eastern Front working as a farm labourer.

'Do the Americans know who you are?' Werner asked.

'They have no idea. Because so many SS men went to the Salzkammergut, they made an intensive search of the area. When they saw my tattoo, they knew I'd been an SS officer, so they arrested me, too.'

'God, man, why didn't you escape, while you had the chance?'

Otto hesitated before replying. He could have escaped. Others had. In those last chaotic weeks of the war, it had not been difficult to get to Italy and he had possessed the funds to buy his passage to some distant land: a small bag of jewels he had taken from the strongroom at Schlachtenhausen, jewels which were still buried under the cow byre at the farm. But he had not been able to bring himself to make that move. Eventually he said, 'I believed we would make a last stand. I thought that the Western Allies would join forces with Germany for a war against the Soviet Union.'

Werner nodded. For a short time, he and the Baron had also hoped the Allies would continue Germany's war against Russia, but they had been swiftly disabused. 'By the time you realized your mistake, it was too late?'

Otto struggled to express his thoughts. He was a man of action, not of words. 'The war isn't over, not the war against the Soviet

44

Union, not so long as there are men like myself alive, who have been fighting the Communists since 1917.' On an impulse, he reached in his pocket and pulled out a much-fingered pencil drawing. 'This is my son, Adolf Alois Tobisch. He's five in November. I owe it to him to continue the fight. Adolf is the main reason I stayed in Austria and did not run away.'

It was a never-ending source of wonder and pride to Otto that he should have sired this child. His fat, stupid lump of a wife, Anna, who had never been very important to him, had faded into complete insignificance after Adolf's birth. At the age of nearly fifty, Otto had finally found a real purpose in life: to make a new world for his son.

Werner glanced at the sketch and mumbled, 'A fine boy.'

Otto put the portrait back in his pocket. 'He takes after me.'

'However, if somebody should give you away? Your wife might be pressurized into betraying you. Your neighbours could identify you.'

'My wife would never give me away and I never mixed with the villagers.'

'Or one of your colleagues from Schlachtenhausen?' Werner insisted.

'Schlachtenhausen is behind Russian lines now. So far as I can gather, the Russians are giving as little information as possible to the Americans and, in any case, most of the camp's records were burnt before I left. It will be difficult for anyone to try and incriminate me.'

Yes, Werner reflected, and the prisoners who could have identified him were now dead. In fact, there was possibly only one person other than Otto's wife and son who knew who Otto Tobisch really was – Werner himself.

As if Otto could read his thoughts, he said, 'I would suggest you don't do anything stupid to try and save your own neck. I know your involvement with Schlachtenhausen was very much more than building a factory alongside the camp. What's more I have papers hidden that prove it. I can plead that I simply obeyed Himmler's orders and did nothing beyond my normal duty. *You* might find yourself in a rather different situation.'

At that moment, a guard broke up their conversation, ordering

Werner back to his potatoes and marching Otto off to join a group of prisoners making mail bags. As Werner got on with his tedious task, Otto's chilling words continued to haunt him. He thought of the narrow gauge railway Kraus Rail had installed at Schlachtenhausen and the very profitable weekly deliveries of chemicals from Kraus Chemie in Cracow. Until now, he had believed that if these were ever discovered, he could claim his grandfather had made a deal with the SS of which he knew nothing. But Otto knew of Werner's involvement and, therefore, as his veiled threat suggested, he held his life in his hands.

One thing was certain. It would be against all Werner's interests if the Americans discovered the true identity of Otto Tobisch.

In the Austrian Salzkammergut, the cows came down from the high summer pastures. Dolfi Tobisch ran in front of the herd, springing from rock to rock like a mountain goat. His mother, Anna, followed slowly, easing her bulk down the mountain side with the help of a gnarled *Alpenstock* watching Dolfi with an anxious, maternal eye. As a child, she had loved taking the cattle up to the *Alm* in the spring and bringing them back again in the autumn. At last, Dolfi was experiencing the same pleasures, very different from the first years of his life at the vast camp Otto had superintended at Schlachtenhausen in Poland.

Anna had not liked Poland with its marshy, gloomy forests. She had tried to improve her house there with window-boxes, hanging baskets and carved wooden shutters, but it had never replaced her real home in the Salzkammergut. Homesick and lonely, she had tried to show an interest in the camp, but Otto had refused to allow her to have anything to do with it.

Then, in her forty-ninth year, when Anna had believed herself past child-bearing age, Dolfi had arrived. It had seemed nothing short of a miracle, a sign of favour from the Blessèd Virgin herself. And Otto doted on the baby, which was blond and blue-eyed, just like himself.

Dolfi, however, thrived no better at Schlachtenhausen than she did. He had trouble with words and was still wetting the bed at the age of four, when Otto had suddenly decided they must return to Austria. Yet since being in the mountains, Dolfi had changed, growing into a normal little boy.

Even Otto's arrest in June, which had come as a great shock to Anna, had disturbed Dolfi less than she had feared. She had told Dolfi that his father had been a great general, with important friends in Berlin, and that his arrest by the American Military Police was a mistake.

In the mean time, she had worries enough with the farm, which had been neglected during their absence. The house and barn were much in need of repairs, few of which Otto had been able to carry out before his arrest. Anna had cut the hay by herself, work she had managed easily in her youth but now found very hard, hampered by the weight she had put on during her years of enforced idleness. Instead of the usual three hay crops, there had only been two and those of poor quality, boding ill for the winter, as did the small amount of timber she had been able to fell for fuel.

Fortunately, the cattle were in good condition and the chickens laying well. With the grain she had stored in the ramshackle barn and provided the winter was not too harsh, they should be able to get through. Well, Anna thought, clambering heavily over an outcrop of rock, as her old father had always said, life was hard in the mountains . . .

Dolfi was the first to reach the farm. At his approach, a low growl came from the long grass and Wolf rose to his feet, towering high above the small boy, his teeth bared in his grey muzzle. Dolfi stopped, his heart pounding and his palms sweating, not just from the exertion of running down the mountain, but from fear. Wolf might be twelve and stiff with rheumatism, but Dolfi was more frightened of the Doberman Pinscher than of anything else in the world. And Wolf knew he was afraid.

Carefully, Dolfi backed away until the dog lay down again, then he ran back through the meadow towards the cows and his mother. He liked life here at Traunsee, even though he missed his father. But he would like it better if Wolf went away.

That night, the nightmare returned. It was not just a bad dream, but something Dolfi had actually experienced at Schlachtenhausen when, unknown to his mother, he had

47

followed his father and Wolf into the camp early one morning. A child was there, a girl of about his own age, dark haired and very thin. Wolf had jumped on her, pinned her to the ground and ripped her body apart. Dolfi had screamed and his father had run back and picked him up, burying his head in his shoulder, murmuring endearments. Then he had lifted his whip and beaten Wolf until the blood had poured down his gleaming coat.

Life in Berlin continued with a nightmarish quality. And ahead lay winter. That was the thought that obsessed Viktoria.

Disease was rampant. Water, electricity and gas continued to be rationed. Fuel was often limited to timber which could be salvaged from the ruins. Fresh food did find its way into the city but, although farmers were supposed to hand over all their produce to the occupying forces, most kept some back to sell on the black market or hoard against worse years ahead. Parks and gardens had been planted with vegetables. Sheep and goats grazed in the Tiergarten, to supplement the critically low milk supply.

The single greatest source of supply remained the black market. Café Jochum certainly depended upon it for its survival. Hasso had established good relationships with the city's main black market agents, who could supply nearly everything the café needed, including meat, chocolate, tea, coffee, wine, spirits, coal, candles, soap and even nylon stockings. Many of these goods were American in origin. The black market dealers accepted in payment anything except rapidly devaluing Reichsmarks – cameras, watches, antiques, carpets, furniture, gold and jewellery, silver tableware or porcelain – items that the occupying troops could send home and get a good price for.

Or one could pay in cigarettes. Cigarettes were becoming the new currency. A Leica camera was worth two hundred Chesterfields, a Dresden tea-set, one hundred Camels. Fifty cigarettes bought half a pound of butter or a bottle of wine and a bottle of schnaps.

There was scarcely a plot of land, balcony or window sill in Berlin on which tobacco plants had not been planted. Seven cigarette butts could be made into one whole cigarette. To supplement their income, the staff at Café Jochum collected butts, which they sold to a woman in a nearby cellar who had set up her own cigarette factory. But the cigarette exchange rate could rise overnight by anything up to 30 per cent, meaning a corresponding increase in the cost of food.

At Hasso's suggestion, Café Jochum had introduced its own system of barter. The early barriers between the British and American troops and Berliners were breaking down, and they were now on familiar terms with many of their regular customers, who were only too pleased to pay for an evening out with cigarettes that cost them next to nothing at the NAAFI or the PX. But although this improved matters, it was not enough to keep Café Jochum going through the winter.

It was Hasso who came up with a solution. The Allies had finally rescinded the non-fraternization order, with the result that, although there was still a ban on sharing accommodation, American and British soldiers could have German girlfriends. Hasso proposed that they sell one or two of Viktoria's smaller pieces of jewellery and use the proceeds to turn the cellar into a proper restaurant, serving a high class menu. At the same time, they would engage a small orchestra and take on some carefully selected girls as escorts and dancing partners.

Viktoria was not naive: she knew Hasso hoped the girls would attract officers who would pay well for an evening's wining and dining in female company. 'But a soldier is going to expect something more than a kiss in return for buying a girl a meal in our new restaurant,' she objected.

'I know a lot of girls who would be willing to give considerably more than a kiss in return for a square meal,' Hasso replied bluntly. 'Don't forget that many girls have ageing parents, crippled brothers, or other dependants who can't work and have to be looked after. The only way they can survive is to find an Ami or Tommy boyfriend. If they go to bed with them in exchange for a carton of cigarettes, who can blame them?'

Viktoria sighed. In the end, everything came down to survival. If she were twenty again, would she be prepared to sell her body for a meal and a carton of cigarettes? Probably yes, if she were hungry enough – or if that were the only way to keep her family alive. In this new Berlin, it was not how you lived, but whether you lived, that was important. Morals were like everything else –

a luxury few could afford. But she was not that desperate. 'No, Hasso! I'd rather sell all my jewellery.'

That was exactly what Hasso did not want her to do. Diamonds, in particular, were commanding a high price on the black market, but he was determined not to fritter away their only real asset. 'What shall we use for capital when the time comes to rebuild?' he asked.

'Perhaps it would be better to forget about rebuilding . . .'

'Frau Viktoria, there is not only yourself to consider. You have other responsibilities. There is Lili. Café Jochum is her inheritance, too.'

She felt herself weakening. 'A restaurant would mean more staff.'

'You'll have people queuing to work for nothing, provided you feed them.'

'And the police?'

Hasso shrugged. 'They'll probably be among our clientèle.'

He was undoubtedly right. The Military Police had too many other problems on its hands to bother about the affairs of Café Jochum, while the newly reformed Berlin police had troubles of its own. Each sector had its own local police force, supervised by that particular Occupying Power, but actually dominated by the Soviet Secret Police. The Chief of Police was a Nazi-turned-Communist, loathed and feared by the entire population.

Viktoria was silent for a long while, wondering what her parents and Benno would have thought of Hasso's suggestions. But did it actually matter? They were dead. Nothing could hurt them any more. 'All right,' she said, 'I don't like it, but we'll do it.' Yet as she spoke, she was conscious of a sense of betrayal, not only of Café Jochum, her parents and Benno – but of herself.

One of the most memorable occasions Mortimer Allen attended that autumn in Berlin was a banquet given by the Soviet City Commandant, to which high-ranking officers from the other Occupying Powers were all invited. The tables were lavishly spread with food, there were small mountains of caviare, the vodka flowed freely and the Russian hosts were in excellent form, gushing bonhomie.

Mortimer tried to convince himself that there was some

50

purpose to the extravaganza, but all he could think of were the refugees at the Stettiner Bahnhof, and slipped away from the banquet as early as he decently could.

He was also permitted to sit in on a meeting of the Allied Control Council, the supreme authority over all Germany, and to attend a meeting of the Allied Kommandatura to see how the four military governors and their staffs were trying to resolve the future of Berlin.

What he learned did not make him feel any easier. The Americans and British worked reasonably well together and were agreed on most issues, but the French were far less cooperative and, while the Western Allies made every effort to work with the Soviets on a friendly basis, the Russians did not reciprocate. There were even problems over Nazi war criminals: the Western Allies shared their findings, but the Soviets kept theirs to themselves.

In Berlin, there was even more ominous friction. Although the Kommandatura operated in superficial harmony, the Russians continued to claim prior right to the city and make difficulties for their allies.

Mortimer had most contact with members of the American occupying forces and from these officers and men he heard muted, rebellious murmurs. Although most of them were living better than ever before, they very naturally wanted to go home. To them, Berlin was a city in the last throes of death. If the Russians wanted it, let them have it.

When he had first arrived, Mortimer might have agreed, but already his opinions were changing. The situation in Berlin was fraught with complex political, economic and human problems, which were going to be only partially resolved by denazification and not at all by handing the city over to the Russians. In his articles, he began to take a contentious line, urging his readers to recognize the strategic importance of the city and have pity upon the miserable circumstances of its inhabitants.

To find out more about conditions in the Soviet zone, Mortimer applied for information to the Soviet Political Information Department and found himself in the office of Basilius Meyer.

The moment he heard the name, it rang bells in his mind. And as soon as he saw Basilius, he knew he was right, for there was a striking similarity between the young man and his mother, Olga Meyer, who, along with Karl Liebknecht and Rosa Luxemburg, had been a leader of the failed 1919 Communist Revolution. Olga was Viktoria's cousin, although Mortimer knew that the two women had fallen out at the time of Viktoria's father's death. He was also aware that, after Hitler had come to power in 1933, Olga and her son had fled Berlin for Moscow. He had heard that Olga had died in Stalin's purges. Now he knew what had happened to Basilius.

Smartly dressed in a civilian suit, with a clean-shaven oval face and grey eyes behind steel-rimmed spectacles, Basilius sat behind a large desk. Clever, Mortimer thought. His youth gives him an air of reassuring innocence and his clothes make him look affluent. He is supposed to make the Germans think they'll be well off under the Russians.

At another desk, a man in Red Army uniform was tapping at an ancient typewriter. Although he appeared to pay no attention to either Basilius or Mortimer, Mortimer guessed he was a member of the NKVD, the People's Commissariat of State Security – the Russian Secret Police. The Russians were unlikely to trust any German, no matter how sound his credentials.

Mortimer began the interview by commenting, 'It must have been a momentous occasion for you when you set foot again on German soil after so many years in exile.' He spoke in German.

Basilius shot him a cool glance. 'We will speak in English if that is more comfortable for you. I did not consider myself to be in exile. Moscow became my home. I have spent half my life in the Soviet Union.'

Mortimer continued in German. 'When did you return?'

With a thin smile, Basilius replied in his mother tongue. 'At the beginning of May. I was also one of a specially selected group who returned with Walter Ulbricht, close in the wake of the Red Army, to help set up a new socialist administration here in Berlin.'

'You are a Communist Party member?'

'Yes, a founder member of the KPD, the new German Communist Party authorized by the Soviet authorities this summer.'

52

'It would interest me to learn more about the KPD.'

'Our first aim is to help create a new socialist German Republic.'

'A new republic?' Mortimer was slightly taken aback. 'The Potsdam Agreement allows for the eventual peaceful cooperation by Germany in international life, but it says nothing about a new republic!'

Basilius shrugged. 'You are like most Westerners. You are only concerned with denazification and bringing the fascists to justice. After that, you vaguely assume the Germans will submit to being governed by the Occupying Powers and will never again seek a political identity. The Soviet Union is more realistic.'

'You think the Soviet Union would permit free elections in Germany?' Mortimer asked.

'Certainly. Other parties were licensed in May: Liberal, Christian and Social Democrats. We are talking about a democracy, Herr Allen, governed by the elected representatives of the people. We intend to achieve power by parliamentary means. I am in no doubt that the Communists and Social Democrats will win a majority when the first election is held.'

Mortimer offered Basilius a cigarette and lit one for himself, using the time to formulate his next question. 'What about the deportees? Stalin's treatment of them is hardly likely to make him popular with the Germans.'

Basilius inhaled on his cigarette, remembering how he and his mother had been forced to flee Berlin with only two shabby suitcases, leaving their home and such worldly goods as they possessed behind them. Nobody had cared about them. Why should he care about the German deportees now, who had only themselves to blame for their fate?

He said, 'Poland and the Soviet Union have been ravaged beyond description by the war. Thousands of cities have been flattened. Millions are starving. Those people were living on land and eating food that is needed by the indigenous population and by those who are returning home after having themselves been deported, when Hitler's armies overran their countries.'

'But most of the deportees are women, children and old people . . .'

'Herr Allen, you must realize that, although one war has

ended, another still continues: the sacred war of the people against capitalism. In the cause of the revolution, the individual does not matter.'

Mortimer sighed. It was the same old Communist cant. Nothing had changed. He tried another angle. 'Most factories in Berlin have been stripped by the Russians. I was in Wedding recently and saw what is left of Kraus Village. How are German workers to work if there is no industry?'

'If it had not been for companies like Kraus Industries, Hitler would not have been able to go to war. Capitalist greed was responsible for the downfall of our country and the misery of our people.' Basilius helped himself to another of Mortimer's American cigarettes.

Mortimer decided to take a gamble. 'I used to live at the Hotel Quadriga before the war. I seem to remember Viktoria Jochum-Kraus telling me that she and your mother were cousins.'

Basilius stiffened. 'It is a relationship I prefer to ignore.' The only family connection he had renewed since his return to Berlin was with his father's sister, Maria Sommer, and her sixteen-year-old son Rudolf, who lived in a flat in the Prenzlauer Berg, a working-class area in the Soviet sector, very similar to that in which he had grown up in Wedding.

'Nevertheless, you might find you have something in common with Viktoria's son, Stefan,' Mortimer persisted. 'He, too, left Germany because of his anti-fascist beliefs. He was a member of the resistance and, during the war, helped the British in their anti-fascist propaganda campaign.'

Basilius doubted very much that he and Stefan had anything in common. He had scant respect for the resistance put up by the middle class against Hitler, the main purpose of which, in his opinion, had been to salvage what remained of their own bourgeois way of life. Anton Sommer, on the contrary, had died in a concentration camp because he had refused to betray the socialist cause.

'Stefan Kraus may pretend to be anti-fascist but I know the truth,' Basilius replied. 'He is the son of an imperialist, capitalist family. He represents everything I most despise.'

*   *   *

54

At Fuerstenmark, in Lower Pomerania, a scant hundred miles north-east of Berlin, Viktoria's daughter, Monika, stood at the sink, scrubbing the bruised, mealy potatoes and turnips which now formed the family's staple diet, staring absently through the kitchen window of the parsonage across the cobbled courtyard towards the gates of Fuerstenmark castle, now local Red Army headquarters.

How different life was now in Fuerstenmark to when she had married Hans Koenig and set up home here in 1938. Then Pastor Koenig and his family had been important members of the small community. Hans had been newly appointed as village schoolmaster, while Monika had been just eighteen, serenely and naively self-confident about her life and the future.

Then war had broken out and Hans had been called up. That in itself had not been so bad. He had returned home quite often on leave and Monika had given birth to their two children, Heini in September 1939, just after his father had left for the Front, and Senta a year later. In fact, war had not really touched Monika or Fuerstenmark until Hans was taken prisoner of war in 1942. Since then, the only news she had received from him was a short, censored letter forwarded by the Red Cross.

Yet still the stark reality of war had not reached Fuerstenmark. There had been no air raids. Rations had grown more stringent, but affected clothing and household goods more than food. Not least among the advantages of living in the country then had been an abundance of fresh produce. Nor had there been any shortage of servants. Throughout the war, the Koenigs had had Polish or Ukrainian maids to prepare their meals and clean the house.

Then had begun the exodus of refugees from the east and Russian troops had crossed the German frontier. Incredible though it seemed, Germany was losing the war. Terrified by the stories of Russian atrocities the refugees brought with them, Monika had pleaded to be allowed to take the children to her parents in Berlin, but Arthur and Gerda Koenig had reasoned with her that they would be safer at Fuerstenmark, and in the end she had allowed herself to be convinced.

Wishing, as she did every day, that she had some salt, Monika put the diced potatoes and turnips into a pan of boiling water on the stove. Then she took a lump of fatty ham from the larder and cut off a few pieces. That was the family's entire meat ration for a fortnight. As meat, it was inedible, but the fat was good for flavouring the so-called vegetable soup.

As it turned out, the Russians were not the rampaging beasts everyone had feared. One or two cottages and barns were set fire to and a couple of girls raped, although most villagers believed the girls had only themselves to blame for letting the soldiers see them. All sensible women, including Monika, had hidden in cellars and attics, until they had been given assurance that it was safe to come out. The storekeeper, who had been promoted to Mayor under the Nazis, was arrested. The body of an SS man was found in the street, riddled with machine gun bullets. Several other Nazi Party members disappeared, but whether they were prisoners, dead, or had been deported to Russia nobody knew. Neither did anybody ask. Asking questions, the villagers had long ago learned, was a sure way to get into trouble oneself.

Russian policemen moved into the police station and it was rumoured that there was a secret police force in operation similar to the former Gestapo. Their presence was mutely accepted. After twelve years, a secret police had become a fact of life.

There had been other new arrivals during the course of the summer. Most were deportees from the east, who came with very few belongings, no provisions and little money, and introduced new tensions into village life. It was one thing sharing their homes with neighbours whom the Russians had evicted, but quite another to relinquish their privacy and dwindling supplies to total strangers. However, Gerda Koenig, a trained nurse and a long-time member of the Red Cross, spent a lot of time with the deportees, many of whom were suffering from chronic ill-health.

Apart from that, life went on with a strange semblance of normality. During the day, the entire village worked on the land, tending the remaining livestock, gathering in the harvest, gleaning the fields to supplement their meagre rations. Pastor Koenig continued to hold church services, although he was careful to drop all innovations introduced under the Nazis. A new schoolmaster arrived and was billeted at the parsonage, a thin, beak-nosed socialist called Guenther Rauch, who seemed to suffer from a perpetual cold, spoke fluent

56

Russian and had spent most of the war in a concentration camp.

Arthur and Gerda Koenig tried to make him feel at home, hoping that his was only a temporary assignment and that when Hans returned, he would take up his old job again and Guenther would move on. Because of Guenther Rauch, Heini and Senta had to give up their bedroom and sleep with their mother in the double bed she had once shared with Hans.

There was a sound of voices outside and Monika glanced out of the window again. From the schoolhouse next to the church, the children were emerging, their lessons finished for the day. Heini was among the first, swinging his schoolbag round his head, then letting it go, so that it flew wildly through the air. The boys laughed and the girls gazed at him admiringly.

Monika smiled. She was very proud of her 6-year-old son and felt much closer to him than she ever would to her daughter. Perhaps this was because Heini, being blond and sturdy, clearly took after herself and Hans, while 4-year-old Senta was a delicate, sensitive child, with reddish hair and blue-green eyes. But maybe the true reasons ran deeper. When she was young, Monika had always suspected that her mother preferred Stefan to her. Certainly Viktoria had not been nearly so upset when Monika had married Hans and come to live at Fuerstenmark as she had been when Stefan had gone to England. As a result, instead of over-compensating with her own daughter, Monika subconsciously exercised her old grudge upon her.

Heini retrieved his bag, said goodbye to his friends, then sauntered towards the castle. Monika knew he was going to see Mischa, one of the castle sentries. How they conversed Monika wasn't sure, but they seemed to make themselves understood. It was strange how fond the Russians were of children. The soldiers were always giving them presents, sweetmeats or toys.

Monika turned her attention again to the soup, on the surface of which a layer of grease was forming. It wasn't, she reflected, that life was bad in Fuerstenmark – it could just be very much better. If only Hans would return. If only there was more to eat . . .

She still often thought about going to Berlin. People said the whole city was in ruins but, having seen only the few pictures

57

the Russians allowed to be reproduced in the papers, Monika found that difficult to believe. There was no postal service and certainly no telephone link between Fuerstenmark and Berlin, so she had heard nothing from her parents since before the war's end, but she was convinced that they were still living in relative luxury at the Hotel Quadriga. Not for them the deprivations she was suffering.

Once, it would have been simple to get to Berlin. She could have taken a bus to Stettin and caught a train. But since the end of the war Stettin was in Poland. Now, Prenzlau, twenty miles away, was the nearest station, but few trains seemed to run from it.

There was a clatter of hooves and the rumble of wheels on the cobbles. Monika glanced through the window again and recognized the cart belonging to Gustav Matzke, a short, stout man in his fifties with a wart on his nose, a farmer, whom the Russians had permitted to retain his smallholding. Gustav showed his pass to Mischa, nodded at Heini and entered the castle courtyard. All farm produce went to the Russians. There is food enough for them, Monika thought bitterly, but none for us.

Half-an-hour later, the cart re-emerged and drew to a halt outside the parsonage. 'Anybody home?' Gustav called.

Monika grimaced. Once she had made the mistake of accompanying the farmer into one of his barns where he said he had some new-laid eggs. If there had been any eggs she had never discovered, for Gustav's real intentions had quickly become clear. 'You must miss that husband of yours,' he had said in a thick voice, ogling her breasts.

'Of course I miss Hans,' Monika had said, edging back towards the barn doors, which Gustav had shut behind them.

He had grabbed her arm and pulled her to him, forcing his mouth onto hers. She had struggled, trying to pull away, and he had laughed. 'Fancy a bit of rough, do you? Well, I like my women to have spirit.' Then, with a slight push, he had sent her backwards onto a bale of hay, and he was lying beside her, one hand reaching up her skirt, the other fumbling with his flies.

She had been saved by the sound of his wife's voice, calling impatiently, 'Gustav, where are you? Your supper's ready.'

58

Since then she had not gone again to the Matzke farm.

Gustav peered in through the kitchen window and mouthed something at her. Monika sighed, wiped her hands on her apron, and went to the door.

He looked around him, to make sure nobody else was in earshot, then he said, 'The Russians have just ordered me to take supplies to Berlin. I thought you might like to come with me.' He leered suggestively.

If it had been to anywhere but Berlin, Monika would have said no. But the prospect of returning to civilization, of having lunch at the Quadriga, of seeing her parents – especially her father – again, of receiving their sympathy and admiration for her courage, and of coming back to Fuerstenmark with bags of provisions, clothes and money, was too enticing. No doubt Gustav would expect to be rewarded for his trouble, but she was confident she would be able to deal with him. 'How thoughtful of you,' she said, choosing her words carefully. 'I would very much like to go to Berlin.'

Monika's return to Berlin would remain indelibly etched in her memory as one of the most shattering experiences of her life. It was still dark when Gustav Matzke drew up outside the parsonage in an ancient, rusting truck, reeking of onions, manure and exhaust fumes. Its windscreen was cracked and the driver's window non-existent. The springs were coming through the cracked upholstery of the passenger seat and Gustav spread a dirty sack for her to sit on. Then he pinched her thigh and, with a crashing of gears, they lumbered off down the main street.

To Monika's relief, Gustav's attention was concentrated less on her than on the truck, which was incapable of travelling at more than twenty miles an hour, slewed to the left whenever he braked and showed a tendency to stall whenever he let his foot off the accelerator. Also, the racket it made going over the pitted road surfaces gave little opportunity for conversation. Monika huddled into her coat. Soon it grew light and she was able to watch the passing countryside, while she dreamed of the day ahead of her.

Eventually, they reached the outskirts of Berlin and there she received her first intimation of what awaited her. Ruined

59

houses. Gaping craters filled with rubble. Makeshift shelters. Queues of people in tattered clothes, buckets in hand, waiting at standpipes. 'What were you expecting, girl?' Gustav asked, noticing her shocked expression. 'There's nothing left of Berlin. People here haven't got anything. No homes. No work. No food. That's why I'm here. The whole city's starving.'

He gave a crude laugh. 'Not that I intend handing over all my load to the Russians. First I'm going to see some of my old cronies near the Alexander Platz. I'll get a better price on the black market than I'll get from the commies. Where did you say you want to go? To Unter den Linden?'

'You can drop me at the Alexander Platz,' Monika said weakly. 'I'll take a tram from there.'

But there were no trams. And when she reached Unter den Linden, there was no Hotel Quadriga. In fact, there was little that she recognized at all from the Berlin she had last seen seven years earlier, no fine shops, no pavement cafés, no embassies and ministerial buildings, nothing except the battered remains of the Brandenburg Gate towering over the rubble.

As Stefan and Mortimer had, a few weeks earlier, she set off towards the Kurfuerstendamm, but her footsteps dragged. Had it not been that she was not meeting Gustav until four o'clock and it was then only ten, she would have been tempted to return immediately to the truck. Already she knew that, whatever awaited her at Café Jochum, it would not be what she had hoped for.

In fact, it was far worse. Above all, Monika had been looking forward to seeing her father, her dear, gentle, Papa, who had always spoiled and indulged her, always taken her side against her mother and brother, who could be guaranteed to show her sympathy, comfort and understanding. But Papa was dead. Papa had died when the Quadriga was burned down.

In the cellar of Café Jochum, there was only Viktoria, getting the tables ready for lunch. True, her mother stopped working the moment she saw Monika, taking her in her arms and saying, 'Thank God, you're all right. I've been so worried about you. The Russians did such awful things – and I thought – you're so pretty – they might have . . .'

She let Hasso and the other waiters take care of the restaurant and sat with Monika while she ate. But although as the restaurant filled, waiters hurried back and forth from the kitchen, with plates of succulent-looking roast chicken, potatoes and cabbage, glasses of frothing beer, and cups of real, aromatic coffee, Monika was given a dish of *boulette*, while Viktoria had a bowl of bouillon and a slice of dry bread.

Disgruntled, Monika pushed her fork around her stew, which actually contained quite a generous helping of meat, and gazed enviously towards the uniformed clientèle enjoying their roast chicken. 'Farmer Matzke said Berlin was starving, but things can't be that bad, not if you can obtain all this food,' she commented. 'We're lucky to get hold of a few rotten potatoes.'

'So are we,' Viktoria said gently. 'It's only our customers who can afford to eat well.'

But Monika did not believe her. She was sure her mother preferred soup from choice not from necessity. And, as the meal continued, all her childhood resentments resurfaced. When she described the hardships she had to put up with at Fuerstenmark, Viktoria said, 'Darling, I do sympathize, but be thankful you have a roof over your head and that you are all well.' And when she complained about having received no news from Hans, Viktoria said, 'At least he's a British and not a Russian prisoner of war, darling, so you know he'll be well treated. Stefan says a lot of British prisoners of war are now arriving in Westerstedt . . .'

'I know she never really loved me,' Monika complained to her mother-in-law, Gerda, late that evening, when she was back in Fuerstenmark, 'but until today I never realized quite how hard she was. Surely she must have known how much I loved Papa? Did she have to say, "Your father's dead," as if it was something that didn't matter at all? The truth is, she never did care about me and she still doesn't. She seemed more concerned about Lili than Senta and Heini. She sends food to Lili, but she didn't give me any to bring back here . . .'

Monika told Gerda all about her mother and Café Jochum, but she could not bring herself to tell her about Gustav Matzke. She was too shocked and too ashamed to tell anybody what he had done to her.

As arranged, she had met him at four in a side street off the Hackescher Markt. He was waiting for her in the truck, his face

61

flushed and his voice slurred, as he asked, 'Had a good day, girl?'
The lorry lurched into motion, rattling even more than it had on
its outward journey now that it contained no load. Once they had
left the city behind them, he reached in his pocket, took out a
bottle of vodka, undid its cap with his teeth, took a large gulp,
then handed it to her.

Monika shook her head, drawing as far away from him as
possible.

He shrugged and tipped more vodka down his own throat. By
the time they reached Angermuende, the bottle was empty and
night was falling.

Without warning, he turned off the road and drove up a
narrow track, pulling to a halt in the lee of a cluster of trees.
The countryside stretched bleak and flat around them with not
a person or a building in sight.

'And now you're going to say thank you.' He reached across,
grabbing her shoulder, pulling her towards him.

She struggled and succeeded in getting out of the cab, but he
caught up with her as she ran back towards the main road, and
threw her to the ground. He was bigger than her and strong
with drink. No matter how much she twisted and turned and
pummelled at him with her fists, she could not push him off
her. In the end, there was nothing she could do but let him
take her.

Gradually, the bruises caused by Gustav Matzke's brutal
treatment of her healed, but the trauma of her rape would never
leave her. In many ways, it supplanted in her mind the shock she
had received in seeing Berlin, learning of her father's death and
recognizing once and for all her mother's true nature. One thing
it did for sure. It cured her of any desire to visit Berlin again.

Mortimer telephoned Stefan to tell him about his meeting with
Basilius Meyer and the news he had received from Viktoria
of Monika's visit to Berlin. Stefan took the call after yet
another gruelling day at Westerstedt, listening to poignant
stories of how German deportees had trekked cross-country,
to distracted demands that they be set free, to impassioned
pleas that something be done to find out what had happened to
other members of their families. And, as always, he had heard

a note in their voices and a look in their eyes that accused him, a German working with the Allies, of being partly to blame for their plight.

In Westerstedt Stefan was neither fish nor fowl. Most of his British colleagues accepted him now, but their acceptance would never be complete. To them, he would always be a German. They had no idea of his inner turmoil: his admiration for Britain's staunch opposition to the Nazis, but his wish that she could take a less colonial and more compassionate attitude towards the refugees, displaced persons and the civilian German population; the conflict that had long plagued him between his admiration for Britain and his loyalty to Germany.

Even harder to bear was the knowledge that he was doing a job for which he was ill-suited by training and experience. Instead of trying to right wrongs and creating a new Germany, he was being employed as a kind of policeman. He said to Mortimer, 'I returned to Germany with such brave ideals. When am I going to be able to do something about them?'

Mortimer listened to Stefan's heartfelt plea echoing tinnily down the telephone line and promised, 'Be patient, son, and I'll see what I can do.'

At the end of October, postal services were resumed to places outside Berlin. Huddled in a blanket, her fingers numb with cold, with only scrap paper to write on, Viktoria sat up late into the night writing letters to Stefan and Monika, to Norbert, to other friends in different parts of Germany. In many cases, she had no idea whether her correspondents were dead or alive, whether their houses still stood or whether she was writing to a bomb crater. But it didn't matter.

When she queued at the post office the following morning, she felt an almost childish excitement. Once more she was in touch with the outside world. The long months of isolation were finally over.

Chapter 4

Viktoria's letter was the first personal news from the outside world Norbert Kraus had received since his arrival in Luebeck in May, after he had fled from Berlin, just before the Russians reached the city.

He had left with Reinhild Pacher, a receptionist from the Hotel Quadriga, with whom he had been enjoying a light-hearted affair for the last two years. Reinhild had been one of the many girlfriends he had had throughout Europe, wherever his duties with the Todt Organization had taken him, building fortifications and defences. A plump, not very intelligent young woman in her early twenties, with dark hair and brown, cow-like eyes, Reinhild was not the most glamorous or exciting of his amours, but she had the decided advantage in that spring of 1945 of having grandparents who lived in Luebeck. Faced with the alternative of being taken captive by the British or the Russians, Norbert preferred the former.

When they had reached Luebeck, however, bad news awaited them. Reinhild's grandparents were both dead and their house razed to the ground. Fortunately the cellar, in which the old people had spent the last few months of their life, was still habitable, so Norbert and Reinhild had taken up residence there.

Soon life had resumed a semblance of normality. Shops opened, although they had little to sell and what they did have was strictly rationed and only available after waiting for hours in long queues.

Since the only way to obtain a ration card was to register for work, Norbert had to admit to having worked for the Todt Organization, with the result that he was tried before a British denazification court. However, because he had only been involved in construction work and not in arms and munitions, the court was lenient towards him. Similarly, since he had never worked for Kraus Industries, it decided to overlook the fact that he was a member of the Kraus family. He was not sent to prison but ordered to work clearing rubble. Reinhild fared slightly better and was given a cleaning job at a British mess.

Rations were pitifully inadequate and the work hard, but Norbert was only twenty-five years old, tall, strong and fit. He was also a trained architect with practical experience of building. During his free time, he started to clear the site of the ruined house, keeping whole bricks and discarding damaged ones, then hand-cleaning them, chipping away the old mortar with a trowel. It was a time-consuming process, and he thought longingly of a set of interlocking bricks he had owned as a child. Building a house with those would indeed be child's play compared to this – and, what was more, he would not be left with a mountain of useless, shattered bricks, tiles, wood and pieces of plaster.

After that, he could not rid himself of the image of those toy bricks and slowly an idea formed in his mind. What was needed was a method of processing the rubble into building blocks, which could be dried in the open air instead of being heat-dried like bricks. Taking some pieces of wood, he made a carefully designed mould. With a club hammer, he smashed some of the rubble into small fragments and mixed them with cement and water. Then he poured his aggregate into the mould and left it to dry. A few days later, when he knocked it out of its shuttering, he had a building block, much larger than a conventional brick.

From then onwards, he concentrated on rubble. By the end of a fortnight, he had fifty identical moulds. As each was completed, he filled it with aggregate. As each block dried, he refilled the mould, so that he had a continuous production line. By the end of July, he had a small brick factory. Instead of trying to rebuild the old house, he began to build a new one on the site, a four-roomed dwelling, single-storeyed and flat roofed, with a chimney and an open grate at one end.

At the beginning of October, Norbert and Reinhild transferred their possessions out of the cellar into their new home. It was then Reinhild sprang her surprise. That evening, when they went to bed, she cuddled close to him and whispered, 'Norbert I'm pregnant.'

Norbert had been thinking only of his achievement in building the new house. Reinhild's news was the last thing he had expected.

'I've known for a week,' Reinhild continued, 'but I wanted to wait to tell you until after we moved. The doctor says the baby will be born next May.'

Norbert stared into the darkness. The last thing he wanted was a baby. Why the hell, he asked himself, hadn't Reinhild been more careful?

Reinhild began to cry. 'Norbert, tell me you love me. Tell me you're pleased about the baby.'

He had drifted into his relationship with Reinhild. He did not love her.

'Now we've built the house, it will be all right,' Reinhild sobbed. 'Lots of other families manage with much less than we have.'

Families . . . Norbert drew in his breath, as the full realization of the word dawned upon him. His immediate instinct was to get out of bed, get dressed, pack his bag and get out of Reinhild's life for ever. But that would mean leaving the home he had built with his own bare hands. Even more importantly, it would mean giving up the plan which had been forming in his mind throughout the summer.

It was estimated that more than half the houses in the British zone were damaged and many of these were beyond repair. An already acute accommodation problem was becoming rapidly exacerbated by the ever-increasing number of refugees pouring in from the east. Although the British had established housing committees to speed up the rebuilding programme, work was progressing very slowly. As winter approached, millions were still homeless.

During the war Norbert's brother Werner had formed a company called Landgut AG, totally separate from Kraus Industries, with himself and Norbert as the only shareholders. Landgut's function was to acquire bombsites, on the premise that no matter what happened at the end of the war, land would keep its value. By the end of the war Landgut owned bombsites in major cities throughout Germany. The title deeds, Norbert knew, were safely in the vaults of the Liegnitzer Bank in Zurich.

If the British saw what he had achieved with reconstituted rubble, it was possible they might give him the equipment to build more houses like his own, on sites that belonged to Landgut. But if he left Reinhild, there would be no prototype to show . . .

Reinhild was weeping now as if her heart would break. In a gruff voice, Norbert said, 'I suppose we'd better get married.'

When he replied to Viktoria's letter, it was to tell her, among other things, that he and Reinhild were now husband and wife and that their first child was expected in the spring.

The Kraus case reached its climax on Monday 12 November 1945, at a preliminary open session of the International Military Tribunal in the Courtroom of the Palace of Justice at Nuremberg, presided over by the British judge, Lord Justice Lawrence.

From the press gallery in the Court House, Mortimer was an intent observer as the American Chief Prosecutor, Robert H. Jackson, and Dr Eckhardt Jurisch, the lawyer representing Baron von Kraus, presented their petitions to a panel of international judges.

Joachim Duschek had not been idle during the weeks since their visit to Castle Waldesruh. Recognizing that he was too young and lacking in knowledge of international law to give the Baron the expert defence he required, he had asked for help from Dr Jurisch, an extremely astute lawyer and partner in a far bigger legal practice than Joachim's, who had, in the past, handled certain legal transactions for Kraus Industries.

Eckhardt Jurisch, a man in his mid-forties, who specialized in business law, had been swift to identify the manifold possibilities lying ahead if he succeeded in saving the Baron from imprisonment. He agreed to represent the Baron and also to take Joachim as his assistant during the proceedings.

A short, tubby man, with a deceptively jovial, round face, betrayed only by slightly close-set, hard eyes, Eckhardt Jurisch informed the court that at the end of October doctors from each of the Occupying Powers had examined Baron von Kraus and unanimously concluded that his physical condition was so poor that to expect him to undergo the rigours of a long trial and that imprisonment might endanger his life.

Unable to refute medical evidence, Justice Jackson argued that the Baron should be tried *in absentia*, at which Dr Jurisch protested that this was contrary not only to all recognized legal practice but to the provisions of the Statutes of the Court. Furthermore, he added, his client was not deliberately avoiding standing trial, but nature had rendered it impossible for him to do so. After considerable discussion, Dr Jurisch's petition was upheld by the judges.

Justice Jackson next proposed that Ernst Kraus be tried in place of his father.

Eckhardt Jurisch asked quietly, 'Are you suggesting that Ernst Kraus be named as a principal war criminal simply because his father cannot be tried?'

'Not at all,' Robert Jackson replied. 'Ernst Kraus had responsibility for the gunshops of Essen. There is evidence that he is guilty in his own right of war crimes and crimes against humanity.'

'However, in view of the fact that Ernst Kraus is not named in the Bill of Indictment, I contend that you are now proposing to substitute one name for another.'

At the end of the hearing, which spilled over into the next day, the Tribunal ruled in favour of the defence motion and against the two petitions brought by the prosecution. Ernst Kraus, however, it was ruled, was to remain in prison and the Baron under house arrest.

As the two lawyers left the Court, Eckhardt Jurisch turned to his young colleague. 'Now we must start looking to the future. First, we must move the Baron off that godforsaken mountainside and back to Germany. Then we must set our minds to seeing how much of Kraus Industries' business we can salvage.'

At Castle Kransberg, the black gaoler could not wait to break the news to Ernst. 'Snow White, no public appearances for you at Nuremberg! Your friends are going to get all the glory!'

Ernst did not react. He just lay motionless, curled up in the foetal position under the bedclothes. Used though he was to Snow White's moods, the warder stared at him anxiously, wondering for a moment if his charge had died in the night. But there was a reassuring slow movement of the blankets. 'Did you hear me, Snow White? You've been let off the hook!'

Ernst heard him but the words did not really mean anything. Vaguely he had been aware of the sudden departure of Professor Speer and Dr Schacht for Nuremberg, but he was not sure any longer what Nuremberg signified.

The gaoler sighed. It had been fun goading Snow White, but now the old goat seemed to have gone completely round the bend, there was no pleasure in it any more. When he was told, a few weeks later, that Ernst was being transferred to another camp, he felt quite worried as to how he would survive.

The French did not want the expense and responsibility of keeping Baron von Kraus and his daughter-in-law in Austria and were only too pleased to give him back to the Germans. A French military ambulance took the Baron and Trude to the top of the Achenpass, where they were transferred to an American ambulance and brought to Munich.

The task of finding suitable accommodation for them had not been easy, but eventually Dr Jurisch had located an elderly nurse living in a cottage in a small village just outside Munich who was prepared to give them lodgings and the Baron medical care.

Although the Baron showed neither gratitude to Dr Jurisch nor any sign of pleasure at his improved circumstances, he was inwardly exultant. Now must start the next stage in his campaign: his gradual recovery, so that when the Allies were finished with retribution and ready to start on reconstruction, he would be ready.

From then on, he devoted his days to self-styled physiotherapy, trying to make paralysed muscles bend to his will, endeavouring to make his mouth utter the sounds he heard in his head and which he had once succeeded in transforming into speech. This was his final battle. And it was one he was going to win.

Norbert knew none of the details of the decision not to try his father or grandfather at Nuremberg. To him, it was simply further proof of the feeling he had long had that, unlike the Russians and Americans, the British were less intent on vengeance than on restoring order. He knew of several instances where even Nazi Party members had been exempted from the purge because they were considered useful for the administration or economy of the zone.

Optimistic that he had little to fear, he requested an interview with Major Peter Graves, the British officer responsible for housing in Luebeck. He had no intention of telling him immediately about Landgut. First, he had to prove himself as a building contractor.

A handsome, grey-haired man, a civil engineer in civilian life, Major Graves listened carefully to Norbert's very accurate assessment of the housing situation in the British zone and his solution for dealing with it. Although he felt a certain misgiving at dealing with a member of the Kraus family, he was drawn towards the tall, lean young German with the rather plain face, and was impressed by his articulate command of English and the ingenuity he had shown in setting up his brick factory and building his own house. He was even more impressed when he saw Norbert's house for himself and went over the projected costings and timings.

In November, Norbert was given a contract to build one hundred houses on a field outside Luebeck, with the promise that, if these were finished on schedule, further commissions would be forthcoming. Norbert had to provide the labour force, which, since manpower was one thing of which there was no shortage, presented no problem. Space would be made available to expand the brick factory and all building materials and equipment, apart from rubble, would be supplied by the British.

It was exactly what Norbert had hoped for: the first step towards founding the fortunes of Landgut AG.

Café Jochum closed on the evening of Sunday 25 November, and opened again on Monday 3 December. Hasso, through his many contacts, had succeeded in fitting it out with pink table linen and pink-shaded, electric table lights. In the centre of the floor a space was left clear for dancing to a quartet of talented but hungry musicians.

The kitchen, now in the hands of another of Hasso's acquaintances, Carl-Heinz Kaftanski, and two kitchen girls, Lotte and

Inge, had a gas stove, to supplement the old coal range. Pipes brought cold running water into newly fitted sinks and there was even an old refrigerator, which Hasso had acquired in a complicated series of deals on the black market.

Four more waiters had been employed, including Ulrich Kleinschmidt, a former waiter at the Hotel Quadriga, freeing Viktoria to manage the café and Hasso to run the bar. Viktoria had a desk at the foot of the stairs from where she had an overview of the restaurant. Except in the bar, which was Hasso's domain, she alone issued bills and took payment. The role of *maître d'hôtel* might traditionally be a male preserve, but she trusted nobody – not even Ulrich – to do the job. The temptations were simply too great.

Only Hasso was permitted to earn money over and above his basic wage. His new cocktail bar was an intimate area to the right of the stairs and here the dancing partners sat, modestly but cleanly dressed, in old-fashioned evening gowns and black-market nylons, smiling invitingly at the soldiers as they entered. As he had foretold, there had been no shortage of girls applying for the work.

Hasso managed the dancing partners and determined their rate, taking a percentage from both the client and the girl. It was a lucrative sideline but Viktoria did not begrudge it him, any more than she did the profits he made from marked-up bar prices. Hasso was the best friend she had. He deserved every pfennig he made.

It was rapidly apparent that the new enterprise would be a success. The select surroundings attracted the best type of officer, well-spoken, well-educated, middle-class men, who were heartily sick of mess food and could afford Café Jochum's prices. They accepted unquestioningly the unwritten conditions that drinks were only served with a meal and that payment was preferred in dollars or cigarettes.

Those two conditions were vitally important for Café Jochum. The high margins charged on food enabled them to keep up with the inflationary prices demanded on the black market. Café Jochum did not make a profit but neither was it running at a loss.

Just as crucial were the left-overs from the meals. Some of

these went to augment staff rations. But as word spread, people took to queuing at the service door, begging for food, and at night, children went through the dustbins for scraps. Soon another sub-economy evolved, in which potato parings, chicken bones and slops acquired their own values for the very poor. Even though Viktoria often gave away all her own portions of left-overs, making do with a bowl of weak potato soup and a hunk of dry bread, she felt guilty about her apparent affluence.

The café's clientèle knew nothing of this. Their stomachs full, they were hungry for female company, for a girl to dance with, to hold in their arms, to kiss and to take to bed.

Christmas drew near and with it, to everyone's relief, the weather turned unseasonably mild. Instead of snow, a light drizzle was falling when Viktoria took Lili to the Christmas Fair in the Lustgarten in the Soviet sector. It was Lili's first Christmas Fair, for none had been held since before the war, and her first taste of what life had been like before black-outs and bombs had turned Berlin into a city of darkness.

With an awe-struck expression in her big green eyes, she gazed at the Christmas tree, festooned with coloured lamps. They wandered among the few booths selling sweetmeats and baubles, unappetizing replicas of the richly iced marzipan hearts and logs essential to every traditional German Christmas; tawdry imitations of the exquisitely hand-made and painted wooden figures of angels, animals, trees and stars, glass balls and bells, toys and trinkets, which had so entranced Viktoria as a child and her children in subsequent decades, but which, to Lili, who had nothing to compare them with, had a magical quality.

Most wonderful of all, however, was the brightly lit round-about, its gaily painted horses prancing round to the cheerful blast of mechanical organ music. Lili squeezed Viktoria's hand. 'Please can I have a ride, Aunt Vicki?'

They had to queue for Lili's turn, as one had to queue for everything in Berlin, taking their place with other drably clothed, grey-faced women and children, but it was worth it to see Lili's face when she mounted the white stallion, decked out in blue, scarlet and gold. The roundabout gathered speed and Lili became little more than a blur when she passed, her thin shoulders hunched in a too tight, threadbare brown coat, her lips parted in exhilaration, her red hair streaming out behind her.

The organ gave a triumphant fanfare, the roundabout slowed down, the music died away and the riders reluctantly dismounted. A glow radiating from her normally pale cheeks, Lili gave her charge a final pat, jumped down from the platform and ran towards Viktoria. 'Oh, Aunt Vicki, that was marvellous!'

Viktoria caught her in her arms and hugged her close. She loved this child so much and there was so little she could do to show it, except send Hilde money to feed and clothe her and to work as hard as she knew how in order to provide her with a future.

Again that evening, when Viktoria returned her to the Webers, Lili begged to come and live at Café Jochum and again Viktoria had to refuse. 'It isn't long till Christmas. I'll see you again then,' she said, and with this promise Lili had to make do.

The café closed early on Christmas Eve and, while Hasso went to spend a couple of days with his sister in Wedding, Viktoria made her way to Heiligensee, laden down with bags including one containing a scrawny old goose, which Hasso had acquired for an inordinate sum on the black market. Hilde Weber exclaimed in delight when she saw it, then proudly exhibited her own showpiece – a carp, sculpted from potato. 'This year we shall have a proper Christmas!' she declared. 'And no bombs!'

Viktoria had hoped Stefan would join them for Christmas, but his duties kept him in Westerstedt. There was a letter on very poor quality paper from Monika, with PSs from the children.

Fritz had found a large pine branch, which he had planted in a pot and decorated with ornaments made from newspaper, meticulously cut and made into shapes resembling bells and stars. They stood round this improvised Christmas tree, Hilde and Fritz, Viktoria and Lili, their hands joined as they sang, 'Stille Nacht, Heilige Nacht . . .' Outside, beyond the steadily falling rain, the night was very, very still.

At Traunkirchen, Anna had lost weight and Dolfi was no longer the sturdy little fellow he had been in the summer, but once more frail and rather fretful, back to bed-wetting and prone

73

to long periods of moody silence, as he had used to be at Schlachtenhausen.

The poor quality hay crop was reaching its end and rats had got at the grain as well as stealing the eggs. The chickens were moulting and laying badly anyway, while the cattle had grown lean, their coats harsh and their milk yield decreasing. Anna and Dolfi were ekeing out an existence on potatoes and turnips. Most of their meat ration went to Wolf. Wolf had always been fed raw meat: Otto had insisted upon it.

Old Farmer Austerer arrived one crisp morning in early January, when Anna was giving Wolf his breakfast. He and his wife felt a certain responsibility towards their neighbour, trying to run the farm without a husband, for they knew what it was like to lose a loved one. Their son, Helmut, had been taken prisoner of war in 1942, since when they had heard nothing more of him.

The farmer filled his pipe with some home-grown tobacco and, after several attempts to light it, eventually puffed out a cloud of foul-smelling smoke. Then he said, 'For God's sake, Frau Feldmann,' – to the people of Traunkirchen, she would always be Farmer Feldmann's daughter – 'why don't you let that dog catch his own food? I'll warrant you've got rats enough in that barn to keep him from starving.'

'And chickens,' Anna said tartly.

Farmer Austerer looked significantly at the cattle stall that occupied half the ground floor of the farmhouse. 'Put the hens with the cows and let the dog loose in the barn.'

Dolfi hovered behind them, out of line of Wolf's vision, watching in dreadful fascination as the big dog's fangs crunched on a bone.

Farmer Austerer caught sight of him and added, 'Looks like the boy could do with some proper food.'

For days after that, Anna pondered on Farmer Austerer's words. There was another solution to their problem, of which the farmer was unaware. Buried under the cowstall was a waterproof bag containing precious stones, which Otto had brought with him from Poland. For use in an emergency, he had said. Hunger seemed like an emergency to her.

In February 1946, the Russian prosecutors presented their

74

evidence to the court at Nuremberg. They showed a captured film shot by a German film crew at Majdanek concentration camp, a gruesome documentary of the SS in its heyday, showing warehouses neatly stacked with shoes and clothes, piles of skulls and bones, and women being driven live to their graves, while guards grinned into the camera. And they called witnesses to the stand, survivors of the death camps – among them Szymon Lewinski, twenty-five years old, with a thin, pinched face, old beyond his years.

Even as he heard it, Mortimer knew he would never forget Szymon Lewinski's story: his description of the desperate conditions under which he and his family had existed in the Lublin ghetto; and the terrible night in July 1943, when SS men had burst into their room, ordering them at gunpoint through the streets to the railway station, where they had been packed into a cattle train with thousands of other Polish Jews.

During the four-day journey that followed, in airless, insanitary conditions, with no food or water, many perished. Just as Szymon Lewinski was fearing for the lives of his family, the train drew to a halt, the doors were thrown open and the inmates were ordered out. It was a pretty station, Szymon Lewinski said, painted white, with hanging baskets of flowers and light music playing. Prisoners in striped canvas suits offered them water, while a voice from a loudspeaker welcomed them to Schlachtenhausen resettlement camp.

SS guards with dogs urged the new arrivals into a long queue and slowly they made their way up a path between neatly mown lawns and herbaceous borders towards a big building bearing the sign RECEPTION. In the distance were factory buildings, from which came the din of machinery. In the other direction, tall chimneys belched forth smoke. Szymon Lewinski's father had brightened a little, muttering, 'It does not look a bad place.'

They were the last words Szymon Lewinski heard him say. An SS guard brought a stick down across his back and shouted, 'Silence!' Before Szymon Lewinski knew what was happening, he himself was seized by the shoulders, dragged out of the queue and marched off to another part of the camp. He turned his head for one more glimpse of his family: his mother and sister lifting his father from the ground.

For the next year and a half, Szymon Lewinski slept in a filthy crowded barracks and worked in a steel factory, making railway tracks and parts. Many of his fellow inmates died from starvation, maltreatment, disease and despair. Others, too weak to work, were taken away, never to be seen again.

That Szymon Lewinski survived was due not only to his stubborn, youthful resilience, but to his artistic talent. With scrap paper and pencil stubs that he found at the steel factory he sketched his surroundings: the buildings, the prisoners and their guards; concealing the results in his straw mattress. Inevitably, he was discovered, drawing an SS guard. But, instead of being angry, the SS man was flattered, seeing only what he wanted to see in the picture, mistaking the brutality Szymon Lewinski had portrayed in his features for virile power. When he showed it to his colleagues, they all wanted similar drawings of themselves.

In due course, Szymon Lewinski's ability reached the ears of the Commandant himself, who ordered the young Jew to do a portrait of his little boy. That sitting – the only time he ever saw the Commandant's family, who lived in a house outside the camp – was one of the most nerve-racking occasions in Szymon Lewinski's life. But his talent did not let him down. The picture turned out well.

By the early winter of 1944, however, the atmosphere at Schlachtenhausen had changed beyond all recognition and there was no more demand for portraits by Szymon Lewinski. He was taken from the steel factory and made to do a new job in the extermination block. Total silence reigned in the court as Szymon Lewinski described his final weeks at Schlachtenhausen.

After the gassings, Jews, wearing gas masks and rubber boots, dragged the bodies from the gas chambers into lifts which took them back up to ground level, where more Jews went through their body orifices for hidden jewels and extracted gold fillings from their teeth. Szymon Lewinski's job was to help pile these mutilated corpses onto a narrow gauge electric railway and transport them to the gas ovens in the crematoria.

Szymon Lewinski's thin fingers twitched convulsively against the side of the witness box. To begin with, he said in a voice so low it was difficult to hear, he handled the bodies carefully, saying a prayer for each one, but the SS complained he was working too slowly, his rations were cut and he was threatened with being sent 'up the chimney' himself. After a while, he learned to think of the bodies not as people but objects, closing his mind to everything except the hope that, one day, he would get his revenge.

He paused, shook his head as if to clear it of agonizing memories, then continued with his testimony. Several thousand people a day were being gassed at that time, apart from the thousands who died before reaching the gas chambers, in the medical experimental station or from the diseases which plagued the camp. And the numbers of deaths rose steadily to ten or twelve thousand a day in January 1945. Then the Russians liberated the camp and the nightmare was over.

As Mortimer wondered whether the nightmare could ever be over, the Russian prosecuting counsel said he had no further questions, while none of the defence counsel wanted to cross-examine. For a moment, Szymon Lewinski made to step down, then he turned to the judges. In a hollow whisper, he said, 'It would have been better if I had died at Schlachtenhausen. Awake or asleep, I smell the stench, I taste the rotting flesh – I see the bodies of my people. I do not know how to live with the burden of my guilt.'

In the room at the Grand Hotel, where Szymon Lewinski had been staying until he had decided upon suicide as the only release from his memories, the table and the floor were strewn with sheets of hastily executed sketches, in which the young Jew had reconstructed from memory the drawings he had produced at Schlachtenhausen. While the other journalists stared at the curtain cord by which Szymon Lewinski had hanged himself, murmuring quietly amongst themselves about the fact that the young Jew had ultimately chosen death rather than live with his self-assumed burden of guilt, whereas the Germans – the perpetrators of the evil – showed no sign of remorse, Mortimer sifted through the pictures, until, suddenly, he came upon one entitled: 'The Commandant of Schlachtenhausen'.

Such was Szymon Lewinski's talent that, despite the restrictions of drawing in black and white, he had been able to put across the grey-blond of the SS Oberfuehrer's hair, the paleness of his eyelashes, the icy blue of his eyes, the cruel thin twist to

77

his lips and the remains of a faint scar running down the man's forehead.

It was a face which was very familiar to Mortimer from the past. He left the room, found a telephone and contacted David Wunsche. 'I know the identity of the Commandant of Schlachtenhausen,' he said curtly.

Werner Kraus and Otto Tobisch had been at Nattenberg for six months. They had both lost a lot of weight but, in their different ways, they had adapted to their circumstances. Discipline and security were considerably more lax than they had been on their arrival. The Americans were bored with their duties and restless to go home. There were no chances of glory or promotion in administering a prisoner-of-war camp. Everyone knew that, sooner or later, Nattenberg would be closed down and the inmates freed.

For this reason, few tried to escape, although there was an escape committee and several unimportant prisoners had successfully got away. But to men such as Werner and Otto, the camp provided the security of anonymity.

Werner now had the task of supervising Nattenberg's potato supply. His duties included unloading the sacks of potatoes from the farmer's cart, weighing them, checking them to ensure that Potato Hansl – as he was popularly known – had not made up the weight with earth and rotten tubers, storing them, peeling them and delivering them to the kitchen for cooking. Werner always managed to keep back some to sell on the black market, which operated illicitly within the camp and on which potatoes commanded a good price, since they could be distilled into crude alcohol.

His job had an even greater benefit. Prisoners were allowed no letters or visitors, and were forbidden to listen to the radio or read newspapers. Potato Hansl acted as Werner's postman. While they were unloading the cart, Werner slid him a letter to take to Joachim Duschek's office in Munich when he went on his weekly trip to market. There, the lawyer's secretary paid him in cigarettes and gave him a reply from Joachim in Nuremberg to take back to Nattenberg, which Werner later read in the relative privacy of the latrines. For Potato Hansl, it was a much

78

more profitable trade than selling potatoes to the Americans for worthless Occupation Marks. For Werner it was a vital link with the outside world.

Joachim's letter, already a week out of date by the time it reached Werner at the end of February, brought the chilling news of Szymon Lewinski's damning evidence, his testimony to the court and the drawings he had made of Schlachtenhausen. Werner did not need to read the final paragraph to appreciate the danger to himself. 'They know the name and have an accurate picture of the Commandant, copies of which American Military Intelligence is sending out to all prisoner-of-war camps. According to the Russians, most records at Schlachtenhausen had been burned before their arrival, but I must warn you that if the Commandant is found and brought to the witness box, he may attempt to shift blame from himself by inculpating Kraus Industries.'

Werner shredded the letter and dropped the pieces into the earth closet. Then he leaned against the wooden wall of the latrine, wondering what he could do to prevent the Americans discovering the true identity of Otto Tobisch. He considered bribery, blackmail and even murder. Finally, he thought of escape.

Otto's reaction to Werner's news was unexpected. He pulled the picture of Dolfi from his pocket, stared at it and growled, 'The scum. I let him live and he betrayed me.' At first, Werner thought he was referring to his son, then he realized he meant the artist.

Otto needed no convincing as to the wisdom of escaping. The escape committee, all former Nazis, planned his get-away. One member had a brother-in-law in Munich, a printer by trade, who was also a skilled forger. It was arranged that Potato Hansl should obtain false documents from him for Otto, with money organized by Werner via Joachim Duschek. While he was waiting for the papers, Otto could hide in Potato Hansl's barn. Then, with the help of one of the organizations who were helping wanted Nazis escape through Austria, Switzerland and Italy, he should go to Egypt, South Africa or South America.

However, for a reason of which only Werner was aware, Otto adamantly refused to go abroad. First he insisted that he could hide out in the mountains near his farm in Austria, disguised as a forester. Then, convinced of the folly of this, he said that his wife's brother-in-law owned an inn in the Black Forest. Hubert Albers was sure to know of somewhere he could be concealed until the hue and cry died down and he could return home. But Werner argued that this was too near. Otto had to leave southern Germany.

Finally, a compromise was reached. At Werner's suggestion, it was decided that he should head north to Luebeck in the British zone, where Werner's brother would certainly take him on as a building labourer.

Otto saw the wisdom in this. Luebeck might be a long way from Traunkirchen, but it was not so far from his son as Cairo, Johannesburg or Buenos Aires.

Two mornings later, Werner slipped on an icy patch and dropped the bag of potatoes he was carrying. The sack split open and its contents rolled in all directions. With shouts of joy, prisoners started gathering up the potatoes, hurrying away with their unexpected windfall. Potato Hansl, who was only paid after his sacks had been weighed in the kitchen outhouse, waved his arms and shouted at the guards, 'The pigs! They're stealing my potatoes! Stop them!'

Grinning broadly at the farmer's indignation and Werner's discomfort as he struggled to get to his feet, the soldiers ambled across. Krauts stealing from Krauts. Entertainment of this sort helped to alleviate their boredom.

Nobody noticed Otto sidle along a wall, clamber into the cart and hide himself under the pile of empty sacks.

A quarter of an hour later, still grumbling loudly to the effect that all Germans and all Americans were pigs, Potato Hansl geed up his old mare and clattered through the gates of Nattenberg. Only when they were a mile down the road, did he call out, 'You all right in the back, sir?'

Dolfi fell ill. He became feverish and delirious, he would not eat and he vomited the herbal teas Anna gave him. In desperation, Anna went to the village and asked the doctor to come and examine him. But the doctor could find nothing the matter. 'Children get these funny turns,' he said. 'Keep

80

him on a milk diet for a couple of days and he should get over it.'

Indeed, Dolfi's temperature dropped the next day. Anna lit a candle at the crucifix in the kitchen and offered up a brief prayer to the Blessèd Virgin. Then she did what Farmer Austerer had recommended. She moved the chickens to the cow byre under the house and put Wolf, on a long chain, in the old barn. The dog growled menacingly as she closed the doors on him, but Anna ignored him. Otto was not here to give orders any more. From now on, Wolf must catch his own food. The meat ration was going to Dolfi.

Dolfi gradually recovered his physical strength but his nightmares grew worse. They started as soon as he got into bed, almost before he fell asleep, and they all centred around Wolf. Dolfi saw him waiting in the barn, his fangs bared and his eyes gleaming silver in the dark. He imagined a little rat scampering out of the straw, to find itself confronted by the huge dog. But, as Wolf pounced upon it, his teeth sinking into the rat's throat, his claws tearing at the flesh, there was no Otto there to lift Dolfi up and murmur endearments, no Otto to beat Wolf into submission . . .

Night after night, Dolfi woke up, his mattress wet, a scream on his lips. But the scream never came out. Terrified that his mother might somehow get in touch with his father, Dolfi always managed to stop it just in time. He could not bear that his father, the great general, should think he was a coward.

It was Farmer Austerer, lighting his foul-smelling pipe one frosty, February morning, who unwittingly gave Dolfi the idea as to how to put an end to his night-time horrors.

That night, Dolfi forced himself to stay awake until after his mother had gone to bed and he could hear her snores from the neighbouring room, then he crept downstairs to the kitchen, took a box of matches from beside the kitchen range, let himself into the cow byre and out into the farmyard.

There was a bright moon and the old barn was silhouetted black against the sky, logs and piles of old sacking stacked under the shelter of its overhanging roof. His heart pounding so loudly that it seemed to echo across the valley, Dolfi approached the sacks, crouched down and struck his first match. The sacking glowed red, fizzled and died out. He tried again. Inside the barn, Wolf growled.

Remembering how his mother lit the kitchen stove, Dolfi gathered together some wood shavings, bits of bark and pieces of paper, and lit his third match. For a long time, the sacking seemed undecided as to whether it would catch light or not, but it was dry, like the logs around it. Dolfi drew back across the yard to the lee of the house and watched fingers of flames leap to the firewood, then creep up the wooden walls of the barn. Eerie shadows danced out towards him and the heat of the fire warmed his cold fingers and cheeks.

Sparks caught hold of the dry straw and hay in the barn, reaching up towards the loft where the grain was stored. Wolf let out a howl and jumped up at the doors but, old though they were, they held fast.

With a sudden whoosh, the whole barn ignited, sending a funnel of flame up through the tarpaulin covered hole in the roof. Wolf screamed, a piercing shriek that rent the night and had Anna rushing from her bed to the window. But, by the time she arrived downstairs, Dolfi had slipped back through the cow byre, into the kitchen and up to his room. And Wolf was a mound of charred, smouldering flesh.

That morning and for all the mornings that followed, Dolfi's mattress was dry, but Anna was too preoccupied with the disaster of losing her barn with its precious store of grain and hay to notice.

One dark night, she made her own nocturnal excursion – to the cow stall. There, by the light of an oil lamp, with the cows watching her curiously, she dug deep down into the earthen floor and eventually retrieved the waterproof bag Otto had buried. Bigger than she remembered, it contained not only the small pouch of jewels, but some papers. She was not interested in papers, so she put them back in their hiding place and covered them again with earth. When the cattle had trodden the floor down, there would be no sign of her excavation.

82

Up in her bedroom, she let the precious stones slide through her fingers. These were riches beyond her wildest imaginings. Now she had them, she and Dolfi would not starve. She concealed the bag under her mattress.

Otto Tobisch's absence was noticed at roll-call on the evening of his disappearance but, although the prisoners were made to stand to attention for three hours on the parade ground and forgo supper as punishment, nobody volunteered any information as to what had happened to him. Several days later, they had to endure another protracted roll-call, while American Military Police walked up and down their ranks, comparing their faces to a photographic copy of a drawing. One or two were taken for interrogation, but they all returned to their barracks during the evening. Clearly, whoever the MPs were looking for was not at Nattenberg.

Otto, learning of both these events from Potato Hansl, felt increasingly confident of his chances of avoiding detection. The American security service lacked the dedication of the Gestapo. With his new papers and certain changes to his appearance, he would never be identified.

Otto was by nature a hirsute man, with a mat of grey-blond hair on his chest and shoulders, and a plentiful head of hair which had needed frequent cutting in the past. Now he let it grow, as he did his beard and moustache. In a painful operation with a branding iron, the farmer burned away the SS tattoo mark under his left armpit showing his blood group. Even if the scar never completely disappeared, it would soon be hidden by body hair.

Finally, Otto ordered Potato Hansl to punch him several times on the face. The results were excellent. Otto's left cheekbone and nose were broken. When they mended, they would totally alter the shape of his face. The vertical scar on his forehead would no longer be a striking feature. With a pair of spectacles, his disguise would be complete.

Chapter 5

It had been a long journey from North Africa for Hans Koenig, where he had been taken prisoner in 1942 by the British. The last three years had been spent in England, first in a prisoner-of-war camp, then as a land worker in Worcestershire. Had it not been for his family, he would have been happy to remain at Pershore. People had treated him well and, once his English had improved, he had grown to feel almost at home.

He had naively imagined that, once back in Germany, he would be able to travel immediately to Fuerstenmark. Nothing was further from the truth. Since his arrival in early January, he had spent over two months in transit camps, waiting for a travel permit to cross the border into the Soviet zone.

The 'green border' local people called it. Winston Churchill, the former British Prime Minister, gave it a more explicit title. On 5 March 1946, in a speech at Westminster College, Fulton, Missouri, and widely reported in the international press, he expressed his dismay at the behaviour of the Soviet Union in Occupied Europe, mourning that 'this is certainly not the liberated Europe we fought to build up,' and going on to say, 'an iron curtain has descended across the Continent'.

It was a border patrolled by tanks and manned by armed Soviet guards, who shot on sight, whose prisoners, if they were fortunate enough to live, were sent to labour camps in the far freezing wastes of the Soviet Union. Yet crossing it was a risk Hans decided to take.

He escaped from the transit camp and crossed the border one cold, frosty night, navigating by the stars, until he was certain he was well inside the Soviet zone. But it was six weeks before he reached Prenzlau and by then the weather had deteriorated considerably. For the last twenty miles, snow beat horizontally

84

across the flat countryside, stinging his face and buffeting his gaunt figure.

It was dusk when he reached Fuerstenmark. The village street appeared deserted, except for a cat which slunk away at his approach and a chained dog that barked, then fell suddenly silent. Then there was the sound of steel-tipped boots on the cobbles, the familiar noise of rifles being cocked, a spotlight shone in his face and a foreign voice shouted, 'Hands up!'

Hans obeyed. Two Russian soldiers pushed him roughly against a wall, while a third searched him expertly for weapons, then extricated his papers from his breast pocket. He studied them briefly, issued a guttural command, and Hans was frog-marched towards the castle. As they passed the parsonage, he gazed longingly towards its shuttered windows.

Tanks guarded the gateway to the castle. Hans was taken past them through the courtyard and into the castle. A heavy door was unlocked and his guards propelled him down stone steps. Another door clanked open. Hans was pushed through it and fell headlong onto the floor. Behind him, the door was locked. He spent that night in a dark, damp dungeon, shivering from cold and exhaustion, with fear gnawing at his heart.

At last, the door opened again and Hans was taken upstairs, through the raftered, galleried hall, into a study, where a Russian officer sat esconced behind a magnificent, leather-covered desk under a portrait of Stalin. Standing, with a table light glaring in his eyes, Hans attempted to answer as best he could the questions hurled at him through an interpreter. Questions about his family, his education, his training, his political allegiances, his career, his army service, his time as a prisoner of war.

Hans stammered his replies. He had been brought up in Fuerstenmark. His only ambition ever had been to be a teacher. He had never been a Nazi. He had been conscripted into the army. He had served in North Africa, until he had been taken prisoner by the British. He had run away from the transit camp before being properly discharged. He was prepared to do anything, provided he could be reunited with his family again . . .

On and on, the questions went, until his mind reeled and his body, already weak, felt as if it must collapse. And then, just when he knew he could take no more, the officer made a terse statement. 'You are permitted to rejoin your family,' the interpreter translated. 'However, your teaching qualifications are now invalid. You will work as an agricultural labourer.'

It was dusk again when he was let out of the castle. Stumbling up to the parsonage door, he leaned against the wall and rapped feebly. After a while, a voice called, 'Who's there?' Dimly, Hans recognized it as his father's.

'It's me – Hans.'

There was a rattle of chains and the door opened a crack. Hans heard a gasp and felt a hand clutch at his arm to steady him. 'Hans! Hans, dear boy . . .' His father led him to a chair and sat him down, then called out, 'Gerda! Monika! Hans is here!'

There were footsteps on the stone flagging. Hans opened his eyes to find a group of people staring at him: his father, smaller and greyer than Hans remembered, in his threadbare cleric's suit; his mother, her white hair tied back in a bun, wringing her hands in her apron; Monika, her mouth open in shock; and a little girl, presumably Senta, gazing at him from big eyes.

Then, hurtling downstairs with a whooping battle-cry, came a small boy in leather shorts, his arm outstretched and in his hand, a toy, wooden gun. Charging past the others, he drew to a halt in front of Hans, lunged his weapon towards him and shouted, 'Hands up!'

For a moment there was silence, then Gerda screamed, Senta burst into tears and Arthur leaped forward and seized the child by the shoulders, dragging him away. 'Heini, that's your father!'

Without letting go his gun, Heini stared at Hans from disdainful grey eyes and announced, 'That isn't my father. My father is a soldier.' Then he turned on his heel and marched back upstairs.

The world blacked out and Hans keeled over onto the floor.

The following morning, after a long sleep, a hot bath and a shave, Hans looked more like his old self, but the differences which separated him from his family were more than skin-deep, as became apparent when they met together for the midday meal.

None of them could bring themselves to ask Hans about his

war and Hans could not bring himself to tell them, knowing it would be as difficult for them to visualize the battlefields of North Africa, followed by three years in England, as it was for him to imagine spending the last seven years in Fuerstenmark.

Monika was strained, Heini glowered sulkily, while Senta picked nervously at her food. Gerda piled his plate high with potatoes and kept saying fondly how glad they were to have him back, but it was left to the pastor to explain the realities of village life.

Life was growing progressively harder at Fuerstenmark, although it was better than in the towns, where disease was rife and rations in even shorter supply. The land was frozen hard and there were no gleanings from the fields. Like the rest of the village, except for those who had food hoarded away, the Koenigs were utterly dependent upon rations.

Still the refugees poured over the border and a special camp had been set up to house them. Arthur and Gerda spent most of their days there, trying to ease conditions, but this did not improve their status so far as rations were concerned. Monika fared slightly better. She now had a clerical job working for the Russians, which entitled her to a higher ration grade.

When the meal was over, both children quickly left the room. As always, when she was upset or frightened, Senta went to find her cat Mimi. Although the large tabby could not talk, she seemed to understand Senta's feelings.

Heini went to see Mischa, who was pleased to have the tedium of his sentry duty relieved by a visit from his young friend. Heini described his charge with gun, saying in a tone of utter contempt, 'No wonder we lost the war, if that's the kind of soldiers we had. I'm going to be in the Red Army when I grow up.' Mischa seemed to get the gist of Heini's words.

That night, Gerda tactfully arranged mattresses for Heini and Senta to sleep with her and Arthur, and the whole family went to bed early. As Hans watched Monika undressing and saw for the first time in nearly five years her big firm breasts and generous hips, he felt a stirring of the old familiar desire. He caressed her for a while, then waves of tiredness swept over him and, before he knew it, he was asleep.

Monika lay awake beside him, trying to adjust to the fact that

87

this gaunt stranger was her husband returned, wondering how they would get on together, worrying about what would happen if he found out about Gustav Matzke. Fuerstenmark was such a small community that it was inevitable the two men must soon meet. If Gustav should choose to brag . . .

Next day, Hans started his new job. The work he was doing was not dissimilar to that which he had been doing in Pershore: repairing roofs and cattlesheds, felling trees and mending fences neglected during the war. Working on the land, he soon discovered, had certain advantages. Grain and root vegetables, salt and animal fodder were stored in barns around the estate and, although these were guarded by Red Army soldiers, Hans soon learned that it was possible to smuggle small quantities of them out, concealed about his person. Grain could be hidden in his oversized boots. Potatoes and turnips could be concealed inside the sacking he wore under his jacket. Fresh eggs could be brought home in his pockets.

Within a few weeks, Hans's health was fully recovered and he was able to satisfy all his and Monika's longings in an intense session of love-making. By then, Gustav Matzke had stopped Monika in the village street, the first time they had spoken since that disastrous visit to Berlin. 'Don't worry, girl,' he had said, 'I won't tell your husband about our little fling. But I'm afraid I won't be able to take you with me next time I go to Berlin. Can't risk attracting the attention of the Russians . . .'

Monika nodded coolly, thankful that, for whatever reason, her shameful secret was safe.

Gradually, Hans seemed to settle into his new existence. Arthur and Gerda were disappointed their son could not have his old position back, but they consoled themselves with the thought that there was nothing shameful in working on the land. Senta realized that she had nothing to fear from her father. She and Mimi took to waiting for him in the evening, keeping him company as he trudged home. Even Heini's resentment seemed to fade.

To none of them, however, could Hans bare his troubled soul: his bitterness at the Russian occupation of his village; the omnipresence of Red Army tanks and soldiers; his distaste at having to share his home with strangers and the marital bedroom with his children; and, above all, the humiliation he felt at the loss of his job.

Strangely, it was Guenther Rauch who best understood Hans's inner turmoil. His first reaction to Hans was the antipathy he felt towards all Germans who had gone along with the Nazis. But the thing Guenther missed most in Fuerstenmark was debate with people of his own age, and since he and Hans lived in the same house, it was inevitable that the initial barriers between them should fall.

It was forbidden for civilians to own wireless sets. Newspapers contained little more than propaganda. Books were impossible to buy and Guenther had soon read the pastor's small library. He turned towards Hans, a former schoolteacher, for intellectual stimulus.

Chess was the pastime which drew them together. After Hans had finished work and Guenther had finished marking homework, they met in Guenther's room over the chessboard. Neither were skilled players, but that did not matter. Indeed, frequently not a single chessman moved throughout the evening, so engrossed did the two men become in their conversation.

'Would you like to teach again?' Guenther asked Hans, a month or so after his return.

'Of course I would.'

'There is no reason why you shouldn't. There is a shortage of teachers in the Soviet zone. Unlike the Americans, the Russians aren't making life difficult for former Nazis who can be of use to the State.'

'I was never a Nazi Party member.'

'You must have been a member of the Nazi Teachers' Association?'

'If I hadn't joined, I'd have lost my job.'

'You were in the army. You swore an oath of allegiance to Hitler.'

'Again, I had no choice. To have disobeyed would have meant being court-martialled, imprisoned or even shot.'

'Did you never consider the rightfulness of what you were doing?'

Hans looked at him with genuine perplexity. 'It's difficult

to explain. At the time, I thought I was doing the right thing. Since then, I realize that we were all badly misled . . .'

Hans Koenig was typical of many Germans, Guenther reflected, in that he had been brought up in the concept of total subservience to political authority, accepting unquestioningly everything he was told. He had never been a convinced Nazi, but under Guenther's instruction, he might become a convinced socialist. He wiped a drip from the end of his long nose with the back of his hand, and asked, 'Would you like to learn Russian? Would you be interested in learning about Marxism?'

'Yes, I should.' Hans paused, then added hesitantly, 'That is, if you would be willing to teach me.'

Guenther found a grubby piece of rag and blew his nose. 'Of course. As well as playing chess, we'll read *Das Kapital* together – in Russian! What interesting discussions we'll be able to have!'

The very next evening, Hans had his first Russian lesson.

On Friday, Guenther compiled his weekly information report for the local NKVD officer. Farmer Matzke, he wrote, was still selling half the produce from his smallholding into the Berlin black market. 'Carpenter' Warrink had recently been heard boasting that he had been in the SS during the war. Grete Kriege had a radio hidden in her attic on which she and her daughter listened to the BBC World Service. He also included a brief account of his conversation with Hans Koenig. Guenther did not enjoy informing on his fellow villagers, but it was the only way he could prove his loyalty to the State – and, in due course, hopefully obtain promotion.

Nowhere were the implications of the 'iron curtain' more obvious than in Berlin, which was at the centre of a controversy regarding the future of the Social Democratic Party.

Two political parties were emerging to the fore in the Western zones: the Christian Democratic Union, the CDU, and the Social Democratic Party, the SPD. The CDU was led by the former Roman Catholic Lord Mayor of Cologne, Konrad Adenauer. The SPD, however, had two contenders for power. One was Kurt Schumacher, who was based in Hanover; the other Otto Grotewohl, based in the Soviet sector of Berlin. Grotewohl wanted a merger of the SPD with the KPD, the

German Communist Party – an idea to which Schumacher was utterly opposed. It was finally decided that a referendum should be held among SPD members to decide the issue.

Mortimer returned to Berlin for the referendum being held on Sunday 31 March and, on the Saturday evening, paid his first visit to Café Jochum since the previous autumn. For a moment, he stood, surveying the scene: a quartet playing American dance music; a cocktail bar, with several attractive girls clustered round a table, smiling invitingly at him; Hasso, dispensing drinks; Viktoria, even thinner than he remembered her, in a definitely prewar costume, talking to two American officers.

Mortimer gave a wry grin and made his way across to her. 'Do you have a table free for this evening?'

Recognizing his voice, she spun on her heel. 'Mortimer!'

'There have been changes here during my absence.'

'One has to move with the times.' There was a defensive edge to her voice. 'Above all, one has to survive.'

The quartet stopped playing and an attractive young girl stepped on to the podium. Mortimer expected her to churn out the normal repertoire of popular songs, but he was in for a surprise. Singing in English and German, Lina Paff took the referendum as her theme for the evening and missed no opportunity to vilify the Russians. It was extremely clever satire. 'She's very good,' he whispered to Viktoria.

'Cabaret is her way of alerting people to the dangers of Communism. In fact, it's the only way so long as the Russians continue to control broadcasting and newspapers in Berlin.' Viktoria looked at him angrily. 'When *will* the British and Americans stop being so afraid of upsetting the Russians and do more to help us?'

He sympathized with her, but his sympathy did not extend to her entire nation. 'Why should we risk provoking another war just to help you Germans?'

Viktoria looked him in the eye. 'For your own sakes, as well as ours. The Soviet Union is a more formidable power than Nazi Germany ever was.'

The following day, the referendum took place. Despite Viktoria's comments about the Western Allies' unwillingness to help Berliners, polling stations in the Western sectors were heavily guarded by British and American soldiers to prevent Russian intimidation, and SPD members like Hasso were able to cast their vote unmolested.

It was a different story in the Soviet sector, as Mortimer discovered. At the last moment, the Russians had banned the ballot and, in the few districts which defied the ban, polling stations were closed after an hour. 'Because the regulations have not been complied with,' an armed Russian soldier in Friedrichshain informed him brusquely, when Mortimer persisted in wanting to know why the ballot box was being removed. Some Russian Military Policemen converged threateningly upon him and Mortimer decided discretion was the better part of valour. It was not unheard of for American journalists to be arrested in the Soviet sector. He beat a hasty retreat, back past the sign which read: START OF THE DEMOCRATIC SECTOR OF BERLIN.

When the results from the Western sectors were announced, it transpired that 82 per cent of the SPD members who had gone to the polls had voted against a merger with the KPD. There was a triumphant atmosphere in Café Jochum that evening.

Hasso said, 'You must agree, Herr Allen, there can be no clearer indication that "Red Berlin" wants nothing to do with Red Moscow.'

Viktoria, too, was very relieved, but she warned Mortimer, 'We still have a long battle ahead of us. Stalin won't give up this easily.'

If only they had shown this fighting spirit towards Hitler, Mortimer reflected. But at least they were determined not to make the same mistake twice. When he left Café Jochum, he kissed Viktoria on the cheek. She took the gesture for what it was: an apology for his past mistrust, a sign of an old friendship revived and admiration for her courage.

On 21 April, at an impressive ceremony in East Berlin, the formation of a new party was announced with Otto Grotewohl as its leader, comprising both the KPD and the SPD, and called the SED – the Socialist Unity Party.

Socialists in the Western zones, including the Western sectors of Berlin, however, refused to recognize the SED and retained their old identity as the SPD, with Kurt Schumacher as their now undisputed leader. Like Germany itself, the Social Democrats were a party divided by an iron curtain.

On May Day, the entire village of Fuerstenmark lined the main street to watch a parade of Russian tanks, Russian armoured cars, Russian artillery, Russian cavalry and Russian infantry. That evening, everyone attended an open-air ceremony in the castle courtyard, during which the Russian commander gave a speech, describing the dreadful conditions still pertaining in other parts of Germany and extolling the benefits of living in a socialist society. Thanks to Guenther Rauch's tutellage, Hans was now sufficiently fluent in Russian not to need to listen to the German translation.

'This alliance between the SPD and the KPD is a good thing,' Guenther said, when the applause had died down. 'It provides a firm basis from which to fight capitalist influences and to work towards peace and unity.'

Hans agreed, adding in a low voice, 'Furthermore, if the Russians were after absolute control of Germany, they wouldn't allow Grotewohl – a German – to lead the new party.'

He and Guenther had spent many evenings debating Marx's theory of dialectical materialism and its effects upon a new socialist Germany. He did not fully understand everything he had learned, but it had been sufficient to get him accepted by the SPD, which meant he was now a member of the SED. With Guenther's help, he was confident that he might yet be permitted to go on a retraining course and become reinstated as a teacher.

Back at Nuremberg, Mortimer met Richard Holtom, the son of an old friend who ran a small newspaper group in the south of England. Richard was with British Military Intelligence, in Nuremberg to give evidence about German Military Intelligence during the war. For a while they discussed the trial, then went on to chat about wider implications of the Occupation.

'Do you remember my brother Graham?' Richard asked. 'Used to edit the *Brighton Chronicle*. He's working now for Information Services Control in Hamburg – you know, interrogating would-be press barons to make sure licences are only given to non-Nazis, that sort of thing.'

Mortimer became instantly alert. 'He couldn't do with another member of staff, by any chance?'

Richard laughed. 'Surely you're not looking for a job?'

'No, but I have a friend who is ideally suited for that kind of work.'

'Doesn't speak German, does he? Poor old Graham is always bemoaning the difficulty of finding an interpreter he can trust.'

'He is German.' Mortimer told him about Stefan, finishing with a description of the work he was doing at Westerstedt.

Richard sighed. 'Sometimes I'm surprised we won the war, the number of incompetents there are in high places. Graham's been agitating for months for someone like your chum to help him, but the powers-that-be say such people don't exist. I'll get in touch with Graham and tell him to pull a few strings. Of course Jochum will have to attend an interview, but it should just be a formality. ISC has high priority.'

Wearing a pair of steel-rimmed spectacles, one of Potato Hansl's old suits and a stout pair of boots, Otto Tobisch set off on his journey north. His bruised face had healed and set in its new shape, his beard and moustache had attained a reasonable growth and his hair hung shaggily to his ears. His identity card and ration book showed him to be Alfred Tobler, aged fifty-three, a butcher by trade, born in Berlin-Pankow, while a British-issued denazification certification – a genuine document, with the details falsely completed, acquired at great cost on the black market – proclaimed him to be free of any Nazi connections.

Lacking the necessary permits to travel by train, Otto went on foot, keeping to minor roads, sleeping in barns or under hedges, inconspicuous among the refugees and displaced persons still trudging across the country. Most of his food was obtained by breaking into farmhouses at the dead of night, grabbing as much as he could and making off into the darkness before the terrified occupants raised the alarm. He made rapid progress, avoiding big towns, particularly Nuremberg, and within three weeks he was near the border between the American and British zones.

He bought a newspaper and peered at it through the distorting lenses of his spectacles. His old face stared back at him under the headline: WANTED – THE SLAUGHTERER OF SCHLACHTENHAUSEN. Yet nobody he met so much as cast a curious glance in his direction. Certainly no one in authority stopped him and asked to see his papers. That night, under cover of darkness, he crept stealthily through thickly wooded country into the British zone.

Three American Military Policemen in distinctive white helmets and an army officer jolted up the stony mountain track in a jeep to the Feldmann farm above Traunkirchen. While two MPs searched the house, the army officer, who spoke German and gave his name as Major Wunsche, ordered Anna into the kitchen. Then, while Dolfi remained in the yard, the third MP found a pencil and opened his notebook, and the Major started his interrogation.

It went on for hours. He told Anna horrific stories about things which were supposed to have taken place at Schlachtenhausen. He hurled questions at her about the running of the camp. He tried to make her confess that she had helped Otto with his work. Again and again, Anna vowed that she had known nothing of Otto's work, that she had never even been allowed inside the camp, that she had had no idea the prisoners were being sent to their death. If she had known what was happening, she cried, she would never have stayed at Schlachtenhausen.

Major Wunsche glanced at his colleague. It would require a very clever person indeed to extricate themself from the tangled web of his questioning and it was clear that intelligence did not rate high on the list of Anna Tobisch's personal attributes. How else could the woman have spent four years at Schlachtenhausen without realizing it was a death camp?

At this moment, the other policemen returned without having found any trace of Otto on the farm. 'Do you want to take her with us?' one of them asked in English.

Major Wunsche shook his head. There was no point in arresting Anna Tobisch. Much better to leave her at liberty, in the hope that Otto would, one day, return. He stood up and told her, 'That is all, except to say that if your husband comes back, you must tell us immediately.'

On his way back to the jeep, he took another look at Dolfi. The boy stared back at him from white-lashed, pale blue eyes, then dropped his gaze. With an unexpected feeling of compassion, David Wunsche wondered what the future held for the son of the Slaughterer of Schlachtenhausen.

When the MPs had gone, Anna went up to the bedroom and sat down heavily on the bed. A death camp. All those people had been going to their death. And her husband had given the orders. She shook her head uncomprehendingly. The American could not have been telling the truth. She had been married to Otto for twenty years. She knew him. He had been a great general, a kind husband and a doting father.

Slowly, her mind moved forwards. Otto was also an intelligent man. He must know that the Americans were looking for him. He would never come back to Traunkirchen.

Dolfi appeared at her side. 'Mummy, why did the Americans come here?'

She could not repeat what they had said, but she had to prepare him for never seeing his father again. She put her arms round his shoulders and held him to her. 'They came to tell me that they believe your Daddy is dead.'

Later, when Dolfi had overcome his shock and gone back out into the sunshine, Anna looked under the mattress where she kept the little pouch of jewels. It was still there. But what use was it to her? She stared out of the window at her lean cattle grazing in the paddock and her scraggy chickens pecking for grain in the blackened remains of the barn. She could not go into the village and exchange a diamond for food. Possibly in Salzburg there was someone who would buy the precious stones from her. But they might easily inform the police and then she would be arrested. Everything she did now would be suspect.

Reinhild Kraus's pregnancy was not easy. Although Norbert's workforce completed the hundred prefabs within the strict financial conditions of the British Government contract and made a small profit, the standard of living in the Kraus household improved little. The profit was ploughed straight back into the next construction project.

Norbert paid little attention to Reinhild's state of mind – or health. He was preoccupied with his work and was not at home when her labour pains commenced, one sunny morning at the beginning of May. Instead, he was watching the walls going up on his latest site of prefabricated houses, in the company of a man called Alfred Tobler.

Not for a moment was Norbert taken in by Tobler's cock-and-bull story of having fled south from Berlin in the last weeks of the war and being wrongfully arrested as an escaped prisoner of war. He had met enough men of Tobler's type to recognize a former SS man when he saw one. For all his new identity, Tobler was clearly a man on the run. But that thought did not trouble Norbert.

While they were talking, an argument broke out among a gang of builders putting the asbestos roof on a nearly completed house, the kind of stormy exchange that took place all the time among men who were ill-trained, underfed and working under constant pressure. Tobler stood for a moment, studying the situation, then marched across the site and issued a few, terse orders. The builders stopped arguing and hurriedly did as they were told. Norbert nodded appreciatively. Tobler would make an excellent foreman.

He arrived home at sundown to find the house in a considerable state of excitement. One of his neighbours greeted him at the door, wiping her hands in her apron, calling, 'Herr Kraus! Your wife's had her baby!'

Norbert stopped and lit a precious cigarette to give himself time to adjust.

'She had a dreadful time of it, poor dear,' the neighbour went on. 'She was in labour for hours. We thought the baby was never coming. But who could blame him, poor little chap, coming into this world . . .'

Norbert inhaled deeply on his cigarette, then resolutely entered the house, to look at the child he had never wanted.

In June, Guenther Rauch's intercessions with the Soviet authorities on Hans's behalf prevailed and Hans was summoned to an interview at the Marx-Engels College in Leipzig. It was a gruelling experience before a stern-faced committee, who subjected him to a long and thorough interrogation.

When the questioning had finished, the chairman stated, 'You must realize that teachers in our new Germany will be more than teachers, Comrade Koenig. They will be leaders, educating their pupils into becoming physically and intellectually healthy men and women, so that they can participate usefully in service to the State.'

He paused significantly, then continued, 'If you become a teacher again, you, too, will have to accept that your responsibilities to your country must come before all other considerations – including your relationships with your family and friends. If you should find their views threatening State security, it will be your duty to report them. Do you understand?'

Hans understood only too well. Under the Nazis, neighbours had been encouraged to inform on neighbours, and children to inform on parents and teachers. Now the same was happening under the Communists. The new society was pandering to all the vices of the old. Hans did not like it but if it was a condition for becoming a teacher again, he knew he had to accept it.

'Your father is a pastor, your wife has family in the West.' The only woman on the committee spoke grimly. 'Will you admit the possibility that you might find yourself torn between divided loyalties?'

Hans took a deep breath and replied, 'My first loyalty will always be to the State.'

A fortnight after his return to Fuerstenmark, a letter arrived, informing him that he had been accepted for a teacher retraining course starting in September.

Major Graham Holtom was in his early thirties, stocky and sandy-haired like his younger brother Richard. He took his position as Press Control Officer for Information Services Control in Hamburg extremely seriously. He believed that a free press should also be a responsible press, which ensured that its articles were accurately researched and truthfully reported, and he was determined that any new German papers formed under his authority would comply to his strict principles.

However, apart from *Die Welt* which attempted to follow the tradition of the London *Times*, and would soon be selling a million copies a day, such other papers as had been licensed were poorly written and badly produced, even allowing for the severe shortage of newsprint.

Major Holtom himself was hampered in his work by a certain suspicion regarding some of the interpreters on whom he had to rely, several of whom were of German-Jewish extraction and were, he feared, motivated more by a lust for revenge than a sense of fair play. The difficult business of deciding who had or had not been a Nazi should not, he thought, be left in their hands.

After an hour or so talking to Stefan Jochum, he knew him to be the assistant he was looking for. In addition to Richard's recommendation, Stefan's Rhodes Scholarship, his resistance to Hitler, his wartime work for the Political Warfare Executive, his friendship with Mortimer Allen and his job with the Control Commission at Westerstedt were all impeccable qualifications. He was articulate and almost transparently honest. Because he had been away from Germany, he could view events more clearly than other Germans. Most important of all, he wasn't weighed down by feelings of apathy or guilt. Not a man normally given to high-flown phrases, Graham Holtom found himself thinking of Stefan Jochum as 'the true German conscience'.

A week later, Stefan was settled in Hamburg, in a barracks that had previously been apartment blocks, from which the former residents had been evicted. His room was hardly luxurious, but it was comfortably furnished. Early each morning, a driver collected him and took him to the office by car. The working day passed swiftly, as Stefan immersed himself in work which interested him, in the company of a man whom he found very congenial. At last, he was doing something useful, in an area he understood.

Alfred Tobler found himself a room in Luebeck old town and settled down with the minimum of fuss, rapidly taking over many of the jobs which had, until then, required Norbert's almost constant presence on the building sites. He not only commanded instant respect from the workforce but also improved their productivity. As one of the builders confided to Norbert, 'He's a military man. We know where we are with him.'

Tobler was not a sociable person. He appeared neither to have nor want any friends, and Norbert was therefore very surprised when his new foreman arrived at the prefab one Sunday morning not long after the baby's birth, asking if he could see him. To Norbert's even greater surprise, he took Tristan from his cot and held him in his arms with great tenderness. It was the very last thing Norbert would have expected.

Sensing Norbert's incredulous stare, Tobler handed the child back to Reinhild, coughed to cover his embarrassment and explained, 'He reminds me of when my own son was a baby.'

'Where's your son now?' Reinhild asked.

Tobler gave that familiar shrug which people gave when they did not know whether those dearest to them were dead or alive and Norbert could only assume that, since Tobler was no spring chicken, his son must have been lost in combat. Feeling an unexpected sympathy, he offered his foreman a cup of coffee. But Tobler refused and, with one last look at Tristan, departed.

Although Norbert invited him to the christening, upon which Reinhild insisted, Tobler did not attend. It was an acute longing for Adolf which had drawn him to the newborn baby, not a desire to become part of Norbert Kraus's social circle, with all the attendant risks of discovery.

Major Peter Graves, however, not only came to the christening but also agreed to be Tristan's godfather. Over the months, he had developed an almost paternalistic feeling towards Norbert, which he explained to himself as a need to 'help these Germans to help themselves'. After the church ceremony, the guests returned to Norbert's house, where the Major had very generously provided the ingredients for a cold buffet, as well as a crate of vintage Rhenish *Sekt* to, as he said, 'wet the baby's head'.

When the other guests had departed and Reinhild was putting Tristan to bed, Norbert accompanied the Major to his car. They stood for a moment in silence, smoking cigars Major Graves had brought with him, then Norbert asked, 'Could I come and see you tomorrow to discuss what I want to do next?'

Major Graves exhaled a cloud of blue smoke. 'Why wait until tomorrow? Now your son's born, I imagine you want to expand your activities.'

Never had Norbert been more aware of the tightrope he was

walking, but he took a deep breath and told Major Graves about Landgut, emphasizing that the company had nothing to do with Kraus Industries and had been funded by money left by his great-grandfather. He said nothing about Werner's part in it.

When he had finished, Major Graves rubbed his chin thoughtfully between his forefinger and thumb. 'Hmm, provided you can get hold of the title deeds, there's no reason why you shouldn't redevelop these properties – apart from finance – and that shouldn't present too much of a problem.'

'The deeds are in Switzerland.'

To his surprise, the Major laughed. 'Well, that's good news! I was afraid you were going to tell me they'd been lost in an air raid! Well, call in at my office tomorrow afternoon and we'll get a letter off to Switzerland, asking them to send the deeds up here to be notarized and so on. Then I suggest you make a survey. Decide where you want to start. I'll get train tickets and a travel pass for you.'

Scarcely able to believe his good fortune, Norbert reached out and took the Major's hand in his. 'Thank you, sir. Thank you for giving me a chance.'

Major Graves winced at the powerful handshake and said gruffly, 'Just make sure you don't betray my faith, Norbert.'

Reinhild raised no objections to Norbert going away. Her world revolved around Tristan. She could think and talk of nothing else except the baby. So, with a sense of freedom and adventure, secure in the knowledge that Alfred Tobler would keep the workforce in order during his absence, Norbert embarked upon his tour of the ruined cities of northern Germany.

He started in Hamburg and for three days, trudged the city, identifying sites acquired by Landgut during the war: a parade of former shops in the old town; a couple of acres of rubble in the suburb of Eppendorf; more in Hamm, Barmbek and Eilbek; and a large, elegant villa set in spacious grounds overlooking the Binnenalster. Astonishingly, this latter had escaped the worst of the bombing, but it had been requisitioned by the British Army and offered no shelter for the night. Norbert had to do the same as every other stranger: rent a space to sleep on the concourse of the railway station.

101

Cologne, Duesseldorf and Essen were as bad, except that here Norbert was treading the streets of towns in which he had spent his childhood. In Essen, he made his way up the road into the low hills overlooking the town, to the ugly red brick and stucco mansion that had been the Kraus family seat since the 1880s. Now, British soldiers guarded the gates, the Union Jack flew from the flagpole and British Army vehicles were parked in the courtyard. From an open window came the sound of a gramophone and Vera Lynn's voice singing 'We'll meet again'.

Norbert turned his back on it. Although it was his childhood home, he had never liked the 'Fortress'. It was a cold and cheerless building, representing money and the very worst in taste. The British were welcome to it. He trudged back down the hill towards the city, the railway station and the train back to Hamburg. There were no fortunes to be made in the Ruhr. Of all the cities he had visited, Hamburg was the most promising. It was there, he decided, that Landgut would commence its operations.

Chapter 6

A clerk from the Liegnitzer Bank arrived in Luebeck with a bulging briefcase containing the deeds of all the properties owned by Landgut AG, together with documents proving that Norbert was authorized to act on the company's behalf. Norbert took them to an English lawyer, who presented them to the Control Commission for approval and Norbert's title was eventually agreed.

Major Graves gave Norbert considerable help in putting together the proposal to the Control Council in Hamburg and, at the end of July, the Control Commission approved Norbert's proposal to build several apartment blocks at Eppendorf, as well as arranging a loan on behalf of Hamburg City Council to finance the operation. Then Norbert announced to Reinhild that he would be moving to Hamburg.

'You're not going without us?' she asked. 'What will I tell my friends?'

He had anticipated this reaction. 'Tell them that it wouldn't be fair to expect Tristan to live in a hut, which is what I shall be doing.'

Mollified, Reinhild said, 'But when your flats are built, we'll join you.'

Norbert grunted non-committally. He intended to delay that moment for as long as possible.

Alfred Tobler seemed more dismayed than Reinhild at the prospect of his prolonged absence, expressing misgivings at having to deal direct with the British and confirming Norbert's suspicions that his foreman had a dark secret in his past. After deliberation, Norbert decided that the time was probably right in any case to take on an assistant or a secretary. Already there was more paperwork than he could cope with and when Hamburg got under way, there would be even more.

Replies flooded in to the advertisement he placed in the newspaper, one of which was from a former Kraus employee now living in Luebeck, a woman in her early thirties, Hannelore Hahn.

She turned out to be a rather forbidding-looking spinster, with hair dragged back in a severe bun and wearing thick-lensed spectacles. After leaving school, she had started work at Kraushaven, where she had developed a strong sense of loyalty for the Kraus family. When the ship yard had been forced to close, she had voluntarily moved to Essen, where she had stayed until the end of the war, at which point she had moved back to her old home in Luebeck. She could type, take shorthand, do book-keeping, and gave the immediate impression of ruthless efficiency. Norbert did not actually decide to engage her. Hannelore Hahn made that decision. She named a very modest salary and announced, 'I'll start tomorrow.'

Within a week, while Norbert was in Hamburg supervising the erection of the single-roomed prefab that was to be his home and office there, Hannelore had his affairs totally under control. She had also sifted through the other replies to Norbert's advertisement. 'I shan't have time to keep running backwards and forwards between here and Hamburg or wherever you find yourself, Herr Norbert,' she told him briskly, handing him a letter. 'In my opinion, you should also engage a personal assistant. This young man, Eduard Wild, appears to have certain qualities to commend him.'

Norbert stared blankly at the application. 'A sixteen-year-old refugee from East Prussia with no work experience? What use is he to me?'

'I've given him a preliminary interview. He's an intelligent young man, who speaks English. And he would be very economical to employ. He and his family were driven from their home by the Russians. His parents were killed on the way to Germany. He's been living in a displaced persons camp. He's prepared to work for just his keep.'

'He could work for nothing and still be a liability. The boy knows nothing about the building trade.'

Hannelore fixed a pair of steely eyes on him. 'Neither did you, when you started.'

104

Norbert gave in. Hannelore Hahn was more than a match for him.

The following day, Eduard Wild arrived at the office, tall, fair-haired and rather shy. When Norbert asked why he wanted to work in the construction industry, he replied simply, 'I've seen enough destruction. I want to help build something.'

'It's going to be hard work. Long hours, low pay, bad conditions.'

'It can be no worse than what I'm used to.'

Norbert suddenly grinned. He didn't know what it was about the kid, but he liked him. They would make a good team: himself and Eduard out in the field; Alfred Tobler, in charge of the workforce; and Hannelore Hahn, running the office.

Next morning, he and Eduard took the train to Hamburg and settled into their new abode. It was rudimentary to an extreme. The living quarters, which contained two mattresses, some blankets and an old chest for clothes, were divided by a curtain from the office, which consisted of a table and some boxes, which served as chairs and storage. A lean-to housed an earth closet and water was supplied by a free-standing pump. Neither of the two men were worried by the lack of comfort. For both of them, it represented freedom.

Only when they tried to get to work did Norbert realize the dreadful conditions pertaining in Hamburg. While the British lived in luxury, the people of Hamburg were crammed into disease-ridden cellars and air-raid shelters. Although the British had given him a contract, they appeared intent on putting obstacles in his path, so that Norbert had difficulty obtaining money, equipment, materials and even manpower. In view of the fact that the second winter since the end of the war was approaching, their attitude seemed unbelievably inhumane.

After weeks of interviewing denazification candidates looking for jobs in the press and in radio, many of whom lied blatantly about their past, falsified their Military Government questionnaires or twisted the truth to serve their own often not very laudable ambitions, it came as a refreshing change for Stefan and Major Holtom to meet Udo Fabian. About six feet tall, thirty-five

105

years old and with hair already grey, Udo walked into their office one mid-July morning, asking for help in setting up a new magazine.

'Before we go any further, tell me about yourself, Herr Fabian,' Major Holtom said.

Stefan did not need to translate. Udo Fabian spoke fluent English.

'I was on the *Hamburger Morgenpost* until I was called up. I then served in the army and had been promoted to lieutenant by the time the war ended.'

'Where were you then?'

'On the Russian front, staring Zhukov's armies in the face.' Udo Fabian gave a thin smile. 'One look was enough for me. I decided I'd rather be court-martialled for desertion than taken prisoner by the Red Army, so I joined the refugees and made my way back home.'

'And when you arrived home?' Major Holtom asked.

'I found that my parents, wife and child were all dead. They had been killed in an RAF air raid.'

His papers confirmed everything he had told them. Major Holtom and Stefan glanced at each other. An honest man at last. No fictitious stories about helping Jews, no self-pitying tales of having been led astray or persecuted by the Nazis.

Udo Fabian continued, 'So I found a space in a cellar to live and started to plan *Aktuell*. I hoped to produce it without any outside help, but I have no printing works, no paper, no money. All I have is an idea.'

And very intriguing that idea was. *Aktuell* was a totally new concept in German publishing, a topical news magazine, bold and investigative, its purpose to expose corruption and injustice, among governments, political parties and individuals. There could have been nothing closer to Stefan's heart. 'It could be the first non-party, non-sectarian opposition in Germany,' he breathed.

'Yes,' Major Holtom agreed, cautiously, 'there is a possibility that the Control Commission would grant a licence for such a publication.'

'Even if I say that I believe there is as much corruption and

106

injustice under the Allied Occupation as there was under the Nazis?' Fabian asked.

Major Holtom attributed Fabian's bitterness to the fact that his family had been killed by a British bomb. 'Provided you were able to prove your allegations, we should not stand in the way of publication,' he said. 'We British believe in a free press.'

Udo knew an elderly printer called Thomas Hartmann, who was prepared not only to print *Aktuell* at a very modest cost on his antiquated press but to let Udo set up office in his cellar. On the strength of this, Major Holtom recommended to the Control Commission that *Aktuell* be granted a licence and be financed by the British, until such time as Udo could afford to run it alone.

At this same time, Stefan received a note from Norbert, saying that he had learned from Viktoria that Stefan was in Hamburg and inviting him to Eppendorf.

His relationship with the Krauses was not one Stefan particularly wanted to revive, but he could imagine the contact could be of interest to Udo, and suggested he came with him.

The meeting turned out very differently from what either of them had expected. Norbert wasted little time on social niceties but launched straight into an account of the housing situation. 'Seventeen thousand Hamburgers have been evicted from the inner city, so that the Control Commission can turn the area into a garden city for the British. Ten thousand labourers are employed on that project, against three and a half thousand creating new accommodation for the hundreds of thousands who are homeless.'

On and on he talked, explaining how ten German families could be turned out of one house, so that one British service family could take it over, without providing any alternative accommodation; how military personnel could confiscate whatever they needed, including furniture and household equipment; how victory clubs and dance halls were being built, while factories were being closed down and dismantled. 'It's iniquitous! The means of production is there, but they won't let us use it. They're even closing down cement works.'

107

Udo muttered grimly, 'It's worse than under the Nazis. *Aktuell* must lead with this story in its first edition.'

'Given the right assistance, I could construct enough prefabs before winter to house at least a thousand people,' Norbert said.

'The purpose of *Aktuell* is to expose issues of this kind,' Udo added.

Stefan gazed across the barren, rubble-strewn site, miserably aware that he was occupying a room that could house a German family and being transported in a chauffeur-driven car while others walked barefoot. 'We'll achieve nothing by composing a hymn of hatred against the British,' he said slowly. 'That will only antagonize them and we'll run the risk having *Aktuell* shut down before it's even launched. We must get our facts right.' Even as he spoke, he realized he was already identifying with the magazine.

The very next day, Major Holtom summoned him to his office. 'I thought you should know about the directive I've just received from the War Office. All NCOs in our department are to be demobilized at the end of the month. Of course, this needn't really affect you. As a civilian, you can continue to work for the Control Commission.'

'As a German civilian?'

'You don't hold British citizenship?' Major Holtom asked, aghast.

'When war broke out, I was considered an enemy alien,' Stefan explained. 'Even though I was allowed to work for the Political Warfare Executive and the Control Commission, I was still banned from becoming a British citizen.'

'That was a wartime ban. There'll be no difficulty now in your obtaining a British passport. For God's sake, apply to the naturalization board. With your record, it will be a mere formality.'

But something in Stefan baulked at taking what he saw as the easy way out, at being allowed the privileges which British citizenship would confer upon him and which would remain unavailable to his fellow Germans. In the end, he confided in Udo, who showed surprising understanding. 'Dual nationality could have its uses, but it isn't going to resolve your personal dilemma, is it? You're always going to feel yourself torn by conflicting loyalties.'

Stefan nodded. 'I have always loved my country. I sided with the British because I hated the Nazis – not the Germans.'

'You could help me run *Aktuell* . . .'

'Thank you,' Stefan said, flattered and pleased by Udo's suggestion. And he suddenly knew that there was nothing he would rather do.

Although Major Holtom was sorry to lose Stefan, he was not altogether surprised by his decision, but he was shocked when Stefan told him that he was proposing to live with Norbert and Eduard in their prefab.

By then, Udo had started interviewing the homeless and the evicted, building workers and contractors, obtaining signatures on a petition and lobbying the German Mayor and Council. Already he had the beginnings of an extremely damning report.

'If I'm to be a German civilian again, I must live like my fellow countrymen,' Stefan told Major Holtom.

At the beginning of August, the first Peace Conference began in Paris, at which the foreign ministers of the countries who had won the war discussed the future of those who had lost. At Nuremberg, the tribunal was reaching its end. Mortimer took the opportunity for a vacation in England to rejoin his wife and see his new grand-daughter.

He came back to Germany as the first postwar local, municipal and state assembly elections were taking place, from which it soon became apparent that Adenauer's Christian Democrats had developed into the largest party in the Western zones.

During September, elections took place in the Soviet zone. Outside observers were not welcomed at these and Mortimer had to rely mainly on press agency reports, which indicated that the Russians were keeping only superficially to their promise of free elections, for in many parishes and towns the choice of candidate was limited to the SED. In others, where Christian Democrats and Liberal Democrats did stand, the chance of swinging the vote was hampered because their candidates did not run jointly, the seats therefore all going to the SED. By the end of September there remained

109

only Berlin, where elections were due to be held on 20 October.

Before then, the first edition of *Aktuell* was published, not looking as prestigious as Stefan or Udo would have liked, for it was merely a single broadsheet of poor quality paper closely printed on both sides, but thanks to Udo and Thomas's unstinting efforts, it was on sale at most news kiosks in the major cities and towns of the British zone.

Stefan himself had written the lead story, which took the form of an open letter to the Control Commission and was written in German and English. It was a well-reasoned plea, in which Stefan started by listing the formidable facts Udo had gathered, then went on to point out that *Aktuell* realized the British were not being wantonly negligent, but that their apparent indifference was doing their reputation no good, at home or in Germany. He also appealed to the British sense of justice, reminding them of Churchill's promise that humanity would be put first when dealing with the vanquished.

Stefan's approach worked. Suddenly, work on the garden city project was halted and Norbert experienced no further difficulty in obtaining equipment, materials and labourers. Alfred Tobler moved to Hamburg in order to supervise the new workforce, which was housed in barracks-like prefabs on the far side of the site. Soon the rubble was cleared and the first dwellings were being erected. Landgut AG had at last started in business.

Stefan, elated by his first success, paid little attention to the work going on around him. When Norbert or Eduard mentioned the name Alfred Tobler, it meant nothing to him and if he had, by chance, noticed the taciturn foreman with the bent nose and broken cheekbone, he would not have recognized Otto Tobisch as the former page boy from the Hotel Quadriga and latter-day SS officer.

Otto's immediate reaction upon learning that Stefan Jochum was sharing accommodation with Norbert was panic. He very nearly jumped on a train and went to Traunkirchen. Then common sense prevailed. Even without his changed appearance, it was unlikely that Stefan would recognize him, for their paths had crossed only a couple of times in Berlin and then a very long

110

time ago. But Stefan's mother was another matter. Otto and Viktoria had been children together at the Hotel Quadriga and hated each other from a very early age. Should Viktoria Jochum come to Hamburg, he would have a very real problem.

If he suddenly left Hamburg, moreover, his abrupt departure would give rise to questions and possibly lead to discovery of his real identity. Better to stay where he was. Where safer than in the eye of the hurricane?

Norbert, Stefan and Eduard got on surprisingly well in their bachelor household, probably because they spent very little time together. On the few occasions when they were all home, Eduard would concoct some kind of meal, Norbert produce some beer, Stefan provide some cigarettes, and they would while away the evening in conversation.

It was Stefan and Norbert who did most of the talking, while Eduard sat cross-legged on his mattress, listening in engrossed silence. In his happiness at being party to their discussions, he forgot the miseries of the past and the gnawing hunger pains in his stomach.

Most of all, Eduard enjoyed Stefan's stories about the Hotel Quadriga and would happily have sat all night listening to descriptions of its elegant rooms and celebrated clientèle, of gala balls and sumptuous banquets. Scarcely able even to imagine such affluence, he could not understand Stefan's attitude towards the hotel: his apparent indifference to it other than as his home. But, as Eduard was already realizing, the material things of life meant little to Stefan. He lived on a different plane from the rest of them.

Norbert's reminiscences were of a different nature, mainly accounts of his love life during the war, including the time when he had had six girlfriends in six different cities, including Reinhild in Berlin. 'And now look at me,' he would sigh. 'A married man . . .'

A married man maybe, but not one who was faithful to his wife or apparently caring about his son. Contrary to Reinhild's worst fears, Tristan, who had been a sickly baby, was proving hardier than he had at first seemed and, although he was still small for his age and very susceptible to germs, he was now putting on

111

weight and the doctor was confident that he would grow up to be a normal, healthy child.

Norbert visited them from time to time, but Tristan was too young for him to feel any sense of identity with him, while Reinhild did not provide either the intellectual or the sexual stimulus Norbert needed. The former he found in his work. The latter he found in the arms of prostitutes.

The International Military Tribunal ended in Nuremberg on Tuesday 1 October 1946, and Mortimer set eyes for the last time on the men who had dominated world history for thirteen years and changed its course for ever. First the verdicts were read out. On Goering: 'Guilty . . .' On Hess: '. . . Guilty.' On Ribbentrop: '. . . Guilty.' And on down the line: 'Guilty.' 'Guilty.' Until Schacht: '. . . not guilty on this indictment . . . shall be discharged . . .'

A gasp of stunned surprise whispered through the court and Mortimer suddenly realized that nobody, including himself, had expected leniency towards any of the defendants.

In the afternoon, the final act was played out. One by one, the defendants entered the dock and received their sentences from Lord Justice Lawrence. Goering, in his blue Luftwaffe uniform was the first. '. . . the Tribunal sentences you to death by hanging.' Then Hess: '. . . life imprisonment.' Ribbentrop: '. . . death by hanging.' And so on, until twelve – including the absent Martin Bormann – had been sentenced to death, three to life imprisonment, and the other four, including Norbert's ex-boss Albert Speer, to prison sentences of between ten and twenty years.

Mortimer was offered a place among the eight journalists permitted to attend the executions which took place on 16 October, but he preferred not to witness the ghoulish spectacle. Instead, he went to Berlin.

Hiram met him at Tempelhof airfield and drove him through streets hung with red flags and plastered with Communist posters. At various squares, speakers were addressing large crowds of people. Above them waved the hammer and sickle. It was an election campaign worthy of any ever staged by Dr Goebbels, making it seem as if there were only one party. But how effective would it prove?

112

Hiram was uncertain. 'Now we have RIAS – Radio in the American Sector – the Russians no longer control the airwaves. But they're still up to all sorts of dirty tricks, like organizing so-called spontaneous Communist protest demonstrations, cutting off the electricity and trying to starve Berliners into submission by stopping the supply of food from the Soviet zone. We're having to bring in extra trainloads of food from our zone.'

When Mortimer visited Café Jochum that evening and discussed events with Viktoria, she said, 'I'm grateful the Americans have finally started to hit back at the Russians and are trying to help us, but, without meaning to sound disparaging, how far do a few trainloads of food go among three million people?'

In his mind, Mortimer took her comments further. He did not know how many million dollars it had cost to stage the Nuremberg tribunal, but he could not help suddenly wondering whether that money might not have been better spent keeping Berlin alive.

What had the Allies achieved at Nuremberg, other than hanging ten men and putting another seven in prison? The purpose of the trial had been to make an example of the Nazi Party leadership, the SS and the Army, and punish them so severely that National Socialism would never again assert itself in Germany.

Yet the German people had been allowed no part in the trial. No German judges had been allowed to participate and very few German journalists even had been permitted to attend the court. How could the Germans have learned anything from it?

And had impartial justice been dispensed in a court where the vanquished were tried by the victors? Throughout the trial, Mortimer had tried to convince himself that it could. Yet now it was over, he was unsure.

The trial had taken no account of those Germans who had opposed Hitler, many of whom had died in the attempt or spent long years in concentration camps. As a result, a collective guilt had been imposed upon the German people, which was not only unjust but could have untold future repercussions.

Furthermore, the Allies, who had sat in judgement, had themselves all been guilty of horrendous war crimes: the firestorms that had razed Hamburg and Dresden to the ground;

113

the atomic bombs which had destroyed Hiroshima and Nagasaki; the wanton slaughter of thousands of German civilians by the Red Army . . . But the Allies won the war and had therefore not been brought to trial. It could be said that those who had been executed at Nuremberg were guilty not so much of starting a war of aggression, but of losing it. What should the Germans learn from that?

Four days later, on Sunday 20 October, a cold, drizzly day, an amazing 90 to 95 per cent of the population of Berlin voted in the first free election they had experienced in thirteen years.

The polling stations were heavily guarded by Allied soldiers and monitored by Allied inspection teams to prevent vote-rigging, but even so, the results were astonishing, particularly in view of the intimidating tactics which had taken place during the campaign. As RIAS triumphantly reported the following morning, the SPD, even though it had failed to gain an overall majority of votes, had been returned as the leading party in all twenty boroughs and obtained 63 seats on the city council. The Christian Democrats gained 29 seats, the Liberal Democrats 11 – and the Communist-dominated SED only 26. Even in the Soviet sector, the SED polled only 21 per cent of the votes. In the latest battle for Berlin, the Russians had suffered an unmitigated defeat.

There was an excited, cheerful atmosphere throughout the city that morning. Wherever Mortimer went, people said, 'Now the Russians will leave . . .'

They were soon disillusioned. Before the day was over, it was learned that at dawn the Russians had launched a surprise counter-attack, in an operation described as the 'Special Administration for the Emigration of Technical Workers'. Tens of thousands of men, engineers and scientists who had been employed in munitions works, arms factories, and in research and development, had been taken with their families from their homes and deported to the Soviet Union.

In the evening, Mortimer went to Café Jochum. Hasso's face was drawn, as he served a rather subdued clientèle, and Viktoria's expression haggard as she accompanied her guests to their tables. Mortimer perched himself on a bar stool, ordered a Jack Daniels and lit a cigarette.

114

A few moments later, Viktoria came and stood beside him. 'You've heard the news?' she asked. As Mortimer nodded, she said, 'The Russians are apparently claiming that the technicians volunteered their services, but of course they didn't. They were kidnapped. Mortimer, for twelve years we lived in fear of being dragged from our beds by the Gestapo. Now it's happening again with the Russians. What are the Allies going to do about it?'

The answer, as Mortimer soon discovered, was very little, other than make a futile formal protest. But there was no doubt the honeymoon with the Russians was reaching its end. Mortimer's account of the spectacular election results and the disappearing technicians appeared on the front page of several international newspapers. In one paper, the headline read: 'THE COLD WAR.'

The sentences passed on the Nazi leaders hit Baron Heinrich von Kraus hard. Worse still, however, was the news Joachim Duschek brought when he came to see him shortly after the end of the trial.

Joachim was surprised to find his client considerably improved. The Baron's speech, although still badly impaired and very slow, was quite intelligible, as witnessed by the first words he uttered when Joachim entered the cottage. 'About bloody time, Duschek!' He waved his stick at Trude. 'Go for a walk, woman, I've got business to discuss.'

When she had gone, the Baron grunted, 'Silly cow. Was hoping I would die. But I cured myself. Can't walk yet, but I can move my right arm. And write with my left hand.'

'A miracle,' Joachim murmured.

'No miracle, boy. Just willpower. Now tell me your news.'

It was clear Joachim did not like the news he was bringing. 'I am in correspondence with Herr Werner, who seems in reasonable spirits. Information on Herr Ernst is rather more difficult to obtain. He was in the Taunus for several months, but now he has been moved to another camp, I don't know where.' The Baron gave a non-committal grunt. Joachim continued, 'Herr Norbert is in Hamburg. I am pleased to report that he has already commenced building work on some of the sites belonging to Landgut.'

115

'What about Kraus Industries?'

Joachim looked down at his case and massaged his crippled arm. 'Herr Baron, I have very bad news. The Allies have ruled that Kraus Industries is to be prohibited from engaging ever again in active business. I have here papers relating to the forced sale of most of your remaining companies under the Allied Decartelization Laws. They are to be placed in the hands of trustees, who will have instructions to sell them to suitable bidders or, as in the case of Kraus Munitions, put them into liquidation. Added to this, all your properties and other personal assets are to be confiscated . . .'

The Baron's face crumpled and he sank back in his wheel-chair. Not just Schloss Waldesruh, but the Fortress and his villa in Berlin were to be taken from him, together with all the valuable antiques, paintings and furnishings he had amassed. And even worse, he was to lose the not inconsiderable fortune which he had amassed overseas: his holdings in the United States, South America and Britain; the Liegnitzer Bank in Switzerland; and the stocks, shares, bonds and gold bars which were residing in its vaults. Never in his worst nightmares had he imagined such a fate overtaking the empire he had spent his life building up from nothing.

Then Joachim said, 'However, Dr Jurisch specifically told me to inform you that, in his belief, all is far from lost. He has been in correspondence with your American lawyers, who report a gradual change in United States policy. The so-called Hoover Committee has publicly declared itself in favour of an end to denazification, seeing Germany as a lesser danger than the Soviet Union. A number of Americans are already starting to believe that a strong, capitalist Germany could provide an effective bulwark against the "Red danger" of Stalin.'

The Baron righted himself awkwardly in his chair. A grimace, which was meant to be a smile, etched itself on his features.

As the second winter since the war commenced, life in Berlin got harder. In August, an order had gone out forbidding Berliners to cut any more wood from the city's forests and parks. The extra supplies of shoes, clothes, tyres, cigarettes, coal and building materials which the Russians, Americans and British had sent

116

in during the election campaign, dried up as suddenly as they had begun, and by Christmas many had ceased altogether. A certain amount of aid, in the form of food parcels, clothing and blankets, trickled into the city from the Red Cross, the Council of Relief Agencies and CARE, the Council for American Remittances to Europe, but it was woefully insufficient. To add to the problems of the Berliners, unlike the previous, exceptionally mild winter, snow began to fall steadily, carpeting the ruins in a white shroud.

Yet, despite the weather, the shortages and the political tensions and uncertainties, that Christmas of 1946, spent at Heiligensee, would remain for ever etched in Viktoria's memory as a small oasis of joy, all the more so because of the miseries, as yet unsuspected, which were to follow.

For one thing, Stefan was there, a Stefan considerably happier than when Viktoria had last seen him, who was finally doing what he really wanted to do and could feel pride in his achievements. *Aktuell*'s readership was increasing and some of his articles had even been reprinted or quoted in such international papers as the London *Times* and the *New York News*.

Lili was overjoyed to see them and very proud of the Christmas 'tree' she and Fritz had decorated. It was only a mis-shaped branch of fir, but from each of its 'branches' were suspended gaily painted, cardboard ornaments and candles made from rolled-up pieces of coloured paper.

Viktoria had again been able to procure a scrawny goose on the black market, which Hilde cooked very slowly so that it was not at all tough, and Stefan had brought with him a couple of bottles of wine, with the result that their mood was very festive.

On Christmas Eve evening, with the exception of Fritz, who was becoming extremely frail, they attended the carol service at Alt-Heiligensee Church. When they returned, Lili discovered a Christmas stocking, sent most unexpectedly by Mortimer, hanging from the mantelpiece, and there was fresh excitement as she unpacked nuts, oranges, chocolates, small toys and even, to their amazement, a couple of lumps of coal.

On 1 January 1947, Bizonia came into existence. The British and American zones were now amalgamated for economic purposes, with plans under way to include the French zone.

A German Economic Council for Bizonia was created to take over the responsibility of economic reconstruction, under Allied supervision. A very real step had been taken towards the formation of a German government – a step bitterly opposed by the Russians.

It was Berlin which felt the full brunt of the Russian opposition, for from that moment on, the Russians dropped all last pretences of any desire to cooperate with the British, French and Americans, and made it absolutely clear that they wanted the occupying forces out and Berlin incorporated into the Soviet zone. Suddenly, their former allies had become 'imperialists' and 'aggressors' and were accused of 'sabotaging cooperation'.

When the snow was several feet deep and temperatures plummeted to well below zero, gripping the city in an icy vice, the Russians reneged on their agreement to deliver the coal for which they had already been paid in steel shipments. With only sparse reserves of coal, the electricity generating company had to restrict supplies to between eight and four hours a day. Life became governed not by day and night but by power.

There was even less fuel for domestic purposes. Households had to get by on meagre supplies of inferior briquettes of brown coal or dig up their own fuel in the form of tree stumps and roots left in parks, for which one 'stub certificate' per family was issued.

At a time when Café Jochum should have been serving piping hot dishes, it could only offer a cold menu. Their supply of candles ran out and such guests as ventured through the snow to the dark, freezing cellar, had to bring their own illumination. The café closed at nine each night, frequently earlier.

Several of the girls and waiters fell ill, while Viktoria herself developed a chesty cold which kept her awake night after night, shivering feverishly under her thin blankets, wrapped up in several layers of clothes. When morning came she was exhausted and it was only by dint of great willpower that she forced herself to get up.

In February, the temperatures fell even lower. Water froze in the standpipes. Wine froze in bottles. Glasses froze to tables. Saucepans froze to their racks. Viktoria, Hasso and their few remaining staff cast conventional morality to the wind and,

118

pushing two mattresses together, slept huddled close to each other, fully dressed, in a communal bed.

Viktoria's spirits reached their lowest ebb yet. Never before had she felt so worn out. Every movement cost her an effort and when the day ended, she could not really remember what had happened during it. It was as if her mind was out of step with her actions, almost as if she were going through life drunk, with everything slightly out of focus.

Worst of all was the feeling of utter aloneness. During the crises of the war, she had had Benno beside her. They might not always have seen eye to eye, but he had always been there to reassure her and give her moral support. Since his death, she had succeeded in ignoring her loneliness by immersing herself in her work. Now, suddenly, she was confronted by the bleak emptiness of her life stretching meaninglessly ahead.

Mortimer came to see them, bringing news of the outside world. Wrapped in a heavy top-coat, wearing a Russian-style fur hat, his cheeks glowing, he burst into the cellar like a stranger from another world. There was enough fuel to heat his billet, sufficient food to keep the mess and the Press Club supplied. 'If it's any consolation, it's not just Berlin that's suffering,' he informed them. 'The whole of northern Europe is caught in the grip of ice. Hamburg, Paris, London. Even Big Ben has frozen!'

'At least they aren't cut off like we are!' Viktoria said bitterly.

'Yes, I realize that and I'm doing what I can.' He opened a copy of a newspaper to an article headed 'BERLIN'S COLD WAR'. Viktoria glanced at the pictures: of twenty people huddled in an unheated room; of bomb-damaged, overflowing hospitals; of grave-diggers drilling holes in the ground in which to plant explosives to break up the frozen earth.

Her eyes skimmed down the printed column: 'Frostbite has become such a common occurrence that hospitals are unable to deal with all the cases ... There is a very real fear that if they do not starve, the people of Berlin will freeze to death ...' She handed the paper back. 'Nothing you write will make any difference. Nobody gives a damn whether we live or die.'

It was the apathy in her voice which startled Mortimer. Until

119

this moment, she had been fighting back. Now she sounded beaten. He turned to take a proper look at her and what he saw shocked him. Her clothes were rumpled and stained, her hair hung white and lustreless, her skin was an earthy colour, there were dark bags under her eyes and her bloodless fingers looked as if they would snap if he took them in his hand.

He had returned to Berlin determined to ignore the ties of the past, to inflict upon Viktoria the suffering the Germans had imposed on others. He had wanted to watch her break. And now that she was breaking, far from giving him the satisfaction he had once anticipated, she aroused in him a sense of deep compassion. 'This cold spell must end soon,' he said with a lightness he did not feel. 'Then things will improve.'

After that, he came as often as he could to Café Jochum, always bringing something from the PX, food, chocolate or items of warm clothing, in an attempt to alleviate Viktoria's wretched existence, but even before he had gone, she had distributed his gifts among her colleagues and prepared a large parcel for Heiligensee.

Things did not improve. By the time the thaw began in the middle of March, there were only six of them left at Café Jochum: Viktoria, Hasso, Carl-Heinz Kaftanski, Lotte, Inge and Ulrich. The others were either hospitalized or dead. One victim of the freeze, Viktoria learned in a letter from Hilde Weber, was old Fritz. The one-legged veteran of two world wars had succumbed to chronic bronchitis. Viktoria's heart went out to Hilde and Lili, but all she could do was send her condolences and a meagre food parcel.

The thaw brought no relief. Roads, weakened by the extreme cold, subsided. Tunnels fell in. Walls, that had survived the bombardment of the war, collapsed. From not having enough water, Berlin suddenly had too much. Frozen pipes burst and, as the snow melted, water poured into cellars. Such conditions would, at any time, have been calamitous. In a city where there was no heat and no refuge, they were catastrophic.

Water cascaded down the stairs and streamed down the walls into Café Jochum, reaching over a foot in depth on occasions. Even when the floods began to subside, there was no reprieve. Clothes, blankets, mattresses, furniture and table linen, all were

120

saturated. Almost worse was the deposit left by the flood: the malodorous, muddy detritus of the city; a dirty, scummy sediment, that fouled every surface and infiltrated every object, even food and drink.

Summoning up their last reserves of energy, the inhabitants of Café Jochum set about the long cheerless task of clearing up: baling out the water by the bucketful; rinsing and wringing out their clothes, blankets and linen as best they could, and hanging them up on lines among the ruins; propping up the mattresses to dry in the March wind; scrubbing and scouring the kitchen, the café and the bar to get rid of the dirt.

Some of the staff returned, recovered from their illnesses, but when Viktoria tried to replace the rest, she discovered few people were interested in a job. As one man said, looking disparagingly round the ruined cellar, 'In return for working here fifty hours a week, you will pay me forty-five marks. I can earn that much in an hour on the black market.' As a result, the remaining staff just had to work twice as hard as before.

Viktoria gave Hasso the sapphire ring and bracelet her father had given her on her eighteenth birthday and he exchanged them for inferior quality – but vital – supplies.

By the time it was back in business at the beginning of April, Café Jochum showed little outward sign of the winter devastation. Viktoria's troubles, however, were far from over.

One night in the middle of the month, she was awoken by strange noises coming from the direction of the kitchen. Muzzy-headed, she lit a candle, got out of bed and stumbled down the passageway.

The kitchen was deserted when she entered it, the service door swinging open, its lock broken and the bolt wrenched off. The intruders had presumably heard her coming and made good their escape. But they had had time enough to find what they wanted – and to leave the room in a complete shambles, the contents of drawers – pots, pans and utensils – strewn over the floor. Worst of all, the larders, store cupboards and refrigerator were empty. Their precious, meagre supplies had all gone.

She wedged the door shut with a chair to keep out the chill night air, then sank down at the table, burying her head in her arms, overcome with a sense of utter futility. After everything

121

else she had been through, this disaster was simply too much to bear. What was the point of continuing? For so long, she had been battling against unconquerable odds. Would it not be best to give up this unequal struggle, take Lili and move out of Berlin to the British or American zone?

There were footsteps behind her and Hasso's voice asked urgently, 'Are you all right?'

'Hasso, look what they've done. It seems that for every step we take forwards we go two back. How long is this going to go on? Will there ever be an end to it? Shall we ever live a normal life again?'

'Yes,' Hasso assured her, 'of course we shall.'

But then fell the most crushing blow of all. It came in the form of a summons from the Soviet Military Administration to report with the deeds of the Hotel Quadriga and it ended with Viktoria being forced to sell the site for a sum of Occupation Marks, which gave the impression that a fair transaction had taken place, but which would at best buy a few packets of cigarettes.

She was heartbroken. Her parents had built the hotel and she herself had been born there, as had her children. Benno had died there. It was not just a building, it was almost a living entity, a part of herself. It had been a landmark, as symbolic of Berlin as the Brandenburg Gate. Even though it had been in the Soviet sector, she had continued to entertain the hope that she might one day rebuild it. And now that hope was gone, she felt as if the last hope for Berlin had gone as well.

At a time when most Berliners were sunk into deep despair, a new storm broke. The city's *Buergermeister*, who had come to office after the October elections and spent his six months in power under severe pressure from the Russians and at constant odds with his own party, handed in his resignation.

The favourite to succeed him was Professor Ernst Reuter. Mortimer, who had met Reuter earlier that year, was greatly impressed by the tall, portly Social Democrat, with his heavy cranium, lined, tired face and mesmerizing eyes.

The Russians felt very differently about him. In his youth, Reuter had been a Communist, in Russia at the time of the Revolution, but subsequent events had disillusioned him and he had returned to his socialist roots. Now, twenty-five years after he had broken with it, the Communist Party still regarded him as a traitor and the Russians went to all lengths to oppose his candidature, publishing one set of lies after another about him, including assertions that because he was anti-Communist, he was an enemy of democracy, and implying that he was a Nazi. Ignoring the fact that one leader after another of Soviet occupied countries was being forced to resign, driven into exile or even executed, the Russians claimed that Reuter was a puppet of the Americans, who were putting him forward for power in order to implement their own divisive capitalist policies.

On 24 June, despite all the Communists' efforts, Reuter was elected as Berlin's new mayor by 89 of the city's 108 municipal deputies. The Russians claimed that he could only take office if all Four Powers formally approved the election, and vetoed his appointment. The other three Powers, rather than provoke the Russians, did nothing to enforce the appointment.

Reuter did not give in. He had visiting cards printed, 'The elected but unconfirmed *Buergermeister* of Berlin', and in the mean time, a deputy mayor, Frau Louise Schroeder – a small, frail-looking woman, with grey hair and kindly, bespectacled eyes – took on his responsibilities.

At the same time, the American Secretary of State, General Marshall, announced that the United States was prepared to give financial aid for a programme of European economic recovery, an offer warmly received by his British and French counterparts. Although it was clearly stated that the Marshall Plan was not directed against any country or political system, but intended to relieve poverty and hunger, the Soviet Union was swift to denounce it as a capitalist ploy to gain political hold over Europe.

At the end of the month, a meeting of Foreign Ministers was held in Paris to discuss the establishment of an Organization for European Economic Cooperation to administer Marshall Aid. After a few days, the Russian delegation withdrew and the Soviet Union forbade all European countries under its control to accept aid under the terms of the Marshall Plan.

The repercussions were felt most acutely in Berlin, where the Soviet-controlled newspapers continued their relentless barrage of anti-American propaganda. Every day, there was an incident of some kind. Cars from the West were refused entry into the Soviet zone because the driver did not carry the right permit. Passenger trains were delayed for hours. There was a spate of arrests in the Soviet sector for crimes as innocent as carrying a Western sector newspaper, while in the Western sectors, several known anti-Communists 'disappeared'.

When Viktoria next went to Heiligensee, she and Lili walked down past the Jochum cottage, still occupied by the French, to where the ferry used to cross to Nieder-Neuendorf.

'You know they stopped the ferry at the end of the war and put up a pontoon bridge?' Lili said. 'Well, now the Russians have blown the bridge up. All the farmers who have land over there are frightened they are going to lose their fields. Can the Russians really do that, Aunt Vicki?'

If they could take the site of the Quadriga, they could take land belonging to Heiligensee farmers. They could take Berlin, too, if they chose. It seemed that nobody else in the world was prepared to defend it and its rights. Except the Berliners themselves, except people like Ernst Reuter and Louise Schroeder . . .

'Look!' Lili exclaimed, 'You can see Russian soldiers over there now.'

Viktoria gazed across the river to the village on the opposite shore, separated from them by just a narrow stretch of silvery water. She had the very real impression of being on an island.

Yet, instead of depressing her, this realization filled her with a sudden sense of determination. Of course she could leave Berlin. Nobody would blame her. But if she did, she would know that she was simply running away. Running away, furthermore, for the very feeblest of reasons – because she was suffering from the effects of a freak winter, from a burglary, from the shock of losing the Quadriga – because she was hungry and tired . . .

That was what the Russians were hoping for, of course. Everyone who left Berlin represented a further victory to them.

No, damned if she would be beaten! She was made of sterner stuff than that. Putting her arm round Lili's shoulders, she muttered, 'I am not going to give in. I'm going to stay – and fight.'

Chapter 7

That summer, Landgut's first apartment house in Hamburg-Eppendorf was completed, a utilitarian building, six storeys high, looking out across churned up, muddy ground to other identical blocks rapidly nearing completion.

Times were improving in the British zone. Vast areas of cities were still in ruins, many people were still hungry and homeless, inflation was still rampant and black market prices were becoming ever more exorbitant, but everywhere one felt an increasing sense of optimism.

After two years of stagnation, the wheels of industry were beginning to turn. Numerous small businesses had started up. Scrap metal and surplus electric components were being put to ingenious use. Domestic goods were being produced. It was possible to buy furniture, cooking utensils and other essentials. The 'Trading with the Enemy' law had been repealed, so that it was no longer high treason for British firms to buy from German companies, and the first postwar trade fair was being held at Hanover in August. Last, but not least, there was the prospect of Marshall Aid.

Norbert's own fortunes had also changed. In April, he had become a father again. A few days after Tristan's first birthday, Reinhild had given birth to a little girl, whom, in a flight of romantic fancy, she had named Kleopatra.

Had it been left to Norbert, he would have let his family remain in Luebeck, while he stayed in Hamburg. He had evolved a very pleasant lifestyle in a city where women vastly outnumbered men, spending more time in other women's beds than his own. However, not only did Reinhild claim that she could not cope with two babies on her own in a primitive prefab and demanded that she join her husband, but Hannelore Hahn added her weight to the argument.

125

Hannelore did not approve at all of husband and wife living apart. And now that Landgut had brand-new apartments available in Hamburg, Norbert's excuses about the lack of proper accommodation no longer held good. She suggested to her employer that since the company's activities were centred now in Hamburg, its head office should be located in the same place. She announced that she was perfectly prepared to leave Luebeck, that the Hamburg site office would serve her perfectly well as an office, and that, if necessary, she would take over the prefab Norbert would be vacating when he and his family moved into their new flat.

In the face of such an offensive, Norbert had no alternative but to take over one of the ground-floor flats, in which he, Reinhild, Tristan and Kleo occupied one bedroom, and Stefan and Eduard the other, while Hannelore was given a bed-sitting room in the cellar, which she called her basement apartment.

Thus far, but no further, did Norbert give in. Once the new household was set up, Hannelore established in her office and Landgut's administration efficiently centralized, Norbert was freed from many of his previous duties. He simply seized every opportunity to leave Hamburg and go elsewhere in the pursuit of business and pleasure.

Hans Koenig had completed his first probationary term as a teacher. Since no Western newspapers were allowed into the Soviet zone and it was forbidden to listen to Western radio, he had little knowledge of the events taking place in the rest of Germany.

He certainly did not invite trouble by trying to find out, for the last thing he wanted was to draw attention to himself. Even now, he was well aware that his future was far from secure. One small mistake could find him back on the land or, even worse, in a Russian internment camp.

In fact, there was little danger of this. Very much as had happened under the Nazi régime, the school curriculum had been carefully thought out and teachers were given exact instructions as to the form and content of their lessons. And Hans had that rare gift of being able to impart information in a manner which made children receptive to what he taught.

Since his classes consisted solely of younger children, he was saved from having to teach some of the more abstruse aspects of political thought.

Not that he went along with everything he was told. As a Christian, he would never accept the philosophy of material atheism, just as he thoroughly disliked the notion of replacing Christmas with a celebration of Stalin's birthday. But he was reassured by other aspects of living socialism: the way in which the authorities were doing everything within their power to help the deprived, the sick and the elderly; the facilities that enabled widowed mothers to work, while their children were taken care of; the feeling that, in this new society which was developing, all people were equal, even if for the moment it meant they were all equally poor and hungry.

He was rewarded with the information that Fuerstenmark school was taking on more pupils and that an extra teacher was being engaged, namely himself. Hans could scarcely believe his good fortune.

In September, back at his old job, he felt happier than he had for many years. Guenther taught the older classes and Hans the younger children up to the age of eleven, including Senta and Heini.

Senta, just six years old and in her first year at school, proved a quick learner, very different from her brother. While Senta was concentrated on her lessons, Heini wasted time gazing out of the window and trying to divert the attention of his fellow pupils.

However, it did not escape Hans's notice that, whenever he asked Senta a question, Heini suddenly grew very attentive. Hans thought he could guess why. Just as he was expected to spy on his pupils and their parents, so his pupils – including his own son – were expected to spy on him. If he showed undue favouritism towards his daughter, word would get back to the school inspectorate. So, hard though it was, Hans treated Senta the same as all the other children, even though her progress was thereby retarded.

Fortunately, the other divisions of loyalties the interviewing committee at the Marx-Engels College had anticipated did not occur. Pastor Koenig still enjoyed a faithful congregation every Sunday, which encouraged him in the belief that Christianity and Communism were compatible. After all, he maintained, the Russian Orthodox Church had not been persecuted. So why should the Lutheran Church be threatened under a Communist regime?

As for Monika, when Hans hesitantly asked her one day if she ever wished she could join her mother in Berlin, she replied adamantly, 'No. Fuerstenmark is my home.'

That autumn of 1947 was proving the final straw for Anna Tobisch. The hay harvest had been even worse than those of previous summers, while the corn yield had been extremely poor. The authorities had taken her so-called surplus, leaving her less than enough to feed her own livestock. In any case, with the barn burned down, there was little storage space.

The chickens were the first to be affected. Each morning when Anna got up, she found another one lifeless. Then the cattle began to suffer from a strange ailment, which none of her herbal remedies would cure. One morning in November, she found her best heifer dead, lying on its side, its empty stomach grotesquely distended.

Distraught, Anna sent Dolfi across to fetch Farmer Austerer's son, Helmut, who had recently returned from captivity as a Russian prisoner of war and, amidst great rejoicing in the village, married his childhood sweetheart.

Helmut dug a burial pit, dragged the heifer's corpse into it and spread it with quicklime to speed decomposition, watched by Anna and Dolfi. When he had finished, he went into the cow byre, wrinkling his nose at the stink from the sparse, unclean straw. After examining the other cattle, he shook his head gloomily. 'It's too late to save them. Best put them all down.'

Anna gazed at him in despair. 'But how shall we live?'

Helmut made his way back into the yard. His father had told him a bit about the bad luck which had plagued Frau Feldmann. He looked up towards the mountain pastures, now covered in snow. This had been good land once, when old man Feldmann was alive. He looked at the house, sadly dilapidated, but sturdily built. He and Elfi should have their own place to live. Where better than here, close enough to his parents, but not too close? It would be hard going to start with, but there would soon be children to help them . . .

On the spur of the moment, before he had time really to consider what he was saying, he suggested, 'You could sell the farm to me, Frau Feldmann. I would give you a fair price. My father has some money put away, and Elfi's parents would help, I'm certain.'

For a long while, Anna's mind grappled with this extraordinary idea, so long that Helmut wondered if she had understood what he had said. Then she nodded slowly. 'We could go to my sister in the Black Forest.'

Once she had made up her mind, Anna felt a great sense of relief. After all, she told herself, if Otto did return from wherever he was and did not find them at Traunkirchen, he would be sure to look for them at Bergtal.

She wrote to Theresia and received a reply by return of post, assuring her and Dolfi of a warm welcome. With the help of the Austerers, the formalities were soon set in motion and a lawyer in Bad Ischl handled the conveyancing. The lawyer also contacted the American authorities on Anna's behalf to obtain approval for her to move to the Black Forest. After a certain amount of prevarication, they agreed, with the proviso that she report weekly to the local Military Police.

Two months later, Anna and Dolfi left Traunkirchen. Helmut Austerer had bought their furniture, household and farm equipment. When the train crossed the border into Germany, the customs officers gave only a cursory glance through the cheap cardboard suitcases containing, apparently, only old clothes and personal items. They did not notice a little leather purse hidden in Dolfi's washbag.

At the end of their long journey, Anna and Dolfi were met at the nearest railway station by Theresia's husband, Hubert, who drove them in the horse and cart he used to collect supplies, up a hilly road, through dense, snow-clad pine forests, to the Gasthof Waldblick.

Bergtal was a lovely little village and the Waldblick a charming inn, with steep roofs, and wide, overhanging eaves. True to her word, Theresia Albers, a buxom, warm-hearted woman, and her big, jovial bear of a husband, did all they could to make her Anna and Dolfi feel at home. Mother and son were given adjoining attic rooms, with a view over a snowy meadow and, beyond that, the forest. Anna discovered an ability for cooking and was able to make herself useful in the kitchen. Freed from the worries of the farm and with other people to help look after Dolfi, she started to relax. Apart from her weekly visit to the Military Police, she enjoyed her new existence.

Dolfi, too, quickly adjusted to his new life. His father, the great general, remained a dominating, if absent influence on his life, but soon he had a new idol. His 14-year-old cousin, Freddy, sporty, good at school, with a cheerful, outgoing personality, took him under his wing, teaching him to toboggan, ski, ride a bicycle, climb trees, play cowboys and indians, and opening up a whole new world to him. For the first time in his life, Dolfi had a real friend.

Helmut and Elfi sat at the kitchen table, gazing at the papers spread out before them, most of them commercial correspondence to and from German companies regarding the supply of chemicals, excavating equipment, railway parts, furnaces, fuel.

It was Helmut who had found them. While Elfi had begun spring-cleaning the house, he had set to work on the cow byre, clearing out and burning the old, infected straw, then digging over the trodden earth and manure, so hard packed it needed a pick-axe to break it up.

Suddenly, his fork had hit a more yielding patch of earth and the prongs became entangled in some kind of material. Sacking, he had thought, tugging at it with the fork. But when he had finally got the object clear, he had discovered it to be a sealed, waterproof bag.

'What are we going to do with them?' Elfi asked.

'I don't know.' Helmut's eyes kept returning to the address at the top of some of the papers: Schlachtenhausen Concentration Camp. And the signature at the bottom: *O. Tobisch, Commandant*.

Suddenly, everything fell into place. The veiled hints his father had dropped, the rumours he had heard in the village, the newspaper reports he had skimmed through . . . Anna Tobisch was the wife of the Slaughterer of Schlachtenhausen.

He shuffled the documents into a pile and pushed them back into the waterproof bag. 'We'd better take them to the police.'

In February 1948, the trial began of the *United States* v. *Ernst Kraus and Werner Kraus*, and father and son met for the first time in years under the watchful eyes of American warders in a cell at Nuremberg gaol. They had never been close: the Baron's policy of divide and rule had seen to that. Now, when their experiences of imprisonment and their fear for the future should have brought them together, they became even more estranged.

Werner scarcely recognized his father when the gaoler brought him in, and for a while he found it hard to believe that this white-haired, pasty-faced old man, who kept bleating about his blood pressure and his pills, could be the same man who had ruled over the quarter of a million workforce in the Ruhr. Ernst Kraus had never been an impressive figure but he had nevertheless been a person of some stature. Now, he was a sad and broken nonentity.

Before their first courtroom appearance, Dr Jurisch and Joachim Duschek were permitted to see them. Joachim, too, was shocked at Ernst's appearance but relieved to find Werner in reasonable health and spirits.

Dr Jurisch was less concerned with their health or morale than about the trial which awaited them. 'The British – and apparently, the Russians and French – say they want no further involvement in a case which they see purely as visiting the sins of the grandfather upon son and grandson,' he told them. 'That's why this is an all-American court. Only the American occupying forces remain determined to make an example out of Kraus Industries. Since the Baron has eluded them, they are trying you. They have even formulated new laws and defined new court procedures in order to do so.

'I don't believe they will hold you responsible for the corporate policies of Kraus Industries, but they may well decide that you were responsible for decisions made in your particular branches.' Eckhardt Jurisch glanced at Ernst. 'For instance your treatment of the Polish slave labour force.' He turned to Werner. 'Or your cooperation with the SS. Papers have been found on the farm which belonged to Otto Tobisch which apparently prove that Kraus supplied the crystals for the gas chambers.'

Joachim massaged his crippled arm. 'Our advice is that you plead guilty to such charges.'

'Guilty?' Werner gasped.

'It will possibly obtain you a lighter sentence.'

'Lighter than what?'

'It may save you from being hanged . . .'

Werner sank back in his chair, the word echoing through his mind. Hanged . . . hanged . . . hanged . . .

'Damn the Poles,' Ernst muttered. 'Nothing but bloody trouble. And look at them now. Living in Silesia. That's German territory.'

'For Christ's sake,' Werner yelled, 'for Christ's sake, shut up! Don't you understand what Joachim said? We might be hanged!'

'We've all got to die some day.'

Werner's eyes bulged with fear. 'One day, maybe, but not yet! Not me, anyway. You're an old man. But I'm only thirty. I'm too young to die!'

Those words gave Dr Jurisch the key as how best to handle their defence. Hardly a day passed when he did not remind the court of Werner's youth and Ernst's advanced years. The Baron had taken advantage of both his son and grandson, he maintained, manipulating them ruthlessly for his own purposes. Although they were pleading guilty on certain counts, there were extenuating circumstances to be taken into consideration.

The trial lasted two months, two months during which Ernst's physical health continued to deteriorate. Convinced that nothing Dr Jurisch said would save him from the hangman, he resigned himself to death and filled with a sudden fear for the fate which might await him in the after-life, he converted to Catholicism.

In the event, the court was lenient. Ernst and Werner were each sentenced to twelve years' imprisonment. In the middle of April they were taken to Landsberg Prison, the same Bavarian fortress not far from Munich in which Adolf Hitler had once been imprisoned and written *Mein Kampf*.

Conditions at Landsberg were better than at Nattenberg, including twice weekly visits from family and friends. Although

132

Ernst wanted only to see the prison chaplain, Werner received regular visits from Eckhardt Jurisch and Joachim Duschek.

Among the journalists who covered the Kraus trial was Mortimer Allen. He did not miss the many references to the evidence supplied by the documents which had been found on the Feldmann farm and, with the help of David Wunsche, traced Anna and Dolfi Tobisch to a remote village in the Black Forest. He did not succeed in interviewing them: Hubert Albers saw to that. But his photographs of the village were published in several newspapers.

Publicity of this kind was not what Hubert Albers wanted. He had been, and remained, a Nazi supporter. To him, as to Anna and Dolfi, Otto was a hero, and he promised Anna that, if his brother-in-law should still be alive and come to him for help, he would do everything possible for him. But sympathize though he did with Otto, he was not prepared to jeopardize his own comfortable existence. So he suggested that Anna apply for a divorce on the grounds of desertion. But this Anna, a staunch Catholic, refused to consider. Even if, as she was beginning to believe, Otto was dead, in the eyes of the Church she remained married. Hubert then proposed that they changed their names by deed poll and to this she eventually agreed. When Dolfi started at his new school, he was registered as Adolf Feldmann.

In Hamburg, Otto was buying cigarettes at a kiosk, when he glanced at the newspapers in the rack and saw the headline: Sanctuary for the Family of Schlachtenhausen Slaughterer. Casually, he bought a copy and slipped it under his arm. He waited until his lunch break to read it, when he had the satisfaction of learning the whereabouts of his wife and son. When the time came to join them, he need not cross the border into Austria. Fate had once again played into his hands.

The Allies set in motion the final dissolution of the Kraus empire and the coal mines, steel works, gun shops, ship-yards, chemical plants and the hundred or so other companies which remained of Kraus Industries were put into the con-trol of trustees, to dispose of in a manner which would

133

ensure that so much power never again rested in the hands of one man.

A lesser man than Heinrich von Kraus might have gone to pieces at witnessing not only the imprisonment of his son and grandson but the wholesale destruction of his own lifetime's work. Not so the Baron.

'In my opinion, fortunes are no longer to be made from coal and steel and certainly not from munitions,' Dr Jurisch told him during a visit in May. 'You have to accept that the days of the "Steel King" are over in more ways than one. I would, however, make one exception. You should try to retain ownership of the Kraushuette.'

The Baron gave him a searching glance and the lawyer explained, 'During the last few months I have succeeded in meeting with most of your managers, including Dr Runge, who managed the Kraushuette. I understand from him that uranium was discovered there during the war, which was used in the Peenemuende experiments to build an atom bomb.'

'That information is highly confidential,' the Baron spluttered.

'And it will remain so,' Dr Jurisch said soothingly. 'In order to keep that uranium, I would strongly advise you not to draw attention to it by fighting the Allied Decartelization order, particularly since I have extracted from the Allies an agreement that you may nominate the trustees to act on your behalf in the disposal of your companies, provided they are approved by themselves. I have already approached Dr Erwin Schulte, President of the Hessische Landesbank, and Dr Hermann Abs, Chairman of the Deutsche Bank. Naturally, I would propose myself as the third trustee. The Allies have agreed in principle to the arrangement.'

Dr Jurisch went on to explain that, with the help of former Kraus managers, he and Joachim had done further calculations which proved that the future was far from bleak. The Baron adjusted his spectacles and ran his finger down the columns of figures Eckhardt produced. Provided dismantling did not continue for too long, the sale of the Kraus subsidiaries might even net a small book profit. The Ruhr coal mines were already in production again and the smelters were processing scrap iron into usable steel, enhancing the value of both these companies to potential purchasers.

There were no bank loans to repay other than to the Liegnitzer Bank, which was owned by the Baron, and since the companies were now no longer the Baron's responsibility, there was no obligation to trade creditors. As for the shareholders, these were all members of the Kraus family.

With growing, albeit reluctant admiration, for he had always prided himself as the mastermind behind all Kraus Industries' transactions, the Baron listened to what Eckhardt Jurisch was saying. Then he asked, 'And if I go along with your proposals, what do you want?'

The tubby little lawyer gave a benign smile. 'A seat on the board of the new company which we shall form in the place of Kraus Industries.'

Norbert followed the reports of his father's and brother's trial and the break-up of his grandfather's empire more with curiosity than sympathy. He had never felt close to any of them and they had always treated him, much as they had his uncle Benno, as a black sheep. Yet for all that he was not a typical Kraus, he still possessed the Kraus business instinct.

Already he had extended his activities to Essen, where the municipal council had given Landgut a contract to build several hundred flats. The Ruhr had the advantage of very cheap manpower, for the industry which had been its mainstay for so long was still in the doldrums. However, people, whether or not they had jobs, still needed homes.

Often Norbert did not go home even at weekends. He knew Hannelore was running the office efficiently. Seven days a week, for twelve hours a day or even longer, he was on site. He was there when the first labourer arrived in the morning and did not leave until darkness had rendered work impossible.

There was another reason why Norbert did not often go home. He was lodging at the house of one of Kraus's former managers, who had a pretty daughter. In return for the little luxuries Norbert was able to obtain on the black market, she was more than ready to give him her body.

Now, however, he decided that it was time to take a look at the Kraus Industries sites in Berlin. He knew them, of course, but he had not been to the city since he and Reinhild had fled

135

at the end of the war. Before the properties were sold off, he ought at least take a look at them.

He had a dreadful journey. His train was subjected to interminable delays, first at Helmstedt-Marienborn, where they crossed from the British into the Soviet zone, and again outside Berlin. Armed Russian soldiers ordered all passengers off, making them stand in a siding while the train was searched and their luggage and papers examined. It was a chill, drizzly day and there were no shelters or toilet facilities. When they were finally allowed to regain their seats, everyone was suffering from cold, fear and exhaustion.

After the rigours of his journey, it was reassuring to find himself in the welcoming company of his Aunt Viktoria and the warm atmosphere of Café Jochum. The evening trade was just starting, so Viktoria had little time to have more than a few quick words, telling him to leave his bag in her bedroom-cum-office and suggesting he take a seat at the bar, which Norbert was more than happy to do. Hasso's girls were already eyeing him speculatively.

It turned out to be an entertaining evening, although disappointingly Norbert found himself an observer rather than a participator. Business was brisk, the restaurant was soon full and the dancing partners were in constant demand. Norbert watched as Hasso conducted a series of low-voiced negotiations with his clients, as a result of most of which they left the premises with a girl on their arm.

During a brief lull, Norbert asked Hasso hopefully, 'Is there any chance of me . . . ?'

The barman shook his head. 'Herr Norbert, I wouldn't advise you going with any girl in Berlin. Too many have VD. It's all right for the Americans. They can get penicillin. Not us Germans.'

'Not even on the black market?'

'You can obtain anything and everything on the black market. But as an indication of the cost of penicillin, it's called "white gold".'

After passing the night in lodgings recommended by Hasso, Norbert spent the following day roaming the city, looking at Kraus Chemie and other Kraus and Landgut sites, appalled at the extent of the devastation. For the first time, he was confronted by the big signs announcing the division of the city. The remains of the Hotel Quadriga, Kraus Haus, Kraus Industries headquarters on the Behrenstrasse, and the Liegnitzer Bank were all in the Soviet sector.

As elsewhere, the military had confiscated all undamaged buildings, including the villa in Grunewald that Baron Heinrich had acquired in 1932, at the same time as the Liegnitzer Bank. Now, judging by the voices coming from the garden, the elegant mansion was the home of an American family. It was all very depressing.

Back at Café Jochum, Viktoria had nothing to say to raise his spirits. 'You should think very seriously before making any kind of investment in Berlin. You could find you've simply been building for the Russians.'

'I must confess I didn't realize how grim things were here until the train,' Norbert admitted. 'I'm afraid, like a lot of other people, when I see something in the paper about Berlin, I just think, "Berlin, again," and turn the page. It isn't until you get here that you see what it's really like.'

'There's no doubt about it,' Hasso said, 'the Russians want the Western Allies out of Berlin and they'll stop at no lengths to achieve their aim.'

Norbert's visit reminded Viktoria that she still had Benno's Kraus Industries share certificates and she asked Norbert what she should do with them. Here, Norbert found himself on surer ground. 'They can't be worth the paper they're printed on. You may as well file them in the waste bin.'

Viktoria frowned. 'No, that wouldn't be right. I'll send them to Dr Duschek and ask him to forward them to Joachim, saying that I relinquish all title to them.'

'You'll be relinquishing all title to nothing,' Norbert laughed.

'Well, I shall feel better for having made my feelings known.'

After Norbert's visit, she did just that and duly received an acknowledgement from Joachim, noting the transaction.

By far the most pleasurable occasion of Norbert's visit was their trip to Heiligensee. 'I hope you don't mind,' Viktoria said, 'but I promised Lili I'd see her before I knew you were coming.'

137

Lili was waiting at the door of Hilde's cottage and when she saw Viktoria coming along the road, she flew towards them. She was wearing an old, carefully patched dress, which was too high at the waist and too short in the skirt, but which accentuated her gamine appearance, and Norbert's heart gave a strange lurch as he watched her, all arms and legs and flaming Titian hair.

Suddenly aware of his presence, she blushed and gazed up at him from big green eyes. Norbert smiled and took her hand in his. 'Hello, Lili. I'm Norbert.'

She studied him with sudden seriousness, taking in his height, uneven features, good-humoured eyes and lopsided mouth. She looked at his big hand, still firmly clasping her own little one. It was brown from the sun and rough from hard work and there were fine hairs along the fingers. It was, she decided, a rather nice hand. Only then did she say, 'I'm pleased to meet you, Norbert.'

They had a simple lunch with Hilde, who was pleased and flustered to have visitors, during which Lili asked, 'Is Norbert my cousin, Aunt Vicki?'

Norbert replied for her. 'Not really. We both have the same Aunt Viktoria, but only by marriage. Your mother was her sister. Uncle Benno was my father's brother.'

Lili tried to work that out, then sighed. 'Oh, well, I suppose we'll just have to be friends . . .'

'Bless the child,' Hilde said. 'She would so like to have some family.'

After lunch, they took deckchairs into Hilde's small garden and sat in the sun. Hilde was soon asleep and Viktoria found her eyes closing.

'Are you tired, too?' Lili asked Norbert.

'Not at all.'

'Would you like to come for a walk? I'll take you to see the cottage. It's not far.'

Viktoria opened one eye. 'Don't let the child trouble you.'

'I'm not a child,' Lili said indignantly. 'I'm nearly eleven.'

Norbert laughed and jumped to his feet. 'She's no trouble. In fact, she captivates me.'

In no time at all, it seemed, Norbert and Lili returned from their walk. 'The sentry let us go into the garden of the cottage,' Lili said. 'He said the Colonel was away, so it was all right.'

'Cottage seems a bit of a misnomer,' Norbert laughed. 'It's a mansion!'

All too soon, the afternoon was over. When they said their goodbyes, Lili asked Norbert, 'Will you come and see us again, soon?'

He smiled at the appealing, upturned, heart-shaped face, then lifted her up in his arms and gave her a kiss. 'Of course I will, sweetheart.'

'She'll break a few hearts before she's much older,' he remarked to Viktoria, as they waited for a tram to take them to Tegel.

'I suppose she will.' It was strange to think of Lili growing up and falling in love. Impulsively, Viktoria turned and kissed Norbert on the cheek. 'Thank you for coming with me and being kind to Lili.'

Long after Norbert had returned to Hamburg, the magic of that day remained in his memory. So, too, did the image of the Jochum cottage. Old and unspoiled, apart from the ubiquitous military presence, with its backdrop of trees and the water lapping gently up to its lawns, that house seemed to him one of the most idyllic spots on earth.

Dr Erwin Schulte was the newly appointed President of the new Hessische Landesbank, whose head office was in Frankfurt. Fifty years old, married, with a 25-year-old daughter, Else, he had spent his career in banking, culminating in a directorial position at the Deutsche Bank, which had come to an abrupt halt with the end of the war. Because he had been a Nazi Party member, he had been interned by the Americans, and although he had been released after six months, it had been some while before he found a job again. Then had come Marshall Aid and the need for German bankers to assist with the distribution of the massive American funds which began flowing into the country. Dr Schulte was one of them.

If Marshall Aid was to work, however, a stop had to be put to the galloping inflation which was already threatening to take on the proportions of the legendary inflation of the 1920s. The black market had to end. The German economy had to be put on a sound financial footing. The only sure way to achieve this, the only means of ensuring that everyone started again from a position of equality, was through currency reform, by abolishing the old Reichsmarks, getting rid of Occupation Marks, and introducing a new currency, the German Mark. And so, in June 1948, Dr Schulte found himself fully re-established in a position of power, at one of the most critical and historic moments in German financial history.

Preparations for currency reform took place in great secrecy, at high speed and not without difficulties. The new notes were printed abroad, but had to be transported to Germany, distributed and counted before they could be stored in the banks. Inevitably, there were discrepancies. Although the old Reichsmark had an exchange value of ten to one, there was to be a cash exchange on a one-to-one basis of forty marks per person. The bank had to be certain there would be enough Deutschmarks for everyone. Dr Schulte had little sleep during the first three weeks of June. When, on the 18th, the Americans gave a press conference announcing currency reform, there was still no absolute certainty that everything would go according to plan.

That weekend, while Dr Schulte and his staff were counting the new Deutschmark notes and coins entering the bank's vaults, the people of Frankfurt went on a spending spree, getting rid of Reichsmarks which were worth little enough already but would be worth nothing the following day. Not that there was much to buy: at best a haircut, a packet of Camels or a couple of bottles of beer.

On Monday morning, everything changed. The shops were miraculously full of goods. Dr Schulte walked home for lunch through the ruined city, witnessing the transformation that had taken place overnight. Shops which had been empty were now full of a bewildering selection of goods. Those who had no shop front had laid out their stock on window sills, on the pavement or in basements. There were leather shoes and handbags, electric light bulbs, bales of material, furniture, kitchen utensils, washing powder, medicaments, even food – bread, butter, meat, coffee and cigarettes.

Finally, German banking was once again fully in the hands of German bankers. The Allies had relinquished control of it. The black market had died its final death. People had the comfort now of knowing what the money they earned was worth and would be prepared to work ever harder in order to achieve the standard of living they wanted. Industry would profit. Unemployment would fall. Mortgages could be granted for new homes. Not that most people were earning much: the average wage was just over 200 Deutschmarks a month and it was unlikely that wages would rise much in the foreseeable future.

For Dr Schulte himelf, the future looked extremely bright. He had a salary of 2,000 Deutschmarks a month and a 500-a-month tax-free expense allowance. He would doubtless find himself appointed to the boards of several companies to whom the Hessische Landesbank afforded loans, with the accompanying director's fees. And, most intriguing and tantalizing of all, was the recent proposition put to him by Dr Eckhardt Jurish, that he become a trustee of Kraus Industries until such time as it could be sold off in separate parts. His star looked very much in the ascendant.

On that thought, he went shopping with his wife and daughter the following weekend and bought them each a new dress and a pair of shoes. Hildegard chose a safe olive green outfit, but Else insisted on having a brightly coloured print dress with big flowers, which did nothing to flatter her far from slim figure and exaggerated the pallor of her plump, rather featureless face. Erwin did not even notice its unsuitability. In his and Hildegard's eyes, Else could do no wrong.

Although they were Roman Catholics, Else was their only child and they had showered her with the love they had once hoped to devote to a much larger family. It was their great dream, even though Else was already twenty-five and had never had a steady boyfriend, that she would marry and produce a family of her own.

The Russian reaction to Western currency reform was immediate. They stopped all traffic from the Western zones to Berlin and announced that the new Deutschmarks would not be permitted currency in the Soviet zone or in Berlin. On 20

141

June, an American military train was stopped at Marienborn and the rails pulled up in front of it. On 21 June, the Russians announced they were introducing their own currency reform in the form of a new East Mark. On 23 June, the Western Powers stated that special Deutschmark notes stamped with a B would be issued in Berlin.

At six o'clock the next morning the Russians stopped all road and barge traffic into West Berlin and halted all supplies from the Soviet sector, including food, milk and coal. West Berlin was an island under siege.

At few times in its history had the city been prey to such rumours, fears and uncertainties as it was at the beginning of the Russian blockade. Because the main generating station was in the Soviet sector, the Russians could regulate the supply of electricity to the Western sectors, which meant they controlled radio and telephone communications. Even when there was power, reliable news seemed impossible to obtain. The Rundfunkhaus, the Radio Berlin broadcasting house, was also in the Soviet sector and this advantage the Russians used to great effect.

So powerful was the American signal that the Russians could not jam RIAS, neither could they stop mobile RIAS loudspeaker vans touring the Western sectors. However, statements made by the Western authorities on RIAS did nothing to reassure Berliners, least of all the promise by the British City Commandant that the people of Berlin would not be permitted to starve – particularly since he gave no indication as to how food was to enter the beleaguered city.

Mobile Radio Berlin vans spread terrifying rumours. They said that due to 'technical difficulties' there soon would not be enough coal to power the small electricity power stations in West Berlin, nor the waterworks and sewage plants. Already, they claimed, there were food riots in the Western sectors, where babies were dying from lack of milk. Within a matter of days, factories would have to close down and public transport grind to a halt. But never once did the Russians admit that they had blockaded Berlin. They wanted Berliners to see them not as malefactors, but benefactors.

From time to time, people came into Café Jochum with grim

news of their own. Shops were empty of food. Long queues were forming outside bakers and butchers, waiting for supplies to arrive. Russian tanks were said to be gathering round the outskirts of the city. Somebody claimed to have heard gunfire. Frequently, during the day, the electricity failed and the café was plunged into darkness. The gas pressure was so low that it took an hour to boil a kettle.

That evening, Hasso took Viktoria to a rally Ernst Reuter was holding at the Hertha Stadium. The stadium was filled to capacity and yet more people packed the surrounding streets. They came from every political persuasion, every class and every walk of life, but in one thing they were united: they were Berliners.

His distinctive beret on his head, Reuter spoke in calm and reasoned terms, explaining that, in his opinion, the Russian reaction had less to do with currency reform than with the city of Berlin itself. He asked the people to be courageous during the ordeal which lay ahead of them and called upon the world to help them in this decisive phase of the fight for freedom.

When he had finished speaking, the voices of the crowd echoed through the stadium: 'Freedom! Freedom! Freedom!'

The following morning, Viktoria queued with other Berliners for her new currency allowance. On this occasion, however, instead of the usual desultory, uncommunicative line, in which each person was intent only on his or her own business, fearful that supplies would run out before they reached the head of the queue, there was an atmosphere of cheerful camaraderie which Viktoria had not experienced since the pre-Hitler days.

'I've heard the new Russian mark isn't worth ten Reichsmarks, like it is in the West,' a man behind her said, 'but fifty Marks. That means it's only worth a fifth of West zone currency. However, if you live in the Soviet sector, it's the only legal tender. Crazy! One city and two currencies!'

'You've heard what's happening over there?' another man chimed in. 'The Russians haven't printed new notes, instead they've printed stick-on coupons. As well as Karl Marx, they now have Coupon Marx!'

'Wallpaper Marks, I've heard them called,' a woman laughed.

143

'Far from rolling, the new Russian currency is going to get stuck.'

'Which is what the Russians will get if they try to starve us out!' the first man said. 'We lived through a thousand bomber raids and firestorms. We can survive anything the Russians do to us now. *Uns kann keener!*'

Nobody can touch us . . . It was an old Berlin saying, typifying the spirit of its people, their independence and their calmness in times of emergency.

When Viktoria returned back up the Kurfuerstendamm, there were new goods in the shops, tantalizingly laid out on view with price tags in new Marks. But how long could they last? How soon before the shortages began again? A brightly painted box containing metal-capped colouring pencils caught her eye. It cost just two Marks. With a feeling of recklessness, she bought it for Lili.

On the steps of Café Jochum, she stopped. The electricity was off. The cellar loomed dark and uninviting. She was confronted again by grim reality. Berlin was an island. There was no way in and no way out. They were held prisoner by the Russians.

Then suddenly, above the noise of the traffic and the conversation of pedestrians, another sound impinged itself upon her consciousness. Automatically, she stared up into the sky. And then she saw it – flying low between the ruins, down towards Tempelhof – an American transport plane.

During the course of that day, 32 planes landed at Tempelhof and, three days later, a British airlift commenced to Gatow. On 28 June, the Americans flew in nearly 400 and the British 44 tons of food and other supplies. Two weeks later, over 1200 tons were flown in. It was far short of the estimated 12,000 tons a day needed to keep Berlin going, but it was one in the eye for the Russians. Basilius Meyer was amused by the idea of supplying Berlin from the air. It was so ridiculous that it did not even bear considering. Everything was on the side of the Russians, even the weather. Day after day, thunderstorms, pouring rain and low cloud meant that flights were aborted because of bad visibility.

Meanwhile, fuel, fresh vegetables and meat could easily be

brought into the Soviet sector by road and rail from the East. The Americans and British might be able to supply their own men for a short while but not the civilian population. The airlift stood no chance of success – which was why the Russians had not bothered even to protest against it. In a matter of weeks, the Allies would simply fly their troops out and the final victory in the Battle for Berlin would belong to the Communists.

Basilius now had somebody with whom to share his thoughts, a young Russian woman, called Irina Volodya, who had recently arrived in Berlin and who occupied the other desk in his office. A year younger than Basilius, with a rather plain face and mouse-brown hair pulled back into a knot at the nape of her neck, she bore a strange resemblance to Basilius's mother, Olga.

Although neither of them said anything, they both knew why Irina was there. It was to keep a surveillance over Basilius to ensure he did not deviate from the Party line. She had orders to report any transgressions, however small or seemingly trivial, to Colonel Tulpanov himself.

However, Irina's respect for her colleague was increasing daily. To begin with, she had mistrusted him because he was a German. Now she was confident that his belief in Communism was stronger than any nationalist feeling. He spoke Russian fluently. He had been brought up in the Soviet Union. He was truly a man made in Stalin's mould.

In the evening, he would accompany Irina through the dark streets to her apartment. He did not do so because of any sense of chivalry or concern for her safety. Irina was more than capable of taking care of herself. He walked with her because he liked her company. And he knew his feelings were reciprocated when, one night, instead of simply saying goodnight, she said, 'I enjoy your friendship, Vasili.'

A month after the commencement of the airlift, the Russians announced that they were willing to supply all Berlin with food, on condition that people registered with ration offices in the Soviet sector.

Although the performance of the airlift improved daily, with food, medicaments, and even petrol, coal and emergency generators being flown in, there had been no immediate corresponding improvement in the conditions of Berliners. For a few days after currency reform, shortages had eased and there had even been a glut of cigarettes. Then, as the true meaning of the blockade dawned, cigarette prices had started to rise again and the black market come back into its own.

Most people were still living in makeshift homes and existing on even fewer calories than they had at the end of the war. They led strange, almost surreal lives, eating their meals, doing their washing and ironing, and opening their businesses at totally different hours of the day and night, regulated by the supply of gas and electricity. As one district was plunged back into cold and darkness, power came on in another – but for only two hours at a time. Candles, when one could get them, became standard lighting.

Food delivered by the airlift arrived in dehydrated form: dried milk, dried vegetables, dried egg, and – perhaps hardest of all to bear for a city whose cuisine centred around the potato – POM, powdered mashed potato. Light though these were to transport, they were unappetizing, lacking in vitamins and protein, and many took longer to cook than the electricity supply allowed.

Yet despite all these considerations; and despite the fact that the Western Allies had made no guarantee that the airlift would continue; although there was still no surety that they would or could provide long-term for the civilian population; and there was no certainty that they would not eventually opt for a political compromise with the Russians and leave Berlin to its fate; their planes filled West Berliners with sufficient confidence to treat the Russian offer with utter contempt. As Viktoria declared, 'I'd rather starve!'

Day and night, from the direction of Tempelhof came the steady drone of aircraft landing and taking off. Little had anyone dreamed that the sound of approaching Allied planes, which had filled them with such fear during the war, would, only a few years later, represent survival. So long as they continued, there was hope. Soon nobody even noticed the noise any more. They only noticed it when it stopped.

On 1 October 1948, the airlift – or the air bridge, as Berliners called it – celebrated its one hundredth day and shortly afterwards the American General Clay announced, 'The airlift will be continued until the blockade is lifted.' The faith of Berliners in the Western Allies had been rewarded. Cognisant of all the dangers and difficulties ahead, the airlift was set to continue throughout the winter.

Constant improvements were made to runways, accommodation, unloading, storage and distribution facilities, weather service and ground control approach. A new runway was planned for Tempelhof. Gatow was being enlarged. Another airfield was being constructed in the French sector at Tegel.

The greatest irony of West Berlin's situation that autumn was that there was no actual shortage of supplies for those who could afford them or had contacts in the right places. On the black market, it was possible to buy anything and everything from caviare to tinned crabmeat, nylon stockings to car tyres, French perfume to petrol, coal to penicillin.

The goods reached the city by a variety of routes. Some were smuggled at night from the Western zones to the Soviet zone, into the Soviet sector of Berlin and across into the Western sectors. Some came directly from the Soviet zone, brought in by peasants anxious to obtain valuable Deutschmarks. Some arrived from the Western zones in lorries supposedly destined for the Russians but which reached the Soviet zone with considerably reduced loads. Some were American goods purchased by members of the Czech, Polish and Yugoslav military missions, sold in Berlin for dollars and sold on again for Deutschmarks. Others were helped on their way by Russian officers, bribed in Deutschmarks to allow private cars carrying smuggled goods through inter-zonal boundaries. Yet more came from airlift pilots not averse to doing private business on the side, by bringing in additional supplies of cigarettes, chocolate, coffee.

No matter how hard the Russians tried to stop the blockade-running, it continued but, as smuggling became more difficult, so prices soared.

Had it not been for Hasso's resourcefulness, it was doubtful that Café Jochum would have survived those first months of the blockade, for in its initial stages the airlift could not keep up with demand and even if she had sold all her jewellery Viktoria could

147

not have afforded the usurious prices demanded by greedy and unscrupulous black-marketeers.

Over the last three years, Hasso's private network had grown to include people in virtually every field of business in both the Western and Soviet sectors of Berlin. When a train load of Silesian coal arrived in Lichtenberg destined for the Russians, Hasso knew the man in charge of the coal yard, who ensured that several sacks were put on one side for him in return for cigarettes which Hasso obtained from another contact who worked in a cigarette factory, whom he paid with fresh meat supplied by a butcher in Niederschoenhausen with a young wife, whom Hasso supplied with nylon stockings, acquired from Lotte's sister, who worked as a maid in an American officer's house. The coal itself reached Café Jochum in a dust cart, driven by a young man from Pankow, whom Hasso reimbursed in West Marks.

Sometimes, the trade did not involve money at all, but consisted entirely of goods. His principal supplier of paraffin, a cheaper source of lighting than candles, expected payment in the form of fresh coffee, which Hasso obtained from an American mess sergeant in return for free beers whenever he visited Café Jochum. The beer came from a brewery in Wedding, where a friend of Hasso's brother-in-law was foreman. The foreman was diabetic and Hasso kept him supplied with saccharine obtained from an elderly woman whose daughter worked in a saccharine factory in Leipzig. The old lady brought the saccharine back concealed in the sleeves of her coat and another contact of Hasso's collected it from her house.

Hasso also did what he could to help Hilde and Lili, who were suddenly far worse off than they had been before. Whereas Hilde had previously been able to make foraging expeditions into the countryside or shop in Soviet zone villages, now the Soviet guards along the border north of Heiligensee had been reinforced and the *Volkspolizei*, the People's Police, harassed shoppers from West Berlin, often confiscating their purchases. Hilde was getting old and was unable to undertake such arduous expeditions. Poor rations, disrupted nights and insufficient heating were taking their toll on her health.

Lili, who had often accompanied her across the 'green border' in the past, could have gone in her stead, but this Hilde forbade.

Lili was too pretty and vulnerable a target for the unscrupulous blockade-runners and the frontier guards. In any case, Lili herself was far from fit, shooting up in height but not eating enough to sustain her growth.

Viktoria increased the frequency of her visits to Heiligensee, often making the journey on bicycle, for buses, the underground and the electric S-Bahn railways ran spasmodically, if at all. She took with her CARE parcels and any little luxuries Hasso was able to acquire on the black market. Provided Viktoria stayed with her while she ate, Lili would devour her offerings with ravenous haste. But Hilde would shake her head. 'They're wasted on me, I have no appetite any more. I feel it in my bones – I shan't see this winter out.'

When Viktoria went to Heiligensee for Lili's eleventh birthday on 4 October, she found Hilde in bed with a severe cold and Lili acting very capably as nursemaid and housekeeper.

'I'm very fortunate,' Hilde told Viktoria. 'My neighbours are being very helpful, but I don't know what I'd do without Lili. Despite her school work, she keeps the place beautifully tidy and she can cook every bit as well as I can – not that there is much to cook . . .'

When Viktoria left, Lili came to the door with her and asked, in a little voice, 'Is Hilde going to die?'

'Of course not, darling,' Viktoria reassured her, 'she'll soon be better.'

Lili shook her head doubtfully. 'Everybody I love dies.'

In November, the Russians showed they still had one last ace up their sleeves. There were rumours that the *Volkspolizei* was increasing in numbers to become 400,000 strong, less a police force than a police army. It could mean only one thing. Since the Russians had found it impossible to drive the Western Allies out of Berlin by the blockade, they were going to launch a land attack.

During the tense days which followed, Russian tanks again rolled towards Berlin, drawing to a halt in a semi-circle around the western perimeter of the city. Rumours spread like wildfire. It was said that Ulbricht had demanded the tanks continue into the city but that Stalin had given orders there should be no shooting. It was said a so-called spontaneous uprising against the Allies was being organized, so that the Russians could take over the Western sectors on the pretext of restoring order. But in the end, nothing happened and it could only be assumed that Stalin was frightened of starting another war, which he had no certainty of winning.

Lili crept out of bed and, as she had done since the new airfield had been opened at Tegel, went to the window, where she stood, wrapped in a blanket, gazing at the planes. Her breath clouded the icy glass and she rubbed it with her hand, melting the Jack Frost pattern, so that the hoary landscape outside glowed eerily white. During November and the early part of December there had been days when the fog was so thick that the planes had been unable to land, dreadful days, when everyone had feared the airlift might not be able to continue and Berlin would starve. But now the weather had improved and the sky over Berlin was once again filled with a constant, distant hum.

Lili shivered and, draping the blanket tentlike around her, took off her pyjamas and pulled on her clothes. With a glance at Hilde's body hunched in the other bed, she padded across the dark room and put some water in a pan. Lighting one of their precious candles, she balanced the pan on a little rack above it. Carefully, she measured a spoonful of ersatz coffee into a pot and waited for the water to boil.

This morning ritual had started when Hilde had fallen ill. No matter whether they had any fuel for the stove or whether the electricity was on or off, Lili got up and made Hilde coffee at seven o'clock. It was an attempt to convince them both that nothing had changed, preserving a sense of normality in an ever less certain world.

'Ah, my cup of Muckefuck', Hilde would say, using the Berlin term for ersatz coffee, although the coarse mixture of dried barley and acorns was unlike coffee of any kind.

The Muckefuck brewed, Lili poured it into a cup and carried it over to Hilde's bed. 'Hilde, good morning.' The old woman did not move. Lili put her hand on her shoulder. 'Hilde.' The shoulder seemed unnaturally stiff. There was no sound of breathing, no movement of the bedclothes. 'Hilde!' Lili's voice was high and urgent.

Hilde's left hand was hanging out the bed. Lili took it in hers. It was cold and lifeless. Lili let out a strangulated cry and started to tremble. She dropped Hilde's hand and sank down beside the bed, huddled into a small ball, consumed by a violent, convulsive shuddering.

She was still in the same position when Viktoria arrived, several hours later.

It was Christmas Eve.

Chapter 8

Viktoria did her utmost to make that Christmas as happy for Lili as it could be under the circumstances. After attending to the various arrangements for Hilde's funeral, she had brought Lili back to Café Jochum the previous afternoon. On Christmas Day, rather than stay at Café Jochum, they went to Tempelhof to watch for the now legendary *Schokoladen Flieger*, an American pilot who dropped handkerchief parachutes containing candy and chewing gum to the waiting crowds of children. They met Clarence, a real camel flown in by the Americans, laden with paniers filled with chocolates and toys. And they went to a party in a British Army mess hall, where there was Christmas pudding and mince pies, and a jovial Father Christmas handed out gifts and kindly sergeants organized games.

But Lili could not enter into the spirit of the occasion. She kept thinking of Hilde, as she had last seen her, being carried away to the undertaker's.

Hilde's funeral took place at Heiligensee immediately after Christmas and was attended by most of the village, for she was not only an old but a much loved inhabitant. Although very pale, Lili remained quite composed throughout the service. Even when Hilde's body, in a flimsy, makeshift coffin, was lowered into its grave next to Fritz, she did not cry.

But she knew a dreadful sense of desolation, which steadily increased during the days that followed. Ever since the end of the war, she had been pleading with Aunt Vicki to allow her to come and live with her. Now she was finally here and life was not at all what she had expected.

From the crack of dawn to late at night, Aunt Vicki was working, and Lili had the choice of either sitting in a corner of the restaurant or remaining in the bedroom which she and her aunt shared. Unlike at Heiligensee, there was no garden, no village to wander in, only the alien ruins of the Kurfuerstendamm. Most of her life seemed to be spent underground.

She was terribly lonely, missing Hilde and the friends she had left behind at Heiligensee. Even when the holiday was over and she started at her new school, things did not improve, for power cuts made school hours irregular and, in any case, she was joining the class in the middle of the school year, when the other children had already formed cliques, into which she found it hard to enter.

She became listless and withdrawn. Her appetite went and, already very thin, she lost even more weight. Deeply concerned, Viktoria took her to the doctor, who took a blood test which showed she was anaemic and recommended that if they had friends or relatives in the Western zones who could look after Lili, she should be sent to them. 'What she needs is a balanced diet and fresh air,' he pronounced, 'two things she won't get in Berlin.'

No longer did the airlift represent a one-way traffic. Now, as well as bringing supplies into the city, planes were carrying cargoes out: mail, empty sacks, manufactured goods and passengers. A lot of children and old people had already been evacuated to the British zone. Before Lili knew what was happening, Viktoria was in touch with Norbert and Stefan, and organizing the necessary travel permits and papers for her to go to Hamburg.

Lili did not understand. She could not help her unhappiness and loss of appetite: it was something beyond her control. 'I don't want to go,' she told Viktoria. 'Why can't I stay here?'

'It's for your own good,' Viktoria replied, kindly but firmly.

But still Lili did not understand.

For the international press, Germany and the Berlin blockade were becoming old news, insignificant compared to events taking place in other parts of the world: in Palestine, South Africa and India. The number of newspaper men in Berlin dwindled, until only Mortimer and a few other old hands remained, of whom Mortimer, at fifty-five, was among the oldest.

As winter commenced, Mortimer found himself wishing he too could leave. He was growing tired of the greyness of roofless buildings against a drab sky; pale, thin children; empty shops; military checkpoints; and the persistent drone of aircraft. He was wearying, too, of the intrigues which infiltrated every aspect of life: the black market, political plots and counterplots, kidnappings and murders. Berlin was becoming a city of spivs and spies.

The black market worried him less than the trade in people and information. Not a day passed when he was not approached by someone wanting to sell him information obtained from the Soviet sector, about life under the Russians, Communist functionaries or the workings of military government departments. Military Intelligence officers asked him to renew his acquaintanceship with Basilius Meyer, in order to find out what was going on in the minds of Ulbricht and his colleagues. Others begged him to find out what had happened to friends or relatives who had disappeared, presumably into the Soviet sector. Mortimer refused them all, saying that he had no desire to endanger his own life or that of other people by crossing the line between West and East, between journalism and espionage.

Yet the truth was that whereas he had once thrived on tensions and conspiracies, now he suddenly felt old and jaded. The momentum which had sustained him for so long was running out. Although the search for Nazi war criminals would never end, the major trials had ended. As for the problems confronting Berlin, Mortimer doubted they would ever be resolved.

During the summer, a West Berlin police force had been set up. Now, a new university was officially opened in Dahlem, named – in the spirit of the blockade – the Free University, the West Berlin counterpart of the old Berlin University on Unter den Linden. The City Council offices were moved from the Soviet to the British sector. Despite Communist efforts to disrupt them, elections were held to select a new City Council and, eighteen months after he had originally been elected, Ernst Reuter finally took office as Mayor of West Berlin.

Berlin had two police forces, two universities, two City Councils, two *Buergermeisters*. Nobody needed the signs which marked sector boundaries to know that it was a divided city.

Mortimer and Lili left Berlin together, one crisp, frosty Sunday in mid-January. Viktoria and Hasso went to Gatow to watch them depart on the first leg of their journey to the British air base at Wunstdorf, from where Mortimer was accompanying Lili to Hamburg, before flying home to Oxford for a much-needed vacation and to see a London publisher who had asked if he was interested in writing an account of his experiences in Germany.

The terminal was a mass of people, while outside the airfield concourse was a flurry of activity with the loading and unloading of planes. Viktoria, Mortimer and Hasso were chatting with strained cheerfulness, each uncomfortably aware of Lili's silent reproachful presence – each certain that what they were doing was for her ultimate good.

Hunched in a shapeless grey coat which accentuated her pallor and emphasized her thin shoulders and bony legs, Lili stood gazing out at the AVRO York in which she was soon to travel.

Viktoria put her arm round her. 'Uncle Norbert and Aunt Reinhild are looking forward to seeing you. Think what fun you'll have with Tristan and Kleo. And it will be warm there. You'll have more to eat . . .'

Lili did not respond.

Their flight was called. Mortimer shook Hasso's hand, took Viktoria in a quick embrace, then picked up Lili's and his own cases. Hasso gave Lili an avuncular kiss and Viktoria crouched down, putting her arms around her, holding her tight to her heart. 'Darling, it won't be for long. You'll soon be back again.'

Lili stared over her shoulder, her eyes bleak, then, as Viktoria relaxed her hold, she drew away and, without a word, followed Mortimer Allen towards the departure door.

The plane journey was very different from what Lili had imagined it would be. It was neither frightening nor exhilarating, just cold, bumpy and uncomfortable, and a lot of people were sick. She wondered why her father had chosen to be a flyer. But like so many things she would have liked to know, it was a question to which nobody seemed able to give her an answer. Nobody wanted to talk about the past. Although both Hilde and Aunt Viktoria had often assured her that her father had been a brave

155

Luftwaffe pilot, they would tell her nothing more about him. His death was shrouded in mystery, like so many other subjects to do with the war about which adults talked in hushed voices and stopped when she entered the room. They did not seem to realize that these events had influenced Lili's life, that she was entitled to know about them ...

Beside her, Mortimer Allen remained motionless, wrapped in his own thoughts. Too short to see out of the window, she sat with her gloved hands on her lap, trying to ignore her fellow passengers and the air pockets, trying to pretend she felt no hurt at the manner in which Aunt Vicki was sending her away.

From Wunstdorf, they caught a train to Hamburg and there, late in the evening, Stefan met them. He took them by tram through streets filled with light and shops filled with goods to the flat, where Norbert, Reinhild, Eduard and Hannelore were waiting with supper.

Dazedly, Lili did as Reinhild told her: put her case in Hannelore's basement room, where she was to sleep; washed her face and hands; and took her place at the table. Norbert urged her to help herself to bread and sausage and jam. Eduard poured her a cup of real tea and asked how much sugar she would like. But despite such long unknown delicacies, Lili still had no appetite.

The adults did not notice. They were too busy plying Mortimer with questions about Berlin and impressing him with their opinions. Soon the warm room was loud with their discussion.

'How much longer can the Allies keep Berlin going?' Norbert asked. 'I sympathize with people like Aunt Vicki, of course, but I can't help feeling it would be best to hand Berlin over to the Russians and make somewhere like Frankfurt the new capital. Adenauer has the right idea, in my opinion. It makes sense to start again with a capital near the Ruhr.'

'And we Germans have to pay for Berlin,' Hannelore sniffed.

'The British and Americans are picking up most of the bill,' Mortimer reminded her.

'We have to pay two pfennigs extra postage into the Berlin fund for every letter we send,' Hannelore complained, 'as well as extra income tax and a compulsory donation from company

156

profits. Why should we have to subsidize the Berliners? I've never liked them. They've always considered themselves superior to the rest of us.'

Reinhild complacently helped herself to more bread and sausage, her plump cheeks mechanically chewing her food. Her body was rounded under her apron with the child she was carrying: her third baby in four years.

Mortimer pushed away his plate and lit a cigarette, their self-centredness and lack of magnanimity increasing his sense of disillusionment.

It was Norbert who noticed that Lili had gone to sleep in her chair, her head awkwardly angled against its hard wooden back. He picked her up and carried her, light as a feather, downstairs to Hannelore's bed-sitting room, where he laid her on the camp bed prepared for her and covered her, fully dressed, with some blankets. 'Goodnight, sweetheart,' he murmured. 'Sleep well.' A teardrop crept slowly over the porcelain skin of her cheek. Very gently, Norbert wiped it away with his finger. A wan little smile formed on Lili's lips.

The next morning, Lili awoke to the sight of Hannelore Hahn struggling into an ungainly corset. Feeling Lili's curious eyes on her, Hannelore snapped, 'Don't stare, child. Get up and make yourself useful.' When Lili arrived upstairs for breakfast, Norbert had already left for Essen.

Gone, too, was Mortimer. He spent that night at the Press Club and returned to England the following day. His temper was not improved when he discovered the British public, including his own family, in a high state of dudgeon because bread rationing had been reintroduced in order that Berlin might be kept supplied with grain.

Lili had known many tragedies in her short life, but never had she felt so utterly miserable as during her first weeks in Hamburg. Everything was so different from Berlin. The flat was warm, they had electric lights and there was plenty of food. But to Reinhild's dismay and Hannelore's disgust, Lili just picked at her food and what she did eat clogged in her mouth. Yet, after she had gone to bed, she would lie awake yearning for bread and jam.

She hated the apartment, where everything was new and

157

Reinhild spent every moment cleaning and polishing. Lili, used to Hilde's old cottage at Heiligensee, where comfort had been put above tidiness, found it difficult to adjust to being constantly ordered to put things back 'in their proper place'. She found Reinhild's furniture and ornaments ugly and soulless and she could not understand her pride in them.

For all that Reinhild pretended to be fond of her children, Lili sensed that she saw them more as possessions than human beings. She showed them off to her friends and neighbours but she seldom showed them any affection. She and Hannelore often talked about the new baby Reinhild was expecting in August, but it was in the same tone of voice that they spoke about the suite of furniture on sale at the newly opened department store in the city centre.

Hannelore Hahn was the biggest thorn in Lili's flesh. No matter what Lili did to try and ingratiate herself, Hannelore found fault. If something was broken or out of place, Lili was to blame. Three-year-old Tristan could throw a tantrum and two-year-old Kleo scream with temper, and Hannelore, despite her grim exterior, would coo endearments and coax them back to good humour. But she seemed to have developed an irrational dislike for Lili upon first sight and remained aloofly immune to her miseries. The fact that Lili was sharing Hannelore's room made things even more difficult.

It was a strange household. Norbert was seldom there and when he did come home he tried to make up for his prolonged absences by bringing presents for everyone. After greeting his family, he would sweep Lili up in his arms with a 'And how's my little sweetheart?' and give her a big kiss. Then, after a few blissful hours, he would be gone again.

Stefan, too, was seldom at the apartment. *Aktuell* was becoming one of the best-known publications in the British zone, read by thousands of people. Major Holtom was returning to England at Easter and, before he left, he was arranging for Stefan and Udo to buy *Aktuell* from the British, with the result that they were planning to move into new premises and take on more staff.

Fortunately, Lili did not have to spend her entire time with Reinhild, Hannelore and the children. There was school, where the standard of her work put her around the middle

158

of the class and where her gentle personality soon encouraged friendship.

But it was Eduard Wild who was really Lili's salvation. Eduard was twenty now, a good-looking young man, with an open face and a kindly nature. An orphan himself, he knew what Lili was going through. Whenever he could spare the time, he and Lili went for long walks, down to the Alster or over the hills overlooking the Elbe towards Blankenese.

As they walked, they talked, and soon, despite the difference in their ages, a very real friendship was forged between them. Eduard plied Lili with questions about Café Jochum and the Quadriga and, to Lili's surprise, she found she could remember more than she would have imagined. Although she had only been four when she had last seen the Quadriga, she could still bring to mind the blue Savonnerie carpet which had covered the white marble floor in the foyer; the blue and gold flecked wallpaper in the restaurant; the deep leather settees in the bar; the figure of a prancing horse carved into each bed-head; the marble baths with gold-plated taps in the bathrooms; the white and gold furnishings in the Palm Garden Room.

In return, Eduard described all the things he had learned during the four years he had been working for Norbert and admitted that, greatly though he enjoyed his job, he didn't think he would ever become an architect.

Lili wrote to Viktoria, letters which were rather stiff and deliberately brave, saying that she missed Berlin, but was sure she would soon grow to like Hamburg. Stefan also wrote to say that she seemed to be settling in well, but most of his letter was concerned with his and Udo's plans for expanding the circulation of *Aktuell*, a copy of which he enclosed, containing a biting article about the attitude of people in the Western zones towards the blockade. Viktoria read it with a sense of perplexity, saddened that the plight of Berlin should arouse such bitterness in the hearts of her fellow countrymen.

Unlike the previous year, there was little snow that January and, although Berliners were given scant information about the performance of the airlift, there was every indication that the amount of supplies being flown in was increasing. Those black

159

days in November and December, when it had seemed that fog might force the airlift to stop, were a thing of the past.

Almost as gratifying was the effect of the counterblockade against the Russians, which had been officially proclaimed in January, banning the export of goods from the West. Industry in the Soviet zone was reliant upon high quality hard coal and steel which had been brought in from the Ruhr and was now no longer forthcoming. Machine tools, ballbearings, motors and optical instruments were among other essential goods for the supply of which the Soviet zone was reliant upon the Western zones. Without them, its already unhealthy economy was starting to suffer even worse. Rumour had it that more and more people were moving from the Soviet zone to the West, because of empty shops, lack of fuel and rising unemployment.

In December, Soviet sector police had started searching people travelling from east to west on Underground and S-Bahn trains and on trams. In February, a barrier was erected in Treptow between the Soviet and American sectors. As the winter continued, more streets were sealed off, although whether that was to stop the people of West Berlin going east or to prevent East Berliners from getting out, nobody knew.

What had dwindled into a very spasmodic correspondence with Monika ceased altogether that winter. She and her daughter could have been living on two different continents, not a mere hundred miles away, so great was the distance that separated them.

Yet, although Viktoria felt an increasing sense of isolation, she did not let it get her down. One thing, at least, was for sure. The situation between East and West was reaching a climax. At some point soon, the Soviet Union would either have to declare war on the Western Allies – or back down. For it was absolutely clear that France, Britain and America were not going to let Berlin go.

At Easter, the airlift surpassed itself by completing its millionth flight and celebrated with a spectacular aerial parade. In the 24-hour period from noon on Easter Saturday to noon on Easter Sunday, 1400 flights flew in nearly 13,000 tons of coal. Virtually the entire population crowded on to the streets, gazing up at the endless stream of aircraft, like a continuous string of silvery

160

pearls, flying into Tempelhof, Tegel and Gatow, unloading and taking off again. It was one plane a minute.

There had been moments during the past nine months, when Basilius Meyer's initial confidence in the blockade and his faith in Russian policies had faltered.

Far from protecting their zone of occupation, the Russians were ruthlessly exploiting it. While the Western Allies poured in Marshall Aid and helped industry, the Soviet Union was stripping its zone and East Berlin bare. While the Western Allies tried to keep the people of West Berlin alive through the airlift, the Russians were bringing the people of East Berlin perilously close to starvation.

The standard of living was dropping. Shops were becoming emptier. Factories were still unworkable. The East Mark was falling in value against the West Mark. Basilius had even heard fellow SED members saying, 'The only place you can live decently now as a Communist is in a capitalist country.' Several Moscow-trained German Communists had become so disillusioned with Soviet rule they had defected to the West.

It did not even occur to Basilius that he might join them and he certainly did not admit his private misgivings to anyone, not even to Irina Volodya or his cousin, Rudi Sommer, for whom he had obtained a post in the People's Police.

Russian policy in the Soviet zone was, Basilius believed, directed at the capitalist West, but unfortunately it affected the Germans most. Soon Stalin would realize what was happening and change his tactics. When, in March 1949, General Chuikov became the new Military Governor of Germany and Molotov was replaced as Foreign Minister by Andrei Vyschinsky, Basilius believed changes for the good must be shortly forthcoming.

He was right. At the end of April, Stalin hinted that he might be prepared to lift the blockade – not that the Russians had ever admitted to a blockade: right to the end they had maintained the fiction of 'technical traffic complications'.

It looked like a defeat but, when one examined the situation closely, it was not. West Berlin was still an island. The access routes could be closed again at any time but, meanwhile, the counterblockade would end and the Soviet zone could stock

161

up with supplies from the West. For as long as they chose, the Russians had the Western Allies at their mercy.

There was one other significant development. The Berlin blockade had lent impetus to the formation of national entities on both sides of the Iron Curtain. In the Soviet zone, the People's Council had in March unanimously approved a constitution for a united German Democratic Republic with Berlin as its capital. Now, in May, the Parliamentary Council which had been sitting in Bonn approved the new constitution needed to establish a German Federal Republic in the Western zones. Interestingly, Berlin was neither included as a twelfth Land in this proposed western republic, nor was it to be the seat of parliament. For that, it was announced, Bonn had been chosen.

This so-called Federal Republic would never survive, Basilius was certain, for it had been born out of desperation and was the product of compromise. No wonder Stalin did not bother even to protest against it. Like a headless chicken, it would founder and then the people of the western zones would join with the German Democratic Republic.

By then, Stalin would have realized that he could trust his German comrades and they would be allowed to run their own country free from Russian supervision, but backed up by the strength of the Soviet Union. And Berlin would again become the capital of a united Germany.

At midnight on 11 May, the blockade was lifted. The first cars and lorries arrived at the American check point after driving unmolested across the Soviet zone and were welcomed by cheering crowds. The first trains arrived from the western zones. The first cars left Berlin for the west bearing banners reading, 'Hurrah! We're still alive!'

At Café Jochum, Viktoria and Hasso threw a party for some of the airport groundstaff and courageous airmen they had got to know over the past eleven months. Most of the men brought bottles and cans of beer with them and those who were not going on duty were extremely drunk by the time the party eventually wound up the following morning with an American style breakfast of coffee, bacon, eggs, waffles and maple syrup. Yet even Viktoria, who drank very little, felt light-headed – from

162

the sheer, heady feeling of relief that the blockade was over and they had survived!

No longer was Berlin a city of darkness. The dreadful days of eating by candlelight were over. At just a flick of a switch, the lights came on. And the new power station, named after Ernst Reuter and completed just before the end of the blockade, meant that never again need West Berlin be dependent on the Russians for power. Public transport was working again. There was food in the shops. There were clothes and shoes. There was coal. Prices plummeted. Cigarettes came off ration.

But before they could properly accustom themselves to living normal lives again, new troubles started. On 20 May, Berlin's S-Bahn workers went on strike. The entire S-Bahn system was under the command of the Soviets and the workers were paid in East Marks, but a large number of them lived in West Berlin, where their wages were worth only one-fifth of their neighbours. The repercussions of the strike were enormous, affecting not only Berlin's transport system, but rail traffic to and from Berlin. Within a fortnight of the end of the Russian blockade, Berlin had blockaded itself.

The German Federal Republic came into existence on 23 May 1949, with Bonn as its provisional capital, but the Russians refused to recognize the new state and Berlin, therefore, remained subject to the Four-Power Agreement.

In the middle of June, the Russians agreed to pay 60 per cent of S-Bahn workers' wages in Western currency and the strike fizzled out. But, once again, the Russians announced 'technical difficulties' on the autobahns and rail routes to Berlin. Berlin remained in a state of semi-blockade. The airlift continued.

Mortimer Allen's sojourn in Berlin had come to an end. He wrote his last article on Berlin, using it to bring up-to-date the stories of some of those people whose lives he had followed since his arrival nearly four years earlier, among them Pastor Scheer and, of course, Viktoria.

Due to his long years of imprisonment, Pastor Scheer had suffered less than others from the privations of the blockade and was uninterested in the sudden plenty of food and goods. Neither did he share in the overall feeling of rejoicing at the end of the blockade. On the contrary, he was concerned that it heralded a widening rift between what were becoming two Germanies.

'I am worried less on a political than on a spiritual level,' he told Mortimer, putting his arm round the shoulders of his grandson, Matthias, now a fine-looking six-year-old. 'Remember what I told you before, Herr Allen. It is of Matthias we must always be thinking, of him and the thousands of children like him . . .'

Mortimer spent his last evening in Berlin at a Café Jochum ablaze with light. Viktoria dined with him, but instead of gorging herself as most other Berliners seemed to be doing, she took only small portions, explaining apologetically, 'I can't get used to having so much to eat.'

'What are you going to do now?' Mortimer asked.

She was silent for a while, then admitted, 'I honestly don't know. I ought to go to Hamburg and bring Lili back. But what kind of life can I offer her here? Ironically, I recently received a notification from the French Military saying that they are vacating our cottage at Heiligensee and that I shall be free to move in again soon. But I can't travel backwards and forwards between here and Heiligensee every day and I couldn't leave Lili there alone. I think the best thing I can do is rent the place out.'

'You yourself could move to Hamburg,' Mortimer suggested.

'But what would I do there?'

That was the crux of the matter. Viktoria had never been a housewife, content with looking after her children.

Eventually, after Mortimer had said goodbye to Hasso and the other staff, they walked up the cellar steps together into the Ku-damm. The streets were cleared of rubble but still the ruins remained, eerie facades, like film sets, lit up in front and with nothing behind. People walked past, talking and laughing. Cars sped by, enjoying the sudden availability of petrol.

Viktoria felt an acute pang of loneliness and a sudden urge to ask Mortimer to change his mind and stay in Berlin. For so long, their lives had been interwoven. It was inconceivable that he would suddenly no longer be there. 'Mortimer, I shall miss you . . .'

164

'Yes, I'll miss you too.' He gave a rueful smile. 'Vicki, if I was unkind to you at times in the past, I'm sorry. I didn't mean to hurt you.'

'I know. Our circumstances have been very strange . . .'

He took her in his arms and she rested her face on his shoulder. His lips brushed her hair and he murmured, 'I shall never forget you, Vicki. You're a valiant and very remarkable woman.'

Then he was gone, striding up the Ku-damm, and Viktoria was left standing alone on the steps of Café Jochum.

Norbert and Reinhild's third child, another girl, was born that August. Reinhild again delved into her limited knowledge of classical mythology and called her Helena, after Helen of Troy. 'Didn't she cause the Trojan War?' Norbert asked.

'She was extremely beautiful,' Hannelore informed him sharply.

Helena showed no immediate signs of being a great beauty. She was a long baby, with rather ugly features and a tendency to cry rather than to smile. Her arrival made life in the cramped apartment even more uncomfortable.

That August, elections were held to select the Federal Republic of Germany's first government, resulting in the Christian Democrats forming a coalition with the Free Democrats. In September, Konrad Adenauer was elected Chancellor, and Theodor Heuss, the cultivated and highly respected Liberal, was chosen as President of the new Republic.

NATO, the North Atlantic Treaty Organization, had come into force, an alliance comprising eleven countries, promising each other mutual assistance should any one member be attacked.

The future looking more secure than it had for many a year, Stefan decided it was a good time for him to move into a flat of his own. *Aktuell* now not only belonged to him and Udo, but was also beginning to make a modest profit. At the end of September, he and Udo moved into a new flat near the University.

Gradually, the number of Allied troops in the Western zones was reduced and the remaining occupation staffs moved into their own purpose-built offices and accommodation. In

September, the British vacated the waterfront mansion on Hamburg's Binnenalster, the last Landgut property in the city which remained to be developed.

Taking Eduard Wild with him, Norbert was able to look round it for the first time. Naturally, Lili accompanied them.

The building dated back to the beginning of the nineteenth century and among its previous owners had been a wealthy Hamburg shipping merchant, who had added several wings during the late 1920s and early 1930s. Despite the damage it had suffered to its facade and roof during the war, it remained a stately town residence, with a semi-circular drive and a flight of steps leading up to a pillared entrance. Inside, they stepped into a spacious entrance hall, at the far end of which a wide staircase curved up towards the first floor. It felt warm and light, although it was lit only by the afternoon sun streaming in through the open door and its floor was littered with debris left by the British.

They wandered round, discussing its possibilities. Nobody could afford any longer to run it as a private home and it would need a lot of work to convert into flats. 'What about an hotel?' Eduard suggested, Stefan's and Lili's descriptions of the Quadriga still vivid in his mind.

'It's an idea,' Norbert said consideringly. 'But there are only thirty upstairs rooms. That's sixty guests maximum. I'm not sure that we wouldn't be wiser to start again with a modern building.'

Eduard knew that skyscrapers were very much in Norbert's mind at that time, as the most economical method of housing people, but it seemed to him a great pity to demolish such a beautiful old house. Hesitantly, he suggested, 'You could add a floor or two. The Quadriga had four storeys.'

'I suppose we could,' Norbert agreed and when he studied the external proportions, he decided that the mansion could take more height.

So it went on. Every modern modification suggested by Norbert was countered by one from Eduard bringing it closer to the classical style of the Quadriga. And the extraordinary thing was that Eduard was right. Despite his lack of formal training, he had an instinctive feel for what was needed. At the end of the day, Norbert laughed. 'You'd get on well with Aunt

Viktoria. You both think in the same way.' Then he clicked his fingers. 'Good God! That's the answer! Landgut owns the hotel and Aunt Vicki runs it!'

The next few days were spent entirely at the villa, Norbert drawing up sketch plans and doing rough costings, and Eduard lost in a dream. Lili could scarcely contain her excitement. If Aunt Vicki moved to Hamburg, she would no longer have to live with Reinhild and Hannelore.

At the beginning of October 1949, the skies over Berlin fell silent. The city had sufficient supplies stockpiled to see it through the winter, even if the Russians reimposed a blockade. The task of the airlift was over.

On 7 October, the Russians proclaimed the German Democratic Republic an independent state. No elections were held. The new Prime Minister was Otto Grotewohl and the President Wilhelm Pieck, but few people were in any doubt that the only man with any real power was Walther Ulbricht, a fervent supporter of the Moscow Party line. The West denounced this so-called republic as illegal and undemocratic. Yet it, unlike the Federal Republic, had kept Berlin as its capital. West Berlin was now an enclave within the German Democratic Republic.

Norbert's letter telling Viktoria about his plans for a new hotel in Hamburg arrived shortly after this latest development. When, a few months earlier, Mortimer had suggested she move to Hamburg, she had dismissed the idea out of hand. Now she gave it serious consideration.

'Obey your head and not your heart,' Hasso said when she discussed the idea with him. 'What do you hope to achieve here? Now the airlift is over, more and more troops and occupation staff are leaving. There is nothing to attract visitors, tourists or businessmen. It could be years before industry picks up again. Who is going to invest in Berlin? But the situation in Hamburg, from everything Herr Norbert says, is very different.'

'What would become of Café Jochum?'

'I'd take care of it. Whatever happens, Berliners will always need somewhere to drink coffee and read newspapers . . .'

Although large areas of Hamburg were still in ruins, Viktoria's first impression of the city was of bustling, pulsating industry. Everywhere new buildings were being erected. People went about their business with an air of determination. Their voices rang with confidence. Their well-fed figures reflected their new affluence. Hamburg was indeed very different from Berlin.

Norbert and Lili met her from the airport in Norbert's new Mercedes. They drove first to Stefan's apartment, where Viktoria was staying during her visit, then to the Binnenalster, where Eduard was waiting for them at the villa. Lili leaned forward in the back seat of the car, chattering non-stop, pointing out city landmarks and Landgut developments, interspersing her commentary with excited descriptions of their plans for the new hotel.

From the moment she set foot inside the villa, Viktoria knew Norbert was right about its potential. She looked around her, imagining guests arriving at an hotel. Commissionaires waiting on the front steps. Hall porter's desk. Reception desk and office. Reception lounge. Yes, with careful arrangement, all these necessities could be accommodated. Most important of all, however, the atmosphere was right. Already, she felt at home.

Norbert flung open a door. 'Come in here. We've decided that if you took down the wall between these two rooms, they would make a beautiful restaurant. And the kitchen is right behind. Look at that view!'

It was indeed a superb view across a road and a wide promenade to the sheltered inland harbour of the Binnenalster. Sunlight was sparkling on the water and the newly planted trees along the promenade were in full leaf.

Impatient to show off the rest of the building, Norbert and Eduard had already moved to another room, followed by Lili. 'What about this for the bar?' Norbert called. 'Doesn't it remind you of the Quadriga?' Viktoria hurried to catch up with them. Yes, the room was remarkably like the Quadriga bar, a little smaller, but the same shape . . .

'Now, look at this! What a ballroom! If we put in French windows, people could dance on the lawn in the summer.'

Viktoria looked out of the window onto an expanse of rutted grass. A garden . . . For one who had spent the last four years underground, it was almost beyond the realms of belief.

168

They went upstairs and Norbert explained how private bath-rooms could be incorporated into most rooms without too much loss of space. 'There are only thirty rooms at the moment, but we could add another couple of floors in due course. There's even room for a lift.'

That evening, when Stefan arrived at Norbert's flat, he found the dining-room table covered in sketch plans, and his mother, Norbert, Eduard and Lili all excitedly talking together, totally ignoring Helena screaming in her cot, Tristan and Kleo playing hide and seek, and Reinhild listening to a radio play.

Stefan grimaced at the hubbub, then kissed his mother and asked, 'What do you think of it?'

'It's a lovely building. And Norbert has come up with some wonderful ideas to make it like the Quadriga.'

'Norbert?' Stefan could not help laughing. 'Mama, credit where credit is due. Norbert wanted to pull it down and start again. It's Eduard you have to thank. It was Eduard, who was determined that your new hotel should be designed as far as possible along the lines of the Quadriga!'

Viktoria turned to Eduard. 'Thank you, Eduard,' she said, gravely. 'My parents would be glad to know their ideas live on.' And at that moment, she knew she had made her decision. She would turn the old mansion into an elegant hotel in the spirit of the Quadriga.

That evening, in her room at Stefan's flat, Viktoria took off the body belt she always wore and spilled the contents on to the bed, gazing at what was left of her mother's, Luise's and her own jewellery: Ricarda's ornate Wilhelmine pieces, Luise's distinctive art deco creations, and the beautiful sets Benno had given her to mark the important landmarks of her life – among them, rubies for her fortieth birthday and a gold and diamond choker to mark her fiftieth birthday and the Hotel Quadriga's golden anniversary in 1944.

The following morning, back at the villa, she and Norbert discussed finances. 'If we use the site as collateral, it should be possible to raise a loan,' Norbert said confidently.

'I don't want to be any more reliant upon you than I have to,' Viktoria stated firmly. 'I still have some jewellery, which I can sell.'

169

'You shouldn't do that!'

'Why not? I'll never wear any of it again. Apart from anything else, it all holds too many memories . . .'

Norbert gave her a searching look. 'You're sure?'

'Absolutely certain. I've had enough experience of being indebted to the Krauses. If I were able to, I'd buy the building from you now. But apart from my jewellery, I don't have any other assets except Café Jochum and the cottage at Heiligensee. I won't sell Café Jochum and I can't even imagine anyone wanting to buy the cottage.'

'You've got the cottage back?'

'From the French, yes. I'm renting it out at the moment. There are three families living there while they wait for new accommodation.'

In his mind's eye, Norbert could see the cottage, a haven of peace beside the lake, the only building he had ever seen and felt an immediate affinity for, even though he had never even stepped inside its doors. 'Would you really consider selling it?'

If her mother, Benno and Luise were still alive, if the Russians and French had not requisitioned it, if Monika and her children lived in Berlin, if Stefan were married with children of his own, then the cottage at Heiligensee would still have a purpose, but Viktoria herself would never live there again, just as she would never again wear her jewellery. 'To the right person,' she said, 'yes, I would sell . . .'

Impetuously, Norbert said, 'I'll offer you a deal. You sell your jewellery and I'll give you the rest of the money you need for start-up capital in exchange for the cottage.'

'You? But why do you want it?'

He gave a rather sheepish smile. 'I like it. It's old, like this place is. It possesses character, a feeling of tradition.'

For a young man who had grown up in the Baron's soulless 'Fortress' and now lived in an overcrowded modern flat, Viktoria reflected, yes, the cottage could appear like that. But – 'It's in Berlin, Norbert.'

'Berlin's future is more secure than it was before the block-ade.'

'I suppose so . . .'

'Think it over, you don't have to make an immediate decision.

170

But I won't change my mind. What's more, if you do decide to go ahead, I'll have my solicitor draw up a lease agreement, which will allow you the option of purchasing the hotel after ten years.'

'No! That's too generous.'

'There can't be many Krauses who have been accused of that! However, what I'm proposing makes sound business sense. If we go ahead, in ten years' time, you own an hotel, while I have the money for the freehold and the cottage, as well as income for the next ten years.'

Slowly, Viktoria nodded. 'All right. And thank you, Norbert . . .'

After that, events moved at high speed. Final planning permission was granted. Norbert received his loan. Viktoria's jewellery was sold. Solicitors in Hamburg and Berlin were busily engaged in drawing up lease documents in respect of the new hotel and contracts for the transfer of title of the Heiligensee cottage. At the beginning of November, an army of builders descended on the hotel and work commenced.

It was then that a disturbing incident occurred. Viktoria was standing watching some workmen erect scaffolding under the supervision of the foreman who, with a trace of a Berlin accent, was barking staccato orders, interspersed with profanities. A chill wind was blowing in from the North Sea. Viktoria shivered, pulled her coat closer around her and, as the scaffolding reached the second storey, decided to go indoors. There was a crash and a pole landed just where she had been standing.

White and shaken, she peered up through the trelliswork of tubes and boards to find the foreman looking down at her. He uttered no word of apology, merely stared at her with insolent hatred in his pale-lashed eyes.

Later, describing the event to Norbert, she said, 'If I hadn't moved when I did, that pole could have killed me. From the way that man looked at me, I think he was hoping it would.'

'Alfred Tobler's a strange fellow. But why should he want to kill you?'

Viktoria frowned. 'I have the feeling I know him from somewhere. His voice and his eyes, they are strangely familiar to me . . .'

*   *   *

171

It had been dangerous enough for Otto Tobisch when Stefan Jochum came to Hamburg. When Viktoria arrived, he knew he was in grave peril, for she was one of the few people in the world who knew him well enough to identify him. He took the first opportunity which presented itself to kill her and, when the scaffolding pole failed to hit its mark, he knew he must leave Hamburg.

That night, he packed his few belongings into a bag and, wearing the shabby suit in which he had arrived in Hamburg, made his way to the railway station. The first train leaving the station was going to Cologne, so he took that. Nobody paid any attention to him as he travelled third class, his old holdall on the rack above him and his face shielded by a newspaper as he dozed. No police searched the train. Nobody asked to see his identity papers. From Cologne, he caught a train to Frankfurt, and from there, after several changes, to Triberg in the Black Forest. He walked the last few miles to Bergtal, keeping to the shelter of fields and woods. On the outskirts of the village, he found a deserted barn and waited for night.

At last, the church clock chimed midnight and he decided he could risk approaching the Waldblick. The village was deserted, all the houses shuttered and their occupants asleep. Otto crept round to the back of the inn and immediately a dog began to bark. A door opened and a beam of light shone across the courtyard. Under shadow of a large dustbin, Otto froze. 'Who's there?' a voice demanded and the silhouette of a big, shambling man with a huge beer gut appeared in the doorway.

'Hubert.' Otto's voice was scarcely more than a whisper.

'Come out of there, or I'll loose the dog on you.'

'It's Otto Tobisch.' He stepped forward so that Hubert could see him.

'Dear Lord God – Otto!' Hubert propelled him through the door into the empty kitchen. 'Good heavens, man, I hardly recognize you!'

For a long time into the night, the two men sat talking, while Otto hungrily devoured a large plateful of *Bratwurst* and potatoes, washing it down with several tankards of beer. Finally, after catching up on the other's experiences since the end of the war, Otto said, 'I don't care what I do, but I must be near Adolf. I could do forestry work. Then, when we see if the Jochum woman has set the police on my trail, I can decide what to do next.'

Hubert took a long draught of beer. 'I'm prepared to help you as far as I can, but you have to understand, I can't endanger my family and my livelihood by harbouring a wanted war criminal. Anna has to report to the Military Police every week. As you know, Otto, she's not very quick. She might easily give you away.'

Otto's eyes narrowed. 'And Adolf?'

Hubert hesitated. 'He believes you're dead.' When anger glinted in Otto's eyes, he went on quickly, 'The boy had to be given an explanation after you went away. But Anna's always told him you were a great general and he holds you in tremendous admiration. His ambition is to grow up like you. And he looks very like you, Otto. He's a fine kid. But he's only eight. You can't expect him to hold his tongue.'

Because it was out of season, there were no guests staying at the Waldblick, so Otto was able to spend the night in a first-floor bedroom. When he awoke, a winter sun was shining and children's voices were calling outside. Keeping back from the window, he gazed down into the street. A woman and a child were standing in front of the inn. One was Anna, the expression on her fat face as stupid as ever. The boy, however, looked bright, his hair a light blond, his clear skin tanned. Adolf . . .

Human relationships had been of small account in Otto's life. To the thousands who had died under his command, he had never given a thought. They had been objects, not people.

Only Adolf had ever aroused in him the feeling of love. Otto had never questioned why this should be. He simply knew that his son gave a purpose to his life. Adolf was his hope for the future. Adolf was a part of himself.

Hubert brought a breakfast tray up to the room and sat with Otto while he ate it. 'I've talked things over with Theresia and we've decided you can stay for a few days. But we can't keep you here, Otto.'

'There are huts in the forest. I could hide in one of them.'

Hubert shook his head. 'It's too dangerous. You'd need provisions, clothes and proper heating. There are foresters and

173

hikers who would notice you. No, I tell you what I suggest. I have a contact in Baden-Baden, a Party member, who used to be a printer on a newspaper. Now he prints public information brochures for the French. Unknown to them, he is also an excellent forger. He'll make up documents for you in another name. Because of who you are, it won't cost you anything. Then you'll be able to go elsewhere . . .'

For a long time, Otto was silent. The village community of Bergtal was very different from the isolated farmstead above Traunkirchen. Hubert was right. If he remained here long, there was bound to be speculation about him. Even if Anna did not inadvertently betray him, someone else could.

Perhaps he should do what the Nattenberg escape committee had originally suggested and go abroad. So far, he had been lucky, but his luck would not hold for ever. He thought of the bag of jewels he had buried in the cow shed. Were they still there? Or had Anna found them? Those precious stones could make all the difference to his future. If he had those, he could afford to start a new life wherever he chose.

'You're right,' he eventually told Hubert. 'I don't want to be a burden to you. But first, I have to see Anna.'

Hubert could not keep husband and wife apart. Reluctantly, he agreed.

Anna's shock at discovering that the husband she had convinced herself was dead was still alive was painfully apparent. 'Where have you been?' she asked reproachfully. 'Why didn't you contact us? The Americans told me dreadful things. They said you killed millions of people.'

I should have killed you, too, Otto thought, but he said, 'During the war, I had to obey orders like every other soldier, Anna. Sometimes, that meant killing people.'

He told her that the Americans had done him a terrible injustice, but that so long as the Allies continued to occupy Germany he stood no chance of proving his innocence. 'Which means I have to leave here again soon,' he said. 'But before I do, I should like to take with me a few memories of the life I once knew.' His fingers pinched her capacious thigh.

That night, when she was sure everyone must be asleep, Anna crept downstairs from her attic bedroom, as quietly as

174

her ungainly bulk would allow. If she did not go to Otto, he might come to her and Dolfi, asleep in the next room, might be disturbed. She agreed with Hubert that Dolfi and Freddy were too young to keep such a momentous secret as Otto's return.

Otto's door was slightly ajar, and Otto himself naked on the bed. 'Where the hell have you been?' he asked thickly. After getting up and locking the door, he pushed her dressing gown and nightdress up round her waist and forced her over the bed, entering her from behind.

The next few days were tense. Since there was no visit from the police, it seemed increasingly likely that Viktoria had not reported him, but there was no certainty. Otto remained in his room where, during the day, he watched out of the window to catch sight of his son, and, every night, Anna willingly subjected herself to him. Hubert visited his printer friend and put in hand arrangements for Otto's new papers. On Saturday, he returned home with an identity card showing him to be a Czechoslovak called Rudolf Tatschek, a bachelor, fifty-six years old, a Roman Catholic by religion and a construction engineer by profession.

'If you take my advice, you'll go abroad,' he told Otto. 'My friend has given me contact addresses of Nazi cells in Austria and Italy. Sympathisers there will help you get to the Middle East or South America.'

Again, to his relief, Otto did not argue. Hubert had feared he might insist upon taking Anna and Dolfi with him. He was familiar with every creaking floorboard in the inn and Anna's nocturnal visits had not escaped his notice. But it appeared that Otto had resigned himself to going alone.

That night, when Anna came to his room, Otto was fully dressed, a rucksack Hubert had given him waiting by the door.

'Otto, what's the matter?' she cried. 'Where are you going?'

He did not answer her question. Instead, he said, 'When we came back from Poland, I buried some things in the cow shed at Traunkirchen. Do you remember?'

She stared at him blankly. Upon her arrival at Bergtal, she had again hidden the pouch of jewels under her mattress, looking, every night, to make sure it was safe. While it was there, she felt secure. It had become a kind of talisman now.

'Do you remember?' Otto's expression and the tone of his

175

voice were very different from the previous nights. 'What happened to the jewels? Are they still there?'

He did not give her time to reply, but moved threateningly towards her. 'Where are they?'

She shook her head, trying to control a feeling of panic.

With the expertise of one who had strangled many people during his life, Otto put his hands round her neck and pressed his thumbs into her windpipe. 'Tell me where they are.'

Never had Anna known such fear or such pain. 'In my bedroom,' she gasped. Otto relinquished his hold slightly. 'Under the mattress . . .'

'Show me.'

Trembling in every limb, she led him up to her room, opened the door and kneeling down beside the bed, took the little purse from its hiding place.

Otto was seized by a wild, uncontrollable fury. How dared she try to steal his jewels? He stared with distaste at the massive rump, upon which he had exercised his sadistic pleasure for the last few nights, then glanced at the capacious undergarments piled on a chair beside the bed. On the top of them lay, incongruously, a pair of nylon stockings. The thought of Anna cladding her lumpy, veined legs in such fripperies made him want to spew.

Well, let her wear her nylons, but not in the way she had envisaged. While she still fumbled under the mattress, he took one of the stockings, wound its ends expertly round his hands, stepped forward and slipped it swiftly in front of her face and round her neck. He had no use for her any more. While she was alive she remained a liability.

For a few moments, she struggled feebly, then her face went puffed and red, her eyes bulged and she sagged limply onto the bed. Otto gave one final tug. Then he let go the stocking and lowered her body to the floor.

Satisfied that she was dead, he took the jewels and left the room. For a moment he paused outside the next door room, where he assumed Adolf was asleep, tempted to seize the boy from his bed and take him with him. But it was too dangerous. Later, when Adolf was older, he would write to him and Adolf could join him. Or maybe, one day, when the witch hunt stopped, he could even return to Germany himself.

As silently as he could, he made his way downstairs, stopping off to pick up his rucksack. The bedclothes had been changed the previous day and were unslept in. There was no evidence that he had ever been there. He let himself out of the inn, growled, 'Shut up!' as Hubert's dog barked, and set off through the sleeping village towards the south.

At dawn, a farmer on his way to market, offered him a lift. 'You're out early,' he commented curiously. Otto explained that he was a newly released prisoner of war, trying to return to his family. His unshaven face, shabby clothes and dusty, scuffed shoes lent credence to his story. The farmer went out of his way to take him as far as Donaueschingen. Several other people took pity on him after that and eventually he arrived at Lindau on Lake Constance, where he went to the first of the addresses supplied by Hubert's friend.

From there on, his escape proved ridiculously simple. As Rudolf Tatschek, a Czechoslovak refugee born in Pilsen, he passed through first the German, then the Austrian frontier controls. The guards, sympathetic to people who had escaped from the Russians, even wished him luck.

It was Dolfi who discovered his mother's body. When Anna did not wake him as usual in the morning, he went into her room and found her lying on the bedside rug. His screams rent the building from top to bottom and had not only Hubert, Theresia and Freddy racing from their beds but passers-by rushing in from the street. Soon sirens were blaring through the village and the inn was crawling with policemen. Photographs were taken of Anna's corpse, then she was covered with a rug and taken away by ambulance to the mortuary. White and shaken, the family sat in the kitchen under the eagle eye of a police constable, waiting to be questioned.

Never had Hubert had to think so quickly as he did that morning. There was no doubt at all in his mind that Otto was the murderer. But why? For a week he and Anna had been sleeping together as husband and wife. Why should Otto then kill her?

177

But that was far from foremost among the questions in Hubert's mind. Most important was his and his family's involvement. If he was not careful, the very thing he had been at most pains to avoid would happen. The police would discover that he had been giving refuge to a notorious war criminal. But if he did not confess about Otto, he or Theresia might find themselves accused of murder.

However, although the police cross-examined them all regarding their relationships with Anna, it was soon evident that they did not suspect Theresia or Hubert of murdering her sister. There were witnesses in the village to testify that the Albers had always treated Anna and her son well. Above all, they had no motive to kill her. Anna had arrived penniless: she had worked for them in return for food and shelter. The arrangement had been mutually beneficial.

Every room in the inn was searched but nothing suspicious was discovered, although the kitchen door was found to be unlocked. Freddy and Dolfi could confirm that there had been no overnight guests for more than a fortnight. Anna's room was finger-printed but the only prints were hers, including on the doorknob. Nothing appeared to have been stolen. Even her silver crucifix was still on the bedside table.

It was Freddy who remembered hearing the dog bark during the night and a villager recalled waking up from a nightmare and looking out of the window on his way to the bathroom and seeing a figure with a rucksack walking down the street. But he had been too concerned with his nightmare and anxious not to disturb his wife to wonder what the nocturnal hiker was doing.

In due course, an inquest was held and a verdict of murder by a person or persons unknown was returned. The Inspector in charge of the case had his own suspicions as to what had occurred. From the police files, he knew who Anna Feldmann had been. More and more refugees from the East were arriving in Germany, including many former concentration camp inmates. Various Jewish organizations were demanding that the Allies continue the war crimes trials and some hotheads were even threatening to execute summary justice on former Nazis allowed to remain at large. One of these, the Inspector privately believed, unable to find Otto Tobisch, had tracked down Anna, found the

178

back door to the Waldblick accidently left open and taken the opportunity to wreak his revenge on her.

Since Hubert and Theresia Albers said that, although they would like the murderer found, for Dolfi's sake they would prefer the case not to be given too much publicity, Anna Feldmann's murder passed unresolved into the annals of Baden-Wuerttemberg history.

Otto travelled through Austria and crossed into Italy, where he was directed to a Red Cross refugee camp and given food, a bed for the night and money to help him on his journey. Within a week, he was in Milan, at the home of a Franciscan priest.

Father Peter Hofer was an urbane, cultured man, who kept an elegant house, spoke German as fluently as he did Italian and sympathized deeply with Otto's predicament. Their personalities and backgrounds were so different that Otto never felt at ease in his host's company, but he did come to understand why the priest was helping him.

Father Peter had been born in Meran in the South Tirol, an area which had been part of Austria until it was ceded to Italy in 1919. In Hitler, he had seen a compatriot and a Catholic, albeit a lapsed one, who alone among European leaders had attempted to stop the spread of Bolshevism. He held Jews in as great a contempt as he did Communists and was bitterly outspoken against the new State of Israel, which he claimed, as the birthplace of Christianity, should never have been permitted to become the homeland of the Jews.

It was Father Peter who suggested Otto went to the Middle East, to Egypt or Syria. The Arab states, defeated in their invasion of Israel in 1948, had spent the time since in building up their armies, so that their next attack should be successful. Otto's particular talents, Father Peter was sure, could be put to good use by the Arabs in their on-going battle against Israel.

Following a letter from Father Peter to the Vatican Displaced Persons Relief Centre, Otto received a refugee passport and an entry permit to Syria. In December, he embarked on the last stage of his journey to the port of Bari and thence by ship to Syria.

In Damascus, he discovered men from all branches of the

179

German armed forces, including the SS and the Gestapo, whose expertise was being very productively used in creating a military system based on the Nazi pattern. He was given a Syrian passport to protect his true identity, should anyone still be on his tracks. Although his new identity was respected for his own personal security, Otto was recognized by several former colleagues and immediately given his own area of responsibility – that of establishing Syrian army units in the style of SS *Einsatztruppen*.

Traffic between Germany and Syria was by no means one-way. The Nazi Party might have been banned, but the Socialist Reich Party kept alive Nazi ideals in Germany. There was a regular courier network between Syria and the Federal Republic, transmitting funds, letters of support and articles for inclusion in the extreme right-wing German press. If Otto wished to keep in touch with his family and friends at home, he too could use the courier service. A former official in the Nazi Propaganda Ministry ran the SRP office in Stuttgart, and would ensure Otto's letters reached his son.

The heat was the main problem Otto encountered in Damascus. Otherwise, the city was very congenial to him. He sold the jewels and deposited the proceeds in a bank under his assumed name. When Adolf was older the money could be used to buy his passage to Syria and set him up in a new life. In the meantime, Otto was established in comfortable quarters, living among fellow countrymen and doing the same job which had occupied most of his lifetime – the planned extermination of the Jewish race.

That Christmas, Uncle Hubert gave Dolfi a puppy, a chestnut short-haired Pointer with white markings, whom he christened Prinz. From the moment Prinz joined the household, he showed his single-minded devotion to Dolfi. Intelligent and tenaciously loyal, he slept in a basket beside Dolfi's bed and, had he been allowed, would have accompanied his young master to school. Finally freed from the fear of dogs which had haunted him ever since Wolf had so terrified him as a child, Dolfi lavished Prinz with affection.

Around that same time, he made another friend. Tobias

Mueller was twenty and helped his father run the local petrol pump and car repair workshop in an old wooden building on the outskirts of the village. Although the forecourt was clean and neat, behind the scenes was a veritable wonderland of oil drums, discarded body parts, bits of engines and other rusting objects which Herr Mueller said 'might come in useful one day,' and, indeed, often did. Above the garage was accommodation, where the Muellers had lived while Tobias was very young. When their fortunes had improved before the war, they had moved to a cottage near the Waldblick, and these rooms over the garage, smelling rather of sump oil, formed additional storage.

Mad on cars, Tobias could talk for hours on end about twin overhead camshafts and multiple carburettors and Dolfi, with Prinz at his side, proved a willing audience. When a car came in for repair, Dolfi watched closely, passing Tobias and his father tools, while they tinkered with the engine. He learned quickly and Herr Mueller laughed, 'There's no doubt what you'll be when you leave school, young Dolfi. A mechanic.'

Although he had friends of his own age, Dolfi was drawn to the company of people older than himself, like the Muellers. Gradually, they, Freddy, Hubert and Theresia came to replace the parents he had lost, and with their help, he recovered from the shock of his mother's murder, although for years his dreams were haunted by the image of her distorted features and the noose around her neck.

It was on Dolfi's tenth birthday on 14 November 1950, that the letter came. Dolfi was sauntering down the village street towards Tobias's petrol station, when a car drew to a halt a few yards ahead of him. Assuming the driver wanted to ask directions, Dolfi went to his assistance. But the man, dark glasses concealing his eyes, asked, 'You are Adolf Feldmann?' When Dolfi nodded, he thrust an envelope into his hands. 'This is for you. Don't tell anyone about it. Understood?' Then he sped away.

Dolfi put the envelope in his pocket and, instead of going to see Tobias, went into the forest, where he was unlikely to be disturbed. There, he read his letter. It appeared to have been written in a place called Damascus, it was very brief, and its contents were a bolt from the blue.

181

'Dear Adolf,' it read.

I was a comrade of your father during the war. He was a brave soldier and a great military leader. In fact, I was serving with the General, when you were born. I remember the day as clearly as if it was yesterday. There was a great celebration in the officers' mess. The General was very proud of you. So I am writing to wish you a happy birthday.

Perhaps one day, it will be possible for us to meet. In the meantime, you must not mention to anyone that you have received this letter, which you should destroy immediately. But you can reply to the address given below, from where the letter will be forwarded to me in Syria. I should like to hear all about you and your life in Bergtal. But I stress that, for security reasons, our correspondence must be kept secret.

Yours sincerely, Rudolf Tatschek.

Underneath was a *poste restante* address in Stuttgart.

Again and again, Dolfi re-read the letter, trying to work out what it really meant. Did it mean that his father was still alive? Or was Rudolf Tatschek trying to tell him his father was dead? It wasn't clear. But one thing was certain, Rudolf Tatschek had known his father, the great general.

Reluctantly, he did as the Syrian instructed. If he kept the letter he knew he would have to show it to his uncle and aunt, Freddy and Tobias. After tearing off the Stuttgart address, he tore it into shreds and buried them under a pile of leaf mould.

The very next day, he replied, telling Herr Tatschek about himself, Prinz, Tobias and all his other friends in the village, and asking for more information about his father.

Rudolf Tatschek, however, proved a disappointing correspondent. Not until his next birthday would Dolfi receive another letter. But those few lines had served to fill his young heart with hope. His mother might be dead, but there was a remote possibility that his father was still alive!

PART TWO

1950–1961

We were young, we were merry, we were very, very wise,
And the door stood open at our feast,
When there passed us a woman with the West in her eyes,
And a man with his back to the East.

Mary Coleridge

Chapter 9

The Hotel Jochum-Hamburg opened on Viktoria's fifty-sixth birthday, 15 June 1950, and she adopted the same philosophy for running it as she had at the Quadriga. Other hotels might be bigger, but hers would be the best.

Under the Chancellorship of Dr Adenauer, his Finance Minister Dr Fritz Schaeffer and the ebullient Economics Minister Professor Ludwig Erhard, the economy was continuing to expand. In years to come, people would describe this period during the early 1950s as the 'Economic Miracle'.

Exports were growing at an amazing pace, bringing in vital foreign currency and encouraging foreign businessmen, eager to take advantage of Germany's low prices. Close to the railway station and within easy access of the airport, the Hotel Jochum-Hamburg was where most of them stayed. Refurbished to give the impression of the secluded atmosphere of a private house, its rooms and suites tastefully decorated, it was rapidly becoming recognized as the city's most exclusive hotel.

New Year's Eve gala balls at the Hotel Quadriga, originally hosted by Karl and Ricarda Jochum, then by Viktoria and Benno, had been a traditional high point in Germany's social calendar. Under the austere circumstances pertaining in 1950, it was not possible to provide the same sumptuous facilities at the Jochum-Hamburg's first New Year's Eve dinner-dance. Nevertheless, Viktoria made every effort to make this start to a new decade an unforgettable occasion.

Slim, tall and stately, her white hair styled in a permanent wave and wearing the first new evening gown she had owned since before the war, she welcomed her guests, as they streamed through into the foyer.

Behind the scenes, Eduard Wild made sure that everything was in order and no last-minute detail had been forgotten.

Eduard no longer worked for Norbert, but was now assistant to the hotel's General Manager, Dirk Kaiser. It was inevitable, Norbert had said laughingly, that since he had been so involved in building the hotel he should want to stay there.

The friendship between Eduard and Lili was closer than ever. Indeed, Eduard thought of Lili more as a young sister than a friend. The change in her since Viktoria had come to Hamburg and she had left Hannelore to live at the hotel was quite phenomenal. She remained thin and under-developed for her age, but she had lost her tragic air. Now, her green eyes shone more often with laughter than glittered with tears.

Viktoria encouraged their relationship. Indeed, she herself treated Eduard as part of the family, talking to him much as she did to Stefan and Norbert, as an equal rather than an employee.

The New Year's Eve ball provided an opportunity for a family reunion of sorts and Eduard had taken his place with them at the family table the previous evening, saying very little but enjoying the feeling of being part of a whole.

Monika and Hans had been unable to obtain the necessary inter-zonal passes to come to Hamburg, and Viktoria had had to content herself with sending them a food parcel. However, Norbert and Reinhild were there (the children left with a babysitter for the evening) and so were Stefan, Lili and Hannelore. So, too, were Baron Heinrich and Trude, much to Viktoria's chagrin, but Norbert – more out of a desire to show off than any real affection – had insisted that his grandfather and mother be invited and Viktoria had scarcely been able to refuse him.

That evening, Eduard and Viktoria were too busy to join the family for dinner. After welcoming their guests in the foyer, they had time for only a kitchen snack before making their way to the ballroom. They arrived just as the Ted Starr Band was launching into their signature tune, Hoagy Carmichael's 'Stardust'. Ted Starr, sporting a Harry James moustache, stepped forward, the mellifluous notes of his trumpet wafting through the room. An American led his partner onto the floor and danced with her in close embrace, his hand on her buttocks. Others followed suit and soon

186

the floor was thronged with a slow-moving mass of dancers.

'I can't understand what Viktoria is thinking of!' Trude complained. 'An English band, playing American music. What's the matter with Strauss?'

'Always thought dancing was a waste of time,' the Baron grumbled, as a waiter wheeled him towards the family table.

A small hand slipped itself into Eduard's and Lili sighed, 'Isn't that a lovely tune?'

Eduard looked down at her and smiled affectionately. She was wearing the emerald green dress and matching pumps that Viktoria had given her for Christmas and her thick auburn hair was tied up with a bow on top of her head. Little Lili was turning into quite a young lady.

As the evening progressed, the air in the ballroom became heavy with smoke, the room loud with music and conversation, and the dance floor a mass of people. The music changed tempo and embarked on a series of popular jive hit tunes. Their feet keeping to the constant rhythm, the dancers moved towards and away from each other, the girls spinning round under their partners' arms, pirouetting away from them, coming back to meet them, their skirts flying, their cheeks glowing, their eyes full of laughter. In their midst Eduard and Lili were having delightful fun trying to follow the steps and Norbert was partnering an attactive blonde with an expertise which proved this was not the first time he had jived.

'It's disgusting,' Hannelore muttered. 'You can see that girl's knickers.'

Viktoria, taking her seat at the table just in time to hear this remark, sighed. She thought these new dances were fun and wished she were young enough to jive and jitterbug.

'What else would you expect from a dance introduced by the Americans?' Hannelore continued. 'They're so brash. They're trying to take over our lives with their tasteless habits, their immoral dancing, their chewing gum, their Coca Cola . . .'

'And so rich,' Trude complained. 'The British are bad enough, but the Americans have no idea what hardship is.'

Viktoria bit back angry words. The tide of anti-British and particularly anti-American feeling she encountered in the Federal

187

Republic infuriated her, where everything British and American was suspect, including the Berlin airlift and Marshall Aid. Now they were on the way to becoming self-sufficient, people preferred to forget the enormous debt they owed the Allies.

Even Stefan was becoming anti-American, although for different reasons. He was deeply disturbed by Senator Joseph McCarthy's campaign against American intellectuals, accusing them with little or no evidence of being Communists. Having himself seen Hitler conduct a similar campaign, Stefan's editorial in the December issue of *Aktuell* had sweepingly condemned McCarthyism.

Seated in his wheelchair at the head of the table, Baron Heinrich was waving a large cigar and discoursing to Stefan on the Korean War, which had broken out exactly six months earlier. 'This war could reach Europe,' he said. 'If the Americans lose in Korea, and they're doing badly at the moment, the Russians could take advantage of the situation by marching into the Federal Republic.'

Then they would again be in the throes of a world war, Stefan thought bitterly, but a world war which would be very different from the last one. Despite the Peace Congress which had taken place in Stockholm the previous March calling for a ban on all nuclear weapons, the threat of the bomb still remained.

'As the Americans well realize,' the Baron went on, 'what they need in Korea are German arms.'

The argument about German arms production had been raging since the autumn, when the foreign ministers of Britain, France and the United States had all recommended an arms contribution from the Federal Republic. At the same time, NATO had adopted the idea of an integrated European defence force, including the Federal Republic.

'I'm glad the Russians are winning in Korea,' Trude said. 'It's about time the Americans learned that they're not the only ones in the world.'

This time Viktoria could not keep quiet. 'If you had spent the last few years in Berlin, you wouldn't dream of saying such a stupid thing. Trude, when will you realize that the Americans are the best friends we have?'

'Some friends!' Trude retorted bitterly. 'Thanks to them, my husband and my son are in prison, and thanks to the British, I'm not even allowed to live in my own house.'

'I object to the fact that we have to finance the Occupation,' Hannelore said, 'and bear the costs of keeping Allied troops on German soil.'

'Yet we're not allowed to have an army of our own,' Trude added.

'We are benefiting from Marshall Aid,' Viktoria pointed out, 'and we do profit from the money spent by the Allied troops. Be thankful you don't live in the Soviet zone. The people there have no advantages at all.'

The argument was threatening to become quite hostile, when fortunately, the music stopped and it was time for Viktoria to step onto the podium and announce, 'Ladies and gentlemen, it is midnight! On behalf of the Jochum Hotel, I wish you all a happy and healthy new year.'

'A happy new year!' *'Prost Neu Jahr!'* Husbands embraced wives. Soldiers kissed girlfriends. Diplomats, politicians and businessmen shook hands with colleagues and old friends. The Baron added the word 'prosperous' to 'new year'. Stefan thought of absent friends. Trude and Hannelore clinked glasses and drank to the end of the Occupation. Lili planted an excited kiss on Eduard's lips, upon which he turned quite pink. Reinhild turned to her husband, but he was not there. Norbert was on the dance floor holding in an enthusiastic embrace a nubile young blonde, ten years younger and twenty pounds lighter than herself.

At the end of January 1951, the American High Commissioner, John J. McCloy, issued a general amnesty. The order to confiscate Baron von Kraus's properties was annulled and Dr Jurisch was informed that his client's personal financial assets would also be restored. The only ruling which still stood was the break-up of Kraus Industries and even that was not as dire as it seemed, for those very companies which the Americans had most wanted to cease trading were now the very ones they most needed in order to produce tanks and munitions for their war in the East.

It was one of the most satisfying moments of the Baron's life.

Again he would possess the means to make another fortune. And he, Eckhardt Jurisch and Joachim Duschek were very clear as to how it would be made. The Baron would no longer be an industrialist, but an investor in industry. Out of the ashes of the old Kraus empire, a new one would arise. And, at its head, would be the indomitable figure of Baron Heinrich von Kraus.

The Baron would not, however, be managing it alone. Again, he would have Werner to help him. As part of the amnesty, McCloy had agreed the release of a large number of prisoners of war and among those whose sentences were suddenly curtailed were Ernst and Werner. On 4 February, Joachim met them at Landsberg Prison gates and took them back to Munich.

Werner was only thirty-three, young and healthy enough to have survived imprisonment well. Ernst, however, was a different matter. He was nearly sixty-five, but he looked twenty years older: his remaining hair was snow-white and his hands trembled convulsively.

The Baron left his son to Trude's ministrations and set about bringing Werner up to date with the latest developments. Quietly, he, Joachim, Eckhardt Jurisch and Werner discussed the future, while, on the other side of the room, Ernst asked querulously, 'When are we going back to the Fortress?'

'We're not,' Trude told him, bitterly. 'This is our home now.'

'And Kraus Industries?'

'It does not exist any more.'

Ernst took his rosary from his pocket and shook his head in utter bewilderment.

The Baron did not attempt to enlighten him. He was not going to inform Ernst or Norbert about his plans for the future. They might be shareholders in Kraus Industries, but he still retained absolute control.

Shortly after this, Werner went to see Norbert in Hamburg, where they lunched at the Jochum Hotel. The two brothers had never been close and, after long years of separation, they now met as virtual strangers. Norbert tried to make Werner feel welcome, ordering a bottle of vintage claret to accompany their meal and enquiring solicitously after his family's welfare.

190

Werner, however, was in no mood for a social chit-chat, but launched directly into the purpose of his visit. 'According to Grandfather, Landgut is doing very well.'

Norbert cut through a thick salmon steak. 'It's growing at a very satisfactory pace. My latest development is in Frankfurt, in a highly desirable residential area near the Zoo.'

'You realize that, as the other shareholder in the company, I am entitled to half the profits?'

His fish halfway to his mouth, Norbert stuttered, 'Half the profits? For God's sake, Werner, you haven't done anything!'

'Because I was unable to, not because I was unwilling.'

'Nevertheless, it's through *my* efforts that Landgut has grown into the company it is. Without me, it wouldn't exist. In any case, there aren't any surplus profits. Everything I make is put back into the company to finance the next development.'

Werner glanced pointedly round the restaurant. 'You still manage to live in a degree of style, unlike the rest of your family in Essen. From what I hear, you can also afford girlfriends, as well as a wife and three children.'

Norbert put his fork down on his plate and leaned back in his chair. 'Come to the point, Werner. What do you want?'

'I am prepared to offer you a deal: my shares in Landgut in exchange for your shares in Kraus Industries.'

'You're crazy! Grandfather told me that Kraus has two thousand million losses. Whatever the proceeds are from the sale of the remaining companies they'll never be sufficient to recoup those losses!'

Werner did not tell him how mistaken he was. All he said was, 'Do you agree? Your thirty-five per cent of Kraus Industries in return for my fifty per cent in Landgut?'

Norbert shrugged. 'I think you're a fool, but I'd be an even greater fool if I refused.'

Kraus Industries was put into liquidation, its capital revalued and a new company, a limited partnership called Werner Kraus Holdings KG, was formed. Although Eckhardt Jurisch was a partner, he owned none of the hundred voting shares: they were held solely by Werner.

Their sudden, if long awaited, affluence meant that several

important changes could finally be made to the circumstances under which the Kraus family was living. Most importantly, they need not remain in Munich. Both Werner and Ernst, who had spent far too much time in a Bavarian prison, wanted to get as far away as possible from Bavaria. Essen was their obvious choice. It was the Baron's, too. Essen was where he had been born. In Essen he intended, when the time eventually came, to die. Although occupation of the Fortress was still denied to them by the British, Norbert was able to provide them with Landgut flats conveniently near the town centre, fully furnished and fitted out with modern appliances. The Baron's apartment was on the ground floor to allow easy access for his wheelchair and with accommodation for a nurse.

So it was that, living in these modest surroundings, from which none of their neighbours or acquaintances could have received any intimation of their true wealth, the Baron and Werner commenced the establishment of the second Kraus empire.

Stefan was among the newspaper, film, radio and television reporters who received an invitation to the World Festival of Youth and Students for Peace being held in August 1951 in East Berlin. 'The Russians are up to their tricks again,' Udo Fabian commented cynically. 'They're using the peace movement as a political weapon to strengthen the cause of bolshevism and weaken the free world. The more dissension there is in the West the better it suits them.'

Stefan feared he was right. But, he argued, if everyone took that attitude, there would never be peace. At least the Youth Festival offered a glimmer of hope.

It also presented Stefan with an opportunity to return to Berlin. With Bonn the seat of government and Frankfurt-am-Main turning into the new financial and commercial centre of the Federal Republic, Berlin seemed to have lost its *raison d'être*.

'Berlin is becoming a forgotten cause,' Viktoria constantly complained. After nearly two years in Hamburg she still felt like a foreigner. People talked about Berlin as if it were in another country. They felt closer to New York and London than they did to their own capital. 'When are you going to

192

make people realize that Berlin is central to so many issues which concern all of Germany – and all the world?'

The only way to do so was for *Aktuell* to have a correspondent permanently based in Berlin, filing regular reports. Udo Fabian agreed. 'And who better,' he asked Stefan, 'than a Berliner like yourself? What's more, your sister still lives over there.'

Nobody in the Federal Republic referred to the Soviet zone as the German Democratic Republic. To do so would be to recognize it as a separate state. Most people referred to it as 'over there'.

'There's no difficulty in my setting up a base in Berlin or, from what my mother tells me, visiting the Soviet sector of Berlin,' Stefan replied. 'But if you're hoping that I'll be able to travel freely in the Soviet zone, you'd better think again. Western journalists aren't exactly encouraged over there, as you know.'

'You're not exactly typical of most Western journalists. You're pretty left-wing, Stefan.'

'I'm certainly not! If anything, I'm a neutralist . . .'

Udo grinned. 'You're an idealist!' He lit a cigarette and pensively watched its smoke spiral upwards. 'Look at yourself from an outsider's point of view. You're anti-war, anti-bomb and anti-remilitarization. You don't think much of the Bonn government and you like certain aspects of current American policies even less. One could assume that you're pro-Communist.'

'I respect the theory of Communism, but I detest the practice. All forms of dictatorship are abhorrent to me, be they Nazism or Stalinism.'

'Of course,' Udo said soothingly. 'However, the point I'm trying to make is that from your articles in *Aktuell*, the Russians and German Communists could well think you are a fellow traveller, which could give you certain advantages.'

'I see what you mean.' Stefan nodded slowly. His campaign against war criminals would not be adversely affected if he worked from Berlin and he could well find himself in an even better position to attack the capitalist and militarist policies of the West. Where better to fight the horrors of Communist dictatorship than from the city over half of which Stalin already ruled? Where better to sue for peace than from a city of bomb craters and ruins?

193

When Viktoria learned that Stefan was going to Berlin, she decided to accompany him. The Jochum Hotel-Hamburg continued to do well and she could confidently leave it in the capable hands of Dirk Kaiser and Eduard. In the middle of July, she, Lili and Stefan flew to Berlin.

West Berlin had changed greatly during her absence. Everywhere, new buildings were going up and, on the scaffolding, were signs showing the symbol of the Berlin bear, reading: Berlin Emergency Programme with Marshall Aid.

Café Jochum, too, had undergone a transformation. The rubble had been fully cleared and part of its wide frontage was now occupied by a single-storey prefabricated building. A glass-shielded verandah was furnished with white-painted wrought iron tables and chairs, and filled with guests, drinking coffee and beer, eating cakes and ice cream.

It was a sunny afternoon, with scarcely a cloud in the sky, as they stepped out of the taxi and stood for a moment gazing at the scene: girls in summer dresses, men in shirt sleeves, waitresses hurrying between the tables, trays balanced at shoulder height.

They dined that evening on the typical Berlin dish of knuckle of pork with pease pudding and sauerkraut, washed down with real Berlin beer. For dessert, they had Berlin almond cake, followed by fresh Berlin coffee. Lili ate everything on her plate and amused them by saying, 'Real food again. Oh, it *is* wonderful to be home!'

Hasso ate with them and it was then Viktoria learned that he had paid for the alterations to the café out of his own savings, from the money he had earned on the black market. Overwhelmed with affection for this elderly man, who had time and time again demonstrated a loyalty far beyond the call of friendship, she thanked him and insisted that she would repay his costs immediately.

He shook his head. 'What use is money sitting in the bank? The best way you could repay me would be by building another new hotel – the Hotel Jochum-Berlin. Industry is starting to pick up. Businessmen are visiting Berlin and American Express is even organizing tours to Berlin, but there aren't any decent hotels. People in the West refer to Berlin as a bottomless barrel, resenting the subsidies they have to pay us, but we are determined to survive – and become self-supporting. Building a first-class hotel would be one very good way of bringing our facilities up to the level of the rest of the Republic.'

He was right. Returning after an absence of nearly two years, Viktoria found herself looking at Berlin with an outsider's eyes. It was as if West Berlin was lagging five years behind the rest of the Federal Republic.

Yet the spirit of Berlin still remained, that unique determination to survive despite unconquerable odds, and of this Viktoria was reminded throughout her visit. Shortly after their arrival, Mayor Reuter unveiled a memorial at Tempelhof Airport dedicated to the heroes of the airlift, a towering three-pronged monument symbolizing the three air corridors. Viktoria, Lili, Stefan and Hasso were among the thousands who gathered to hear Reuter speak.

Hasso also took them to the Town Hall at Schoeneberg, the seat of the West Berlin city government, to see the Freedom Bell, inaugurated the previous year by General Clay before a crowd of more than 400,000 and donated by the citizens of the United States as a reminder that the defence of freedom is the basis of human existence.

'The Russians are constantly saying that we have the alternative of bread or freedom, but that's untrue,' Hasso said, bitterly. 'As we can see with our own eyes every time we go over there, the Russians do not offer bread. They cannot even feed their own people, let alone the Germans.'

There were rumours that the Russians were planning another blockade. Trains and lorries were constantly being stopped and sometimes it was weeks, if not months, before products made in Berlin reached their destination.

Every day, refugees from the Soviet zone crossed into West Berlin. In the last year alone, there had been an estimated hundred thousand, many bringing nothing with them except an overnight bag, and causing tremendous headaches for the West Berlin authorities, since the refugees were unable to obtain entry permits to the Federal Republic and drained the city's limited resources even further.

One of the things which shocked Stefan most was hearing

195

some visiting West Germans refer to the refugees as Russians. Had relations between the two parts of Germany really deteriorated so greatly that Germans thought of their fellow Germans as foreigners?

Stefan remained in Berlin. Hasso found him a furnished, two-roomed apartment not far from the Kurfuerstendamm. Before Stefan quite knew what had happened, *Aktuell* not only had a Berlin correspondent but a Berlin office.

Viktoria and Lili returned to Hamburg and, at the first opportunity, Viktoria talked to Norbert about building a new hotel in Berlin. 'My father built the first de luxe hotel ever in Berlin,' she said. 'I'd like to build the first postwar one.'

Norbert smiled. 'So you're going to do what you once warned me against – invest in Berlin? Well, at least you don't have to buy a site. Provided we build upwards and not outwards, Café Jochum's site is ample. And I'm willing to risk some time drawing up plans. I'm bored stiff with apartment blocks. I'd love to create something ultra-modern.'

'What about money?' Viktoria asked.

'Under the "Emergency Building Programme" you should be able to obtain financial assistance, either in the form of a grant or a loan at favourable terms. I'll do some preliminary drawings and we'll submit them to the planning authority. Agreed?'

Viktoria agreed. For all its faults and problems, Berlin was her home. It was where she wanted to spend the rest of her life.

In East Berlin, massive posters, depicting athletic children of every race and colour, concealed the ruins. Banners stood amidst the rubble, reading: 'The youth of the world fights for peace. We greet the participants of the World Youth Peace Festival in Berlin.'

Down Unter den Linden they marched, the youth of the Communist world, an estimated million strong, singing revolutionary and socialist workers' songs, carrying huge portraits of Stalin, Mao Tse-Tung, Wilhelm Pieck and other Communist leaders. How different that broad avenue was now to how it had been in its heyday. Only the Soviet Embassy had been rebuilt. Of the Hotel Quadriga there was no vestige left. The site had been cleared and a new ministry building was in the process of being erected. Neither was there any evidence of the bronze statue of the four-wheeled chariot after which the hotel had been named. Its remains had been removed from the top of the Brandenburg Gate. The Soviet sector lacked the funds to restore it and the West Berlin authorities refused to hand over the casts of Schadow's original sculpture so that a new one could be made. Only the Red Flag remained.

The long procession entered the flag-bedecked arena of the Central Stadium where, on a high podium, the Russian military and German Communist Party hierarchy was seated. Distinctive among the marchers were members of the FDJ, the Free German Youth. They looked, Stefan thought dejectedly, from his place in the press stand, dreadfully reminiscent of the Hitler Youth.

From the podium, speeches were made, calls for peace and denunciations of 'Western warmongers' and the boys and girls lined up in the arena cheered obediently. There followed a series of human tableaux. In one, thousands of young people in bathing costumes arranged themselves to form a giant, recognizable head. 'To the greatest friend of the world's children, the great Joseph Vissarionavich Stalin. Hurrah! Hurrah! Hurrah!' they shouted.

At last, the parades and demonstrations ended. The Western journalists were loaded back into the coach which had brought them from West Berlin. They had seen what the East Berlin authorities wanted them to see.

Several times, Stefan applied for an inter-zonal pass to visit Monika and, every time, his application was refused. He was not altogether sorry. Even as children, he and Monika had not been close. When Monika had gone to live at Fuerstenmark and Stefan had fled to England, all contact between them had ceased. Since the war, they had kept in contact through Viktoria. Now Stefan doubted if, when they met, they would have anything in common. If he was honest with himself, the main reason he wanted to go to Fuerstenmark was to see the conditions under which his sister was living.

The authorities could try to prevent people travelling between the Western and Eastern zones, but it was impossible to stop communications between the Western and Soviet sectors of Berlin. There were still many people who lived in one sector and worked in another, and it was easy to travel from one side of the city to the other.

Hasso went to a barber in the Soviet sector. 'Why pay Ku'damm prices when you can get a haircut over there at a sixth of the price?' he asked.

He took Stefan with him on his trips to the Soviet sector and introduced him to a number of people who were only too delighted to enlighten him about life under the Russians. 'Berlin is a city of spies,' Hasso explained. 'Selling information is the best way to make money here. Espionage has taken over from the black market.'

One of Hasso's friends with whom Stefan established an immediate rapport was not a spy, but a man in his early sixties, a former secondhand bookseller called Paul Drescher. After the book-burning in 1933, he had been imprisoned for being a Communist. Suffering from malnutrition and chronic rheumatism, he had returned to Berlin after the war to find that his wife had been killed in an air raid and his shop and house had been razed to the ground.

Now, bent and stiff-jointed, Paul Drescher lived with his 28-year-old daughter Erika in an old flat near the Frankfurter Tor. Erika paid the rent from her salary as a shorthand-typist at the Foreign Ministry.

Paul's daily exercise was walking to the Stalin-Allee, a new, very wide, long street being cut through the ruins, to either side of which new buildings were being erected. Many of the bricks had been recovered from the rubble and were still caked with old mortar. The labourers, intent on achieving their norms, slapped them together, regardless of the cracks between them.

The norm system was one of the most resented innovations in the GDR. A norm was a standard day's work, be it for a builder, a factory worker or a farmer. Workers who achieved their norm were paid the standard wage, while those who failed to achieve it could lose up to 30 per cent of their pay. Since norms rose to keep pace with the fastest worker, there were few who achieved and even fewer who exceeded them. 'The houses will fall down before the street is even finished,' Paul forecast. 'However, by then Stalin will hopefully be dead, the Russians will have gone and we'll be free again.'

Yet although Paul Drescher said this, he did not really believe it. In his more honest moments, he would admit, 'The Russians will never leave.'

Once, Stefan asked him why he stayed in the Soviet sector, when he could easily move across to the West. 'If it weren't for Erika, I'd go,' Paul replied. 'But Erika insists we stay.'

But when Stefan asked why, Paul would only say, 'She has her reasons.'

Gradually, Stefan began to compile a comprehensive dossier on life in East Berlin, but he was extremely careful as to what he included in his reports for *Aktuell*. He was also careful never to carry a camera. More than 800 people were now estimated to have 'disappeared' in East Berlin or been arrested on charges of espionage or anti-Communist activities. The East Berlin authorities would go to all lengths to prevent evidence of any kind reaching the West of their growing military strength, the lack of progress they were making in rebuilding their part of the city, or the queues outside their shops.

Chapter 10

It was not until Paul invited him to Sunday lunch that Stefan met Erika. Paul opened the door that Sunday, unusually spruce in his best suit, rather shiny around the knees and elbows and slightly frayed at the cuffs. Stefan handed over his contribution to the meal, a bag containing a joint of smoked loin of pork, cured in the traditional manner for that very special Berlin dish, *Kassler-Braten*. It was Paul's favourite dish and one long absent from the tables of most East Berliners, whose meat rations were dwindling, the meat often horsemeat or even replaced by fish.

Paul peered into the bag and his eyes lit up. 'Not just pork, but beer as well! And what's this? Coffee! Oranges and bananas! Wait till Erika sees these!' He raised his voice and called, 'Erika, come and see what Stefan has brought!'

The kitchen door opened and Erika appeared. She was of medium height, with an attractive, well-formed figure, which even the shapeless pinafore she wore could not conceal. Blonde hair curled about her ears, framing a pert, round face. But her most striking feature was her eyes, which were shaded by long lashes and of the most startling blue.

Stefan stood rooted to the spot, caught totally unprepared. Erika bore an almost uncanny resemblance to Christa von Biederstein, the girl with whom he had been so deeply in love in those far-off days before the war and who had died so tragically at the end of the war. True, Erika was taller and lacked Christa's delicacy. But her face and especially her eyes were amazingly like Christa's.

She crossed the room and held out her hand. 'I am so pleased to meet you, Herr Jochum. Papa has told me so much about you.' Her voice was different, lower-pitched than Christa's, and she spoke with a Berlin accent.

Stefan took her hand and mumbled a greeting.

Paul laughed delightedly. 'You didn't realize I had such a pretty daughter, did you?' Then he said, 'Erika, put the kettle on! Stefan has brought us some real coffee.'

Erika cooked the *Kassler* to perfection, with a hint of bay leaf in the sauce, and accompanied by red cabbage and potato purée. Stefan ate, but he had little idea what he was eating. He spoke, but it was as if the words came from somebody else. Meeting Erika had brought the past rushing back. Memories of Christa, which he had thought buried deep in his subconscious, suddenly returned to haunt him. Erika was not Christa. Indeed, the more he observed her, the more he realized that the similarity between the two young women was literally only skin-deep, but it was sufficient to make him feel something he had not felt for a very long time. It could not be love. That was impossible. They had known each other only a few hours. But it was certainly a very strong attraction.

The autumn day was exceptionally mild and in the afternoon Erika suggested they went to Treptow. The Treptow Park, with its river walks and beer gardens, had always been a favourite spot for Sunday afternoon outings. Now, one of the first areas to be restored by the Russians, it was dominated by the Soviet Memorial.

Paul glanced with hatred towards the memorial as they passed the gates. 'Only the Russians would think of building such a thing. Well, once they go, we'll have it down soon enough.'

Erika took his arm. 'Papa, it's a beautiful afternoon. Let's forget the Russians for once and look at the river.' Before he could respond, she turned to Stefan and said, 'When I was a child, we often came to Treptow. There was an astronomical museum over there, with the longest telescope in the world. It was twenty-one metres long . . .'

Stefan nodded. 'I remember it. We used to come to Treptow, too. There was a restaurant by the Carp Pond, where we had coffee. Sometimes we took the steamer down the Spree.'

'We did, too! Once we went all the way to the Spreewald! I loved the Spreewald, with its forests and rivers . . .'

Paul had no alternative but to forget his bitter thoughts and join in their reminiscences. By the time they reached the sadly neglected remains of the formerly beautifully laid-out

201

Plaenterwald Park, he was his old self again. Erika had that effect on people. In her presence, it was impossible to remain gloomy for very long.

After he left the Dreschers' that evening, Stefan did not return immediately to his own flat, but went to Dahlem. It had been at this season of the year that he and Christa had fallen in love, thirteen years earlier. She had been eighteen. He had been twenty-three. They had walked, hand in hand, over carpets of russet leaves, to the music of the wind soughing through the pine trees . . .

The former von Biederstein house still looked the same, but the high hedges which had protected it from the curious gaze of passers-by had been ripped out. On the driveway stood a Chevrolet with American military number plates. Through the window, Stefan could see the eerie glow of a television screen.

He tried to imagine Christa's face tilted up towards his for a goodnight kiss. He tried to remember her voice telling him she loved him. But all he could see was Erika's face. All he could hear was Erika's voice.

Herr Domke, the janitor at the Dreschers' apartment block was soon giving Stefan a knowing leer when he arrived. A man of about fifty, he had lost an eye in the war and wore a black patch, which gave his smile a grotesque twist. Despite his disability, however, very little happened in the house which escaped his attention and he had been quick to notice that, whereas Stefan had used to visit Paul Drescher during the day, now he came in the evenings or at weekends, when Erika was there.

'She got back about five minutes ago,' he would inform Stefan. Or, 'She must be working late this evening. She's usually home by now.'

'Domke's an officious old busybody,' Paul would complain. 'He can't keep his nose out of anything. If you make a telephone call from the booth in the hall, you'll find his office door is open. I'm certain he steams open our mail and I'm not sure that he doesn't come snooping round the flats when we're out. He has a master key.'

Erika was more tolerant. 'Poor Herr Domke. He has nothing

202

else to think about, except what goes on in the house. He's always very nice to me.'

Stefan, who had grown up in an hotel, where it was the business of the staff to know which guests were in or out at every minute of the day, was unconcerned about Herr Domke. Indeed, if it hadn't been for the eye patch and the fact that Paul kept complaining about him, it was doubtful that he would have paid any attention at all to the caretaker.

Erika absorbed his every waking thought. Not a moment passed when he did not think of her. Wherever he was, he was conscious of her. Whatever he wrote, it was with Erika in mind.

It was by no means a one-sided attraction. Erika swiftly made it clear that she was as attracted to him as he was to her. After he had taken her out a couple of times, she responded to his rather hesitant embrace with an ardent kiss. Soon, they were behaving more like teenagers than adults, seeking every opportunity, when Paul left the room, to caress and touch each other.

One evening, instead of going home, Erika came to Stefan's flat. He had spent the afternoon tidying up. The table was ready laid for the cold meal he had prepared, with an arrangement of white and gold chrysanthemums as the centrepiece. A bottle of white wine was in the fridge. The room was illuminated by a single table lamp, which cast a golden glow.

No sooner had they closed the door behind them than they were in each other's arms. Tremulously, Stefan cupped his hands around Erika's face. 'Are you sure you want this?'

Her blue eyes gazed unfalteringly back into his. 'Yes,' she replied huskily, 'I have never been more sure of anything in my life.'

She undressed without any shyness, taking off her clothes with a natural grace, putting them tidily on a chair, as if she were going to bed in her own room. With awkward haste, Stefan clambered out of his own clothes. Erika lay back on the bed and held out her arms to him. 'I want you, Stefan, I want you so much . . .'

'I know. I want you too.' Not since Christa, had he felt such a longing to hold and be held, to touch and be touched, to love and be loved. There had been few women in his life during those barren, intervening years and certainly none who had aroused in him such desire.

He was afraid that he might hurt or disappoint her, that he might not live up to her expectations and so he took care to be particularly gentle. Yet their love-making, although tender, did not lack in passion. As they grew more confident, they took a fierce delight in raising each other to scarcely bearable pitches of pleasure, until finally they could endure no more and, clasping Erika in a tight embrace, Stefan made her his.

Later, with the eiderdown around their shoulders, they sat up in bed drinking wine.

'Why have you never married?' Erika asked.

'I was engaged,' he said. 'My fiancée died during the war.'

'I'm sorry.' Erika gazed down at her wineglass. After a long silence, she went on, 'There is something you should know about me. I'm married. My husband was a soldier. He was sent to the Russian Front in 1943. We had only been married six months. That was the last time I saw him.'

'Married . . . ? I had no idea. Your father never said . . .'

'Papa refuses to talk about him. He was in the concentration camp when I met Kurt. He says he would have opposed the marriage if he had known. But Kurt was just a conscript. And he seemed so handsome – and so brave. It was at the time that the British really began bombing Berlin. My mother had just been killed in an air raid. I was lonely and frightened. I wanted to live before I died . . .'

'I understand. You don't have to make excuses.'

'Papa says he must be dead now. But I'm not so sure. There are still thousands of German soldiers in Russian captivity. Kurt could be one of them. That's why I have to stay in the Soviet sector. If Kurt is still alive and he is ever released, he must be able to find me.'

Stefan lit two cigarettes and handed one to her. 'So you still love him?' It was as much a statement as a question. The mere fact that she cared enough to remain must mean that she loved him.

'I don't know. It's eight years since I last saw him. We must both have changed a lot in the mean time. But he is still my husband.' She inhaled deeply on her cigarette, then sighed, 'I suppose now you know the truth you won't want to see me any more?'

'Why not?'

'Because I don't think you're the sort of person who has affairs with married women. That's why I didn't tell you before. But you would have found out sooner or later and I'd rather you heard about Kurt from me, even if it means that I lose you.'

She was right. He had always disapproved of Norbert's affairs. Yet this was different. Erika's husband could well be dead and, if he were still alive, after a separation of eight years, she was legally entitled to a divorce. It said a lot for her moral character that she was prepared to sacrifice freedom for a man whom she no longer knew whether she loved. He put his arm round her shoulders. 'So long as you want to go on seeing me, I shall always want you,' he said, gently.

She stayed with him that night, but long after she had fallen asleep, Stefan lay awake. Her face, dimly illuminated by the street lamp outside, appeared very young and vulnerable. She moved in her sleep and her arm, resting across his stomach, drew him closer to her. You have to trust someone very much, he thought, to sleep with them. He brushed his lips against her cheek. And, in that moment, he knew that a capacity for love, which he had thought had died for ever with Christa's death, was still alive within him.

Paul made no attempt to conceal his joy at the way their relationship was developing. 'There's no one I would rather Erika fell in love with,' he said. 'I gather she's told you about her nonsensical marriage to Kurt Quanz. Well, now she has a second chance of happiness. Not many people are given that.'

It was Erika who suggested that, instead of Stefan visiting Fuerstenmark, his reunion with Monika and her family should take place at the Dreschers' apartment. There should be no difficulty in the Koenigs travelling to East Berlin to meet old friends and the presence of herself and Paul should alleviate any awkwardness between Stefan and his sister. Not, she said brightly, that she expected any awkwardness. The six-year age gap which had separated them as children would be scarcely noticeable now they were both in their thirties.

205

She proved right and the meeting, which took place at the beginning of December, was a far more enjoyable occasion than Stefan had anticipated. Monika, far from being the silly, rather spiteful little girl he remembered, had turned into a mature wife and mother. Hans, whom Stefan had only met on a couple of occasions, proved, to his surprise, to be quite an Anglophile, delighted to have someone with whom to share his memories of England.

For the first time, Stefan met his nephew and niece. Heini, now twelve, reminded Stefan greatly of Monika at the same age, not just in looks but in temperament. He wanted, he told them, to join the Free German Youth as soon as he was old enough, and after that, he was going to be a soldier.

Monika explained, 'It's been his ambition ever since he was a baby and saw Hans in his uniform. He'll grow out of the idea when he's older.'

'He'd better, since we don't have an army any more,' Hans said.

Senta was very different. Like Lili, she had inherited Ricarda Jochum's red-gold hair and green-blue eyes. Shy in the presence of strangers, she said little throughout the visit, but she endeared herself to both Stefan and Paul by asking to look at the latter's books. 'She's like you, Stefan,' Monika sighed, 'a real bookworm. She'd read all night, if we allowed her to.'

Erika took the children for a walk in the afternoon, in order to give the adults an opportunity to talk. Hans and Monika needed little prompting to talk about their lives. Guenther Rauch, Hans told them, had recently been transferred to Dresden, and he hoped soon to receive promotion himself.

'I've just been given a supervisory job at the new nursery for children under school age whose mothers are at work,' Monika said proudly.

'My parents are finding life rather more difficult,' Hans admitted. 'My father is growing disillusioned about the philosophy of so-called "Christian Realism", with which the government is trying to reconcile Communism and Christianity. As a result of his outspokenness, my mother, who is chairman of the local committee of the Red Cross, is having a rather unpleasant time with the local Party office. The villagers think she's wonderful. We have no doctor, you see, so a Red Cross nurse is invaluable. But the Party is of the view that such a position should not be held by the wife of a dissenting pastor, and someone who, moreover, is not an SED member.'

'For God's sake!' Paul Drescher snorted. 'Since when has the Red Cross been a political organization?'

'The people to suffer most are farmers,' Hans continued. 'A lot of farmers have fled. Farmer Matzke and his wife left the other week. They came to Berlin to buy fertilizer and never returned. But people like them make things all the more difficult for those who remain. If enough farmers go, the Russians will simply carry out their threat to introduce collective farms and that will be truly disastrous. As it is, I don't know what we'd do without the food parcels your mother sends every month.'

The departure of Gustav Matzke had come as a great relief to Monika, finally freeing her of the burden of guilt and fear which had weighed on her since her first disastrous visit to Berlin and Hans's return from the war.

'Have you ever thought of leaving?' Stefan asked.

Monika shook her head, but Hans said, 'Of course. But to begin with, there was no point. On my way back from England I had seen the state the rest of Germany was in. At Fuerstenmark we did at least have a roof over our heads. There are also my parents to consider. My father feels he owes a loyalty to his congregation and my mother has a loyalty to the village.'

'Presumably as a teacher, you're expected to put over a certain amount of Russian propaganda? Don't you find this difficult?'

Hans nodded. 'Particularly when it comes to glorifying Stalin. But so far as I am able, I concentrate on the more positive aspects of socialism. It's certainly preferable to fascism or Western militarism and capitalism. I'm extremely fearful of the Americans. I'm sure they're intent on gaining world power and don't care by what means they attain it.'

'And if all else fails, they'll use the bomb,' Monika went on.

'The Russians have the bomb, too,' Stefan commented.

'The Soviet Union had to develop their own atom bomb in self-defence,' Hans said. 'If America hadn't started the arms race, the Soviet Union wouldn't have had to join in.'

'Personally, I would say both sides are as bad as the other,'

Stefan said. 'But, at the final count, we Germans are in the middle.'

'The worst aspect of living in the GDR, apart from norms and rationing, is the lack of freedom,' Hans said. 'In many respects, life is not that different from under Hitler, but at least the Nazis were Germans. I hate having my life ruled by Russians.'

'But from what I've heard, the Americans don't treat people much differently,' Monika said. 'In the newspapers we read how Americans are being persecuted for being artists, intellectuals or Communists, and that American concentration camps are filled with innocent people arrested by the FBI.'

'When Stalin dies, things will improve,' Hans stated confidently.

Shortly after this, Erika returned with the children and the conversation centred on more mundane matters until it was time for the Koenigs to catch their train home. They departed with a bag full of Western provisions and some books from Paul's bookcase for Senta.

'It's been a lovely day,' Monika sighed, as they took their departure.

'You must all come again,' Erika insisted.

Monika whispered to Stefan, 'She's sweet. Why don't you marry her?'

Basilius Meyer was one of the few people in the GDR who saw *Aktuell*. Apart from high Party officials like himself and Irina Volodya, whom he had married the previous year, listening to Western radio or reading Western newspapers was forbidden. But there was still enough contact between the Eastern and Western zones for ordinary people to know that their counterparts in the West were far better off than themselves. Because of that, thousands were fleeing to the West, causing serious economic problems, for they tended to be professional men and skilled workers, the very people who were most needed to build the new state.

That was why Basilius took a great interest in Stefan Jochum's articles in *Aktuell*. To his surprise, Stefan was proving to be neither a scion of the imperialist Jochum nor the capitalist

208

Kraus families. From his writing it was clear that he deprecated the Bonn government's policies; that he wanted Germany to unite in the cause of peace; and, most importantly, that he was anti-American. Even Basilius had to admit that Stefan's most recent article in *Aktuell* was a well-reasoned and very fair summary of the advantages and disadvantages of living in the GDR. More than most Western journalists, he appeared to appreciate the fundamental ideals towards which German Communists like himself were striving.

If he were to write more articles in an even more positive vein, he would have a tremendous propaganda value, not only in the West – but in the GDR itself. If the people saw their government's policies endorsed by a Westerner of Stefan Jochum's reputation, they would be more tolerant of the hardships they were expected to undergo while their socialist state was in its infancy.

Basilius knew about Stefan's past history. Now he set out to discover all he could about his present activities. He was helped by his cousin, Rudi Sommer, who was now twenty-two years old and had proved to have such a quick mind that Basilius had been able to recommend his transfer from the People's Police to the State Security Police.

A plainclothes SSD man followed Stefan on his visits to East Berlin and found Comrade Domke, the janitor at the Dreschers' apartment block, extremely forthcoming. Soon Basilius and Rudi knew all about Stefan's affair with Erika and about the Koenigs' recent visit to East Berlin. In addition, Fuerstenmark Party Office sent him a detailed report on the Koenig family.

For Basilius, it was a tailormade situation. He found himself presented with a full cast of characters, whom he could manipulate, to achieve his propaganda aims and further his own political career.

One evening, when Erika Quanz left work, a police car was waiting to take her to Police headquarters on the Alexander Platz. Basilius sat at the back of the interrogation room, while, a spotlight shining in her eyes, Rudi accused her of being a West German agent, passing confidential information acquired in the course of her job at the Foreign Ministry to the journalist, Stefan Jochum.

209

Although she was clearly frightened, Erika Quanz was not lacking in courage. In a low but steady voice, she said, 'My relationship with Stefan Jochum is purely personal.'

The young SSD officer did not spare her. She was made to describe all, including the most intimate details of their affair.

'You are a married woman. How do you justify betraying your husband by having an affair with another man?'

With quiet dignity, she replied, 'I love Stefan Jochum. If my husband returns from Russia, I shall ask him for a divorce.'

'Does Jochum know of your decision?'

'There's no point, not while I don't know whether my husband is dead or alive.'

'You are in love with Jochum. What do you know about him?'

Her knowledge about Stefan's life turned out to be sketchy. She had never, she said, seen a copy of the magazine he wrote for. As for his family, she had met Monika and knew his mother ran an hotel, but apart from that, he had told her little about his background.

'You are not then aware of the identity of his grandfather?'

Erika shook her head.

'He is the former munitions manufacturer, Baron von Kraus.'

She was obviously shocked.

After an hour or so, Basilius drew his chair up to the table. The spotlight still shone in her eyes, so that she could not see his face. 'You may continue your relationship with Jochum. In fact, you may spend more time with him. Your duties at the Foreign Office will be extended so that you accompany him on various visits within the GDR.'

Erika stared uncomprehendingly back at him.

'It will be your responsibility to ensure that nothing he writes contains anything detrimental to the State.'

Erika's expression changed only slightly as she realized the implications of what he was saying.

'Furthermore, you will obtain information from Jochum on the present activities of Baron Kraus and other Western industrialists and politicians with whom he is in contact. Every week, someone will come to your office and give you your instructions.'

Erika remained motionless.

'If you should fail in your duties, the consequences will be extremely serious, not only for yourself and Jochum, but for your families. Shall I describe them?'

Erika shook her head. She could imagine only too well what they would be.

'Do you accept your assignment, Comrade Quanz?'

In a voice little more than a whisper, Erika replied, 'Yes, I accept.'

Stefan wanted to spend Christmas with Erika, but she persuaded him that he should be with his mother and Lili on that particularly family occasion. It was typical of her generous nature, he thought, as he flew to Hamburg on the morning of 24 December, but he did dearly wish she could have accompanied him. However, unless she left the GDR for good, that was impossible.

Christmas Eve was celebrated in the traditional Jochum fashion. Lili decorated the tree, they sang carols and gave each other presents. After their meal, Stefan told them about Erika.

Although she was delighted that Stefan should have fallen in love again, Viktoria found herself feeling strangely apprehensive. Perhaps it was because Erika lived in East Berlin and, even if her husband were dead, the affair was therefore bound to be fraught with difficulties. Or maybe it was because of her apparent similarity with Christa, and Viktoria feared Stefan was trying to reinvoke his old love. 'She sounds a wonderful girl,' she said, hoping her voice did not betray her uneasiness. 'I do look forward to meeting her.'

Lili, who was fourteen that year and spent her every free moment devouring classic romantic novels, found his story spellbinding. 'I don't want her husband to be dead,' she said, 'but I hope he has fallen in love with someone else. Then you'll be able to marry Erika. When you do, can I be a bridesmaid?'

During the holiday, Norbert came to dinner with them. He had just paid a duty visit to Essen and was full of indignation at Werner's underhandedness. 'Father received half a million Marks for his Kraus shares!' he expostulated. 'And he only had a ten per cent holding in the company. I had thirty-five per cent.

If I hadn't exchanged my shares in Kraus for Werner's shares in Landgut, I'd be one and three-quarter million better off today! I should have known there was a catch when Werner offered me that deal!'

Stefan frowned and turned to Viktoria. 'What happened to Papa's shares? You inherited them, didn't you?'

'I sent the certificates back to Joachim Duschek a long time ago, relinquishing all title to them.'

Norbert groaned. 'On my advice, if I recall! I'm sorry, Aunt Vicki.'

'Don't be. I'd rather starve than be reliant on money which was earned from selling the weapons of war and gassing Jews in concentration camps.'

'I don't understand,' Stefan said slowly. 'If Kraus Industries went into liquidation, where did the money come from?'

Norbert shrugged. 'Apparently, Kraus only went bust on paper. The sale of the remaining companies netted millions. Werner's playing everything very close to his chest, but Grandfather couldn't resist showing off. The new company, Werner Kraus Holdings, is investing world-wide in everything from radio sets to tanks. Before he dies, the Baron is determined to be once again the richest man in Europe.'

Before Stefan left for Berlin, he had a long meeting with Udo Fabian, during which he handed over the copious notes he had made so far in Berlin, told him about Erika and repeated Norbert's account of the latest Kraus developments. 'It's immoral that the Krauses should already have that kind of money and power again,' he argued. 'So much for the integrity of the Bonn government! Hans Koenig is right to prefer socialism to capitalism!'

Udo looked at him shrewdly. 'Corruption isn't the sole prerogative of capitalist governments, Stefan. In the so-called Democratic Republic, it is just as rife.'

Nevertheless, Udo did try to investigate the activities of Werner Kraus Holdings KG but his enquiries did not get him very far. The company's status as a legal partnership meant it did not have to make public its activities. No matter what avenue Udo followed, each time he came up against the ubiquitous lawyer, Dr Eckhardt Jurisch.

*   *   *

212

Stefan's anger was fuelled still further when he returned to Berlin and compared the expanding, bustling affluence he had left behind in Hamburg to the poverty which confronted him in the Eastern parts of the city. Erika spent New Year's Eve with him at Café Jochum, but he could not enter into the spirit of the festivities. Shortly after midnight, they went back to his flat. She asked, 'Stefan, what's the matter?'

Erika had become closer to him than any other person. She was not only his lover, but his friend. He could talk to her as he could to nobody else, not even his mother or Udo. As the city around them continued its revels into the early hours of the morning, Stefan told her about the Baron.

She showed no surprise at learning he was related to the Krauses, neither did she seem unduly shocked at his revelations about the Baron's current activities. 'There are some people for whom the acquisition of money and power is a compulsion,' she said gravely. 'Baron Kraus is one of them. I am just thankful you don't take after him.'

The following day, a stranger came to Erika's office and, after showing her his SSD identity card, asked, 'You have information for me, Comrade?'

She repeated everything Stefan had told her about the Krauses. She hated herself for betraying Stefan's trust, but consoled herself with the thought that he might even be pleased if he knew that the matters which troubled him so greatly were of deep concern to others than himself.

A week later, he was invited to a performance of a visiting Russian ballet company, the only Western journalist, so far as he could ascertain from his colleagues, to be so honoured. 'Why me?' he wondered aloud to Erika.

'I don't know. Journalists are the responsibility of the Political Information Office. But I'm delighted, because I shall be there, too. My department is greatly involved in cultural activities.'

It was, in fact, a marvellous evening, not least because Erika was sitting beside him. The ballet was superb and, at the reception held afterwards at the Soviet Embassy, Stefan met a number of her colleagues, all of whom were extremely courteous towards him. One even asked them both to his birthday party the following weekend.

213

Stefan hesitated, but Erika answered brightly, 'We'd love to come.' She turned to Stefan, 'Franz lives in an old cottage on the Mueggelsee! Franz, is the ice thick enough for skating?'

The ice was thick enough, although there were not skates enough for all the guests and most of them had to make do with throwing snowballs or pulling each other across the snow on makeshift toboggans. When it grew dark, a camp fire was lit and they gathered around it, sipping soup and talking. They were a mixed gathering: several were artists and writers and one was an extremely talented musician, who had formerly played with the Philharmonie. Inevitably, the conversation started with politics, but soon it had diversified into art, literature, religion and philosophy.

The fire died down. Someone threw a few more logs onto it and sparks flew into the frosty night. A girl began to sing and the others joined in. Stefan realized he had not enjoyed such simple pleasures for more years than he could remember.

On their way home, Erika asked casually, 'Will you write about today for your newspaper?'

'I should hate to get you or your friends into trouble,' he replied.

'You needn't mention any names,' she said. 'But mightn't it show your readers that, although we lack their material comforts, life over here is not as bleak as they imagine?'

'Congratulations, Comrade Quanz,' her visitor from the SSD said on his next visit to her office. 'Your friend's article was in exactly the right tone, praising our cultural activities. Next weekend, you may accompany him to Weimar, to see the Goethe House and visit the Opera.'

'He has no travel permit . . .'

'That will be arranged. His will be an official invitation. In return, when you see him next, find out what progress his partner has made in his investigations into the affairs of Werner Kraus Holdings. We want the names of the companies in which it has investments . . .'

Stefan believed Erika's story that she had arranged things with her boss so that they could visit Weimar and that she had managed to pull strings so that she could become his guide. As winter turned into spring, they took other trips inside the GDR and, although Stefan saw and heard many things which filled him with disquiet, he recognized that it was due to Erika that he was allowed freedoms and privileges granted to very few other West German journalists and took care never to write anything in his articles which might get her into trouble.

He found nothing strange in the questions she asked about his work and his family. They were lovers: they hoped one day to marry. What could be more natural than that she should be interested in his life?

In January, Norbert went to Berlin for an exploratory meeting with the West Berlin Planning Authority. He could have stayed with Hasso or Stefan, but he did neither. Instead, he stayed at Heiligensee. Often, in the intervening two years, during which his path had taken him nowhere near Berlin, he had wondered if he had done right in making that rash deal with Viktoria, but he had consoled himself with the thought that the property represented a long-term investment and, while it was let, it was at least bringing in an income.

However, in Berlin as elsewhere, as new buildings were erected, people were moving out of temporary accommodation into homes of their own, and the cottage had recently been vacated by the tenants to whom Viktoria had let it.

A set of keys was waiting for Norbert with Alfons and Waltraud Breschinski, who had taken over Fritz and Hilde Weber's former jobs as non-resident caretakers. A middle-aged couple, they were pleased at the thought of the cottage having a proper owner again, even though Norbert warned them he would not be spending much time there.

Heiligensee looked even more beautiful than on that summer's day in 1947, when Lili had taken him to see the cottage. Snow blanketed the ground. The lake was thick with ice. Before Alfons and Waltraud left Norbert alone in his new domain, Alfons stoked the stove in the kitchen and put another log on the fire in the living room. 'If you need anything, just let us know,' Waltraud said.

Norbert assured them he would, then poured himself a whisky

from the bottle he had brought with him and, glass in hand, set off on a journey of exploration. The house showed little sign now of its original owners. Patches on the wallpaper indicated where pictures and mirrors had once hung. The occasional piece of heavy furniture hinted at what the furnishings had been like. Only in the cellar, still equipped as an air-raid shelter, had time stood still.

Yet, despite the cottage's state of disrepair, it had a homely atmosphere and Norbert could not help wondering why Viktoria had relinquished it so easily. Then he remembered that most of the people with whom she had enjoyed happy times there were now dead. Probably that was the reason.

He stayed just two nights, eating at the local inn and spending his spare time drawing up a list of essential repairs, which he handed to the Breschinskis before he left, together with instructions to give the place a coat of paint.

His meetings with the Planning Authority went extremely well. The city architects agreed that a first-class hotel was an amenity greatly lacking in Berlin and Norbert's preliminary sketches convinced them that he possessed the vision and ability to create an hotel exemplifying Berlin as 'the window of the free world'.

For the rest of the winter, his every spare moment was devoted to producing drawings for the new hotel, and gradually, on paper at least, it began to take shape. Detailed plans were drawn up, costings assembled and an artist's impression of the hotel prepared.

At Whitsun 1952, Norbert and Viktoria, with Lili who, because it was half-term, was able to accompany them, went to Berlin to present the plans. At Norbert's insistence, they stayed at Heiligensee. Afraid of invoking too many old memories, Viktoria had not wanted to go to the cottage, but since January, Alfons and Waltraud had achieved miracles with scrubbing brushes and paint. Inside and out, the house gleamed with fresh, white paint, with the result that it had taken on a completely new atmosphere and Viktoria felt as if she were staying at a place she had once visited or maybe only dreamed about, but not one she had ever owned.

However, when they wandered through the garden to the

lake, Lili shivered and said, 'Let's go back to the house.' For her, one abiding memory would always remain of the cottage: of Christa's body lying in the lake.

Fortunately, there were a lot of other things to occupy Lili's mind, not least the hotel. She had expected the planning authorities to make an immediate decision, but Norbert was more realistic. 'By the time the plans are put before the committee – who will then come up with modifications which will in turn be considered – it will take at least six months,' he told her.

'But they're calling it an emergency building programme!' Lili exclaimed indignantly.

Norbert laughed. 'Even in emergencies, bureaucrats must earn their keep!'

On their first evening, they had dinner at Café Jochum with Stefan and Erika. Lili, who had been tremendously looking forward to the meeting, felt rather let-down when she actually met Erika. There was a resemblance between her and Christa, she supposed, but it was only skin-deep. What struck her most about Stefan's girlfriend was how nervy she was. Erika picked at her food, smoked too much and there was something forced about her bright chatter.

Later, when they were back at Heiligensee and Viktoria came to her room to say goodnight, Lili was sitting up in bed, her knees hunched between her arms. 'Did you notice how jumpy Erika was?' she asked.

Viktoria considered the matter and agreed, but pointed out, 'It's understandable that she should be nervous, meeting us for the first time. And she is running quite a considerable risk, visiting West Berlin and having a West German boyfriend.'

Lili's eyes gleamed. 'I think there's more to it than that. I think there's some dark and mysterious secret in her life.'

'You've been reading too many novels,' Viktoria remonstrated fondly.

Erika's nerviness might be apparent to Lili and Viktoria, but if Stefan was aware of it he gave no sign. Indeed, although he was very attentive to Erika, his mind seemed more preoccupied with politics than with her and, to Viktoria's dismay, his ideas seemed to have become even more extreme.

217

During one of their evenings together he launched into a diatribe against the West German government, accusing it of being composed to a very large extent of former Nazis. 'Do you realize that eighty-five per cent of employees at the Foreign Ministry were Nazi Party members?' he demanded angrily.

'Then there are men like your brother and grandfather,' he informed Norbert, 'war criminals, who have had their fortunes restored to them, so that they can produce munitions for the Americans. Next thing we know, we'll have an Army again – and guess who will be in charge of it? – the same generals who commanded Hitler's army.'

Norbert shrugged non-committally, reluctant to provoke an argument, and Stefan turned his attack onto Adenauer, accusing him of totally disregarding Germany's interests on a domestic and international level and siding unconditionally with the Western Allies. Adenauer, he claimed, believed that only when Europe was united could Germany be reunited and freed from the Occupation forces. 'A united Europe is more important to him than a united Germany, and I do not agree with him that a united Europe, backed by America, is the only way to prevent the Soviet Union embarking upon an aggressive war.

'In fact, I'd go so far as to say that any danger of war comes from the Americans. If you remember, in March, the Soviet Union announced that it was prepared to consider German reunification on condition that Germany was neutralized. But the Western Allies and Dr Adenauer turned the proposal down out of hand.

'I'm not saying we should cooperate unconditionally with the Communists, certainly not while they suppress human rights and run a totalitarian state. However, I remain passionately against any idea of Germany becoming remilitarized – and that is what Adenauer really wants.'

'For all that Adenauer is criticized by his opponents and even, on occasions, by members of his own party, he has achieved a great deal in a very short time,' Viktoria pointed out mildly.

Erika looked uncomfortable and put a restraining hand on Stefan's arm and, with obvious reluctance, he let the matter drop.

While Viktoria and Lili were in Berlin, Monika and her family

218

made another visit from Fuerstenmark. Norbert had returned to Hamburg by then, but the rest of them met at the Dreschers' flat. They travelled by underground to East Berlin and could not help but be conscious of the plainclothes policemen on their train and the very different surroundings when they emerged from the station. There seemed to be little rebuilding work taking place and there was certainly none of the bustling activity of West Berlin and Hamburg.

The first thing that struck Viktoria when she saw Monika was her shabby appearance. She experienced a sudden sense of compunction. Although Monika complained in her occasional letters about shortages, she had assumed her daughter was exaggerating. She had sent the food parcels Monika had requested, less because she felt they were needed, than because Monika seemed to expect them. Now, from the comments Monika and Hans let drop, she realized how very mistaken she had been. Even in the countryside, people in the Soviet zone were suffering very real hardship.

Lili was less interested in conditions in the Soviet zone than in meeting Senta and finding in her a younger, mirror image of herself. 'It's incredible,' she kept saying, 'you could be my sister!'

Paul Drescher was captivated by the two girls, especially when he discovered they both loved books. Bored with the adults' conversation, they leafed through his treasured volumes. 'Wait till I open my new bookshop in West Berlin,' he told them, 'then you'll think you're in paradise.'

'Are you going to move to West Berlin?' Lili asked.

Paul glanced in the direction of Erika, seated at the table, talking with the others, and lowered his voice. 'I hope so, yes. When Erika and Stefan get married, we'll live in the West.'

During the afternoon, he took the three children for a walk to the Stalin Allee, still in the process of construction. Heini was tremendously impressed. 'I've never seen such a wide street,' he exclaimed. 'It's going to be six carriageways wide – and look at the pavements! They're even wider than the road. I bet there isn't anything like it in the West, is there?'

Soberly, Paul replied, 'No, I expect you're right.'

While they were out, Viktoria asked Monika, 'Why don't you

219

leave Fuerstenmark? You could all stay with me in Hamburg until you found a place of your own.'

However, Monika did not want to move to Hamburg, a city she had never even visited, and she certainly did not want to be beholden to her mother.

'Why don't you leave?' Erika asked, with unexpected intensity. 'In the West, you'd all have enough to eat; your children wouldn't be wearing old clothes; they'd go to good schools – and have opportunities they'll never have in the GDR. You should seriously think about it, before it's too late!'

'If you feel so strongly, why do you stay?' Monika retorted.

The colour drained from Erika's face. 'I'm in a rather different situation. My husband is a Russian prisoner of war . . .'

Viktoria knew that was true but instinct told her it wasn't the whole truth. What was it about the girl? she wondered. Lili was right: there was some mystery surrounding Erika. However, curious though she was to find out more, now was not the time or place to ask searching questions.

Instead, she told Monika, 'If you change your mind, please know I'll do all I can to help you.'

But although Monika thanked her mother for her offer rather more graciously than she would have done in the past, she said she was convinced that things would soon get better in the Soviet zone and that she would never need to leave Fuerstenmark. However, she did add that if Viktoria could manage to include in her parcels clothes and things like soap, skin cream and basic medicaments, like aspirin, as well as food, she would be grateful.

On 1 June 1952, just after Viktoria and Lili returned to Hamburg, the Soviets announced that as from midnight that night all West Germans would need a special permit to enter the East zone. A three-mile security belt had been set up to reinforce existing frontier crossings, including a ten-yard deep 'shoot on sight' strip. Road and railway links between West Berlin and West Germany were not affected, but since crossing the East zone between Berlin and Helmstedt had long been a hazardous undertaking, that meant very little. The same restrictions, of course, applied to East Germans travelling to the West.

It was clearly meant to be seen as a retaliatory measure against the Western rejection of the Communist reunification proposals. However, if the Soviet Union hoped its tactics would make the Americans and Adenauer change their minds, it was mistaken. Pacifist, neutralist and socialist movements were vociferous in their condemnation of the actions of both sides. But the net result was that even more refugees fled from the East to the West through Berlin – the single remaining hole in the Iron Curtain.

Stefan was granted one of the new special permits, enabling him to travel fairly freely within the GDR, so long as Erika accompanied him. He and Udo spoke every day on the telephone, and frequently Udo sent drafts of articles he proposed publishing in *Aktuell*, criticizing West German politicians, industrialists and powerful organizations, exposing scandals, corruption and intrigues. These articles were the result of months of investigation and supported by painstakingly obtained facts. Stefan would show them to Erika, never dreaming that she was passing much of the information on to the SSD.

Erika hated the double life she was living and, more than anything, she hated deceiving Stefan. But she was caught in a net from which there was no escape. Even suicide, which she seriously considered on occasions, was no solution. Death would release her from her dilemma, but it would place the Koenigs, her father and Stefan in even greater danger. Little had she dreamed when she fell in love with Stefan that their affair would have such far-reaching and terrifying repercussions.

Even Stefan could not help but notice her agitated state, and aware that he owed his privileged position to her, asked, 'You aren't in some kind of trouble because of me, are you? I do appreciate everything you've done, but the last thing I want is to put you in any danger . . .'

'No,' she insisted. 'I'm just, er, under a bit of strain at work. It's nothing to worry about.' But, as she spoke, she could hear the tremor in her own voice and looked away from him, so that he should not see the anguish in her eyes.

221

Chapter 11

As Norbert had foretold, the Berlin Planning Authority required several modifications to his plans for the Jochum-Berlin, but as he said, laughingly, 'They're more worried about the drains than the design.'

In November 1952, six months after the plans had first been submitted, approval was granted. With the backing of the Emergency Building Programme, Viktoria's bank granted her a very favourable loan. Viktoria and Norbert were both on site to watch the bulldozers move in and work commence, just before Christmas. Café Jochum, of course, had to be closed, and Hasso and the other permanent staff were given paid leave during the initial stages of the construction work. Hasso, rather reluctantly, went to relatives in Wedding. Viktoria and Norbert stayed at Heiligensee.

It wasn't until she actually stood watching the excavator begin to dig out the foundations that Viktoria realized how important this project was to her. When Norbert casually mentioned that she was more than welcome to stay on at the cottage, she jumped at the opportunity. Far more than the Jochum-Hamburg, this was her hotel. She had opened the Jochum-Hamburg because it made business sense, but the Jochum-Berlin was another matter. No matter how she justified it to others, the real motive behind it was emotional. Like the Quadriga had been, the Jochum-Berlin was more than a mere building. It was a symbol of faith and hope in her city's future. She hated the thought of missing out on any stage of its construction.

Dirk Kaiser, who had turned into a loyal and efficient employee, was promoted to General Director of the Jochum-Hamburg and Eduard given his post as General Manager. Viktoria had great hopes of Eduard. Despite his youth, he commanded respect from the hotel personnel, not least because there was no job with which he was not prepared to lend a hand, be it washing-up, waiting at table, or general maintenance. At the same time, he had a quick mind and a pleasant manner, which endeared him to both staff and guests. Viktoria had never seen him lose his temper, no matter how much provoked. Most importantly, he was an able administrator. Once the Jochum-Berlin was completed, Viktoria intended transferring him there.

Lili assumed she would be coming to Berlin to be with Viktoria, but her aunt had decided differently. 'Lili, do be sensible, please,' she said. 'You have less than two years left at *Mittelschule* before you go on to vocational college. Changing schools now would not be a good idea.'

Lili pointed out that she used to go to school in Heiligensee, but Viktoria remained adamant. 'That was a long time ago. You're at senior school now. And the curriculum would be quite different from the one you're following here in Hamburg. In any case, there really isn't any point in your coming to Berlin. I shall be away all day. You'd be alone at the cottage most of the time. You can come during the holidays and see what progress we're making with the hotel.'

'But I wouldn't mind being alone at the cottage . . .'

'It isn't that I don't want you with me, but it just wouldn't work. All the time, I'd be worrying about you. When the hotel is finished, you can come to Berlin, I promise.'

Tears glinted in Lili's eyes and Viktoria sighed. 'Lili, please try and understand. I'm building this new hotel as much for you as for myself. The hotels represent your future . . .'

But Lili did not understand. This was not the first time Viktoria had made her fit in with her own plans. When her mother had died, Viktoria had not kept her with her at the Quadriga, but sent her to Heiligensee with Ricarda and Christa. After the war, she had been made to live with the Webers, instead of at Café Jochum. During the blockade, she had been sent to Hamburg. And now she was again being left behind. It seemed like betrayal of the worst kind.

Until then, she had believed that her aunt loved her as if she were her own child and that it was circumstances which had forced them to be separated. Now she realized that, whatever

223

Viktoria might say, the truth was that she cared more for her hotels than she did for her niece.

Viktoria left for Berlin and the same thing happened to Lili as when Hilde had died. She became tired and depressed. Her appetite went and she lost weight. Her school work began to suffer, the very thing which Viktoria had been at pains to avoid. Concerned, Eduard had a quiet word with Dr Mehring, when he next came to visit one of the hotel guests. The doctor gave Lili a thorough examination, but could find nothing physically the matter with her. He did make a note on his records that, although she was fifteen, she was still flat-chested and had not yet started to menstruate, but this was not unusual for girls who had grown up on wartime rations, quite a number of whom were under- developed for their age. Indeed, it was possible that Lili's condition was due to the onset of puberty. He prescribed a tonic and told her, kindly, to 'pull herself together'.

However, Lili did not get any better. Soon she again resembled the waiflike figure she had been when she first came to Hamburg. Nothing and nobody could rouse her from her apathy. Eduard was at his wits' end to know what to do and was thankful when Norbert paid one of his periodic visits to the hotel, took one look at Lili and said, 'Aunt Vicki must come back immediately. The child's fading away before our very eyes!'

Viktoria was shocked when she saw Lili. She talked to Dr Mehring and to Lili's teachers and it was agreed that, since her business interests clearly took priority over everything else, the best thing would be for Lili to join her in Berlin, where she could keep an eye on her.

Viktoria's attitude, however, made Lili feel even more miserable. She sensed that her aunt was annoyed because she had disrupted her plans. Viktoria was taking her to Berlin, not because she wanted her there, but because she couldn't be trusted alone. Lili was a responsibility, a burden, a nuisance.

By Easter 1953, the outer shell of the Jochum-Berlin was virtually completed. A new Café Jochum had taken shape, very similar to Luise's original café, with a glassed-in terrace and huge plate-glass windows, occupying half of the ground floor of the new building, the hotel itself rising above and around it. And, in the cellar, the bar was again open.

Although the hotel remained in the throes of construction, Viktoria and Lili moved into a small apartment on the first floor. For the first time, Lili had a room of her own and the privacy this room gave her helped mitigate the feeling of hurt created by Viktoria's attitude. In her little haven, Lili could shut out the outside world, read the books she loved, listen to the music she most enjoyed and dream her own dreams.

Hasso, too, moved back from Wedding and into a self-contained bed-sitting room next to Viktoria and Lili's apartment. Not that he was connected with the hotel any more, except by sentiment. Viktoria had transferred the cellar bar into his name: the best way she knew of thanking him for everything he had done for her over the years.

Hasso was deeply touched by her gift, but reluctant to accept it. He was nearly seventy and the past years had taken their toll of him. He was too old, he protested to Viktoria, to start running his own business, and too old-fashioned in his outlook to compete with other new nightclubs, which were turning the Ku'damm into Berlin's version of the notorious Hamburg Reeperbahn. Viktoria refused to accept that the years were catching up on him, but she did take his other point. A new era of permissiveness had begun. As in the Twenties, there were bars and clubs catering for every sexual taste, and Berlin's transvestite community was again offering the public its own particular brand of amusing and controversial entertainment. For Hasso even to try to compete with them was impossible.

Yet not every visitor to Berlin sought sexual titillation. There would continue to be a need for a quieter, intimate bar, offering a more refined and sophisticated entertainment, and presided over by an attentive host. Furthermore, apart from a cocktail bar on the top floor, next to the restaurant and ballroom, the Jochum-Berlin would have no bar of its own. Many hotel guests would spend their evenings in 'Hasso's Bar'.

Hasso had, in fact, underestimated his own popularity. Long before the Berlin-Jochum opened, 'Hasso's Bar' had become one of Berlin's most fashionable nightspots for a more discerning type of clientèle. But Hasso did not run it alone. He was helped by his nephew, who, only in his forties, possessed the energy to work long, demanding hours, which Hasso no longer had.

Once again, Lili started at a new school, but Viktoria's fears proved groundless. Her standard of work was well up to the rest of her class.

She was further blessed with an unusually perspicacious class teacher, who recognized that Lili possessed many hidden abilities. She might not be very good at mathematics or science, but she could draw, had a good ear for music, wrote imaginative essays and showed an aptitude for languages.

Until then, Lili had viewed school as a necessary evil. Under Frau Krickow's tuition, it acquired a purpose. Frau Krickow lent her books from her own library, novels in French and English as well as German, which held Lili's attention and fired her imagination and she responded by wanting to share her enjoyment with others. When Viktoria sent her parcel to Monika, Lili sent a packet of books to Senta, classical novels which would pass the censor's critical eye.

On the morning of Monday, 15 June 1953, Stefan took the Underground to the Frankfurter Tor and made his way to the Dreschers' flat. Erika was at work, but Paul had told him the previous day, while Erika was preparing lunch, that there was someone to whom he wanted to introduce him, a carpenter called Max Finkemayer. 'He used to run his own business, making furniture, but he was forced to close down,' Paul had explained. 'Now he's working on the Stalin Allee.' He paused, then continued, 'You know the government announced a ten per cent increase in norms on 28 May? Well, the workers received their first pay packets on Friday.'

'And . . . ?'

'Most of them were finding it difficult to achieve their norms before they were increased. Now it's impossible. Because Max failed to make his norm, his wages were reduced by thirty per cent. He's urging his fellow workers to go on strike.'

After Stalin's death in March, there had been a surge of optimism in the East zone. There had been rumours of a 'new course' of economic policy and some of the more oppressive regulations had been relaxed. But, as Paul pointed out, shops were still empty, wages low, prices high and rationed goods only obtainable if one belonged to the Party élite. Most of the GDR's agricultural and manufacturing production continued to be sent to the Soviet Union in the form of war reparations. A rumoured two million people had, in fact, had their ration cards withdrawn and the number of refugees fleeing to the West had increased.

That morning, Stefan could not help noticing that there seemed to be more guards than usual on the Underground and, when he emerged above ground, there were even more *Vopos* than normal on the streets.

Paul was waiting ready when Stefan arrived at the Dreschers' flat. 'Let's go,' he said. Herr Domke looked at them curiously as they passed. 'We must be in a hurry,' the caretaker commented, 'not even time for a coffee.'

'I don't trust Domke,' Paul muttered, when they reached the street.

Little work was taking place on the Stalin Allee when they arrived. Gangs of workers were gathered together, angrily discussing what they should do. A larger group was being addressed by a burly man. 'That's Max,' Paul whispered. He and Stefan attached themselves to the back of the crowd.

'The government must be made to realize that we are not going to tolerate the norms system any longer,' Finkemayer was saying. 'But we don't just want the abolition of norms. We want free trades unions! We want fair wages! Support the building workers' strike committee! Down tools, comrades! Strike for freedom!'

A cheer went up from his audience. Along the length of the Stalin Allee echoed the words, 'Strike! Strike! Strike!'

Finkemayer stepped down from the table and made his way through the crowd to Paul and Stefan. 'So you're the journalist Paul has told me about. Well, if you come with me, you'll see something to write about.'

For the rest of the day, Stefan and Max Finkemayer travelled through East Berlin. Paul Drescher did not accompany them. His rheumatism meant that he could not walk long distances. But Stefan and Max attended one meeting after another like the one on the Stalin Allee. 'And meetings like these are taking place

227

throughout the Soviet zone,' Finkemayer said. 'The government has pushed the workers too far.'

It was Viktoria's birthday that day, but Stefan was too late for the small dinner party she was giving that evening. He rang to say he had been delayed, then telephoned a long report through to Udo in Hamburg describing the day's events, including the arrest of three members of a workers' delegation from the Friedrichshain hospital who had presented a petition to the government.

The following morning, dressed in working men's clothes, Stefan caught an early train and was on the Stalin Allee at seven o'clock. There were even more *Vopos* around than the previous day and a large number of members of the Free German Youth. 'They've brought in the FDJ to unload lorries and try to break the strike,' Max Finkemayer explained.

'It's definitely a strike?' Stefan asked.

'Yes,' Finkemayer breathed with satisfaction, 'we're on strike.'

Down the broad length of the Stalin Allee, with its unfinished buildings to either side, they marched, the workers of East Berlin. As they approached the Strausberger Platz, their numbers swelled. By the time they reached the Alexander Platz, there were several thousand of them. *Vopos* tried to stop them, but the angry demonstrators pushed them to one side. Across the Marx-Engels-Platz and into Unter den Linden they marched, chanting: 'Down with norms! Down with norms!'

They halted outside the ministry buildings in the Wilhelm-strasse, a seething, rebellious mass of people, demanding that Ulbricht and Grotewohl come out to meet them, continuing their shouted hatred of the norm. But it was left to a lesser minister to address the crowd with trite words of conciliation which, far from appeasing the workers, made tempers even more heated. In the end, the government representative was pushed from the makeshift platform and his place taken by members of workers' strike committees.

At one point, Max Finkemayer took the stage, reading out from a typed manifesto the demands of his group. After fulminating against the injustices of the norms system, he went on, 'We demand free speech and freedom of the press! We demand the abolition of all zonal boundaries! We demand

228

the withdrawal of the Occupying troops! We demand the end to the war reparations!'

The demonstrators roared their approval, but the blank walls of the Wilhelmstrasse did not respond.

Eventually, the demonstrators began to return to their workplaces, streaming back in the direction they had come, and as they entered the Stalin Allee, a voice boomed down the loudspeakers which were used to make important public announcements, that at an extraordinary Party Action meeting of the SED, Prime Minister Grotewohl had cancelled the order increasing norms. All workers should return to work.

'You appear to have won,' Stefan said to Finkemayer.

But the burly carpenter looked at him from glowering eyes. 'If they think they can appease us by rescinding one order, they are mistaken. The strike will continue!'

At seven o'clock on the morning of 17 June, the workers again marched down the Stalin Allee, through the Strausberger Platz, the Marx-Engels-Platz and down Unter den Linden, far, far more of them than there had been the previous day, despite the pouring rain. From one end of Unter den Linden to the other, they stretched, thousands and thousands of them, their voices raised. 'Down with norms!' 'We want free elections!' 'We want free trades unions!' 'We want freedom!' 'Freedom!' 'Freedom!' 'Freedom!'

Vopos were there to meet them but, to Stefan's amazement, they did not shoot at the demonstrators. Indeed, many marched with the strikers and for a short while, Stefan believed the revolution stood a chance of succeeding. The German People's Police was not going to fire on the German people.

However, the ugly temper of the crowd could not be controlled. The people were no longer content to shout slogans. They wanted action. Windows were smashed. Voices yelled: 'Down with the government!' A building burst into flame. Smoke billowed into the wet air.

Stefan had long been separated from Max Finkemayer. He was still near the front, but to the edge of the procession. From where he was standing he could clearly see the Brandenburg Gate. Some youths swarmed up a long pole and ripped down the Red Flag, hurling it into the crowd below.

The demonstrators moved on towards the Potsdamer Platz, from which dense smoke was also billowing. Word came back. 'They've stormed the Police Headquarters!' 'They've stormed the prison!' 'The HO shop is on fire.' Only Party members and foreigners were allowed to shop at the State-owned HO store. Confidence rose as rumours spread of successes elsewhere in the city. The bastions of Communism were falling.

Then Russian tanks rumbled into the Potsdamer Platz. Loudspeakers ordered the workers to turn back. But the men had come too far to give in meekly. They surged forward, throwing stones and beating on the sides of the tanks, shouting, 'Ivan, go home!' 'Ivan, go home!'

When the tanks moved into the crowd, Stefan was fortunate enough to be able to back into a doorway. But that did not prevent him seeing Max Finkemayer standing, fist raised, in the path of an approaching tank. Neither did it stop him seeing Max Finkemayer's body disappear under the tank's caterpillar tracks and his crushed corpse emerge again as the tank continued to rumble forward.

Unarmed men were no match for the Red Army. As the tanks rolled relentlessly on into the crowd, the workers had no choice but to back away. Slowly at first, then at a brisk walk and finally at a run, they retreated, an angry, frightened mass of people. Around them loudspeakers declared that martial law had been imposed and that a curfew was in force between the hours of nine and seven.

Gunfire continued to echo through the streets of East Berlin as Stefan followed the mainstream of the marchers eastwards, then turned north. He longed to go to the Dreschers' flat, but he dared not, for fear of drawing attention to them.

All public transport had been halted, all bridges over rivers and canals would be blockaded. Stefan's only way back to the West was along alleyways and paths through the ruins. Time and time again, he thought he heard footsteps following him. He waited for the sound of a gun. So it must feel, he thought, to be an escaped criminal. But he was fortunate.

He succeeded in avoiding the border guards and arrived safely back in West Berlin.

In East Berlin, martial law remained in force for over three weeks, during which time travel between the two sides of the city was severely restricted, so that Stefan was unable to get to the Frankfurter Tor to find out how Paul and Erika were, and because telephone communications between East and West had been stopped the previous year, except for official calls and emergencies, it was impossible for him to ring them.

He was desperately afraid for Paul, who was a friend of Finkemayer, even though he had not been with them during the demonstration. 'He'll be all right,' Hasso, who had introduced him to the Dreschers in the first place, reassured him. 'He wasn't involved. There's no reason for him to be in any danger. And the same applies to Erika.' But throughout those interminable weeks of silence, Stefan's apprehensions remained, as did those of thousands of other Berliners, who had friends and relatives in the Eastern part of the city.

There was nothing any of them could do, except wait and pray. From the government in Bonn came only empty words. On 1 July, the Bundestag proclaimed 17th June as a national holiday, 'the Day of German Unity'. A State ceremony was held in West Berlin to honour the victims of the revolt, attended by Chancellor Adenauer, who declared that they had shown the whole world that the Germans did not wish to be slaves and vowed that Germany would not rest until it was once more united in peace and freedom.

The Charlottenburger-Chaussee, that long broad avenue, which ran from the Am Knie square through the Tiergarten to the Brandenburg Gate, was renamed the 'Street of the 17th June'.

But no pressure was put on the Soviet Union. As Stefan was forced to realize, few people in the West really cared about what was happening the other side of the Iron Curtain. They were shocked, they made a lot of speeches, but at the final count, the events of 17th June meant less to them than the forthcoming election. Several West German firms even cancelled their orders to West Berlin companies, because of

231

the disturbances, which they believed could mean deliveries being delayed.

Unable to contain his pent-up emotions any longer, Stefan sought release in his article for *Aktuell*. He bitterly denounced the materialism of the West, but he could not condone the so-called socialism of the East. Workers in the Soviet zone, he wrote, had been rebelling against a system which denied them not only national liberty, but also social freedom. Socialism had been proved to them to be nothing but thinly disguised slavery. So much for the system which boasted: From each according to his ability, to each according to his needs. He took care to lay the blame for the events of 17th June not on Ulbricht, but on the now-dead Stalin.

When Udo Fabian received the article in Hamburg, he telephoned Stefan. 'It's a bit wishy-washy,' he complained. 'Can't you make it more of an indictment?'

Stefan sighed heavily. 'I daren't, Udo. My girlfriend and her father are over there. So are my sister and her family. I can't endanger them . . .'

In the weeks following the 17th June, the people of the GDR lived in a state of terror, as thousands of strikers and demonstrators were arrested.

Fear was not restricted to the people. In government circles too, it was recognized that, as a result of the workers' rising, heads were bound to roll. If Ulbricht was to keep his job, he had to appease the workers and prove to the Soviet Union that he was in control of the country.

Ulbricht acted swiftly. The order to increase norms was rescinded and it was announced that henceforth increases would be voluntary and rewarded accordingly. Once martial law was lifted, travel restrictions between the East and West were to be relaxed. Workers who had taken part in the revolt were assured that they would not be victimized and that the right to strike would be written into the Constitution.

Blame for the 17th June uprising was attributed to Western agents, who were said to have infiltrated factories and building sites and incited the workers. The people were told that the Red Army had been called in to prevent an attempt by the

West to overthrow the regime of the Democratic Republic.

There was little doubt in Basilius Meyer's mind that Ulbricht would survive all attempts to topple him from power. However, he was well aware that more positions than Ulbricht's were at risk, including his own, particularly when he read Stefan Jochum's article in the most recent edition of *Aktuell* and was forced to realize how disastrously he had failed in his attempt to use Erika Quanz to convince the journalist of the socialist ideals of the SED. If the Foreign Ministry or the Ministry of State Security chose to draw attention to the privileges Basilius had insisted upon allowing the West German journalist, he, too, although he was a lifelong Party member, might find himself out of a job.

He talked the matter over with Irina who, four months pregnant with their first child, suggested that he ordered Quanz's arrest. Then she gave a little smile. 'No, wait, I have a better idea. If Stefan Jochum is as much in love with the Quanz woman as you believe, there's another way of winning him over to our side.'

Martial law was lifted on 12 July. That same evening, Erika arrived at Stefan's apartment. 'They've arrested Papa.' Her face was white and there were dark bags under her eyes.

Horrified, Stefan said, 'But Paul took no part in the revolt. He is innocent. Just because he was a friend of Finkemayer ...'

'That isn't why they arrested him.'

'Then why ...?'

Taking a deep breath, Erika told him the whole story, from her first interview at Security Police headquarters through to her last visit from the SSD the previous day. 'They said that if you came back with me, they would release Papa.'

Stefan shook his head in incomprehension. 'I don't believe it. Why am I so important to them?'

'There was another man present yesterday. I think he was the same one who was there the first time they picked me up. I didn't get a chance to see his features properly, but one of the *Stasis* called him Comrade Meyer. Does that name mean anything to you?'

Stefan let out a long breath. 'Meyer . . . Yes, someone called Basilius Meyer is distantly related to me. The last I heard of him he was quite high up in the Political Information Office.'

With sudden hope, Erika said, 'Perhaps he was trying to help.'

'No,' Stefan said shortly. 'If it was Basilius Meyer, he wasn't trying to help. God, why have I been so stupid? I should have realized! We've been manipulated from the very beginning!' He seized her hand. 'Erika, you mustn't go back. You're staying here.'

She shook her head. 'Stefan, I can't. The *Stasis* told me that if I stayed in West Berlin, they would carry out all their threats against you and the Koenigs.'

'Then Monika and her family must leave Fuerstenmark.'

Erika shook her head. 'You heard them yourself. They won't leave. In any case, it isn't just them. There's Papa. Oh, I feel so sorry for him, and so guilty. He's already spent years in a Nazi concentration camp . . .'

For a long time, Stefan was silent, thinking over everything she had said. There was, he realized, one last question to be clarified. 'Do they know you have come to see me this evening?'

In a very quiet voice, she replied, 'Yes. They told me Kurt was dead. They showed me his death certificate. They said that if I persuaded you to come back with me, they would not only release Papa but we could get married.'

He opened his mouth to speak, but she forestalled him. 'No, Stefan. Even if you are prepared to sacrifice your principles, I won't.'

He held her to him. 'Erika, I love you . . .'

'And I love you, too. I love you more than anyone else in the world. And I always shall. But this concerns more people than ourselves. For their sake, as well as for our own, we have to show that we won't give in any more to fear and intimidation. I have done so many things which I now bitterly regret, but I won't make any more mistakes.'

They clung together, then Erika asked, 'Will you promise me something?'

'Of course. Anything.'

'Whatever happens to me, you will continue to fight for justice. You mustn't let your fear for me sway you from your course.'

He could not respond. He did not want to believe that anything would happen to her.

She drew away from him. 'Wherever I am, my love will always be here with you. You will never be able to escape it. It will always be around you . . .'

Stefan did not go to bed that night, but paced to and fro in his apartment, trying to decide what to do. Were Monika and her family in as great a danger as Erika feared? He could not really believe it. As for Paul, he was an old man. The *Stasis* had arrested him only to frighten Erika. If Erika escaped them, they would soon let him go.

Very early the following morning, he went to East Berlin, determined to make Erika change her mind and come back with him to West Berlin. But, with satisfaction clearly gleaming in his one eye, Herr Domke informed him that Frau Quanz had been arrested.

Desperate to do something, Stefan took advantage of the easing of travel restrictions between West and East and risked using his travel permit to go to Fuerstenmark in a last bid attempt to persuade Monika and her family to come to the Federal Republic.

Monika, however, although dismayed to hear about Erika and Paul, did not believe their arrests would have any repercussions upon her own family. 'Neither will anything you write, Stefan,' she insisted. 'Nobody sees Western newspapers over here.'

'The authorities do,' he replied grimly.

Monika shrugged. 'I still can't believe we're in any danger.' To Monika, living in the backwater of Fuerstenmark, Stefan was simply a brother, not a celebrity.

Her father-in-law took Stefan more seriously. After lunch, the two men strolled across the fields together and Pastor Koenig bared his soul. 'I am often tempted to flee to the West,' he admitted. 'But every time, something holds me back. Gerda says it's my sense of duty towards my parishioners. But there's more to it than that.' He paused and stared

235

out across the flat countryside, a short, grey-haired, balding, insignificant-looking man.

'I have a dreadful feeling of seeing history repeat itself twice within my lifetime. In the 1930s, I saw my son don the brown uniform of the Hitler Youth, discarding in the process many Christian values. Then, I consoled myself with the thought that it was for the good of Germany. Indeed, I myself went along to a great extent with the Nazis. I became a fellow traveller. Too late, I saw my mistake. Now the same thing is happening again. Only the colour of the shirts is different.

'I am referring principally to the FDJ, the Free German Youth. Heini will be fourteen in September, which, as you know, is the traditional age for children to be confirmed. But Heini refuses to join the confirmation class. He finds it amusing to mock everything religious. If he does come to church, he and his friends try to distract the attention of the rest of the congregation. They won't stand for prayer and they clench their fists instead of holding their hands together. They deliberately sing out of tune and stamp their feet, as if the hymn tune were a military march. When I accused Heini once of showing disrespect to God, he said, "Who's God? Have you ever seen him? God doesn't exist." '

Stefan frowned. 'Who's feeding him these ideas?'

'Klaus Gutjahr, the new teacher in charge of the upper school.'

'How does Hans feel about it?'

Pastor Koenig sighed. 'He doesn't like what's happening, but he isn't prepared to risk his job by protesting. After all, Gutjahr has the State on his side.'

'And Monika?'

The pastor gave a thin smile. 'From what I gather, your family have never been regular church-goers. Monika adopts the attitude that provided Heini is happy, that's all that matters. But Gerda and I know there is much more at stake. Like your friend Erika said, these things are happening throughout the Soviet zone. If we are not careful, the Church will again be forced into submission to the State. I'm not going to make the same mistake twice in my life. This time, I'm going to stand my ground and fight back.'

'It isn't fair to ask you this, but if you were in my position, what would you do about Erika and her father?'

'I would tell the world the truth.'

'Despite the risk to all of you, here in Fuerstenmark?'

'You have told us the truth about where we stand. It is our decision now what we do about it. But, Stefan, keep things in perspective. We are very small fry. I think it's unlikely that the authorities will bother with us.'

'But you are prepared to accept the consequences?'

Pastor Koenig gave a gentle smile. 'Whatever happens, I shall accept it as God's will . . .'

So, in the August issue of *Aktuell*, Stefan described with simple truth his love affair with Erika and its tragic conclusion. He ended the article with the words, 'Let the Communist regime announce the charges under which Erika Quanz and her father are being held, bring them to trial and allow outside observers to be present in the court.'

The article did not excite the response Stefan had hoped for in the Federal Republic, but it had one unexpected result. Although there was no reaction from the GDR government, somehow people in the Soviet zone obtained copies of *Aktuell* and soon Stefan's office was filled with men and women who had stories of friends and relatives who had disappeared under circumstances very similar to those of Erika and Paul.

'Tyranny must be opposed whatever the cost,' Stefan wrote in the next edition of *Aktuell*. 'We must stop at nothing to obtain the release of all those who are wrongly imprisoned. We must knock on the prison door until it opens.'

In the meantime, the Soviet Union exploded its first hydrogen bomb and, a few days later, made the announcement that the GDR would be freed from war reparations payments with effect from 1 January 1954. In September, elections took place in the Federal Republic, resulting in an overwhelming victory for Adenauer. In Moscow, Khruschev became First Secretary of the Communist Party.

From Fuerstenmark, Monika wrote, saying that Heini had passed his initiation tests with flying colours and was now a member of the FDJ. Stefan's sympathies went out to Pastor Koenig, but he also felt a sense of relief. If the Koenigs' safety

237

was under threat because of his articles, Heini would not have been accepted into the FDJ.

On 29 September, the totally unforeseen occurred, a tragedy which affected all Berlin, West and East. Ernst Reuter had a heart attack and died.

Stefan was at his desk when a member of Reuter's press office rang through with the news. Almost immediately afterwards, Udo telephoned, asking him to write an obituary. Then Viktoria rang. 'Reuter's dead,' she said shakily. 'Stefan, Reuter's dead . . .'

Stefan understood her grief. Reuter was the man who had led Berlin throughout its fight for freedom, who had stood strong during the blockade and who had inspired the workers during the June uprising. To Berliners, he had been far more than a mayor. He had been a friend.

Dusk fell and Stefan remembered something Reuter had said the previous Christmas. He had suggested that all Berliners put candles in their windows to demonstrate their sympathy with the many German prisoners in Russian hands, and as a pledge of faith and solidarity to everyone who was dearest to each of them. Stefan took a candle, lit it and carried it over to his window sill.

All day and all night, until Reuter's funeral, candles burned at windows throughout Berlin. Reuter's coffin was placed in front of the town hall and hour after hour, day after day, Berliners from West and East filed past it to pay their last respects. Seldom in its history had the city seen a greater funeral. In Reuter's honour the Am Knie square was re-named the 'Ernst-Reuter-Platz'.

The lasting effect upon Stefan of Reuter's death was to imbue him with greater moral strength. Reuter had never doubted the victory of Freedom and had inspired everyone who worked with him with hope and confidence. Stefan determined that, at no matter what cost and danger to himself, he would – as he had promised Erika – continue that fight for freedom.

When Erika Quanz was arrested, Basilius had expected Stefan to be afraid of drawing too much attention to her case for fear of worsening the conditions under which she and her father were imprisoned, and of harming those members of his family who lived in the GDR. Instead, the opposite seemed to be true.

As a result of Stefan's articles in *Aktuell*, Basilius had been questioned by his Minister and senior officers in the SSD about his role in the Quanz affair. It was agreed that Quanz and her father should be tried as soon as possible on charges of espionage and anti-State propaganda. Their trials took place in November at Potsdam, and both were given six-year sentences. Quanz was sent to Leipzig prison, Drescher to Jena.

Stefan Jochum retaliated with his most virulent attack yet on the iniquities of the justice system in the Soviet zone and, to make matters worse, his report was taken up by several reputable international newspapers.

Basilius found himself again under attack not only from his own Minister and the SSD, but also the Ministry of Justice. On this occasion, he did not like to worry Irina with his problems. Their baby was due any moment and she was understandably tetchy. He thought of ordering the arrest of the Koenigs but, upon reflection, concluded that, since Paul and Erika's arrests had failed in their desired effect on Stefan, there was little point. Better to keep them as an ace up his sleeve.

In the end, he decided to adopt the one certain course of action which would ensure Stefan Jochum's silence.

Early on the morning of 29 November, Stefan set off from his flat in Wilmersdorf to make his usual Sunday visit to his mother. As he turned into the Paulsborner Strasse, a man tapped him on the shoulder and asked him for a light. While Stefan searched in his pocket for his lighter, the man grabbed him by the shoulders, kneed him in the groin and shoved him towards a waiting car. Stefan struggled, but the man was too strong and too quick for him. The back door of the Opel opened, hands reached out to grab him. Stefan sprawled across the seat, felt an excruciating blow across the head and sank into unconsciousness.

The driver of a Volkswagen, who had seen the incident occur, gave chase, but although he drove like a madman and crossed several sets of red traffic lights, the Opel gained steadily on him. Police sirens suddenly sounded and the Volkswagen driver gesticulated wildly to the car in front, hoping the police would understand. It appeared that they did, for instead of stopping him, as he had feared, the police car overtook him.

The back window of the Opel shattered and a barrage of sub-machine gun bullets hurtled in their direction. One hit the Volkswagen's windscreen on the passenger side. The driver swerved. From the police car, a volley of pistol shots rang out.

But the police car could not get close enough to inflict any damage on the Opel. Unscathed, it reached the border with the Soviet sector. *Vopos* lifted the barrier to let it through, then dropped it again in front of the police car and the Volkswagen, forcing them to screech to a halt.

The Volkswagen driver told the police what had happened and gave them as good a description as he was able of the man he had seen abducted. Before the day was out, Stefan Jochum had been identified and his name was hitting the headlines in newspapers throughout the world.

Stefan himself was taken to the MVD prison at Soviet headquarters in Karlshorst, where he was placed in solitary confinement, in a dank underground cell, lit by a weak electric bulb, which intermittently went out, plunging him into total darkness. His head was shaved and he was dressed in prison garb. His bed was a thin straw mattress and his toilet a bucket, which all too often was not emptied for days. The food was dreadful: coffee, almost too foul to drink, stale bread, potato soup with unidentifiable objects floating in it.

From time to time he was taken from his cell to an upper room, where he was subjected to violent verbal abuse and harsh interrogation. Despite Pastor Koenig's reassurances, he was terrified of the danger in which he could be placing not only Erika and Paul but his own family, so he refused to be provoked by his captors and maintained silence. The result, however, was that his interrogators resorted to crueller, physical methods to extract the information they wanted. When his thumbnail was pulled out, Stefan could not resist the pain and gave in.

He gave his captors the information they wanted but refused to implicate others. The blame for the crimes of which he was accused he took upon his own shoulders. When he did not have

240

the answers they demanded, he made up stories, but whether or not they believed him he had no idea.

Hardest of all to endure was the solitude, broken only by a warder bringing food, with not even a window to look out of onto the outside world. Sometimes the loneliness overcame him and he would lie on his mattress, weeping from sheer hopelessness, tears that streamed unbidden and unstoppable down his cheeks. And on occasions, he felt a despair so great, that he would pray for death to rescue him from his existence.

The flesh fell from him and, with his fingers he could trace the gaunt lines of his face, sunken cheeks under a growth of stubble which, like his head, was shaved weekly by the prison barber. Once, he dreamed that he had been reduced to a skeleton and that his body was powered only by his spirit, which he could see – a shadowy wraith, like a wisp of smoke – that suddenly evanesced and, with its passing, extinguished his life. Long after he awoke from that dream, it continued to haunt him and he found himself hoping that it heralded his end.

That was his darkest moment, when he nearly gave up hope and even his innermost faith was almost overthrown.

It was then, when he was on the verge of utterly succumbing to despair, that the little miracle occurred. A new warder came on duty and, with the plate of food passed silently through the hatch in the door, Stefan found a note. 'I am in the cell next to you. Knock twice on the wall to show you have received this.'

Although fearful that it might be a trap, Stefan did as his neighbour bade and was rewarded by two taps in return. A little later, the tapping started again and Stefan realized he was being sent a message in Morse code. But he was unfamiliar with Morse and all he could do was tap back: SOS.

Next day, with his food, the warder brought another piece of paper listing the Morse Code.

When he had gone, Stefan slowly tapped on the wall: Thank you.

This marked the beginning of the strangest friendship ever in Stefan's life, with a man whose name and background he would never know, whom he would never see face to face, but whose mind he gradually came to know intimately. Never once in their strange conversations through the wall did they

241

discuss their personal circumstances or the reasons for their imprisonment.

And as the weeks went by, it became clear that no trap had been set and the warder was not a plant. The interrogations and the torture continued, but no mention was ever made of messages tapped in Morse Code. For some reason Stefan never discovered, the warder had taken pity on them.

Even in that hell-hole, humanity existed.

Reinhardt Meyer was born on 1 December 1953 in a private room of the Charité Hospital reserved for Party officials and their wives. Basilius named his son after his own father, who had died during the Spartacist Uprising in 1919. On that occasion, German Communism had failed to win a victory. Now, more than ever, Basilius was convinced that it would succeed.

Irina quickly recovered from the birth and Reinhardt proved to be a strong, healthy baby. After a week, Basilius was allowed to bring them home. They travelled in a chauffeur-driven Chaika limousine to their new home in the officials' colony at Pankow, where the Republic's leading politicians were close neighbours.

This move and his promotion to a senior position in the Foreign Ministry was Basilius's reward for the skilled manner in which he had dealt with Stefan Jochum. The way had been long and hazardous, but in the end he had succeeded in manipulating Stefan to his own advantage. When all the evidence was assembled and the journalist persuaded to confess his guilt, Stefan would be brought before the Supreme Court, in a trial which would expose how he had tried to undermine the Democratic Republic's social and economic achievements.

If it had not been for Hasso and Mortimer, who flew to Berlin the moment he heard the news, Viktoria did not know how she would have survived the shock of Stefan's kidnap. Hasso, although himself extremely upset, was stalwart as ever, urging her to be strong and have faith, and doing his best to convince her that Stefan was safe and would soon return. Hasso's support was all the more touching because he was clearly not particularly well, although he denied that anything was the matter with him, and said he was just suffering from encroaching old age.

As if her emotional turmoil and her fears for Stefan were not enough to cope with, Viktoria had to undergo police interrogations and interviews with Foreign Ministry officials, the latter telling her to say as little as possible to the press, insisting that silence was the best way to secure Stefan's safety, and pointing out that if too much publicity were brought to bear on him, the lives of Monika and her family could also be in severe danger.

The press, hungry as always for a sensational story, would have subjected her to an intolerable pressure, had they not been confronted by Mortimer Allen, himself an old newshound. Although he did not personally agree with the Foreign Ministry line, Mortimer took it upon himself to protect Viktoria and Lili from journalists, deflecting the glare of publicity towards himself as family spokesperson and old family friend, giving reporters sufficient information to write the human interest story their editors demanded, without intruding any more than necessary on Viktoria and Lili's privacy.

Then, as there were no further developments, as no news came of Stefan's whereabouts and other stories hit the headlines, press interest in Stefan died down. But when *Aktuell* also dropped the story, Mortimer became very perturbed. He telephoned Udo Fabian and asked why.

'The Foreign Ministry,' Udo replied, succinctly. 'I have been advised against drawing too much attention to Stefan, for fear – and here I quote – of damaging the delicate negotiations which are in hand to improve diplomatic relations between the Federal Republic and the Soviet Union and which may ultimately lead to an amelioration of the conditions under which Stefan is being held and even secure a reduction of his sentence when it is passed.'

Mortimer sucked in his breath. 'So it would appear that the Foreign Ministry has some kind of evidence that he is at least still alive.'

'That's about the only consolation one can find.'

'My fear is that, unless attention continues to be centred upon Stefan, he will suffer the same fate as countless others

243

who have disappeared in recent years: he will either be killed by his captors or simply allowed to die,' Mortimer stated.

At the other end of the telephone line, Udo sighed, 'To be honest, I'm in a hell of a predicament. I'm already in trouble with the government for an article I published the other week on neo-Nazis. If I go against Foreign Ministry orders regarding Stefan, I may not only be placing his life in even greater danger, but also risk having *Aktuell* banned.'

Later that evening, Mortimer put the whole matter squarely to Viktoria. 'I'm convinced that if Stefan could be consulted, he would agree that we should not give in to the Communists because of vague Foreign Ministry promises. He has seen for himself, all too often, what happens as a result of appeasement and submission. He would be the first to agree that opting for silence, for fear of upsetting delicate negotiations, has too often proved disastrous in German history. If you need any proof, remember the way he attacked the GDR over Paul and Erika, despite the risks to his own and their safety. But since it isn't possible to talk to him, I must ask you, Vicki. Are you prepared to risk letting Stefan fade into oblivion – or are we going to fight back?'

She shook her head helplessly. 'I love Stefan more than anyone else in the world, but there are Monika and her family . . .'

'Naturally, I've thought of the Koenigs. However, if they were in danger, I think something would have happened by now. Monika may be Stefan's sister, but they've never been close. It's possible that nobody has connected them. Because she's married, Monika doesn't even have the same surname.'

'I know Stefan went to see them after Erika was arrested. If they wanted to, they could get away . . .' Viktoria sighed. 'What are you intending to do?'

Mortimer gave a grim smile. 'Start a campaign. Bring Stefan's case to the attention of politicians, newspapers and individuals throughout the world and keep him constantly in their minds by getting as many other people as possible also to write, asking them to intervene with Khruschev and Ulbricht on Stefan's behalf. In other words, make a bloody nuisance of myself.'

'Do you think it will work?'

'I hope it will force the GDR's hand. Nobody likes bad publicity, not even dictatorships. If sufficient world interest is centred on Stefan, it is just possible that the GDR will decide simply to release him.'

Viktoria took his hand. 'In that case, Mortimer, of course . . .'

'Come hell or high water, Vicki, we're going to get Stefan home again,' he promised her.

Mortimer started his campaign right there in Berlin, and by the time he returned home just before Christmas, had enlisted the support, among others, of Pastor Scheer and a young lawyer called Holger Busko. The pastor, now a figure of international repute, readily agreed to exert his influence on his fellow clergy, the Lutheran and Roman Catholic Church authorities and clergymen abroad.

Holger Busko was a different matter altogether. Mortimer had never heard of him, until he received a letter from him, offering his support. Yet within the first moments of their meeting, he instinctively liked him.

Tall and rangy, with slightly slanting eyes under heavy brows, Holger Busko did not present at all the conventional image of a lawyer, but, with his worn clothes, scuffed shoes and over-long hair, looked far more like the student he had so recently been.

From his accent, Mortimer deduced that he came from the Soviet zone and Holger confirmed that he had been born in Leipzig. 'My brother Volker and I left after the 17th June uprising. My parents stayed behind. Despite the brutal reprisals against the striking workers, they still believed things would change as a result of Stalin's death. They couldn't understand that the system would continue.'

'Do you know Stefan? Is that why you want to help him?'

'No, I've never met him. But I used to read his articles in *Aktuell* and think we probably share a great number of beliefs. Although I am a socialist, I deplore the form socialism has assumed in the GDR. Like Stefan Jochum, I am vigorously opposed to militarism and the bomb.'

'You're not well known. How do you think you'll be able to help Stefan?'

'My brother, Volker, is an art student at the Free University. Through him, I have a lot of friends who are students, most of whom are readers of *Aktuell* and feel very strongly about Stefan Jochum's kidnap. I shall start with them. But I shan't stop there. With your agreement, I intend to petition the City Council, businessmen, bankers . . .'

'You realize that you may be placing yourself in some danger?'

Holger shrugged. 'That didn't stop Stefan Jochum doing what he did. Why should it stop me?'

Mortimer looked at him quizzically. 'Would I be right in thinking that you harbour dreams of becoming a journalist yourself?'

Holger shook his head. 'No, I want to do more than criticize events. I intend to influence them. It's my ambition to be a politician.'

Stefan's disappearance was not the only tragedy with which Viktoria had to contend that winter. December was a relatively mild month, but the January that followed was bitterly cold and Hasso's health visibly deteriorated. He walked very unsteadily from his room to the bar, picked at his food and started to lose a lot of weight. Although he said it was just the weather, Viktoria insisted on calling in Dr Blattner.

Three generations of the Blattner family had looked after the health of the Jochums and their staff. Dr Blattner emerged from Hasso's room with a grave expression. Taking Viktoria's arm, he said, 'It's not good news, I'm afraid, Frau Jochum. Of course, we must do proper tests, but I fear very much that he has cancer.'

Hasso was taken by ambulance to hospital that afternoon and there he stayed for what little remained of his life. His nephew, Detlev, went to see him most afternoons and Viktoria every evening. She talked and read to him, helped him to eat and drink, and sadly watched his rapid deterioration. Hasso himself remained cheerful and optimistic. He had a tumour, he told her, upon which the surgeon was soon going to operate. Then he would get better again.

Viktoria slept with her clothes laid out on a chair and her ear alert for the phone, dreading but ready for the call she knew must come, summoning her to the hospital to be with Hasso during his final moments.

He died a week later, with Detlev and Viktoria at his bedside, but he was unaware of their presence. His breathing was stertorous and painful. Viktoria sat beside him in the single room to which he had been moved, clasping the hand that lay limply on the sheet, her eyes fixed in anguish on his face.

Suddenly, his breathing stopped. Viktoria leaned over and kissed him. With a scarcely perceptible sigh, his life passed away.

With characteristic efficiency, Hasso had left his affairs in good order. His bills were all fully settled. A life assurance policy paid for his funeral. In his will he bequeathed the bar and his small savings to Detlev. There was also a letter to Viktoria, marked, 'To be opened after my death', which Viktoria read in the privacy of her room.

'My dearest Viktoria,' he wrote – the first time, she realized, that Hasso had ever addressed her without preceding her name by 'Frau' – and he used the familiar term 'Du' for you, something, again, which despite the thirty-five years they had worked together, he had never done before.

'For as long as I can remember, you have been the most important person in my life and, in recent years, since the death of your husband, we have become closer than ever. Your family has become my family. The ordeals you have suffered have been my ordeals, too.

Many were the times, when I wished I could express my affection, but I knew it was not necessary. And now I am glad I said and did nothing to upset the balance of our relationship. It is enough that I once saved your life and that, since then, I have been able to do as much as I have to help you.

Without you, my life would have been a poor thing. You have made it infinitely rich. My dear Viktoria, from the bottom of my heart I thank you. I hope that we shall one day meet again. And I say now, what I have never dared to say before. I love you.

Hasso.'

For a long time, Viktoria sat gazing at that single sheet of paper. Then the writing blurred, tears streamed down her face and she wept as she had not wept since the death of Benno and her mother. She was not crying for Hasso, although she knew with his death she had lost one of the best and dearest friends she had ever known. She was not crying for herself, although on few occasions before had she felt so utterly desolate and alone.

She was crying for the regret of things undone, the words it was now too late to say: to Hasso, to Stefan, to all those people she had lost or from whom she had been separated during her lifetime. In a way, she was crying for all the sufferings which were besetting the world. She was crying, not for the anguish of death, but the agony of life.

Yet when she next appeared in public, she appeared utterly composed. Her grief was a deep and very private matter.

Chapter 12

The years Ernst Kraus had spent in prison had taken a deep toll of him. The bitterly cold weather that January of 1954 was simply too much for him. He caught a cold, which developed into double pneumonia, from which he died.

Among the handful of mourners at Ernst's funeral, there was nobody who lamented his passing. Not even Trude felt any real sense of grief. Ernst had been her cousin: their marriage had been prearranged by their parents to combine more closely the interests of von Biedersteins and Krauses. She had done her duty by bearing him two sons, keeping his house and looking after him in health and in sickness. Even during the last three years they had not been close. Ernst had preferred the company of Father Johannis, a Catholic priest, to herself.

The Baron shifted impatiently in his wheelchair throughout the long funeral mass. He was going deaf and, although he had been provided with a hearing aid, he refused to use it except at his own convenience and that did not include the mumbo-jumbo ramblings of Catholic priests. Both his sons had been failures in his eyes. Both were now dead.

So far as Ernst's own sons were concerned, the main effect of his death upon them was the inconvenience of having to attend the funeral.

After Ernst's mortal remains had been consigned to the icy ground, Father Johannis and the family went to Trude's house for refreshments and the reading of Ernst's will.

Joachim extracted the document and began to read and, as he read, the faces of those around him dropped. Ernst had left his entire property to the Roman Catholic Church. It was, he had written, the only way he knew of atoning for his past sins.

Trude let out a rasping sob. 'No, it can't be true!'

Werner ground his teeth in annoyance. 'He was senile,' he growled. 'He didn't know what he was doing.'

Joachim took a deep breath. 'In the opinion of myself and Dr Uthoff, who witnessed the signing of the will, Herr Kraus was of sound mind. He was adamant that it was what he wanted.'

'My mother will contest it,' Werner argued.

'I am sure the Church will be sympathetic to her needs,' Joachim said, glancing expectantly at Father Johannis. 'Father, I assume Frau Kraus will be allowed to continue to live here for the remainder of her life?'

A pious expression on his round face, the priest murmured, 'It was Herr von Kraus's wish that the villa be turned into an orphanage.' He glanced meaningfully in the direction of the Baron, Werner and Norbert. 'I should have thought her family would be able to provide for Frau von Kraus.'

The Baron's hearing aid was switched off, his head was drooping on the back of his wheelchair. Werner found himself attacked by an uncontrollable fit of coughing. Norbert knew to whom the burden of looking after his mother would fall.

He was right. In the end, it was he who provided the flat in a quiet suburb of genteel Wiesbaden, in which Trude was to spend the rest of her days.

Ernst's death and his legacy to the Roman Catholic Church did, however, have one other totally unforeseen repercussion.

A few days after the funeral, Dr Schulte, the President of the Hessische Landesbank, invited Werner to a small dinner party at his house in Frankfurt, when, for the first time, Werner met his daughter, Else.

Erwin and Hildegard Schulte had almost given up hope of seeing Else married. Thirty years old, plain and overweight, she seemed destined to remain a spinster all her life. Because her father could afford to give her an allowance, she did not work, and her life seemed to centre round the Church. When, as had happened on just one occasion, a potential suitor had hovered into view, Else had dismissed him out of hand because he was not a Catholic. Sometimes her parents thought she should have become a nun.

The last thing Dr Schulte had ever imagined was that Werner Kraus would show any interest in her. Although Werner was thirty-seven years old and still a bachelor, Dr Schulte assumed he was staying that way through choice. After all, a man in his position could take his pick of women. Why should he fall for Else? If he had believed there was any possibility of that happening, he would have asked Werner to the house long ago. That just proved, however, how little Dr Schulte knew and understood Werner.

The same evening that Werner met Else, he decided to marry her. Not that he fell in love with her. Romantic love was an emotion which would always be alien to his nature. No, it just happened that Dr Schulte's invitation arrived at a moment when family matters were on his mind, and he had come to the conclusion that it was time for him to marry and have a son.

Marriage to the daughter of one of Germany's top bankers, moreover, offered other untold advantages. For some time, Werner had been considering re-opening a branch of the Liegnitzer Bank in Germany, in order to preserve the privacy of his banking transactions. What better man to have in charge than his father-in-law?

He started the evening off on an auspicious note when, knowing his hosts' religious belief, he accepted their condolences on his father's death with a show of regret, then went on, in a pious tone, to tell them about Ernst's bequest to the Roman Catholic Church.

He could have found no surer way of winning Else Schulte's heart.

The Hotel Jochum-Berlin was completed in May 1954. Fourteen storeys high, it soared impressively above its neighbouring buildings on the Ku'damm, a very different edifice from its elegant sister establishment in Hamburg and its predecessor, the Quadriga. Containing three hundred rooms, it was designed to cater for every kind of guest from businessmen with lavish expense accounts to tourists travelling on a shoestring.

On the very top floor, Norbert had designed a structure which Viktoria thought resembled an airport control tower but which Lili considered the hotel's best feature and immediately christened the 'glass-house', containing a restaurant, cocktail bar and ballroom, with kitchens situated in the middle.

It was in the 'glass-house' that the party to celebrate the opening of the new hotel took place on 15 June, Viktoria's sixtieth birthday.

Never had Viktoria felt less like celebrating. Never would she have been more prepared to let an event go by unnoticed. It was as if some vital spark had died in her with Stefan's kidnapping and Hasso's death, and the hotel, which had meant so much to her at its inception, had now lost its importance, overshadowed by the personal ordeals which had overtaken her.

Furthermore, at the beginning of May, a paragraph in the Communist newspaper *Neues Deutschland* had stated that Stefan had confessed to being an agent of the British Military Intelligence Service and was shortly to be tried for anti-Communist activities.

Viktoria feared, and Mortimer, with whom she discussed the matter on the phone, agreed, that it was most likely Stefan would find himself at the centre of a Stalinist show trial. But at least it meant that, possibly as a result of Mortimer's campaign, the GDR government had realized it had to be seen to be conducting its affairs in a just manner.

Lili refused to be depressed by the news and insisted that it should be regarded as a cause for optimism. Since Stefan had committed no crime, she was confident he must be found not guilty.

That illustrated the difference, Viktoria reflected soberly, between being sixteen and sixty. Lili had been terribly upset when Stefan disappeared and when Hasso died, but her grief had passed much more quickly. It was only natural, she supposed. Youth was looking forward to life ahead. Old age could only look back. Undoubtedly, at Lili's age, she had been just as resilient.

'I'm sure Stefan wouldn't be hurt if he knew we were having a party,' Lili told her, in a well-meaning attempt to make her feel better, 'nor would Hasso. In fact, I think they'd be very upset if we didn't celebrate the opening of the hotel, after all the effort that has gone into building it. Life has to go on, Aunt Vicki.'

'Yes, I suppose so . . .'

'You won't have to worry about anything. Eduard and I will organize it all.' Lili had been delighted that her aunt had transferred Eduard from Hamburg to become the Jochum-Berlin's Assistant General Manager. 'Please, Aunt Vicki. It would be good experience for me . . .'

Very reluctantly, Viktoria allowed herself to be persuaded.

She was beginning to think that Lili might have a future in the hotel, although in what capacity she was unsure. Lili's was a butterfly nature, unable to concentrate long on any one subject, rapidly bored with anything which did not seize her imagination. The attraction to her of hotel life was that it offered constant variety. She was happiest when she was with people and, although she had little patience with paperwork, loved the bustle of reception. Certainly her talent for languages would be an asset in a city, where German, English, French and Russian were in everyday use.

What with the events of the past half year and the completion of the hotel, Lili had forgotten her old resentment towards Viktoria. She threw herself with enthusiasm into the preparations for the party. At least six times a day she would find an excuse to see Eduard and inform him of her latest requirements or her most recent change of plan. Soon, the hotel was fully booked for the night of 14 June and Lili was having to turn people away.

As the star turn of the evening, she decided to invite Emmy Anders to join the Ted Starr Dance Band. She had never met Emmy Anders, but she knew a lot about her. Now one of America's most famous jazz singers, Emmy had been born in Berlin, and her first job had been as a kitchen maid at the Quadriga. She had made her singing début on the opening night of Café Jochum on New Year's Eve 1924, and five years later played the principal part in the musical film, *Café Berlin*, as a result of which she had won international fame and eventually gone to California. Although Viktoria seemed doubtful, Lili was sure Emmy would like to return to Berlin to celebrate the opening of the new Hotel Jochum.

Ted Starr sent her the address of Harper Miller, Emmy's agent in America, who eventually replied, saying that Emmy would be pleased to accept the invitation. Viktoria was very

253

surprised. 'I never thought Emmy would ever return,' she said slowly, 'not after the way she was treated. However, they say time heals and perhaps it does . . .'

When Lili pressed her for a more detailed explanation, Viktoria looked embarrassed. 'She left Berlin because of the Nazis. However, that's history now, thank God.'

It was the first time that Lili had been told the true reason for Emmy's departure and it was another of those references to the past which intrigued and infuriated her. Sometimes she felt that life in Germany between 1933 and 1945 was a closed book, about which all adults had been sworn to silence.

All day long, people arrived to celebrate the opening of the Jochum-Berlin, including Mortimer. Mortimer never seemed to change. That wayward lock of hair, greyer than it had been, still flopped over his forehead. His eyes still contained their old cynical light and his mouth that old sardonic twist. 'If I didn't know you to be a year younger than myself, I'd never believe you are sixty,' he told Viktoria affectionately.

'But I feel it,' she sighed. 'The energy seems to have gone out of me. I can feel no enthusiasm for anything any more, even my hotels. I really don't want to hold this party, but Lili insisted. It seems so unfeeling to be celebrating while Stefan is in prison. I keep wondering what kind of horrors he is experiencing . . .'

Mortimer nodded. 'I do understand. But you have to go on, Vicki. Giving up now won't help Stefan.'

'I suppose not. But sometimes it is so difficult . . .'

In fact, Viktoria enjoyed the party more than she had anticipated. For one thing, most people made sympathetic remarks about Stefan and much to her surprise, she realized that she and Stefan were held in deep affection by a great many people.

There were also a number of guests present, whom she had not expected to see, not least the Koenigs who, to her great relief, were suffering no repercussions because of Stefan. 'The authorities have too much on their plate to bother with the likes of us,' Gerda Koenig told her, reassuringly.

Nevertheless, they had travelled to West Berlin by an indirect route. As Monika explained, 'We went to Neu-Brandenburg and caught the train from there. It has a big station. Nobody paid any attention to us, as they would if we'd come from Prenzlau.'

'I thought travel restrictions had been eased,' Mortimer said sharply.

Pastor Koenig gave a bitter little laugh. 'Not unless you call putting mines along the green border easing restrictions. So far as our neighbours are concerned, we're attending a funeral today in Neu-Brandenburg. You can't be too careful. Everyone informs on everyone else over there.'

Viktoria was touched that they should have made so much effort, at such danger to themselves, to attend the occasion, although she soon realized that, certainly in Monika's case, the reasons were not entirely altruistic, when her daughter announced, 'While I'm in West Berlin, I want to buy Heini some new clothes. Mama, would you mind lending me some money . . . ?'

But Viktoria was so relieved they were all safe, she could not find it in her heart to blame her.

Among the other guests there was one in particular, whose acquaintance she was delighted to renew. Bruno, Graf von der Eschenbach, had been a frequent guest at the Quadriga before and during the war. Now in his mid-to-late forties, the Count was a striking-looking man, with dark hair, greying a little at the temples, an aquiline nose and eyes which crinkled disarmingly when he smiled. Despite the ravages of the war, he remained immensely wealthy, with vast estates in the Franconia region of Northern Bavaria and interests in property, brewing and financial institutions, including a private bank, which had been founded in the eighteenth century.

Bruno von der Eschenbach had remained aloof from Nazi politics. A keen aviator with his own private plane, he had become an officer in the Luftwaffe and served with Lili's father, Sepp Nowak. At the time of the Battle for Britain, they had both been stationed in France. When Sepp had died, Bruno had been deeply upset.

The last time Viktoria had seen him was in spring 1944, when he had come to Berlin on a visit from Paris. Later, she realized that he must have come to liaise with other officers on the plot to kill Hitler, for, after the assassination attempt failed, he had been brought back to Germany under armed SS guard and spent the next ten months in prison. Freed by the Allies, he had returned to his wife and two grown-up sons at his castle in Franconia.

From time to time, Viktoria had seen his name in the papers, sometimes in connection with his business interests or seigneurial duties, but more often linked to charitable work. Unlike the Krauses, Bruno von der Eschenbach was a man of integrity, very conscious of owing a debt to society.

The most recent reference to him, however, had been just over a year ago, when tragedy had unexpectedly struck him, in the form of the death of his wife from a sudden illness.

'It isn't until something like that happens to you personally, that you understand how others feel,' he told Viktoria. 'When I received your niece's invitation, I felt I had to come, to tell you how much I admire your courage in continuing, despite your husband's death and your son's disappearance. I know what it is like to lose one's partner. I have two sons – I hate to think what it would be like to lose them, too . . .'

Viktoria thanked him for his sympathy and took pleasure in introducing him to Mortimer. As she had expected, the two men got on extremely well together and were soon joined by Pastor and Klara Scheer and their grandson, Matthias, now a fine-looking eleven-year-old. As she passed their little group on one occasion, Viktoria heard the Pastor explaining to Bruno, 'Herr Allen is right in saying that we must keep Stefan's name in the public mind . . .'

Deeply touched, she realized suddenly how fortunate she was to have such wonderful friends.

The same could not be said for the Krauses, who for good form's sake had had to be invited. The Essen contingent were among the first to arrive, the Baron with his nurse, with his hearing aid turned up, so that it emitted a constant blasting whistle. Werner was accompanied by a plain young woman, proprietorially holding his arm, whom he introduced as his fiancée, Else Schulte. Trude, despite her recent bereavement, looked better than she had for years.

Neither the Baron nor Werner could travel anywhere without their lawyers, so Eckhardt Jurisch and Joachim Duschek were

256

also present, the latter in the company of his wife, Annelie, and their eleven-year-old son, Dieter. Joachim's father, Oskar, was not there. He had suffered a fatal heart attack the year before.

Reinhild, the children and Hannelore Hahn had come from Hamburg, without Norbert. 'I don't know what people must think,' Reinhild complained. 'Norbert never shows me any respect. I have to do everything on my own.' That last was patently not true. Far from travelling alone, Reinhild and her children had been in the company of Dirk Kaiser and several other employees of the Jochum-Hamburg, as well as Udo Fabian and Thomas Hartmann from *Aktuell*.

Norbert was also very much on Lili's mind for, at six o'clock, he had still not arrived. Downstairs in reception, she was asking Eduard, who was checking through the guest list with Lotte, 'What can have happened to him?'

At that moment the revolving doors spun round and Norbert entered. A grin on his face, he held his arms wide, as Lili ran towards him, her skirt flying. When she reached him, he lifted her off the ground, so that her feet dangled in the air. 'Hello, my little sweetheart! How are you? Missed me while I've been away?'

As she always did, Lili kissed him, then buried her nose in his jacket, breathing in that dear, familiar Norbert smell of tweed, tobacco, aftershave and brick dust. Then, as he lowered her to the ground, she said reproachfully, 'You're late.'

'Sorry. Something cropped up at the last minute.'

Lili took his hand and led him across the foyer to the lift.

Eduard, standing by the reception desk, watched the lift doors shut. There was a strange, tight sensation in his chest, as if his heart were suddenly constricted. Many times in the past, he had seen Lili greet Norbert in that same manner – it had become an accepted routine – a little girl welcoming her favourite uncle. But Norbert was not Lili's uncle. And Lili was no longer a little girl. At some time, and Eduard did not know quite when the metamorphosis had taken place, she had changed – and become a young woman. And, with that change, Eduard's feelings for her had changed.

Eduard was a normal, healthy young man of twenty-four, with a normal young man's appetites, appetites which were not hard to satisfy in Berlin, particularly for one as good-looking as Eduard. But among none of the saucy, pretty Berlin girls he had dated had he met one who had captured his heart. They had been spirited and sexy. They had been amusing. But after a few weeks he had lost interest in them. It was only as he and Lili had been organizing Viktoria's party that he had realized why. Lili might still regard him as a kind of older brother, treating him with the same insouciant camaraderie as had always existed between them, but Eduard no longer saw her as a kid sister. He had fallen in love with her.

'Now that Herr Norbert has arrived, all the guests are here,' Lotte said.

Now that Norbert had arrived, the joy had gone out of Eduard's day.

For as long as she lived, Emmy Anders would never forget the circumstances under which she had left Berlin: her vandalized apartment, the swastikas daubed on the walls and the message crudely smeared above her bed: *Emmy Anders! Get out of Germany! Go home to Africa!* Just because she wasn't pure 'Aryan', just because, from somewhere in the past, she had African blood in her. She had fled to the Hotel Quadriga, sure that Luise Jochum would help her, but instead of finding Luise, she had been confronted by Benno Kraus. Some kind of Nazi meeting had been taking place in one of the reception rooms. Benno had said he dared not give her refuge.

Emmy had gone first to Paris, then to America, where she had married a Hollywood producer considerably older than herself, who had divorced her a couple of years later after finding her in bed with a young film star. After that, she had enjoyed several affairs, but never remarried. Now, an attractive woman of forty-four, she still enjoyed the occasional dalliance, but was, as she was the first to admit, wedded to her career.

It was when her latest affair went wrong that she decided to take up her agent's suggestion of doing a European tour, although she baulked at the idea of returning to Germany, even at the invitation of Luise's daughter. 'I don't care if I never see Germany again,' she said firmly.

'But the Germans love you, darling,' Harper said. 'Your

records are selling better there than anywhere else in the world.'

'But I don't love the Germans.'

'You can't run away for ever, Emmy. One day, you have to lay the ghosts of the past. Berlin is still your home.'

Home, someone had said, is where one has memories. But could she stand the pain of rekindling memories of the sort she possessed? Could she bear to return to the city which had rejected her?

'We don't have to stay,' Harper went on. 'After the party, we'll go straight to Paris.'

Eventually and with a great deal of reluctance, Emmy allowed herself to be persuaded. But, even as she agreed, she made a private vow that she would use her visit to exact some form of revenge for the sufferings which had been inflicted upon her so long ago.

Harper's statement about her popularity in Germany was proved by the chauffeur sent by the Hotel Jochum to meet her and Harper at the airport. He recognized her immediately and shook her fervently by the hand. 'Welcome back to Berlin, Fraulein Anders.' When she was settled in the back of the car, he said, 'I saw you in *Café Berlin* and I still have some of your records. Of course, we weren't supposed to listen to your music after Hitler came to power, but the wife and I still did. My wife was a great fan of yours.' He sighed, then said, 'You've been away for a long time.'

'I left in 1932.'

With that dry understatement so typical of Berliners, the driver replied, 'Twenty-two years. Well, Miss, you haven't missed much in the mean time.'

After champagne cocktails, the guests went through to the restaurant, where family and close friends were seated at a horseshoe shaped table, the other guests at long tables to either side. Only Emmy was missing. Tired after her long flight, she had asked to dine in her room.

The children were grouped together, with Lili in charge of them, ensuring that they ate up their food and minded their manners. Tristan, who was eight, was starting to look like

Norbert, with a cheeky twinkle in his eye. Of the coughs and colds which had plagued him during the winter, there was no sign. Kleo resembled neither of her parents, but with her roundish face and mop of dark curls, reminded Viktoria of the Baron's wife, Julia, now long dead. Dieter Duschek was sitting beside her and Kleo was smiling very prettily at him. On her other side was Matthias Scheer. The four of them made a happy, chattering group.

Only Norbert's youngest daughter, Helena, seemed not to fit in. Helena had inherited her father's angular features and her mother's fine, lank hair. She made no attempt to join in the other children's conversation but studied the rest of the room with a grim little expression.

When Lili wasn't admonishing the children, she was busy telling Senta her plans for the future. 'I leave school at the end of the month,' she was saying. 'I'd really like to start work immediately, but Aunt Vicki says I have to have a qualification. So I'm taking a trilingual secretarial course. I suppose the typing could be useful but nobody is ever going to dictate letters to me! If Aunt Vicki thinks I'm going to be a secretary, she's mistaken!'

Senta looked at her with big eyes, envying her the ability to talk so confidently about deciding her own future. Her parents and grandparents had made up their minds that she would go to university and become a teacher.

Heini was seated next to his great-grandfather. The Baron, tired after the day's exertions, kept dozing in his wheelchair, but suddenly, sensing Heini's curious eyes on him, woke up and turned on his hearing aid. 'Who are you?' he asked. 'Don't think I've met you before.'

'No,' Heini replied, 'but I was named after you. I'm your great-grandson, Heinrich Koenig.'

'Hmmph,' the Baron grunted. 'Thought you had Kraus blood in you.'

'I like guns, too,' Heini informed him.

After dinner, the party moved to the ballroom, but it was not until eleven that the music stopped, the lights dimmed and the dancers returned to their tables. As an expectant hush fell over the room, Ted Starr announced, 'Ladies and Gentlemen, it is time for our guest artiste – Emmy Anders!'

Wearing a flame-coloured, close-fitting dress, Emmy's petite figure stepped into the spotlight. Her black curly hair framed her olive-skinned face with its luminous dark eyes like a halo. She bowed to her audience, glanced at Ted Starr and he led his band into Gerschwin's 'Lady be Good'. Then, throwing back her head, Emmy started to sing.

Her voice had always had an incredible range, growling from seemingly bottomless depths, effortlessly reaching the very highest notes and performing the most amazing vocal contortions. Now age had added an indefinible maturity to her virtuosity. Her audience sat in silent homage as she sang and, when she finished, broke into tumultuous applause.

Her next song was in a very different mood. 'Love for Sale . . .' Her huge dark eyes roamed over her audience, fluttering her long lashes invitingly at the men. Casually, she moved her leg, so that the material of her dress slipped away, revealing a slim, black-stockinged thigh.

Norbert watched her, mesmerized, letting her music waft over him, his eyes never leaving her expressive face and suggestive body. Emmy Anders might be over ten years older than himself but, instead of detracting from, that added to her fascination. This was his sort of woman, sensuous and sophisticated.

As her finale, Emmy sang the most celebrated number from *Café Berlin*: 'Now, What Do I Do Now?' She had been twenty when she had originally sung it. Now she was forty-four, but she still succeeded in conveying the gamine impression of a lost little girl. 'You gave me everything I wanted, except yourself. Without you, I am nothing at all!' She paused, then spreading her arms wide, cried, 'Tell me, what do I do now?'

'I know what you do now,' Norbert thought to himself, as he rose to his feet with the rest of the guests to give her a standing ovation. 'You have an affair with me.'

Emmy joined them at the family table, Harper pulling up a chair protectively beside her. 'I should like to thank you – sincerely – for coming back,' Viktoria said. 'You could have given me no more wonderful birthday present.'

'Oh, yes, I'm so glad you came,' Lili said.

261

'So am I,' Norbert murmured. Close to, with her knee tantalizingly near to his, Emmy was even more attractive than she had appeared on stage. Never had he felt so great a desire to possess a woman as he did her. Totally ignoring Reinhild, he concentrated on impressing Emmy, refilling her glass, lighting her cigarettes and showing an avid interest in everything she said.

It was in the early hours of the morning that the party finally broke up. The children had been sent to bed before Emmy's appearance and the Baron had gone at about the same time. Now the other party guests began to retire to their rooms or make their way downstairs to their waiting cars.

While Viktoria was wishing her guests good night, Emmy walked across to the window and stared out across Berlin's skyline, at the glittering lights of West Berlin, which stopped abruptly at the border with the east.

'Do you have to leave for Paris tomorrow?' Norbert's voice asked softly. 'Why not stay – and let me show you round? Berlin has changed a lot since you were last here.'

She was not surprised to find him beside her. It had been impossible to remain oblivious to his attentions and she was far too experienced to be in any doubt as to his intentions. Norbert Kraus, she reflected, was the kind of man with whom it could be quite amusing to have an affair. He was tall, well-built and almost handsome when he smiled. For a businessman, he possessed unusual charm, and his youth gave promise of a physical stamina lacking in many men of her own age or older. That he was married did not concern her.

However, Norbert was a German and, furthermore, a Kraus. Emmy's father had worked for Kraus Chemie and been one of the first to be sacked by Baron Kraus during the recession in the early 1920s, and it was Benno Kraus who had turned her away from the Quadriga that dreadful night in 1932. Emmy owed much to the Jochums, but she had no love lost for the Kraus family.

Her white teeth gleaming provocatively between her full red lips, she purred, 'I should love to stay on for a few days.'

The following morning, Harper was informed by Emmy, much to his surprise, that she wanted to delay her departure. Mortimer,

Bruno and Norbert also remained in Berlin. Mortimer and Bruno went to meetings Holger Busko had arranged with Willy Brandt and other leading city figures on behalf of Stefan. Norbert said he had business to attend to.

Whatever Norbert's business was, it was quickly dealt with, because for the next three days, he scarcely spent a moment out of Emmy's company. They were seen everywhere together: in restaurants, at the theatre, at the cinema and in nightclubs. The gossip columnists were quick to recognize a good story. Emmy's return to Berlin had been well publicized. Now she appeared to be having a sizzling affair with one of Germany's most prominent, up-and-coming property tycoons, and one who was moreover considerably younger than herself – not to mention a married man. Photographs of the couple appeared first in Berlin newspapers, then in the national press.

Viktoria was annoyed and dismayed, but at a loss to know what to do. Emmy and Norbert weren't children. It wasn't her responsibility to interfere in their lives.

Lili was dreadfully disappointed. She had hoped, when Emmy had announced she was staying on, that she would have an opportunity to talk with her about the past. But Emmy had no time for Lili. What was more, since he had met Emmy, Norbert had paid no attention at all to her either. Lili rather wished she had not invited Emmy Anders to Berlin.

Only Eduard felt a sense of relief. His fears about Norbert and Lili were proving to be totally unjustified.

By Friday, Emmy's last day in Berlin, Norbert had still done no more than kiss her. Yet he was sure his feelings were reciprocated, that Emmy wanted him as much as he wanted her. They could not part on so inconclusive a note, with the desire they both felt left unfulfilled.

That night, they dined by candlelight at an old, romantic restaurant in the Grunewald and, after their meal, strolled beside the Havel. They walked in silence, Norbert's arm around her, her head leaning against his shoulder, her thigh pressed against his.

Then they drove back to the Jochum, collected their keys from reception and took the lift to the first floor. On this occasion, instead of kissing him goodnight outside the door to her suite, Emmy motioned him to enter.

The lounge was lit only by a table lamp. Emmy sat down on the sofa. The dim light emphasized the cleavage between her breasts in her off-the-shoulder gown. Never had she appeared more desirable.

Norbert could no longer restrain himself. Throwing himself down beside her, he drew her to him, covering her bare flesh with kisses, tugging at her dress and ripping the fragile material. As he had hoped, she was wearing nothing underneath and a pertly rounded breast was released from its confinement.

With his other hand he followed the length of her long, slim, stockinged legs, until he reached the warm, naked flesh of her upper thighs. 'Aren't you wearing too many clothes?' Emmy asked huskily.

Norbert was expert at undressing quickly. He shrugged his way out of his jacket, undid his tie, unbuttoned his trousers, slipped out of his shoes, then stood up to discard his superfluous garments. Glancing at her, he saw her gaze fixed on his bulging underpants.

Suddenly, he was extremely confident of what would happen next. He knew he was well-endowed compared to other men. Like all his previous girlfriends, Emmy would gasp when she realized what he had to offer her, moaning and pleading with him to take her.

But it was not like that. As he lowered his pants, she got up from the sofa but, instead of taking off the rest of her clothes as he expected, she gathered up the ripped material of her bodice and, holding her arm across her chest, ran to the bell push used to summon room service. 'If you don't leave my room immediately, I'll press this bell,' she told him in a cold voice.

Norbert couldn't believe his ears. 'What on earth . . . ?'

'If you don't leave my room immediately, I'll press this bell,' she repeated.

He felt his erection subsiding and pulled his pants back up. 'Emmy, I thought you wanted me . . .'

'Why the hell should I want you?' she asked derisively. 'What should I want with a German, with the son of a Nazi war criminal?' Her finger hovered over the bell. 'I mean what I

264

say. I'll tell the bell-boy you tried to rape me. He'll call the police.'

Norbert realized she was serious. He also knew that if she carried out her threat, all evidence would be against him. Never in his life had he felt so helpless and ridiculous, standing there in his shirt, pants and socks. 'Take your clothes with you,' she said. 'Get dressed somewhere else.'

He knew from personal experience that if you rang for a bell-boy in a Jochum Hotel, he would be knocking on the door within ten seconds. He bundled his clothes into his arms and shuffled to the door. With a triumphantly scornful gleam in her eyes, Emmy watched him depart.

Fortunately, his own room was nearby on the same floor and, to his relief, there was no one in the corridor to see him emerge from Emmy's suite in his semi-clothed state – nobody to witness the ignominy of his defeat.

The day after Reinhild and the children returned to Hamburg, Tristan developed another cold and hacking cough and had to stay in bed. On the Thursday, Hannelore Hahn came up to the apartment, brandishing a magazine. 'At least he's tried to be discreet until now!' she exclaimed indignantly.

Reinhild stared at the picture on the front cover of Norbert and Emmy, dancing very close together, their lips almost touching, and her heart seemed to stop beating. 'What do you mean?'

Hannelore gazed at her incredulously. 'Don't tell me you didn't know? Your husband has been fooling around with other women for years. But this is going too far! Now he's flagrantly flouting his infidelity!'

With shaking fingers, Reinhild lit a cigarette.

'I know what I would do in your position,' Hannelore went on. 'I'd divorce him. His son is ill – and where is he? Gallivanting round with some whore! I tell you, I wouldn't want a man like that having anything to do with *my* children! I shall certainly hand in my notice . . .'

Steeped in self-pity, Reinhild spent that night by Tristan's bedside, wiping his fevered brow and trying to soothe his cough with a mixture of butter and sugar. Hannelore's words kept echoing in her mind. How could Norbert treat her like this? How could he behave in such a scandalous manner? And when Tristan was ill. There had been a recent report in the local paper about a whooping cough epidemic and an article in the *Bild Zeitung* about tuberculosis. The more she thought about it, the more certain Reinhild became that Tristan had one or the other of these infections.

First thing in the morning, she called the doctor. The doctor felt Tristan's pulse, took his temperature and applied his stethoscope to his chest and back, then said, 'I don't see any great cause for concern at the moment. His lungs are congested, but his colds do tend to affect him that way.'

'You don't think he has whooping cough or tuberculosis?' Reinhild asked tremulously.

'I don't think so. But it wouldn't do any harm to take one or two precautions in case he does have something infectious. Leave his bedroom window wide open, so that he can breathe more freely. And keep the girls away from him. Whatever it is, we don't want them catching it, do we?'

'But if he does have tuberculosis? Isn't that incurable?'

'Not any more. Most cases can be treated at German sanatoria. Or someone in your position could send him to Switzerland. Mountain air and sunshine effect the best cure. But don't worry. I'm sure what we're dealing with here is just another common cold. I'll pop by tomorrow and take another look at him.'

By the time Norbert arrived back in Hamburg on Saturday evening, Reinhild had worked herself up into a dreadful state. Norbert found her in the living room, wearing her dressing gown, her hair hanging lank and her eyes red and swollen. From one bedroom came the sound of Helena crying, from the other that of Tristan coughing. 'That's all I need!' Norbert thought. 'The bloody kids are ill again.'

Then he saw that on Reinhild's lap was a magazine showing a picture of himself and Emmy. 'How could you do it?' she asked. 'Tristan is critically ill – and you've been having an affair with another woman!'

'He seemed all right when he was in Berlin,' Norbert said evenly.

'That was five days ago. Remember your father. He was alive one minute and dead the next! Norbert, how could you do this to me? I thought you were staying in Berlin on business . . .'

It was difficult to know which was upsetting her most: the fact that Tristan was ill or that Norbert had betrayed her. Tristan coughed again and he asked, 'What's the matter with him?'

'Tuberculosis,' Reinhild whispered tragically.

Norbert strode into the bedroom. Despite the open window, it reeked of eucalyptus. Tristan was awake, lying propped up on pillows. His nose was red from blowing it, but, to Norbert's relief, there was no hectic, feverish light in his eyes or pale consumptive cast to his cheeks. He looked as he always looked when he had a cold. 'So who's a poor old chap?' Norbert asked, bending down to kiss him.

'You mustn't kiss him!' Reinhild screamed. 'That's one of the quickest ways of spreading the infection.'

Tristan gazed fearfully into his father's eyes and Norbert felt a surge of hatred for Reinhild so strong that it was only with the greatest of difficulty that he did not turn and strike her. Instead, he righted himself slowly and smoothed his hand across Tristan's forehead. 'Sorry. Have to obey doctor's orders.'

Tristan nodded wanly.

From the other room, Helena's cries turned to screams. 'What's up with her?' Norbert asked.

'She's frightened her brother is going to die,' Reinhild told him, accusingly.

Norbert went in to the girls' room. Kleo was sitting on the edge of her little sister's bed, her arm round Helena's shoulders. When she saw her father, she was clearly relieved. 'Oh, Papa, please tell her to stop crying. She'll make herself ill. Tell her Tristan's going to be all right.'

'Of course he is,' Norbert said. 'Helena, here's a hankie, now blow your nose and listen to me. Tristan's got a cold . . .'

It was a long night, interspersed with fits of Tristan's coughing, sobbing from Helena and floods of Reinhild's tears. Eventually, Norbert forced Reinhild to admit that the doctor had not actually diagnosed tuberculosis. 'Not that you care,' she wailed. 'You don't care about anyone except yourself. Otherwise, you wouldn't have been having an affair with this whore, Emmy Anders.'

And that, Norbert realized, was the core of the trouble. Having discovered he was being unfaithful to her, she had hoped to make him feel even guiltier by using Tristan's illness. She hoped to trap him, as she had trapped him into marriage and tricked him into fathering her children.

'Hannelore says I should divorce you.'

So Hannelore was at the root of the trouble. Having taken over control of his office, she now wanted to rule his personal life. Probably Hannelore had showed Reinhild the magazine in the first place. But, whatever her intentions, Hannelore was right. He had drifted into his marriage for all the wrong reasons. There had been no passion, no rapture, no ecstasy. Now, there was nothing at all, no guilt, no remorse, nothing, except a sense of tedium – and a sudden, intense longing to be rid of Reinhild. He could not have Emmy. He did not want Reinhild. 'That might be the best solution.'

'But, Norbert, what will people think?'

'Whatever you choose to tell them, no doubt.'

Then Norbert picked up his bag and left the apartment. Outside, he got into his car and drove to the Jochum-Hamburg. As he went, he knew, with a sense of relief, that part of his life was finished for ever. And, at the same time, he was conscious of the irony that, in this particular instance, he was being blamed for an affair he had never had.

Norbert and Reinhild met, in fact, just two days later, at the hospital. Although Tristan's cold did not develop into whooping cough or tuberculosis, it did have quite serious repercussions, for one of his lungs collapsed. The doctors reassured his parents that, although the condition was frightening and painful, it was not dangerous and had probably occurred as a result of some mucus that he couldn't cough up. Reinhild insisted that he go to Switzerland for treatment and convalescence.

As soon as Tristan was declared fit enough to travel, Norbert paid for him, Reinhild and the two girls to go to the Bernese Oberland. Tristan spent a month in a very expensive sanatorium and the rest of the family at an only slightly less expensive hotel.

268

Reinhild sent postcards to all her friends, neighbours and relations with suitably gloomy messages which contrasted with the beautiful mountain scenes depicted on the front. Kleo also sent a card, but she did not let her mother see who it was to, for she was afraid her mother would laugh at her. Kleo had fallen in love at Aunt Viktoria's birthday party. His name was Dieter.

The children saw their father again not long after their return to Hamburg, on Helena's fifth birthday in August, when he took them for tea at the Jochum. Tristan's health had benefited greatly from the mountain air. He did not have so much as even a hint of a sniffle or a cough and, like the two girls, his face was tanned and glowing.

They were rather awkward with their father to begin with and Norbert rightly guessed that Reinhild had been telling stories against him to blacken him in their eyes, but by the time the afternoon was over, Tristan and Kleo, at least, had overcome their nervousness and were chattering away, although Helena was still very quiet. He bought them lots of ice cream, gave them each a ten Mark note and took them for a spin down the autobahn before taking them home. When he left them at the Eppendorf flat, Tristan and Kleo kissed him cheerfully and affectionately, but Helena burst into tears.

'What have you done to the child?' her mother snapped, glaring at Helena.

Norbert shrugged impatiently. 'She was fine up to now.'

Kleo put her arm round Helena's shoulders, but Helena pushed her away and ran, sobbing, into the apartment.

Reinhild duly filed a divorce petition against Norbert on the grounds of adultery and mental cruelty, and the law commenced its lugubrious process. Norbert did not even attempt to defend the action. At his lawyer's suggestion, rather than become burdened with indefinite maintenance payments, he gave Reinhild the block of flats in which she was living as a one-off divorce settlement, together with the income from the rents.

Their parents' separation and eventual divorce affected the children in very different ways. Tristan was of the opinion that it might prove a very good thing, if Father gave them ten Marks every time they saw him. Kleo, although she tried to appear grown-up and keep a stiff upper lip, was inwardly very upset.

Father had always spent more time away from home than with them, but he had been a stable, dependable factor in their lives. For the first time she realized that nothing in this world, not even her parents, was permanent or secure.

Helena, although nobody was aware of it, for she was such a strange, introvert child, was hit hardest of all. She did not understand why her father had left them, but from the way her mother snapped at her, she felt she was partly to blame for the divorce. If Tristan hadn't been ill and she hadn't cried so much, Father wouldn't have been so angry whenever he came home. If only he could have given her the opportunity to explain that she didn't throw tantrums on purpose to annoy him – but he hadn't, he had just gone . . .

Just as Norbert's married life ended, Werner's began. Leaving the Baron with his nurse in the flat in Essen, he bought an apartment in Frankfurt for himself and Else. They were married at the beginning of September 1954 at the Roman Catholic Church of St Mary Magdalene, attended only by close family members. There seemed no point in wasting money on a lavish reception for people who had so recently met each other at Viktoria's birthday party.

Since Norbert and Reinhild's separation, tension between Hannelore Hahn and her employer had mounted. Now that Werner was married and had opened an office in Frankfurt, Hannelore wrote to him, offering her services as office manager. Never one to miss an opportunity to hurt his brother, Werner accepted with alacrity. She quickly proved an extremely capable employee, and Werner soon found himself confiding in her information about his business affairs which he trusted to no other, including his own wife.

Hannelore not only found her new position far more interest-ing and challenging than her previous job at Landgut, but she also saw in it scope for the advancement of her own personal finances. Unknown to Werner, she began to invest part of her modest salary every month in the companies in which Werner Kraus Holdings KG and its now vast list of interwoven subsidi-ary interests were investing. Gradually, she had the satisfaction of seeing her small portfolio increase and rise in value.

270

Norbert appointed a new manager in charge of Landgut, a keen young man called Oskar Stallkamp. He was determined to employ no more women.

The reunion between Lili and Senta at Viktoria's birthday party had sealed the friendship between the two girls. Lili's letters and monthly parcels of books had long been the highlight of Senta's existence. Monika looked forward to the food parcels she received from Viktoria, but provided Senta could stave off the pangs of hunger, she cared little what she ate. She craved spiritual nourishment and this Lili provided.

Senta was not the only one to enjoy Lili's books. When she had avidly consumed their pages, her grandparents would read them and, sometimes, she would find her father leafing through them, with a sad expression in his eyes.

Often, those days, Senta sensed a great unhappiness in her father, reminding her of the time when he had returned after the war. There was a bitterness in him, which would explode in occasional outbursts of temper, usually against her grandparents or her mother and very rarely against herself, although never against Heini. Her mother would excuse them by saying he was working too hard and was disappointed at not getting his expected promotion to the upper school. However, Senta believed there was more to it than that. Her father was at war with his own conscience.

Those days, Senta's parents seldom went to church and Heini had long since refused even to enter the church doors, so it was only Senta who accompanied her grandmother to Sunday worship. She went out of affection for her grandparents and from a sense of rebellion against her brother and Herr Gutjahr. She would be fourteen that October and was developing a stubborn little personality of her own. She did not like being told what to do. She wanted to be free to follow her own instincts. She also went to church for the very simple reason that she believed in God.

Just after her fourteenth birthday, she started attending confirmation classes, looking forward to the day when she would be admitted to full participation in the Church.

That November, however, the State introduced a new measure

271

to secure the souls of young people for itself: the *Jugendweihe*, a lay confirmation. Senta's class all went on visits to factories and State farms and attended special youth lectures in preparation for the dedication ceremony, which would take place at the end of the school term and during which they would swear an oath pledging their lives to service to the State.

Pastor Koenig was put to the ultimate test. He could do as he had done under the Nazis, acquiesce to the State ruling and allow the significance of confirmation into the Church to be belittled. Or he could stand firm and give children and their parents the choice of confirmation or dedication.

All winter, the discussions continued, not only in the parsonage at Fuerstenmark but in households throughout the GDR and in the higher echelons of the Church. In the end, some Church authorities ruled that it was permissible for confirmation to take place within weeks of the *Jugendweihe*; others that at least a year must elapse between the two; yet others, and it was this minority which Pastor Koenig eventually joined, that the two were incompatible. Children who took the *Jugendweihe* could not receive Christian confirmation.

His decision was influenced most of all by Senta, who said she could not reconcile her inner belief in God and what she was learning at confirmation classes with the materialistic doctrines put over by Herr Gutjahr at school. It was impossible to dedicate her soul both to God and to a godless State. If Senta had the courage to take this stand, Pastor Koenig decided, then he must, too.

At Easter, only a very small number of Senta's class took the *Jugendweihe*. Far more were received into the Church.

Local Party offices reported to East Berlin the names of pastors who refused to acknowledge the *Jugendweihe*. Some were arrested but Arthur Koenig was not among them. The parish of Fuerstenmark was considered too small for the influence of its pastor to be considered of any great importance.

As for Basilius Meyer, he was too concerned with other matters to pay much attention to the intransigence of the clergy, even the Koenigs. His entire attention was focused on the forthcoming trial of Stefan Jochum before the Supreme Court.

The trial took place in April 1955, just before Stefan's fortieth birthday and seventeen months after his capture. Although no foreign observers were permitted, journalists from State-approved newspapers and radio were present. So, too, was Basilius, the first time he had ever seen Stefan in the flesh.

Although Stefan was very pale and thin, he was clean-shaven and neatly dressed in a well-fitting suit. He walked unaided to the dock and spoke clearly, if softly, as he gave his oath. There was no visible sign that he had been maltreated in any way during his imprisonment.

The case for the prosecution was short and to the point, and accused Stefan under Article 6 of the Constitution. Jochum, the prosecuting lawyer stated, had worked during the war for the British Secret Service and returned to Germany with the Control Commission. He was related to well-known capitalists in the Western zones, including the notorious Baron von Kraus. He had abused the confidence of Erika Quanz, a young woman working at the Foreign Ministry, to obtain State secrets which he had passed on to the West. He had helped provoke the disturbances of 17th June. From information he had acquired in the GDR, he had published propaganda in Western newspapers which endangered and slandered the State. He had also confessed to passing on information to British Military Intelligence.

The defence lawyer presented a convoluted argument, claiming that his client had been a victim of love. Erika Quanz and her father had wanted to defect to the West and had seen in Stefan Jochum a means of achieving their ambition and earning some money. Jochum, he said, believed in socialist ideals, but had been too infatuated and too weak-willed to refuse their demands. In his confession, which was read aloud to the Court, he expressed his regret at his betrayal of the State.

The trial lasted two hours, during which Stefan was not permitted to speak in his own defence, but various witnesses, who had met him, were subjected to intense cross-questioning. The most credible of these was Herr Domke, the one-eyed caretaker at the block of flats where Quanz and Drescher had lived, who testified that the defendant had paid several visits to the Stalin Allee prior to the 17th June strike and had been

273

seen marching with the demonstrators on that day. Extracts from Stefan's articles in *Aktuell* were read aloud and handed round the Court.

Long before the trial ended, the outcome was obvious. Stefan Jochum was condemned to twenty-five years' imprisonment. Handcuffed to a prison warder, he was led out of the dock and taken to the Soviet military prison in Lichtenberg.

Basilius could have hoped for no more satisfactory outcome. Rudi was promoted to a more senior rank within the SSD, and Basilius himself was rewarded with a two-year course at the Institute of Higher Political Studies. In July, he, Irina and baby Reinhardt went to Moscow.

Chapter 13

Viktoria was not surprised when Stefan was found guilty, but she was horrified at the severity of his sentence, while Lili, who had been so optimistic about the outcome of the trial, was shocked to the marrow.

Mortimer, however, who telephoned immediately upon hearing the news, refused to be downcast by it. 'Don't give up hope, Vicki. I'm positive our campaign has been influential in having Stefan brought to trial and not just sent to Siberia, which is what I suspect happens to most people who disappear inside the Soviet bloc. Now, more than ever, we must keep up the pressure. The trial was unfair, the verdict totally unjust. If enough people create a stink about it, he may be granted a remission.'

Holger Busko concurred. 'Remember what Stefan himself wrote,' he told Viktoria. ' "We must knock on the prison door until it opens." '

Since Holger's first meeting with Mortimer after Stefan's arrest, he and his younger brother, Volker, and several other students from the Free University, had established a *Stammtisch*, a regular table, on the terrace of Café Jochum, where they gathered in the evening for a beer and a chat and to discuss the next stage in the Stefan Jochum campaign.

Viktoria had grown very attached to these young people and found their steadfast devotion to Stefan, whom they knew only by reputation, extremely moving. She was impressed by their determination not to repeat the mistakes of the past and especially not to give in to tyranny.

She liked Holger the best, probably because there was a lot about him which reminded her of Stefan at the same age and, although she no more agreed with some of his ideas than she had done with Stefan's, she could not help but respect his integrity. If he did achieve his ambition to

275

become a politician, she was sure he would make a very good one.

Although the two Busko brothers looked alike, their personalities were very different. Volker was an artist, dreamy, slightly frivolous and rather lazy. Holger was a driver and self-motivating, whereas Volker, Viktoria suspected, relied on his brother and his own, not inconsiderable, charm to get him through life.

Sometimes she and Lili joined the students on the terrace and often, as the evening wore on, the conversation would turn into a political debate, of which Viktoria found the cut and thrust stimulating. But Volker would grow bored with it, and so would Lili, and while the others heatedly discussed current events, they would talk about art.

Whilst Holger Busko and his friends were deeply concerned about Stefan's well-being and determined to get him released from prison, they were far enough removed to be able to see him in the context of events of international importance, being played out on the world arena. Gradually, Viktoria too came to realize that Stefan was, in fact, only one little pawn in a very big and extremely dangerous game. This realization did not, of course, stop her worrying about him, but it gave her hope that if Mortimer and Holger's campaign were successful, the GDR authorities might just decide that Stefan was more trouble than he was worth -- and release him.

That May, exactly ten years after Germany had surrendered at the end of the war, the statute under which the Allies had occupied the country was finally abandoned, except for Berlin, which remained under so-called Four-Power Occupation. The Federal Republic became a sovereign state and, almost immediately, joined NATO. The government cautiously admitted that it was creating the framework for a *Bundeswehr*, new armed forces.

The Soviet response was swift. It announced the formation of the 'Eastern European Mutual Assistance Treaty', known as the Warsaw Pact, in which, like NATO, its member countries pledged to assist each other to meet any armed attack on any other Pact member. At the same time, however, the Soviet Union invited the Federal Republic to a meeting to discuss the resumption of diplomatic relations.

276

In June, the foreign ministers of the six member countries of the European Coal and Steel Community met in Messina and agreed to explore the possibility of forming a European economic community and the establishment of a European Atomic Energy Commission, in which member states would cooperate in the development of nuclear research and the production of nuclear energy.

There was a spontaneous and angry public reaction in the Federal Republic to all these events. A number of peace rallies, in many of which Holger participated, took place throughout the country, supported by members of the Protestant Church, the trades unions, the SPD and even some of Adenauer's own party, the CDU.

It was at one of these rallies that Holger met Pastor Scheer and his 13-year-old grandson, Matthias. The demonstration followed a meeting of the Bundestag at which delegates had voted on rearmament and, to the dismay of all pacifists, the SPD had sided with the government. 'Chancellor Adenauer says that our place in the world is at the side of free people,' Pastor Scheer said, during his speech. He looked old and very frail, but his voice had surprising strength. 'He claims that to be the reason behind the Federal Republic joining NATO. But what he has done is to damage irrevocably the chances of freedom for many of his own countrymen. And by voting with him, the Social Democrats are guilty of an even worse betrayal.'

He paused and put his arm round the shoulders of his flaxen-haired grandson. 'In everything we do, we should be thinking of children like Matthias. We should not be simply considering the events of the present, but the effects of our actions upon the children of the future.'

After the rally, Holger went up to the pastor and for a while they stood talking, then the pastor said, 'Any friend of Stefan Jochum is a friend of mine. Please come and see us in Schmargendorf whenever you like. Klara, my wife, and I always like to meet young people. And it's good for Matthias. His parents are abroad, you see, working for an Evangelical Church mission organization in Africa.'

Holger glanced at the boy. He was staring straight ahead, a stony expression in his clear blue eyes.

277

In September, Chancellor Adenauer finally took up the Soviet invitation to visit Moscow, a meeting which resulted in diplomatic relations being established between the Federal Republic and the Soviet Union; negotiations being started for the development of trade relations between the two countries; and the release of thousands of German prisoners of war, still in captivity from the war. Shortly after Adenauer's visit, the Soviet Union declared the GDR to be a sovereign state.

In January 1956, the first training company of the Bundeswehr was organized. Two weeks later, the GDR announced the establishment of the National People's Army.

All hope of German reunification had gone. What had once been one country was now two sovereign states. And, with the creation of two separate armies, Holger Busko's and Pastor Scheer's worst fears had been realized. Now the possibility existed that, one day, the two Germanies might find themselves fighting each other.

In February, Bruno von der Eschenbach returned to the Jochum-Berlin and, on the evening of his arrival, invited Viktoria to dine with him. During the course of their meal, he made her a most unexpected proposal.

'My eldest son, Konstantin, has just left University,' he told her. 'He has begun to take his heritage very seriously and has just completed a review of all our properties. Our family seat, the Alte Hofburg, is the largest of our estates, but by no means the only one. We have considerable land-holdings in the rest of Bavaria and in other regions, including Hesse and Baden-Wuerttemberg, some of which have been rather neglected.

'I must admit to having left the running of my business and estates to my managers and advisers, while I concentrated on social matters – the problems of the homeless, refugees and war orphans particularly concern me. But Konstantin has persuaded me that I must be more businesslike.'

A twinkle in his eye convinced Viktoria that he had not been quite so lax as he was making out and that he was indulging Konstantin a little.

'We own a building on the Zeil in Frankfurt, where the

278

Eschenbach Bank is situated, and Konstantin is proposing that, instead of leasing out the upper floors, we take them over and centralize the activities of Eschenbach Estates.' He picked up his champagne glass and twirled it, gazing at its glittering facets rather like a fortune-teller staring into a crystal ball. 'He's probably right. Frankfurt is rapidly becoming the financial capital of Germany and, if Adenauer has his way, it will soon be the financial capital of Europe.'

Then he looked up from the glass and into Viktoria's eyes. 'The reason behind my rather long-winded tale is that, just outside Frankfurt, quite near the airport, we have an old hunting lodge, set in several acres of forest. I've been to have a look at it. It's ideally situated for an hotel.' He paused to let his words sink in, then added, 'Another Jochum hotel.'

Viktoria's immediate instinct was to say no. Although Mortimer and Holger had made her feel more confident about Stefan eventually being released, she was still suffering from the same feeling of guilt as she had experienced at the opening of the Jochum-Berlin. Quite simply, it seemed wrong and selfish to pursue her own interests while Stefan was enduring God only knew what kind of hell.

But she did not feel able to explain this to Bruno. However, she could say, with all honesty, 'It's an extremely kind thought but, apart from anything else, I don't think I can afford to expand. Although the Jochum-Hamburg is doing well, the Jochum-Berlin is still far from profitable, even with Berlin's favourable taxation system.'

'We should not be looking for any capital input from you.'

'Then how – why . . . ?'

'Firstly, because Jochum Hotels have a unique reputation and I believe an association between us would be mutually beneficial. Remember, as well as property, we own one of the largest breweries in Bavaria. But, mainly, because I have a great admiration for you personally and would like to help you as much as possible.'

'Thank you,' Viktoria said, deeply touched. 'However, I think it's also only right to point out that the idea of being a tenant, even your tenant, does not appeal to me.'

'I understand that. What I propose is that we form a new

279

company, in which we each hold fifty per cent of the shares. Eschenbach Estates would provide the capital and yourself the management.'

Viktoria frowned. 'But that would mean I no longer had overall control of my own business.'

'If I'm correct, you don't actually control it now. Landgut holds the freehold to the Jochum-Hamburg, I believe.'

'I'm due to purchase the freehold from Landgut this year.'

'Which will wipe out all your reserves,' Bruno hazarded, again correctly. 'Viktoria, you and I have known each other a long time. We are old friends. I have no desire to take anything away from you. I'm not a Kraus. On the contrary, I should like to see you released from the clutches of the Krauses.'

'Norbert isn't typical of his family. He's been very good to me.'

'I'm glad to hear it,' Bruno said drily. 'However, the fact remains that if Eschenbach Estates buys back the freehold of the Hamburg hotel, you can be free of your debt and free to open new hotels. The best way to consider my proposal is in the form of outside investment. You have the expertise. Eschenbach Estates has the money to allow you to realize your ambitions.'

For a long time, Viktoria was silent. Then she asked slowly, 'Whose idea is this? Yours or Konstantin's?'

His smile crinkled the corners of his eyes. 'The hotel was Konstantin's idea. The rest is mine. I'm not quite the fool he likes to make me out. So, will you at least think about it?'

He was very persuasive. 'Yes,' Viktoria promised, 'I'll think about it.'

'And come and see the property?'

Again, it was easiest to say, 'Yes.'

With a wave of his hand, Bruno summoned an attentive waiter and ordered another bottle of champagne.

Bruno had other business in Berlin and remained at the hotel for several days, during which he renewed his acquaintance with Holger Busko, met his younger brother, Volker, and got to know Lili a little better.

Lili was eighteen now and in her second year at secretarial college, at the stage when people like Bruno von der Eschenbach, thirty years older than herself, seemed extremely old and staid. For that matter, Lili, who was younger than both his sons, seemed very young and immature to Bruno. However, he could not help but find her engaging and, with her green eyes and auburn hair, she reminded him greatly of her mother, Luise, of whom he had been very fond.

While Bruno was still in Berlin, some of Volker's paintings were exhibited at a show of student work at the Academy of Arts, and Lili persuaded him and Viktoria to come with her to see them.

'Don't you think they're good?' she asked, blushing slightly as she spoke and pointing to a group of half a dozen rather abstract paintings, all of female nudes, painted in bold, vibrant colours.

Viktoria frowned. She liked conventional pictures and, furthermore, did not consider the subject matter of these very suitable for a young girl.

Bruno studied them critically. The paintings were certainly eye-catching and their apparent simplicity belied the care which had been given to their composition and the rhythmic arrangement of patterns and colours. 'Yes, I do,' he said finally. 'Your friend has talent.'

Lili's colour heightened. 'Would you buy one? You see, Volker doesn't have a lot of money. He only has a small grant and his parents live in the Soviet zone, so they can't help him financially.'

Bruno smiled indulgently. 'I think that can be arranged.'

Later that evening, when he and Viktoria were alone, he commented, 'Would I be right in assuming that young Lili is smitten with Volker Busko?'

'Not that I'm aware of,' Viktoria replied sharply. 'Volker Busko isn't a type I want Lili to become involved with.'

'His brother is doing a lot for Stefan.'

'Holger and Volker are two very different kinds of men,' Viktoria replied.

When Bruno returned to the Federal Republic, Viktoria went with him to Frankfurt. A chauffeur-driven limousine met them at the airport and, after driving for a short while towards the city centre, they branched off up a bumpy, forest track, which came to a halt in front of the old hunting lodge Bruno

281

had described. In the distance was a small lake, overgrown with reeds.

Slowly, Viktoria walked over the rutted grass towards the building. Clumps of daffodils and narcissi danced in the breeze. In the forest doves cooed. In a strange way, the place reminded her of Heiligensee.

'Visualize the building renovated and extended,' Bruno said, 'surrounded by landscaped gardens, tennis courts and a golf course. There's room for a stables and a swimming pool. A country retreat, ten minutes from the airport and the city centre . . .'

'I'm not sure,' Viktoria prevaricated. But, just as she had instinctively known that the mansion on Hamburg's Binnenalster was right for her first hotel, so, in her heart of hearts, she knew this lodge was ideally suited for another Jochum hotel.

Bruno took her arm. 'I think I know how you are feeling. You've suffered so many set-backs and tragedies during the last years, that you are tempted to call a halt and stop where you are. In my opinion, that would be a mistake. All your life you have worked, Viktoria. You have always had some goal to strive towards. Take the challenge of work away, and what is left? Empty years, stretching ahead . . .'

'It's Stefan,' she blurted out. 'I feel so guilty . . .'

Bruno nodded. 'I felt the same after my wife died. It seemed wrong that I should still be alive, when she was dead. But doing nothing will not bring the dead back to life, and neither will it speed Stefan's release. When he is set free, he will not thank you for having given up living for him. More likely, from what I know of your son, he will be angry . . .'

Viktoria gave a wan smile. Bruno von der Eschenbach was not only a kind but a very perceptive man.

It was while Viktoria was in Frankfurt that Volker Busko asked Lili to model for him. Holger was out and they were alone in the old house in Kreuzberg which the two brothers shared. Lili loved Kreuzberg. The oldest part of Berlin, with narrow, cobbled streets, it had an almost foreign atmosphere about it. Kreuzberg was how Lili imagined the Montmartre area of Paris to be.

282

Half in hope, half in fear, Lili had been waiting for Volker to ask her to model for him ever since she had met him. She had been speaking the truth when she had told Bruno that she believed Volker to be very talented. What she had failed to say was that, with his slightly bohemian good looks and gentle temperament, she also found him extremely attractive.

Now that he had asked, however, her courage failed her. It was not modesty which held her back or even the knowledge that Viktoria would be furious if she discovered that she was posing for him. What worried her was that Volker would be disappointed when he saw the underdeveloped little body she concealed under loose pullovers and full skirts.

'Why are you nervous?' Volker asked. 'You know me. I won't hurt you.'

Lili shook her head. 'It's just . . .'

Volker misinterpreted her awkwardness and assumed that she was afraid he would take advantage of her. 'Listen, sweetheart, not all men are rampaging beasts. I give you my word that I shall not so much as lay a hand on you, unless you want me to. I'm an artist, not a rapist.'

Eventually, he persuaded her to shed her inhibitions and her clothes, and she took up position leaning against a wall in a shaft of sunlight. For a long time, Volker studied her before picking up his brush. Nervously, Lili said, 'I'm too thin, aren't I?'

Volker shook his head. 'Not all artists are Rubens, you know. Saskia has never appealed to me.' Then he picked up his brush and painted the first lines on the bare canvas.

For three Saturdays, Lili returned, and each time, Volker seemed unaware of her body except as a subject for his painting. He spoke little and when he did it was to utter only instructions to change her position slightly. Yet during those long periods of silence, Lili was aware of a growing communion between them. Each was seeing the other at their most intimate. She was observing him when he was lost to everything except his work. He was painting her at her most vulnerable.

It was getting late and the light was dying on the third Saturday when he laid down his brushes and asked, 'Want to have a look?'

She went and stood beside him. The picture was less abstract

283

than his previous works and had caught the essence of her boyish figure. Her legs looked longer, her pubic hair more bushy, her hips narrower and her tiny breasts flatter than they really were. Her face appeared more elfish and was surrounded by a halo of fiery hair, but as yet it wore no expression.

He looked up at her. 'Do you know what's missing?'

She nodded.

'Do you know why?'

'I think so.'

'I promised not to touch you unless you asked me to.'

Huskily, she said, 'I want you to. I want you to make love to me.'

Volker was very gentle. His long artistic fingers caressed her body as tenderly as his brush applied paint to canvas. Lovingly, caringly, he guided her into a discovery of his body, while revealing the delights which were hidden in her own, and during this long, tantalizing journey of exploration, Lili gained confidence, forgot her fears, lost her tenseness and soon began fully to enjoy, so that she was moving with him, matching her rhythm to his, laughing and crying, filled with a sense of desire and – eventually – a sense of fulfilment, which she had never imagined existed within her.

Later, when there was no more of herself to give, when she was lying in the crook of his arm, warm and happy and complete as she had never felt before, Volker gazed at her face. 'That's the expression I want.'

When Lili finally saw the finished picture, she knew what he meant. There was a softness to her eyes, a self-satisfaction about her smile. It was the face of a woman who had just made love.

After her decision to accept Bruno's offer, Viktoria was kept extremely busy and, in her work, she found a sense of release from her fear and grief, a positive vent for her emotions. She began to sleep soundly at night, without dreaming, and when she woke in the morning, it was with a feeling of vitality and purpose.

First, she had to see Norbert, who had finally settled in Munich, in an apartment in Schwabing overlooking the

Englischer Garten. He accepted her decision philosophically and, in fact, admitted that he believed she was doing the right thing. 'Leaving the money management to Eschenbach Estates will free you from all your financial worries,' he said.

Then, rather to her amusement, he went on to give some advice which was the exact opposite of what Bruno had said. 'I know you like to think you can do everything, but you're not getting any younger, Aunt Vicki. If you continue as you have been, you'll just wear yourself out. Even I have had to learn to delegate. Oskar Stallkamp and Erwin Hoffmann look after the everyday running of Landgut for me now, while I concentrate on new projects.'

Judging by the obvious signs of a recent female occupant at his flat, Viktoria surmised that his new projects were not entirely to do with work.

Even more generously, Norbert offered to recommend an architect to plan the refurbishment of her new hotel and liaise with the Frankfurt planning authorities on her behalf.

After that, there were countless meetings with Bruno and Konstantin, and with lawyers in Berlin and Frankfurt. Not only did the structure, shareholding and financing of the new company have to be agreed, but Lili's half-share in the business, which she would inherit in 1958, when she became twenty-one, had to be protected.

While she was in Frankfurt, Viktoria felt duty-bound to visit Werner and Else, although she would have much preferred not to. It was not an easy evening they spent together. Else was in the last month of pregnancy, so enormous she could hardly move. Their flat was sparsely furnished, the meal prepared from the cheapest ingredients and, although Werner permitted himself a glass of beer, Viktoria and Else had to make do with tea.

Bruno laughed when Viktoria related her experience. 'His meanness is notorious. Did you know that he has just re-opened the Liegnitzer Bank here in Frankfurt? His wife's father is in charge of it. Everyone says that's the reason he married Else – to have a banker for a father-in-law.'

In May, Else was delivered of twin girls by Caesarian section. During the operation, her life literally hung in the balance.

Viktoria, who had kept herself informed of Else's progress,

went to see her as soon as she was fit enough to receive visitors. Despite her ordeal, she looked quite well and was sitting up in bed, with the babies in a crib beside her. 'Werner says he doesn't care what they're called, so I've decided to call them Margarete and Brigitta,' she said.

'What do you mean, Werner doesn't care?' Viktoria asked.

'He's furious they're not boys. He hasn't been to see me since they were born. But everyone else has been very good. The hospital staff are very kind, and my parents have promised to give me all the support I need. My father is paying for a nanny to help me look after them when I return home. I hope that, when Werner gets over his disappointment and shock, he'll become fond of them. The surgeon told me after the operation that I'll never be able to have any more children.' Sadly, Else added, 'I think Werner would like to divorce me now. But he can't. I'm a Roman Catholic and in our Church marriage is for life.'

At that moment, Viktoria felt extremely sorry for Else Kraus.

Soon, Lili's friendship with Volker was common knowledge, although nobody at the hotel knew they were lovers. Lili would have liked to confide her secret in Eduard, but he had started to behave very strangely towards her and whenever she mentioned Volker, he changed the subject. Volker laughed when she told him. 'What do you expect? He's jealous.'

'Eduard – jealous? Don't be silly.'

'Anyone can see he's in love with you. What's silly about that?'

'He can't be in love with me. He's known me for years.'

Volker shrugged. 'What's that got to do with it?'

Because Eduard showed no sign of being in love with her and, in fact, acted as if quite the contrary were true, Lili decided to ignore him. She could not, however, ignore Viktoria's reaction.

Since meeting Volker, Lili had badly neglected her college work. At the end of June she passed her exams and qualified for her secretarial diploma by the skin of her teeth. 'It doesn't matter,' she said blithely, when Viktoria commented with displeasure on her results. 'You'll still give me a job.'

'Why should I choose you in preference to the other girls in your class who did so much better?' Viktoria demanded.

The trouble was the girl had been spoiled. She had grown up believing that everything she wanted would be handed to her on a plate. Well, life wasn't like that and the sooner Lili realized it the better. Lili could have a job, but not in Berlin. She could start work at the Jochum-Hamburg.

Lili was furious and refused point-blank to go. She went for a number of interviews with other companies but found none who would take her on. With unemployment in West Berlin still at a critical level, employers could afford to be choosy about whom they engaged among college leavers.

Finally, Lili said, 'Then I won't work at all. I'll just marry Volker. We'll get by somehow.'

'You're only eighteen. I'm still your legal guardian. And if you think I'm going to allow you to marry a penniless artist, you're mistaken.'

Eventually, and with a very bad grace, Lili agreed to go to Hamburg. 'But you won't separate me and Volker. He'll come with me.'

Viktoria merely said, 'I doubt very much that he'll do that.'

Volker, too, had just completed his college course but, unlike Lili, he had passed his exams with flying colours and already accepted a job as an illustrator at a Berlin publishing house. Lili did not see this as an obstacle. He was sure to obtain an even better job in Hamburg.

What she failed to take into account were events taking place around her which affected her personally very little but were of great importance to her friends. That July, conscription had become compulsory for all men between the ages of eighteen and forty-five, but because West Berlin remained under Allied Occupation, Berliners were exempt. Volker had no intention of going to Hamburg, where he ran the very real risk of being called up.

'And that is more important to you than I am?' Lili asked, horrified.

He tipped her chin up towards him and kissed her. 'Lili, there are other things in the world besides love.'

Lili was desolate. Not only had Viktoria again betrayed

287

her but, even worse, her first love affair was proving an illusion.

Even Eduard had failed her. At this most critical stage in her life, he showed her no sympathy at all but told her stiffly that he was sure her aunt knew best. When Lili threw her arms round him and burst into tears, he pushed her brusquely away, ordering her to pull herself together.

Lili left Berlin for Hamburg at the beginning of August with the feeling that she was loved by nobody at all in the whole world.

As Lili rapidly discovered, working in an hotel was a very different matter from living in one. Since Viktoria had given no exact instructions as to how she was to be employed, Dirk Kaiser put her in Viktoria's own office, with vague instructions to make herself useful. Within a week, Lili was responsible for accepting room reservations without telling reception, resulting in three rooms being double-booked and angry guests having to be found accommodation elsewhere. When another guest complained that his room was too noisy she moved him to a suite at the back of the hotel but failed to tell him that the rate would be double. She gave away drinks at the bar and invited people she liked to dine with her without realizing that all drinks and meals had to be accounted for.

The situation could not be allowed to continue. Faced with angry complaints from guests and staff, Dirk Kaiser was sorely tempted to send her back to Berlin but, upon reflection, decided he was probably to blame in giving her too free a hand and, instead, moved her in with his secretary, Angela Avermann, a middle-aged widow, known in the hotel as 'the dragon', who was told to teach Lili the rudiments of hotel management, keep her busy and out of harm's way.

Frau Avermann had joined the staff of the Jochum-Hamburg after Lili had moved to Berlin and because she knew little of her background felt she was being given an unfair advantage, which she did not deserve. The girl was unable to concentrate for more than five minutes at a time; often she could not read back her own shorthand; she typed quickly but inaccurately; and, on the slightest provocation, she left the

288

office and wandered off round the hotel to find someone to talk to.

She seemed totally unaware of the rules of proper behaviour and was friendly with the most unsuitable people. One of these was a chambermaid called Magda, who had recently arrived with her parents from the Soviet zone, leaving her boyfriend behind. Lili and Magda were often to be found commiserating with each other over their lost loves. In Frau Avermann's eyes, it was not done for management to consort with menials. Such conduct swiftly led to a breakdown of discipline.

Worst of all was Lili's reaction when Norbert Kraus arrived back at the hotel after a prolonged absence. Frau Avermann's feelings towards Norbert Kraus were ambivalent. On the one hand, he was a prominent businessman. On the other hand, he was a notorious philanderer.

Lili was staring blankly at her shorthand pad in the vain hope of deciphering her hieroglyphics when Norbert strode into the room, peered over her shoulder and read, 'Dear Sir, Thank you for your letter of the 17th ultimate. We are happy to confirm . . .'

'Norbert!' Lili leapt to her feet with such force that she sent her chair flying backwards. She flung her arms round his neck. 'Norbert, you don't know how wonderful it is to see you!'

He laughed and lifted her off the ground, swinging her round, so that her skirt flew out in a most indecorous fashion. 'I don't believe it. You haven't given me a thought in months.'

'I have!' Lili nuzzled her face against his shoulder. 'I've been so miserable. If only you'd been here, it wouldn't have been nearly so bad.'

Frau Avermann clattered pointedly on her typewriter. Norbert lowered Lili to the ground and took her hand. 'Come and have a drink and tell me all about it.'

When they had left the office, Frau Avermann's hands fell to her lap. Never in her life had she witnessed such a flagrantly shameless display. What a hussy! Literally throwing herself at Herr Kraus like that. And not even having the common courtesy to ask Frau Avermann's permission to leave the office. It was disgraceful!

In the bar, Lili sipped a glass of wine and poured out her

troubles. 'I hate working in an office. I get so bored. And everyone's beastly to me because I'm Aunt Vicki's niece. They don't realize she made me come here. I don't know how much longer I can stand it before I go completely mad.'

Norbert could not help laughing. 'Perhaps you should have concentrated a little less on Volker Busko and a little more on your studies.'

Lili's eyes narrowed. 'How do you know about Volker?'

'Aunt Vicki told me.'

'She has no right to discuss my private affairs with all and sundry.'

'She's concerned about you.'

'Rubbish! She doesn't give a damn. Otherwise she wouldn't have sent me away like this. Oh, Norbert, please understand – I love Volker!'

Norbert suddenly realized that for all that she appeared grown-up, she was still only a kid. 'It would never have worked. Your Volker may be a great artist, but he'd have made a lousy husband. Most interesting men are the same.'

Tears brimmed to Lili's eyes and she brushed them away with her hand. In her heart of hearts, she knew he was right, but she still could not bear to admit the truth.

Norbert ordered more drinks, and, while he waited for them to be served, wondered what he would do in her situation. When he came to the end of a love affair, he immediately entered into another. That way he was saved the pain of having to analyse what had gone wrong. 'In my experience,' he said, when the waiter had gone, 'a change of face and a change of place are the best cures for most ills. You speak English. Why not go to London? I'm sure Mortimer Allen would help you find a job.'

The suggestion took Lili utterly by surprise, but after only a few moments' consideration, it appealed to her. She had to get away from Hamburg and Berlin. 'All right,' she said, with sudden decisiveness, 'I'll go to London.'

Norbert clinked his glass against hers. 'To the future, sweetheart.'

'To the future,' Lili said and gave a wan little smile.

* * *

As things transpired, the timing could not have been better. Mortimer's married daughter, Libby Ashbridge, had just resumed her former job as a graphic designer in a London advertising agency and needed somebody to look after her own ten-year-old daughter, Julie, while she was at work. She was more than happy to engage Lili. In the middle of September, Lili packed her belongings once more and took the ferry from Hamburg to London. Norbert was in Munich and Viktoria in Frankfurt, where planning permission had just been granted for the new hotel. Magda was the only person to see her off.

The ship chugged down the Elbe into the North Sea and Lili continued to stand on deck long after Magda had disappeared from view, her coat huddled round her, her eyes misted with tears. Then, resolutely, she turned her back on Germany and looked forwards towards England and her new life.

Mortimer, Libby and Julie were waiting for her in London. Libby and Julie were remarkably similar, with straight, dark hair and big brown eyes. 'There wasn't room for us all in the car,' Julie explained, taking her hand and leading her out of the customs building, while Libby and Mortimer organized a porter for her luggage, 'so Grandma and Daddy stayed at home. Grandma and Granddad are staying the night. Grandma's cooking dinner. I hope you like roast beef and Yorkshire pudding. It's a special treat for you. And I've made a treacle tart for pudding.'

Lili looked down at her new charge and smiled. 'I've never eaten treacle tart.'

'It's very sweet,' Julie informed her.

'Then I'm sure I'll like it.'

'Why do you spell Lili with two i's?'

'It's a pet name. It's short for Elizabeth.'

'What a coincidence! Mum's name is Elizabeth, too. But everyone calls her Libby.'

Soon they were in Mortimer's Jaguar, driving through the East End of London and the City, where bomb sites still remained very much in evidence, past landmarks of which Lili had only previously seen photographs in books. It seemed no time at all before they arrived at the Ashbridges' prewar semi-detached house in Richmond and Julie was bursting out of the car, calling, 'Daddy! Grandma! We're here!'

291

Joyce Allen opened the front door, an older version of Libby and Julie, her once dark hair grey and gently waved. She took Lili in her arms and said, 'How nice to welcome another member of the Jochum family to England. I grew very fond of Stefan, when he stayed with us before the war, and I am sure we shall all grow very fond of you, my dear.'

Libby's husband, Geoffrey, appeared at her side, a nice-looking man of about forty, dressed in a tweed sports jacket and flannel trousers, with a pipe in his mouth. He shook Lili's hand and said, 'I hope you had a good journey and that you'll be happy here.'

'Julie, take Lili up to her room,' Libby said, 'and show her where the bathroom is. I'm sure she'd like a wash and brush up.'

Julie darted up the stairs. 'You're in the back bedroom, next to mine,' she explained, throwing open a door. 'Oh, look, Shadow's sleeping on your bed. I hope you like cats. We have two. Shadow's black and white. The other one's a tabby. She's called Tigger, like in Winnie the Pooh.'

Lili's first weeks were very happy. Geoffrey and Libby left early for work and Lili took Julie to school, then she had the rest of the day, until quarter to four, when school finished, to spend as she liked. Although Libby told her it wasn't expected of her, she did the housework every day and found an unexpected pleasure in the simple domestic chores and the appreciation Libby showed when she returned home to a tidy house. She went shopping, enjoying the novelty of buying strange ingredients with different weights and measures in a different currency. Cooking was another matter, but this art too Lili determined to master, and she and Julie spent many an amusing hour pouring over recipe books and concocting dishes which did not taste quite as they were supposed to, but which Libby and Geoffrey ate with apparent relish.

When the weather was fine, Lili explored Richmond Park and Bushy Park, walked along the Thames, and discovered Kew Gardens. She took the Underground into London and went sightseeing. She visited museums and art galleries. At weekends, the Ashbridges took her into the country. Every so often, they spent the weekend with Mortimer and Joyce.

Lili enjoyed those weekends tremendously. She loved the big garden and the gentle Oxfordshire countryside. She liked the comfortable confusion of 'Fairways', the rooms filled with piles of newspapers, magazines and books, and Joyce's studio, its walls covered with her landscapes, so different from Volker's Kreuzberg room that, despite the smell of turpentine and linseed oil, it revived no unhappy memories.

Above all, she grew to love Joyce and soon an affectionate sense of companionship had developed between her and the older woman. 'Remember, I'm not far away,' Joyce told her on one occasion. 'If ever you feel lonely or unhappy, you can always talk to me. You only have to pick up the phone.'

Lili was so engrossed in her new life that she paid scant attention to events going on in the world outside, to the troubles brewing in the Middle East and the potential revolution stirring in Hungary. Even when the Suez Crisis and the Hungarian National Rising occurred, virtually simultaneously, she had only a hazy impression of what was taking place. Geoffrey, who was a marketing manager for an oil company, scanned the newspapers anxiously every morning and evening and sat with his eyes glued to the television news, but seemed more concerned about petrol rationing and the collapse of sterling than with what was taking place in Hungary.

Lili saw photographs in the papers of British and French planes attacking Port Said and of Russian tanks rolling into Budapest but, in the secure refuge of Richmond, all this action seemed to be taking place a long way away. More interesting to her was her first celebrations with Julie of Halloween and Guy Fawkes Night, of lighting candles inside hollowed-out pumpkins, building a bonfire and setting off fireworks.

The shadow of Suez still lay over the British Isles at Christmas, but that did not detract from Lili's enjoyment of it. On Christmas Eve, she and Julie decorated a Christmas tree and, before she went to bed, Julie hung one of her father's socks up from the mantelpiece. After a couple of sherries with Libby and Geoffrey, Lili played Father Christmas and filled the sock with small gifts. The four of them spent Christmas Day at Richmond, then on Boxing Day went to Oxford.

It was not until then, the first time Lili had seen Mortimer since early November, that she realized something of what had been happening in the world. His face drawn and appearing suddenly old, Mortimer asked her, 'Are you still in touch with your cousin in Fuerstenmark – Senta, wasn't it?'

Lili bit her lip, feeling guilty. After meeting Volker, she had grown very lax about sending her monthly letters and parcels of books and when she had moved to Hamburg she had been so immersed in her own troubles that she had stopped altogether. 'I'm afraid not,' she admitted.

Mortimer sighed. 'The Hungarian Uprising is having repercussions in East Germany, too. For a short while after Khruschev came to power, I thought there was a chance that the SED would become more lenient and even that Stefan's sentence might be reduced, but now I don't believe there's a hope. For Khruschev to survive, he has to take strong measures . . .'

Lili made a resolution to send Senta a belated Christmas present, but within a few days it was New Year's Eve and something had occurred to make her forget all about Senta. The head of the advertising agency where Libby worked threw a Hogmanay party, to which Geoffrey and Lili were also invited. And at that party Lili met Jeremy Harrison-Browne.

Lili looked across the crowded room and saw a man in his mid-twenties, with film-star-ish English good looks, fair, waving hair and laughing blue eyes. 'Who's that?' she asked Libby. 'Is he an actor?'

Libby laughed. 'With those looks, he should be! In fact, he's a photographer. His name is Jeremy Harrison-Browne. He used to work a lot for our agency, but now he works mainly for fashion magazines. He's what we call a deb's delight. His family is very well-off – they own acres up in Lincolnshire – and all the debutantes' mothers want to catch him for their daughters. But, give him his due, he has talent.'

Lili sighed and turned her attention to the other guests in the room. After nearly six months away from Volker, her feelings towards him were reaching the stage where if another man entered her life she could be interested, but she could not imagine that Jeremy Harrison-Browne and she would find anything in common.

Jeremy looked across the room and saw a tall, skinny girl with thick auburn hair surrounding a pale, heart-shaped face with superb high cheekbones and huge green eyes, talking to Libby Ashbridge. He imagined her hair dressed differently and her face properly made up and felt a surge of excitement. For months he had been looking for a new face . . .

Forgetting the model he had brought to the party, who was in any case more interested in a balding American business tycoon than himself, he pushed his way through the guests. 'I'm Jeremy Harrison-Browne,' he said, taking Lili's hand. 'How d'you do?'

Lili's slim hand took his in a delicate but firm handshake. 'Lili Nowak. I'm pleased to meet you, Mr Harrison-Browne.'

'You're not English?'

'I am German.'

'You're on holiday in London?'

'No, I work for Mrs Ashbridge. I look after her daughter, Julie.'

Turning to Libby, he asked with mock formality, 'Will you allow your nanny to dance with me, Mrs Ashbridge?'

They danced together, ate together, talked together and, when the evening was over, Jeremy drove her back to Richmond in his red Austin Healey sports car. 'Don't go too fast! And don't catch cold!' Libby called, as she and her husband got into Geoffrey's new Ford Popular. 'Jeremy, surely you're going to put the hood up? It's freezing out here.'

'Do you want the hood up?' Jeremy asked Lili, opening the boot to produce fleecy-lined, leather flying jackets.

Lili shook her head. She had drunk quite a lot of champagne and was in a mood for adventure. 'Oh, no. Please leave it like it is.'

He grinned at her. 'I knew you were a girl after my own heart.'

She fell in love that night, not so much with Jeremy as with his car, with the exhilarating feeling of freedom as they raced through the virtually empty streets of London, the cold wind stinging her cheeks and making her eyes water. Jeremy drove with none of Geoffrey's caution and regard to speed limits, but pushed the little Healey to the limit, moving expertly through

295

the gears and accelerating round bends and roundabouts, with all the skill of a racing driver. Several times, Lili glanced at him. There was a smile of sheer, naked pleasure on his face, which she felt mirrored on her own.

They reached the Ashbridges' house long before Libby and Geoffrey. Jeremy turned the engine off and the world turned suddenly very quiet. 'You have a key, I suppose?'

Lili came abruptly back down to earth. 'Yes, of course.'

He reached across her to open the car door and she swung her legs over the sill as elegantly as she could. Once she was standing, she started to shrug her way out of the jacket. 'Keep it,' Jeremy said. 'You'll need it tomorrow night when I take you out to dinner.'

He accompanied her as far as the porch and as she put her key in the lock, he took her in his arms and kissed her. Then, before she had time to recover her breath, he said, 'Happy New Year, Lili Nowak,' and was gone, back down the path and into his car.

The following weekend, Jeremy took Lili into Richmond Park and photographed her, her hair tied back in a ponytail and wearing his flying jacket. She returned with him to his studio in a pretty Kensington mews that afternoon and watched as he developed and printed the pictures. Soon, there were two dozen black and white prints hanging up to dry.

Unlike Volker's portrait of her, they showed her as she really was, young, ingenuous and attractive in an unusual kind of way. But when she compared her pictures to others of well-known models pinned to the wall of the darkroom, she sighed. 'They're all so elegant. Look at this one. She doesn't have a hair out of place. But I look a mess!'

Jeremy did not reply. He had one characteristic in common with Volker: when he worked, he had no time for chit-chat; he became all-absorbed. Now he was examining the prints critically. Lili did not have the currently fashionable hourglass figure; she did not know how to stand or move properly; but she had a natural grace. With proper training she could be a model. Satisfied, he said, 'Let's go and find a drink and some dinner.'

He took her to a pub on the river, where they did not need to dress up and where they found a quiet table at which they could talk undisturbed. After a couple of sherries, Lili relaxed and soon he prised from her the story of her affair with Volker. By the end of the evening, he had convinced her that being a fashion model was a very different matter from posing in the nude for an art student.

Next time he came to Richmond, Jeremy brought the prints with him and showed them to Libby, who studied them with a professional eye and agreed that Lili photographed well. 'I'd like her to go on a course with Lucie Clayton or Jean Bell,' Jeremy said.

'Why not?' Libby agreed. 'She has time during the day, while Julie's at school.' Although she feared that the end result of all this would be that she would have to look for another nanny, she was not so selfish as to stand in the way of Lili's future and was delighted with the manner in which the friendship between Lili and Jeremy was progressing. Geoffrey warned her not to anticipate events, but already she saw Lili with a sparkling career and married to one of the country's most eligible bachelors.

Almost before Lili knew what had happened, she was enrolled at Lucie Clayton's model agency. After taking Julie to school, she went to Bond Street, where she was taught the arts of deportment, etiquette, grooming and make-up. For the most part, her colleagues were girls from middle or upper middle class backgrounds. Some wanted to be mannequins or photographic models, but many were there simply to learn the social graces. Quite a few knew Jeremy and seemed surprised that he should be taking any interest in Lili. From them, Lili gained an impression of Jeremy living a wild round of parties, dances, dinners and country weekends, in a social environment in which she stood no hope of being accepted.

If they hoped to hurt her, they were disappointed. Lili was more than grateful for the little attentions Jeremy paid her, for the telephone calls which announced that he would be arriving in half an hour to take her out to a country pub or for a quiet dinner at an Italian restaurant in Soho. Best of all, she enjoyed the sessions at his studio, in which she showed him what she had learned at Lucie Clayton's and

297

watched her achievements taking tangible form in the resulting photographs.

At Jeremy's insistence, she went to André Bernard's salon, where most of Lucie Clayton's pupils and models had their hair done. She entered with trepidation, fearful of the famous *coiffeur*'s reaction to her unruly shoulder-length mop of curls. She need not have worried. Bernard took one glance at her and announced that he would look after her himself. He was in love with Audrey Hepburn and in Lili's gamine looks, he saw an opportunity to re-create another in her style. 'By the time I've finished, you won't recognize yourself,' he declared, as his scissors expertly snipped a few soft tendrils of fringe. From his name she had expected him to be French, but his accent revealed him to be a Londoner.

He piled her hair on top of her head and, as his fingers deftly coaxed her curls into shape, advised her about the make-up she should use. 'Accentuate your eyes and eyebrows, and use a little, just a very little rouge to emphasize your cheekbones . . .'

Lili stared at herself in the mirror, scarcely able to believe the transformation which was taking place.

Jeremy met her from the salon not in the Healey but in a taxi and after nodding approvingly at what Bernard had accomplished, took her to his studio. In the changing room, he showed her a black, tunic-like dress. 'This is Balenciaga's latest creation, which I've managed to borrow.'

Even before she put it on, Lili knew that the dress's straight simple lines demanded a slim figure to show it to its best advantage. It was the exact opposite of the tight figure-hugging clothes which were all the rage. This was a fashion which could have been created expressly for her.

The spreads which were commissioned by *Vogue* as a result of this test session not only established Balenciaga's chemise as a new fashion trend, Jeremy as a photographer and Lili as a model, but also had much further-reaching effects.

Until then, Jeremy had kept Lili away from his other friends and very few people in his circle had been aware even of her existence. Suddenly, she was hot news. World-famous couturiers wanted her to model their latest designs. World-famous photographers asked her to work for them. But Lili was aware

298

that she owed everything to Jeremy and would work for nobody but him.

Jeremy knew better than to hide his light under a bushel and took advantage of the opportunity to launch Lili upon society. Libby had to find a new nanny in a hurry, as Lili embarked on a mad social whirl. What had been purely a working relationship developed into something more personal, and rumours spread that the couple were having an affair. Inevitably, what had been rumour in due course became fact. Returning to Jeremy's flat above his mews studio early one morning after a wonderful night listening to jazz at Ronnie Scott's, Lili and Jeremy became lovers.

It was the beginning of the happiest period of Lili's life. Jeremy was not only handsome, but he had a personality to match. Debonair, charming and extrovert, his high good spirits were infectious. He was also extremely generous. Lili only had to say she liked something and he bought it for her. She herself was earning more money than she had ever imagined possible and had nothing to spend it upon but herself. She purchased a white Morris Minor and, with Libby's blessing, rented a small apartment in Chelsea. Not that she was there much. If she wasn't working or shopping, she was at parties, cinemas, dances or jazz clubs. And she spent her nights in Jeremy's bed.

The building of the Jochum-Frankfurt was in the final stages of completion and the full-time presence of a competent person was needed on-site to oversee the decorating, furnishing and fitting out under the architect's supervision and then take over its management. Viktoria's first choice was Eduard and, to her delight, he accepted her offer with alacrity.

The opportunity to make a break with Berlin and all its memories of Lili could have come at no better time for Eduard. It was over a year since she had gone to England, during which time she had not written to him once and the only news he had had of her were hurried letters and magazines she sent to Viktoria. She had, it appeared, not only become a celebrated model, but was in love with an aristocratic English photographer.

First there had been Volker Busko. Now there was Jeremy

Harrison-Browne. Even if that affair went wrong, somebody was sure to be waiting ready to step into Jeremy's shoes. In a year's time, Lili would be twenty-one and inherit half the Jochum empire. As an heiress, she would be an even more attractive prospect for marriage and Eduard's chances of winning her even more remote. Finally, he forced himself to accept the bitter truth that his love for her was doomed never to be reciprocated.

The Jochum-Frankfurt opened at Christmas. It was the smallest of the three Jochum hotels, with only thirty rooms, but its facilities were superb. Log fires burned in the foyer, the lounge and the bar. All the rooms were furnished traditionally, their walls wood-panelled. The bedrooms all had private bathrooms, radio, television and telephone. There was a ballroom, a fitness room with a sauna, an indoor swimming pool, and, in the grounds, there were tennis courts and stables and, of course, the lake with its own terrace restaurant. Had it not been for the loneliness in him, Eduard would have been very happy there.

At Christmas, Lili met Jeremy's parents for the first time, when they went to Tillbridge Manor, his family home in Leicestershire. They did not leave London until late on Christmas Eve and the manor was in darkness when they arrived, except for lights shining in the hall and the library. Jeremy's father opened the door to them and, from the moment she saw him in the doorway, tall, greying, with a stiff military moustache and a stiff military stance, and a Red Setter at his heels, Lili had a premonition that the visit was going to go wrong.

'Thought you said you'd be here in time for supper,' he barked. 'Your mother invited the Buckleys and the Lyttons over for the carol singing.'

'Sorry, Pater,' Jeremy replied, opening the boot of the Healey and unloading their weekend cases and a Harrods bag full of presents, which he had ordered by telephone. 'We got a bit tied up in town. You know how it is.'

Lili stood awkwardly, waiting to be introduced, but when Jeremy showed no sign of so doing, she went up the grey, stone steps with her hand outstretched, and said, 'Hello, Mr

Harrison-Browne, I am Lili Nowak. Thank you so much for inviting me to spend Christmas with you.'

Jeremy's father did not take her hand, but fixed upon her a pair of steely grey eyes. 'Major-General Harrison-Browne. Jeremy, for God's sake, how much longer are you going to fiddle about in that car? It's already an hour past bed-time.'

They went through a wide hall in which stood a decorated Christmas tree and up a staircase to the first floor. The Major-General waited while Jeremy showed Lili to her room and, under his scrutinizing gaze, she did not have the nerve to kiss Jeremy good night. From behind the closed door of her bitterly cold bedroom, she heard their footsteps recede down the uncarpeted corridor and the Major-General snort, 'You didn't say she was a damn foreigner, boy!'

The truth that she was German emerged at breakfast time when Jeremy's mother, a pleasant, rather nervy woman, asked Lili where she came from. Lili answered simply, 'Berlin.'

The blood rushed to the Major-General's cheeks. 'A German!' he thundered. 'What do you mean by bringing a German to this house, Jeremy?'

'Lili can't help it,' his wife murmured. 'I'm sure she'd much rather have been born somewhere else, wouldn't you, dear?'

The four of them went to church in the morning, although it was clear from the Major-General's outraged expression that he felt Lili's presence in the House of God to be a desecration. During their absence, the housekeeper prepared lunch, which was consumed in an atmosphere of unnatural formality. They then had to listen to the Queen's speech on the radio, at the end of which the Major-General stood while the National Anthem was played.

The day was saved by the arrival of the Buckleys and the Lyttons, who appeared to be the Harrison-Brownes' only near neighbours, for madeira, Christmas cake and bridge. Assuming – rightly – that Lili did not play, she was not invited to the game. Promptly, at half past ten, the Buckleys and Lyttons departed and the Harrison-Browne household went to bed.

The following morning, Boxing Day, the meet gathered at Tillbridge Manor and Jeremy and the Major-General rode to hounds. After lunch, Jeremy took Lili into the conservatory, the first time they had been alone together since their arrival, and said, 'I have to stay on for a bit and talk a few things over with the Pater. I'll drive you into Lincoln to catch the train back to London.'

'Jeremy, I don't understand. Why does your father dislike me so much? Surely not just because I'm German?'

He looked rather embarrassed. 'Well, you see, he had rather a hell of a war. His sister and her children were killed in the Blitz. He took part in the D-Day landings and later he was one of the officers who helped liberate Bergen-Belsen. His best friend died in Colditz.'

'I lost most of my family in the war,' Lili pointed out.

'I told him that, but he said he couldn't give a damn. He hates the Germans. I'm sorry, Lili. I should never have brought you here.'

'Then perhaps it is better if I leave,' Lili said in a little voice.

New Year came and went and she heard nothing from Jeremy, and when she telephoned his studio his assistant said he was still at Tillbridge. New Year's Eve she spent with the Ashbridges. Eventually, in the middle of January, Jeremy rang and asked her to tea at the Ritz. There, surrounded by genteel English people drinking China tea and eating cucumber sandwiches, he told her that his father had issued an ultimatum. Either he stopped seeing Lili or he would be disinherited. 'You see, I actually owe the old man quite a lot of money,' he said. 'He helped me set up my studio and bought most of my equipment. And I've run up quite a few other debts, one way or another . . .'

Lucie Clayton's training stood Lili in good stead. With perfect poise, she made her way out of the Ritz and into her Morris Minor. Not until she was back in her Chelsea flat, did she burst into tears.

It was much later that she realized she still did not know of what she was guilty, except that she was a German. Although she had lived through the war, she had no idea why it had started. Her own school history lessons had ended in 1888, with the death of Wilhelm I. She had only the scantiest knowledge of what had happened since and she certainly did not know what had taken place at Bergen-Belsen or Colditz.

Two weeks later, she accompanied the Ashbridges on a weekend visit to Oxford. She and Joyce wandered round the garden at 'Fairways' while the rest of the family listened to a radio programme and Lili said, 'Mrs Allen, will you tell me about Hitler and what we Germans did during the war?'

Joyce saw the hurt in Lili's big, green eyes. 'Have people been saying things to you?'

Lili nodded. 'I wouldn't mind so much if I knew the truth. But nobody at home would ever talk about those times. And now I have to know . . .'

It was a mild winter afternoon which seemed to promise that spring was just round the corner. Under the silver birch trees at the end of the garden, snowdrops formed a carpet of white. The green tips of daffodils were thrusting up through the grass. The war suddenly seemed a very distant memory to Joyce. Was it necessary for Lili to know about it, she wondered. And then she realized that it was. If those horrors were never to be repeated, there must be no forgetting. 'Let's go for a walk,' she said. 'And I'll do my best to explain.'

The curtains were drawn at 'Fairways' when they returned and the porch light turned on. 'You must have walked a long way,' Libby exclaimed. 'We were about to send out a search party! Lili, you look quite exhausted. Come and sit by the fire and I'll get you a cup of tea.'

As in a daze, Lili sat down and looked unseeingly at the sparks flying up the chimney. Around her, the conversation went on, but she was unaware of it. The terrible events which Joyce had described were still echoing in her ears. Everything had fallen dreadfully into place.

Now she understood why Viktoria had refused to talk about certain subjects and why Emmy Anders had left Germany. Vague recollections of people she had known when she was a child suddenly returned, people who had disappeared never to be seen again. Worst of all was her realization of her father's role in the war. Although she had scarcely known him, she had always loved his memory. Now she had discovered that he had possibly taken part in bombing raids on Warsaw, Rotterdam – and London. Although Joyce had stressed that nobody in their right mind held Lili's generation responsible for the

303

atrocities of the past and that Major-General Harrison-Browne was ridiculous to take his hatred to such extremes, Lili knew that she could not be absolved from her country's guilt. She was a German, a child of the Nazi era. She deserved to be hated.

Chapter 14

Word quickly spread around London that the partnership between Lili Nowak and Jeremy Harrison-Browne had broken up and offers of work flooded in to Lili. To begin with, she accepted them, but the resulting pictures were wooden and the photographers blamed Lili. They were right. Some special chemistry had operated between her and Jeremy. Without him, she was useless.

As the telephone stopped ringing, she fell prey to an old, familiar depression. If she had known everything she knew now, she would never have come to England and then she would not have had to suffer the heartbreak of losing Jeremy. It should not have been left to Joyce to explain what had happened under Hitler. Viktoria should have told her. Her aunt shouldn't have allowed her to wander off, totally ignorant, into the world. The Germans might prefer to forget the war, but the English never would . . .

She lost her appetite, could not be bothered to cook for herself, and started to exist on biscuits, cigarettes and instant coffee. For days on end, she did not leave her flat. She did not open her mail. She lost all interest in her appearance. She dressed in jeans and sloppy pullovers and did not put on any make-up. Her hair hung to her shoulders, lank and lifeless.

It was like this that Joyce, worried not to have heard anything from her, found her when she came up to London. Taking one look at Lili's unkempt figure and the chilly, untidy apartment, she announced briskly, 'Right, my girl, you're coming home with me.'

Slowly that summer, in the mellow Oxford house, Lili recovered her health and self-confidence. She gave up her London flat and sold the Morris Minor. Upon Joyce's suggestion, she took up watercolours and found a simple pleasure in painting the flowers which blossomed in profusion in the Allens' garden. Often, she went for long walks in the surrounding countryside and sometimes, on these, she was joined by Mortimer.

He would stride along the lanes with amazing energy for a man in his mid-sixties, his mind even more extraordinarily active. Not for Mortimer the bigoted attitude of Major-General Harrison-Browne. Although, like Joyce, he agreed that the past should not be forgotten, he was preoccupied with the present and, finding in Lili a captive audience and one, moreover, who shared his knowledge of Berlin, would discourse for hours on current events. He possessed a seemingly endless fund of information and he brought things alive, so that Lili could visualize the events he was describing.

She began to realize how out of touch she had become. Some of the people she and Jeremy had met at parties and dinners had been part of the Ban-the-Bomb movement and some had even taken part in the Easter Aldermaston Marches, but she had been more concerned with having a good time. Now, Mortimer explained to her the pros and cons of atomic weapons and, in particular, how they affected Germany, where the Bundestag had recently agreed that, in the face of Russian nuclear armament, the Bundeswehr should be equipped with nuclear weapons, and a massive protest movement was gaining hold.

She began to understand better the division of her country and how hopeless the possibility that it could ever be reunited. For the first time, she heard about the so-called 'passport law' which had been introduced in the GDR the previous December, making it a punishable offence for people to leave the Soviet zone. 'Until then, the East German government had at least preserved the illusion that people were free to emigrate,' Mortimer said. 'But now that thousands, if not millions have fled, the Communists are worried they will lose the vital manpower necessary to keep the country going.'

He continued his campaign for Stefan's freedom and remained in correspondence with Holger Busko. 'Willy Brandt appointed Holger Busko to his staff, when he was elected Mayor of Berlin last October,' he told Lili. 'I shouldn't be surprised if Busko doesn't become an SPD deputy very soon.'

306

Strangely, Lili discovered the name Busko no longer had any power to move her. She could look back on her affair with Volker with complete equanimity.

She found it harder to accept that Jeremy had not only forgotten her but married someone else. Although Joyce concealed the news from her, Lili saw photographs of the wedding in *The Tatler* when she went to the hairdresser. His bride, it appeared, was the daughter of a Lord. She hoped Major-General Harrison-Browne was happy now that his son was married to a true-blue English girl. One day, she knew, she would also hope that Jeremy was happy. But at the moment, that was still rather difficult.

In early September, she received a long letter from Viktoria, asking her to come back to Germany for her twenty-first birthday. She explained that provision had been made in the articles of Jochum Hotels KG, the new company she had formed in conjunction with Eschenbach Estates, for Lili to take her place on the board, when she came of age. 'I realize that I over-reacted when I sent you to Hamburg,' she wrote. 'Now Eduard is in Frankfurt, I wonder if you would like to take over his former position here in Berlin.'

Even Lili realized how much this offer must have cost her. 'But Aunt Vicki needn't worry,' she told Joyce, 'I shan't take the Jochum-Berlin away from her. My experiences in Hamburg were enough to prove to me that hotel management is not the right career for me.'

'Your aunt isn't getting any younger,' Joyce said. 'She must worry about who is going to take over from her.'

Lili was unsympathetic. Even though Mortimer and Joyce tried to persuade her that Viktoria had always tried to do her best for her, she remained unconvinced. In her opinion, Viktoria had failed her, not just once, but time and time again.

'Dirk and Eduard will do a much better job than I ever could,' she said. 'And now she has the Eschenbachs as well.'

'But they're not family,' Joyce pointed out.

Lili shrugged. 'Yes, it's strange, neither Stefan nor Monika ever wanted to work in the hotel business – and now I'm the same.'

'However, you must do something with your life. The money

you earned modelling will soon run out. You can't drift for ever.'

Lili certainly realized that she could not prolong her stay with the Allens indefinitely and, finally, she agreed to return to Germany for her birthday and to have a frank discussion with Viktoria about the future.

As the evening of Baron Heinrich von Kraus's life moved inexorably towards night, one final objective remained the dominating motivation behind his continued existence. He wanted to be a hundred.

Vaguely, he was aware of events taking place in the world around him. He knew that the Russians had launched a sputnik into space containing a dog. He had heard of the bitter controversies raging over nuclear weapons. He was aware that the assets of Werner Kraus Holdings could now be counted in billions rather than millions. But these developments meant little to him.

Even his family had ceased to matter much. Else and the twins came regularly to visit him, but he had never had any patience with babies. Norbert's three were little better, despite being older. Out of some sense of misplaced duty, or perhaps because she hoped they stood to inherit from him, Reinhild occasionally brought them to see him.

When they had gone, he could no longer remember the children's names. His main preoccupation was with himself, with his bodily functions, with the food and drink he consumed, and the movement of his bowels.

In his imagination, he planned his centenary celebrations in October. The new Hotel Jochum-Frankfurt would make an ideal venue. As well as his family, aristocrats, business tycoons and the country's leading politicians would be present . . .

But in this, his final goal, his ambitions were thwarted. On the night of 15 September 1958, exactly one month before his hundredth birthday, he suffered a massive heart attack. In the small hours of the morning, Baron Heinrich von Kraus breathed his last.

A week later, the coffin containing his earthly remains was consigned to a furnace and reduced to ashes at Essen crematorium. There was no ostentatious funeral ceremony and no extravagant obsequies. Werner made sure of that. He had been spared the expense of a hundredth birthday party and had no intention of wasting money on a wake. After the funeral, the mourners had to cater for their own refreshments. Werner had inherited his grandfather's entire fortune and was now in absolute control of Werner Kraus Holdings KG. He had no intention of frittering away his inheritance.

After the Baron's funeral, Norbert took Viktoria to lunch at a small restaurant he knew on the Baldeney Lake. Even though their ways had parted, they remained good friends. For a while they discussed the Baron, Werner's meanness and the unlikelihood of Norbert inheriting any of his estate, then Viktoria changed the subject and unburdened her heart about Lili.

'When's her birthday?' Norbert asked.

'Saturday, the fourth of October.'

'The last weekend of *Oktoberfest*! That's easy! Come and stay with me.'

In Munich, Norbert had found his spiritual home, an architect's dream, with its mixture of ancient and modern buildings, a culture lover's heaven, with its art galleries, concert halls and theatres, and a *bon vivant*'s paradise, with its restaurants, bars and beer gardens. A wealthy bachelor in his late thirties, he had been quickly adopted by Munich society.

Viktoria frowned. 'That's a kind suggestion, but not exactly what I had in mind.'

'Aunt Vicki, don't be a stick-in-the-mud. It's Lili's birthday. Let her have a good time at the beer festival, before you get dug into the serious discussions.'

Viktoria could see the advantage of meeting Lili on neutral territory, but still had misgivings about the venue. Against her better judgement, she agreed.

Two weeks later, on the Thursday before Lili's birthday, she arrived at Norbert's apartment. Tired after her journey, she did not join him at the beer festival. He came home, extremely drunk, in the early hours of the morning, and was still in a comatose state at noon when she awoke him, with a cup of black coffee, and informed him, rather coldly, that Lili's train arrived in half an hour.

Suffering from a blinding hangover, he stood watching the train disgorge its passengers. 'There she is!' Viktoria exclaimed and, with a porter in tow, hurried along the platform. 'Where?' Norbert asked blankly. Since English fashion magazines did not feature among his reading material, his image of Lili was still of a woebegone little figure at the Jochum-Hamburg. None of the passengers resembled the Lili he remembered.

Then he saw her, tall and chic, in a navy blue costume, her hair swept up and back from her immaculately made-up face. She allowed Viktoria to take her in an embrace, kissing the air to either side of her aunt's cheeks, after which, with a graceful wave of an elegantly gloved hand, she indicated her luggage to the porter.

Viktoria pointed in Norbert's direction and Lili's joyful exclamation of 'Norbert!' could be heard above the bustle of the station. But, whereas in the past, she had rushed to him when they met, now she stood still, waiting for him to come to her.

Dazedly, Norbert found himself walking down the platform. Then Lili was in his arms, her perfume in his nostrils and her lips briefly, much too briefly, on his. 'Oh, Norbert, it is wonderful to see you again!' Then she stood back and studied him more critically. 'On closer examination, however, you don't look too good. Your eyes are bloodshot and you haven't shaved.'

An Underberg and a cold shower cured Norbert's hangover and the three of them went that evening to the beer festival on the Theresien Meadows. Although Norbert had feared this new, transformed Lili might consider the rowdy celebrations beneath her, she entered into them with enthusiasm. She admired his Bavarian *loden* suit and hat, and complimented him on how well it set off his tall figure. She was polite to his friends and the many acquaintances they met in the beer tents. She went on the roundabouts, the dodgems and the big dipper. She danced and joined in the singing, her arms linked through his and Viktoria's as they swayed to and fro to the old familiar tunes. She drank enough beer to make her merry but not drunk. And throughout the evening, Norbert

310

had the satisfaction of seeing people looking enviously in his direction.

At Lili's request, they spent her birthday not in Munich but in the country. They got up early, breakfasted at an inn by the Ammersee, then drove through the golden, autumnal countryside to Garmisch-Partenkirchen, where they lunched under the shadow of the Zugspitze, after which they took the cable car to the top and walked through the snow to the weather station on the summit.

Lili leaned on a railing and gazed out across the Alpine panorama, breathing in the crisp clear air. 'How wonderful to live up here and have this view every day,' she murmured.

'A bit impractical in the winter,' Norbert observed.

'I wouldn't care. It's so beautiful, it seems unreal.'

'Have you ever been skiing?'

Lili stared at him. 'How could I? This is the first time I've ever seen a mountain.'

She was very quiet as they returned towards Munich, gazing back out of the car window until darkness concealed the mountains from view. It was as if she had been given a tantalizing taste of something exquisite, only to have it taken away from her again and, although she did not realize it at the time, she had fallen under a spell, which was to haunt her her whole life long.

'Thank you for a lovely day,' she yawned, as they returned to Norbert's flat.

Yet although Viktoria went to bed, Lili stood by the window, staring out into the night.

'A brandy?' Norbert suggested. 'Or a glass of champagne?'

'Mmm, champagne, please.'

Norbert opened a bottle and poured two glasses. 'Here's to you, birthday girl.'

Lili smiled at him and clinked her glass against his.

'So how does it feel to be twenty-one?'

'It feels stranger to be back in Germany, although in a funny way I feel almost as if I were still abroad. I like Munich.'

'So you're glad you came?'

She nodded, looking up at him from beneath her incredibly long lashes, her lips very slightly parted.

311

Norbert could resist her no longer. Taking the glass from her hand, he put it on a table and took her in his arms. She seemed fragile, almost insubstantial, more delicate than any woman he had ever held. She laid her head against his shoulder and he kissed her sleek hair. Then, gently, he lifted her chin and kissed her on the mouth. Her lips yielded softly to him.

Norbert had kissed hundreds of women but never had he experienced a kiss which filled him with such a sense of tenderness and love as that one did. He had the feeling that everything in his life had been leading up to this moment, that the past thirty-eight years had merely been a rehearsal, and that now his life was finally beginning.

A host of emotions, utterly alien, raced through him. He felt nervous, like a teenager on his first date, frightened of doing or saying something wrong which would ruin everything.

Then Lili drew her lips away from his and buried her face in his chest. 'Oh, Norbert, I've been so unhappy.'

'I know.' He did not know, but he felt as if he knew. 'I shall never make you unhappy, darling. I promise you. I love you, Lili.'

And, as he said the words he had repeated scores of times before to scores of other women, he knew that, on this occasion, they were finally true. What he felt for Lili was not simply desire or lust, but love. He had loved her ever since their first meeting at Heiligensee, when she had been an engaging little ten-year-old in a let-down dress and, although he had not recognized his feelings for what they really were, he had continued to love her during the years of her growing-up. And now, like the ugly duckling in the Hans Andersen fairytale, she had gone away and returned – a swan.

She lifted her head and gazed at him wonderingly, then she gave a smile of pure happiness. 'Oh, Norbert, what a fool I've been. I never realized . . . All the time, you were there . . .'

'Hush . . .' He silenced her with a kiss, longer and softer than the first one. Then he took her hand and led her down the hall into his bedroom.

By the light of a single table lamp, he unzipped her dress and helped her out of it. Unlike most other women, she had no need of rubber girdles and supporting brassieres. Indeed, she was boyishly slim, her breasts scarcely developed, her hip bones jutting out beside her flat stomach – the very opposite of the kind of female figure he usually preferred.

With the shedding of her clothes, she seemed to lose her sophistication. With almost childlike naivety, she asked, 'Do you really love me, Norbert?'

He sat on the bed and drew her to him, so that her hard little brown nipple was in his mouth and murmured, 'I love you, Lili, more than anyone else in the world.'

A couple of hours later, Viktoria awoke, experiencing the need to go to the bathroom. Quietly, she made her way down the corridor. The door of Lili's room, next to hers, stood slightly ajar. The curtains were unpulled and by the light of the street lamp outside, she could see the bed was unoccupied. From Norbert's room came the sound of movement and a swiftly muffled cry.

Viktoria continued to the bathroom, locked the door, sat down on the edge of the bath and buried her face in her hands. 'Oh, no,' she muttered aloud, 'please don't let it be true. Not Norbert and Lili . . .'

The following morning, Norbert went out early, leaving Viktoria and Lili free to breakfast and talk in private. When they had finished eating, Lili said, 'I've given a lot of thought to your proposal, Aunt Vicki, but I must be honest with you and say I don't want to work at Jochum Hotels.'

Viktoria sighed. 'Most young people in your position would give anything for such an opportunity.'

'Maybe I'm different from most young people.'

'Now you're twenty-one, you are a director of the company. You should know what goes on in it.'

'I don't want to be a director. I don't want anything to do with it.'

'Lili, don't be silly. Under the terms of your grandmother's will, you have a legal and moral entitlement to half the business.'

'When Grandmama made her will, I was only a baby. She had no idea of all the things which would have happened by the time I was twenty-one. She certainly didn't imagine you would have had to start again from nothing. The Jochum Hotels aren't my

313

inheritance. You've built them. They're yours. I've contributed nothing to the business. If you like, I will sign a document and renounce my inheritance.'

Viktoria shook her head uncomprehendingly. 'What has happened to make you feel so strongly? Or has someone talked you into this?'

Lili could have explained but she had no desire to become involved in a long discussion which would get them nowhere. 'Aunt Vicki, your obligations towards me are over. You've fed me, educated and clothed me. Now I'm twenty-one and it's up to me what I do with the rest of my life.'

'So what do you intend to do?'

Lili lit a cigarette. 'I'm still not sure. For the moment, at least, I shall remain in Munich.'

Viktoria took a deep breath. 'Are you thinking of staying here with Norbert?'

'It's possible.'

'Well,' Viktoria said, 'it seems there is nothing more to discuss.' Looking suddenly old, she began to gather together the breakfast things and carry them into the kitchen.

Upon her return from Munich, Viktoria threw herself into her work, getting up at dawn each morning and not going to bed until the last guests had retired to their rooms. Work had proved a sound palliative to prevent her from going mad with fear about Stefan. Now, work stopped her fretting about where she had gone wrong with Lili and how she had failed her.

Then, on 10 November, something occurred which pushed her worries about Norbert and Lili to the back of her mind. In the Moscow Sports Palace, Khruschev made a speech in which he announced that it was time to be freed of the obsolete obligations which had resulted from the Potsdam Treaty and to bring about a 'normal situation' in Berlin, the capital of the GDR.

It was exactly ten years since the Blockade, ten years since Berlin had started to be torn in two, ten years since the first barriers had been erected between the divided halves of the city. For seventeen days, their nerves stretched to the limit, Berliners waited to discover what he had in mind.

314

On 27 November, Khruschev delivered his ultimatum to the Western Powers. He demanded that within six months all Occupation troops should be withdrawn from West Berlin and that West Berlin be dissociated from the Federal Republic. As a result of this, Berlin would be given the status of a 'Free city', in the life of which no state, including the two German states, would be permitted to interfere. He proposed that discussions be held regarding the city's demilitarization and that West Berlin should have its own government and economy. He blamed the need for such action upon West German rearmament, through which the Western Powers were using the Federal Republic as a tool for their own anti-Soviet policies, thus breaking the terms of earlier peace treaties.

He did not say what would happen if the Western Powers did not agree to his terms. But everyone feared the worst. As had happened at the time of the 17th June uprising and during the Hungarian National Rising, the tanks would surely roll in . . .

Yet strangely, once the truth was out in the open, the incipient panic died. A few people left the city, but most remained. For the most part, life continued as normal, although once again, West Berlin companies experienced difficulties with their trading partners in the Federal Republic, some of whom cancelled orders and others refused cheques drawn on West Berlin banks. The number of visitors to Berlin again dwindled.

But, as they had so many times before, when confronted by disaster, Berliners showed their inner strength. The first part of the new inner-city autobahn was opened for traffic. In Charlottenburg, the opening was celebrated of a big new housing estate. On the radio, Mayor Willy Brandt said, 'Here in our Berlin the facts speak for themselves . . . That which we have achieved in these last years is visible to everyone, even to those who live today on the shadow side of the economic ascent . . .'

Not until the end of December did the Western Powers notify Moscow that its proposal to make Berlin into a 'Free City' was unacceptable. By that time, Norbert and Lili were married.

Although Landgut's head office remained in Hamburg, Reinhild had not seen Norbert since their divorce. When she needed

315

anything, her lawyer wrote to Norbert, who always responded by sending a cheque. She and the children no longer lived in Eppendorf. The block of flats, which Norbert had given her in lieu of alimony, had gone up so much in value that she had recently been able to sell it and buy an apartment just off the Alsterufer, a much finer area, with a much better class of people as neighbours.

To begin with, it had been difficult to be without a husband, more because of the social stigma attached to divorce than because she had missed Norbert personally. However, Norbert's philandering had attracted such attention that few of her acquaintances and none of his family blamed Reinhild for what had happened.

Reinhild had taken great care to remain on good terms with her ex-husband's family. Until his death, she had visited the Baron regularly, even though he had terrified her. Every year, at Christmas, she took the children to visit their grandmother in Wiesbaden. She had become close friends with Else, especially since the birth of the twins, and the two women wrote each other long, confidential letters and talked for ages on the phone.

Reinhild had also fostered her relationship with the Krauses in other ways. She kept in touch with Hannelore Hahn and made sure the children sent her presents on her birthday and at Christmas. And she encouraged the friendship Kleo had formed with Dieter Duschek at Viktoria's sixtieth birthday. Because of his position as Werner's legal adviser, Joachim Duschek was already becoming a wealthy and influential man. Kleo might be only eleven, but Reinhild was realistically looking ahead to the not-so-distant future, when she would have boyfriends. A pretty little girl, with her bouncing curls and vivacious eyes, she would soon be attracting suitors. Reinhild favoured the idea of her eldest daughter marrying Dieter Duschek.

In view of the misfortunes life had dealt her, Reinhild considered she was doing a very good job of bringing up her children. Tristan was twelve and growing into a nice-looking, sunny-natured boy. His teachers complained that he did not devote enough attention to his schoolwork, but Reinhild was worried that, if too much pressure was put on him, he would fall prey again to the illnesses which had plagued his early years.

When Tristan had started at senior school, he had insisted that he be known as Kris. Tristan, he said, was a soppy name and all his friends teased him about it. Reinhild indulged him in this as she did in everything else. He was mad about cars and when he said he wanted to be a racing driver when he grew up, she recklessly promised that he would. Norbert might have evaded all responsibility for his son's upbringing, but he possessed money enough to see his ambitions fulfilled.

The only one of Reinhild's children to cause her any concern was Helena. With only a year between them, Kris and Kleo were almost like twins, and did a lot of things together. They tried to get Helena to join in their activities, but she preferred to stay alone in her room and read. Unlike Kris and Kleo, who were popular with their schoolmates, she had no close friends. Again, unlike her brother and sister, she had a violent temper and would throw dreadful tantrums, after which she would sulk for hours.

Reinhild laid the blame for Helena's dark moods firmly on Norbert. 'It was a terrible thing to do, to go and leave three young children,' she would tell all and sundry, often within her children's hearing. 'Kris and Kleo were old enough to adjust, but Helena was only five. She didn't understand what was happening.'

When the news broke that Norbert was marrying Lili, Reinhild's indignation knew no bounds. 'There's gratitude for you!' she exclaimed, as she scoured the gossip columns voraciously. 'During the Blockade, I took Lili in and treated her like my own daughter. And this is how she repays me. Now I think of it, she was making eyes at him even then. As for your father, this just proves what I always felt. He's one of the most selfish, unscrupulous men who ever lived. Well, he's going to pay for this.'

That same morning she was on the phone to her solicitor. Within a week, a cheque arrived from Norbert. Reinhild bought herself a mink coat.

Norbert and Lili were married on Saturday 6 December 1958. Viktoria flew to Munich for the event, but she was too sick with worry about the possible repercussions Khruschev's ultimatum

317

could have on Stefan, the fate of her city, and what must inevitably be a disastrous marriage between a 38-year-old womanizer and a 21-year-old *ingénue*, to enjoy herself.

She was the only member of either of their families to be present. She was Lili's only near relation and the Krauses had all closed ranks with Reinhild and boycotted the event. It did not matter. Norbert's social circle was so wide that their absence was scarcely noticed.

Lili floated through her wedding incredibly beautiful in a haze of lace and radiating happiness. That evening, she and Norbert drove to Garmisch, then the following day crossed into Austria to Lech-am-Arlberg. They stayed at an hotel owned, Lili discovered to her amazement, by a family called Jochum, who extended her a very warm welcome when they discovered her grandfather had been an Austrian Jochum. It was an auspicious beginning to a wonderful honeymoon in some of the most beautiful mountain scenery in the world and enjoying some of Europe's best winter sports terrain.

Lili was duly kitted out with an anorak, ski pants, locally handmade boots and skis, and embarked on her first skiing lesson. She approached it with all the fearlessness and impatience of a child, determined that, before the week was out, she would be able to accompany Norbert on his more advanced runs. In this she succeeded. She possessed a natural sense of balance and, despite aching muscles and numerous tumbles in the snow, was soon pronounced good enough to leave the nursery slopes.

While Oskar Stallkamp minded Landgut's business, Norbert and Lili stayed four glorious weeks in Lech. During the daytime, they skied. In the evenings, they danced. At night, they clung together under their voluminous eiderdown and made love.

But the most treasured moments of Lili's honeymoon were when she and Norbert stood poised on their skis at the top of a mountain peak under a peerlessly clear blue sky, prior to gliding over crisp powder snow into the valley below. That was true happiness – and happiness was an emotion which had been sorely lacking in Lili's life until then.

In due course, Senta received one of the cards Norbert's

secretary sent out on his and Lili's behalf, announcing that the marriage had taken place. Senta made a card on the front of which she pasted dried, pressed, wild flowers and in which she offered her congratulations and best wishes. She wished she could send a wedding gift, but, although rationing in the GDR had ended the previous year, everyday goods were still in short supply and there was nothing suitable in Fuerstenmark's Cooperative store. In fact, there was very little at all to buy, unless one was a Party boss, in which case one could shop at HO stores.

Some time later, Lili sent a postcard from Austria, showing a small village nestling under towering snow-covered mountains. 'Norbert and I spent our honeymoon here,' she wrote, 'and have just returned for a few days' skiing. We are wonderfully happy. Although I never seem to have time to write letters, I often think of you. Loving greetings, L.'

Although her father told her to burn the postcard, as the family did all letters from the West, Senta used it as a bookmark, transferring it from one book to another, until its corners were bent and the ink started to fade.

Despite her long silence, Lili had continued to be an inspiration to Senta, who shared her gift for languages. In her final year at school, she was working hard towards the examinations which she expected would win her a place at the Humboldt University in Berlin.

She was certainly intelligent enough. But as the granddaughter of a clergyman, a practising Christian and a girl who preferred her own company to that of members of the Free German Youth, Senta had many black marks against her name. However, there were points in her favour. Her father was a teacher. Her mother worked at a kindergarten. And Heini had just completed his first year's service in the National People's Army at Karlshorst in East Berlin. So, when Senta sat her examinations, she was reasonably confident that she would not only pass them with flying colours but gain that coveted place at the Humboldt.

It was not to be. She did every bit as well as she had expected in her *Abitur*, but the school committee informed her curtly that she was not suitable for university or higher education. She

319

had sealed her own fate at the age of fourteen by choosing confirmation instead of *Jugendweihe*.

The committee's decision hurt less than she had imagined. It had always been taken for granted that she would be a teacher like her father, but Senta herself had entertained private misgivings about the idea. Now that was not to be, she could consider other means of earning a living. Her greatest disappointment lay in the fact that she was not going to Berlin, where she had hoped that she would have the opportunity to cross the border and visit Grandmother Jochum and maybe even see Lili again.

Pastor Koenig, however, lacked Senta's stoicism. For a few weeks, he underwent a severe moral crisis, reproaching himself for having encouraged Senta to be confirmed and thus denying her the opportunity she deserved to attend university. Then, when Senta finally convinced him that it was not his fault, his anger turned towards the State.

'I can't remain silent any longer,' he told his wife, one evening in the privacy of their bedroom. 'No matter what the consequences, I have to speak out. It is wrong that a child should be persecuted and have her future ruined because she refuses to give her soul to the Communist State.'

Gerda nodded. 'But if you are arrested, will that help her?'

Early the following morning, the pastor went into the church and knelt at one of the pews, gazing at the altar. For a long while, he remained in silent prayer and contemplation and by the time he re-emerged from the church, he knew the course of action he must take.

Although the 'passport law' made it illegal, it was still possible for inhabitants of the Soviet zone to travel to East Berlin and escape across the sector boundary into the West.

'I have decided,' he informed Gerda, 'that we must go to the West and take Senta with us. I hope Hans and Monika will come too.'

Gerda nodded. She, too, after much soul-searching, had come to the same conclusion. 'And Heini?' she asked.

The pastor sighed. 'I don't know. It's possible that he won't want to come. But we have to tell him. He must be given the choice.'

Their eyes met. 'How dreadful,' Gerda murmured, 'not to be able to trust one's own grandson . . .'

Hans needed surprisingly little persuading. Senta was his favourite child and he was heartbroken that she had been refused a university place simply because she believed in God. Monika, however, took more convincing. She had lived in Fuerstenmark for twenty years. To flee meant leaving behind everything she held most dear: her home, possessions and her friends. 'And for what?' she asked Hans. 'What guarantee do we have that things will be any better over there? How do we know that Senta will be accepted at university – or that you will get another job? And what about Heini? He can't just walk out of his barracks. No, Hans, it's too dangerous . . .'

'We have to take the risk,' Hans said. But, although he did not say so to her, he agreed with his parents that the biggest risk would be telling Heini of their plans. Heini was a child of his time, a product of the Communist regime: his loyalties lay not with his family, but with the State.

During the next month, the Koenigs organized their departure. The pastor wrote to an old friend, a lawyer in Leipzig, asking if he would consider offering Senta a job in his practice. The lawyer replied, saying that he would like Senta to attend an interview and suggesting Friday 16 October as a suitable date. Since the journey was too far to make there and back in a single day, he offered to arrange overnight accommodation for her and her father. Hans asked for two days off from school to accompany her.

On Saturday 17 October 1959, the German Democratic Republic was celebrating its tenth anniversary, with festivities being held throughout the country. Learning that a performance of her favourite opera was taking place at the State Opera House in honour of the occasion, Gerda sent for tickets for herself and Monika. Because it would be too late for them to travel back from Berlin after the performance, she booked a room at a small guest house and wrote to Heini, saying that she hoped it would be possible for him to obtain leave to meet them. Heini duly replied, agreeing to see them at noon at the café in front of the Opera House and explaining that he was on duty that afternoon.

In order not to arouse suspicions, Pastor Koenig would remain in Fuerstenmark. On the Sunday morning, however, Gerda would telephone him from East Berlin, saying that Monika had been taken ill and asking him to come and bring them back to Fuerstenmark. This would also be a signal that the family had arrived safely at the Hotel Jochum in West Berlin.

Finally, the day for Hans and Senta's departure arrived. Both wore their best clothes and carried small overnight bags. With one final look at the parsonage, the church, the school and the castle, they caught the bus to Prenzlau. From there, they took the train to Berlin, where they had to change trains. In the afternoon, they arrived in Leipzig, Senta duly attended her interview and the lawyer promised to consider her application. The following morning, they returned to Berlin.

Because the train was crowded, they were unable to sit together, which was fortunate, otherwise Senta feared she might have betrayed her inner agitation to the other passengers and any plainclothes policemen on the train. Hans read a newspaper and Senta buried her nose in a book, but if either of them had been asked what they were reading, they would have had not the slightest idea.

They remained separated after they left the train, Senta following a discreet distance behind her father, as he crossed the station concourse and delved down into the Underground. This was part of the plan. One person was less conspicuous than two. Every precaution had to be taken not to alert the attention of the *Stasis*.

'Look natural, act normally.' Her father's instructions kept echoing in Senta's ears, as they waited for the train to arrive which was to take them to freedom. Plainclothes *Stasis* travelled all the time on the U-Bahn, he had told her, on the lookout for people fleeing from the East.

The train stopped at four stations, at the last of which, the Friedrich Strasse, a loudspeaker announced, 'Last station in the Democratic Sector.' *Look natural, act normally*. Her heart in her mouth, Senta clutched her overnight case and stared across the shoulders of the people around her at the posters on the platform. After what seemed an eternity, the train set into motion again. Several times, it slowed down, as if it would

322

halt, but each time it gathered speed again, until it finally pulled into into another station, crowded with people and with posters advertising products unknown in the Soviet zone. Hans stepped off the train and waited for Senta to catch up with him. He seized her hand and squeezed it very tightly.

Up on the street, they fell into each other's arms. They were in West Berlin. They had made it! They were free!

The following morning, Gerda and Monika set off on their journey, also with overnight bags. In case anyone searched them, these contained, besides their night things, dresses and shoes suitable for the opera. The pastor accompanied them to the bus stop, kissed them both goodbye and called, 'Enjoy yourselves! See you tomorrow!' as the bus departed.

'I do wish he could have come with us,' Gerda murmured, looking back out of the bus window.

Heini duly met them outside the Opera House on Unter den Linden. He swaggered slightly as he crossed the square in his field grey uniform, arousing anxious and slightly hostile glances from passers-by. 'Heini, darling!' Monika cried, hurrying towards him, her arms outstretched, while Gerda secured a table. But Heini was not going to be embarrassed by demonstrations of maternal affection. 'Hello, Mother,' he said coolly, avoiding her embrace.

Gerda ordered beers and Heini looked at the clock. 'I have to be on duty in an hour.'

'Heini, we have something to . . .' Monika said.

'Let's enjoy our beers first,' Gerda interrupted. 'Heini, tell us what you've been doing in the Army.'

It was then the shock came, when Heini, unaware of the effect his words were having, described how he had recently been posted as a border guard on the Bernauer-Strasse crossing between Berlin-Wedding and Berlin-Mitte and bragged about the would-be escapees from the East he had succeeded in apprehending. Fortunately, he ran out of cigarettes and, while he was buying some more from a kiosk, Gerda whispered to Monika, 'We mustn't tell him.'

Monika, too, was looking shaken. But, 'We have to,' she insisted, 'he may still want to come with us. If not, I can't go without saying goodbye.'

'He'll report us,' Gerda muttered urgently.

'Of course he won't. Heini wouldn't inform on his own family.'

It was no place to argue. Gerda had to hope Monika was right. They finished their beers and strolled along the wide promenade of Unter den Linden towards the Brandenburg Gate, where the statue of the Quadriga was once again in place. No longer did Viktoria, goddess of victory, face West as she had done since the Franco-Prussian war, to bring victory to the Prussian armies as they marched to war. Now, she faced eastwards, to – according to the Communists – bring peace to the city.

In a low voice, Monika told Heini of their plan and begged him to accompany them.

Heini stood stock-still and, for a moment, Gerda thought he was going to denounce them publicly. But instead, he asked, 'And Father and Senta?'

'They are already in West Berlin.'

'And Grandfather?'

Before Gerda could stop her, Monika said, 'He is following us tomorrow.'

For a long time Heini was silent, then he said, 'The Friedrich Strasse Underground station is just up there. Go quickly, before I change my mind about what I'm doing.'

'Heini, come with us,' Monika pleaded.

But her son was already striding away towards the Marx-Engels-Platz.

Gerda took her arm. 'Monika, don't create a scene. We have to do as he says. We must go, quickly.'

Possibly, Monika's distraught state helped them as they passed the guards in the underground and boarded the train. Few people who fled from East to West did so in such obvious distress.

The following morning, Gerda travelled back to East Berlin and, from a public telephone, rang Arthur as they had agreed. Then, instead of returning to West Berlin, she waited at the main railway station for the arrival of his train. She was reasonably sure that she was safe. Old women of seventy, like herself, were the least important members of society in the GDR. They did not work or produce children: they were merely a drain on the State.

Before Pastor Koenig left Fuerstenmark, he had one last sermon to preach. From the pulpit in which he had taken his stand for some fifty years, he announced: 'Marxism-Leninism is not the truth. God is the only truth.' The few, faithful, familiar figures of his congregation hung on his words with rapt attention.

The pastor reached Berlin without difficulty, where he saw Gerda waiting on the station concourse. She showed no sign of recognition but turned and led the way towards the Underground station. Keeping a safe distance, he followed her. A train entered the station, but she did not board it. Two more came and went and still Gerda glanced around her. Finally, upon the arrival of a fourth train, she gave a little nod and entered it. Further down the same carriage, Arthur did the same.

All went well until they reached the Friedrich Strasse station. There, they halted for an interminable period, as policemen entered the train and subjected its passengers and their papers to minute scrutiny. Arthur Koenig was one of the people who were taken off the train. Before the *Stasis* reached her, Gerda alighted. The children were safely in the West. For herself, freedom was of no importance compared to Arthur.

They were taken to the Ostbahnhof and there they were separated. Gerda had a brief moment to embrace her husband before he was marched away. She was put in a train with a number of other would-be fugitives and eventually ended up in a hostel for old people in Dresden. Although she never ceased in her efforts to find out what had happened to Arthur, she heard nothing from or about him. Early in 1961, she contracted cancer, and six months later died. Pastor Koenig himself was imprisoned on the charges of anti-State propaganda and attempting to flee the Republic. He died from pneumonia before the date for his trial was even fixed.

For several weeks, Monika, Hans and Senta remained at the Berlin-Jochum. Day after day, they went to the refugee reception centre at Berlin-Marienfelde, hoping to find Gerda and Arthur there. But, after a while, they were forced to accept that something had gone wrong. Either the old couple had changed their minds and returned to Fuerstenmark, or they had been stopped by the *Stasis*. Deep in her heart, Monika feared Heini had betrayed them.

Senta began a degree course in German, French and English at the Free University. Although Viktoria offered to let her have Lili's former room, she found her grandmother and the Hotel Jochum rather daunting after the simple life to which she had been accustomed in Fuerstenmark, and said, tactfully, that she would like to live on campus where she would stand a better chance of getting to know her fellow students.

It did not take her long to become assimilated. Berlin itself had been formed from a hotchpotch of nationalities. Its student community was just as cosmopolitan and, although Senta suffered a little to begin with from the disadvantages of having been brought up in the Soviet zone, she was young and adaptable. Before long, she had forgotten her inhibitions and did not feel in the least intimidated when she visited her grandmother.

The West Berlin authorities encouraged students to remain in the city but, because of the high level of unemployment, persuaded adults to look for jobs in the Federal Republic, where the 'economic miracle' had been so successful that there were fears of a labour shortage. Hans obtained a teaching position at a junior school in Worms, where he and Monika settled down, although not without initial difficulties.

Because they had Viktoria to help them financially, they were better off than most of their fellow refugees, but nonetheless, they spoke with Pomeranian accents and had old-fashioned, countrified habits and values, which set them apart from their smart new neighbours and colleagues. Coupled with their anxieties about Hans's parents and Heini, it took them much longer to adjust to their new life than it did Senta.

The military career of Heini, or Heinrich as he preferred to be known, did not suffer because of the flight of his parents and sister to the West. The State did not punish the families of those who betrayed it, especially those who informed against their own kin. Heinrich Koenig's information had come too late to prevent the apprehension of his parents and sister, but it had been in

326

time for the police to arrest his grandfather. In recognition, he was promoted to the rank of corporal.

In November 1959, in exact accordance with her six years' sentence, Erika Quanz was released from Leipzig prison. The clothes she had been wearing at the time of her arrest, her handbag containing a few personal possessions and her identity papers were returned to her. They were all she had in the world. While she was in prison, she had learned from another prisoner of Stefan's kidnap and trial and, in October 1956, a letter from the Governor of Jena Prison had informed her that her father was dead. Because she had no family and no home, she was ordered to go to the town hall, where she would be allocated accommodation and given help in finding work.

For Erika Quanz, during the first weeks of her freedom, the socialist system proved its value. She was given a room, food and money to tide her over. Within a week, she had a job in the records department at the hospital. Qualified women, even those with a criminal record, were badly needed in the GDR. Due to the number of people who had fled to the West, the department was severely understaffed, as was the rest of the hospital. Erika's arrival was warmly greeted.

Aware that she would still be under surveillance, she kept herself very much to herself, working efficiently and conscientiously. Even though there was a great element of routine monotony about her work, she found a simple pleasure in it, as she did in the novelty of being able to wear the clothes she chose, going to the bathroom unaccompanied, washing her hair when she wanted, reading books and going for walks, all things she had once taken for granted, which had now become very precious.

'When you get out, you must go to the West as soon as you can,' Anja Nuschke, her cellmate for the last six months of her sentence, had insisted when they had discussed what they would do when they were set free. The fact that Anja had been caught escaping to the West had not stopped her from trying to persuade Erika to flee. 'Take a job, earn enough money to pay your fare, then go to Berlin.'

But Erika had had six long years with little else to think about apart from the dreadful repercussions of having deceived Stefan.

327

Because of her, her father was dead and Stefan in prison. If she tried to leave the GDR now, she dreaded to think what would happen. If she were caught, she would face a far harsher sentence than that which she had just served. But even worse would be Stefan's fate. She dared not jeopardize his chances of freedom.

So she remained in Leipzig and, gradually, began to make a new life for herself. In this she was greatly helped by the friendship of one of her neighbours, Karsten Schwidinski, a widower in his mid-fifties.

Karsten had been a general handyman until lack of materials had driven him out of business, and now he worked for the Department of Municipal Works. The apartment block where he and Erika lived had, like much of Leipzig, been built around the turn of the century. Since the end of the war, its ownership had passed into State hands and it was suffering the ravages of time. As Karsten said, Leipzig had not suffered the bomb damage of Berlin and Dresden, but years of neglect were achieving the destruction the air raids had failed to inflict.

He had kept his own flat in a good state of repair, by reusing old materials – Karsten never threw away a nail or a screw, no matter how bent and rusty it was – and taking advantage of his position in the Department to jump the queues and buy paint, wallpaper and timber as soon as any became available.

Erika's room was very dingy when she moved in, the furniture dilapidated, the wallpaper peeling, the windows cracked, the sink stained, and black mould growing on the wall behind it, where the pipe leaked. She cleaned the place as best she could, but it was Karsten who made it properly habitable, repairing the furniture and the leaking pipe, mending the window and cheering everything up with a coat of precious paint.

In return for his kindness, she would cook for him and often they would spend the evening together, playing cards, reading aloud to each other, or, as trust developed between them, talking about themselves. Karsten told her about his wife, whom he had adored and who had died from cancer six years earlier, and Erika confided in him about Kurt and Stefan and the tangled web of deceptions which had ended in tragedy.

In due course, she also met Karsten's son, Wolfram, a

328

20-year-old law student at the Karl-Marx University, a gentle, kindly young man, like his father, of whom he was clearly immensely fond. Far from resenting his father's new friendship, Wolfram seemed to welcome it and on one occasion even told Erika that if his father should decide to marry again he would not stand in his way. 'I loved my mother,' he explained, 'but I'm sure she wouldn't have wanted my father to spend the rest of his life alone.'

However, Erika had no intention of hurtling headlong into another relationship and, although Karsten was clearly growing quite attached to her, he did not try to rush her. For the moment at least, their easy friendship was all either of them desired. It was a simple, uneventful existence, and one which was fraught with no danger.

In 1958, following his return from Moscow, Basilius Meyer had been elected to the Central Committee of the SED and become a full member of the Politburo. In 1960, he was given a seat on the newly formed State Defence Council, the Chairman of which was Walter Ulbricht. The Secretary was Erich Honecker, a man in his mid-forties, just a few years older than Basilius. Meyer and Honecker were of the new, younger generation, rising to step into the shoes of the Party grey-beards, when they inevitably retired or died. As a result of his position, Basilius was again able to further Rudi's career by obtaining him a more senior posting to the State Security Service in Leipzig.

So far as Basilius's personal life was concerned, he had never been happier. He, Irina and 7-year-old Reinhardt lived in a fine, modern apartment in Pankow, with a garden where Reinhardt could play. The little boy was doing well at school and Irina occupied her spare time on the committees of the German-Soviet Friendship Society and the Democratic Women's League. When Rudi, who showed no sign of marrying, had leave, he would occasionally come and stay with them. They were a close and united family.

So far as the GDR was concerned, however, prospects looked bleak. Despite the 'passport laws', farmers, skilled workers and professional people continued to flee to West Berlin, joining the two million who had left the Republic since 1948. In

329

March 1960, to stop the deterioration of deserted farms, the compulsory collectivization of agriculture was introduced. In 1961, another new law abolished the rights of workers to choose their place of work and introduced a policy of direction of labour. Still the stream of refugees into West Berlin continued, reaching an estimated 20,000 a day, when the school holidays began in July.

A meeting in June 1961 in Vienna between Khruschev and America's President Kennedy had not resolved the stalemate over Berlin. Khruschev still insisted it be given the status of a free city: Kennedy still insisted upon unrestricted access to the city, the ongoing presence of Western troops and a close connection between West Berlin and the Federal Republic.

In the opinion of the Defence Council, there was only one thing to do. West Berlin must be sealed off from the GDR. The blockade of 1948 had not worked and so another means must be found, one moreover which prevented the lemming-like exodus. The hole in the Iron Curtain, the sector boundary between East and West Berlin, must be sealed.

During the night of 12 to 13 August 1961, the pavements at the sector crossing points between West and East Berlin were ripped up, underground railway links cut, houses on the boundary occupied by State Security Police, and barbed wire fences erected the length of the border.

Three days later, workmen began to build a wall. Basilius took Reinhardt to the Bernauer Strasse to watch it going up. The sector demarcation line ran down the middle of the road and that was where the wall was being erected. On both sides, small groups of people had gathered, their faces anxious and full of despair. Even Basilius's expression held a hint of sadness. He had grown up in Wedding, just the other side of the street, but from now on even he would be unable to visit his childhood haunts.

Reinhardt asked, 'Why is the wall being built, Father? Is it to keep us in or to keep them out?'

'It's to protect us against the capitalists and fascists in the West,' Basilius told him.

Reinhardt nodded uncertainly. He was too young to understand what capitalists and fascists were, but although the people on the

330

other side looked harmless, they must be dangerous, since the soldiers patrolling the border and guarding the workmen were heavily armed.

Every weekend after that, he and his father monitored the progress of the wall, which in a remarkably short time stretched across the city from north to south and surrounded West Berlin's outside boundaries with the GDR. It quickly rose in height and soon Reinhardt was unable to see over it. The wicked capitalists and fascists on the other side were hidden from his view.

PART THREE

1961–1972

Children begin by loving their parents. After a time they judge them. Rarely, if ever, do they forgive them.

Oscar Wilde

Chapter 15

A few days after its erection, the Wall took its first victim: a student, who jumped from the window of a house on the Eastern side and missed the blanket held out for him in the West. In West Berlin, 40,000 demonstrators, many of them students, staged a silent protest march.

One of the march leaders was Holger Busko. Holger's professional and political career was making steady progress. He had formed his own legal practice. He was on the committee of the Berlin Social Democratic Party and hoped one day to become a Bundestag Deputy. He also lectured on law and political science at the Free University.

Among Holger's students were Dieter Duschek and Matthias Scheer, both in their first year and both taking part in the demonstration. Just as Dieter had remained friends with Kleo Kraus since Viktoria's sixtieth birthday party, he had also kept in touch with Matthias Scheer.

They were two very different kinds of friendship. For one thing, Kleo was five years younger than himself. When she had first started writing to him, Dieter had been embarrassed, but his mother had insisted that he reply and, in due course, asked Kleo to stay with them in Essen, after which Reinhild had invited him back to Hamburg. Now he was nineteen, however, his attitude towards girls had changed. Although she was still very young, Kleo was remarkably grown-up in character and developing a mature womanly figure.

His parents had not encouraged his friendship with Matthias in the same manner. Joachim described Pastor Scheer derisively as 'the Peace Pastor' and was scornful of his campaigns against remilitarization and the atom bomb, but on this subject, as on many others, Dieter disagreed with his father.

Annelie and Joachim Duschek had to be careful, however,

what they said against the Scheers. Pastor Scheer was universally venerated and his son and daughter-in-law were still working in South Africa at a Church mission. When ill-health had forced the pastor to give up preaching, the Church had provided him and his family with a spacious new apartment in Schmargendorf. Upon his death in 1960, people from all over the world had attended his funeral. Annelie and Joachim might disapprove of their son's friendship with the grandson of such a man, but it was almost impossible for them to forbid it.

When Matthias announced that he was going to the Free University to read Political Science, Dieter seized the opportunity to leave home, applied for a place there and was accepted. His parents consoled themselves with the fact that he was at least following in the family tradition by reading law, and, with bad grace, let him go.

Most students whose family homes were not in Berlin were not in the city when the Wall went up, since the summer semester had already ended, but Dieter was staying with Klara Scheer and Matthias.

After the march had followed the route agreed with the police, most of the demonstrators dispersed. A thousand or so students, however, headed towards the Wall, shouting, 'Down with the Wall! Away with Ulbricht!' The Wall loomed up ahead of them: fifteen feet high, built of smooth blocks of concrete, overlooked by machine gun towers, manned by the National People's Army. And behind it, a stretch of mined ground, patrolled by armed border policemen with dogs.

It was not the East Berlin guards who broke up the demonstrators as they tried to storm the Wall, but West Berlin policemen who drove them back with truncheons and tear gas. Matthias and Dieter were furious, as they returned to the Scheer apartment. 'Whose side are the police on?' Dieter demanded.

'What we need is action!' Matthias agreed. 'All anyone does is talk. Words won't bring down the Wall. If the government and the Allies won't do anything, we must blow up the Wall . . . !'

Before a week was over, President Kennedy had sent a personal emissary in the form of American Vice-President Lyndon Johnson to Berlin, with the reassuring message that

West Berlin was more important than ever, its citizens not only an outpost of freedom but an important part of the free world. Johnson and Brandt toured Berlin in an open car and during an address to the crowds gathered to hear him, the American repeated Roosevelt's famous words: '. . . the only thing we have to fear is fear itself.'

Gradually, the panic which had greeted the erection of the Wall subsided, but Holger could not forget Stefan, incarcerated in a prison on the other side. What were the chances now for his release?

Otto Tobisch was sixty-eight that summer when the Berlin Wall went up. No longer was he the stocky figure he had been when he arrived in Syria. His frame had shrunk, his remaining hair and his beard were grey, and his face was deeply lined, so that the scar on his forehead was barely distinguishable. Only his eyes were the same, retaining their distinctive, icy blueness, but they now required the spectacles he had once assumed as a disguise.

Although he was still called in occasionally for consultation, he had been forced to retire from active service in the Syrian Army. Younger men, whom he had helped train, now did his work, launching terrorist raids into Israel and bombarding Israeli settlements. Most of his time was spent in a German bar, drinking, reminiscing with other former Nazis and dreaming of the success of the neo-Nazi movement in Germany, when they would return home in glory and force the Soviet invaders all the way back to Moscow.

It was a relatively easy matter to visit the Fatherland now. Several of Otto's fellow exiles had made the journey, some openly addressing neo-Nazi meetings in the Federal Republic, inspiring their audiences with reminders of Germany's past glories and stirring exortations to future triumphs.

In 1958, the government had set up a central office in Ludwigsburg with the sole purpose of tracking down war criminals, and several former Nazis had been arrested and tried, but in such cases as had come to court, judges and juries had both proved extremely lenient in their sentences and Otto suspected that the Ludwigsburg office had been set up, less to wreak vengeance on the Nazis, than as a conciliatory gesture towards America and Israel.

It was the Israelis, a very different breed from the submissive Jews Otto had known in Germany and Poland, who were determined to bring to justice the perpetrators of what they called the Holocaust. One of their most fantastic feats had been in 1960, when they had kidnapped Adolf Eichmann in Argentina and flown him to Israel, where he had been tried, sentenced to death and, in May that year, hanged. So long as the Israelis continued their relentless witch hunt, Otto dared not leave Syria. If ever he fell into Israeli hands, he was doomed.

Only one dream continued to sustain him: that of seeing his son again. Every year, on Adolf's birthday, he wrote to him, and every year Adolf replied. But, to Otto's disappointment, the boy had still not worked out that Rudolf Tatschek was actually his father.

Nevertheless, his letters gave Otto an insight into his son's life. At sixteen, he had left school and started work as an apprentice mechanic at the village garage. At eighteen, he had been conscripted. 'I feel proud,' he had written to Rudolf Tatschek, 'to be following in the footsteps of my father, the general.' Briefly, Otto had hoped he would take up a military career, but that hope was soon dashed.

Adolf had enjoyed his national service, but his ambition was to work with cars. His friend, Tobias Mueller, it appeared, had now taken over the management of the garage where Adolf worked and was gradually enlarging and improving the place. He had two petrol pumps and the workshop housed a motley collection of vehicles in various stages of repair, among them a dilapidated red VW Beetle, which belonged to Dolfi and with which he tinkered whenever he had a spare moment.

Finally, on the occasion of his son's twenty-first birthday, on 14 November 1961, Otto was able to write the letter he had looked forward to writing ever since his flight from Germany over eleven years ago. At last, Adolf was of age. He was no longer bound by the guardianship of Hubert and Theresia. He was free to come to Syria.

Dolfi had grown almost to dread his annual letters from Syria.

338

The brief hope he had known when he received the first letter had long since died, although he had continued to reply, because Rudolf Tatschek was the only link he had with the past. Simple logic dictated that if his father was alive, he would by now have found a means of contacting him personally and not left it to Tatschek. His father must be dead.

The letter Dolfi received on his twenty-first birthday started, as always, with Tatschek's memories of the day Adolf had been born and the hopes 'the General' had entertained for their life together. Then he continued:

> I have some money saved up, which I would like to spend on my old comrade's son. I'm an old man now, and I would like to see you again before I die. It would give me great pleasure, if you would visit me in Damascus. I will, of course, pay your fare . . .

Dolfi shook his head. Tatschek must have a screw loose. There could be no other explanation for this crazy invitation. The situation had finally gone too far. Now was the time to end this clandestine correspondence.

He wrote there and then, before he had time to change his mind, thanking Tatschek for his offer, but pointing out that he was very happy in Bergtal. 'I am grateful for your interest in me over the years,' he finished, 'but I would prefer you not to write again.' Then he destroyed Tatschek's letter, as he had all the others, and continued leading his own life.

Just after his birthday, Dolfi met Gabriele Mueller. He had long been quite a heart-throb with the village girls, although to Theresia's disgust, he was less interested in them than in cars. However, Gabi was different from any other girl Dolfi had met. A year younger than Dolfi, she was Tobias's cousin and could converse almost as knowledgeably as he could about cars and, according to Tobias, could change a tyre or a set of sparking plugs as well as any man. Her father had, until recently, run a garage in Frankfurt-am-Main, but ill health had forced him to sell the business and he had decided to move near to his brother in the Black Forest.

Of medium height, with a plumpish figure and short, light

339

brown hair cut in a fringe which did nothing to flatter her rather long face, Gabi was by no means a beauty, but her personality more than made up for her looks. Prinz showed that he had fallen in love at first sight, by rolling over on his back and inviting her to tickle his tummy.

The following Sunday, Gabi came to Bergtal again and spent the whole day with Tobias, Dolfi and Prinz, repairing the exhaust system on the Beetle. 'I wish I was a man,' she sighed, as she wriggled out from under the car, clad in a pair of Tobias's greasy dungarees, 'then I could be a mechanic.'

Tobias glanced at Dolfi and grinned. 'I think I know someone who's glad you're not.' To his dismay, Dolfi found himself blushing. Prinz, with none of Dolfi's inhibitions, licked a spot of oil from Gabi's nose.

Under Tobias's expert eye, he and Gabi succeeded in getting the Beetle running again and, whenever possible, they met in the evenings and drove out to some isolated spot, where, on the back seat of the VW, the windows steamed up, they indulged in heavy petting.

Erika Quanz and Karsten Schwidinski were married in January 1962 in a simple, civil ceremony at Leipzig Town Hall, attended by Karsten's son Wolfram and his fiancée, Ilona, a sweet, rather delicate girl of whom Karsten and Erika both thoroughly approved, who was a chemistry student at the Karl-Marx University.

The first time Karsten had asked Erika to marry him, about a year after they had met, she had refused. Emotionally she was still unbalanced. Her years in prison had left a mental scar which was far from fully healed. She was still possessed by a deep and abiding guilt about Stefan. Already she had deceived him once. Even to think of loving another man seemed like compounding her sin in the most heartless fashion.

She heard her own voice saying, 'I love you more than anyone else in the world. Wherever I am, my love will always be here with you.' Yet what were the chances of their ever meeting again? If and when Stefan was released, he would not remain in the East and she could never go to the West.

She was terrified that she might one day again be drawn into another such situation beyond her control, where the lives of other people would be in danger, and she was frightened of the repercussions her past might have upon Karsten and especially Wolfram, who was now in the final year of his legal studies. Wolfram knew she had been in prison, but they had not told him the reason. Although it was unlikely that the authorities would hold Erika's criminal record against him and not allow him to practise as a lawyer when he graduated, Wolfram had become increasingly critical of the State and was quite capable of sealing his own fate, by speaking out in her defence. So, since she had been arrested after the 17th June uprising, they let him assume she had been punished for participating in it. But even this was apparently sufficient for him to accord her a respect of which she felt far from deserving.

Then there were her feelings for Karsten. Never again would she love anyone with the same passion she had felt for Stefan. But was passion so important? After all, she was approaching forty and Karsten nearing sixty. They were middle-aged. Did it matter that they would never experience together the agonies and raptures of passionate love? Were not affection, understanding, companionship and mutual trust far more important to any happy and lasting partnership? Yet she still felt that Karsten deserved more than she could ever offer him.

The last thing she wanted was to hurt Karsten and she tried to explain her feelings in such a way that he would not feel himself in any way to blame, but she need not have worried. 'I understand,' he said soothingly. 'You need more time. Well, I can wait.'

When, a year later, in November 1961, he again asked her to marry him, the Berlin Wall had gone up and she knew that there was no longer any possibility of her ever seeing Stefan again. More settled in her mind and her emotions, she realized that not only was she denying Karsten his happiness, but throwing away her own last chance of achieving self-respect and tranquillity.

So, a couple of months later, she found herself becoming Frau Erika Schwidinski. And, as they emerged from the town hall onto the cobbled square, into the hazy winter sunshine, she was sure she had done the right thing. Karsten stood tall and proud beside her, his arm through hers, a carnation in his

341

buttonhole. Wolfram and Ilona showered them with rice. The photographer from Foto Schmidt told them to smile into the camera and informed them that the prints would be ready in three days' time.

Erika looked up at her husband and made a silent vow, that for as long as they were together, she would give her life in his service and do everything in her power to make him happy.

In February, there was an amazing new development in East-West relations, when an American pilot, Gary Powers, who had been shot down by the Soviets and charged with espionage, was exchanged for a KGB spy, Colonel Rudolph Abel. The exchange took place on the Glienicke Bridge, the frontier post between West Berlin and Potsdam, and had, according to the papers, been effected by an East Berlin lawyer, Dr Wolfgang Vogel.

Optimistic that Dr Vogel might be able to negotiate Stefan's release, Viktoria asked Holger whether it was possible to contact him.

'The short answer to that is no, I'm afraid,' Holger replied. 'Since the Wall went up, Dr Vogel has not been allowed to enter West Berlin. However, I do know a lawyer over here, Dr Juergen Stange, who was at law school with Dr Vogel. He's already told me that, provided he can resume contact with Dr Vogel, he will ask if it would be possible for Stefan either to be exchanged for another political prisoner or bought out for a ransom. He thinks a ransom is the most likely way. You see, since it's shut itself off from the West, the GDR is badly in need of Western currency.'

Viktoria's mind raced ahead, wondering how quickly she could raise the sort of sum the GDR government would demand. But, as if he could read her thoughts, Holger said, 'Dr Stange is of the opinion that the government would probably provide the ransom.'

'I would pay anything to have Stefan back,' Viktoria insisted.

'I know. But you won't be allowed to. If things reach that stage, Stefan and other West German hostages will have become political pawns.'

That weekend, Senta came to see her grandmother, as she often did, and Viktoria told her the news. 'I'd rather you didn't tell anyone else,' she said, 'but I thought you'd like to know what's happening.'

She and Senta had grown very close during the past three years and Senta had already decided that, when she left university, she would like to work at one of the Jochum hotels. To Viktoria's delight, the opportunity which Lili had refused, would, it seemed, be taken up by Monika's daughter.

After expressing her hope that the two lawyers would be able to do something on Stefan's behalf, Senta asked, 'Do you think this Dr Vogel could find out about my grandparents?'

'I asked Holger the same thing,' Viktoria replied. 'But he pointed out that because Stefan is a West German, he's a different category of prisoner from your grandparents.' She paused, then said gently, 'Senta, I'm not suggesting you give up hope, but, unless a miracle occurs, I think it's very unlikely you'll ever see your grandparents again.'

Senta blinked, then nodded bravely. 'The worst part is not knowing. If only I knew whether they are alive or dead . . .'

Viktoria understood exactly what she meant. She had lived with uncertainty for much of her life.

At least twice a year, during her vacations, Senta went to see her parents in Worms, but, fond though she was of them, she found their company trying. Her mother moaned about the small flat, which was all they could afford on Hans's salary, and continually said she wished they had stayed at Fuerstenmark; while her father was becoming increasingly disillusioned with the materialistic attitude of West Germans, and complained about the cost of living, including basic social services which they had taken for granted in the GDR.

In fact, they were doing very well. They had a washing machine and a television and were buying a car on hire purchase. The real reason behind their discontent, Senta realized, was their concern for Heini and Hans's parents. But that did not make them any easier to be with.

She much preferred staying with Lili in Munich, with whom she had revived her old friendship. Norbert's fortunes had continued to flourish and Landgut was among Germany's biggest property development companies, although, according to Lili,

343

Norbert had little to do with its day-to-day running now, but left this to his managers in Hamburg. The couple lived in a lovely villa on the banks of the Isar, where they entertained lavishly. Lili had her own red Mercedes Roadster. They travelled extensively. Although the press insisted on calling Norbert 'the playboy tycoon' and photographers delighted in catching him surrounded by beautiful women, their sly innuendoes appeared to have no foundation. Norbert and Lili were golden people and theirs appeared to be a golden marriage.

That appearances could be deceptive, Senta did not realize until the Easter of 1962, when Lili telephoned, saying Norbert was away and asking Senta to spend the vacation with her.

When Senta first arrived, she assumed Lili was subdued because Norbert had gone away without her. On the Saturday, they wandered round the shops, but Lili was not in the mood for looking at clothes. On Sunday, they went to the Pinakothek, but the tourists irritated Lili. On the way home, they were held up by a peace march and Lili exclaimed, 'These bloody demonstrators get on my nerves! They should ban them, not the bomb!' On Monday, they sunbathed in the garden, but Lili could not concentrate on her book and chain-smoked, gazing vacantly into space.

On Tuesday, she suggested they went into the country. Usually, she drove fast but carefully, giving a non-stop, humorous monologue on her fellow drivers. This time, she said scarcely a word, except – when the Alps came into view – 'I need to see a mountain.'

They drove to Mittenwald, on the border with Austria. Lili parked the car and took off her headscarf, standing for a moment, tall and slender in a sleeveless turquoise dress, a pullover draped over her shoulders, gazing up at the snow-covered Karwendel peak towering above them. Then, with a grim set to her mouth, she set off along a path beside a small, gushing river, until they reached a lake, where she sat down, cradling her knees in her arms.

'Norbert's having an affair,' she announced. 'She's an English fashion model. She has black hair and blue eyes and her name is Jill Grenville. Norbert met her earlier this year in Milan. He's

344

in London at the moment – with her.' Lili stared bleakly across the lake. 'She's very beautiful.'

'So are you,' Senta blurted out. She did not understand what could possibly have gone wrong. What did Norbert see in this raven-haired Jill Grenville that he did not already have in Lili?

'I expected too much of him,' Lili said, ignoring Senta's loyal interjection. 'I wanted him to be something he wasn't. I wanted us to have a proper home and be a proper family. I wanted the security I had never known as a child. Above all, I wanted children, lots of children . . .'

This Senta could understand. When she married, which she could not imagine happening for quite a while, since although she had dated several boys at university, she did not have a steady boyfriend, she too wanted to have children. Norbert, however, already had three from his previous marriage. 'But Norbert didn't want any?' she hazarded.

'No, that wasn't the problem. In fact, in the early days of our marriage, he used to talk about us having a little girl who looked like me. The problem was that I couldn't get pregnant. And the more we tried and the more we failed, the more tense I became. I knew it must be my fault. And then I convinced myself that I would lose Norbert because I couldn't conceive. I started to get jealous. Every time he looked at another woman, I created a scene. We began having the most dreadful rows.'

'Have you seen a doctor?'

'Yes, Norbert made me see a gynaecologist.' Lili gave a brittle little laugh. 'You probably won't believe this, but until then it had never occurred to me that it was not normal to have a period only every three months or so.'

'Every three months?' Senta gasped.

'According to the gynaecologist, there are quite a number of girls my age with the same problem. He said that if I relaxed, my body rhythm should adjust itself. Then he told me I was much too thin and should put on at least a stone in weight, but that my hips are so narrow I should have difficulty in giving birth. Finally, he said that it was probably better for me not to get pregnant and offered to prescribe me the new anti-baby pill, which would regularize my periods and stop me getting pregnant.

'Norbert agreed with the doctor,' she went on tonelessly, 'so now I'm taking the pill and, sure enough, I have periods as regularly as clockwork. But any hope of having children has flown out of the window. And, worst of all, the very thing I was most afraid of has happened – I've lost Norbert.'

'But why? He can't blame you for something that isn't your fault.'

'Norbert doesn't blame people. He just grows bored with them. That's what happened with all his girlfriends – and with Reinhild. Once the novelty wore off, he discarded them. Now he's bored with me. It's months now since we've done anything together, gone on holiday, gone to the theatre – even gone to bed together.' Tears welled in Lili's eyes. 'Ever since I was a little girl, I've loved Norbert. I was so happy when I came back from England and discovered that he loved me too. I can't bear the thought of having to live without him. What am I going to do?' Her self-control suddenly broke. Tears poured down her cheeks and she buried her face in her arms.

Helplessly, Senta put her arm round her thin shoulders and murmured words of comfort, until Lili's fit of weeping abated. Then, when Lili had collected herself, they continued their walk. But Lili had no energy left and, upon Senta's suggestion, they returned to the car and drove back to Munich.

As soon as they arrived home, Lili went to bed. Senta sat beside her, holding her hand, until she fell asleep. Then, too restless to settle down to anything, she wandered round the house. There had been occasions, if she were honest, when she had almost envied Lili her glamorous existence, but now she saw that these outer trappings were nothing compared to inner happiness. Norbert had given Lili everything she could need, but he had not given her the one thing she wanted most: himself.

And at that moment, Senta made a solemn vow. She would never allow any man the power to hurt her as Norbert had Lili. She would build a wall round her heart to protect it, a wall so strong that nobody would be able to pierce it and discover how vulnerable she really was. She and Lili were similar in many ways, but in this they would be different.

During the next few days, Senta came to realize a lot of things

346

about herself. She might be three years younger than Lili, but she was the stronger person, and it was due to her willpower and common sense that Lili did not lapse totally into the state of depression which had overtaken her in London. Senta did not let her stay in bed as she would have liked, but made her get up and go out. Experience had taught Senta that problems did not go away if one ignored them: they had to be confronted and resolved.

She had no personal experience of marriage, but from what Lili had said, her situation seemed far from lost. Since Norbert did not mind one way or the other about having children, provided Lili could reconcile herself to a future without them, there seemed no reason why they could not start again.

But Lili seemed to have no fighting spirit. When Senta urged her to make every effort to woo Norbert back again, she said apathetically, 'He's been in London for two weeks and I haven't heard a word from him. Senta, our marriage is over. I've destroyed it.'

Senta tried another tack. 'Perhaps a change of scene would do you good. Why don't you come back with me to Berlin?'

'And give Aunt Vicki the satisfaction of knowing she was right? Never!' To Senta's surprise, all the resentment towards Viktoria which had been building up within Lili over the years came spilling out, the feeling that Viktoria had never loved her, had used her, lied to her and, no matter how hard Lili had tried to please her, had always found fault with her. 'She's never cared about my happiness, only ever about herself. She's totally and utterly selfish – and ruthless.'

'Lili, you're not being fair. I know she loves you very much.'

'You weren't brought up by her,' Lili said dully. 'You don't know what she's really like.'

A month after Senta had returned to Berlin, Lili sent a telegram saying: ALL OVER STOP HAVE DECIDED TO LOOK FOR A COTTAGE IN THE MOUNTAINS. LOVE LILI. In the middle of July, she sent a card, giving an address and telephone number in Riezlern in the Kleinwalsertal. She had reverted to using her maiden name of Lili Nowak.

As soon as the summer semester ended, Senta went to

347

see her. Viktoria, who was not surprised the marriage had gone wrong, but was nevertheless very distressed, wanted to accompany her, but Senta persuaded her, diplomatically, that it would be better if she went on her own.

Lili met her at Oberstdorf station and they walked up to Riezlern, where she had rented a charming chalet. Superficially, she appeared to be the old Lili. 'Do you realize the Kleinwalsertal is really in Austria?' she asked. 'But the only way into the valley is from Germany. There's no way out into Austria except by foot over the mountains. The postage stamps are Austrian but you pay for them in German money. If I decide to buy a house here I shall be a foreigner. Don't you think that's romantic?'

Throughout Senta's visit the weather was beautiful and they went for long hikes through the magnificent Alpine scenery. Lili dressed for the part in climbing boots and breeches, and carried a rucksack on her back. Her hair was drawn up in a ponytail and her face was lightly tanned. 'I feel better than I have for years,' she kept telling Senta gaily. 'I love it here. The air is so fresh and the people are so nice. For the first time in my life, I feel really at home.' Yet there was a defensive note in her voice, as if she was daring Senta to contradict her.

'What are your plans for the future?' Senta asked on the evening of her departure.

'Why do I have to have plans? Norbert's agreed to make me a generous divorce settlement. I don't need to do anything.'

'Once the novelty wears off, you're going to be very bored and very lonely here, particularly in the winter. And aren't you conscious of the mountains looming up all around, blocking you in?'

For a moment, the thin veneer of Lili's self-confidence almost cracked. 'My life has reached a dead end,' she said. 'Where better to spend the rest of it than here?' And nothing Senta said would convince her otherwise.

On Dolfi's twenty-second birthday, in November, he and Gabi announced their engagement and set the date for their wedding for the following June. Tobias very generously told the young couple that, if they were prepared to clear them out and

348

renovate them, they could have the rooms above the garage at a peppercorn rent. Dolfi was good with his hands and found great pleasure in painting, decorating and furnishing the loft.

Despite Dolfi's letter the previous year, saying he did not want to continue the correspondence, Rudolf Tatschek wrote on his birthday, repeating his invitation to Damascus. Dolfi was tempted simply to ignore the letter, but, in the end, sent a brief note saying he was getting married. That, he was sure, would shut Tatschek up.

During the Christmas holiday, he and Prinz moved into their new home. Gabi would remain with her parents in Triberg until they were married, but when the garage closed, she often slipped up the outside staircase to see how Dolfi was progressing with his handiwork.

It was a situation in which everyone was happy. Everyone, that was, except Prinz, who found himself rather neglected. However, the dog was more than capable of providing his own entertainment. When his master was occupied with other matters, Prinz took himself into the forest on wonderful, solitary, hunting expeditions.

At the beginning of February, Prinz returned from one of these excursions in a more than usually bedraggled state. A fine early morning had degenerated by noon into a blustery day, with sleet mingled in the rain. His pelt was soaking wet and his paws covered in mud. He limped slightly as he entered the garage and when Dolfi examined him, he found a deep wound in the dog's shoulder and another in his front leg. It looked very much as if he had been in a fight. But although the wounds were clearly painful for several days, they were clean and healed quite quickly, and Prinz had soon resumed his normal exuberant spirits.

Suddenly, in April, Prinz refused to sleep in the basket beside Dolfi's bed, but wandered listlessly round his new home and eventually settled down in a dark corner. He allowed Dolfi to examine him, but Dolfi could find no evidence of any cuts, bites or abscesses. His nose was dry and he had no appetite. Because the dog had difficulty in swallowing, it seemed possible that he had something stuck in his throat. Dolfi decided that if he didn't get better he would take him to the vet in Triberg.

349

The following morning, Dolfi was woken by Prinz clawing furiously at the door mat to be let out. He opened the door and let him go. Prinz rushed down the steps, into the forest and disappeared from sight. Dolfi felt a sense of relief. The dog had clearly recovered from whatever had been ailing him.

It was that day the telephone call came. Gabi answered the phone and shouted from the small office, 'Dolfi! Telephone for you!' Then she stood, waiting curiously, while he took the call, wondering who it was that had asked for him by name.

The conversation was very one-sided. Dolfi said, 'Yes, I understand.' Then, after saying, 'Yes,' several times, he said, 'Yes, I know where that is. All right, I'll see you there,' and replaced the receiver. For a few moments, he stood looking dazed, then turned and left the office.

'Dolfi, who was that?' Gabi asked, running after him.

An almost vacant expression on his face, as if he was not really aware of Gabi's presence, Dolfi replied, 'I have to meet someone. I may be late, so you'd better catch the bus home.' Before she could ask any more, he took off his overalls, got into his Beetle and drove away.

The garage closed at six and still Dolfi had not returned. Gabi went up the outside staircase to the loft, intending to wait for him, but when she reached the door, Prinz was lying there, panting heavily, his coat covered in mud and matted with grass seeds and weeds. She crouched beside him. 'Prinz, what's the matter, you poor old thing?' But when she made to stroke him, he bared his teeth and gave a deep, menacing growl. Gabi stood up and backed away. She could only assume that he was guarding the property in his master's absence. Shakily, she went back down the staircase and did as Dolfi had said – caught the bus home to Triberg.

When Dolfi returned to Bergtal, late that night, he was still in a state of shock. The telephone call from Rudolf Tatschek saying that he was in Germany and wanted to meet him had been surprise enough, but to discover that Tatschek was actually his father, that had stunned him into a state of bewildered stupefaction. They had met in the car park at the foot of the Triberg waterfall, but Otto had insisted they leave the popular tourist haunt swiftly and drive to a less frequented spot to talk.

Dolfi had taken him to an isolated lane leading to a deserted farmhouse, where he and Gabi used to go during the early days of their courtship, and there his father had explained that he had had to leave Germany after the war, take a different name and start a new life. He had had to pretend to be Rudolf Tatschek, even to his own son. He was sure Adolf understood why.

Dolfi had no idea why his father had to pretend to be someone else, but, for the time being at least, he did not really care. The main thing was that he was still alive. He was very different from the memory he had retained of him since his childhood – tall, strong and commanding, an older version of himself, but with the authority of a general. But over twenty years had passed and, in that time, people change.

Long after darkness fell, Otto reminisced about the celebrations in the officers' mess on the night Dolfi had been born, and the way he celebrated the event each year with German comrades in Syria who shared his own memories and experiences.

Eventually, he shivered. 'It's cold here and I'm hungry. Is it safe for me to come home with you? Will anyone see me?'

Dolfi shook his head. The garage was on the very outskirts of the village, overlooked only by hills and forests. At night, when it was shut, apart from the sound of occasional passing traffic, he could be living in the middle of nowhere.

He drove back to the main road and on to Bergtal. 'Bit of an old wreck, this car,' Otto commented. 'You could have a Mercedes if you came to Damascus.'

Lights were still on in the Waldblick and one or two houses, but most of Bergtal was asleep. Dolfi parked in deep shadow and led his father up the outside staircase to the loft, opened the door and let him in. From a cupboard he took some bottles of beer, bread, sausage and cheese and put them on the table he had made himself.

His father opened a beer, took a long draught from the bottle, then looked round him. 'Not much of a place, this. My son shouldn't be living above a garage in a godforsaken hole like Bergtal. I could buy you something much better in Damascus.'

At that moment, there was a strange scuffling noise at the

door. Quick as a shot, Otto grabbed the bread knife and leaped to his feet. But it was only Prinz. He staggered in, circled aimlessly for a few minutes, then went to his water bowl and drank thirstily, sagging slightly on his haunches.

Otto sank back into his chair. 'I'd forgotten you had a dog. Sorry-looking cur, isn't it?'

'He's not well,' Dolfi explained. 'I thought he was better this morning, but he doesn't seem to be.'

'It looks old,' Otto commented. 'I'd have it put down.' As if he had understood, Prinz gave a low growl and slunk away into a corner.

Otto cut a wedge of bread and cheese and started to eat. With rather less appetite, Dolfi followed suit. When his father finished eating and announced that he was tired, Dolfi was not sorry. Some instinct told him that his father was not the man he had built him up to be in his mind, but he needed time to sort out his impressions. He allowed Otto to have the bedroom and made a makeshift bed for himself in the living room.

He slept fitfully, his mind over-active from the day's events and his night disturbed by Prinz's restlessness. Dawn was scarcely breaking when Prinz again started clawing and chewing at the door mat. Dolfi got up and let him out. With a curious gait, the dog ran into the forest. Dolfi pulled on his boots and followed him, but when he called, Prinz paid no attention.

Otto was up and dressed before Dolfi left for work. 'Nobody must know I'm here,' he said. 'I mean that, Adolf – nobody. If you tell anyone about me, you'll put us both in mortal danger.'

Dolfi agreed, but not without wondering why his father's presence had to be kept so secret.

The first customers to arrive at the garage that morning were two foreigners on a touring holiday in a hired Mercedes. The car chugged up the hill and ground to a halt on the forecourt. 'It kept misfiring yesterday,' the driver told Tobias, in accented German. 'This morning, it didn't want to start. Now listen to it.'

New plugs and cleaning the distributor cap didn't work, so Tobias suggested they left the car there, had a coffee at the Waldblick, and returned in a couple of hours. Glad of something to keep his mind off his father and Prinz, Dolfi set to work, but the fault was far from easy to find and when the men returned at lunchtime, he had still not located it. The driver was not concerned. He chatted to Tobias and Gabi, saying how delightfully unspoiled the village was. 'Do you get many tourists here?' he asked casually.

Dolfi stiffened, but Tobias said, 'No, you're the first strangers we've seen this year.'

'My friend and I are keen walkers. While your mechanic sorts out the car, we'll explore the surrounding countryside.' They took rucksacks from the car boot and set off on foot into the hills.

Dolfi was very quiet that day and nobody, not even Gabi, could get much out of him. When she asked about the friend he had gone to meet the previous afternoon, he did not reply but reached for a screwdriver and peered back into the Mercedes' engine. By six, he had repaired the fault and the two men were in possession of their car again. When he locked up for the evening, however, they had not left the village, but were sitting on the garage wall, smoking and enjoying the last rays of the sun.

Otto's first words when Dolfi came in, were, 'Who are those men?' When Dolfi told him they were tourists, he shook his head. 'They're Israeli agents. They're looking for me.'

'Why should they be looking for you?'

Otto's astonishment was clearly etched on his face. 'You mean to say you don't know?'

'How can I? Herr Tatschek – I mean, you – never said anything in your letters. And here, nobody ever speaks about you. Apart from the fact that you were a general in the army and you left us when I was a little boy, I know nothing about you.'

Otto gave a harsh laugh. 'I wasn't in the army. I was in the SS. You mean nobody has told you about the crimes I'm supposed to have committed . . . ?'

Before he could continue, however, there was, as on the previous evening, a scratching at the door. Again, as Dolfi went to open it, Otto grabbed the bread knife. Prinz staggered in, his coat filthy, saliva frothing at his mouth. Dolfi fell to his knees and reached out to the dog. 'Prinz . . .'

Prinz peered up at him, his eyes glazed and unfocused, then his hackles rose and he snapped at him.

353

Before Dolfi knew what had happened, Otto had pushed him out of the way, knocking him to the ground. Then, knife poised, he approached the dog.

Prinz gave a savage growl and hurled himself against the assailant, sinking his teeth deeply into the arm that thrust itself towards him, clinging on tenaciously, even after the sharp blade of the knife had entered his throat. Then, he sank down, jerking convulsively, onto the floor.

Otto prised the dog's jaws from his wrist, tore off his jacket and ripped open his sleeve. Its incisors had penetrated deep into his flesh. He aimed a kick at the animal's belly, as he hurried to the sink to wash the bite clean.

Dolfi crouched down, gazing in horror at the dog's writhing body and the knife handle sticking out of him. The Pointer's last throes did not continue long. Within minutes, the life blood had ebbed out of him and he lay, stretched out, dead, on the kitchen rug. Slowly, Dolfi turned to his father. 'Why did you do that? Why did you have to kill him?'

'For God's sake!' Otto shouted. 'The beast was vicious. He'd have killed you if I hadn't got him first.'

'Of course he wouldn't. Prinz never hurt a soul in his life.'

'I've just saved your life and been bitten in the process, and all you do is defend the brute!' Otto exploded. 'Are you telling me that you care more for that dog than you do for your own father?'

Yes, Dolfi wanted to say. Prinz had been his loyal and constant companion for the last ten years. Prinz had been closer to him than the father who had left him and his mother alone when he was only four could ever be.

He wrapped Prinz in a blanket and carried him outside. At dawn, he went into the forest and buried his old friend, marking his grave with a simple, wooden cross.

Dolfi's life took on a nightmare aspect, far worse than the days following his mother's murder. The wound on Otto's wrist healed quickly, leaving a clean, pink scar. But the hurt inflicted on Dolfi by his father's revelations about his past life was something from which the young man would never recover.

Dolfi knew now why his father had had to flee to Syria and live under a pseudonym. He knew now why his father had picked up the knife when Prinz had scratched at the door.

After Dolfi had carried Prinz's body downstairs that evening, Otto had described the circumstances leading up to his exile in Syria. 'When you were born,' he said, 'Germany ruled most of Europe. The Empire reached from France to Poland. Our army was in sight of Moscow. If it hadn't been for the Americans, we would have conquered Russia. The Bolsheviks and the Jews wouldn't exist any more. At Schlachtenhausen, they were being killed at a rate of five thousand a day. I was commended by Himmler.'

Dolfi looked at him numbly. In the deep recesses of his mind, a memory stirred of Wolf savaging a little girl, while, in the distance, tall chimneys belched out smoke. The foul odour of that smoke had permeated his early childhood. Suddenly, he could taste it again on his lips. 'You were killing five thousand people a day?' he asked in a small voice.

'They weren't people. They were animals, the scum of the earth. That has always been my mission, Adolf, ever since you were born, that you should grow up in a world free from Bolsheviks and Jews.'

Dolfi shook his head in blank, uncomprehending horror.

Otto snorted in exasperation. 'Adolf, don't tell me you've been taken in by American propaganda. Believe me, the Jews are vile and corrupt. They want only one thing – to dominate the world. Even now, the United States is subsidizing Israel. It has forced Germany to make reparations. God, it makes me puke. They put me in prison. The newspapers called me the Slaughterer of Schlachtenhausen. They hounded me from my own country and I'm forced to live in exile. And the Israelis are still hunting for me, hoping to make me stand trial. But I was doing the world a great service. You're my son, Adolf, you must understand.'

Dolfi was scarcely hearing his words any more. He only heard the cruel, arrogant note in his voice. He saw only the cold, evil light in his eyes.

As he lay on his makeshift bed that night, he tried to make sense of everything his father had told him, but the over-riding

355

image in his mind was of Prinz's corpse. His father had killed Prinz without a moment's hesitation and with no regret. If he could do that, he was capable of killing people, too.

Otto's secret presence in his home put a tremendous strain on Dolfi in more ways than one. Not only did he have to live with the knowledge that his father was a cold-blooded mass murderer, he also had to engage in subterfuge with Tobias, Gabi and the Albers. He longed to tell them the dreadful secret he was guarding, but he dared not. If he did, they would almost certainly insist he told the police. And no matter what his feelings towards his father, Dolfi could not bring himself to betray him.

Even worse, was the fear that he might have inherited his father's characteristics. His mother had always told him how like his father he was. Imagining his father to be a war hero, the great general she had described him as, Dolfi had taken pride in the comparison, had tried to become more like him. Now he hated the thought that Otto's tainted blood ran in his veins.

Never in his life had he felt so utterly helpless and alone.

For fear that Gabi might somehow coax the truth out of him, he stopped taking her out after work and, for obvious reasons, she could not come up to the loft. He could not tell her the true circumstances of Prinz's death and had to pretend the dog had died in its sleep. Gabi could only assume that his sudden change of mood meant that he didn't love her any more and that he was plucking up the courage to say he did not want to go ahead with the wedding.

Evening after evening, Otto tried to persuade Dolfi to accompany him back to Damascus. He pleaded loneliness. He tried to convince Dolfi that it was his filial duty to be with his father. But Dolfi adamantly refused.

Otto did not know what to do. His plans were going catastrophically wrong. With every day that he remained in Bergtal, the danger to himself increased. Although the two strangers had taken their car and gone, he had no way of knowing whether they had left the neighbourhood. If, as he feared, they were Israelis, then they were undoubtedly still out there, somewhere. The Jews were as tenacious as they were unforgiving. Sometimes, he thought he saw the sun glint on glass in the forest and wondered if they were watching him through binoculars.

356

Yet he could not bring himself to leave. He could not bring himself to admit defeat. He would not go back to Syria unless his son went with him.

He tried everything to convince Dolfi. He belittled Dolfi's life, ridiculed his ambitions and poured scorn on his friends. He emphasized his own influential Syrian contacts and his standing with the Syrian government. But to no avail. In the end, he used his trump card. 'When I left Schlachtenhausen, I took a bag full of gold and precious stones with me, which I sold when I reached Damascus. There's a fortune waiting for you, Adolf, when you come back with me.'

'Who did the gold and precious stones belong to?' Dolfi asked, dully.

'Jews,' Otto shrugged. 'But they weren't any use to them where they were going. Now they're yours.'

His son's mouth set in an obstinate line. 'I don't want them.'

Day after day, as he worked in the garage, Dolfi wondered miserably how long he could continue with this double life. His feelings towards his father had turned into a deep hatred, which was poisoning everything, his work, his sleep, his friends and his home.

When Otto made yet another attempt to persuade him to come to Syria, Dolfi's patience finally broke. 'For God's sake!' he shouted. 'Why the hell don't you get out of my life and leave me alone. I didn't ask you to come here. I don't want you or your money. Go away!'

The strain of his confinement and the fear that he was being watched were beginning to take their toll on Otto. He had always had a short temper. Now it was pushed to the limit. Furiously, he raised his hand and made to strike his son.

Dolfi saw the blow coming. With youth and strength on his side, he seized hold of his father's arm and held it in a firm, unyielding grasp. For a long while, the two men stared into each other's eyes. Then Otto looked away and Dolfi released his hold on his arm. Otto knew he had lost.

During the next couple of days, there was a considerable change in Otto. The bitterness of his defeat weighed heavily upon him. He fell prey to deep fits of depression, when everything in the world seemed black. The Black Forest lived truly up to its name. The hills loomed blackly over him. When he tried to sleep, he had a sense of them spilling down towards him under the black cover of the night, threatening to swallow him up. When he looked out of the window, he had to shield his eyes from the spring sunlight.

He felt hot and feverish. His throat hurt when he swallowed and he was consumed by thirst, but when he tried to drink, the coffee made him retch. He had no appetite and when he tried to eat, the food clogged in his throat. He felt an overwhelming desire to get away from Bergtal, but his mind was unable to concentrate for any length of time and he felt incapable of making any plans, so he resorted to wandering restlessly to and fro in the loft.

Dolfi, with his sullen expression, irritated him almost beyond endurance. He was plagued by a host of grievances, real and imagined. 'God, what did I do to deserve such a son?' he raged. 'Even the army didn't want you. After a year, they were thankful to see the back of you. For twenty-two years, I assumed you took after me, that you were a man. But I was wrong. You're Anna's son, soft, stupid and spunkless!'

The following day, Otto felt worse. His thirst raged more than ever. He grew increasingly depressed and irritable. Catching sight of his reflection in a looking glass, he picked up a stick and smashed the mirror. As his fractured image stared back at him, he knew a sudden, overwhelming sense of terror.

He went back to bed and eventually fell asleep, but his sleep was haunted by dark and terrible images from the past, confused with fears from the present. He seemed to be walking through the forest, which was full of strange sounds, filling him with a wild and uncontrollable dread. All around him were shades, relentlessly hunting him down. He knew who they were. They were the souls of Jews and Communists, intent on vengeance.

Anna was suddenly standing beside him, an expression of gloating satisfaction on her stupid face. 'You can't get away with it this time. Now it's your turn to suffer.'

A huge dog leaped out of the undergrowth, its fangs bared. A voice – his own voice – shouted, 'Wolf, kill!' The dog jumped on

358

to him, its teeth fastened round his neck. Otto tried to scream, but no sound would come.

He felt himself haunted by death. It was there, all around him, huge and black and ghastly, waiting to pounce on him and subject him to inconceivable horrors.

When Dolfi returned from work and found his father in bed, he thought at first that it was a ruse to make him feel sorry for him. But as the evening wore on, he realized Otto was seriously ill. He had a high temperature, he had great difficulty in eating and when Dolfi held a cup for him to drink, the mere sight of water sent him into a convulsion, during which he gasped for breath, almost choking on his own saliva.

During the night, his condition deteriorated and the convulsions grew more frequent. He raved deliriously and thrashed about so wildly that Dolfi had to forcibly restrain him in case he fell out of bed. Light and merely the sight of water seemed to cause him immense agony and threw him into a state of almost maniacal excitement. 'When he recovered temporarily from these fits, he was so exhausted that he could not even sit unaided, but he had moments of complete lucidity and was able to talk quite rationally.

When he spoke, it was of death. Suddenly, all the bombast had gone out of him, and the evil deeds of which he had boasted so proudly upon his arrival, now filled him with an unholy fear. He was, Dolfi realized, desperately afraid of dying and even more terrified of retribution.

'They made me do those things,' he muttered on one occasion, his eyes glazed and sunk deep into their sockets. 'Adolf, believe me, I didn't want to kill anyone. But I had to obey orders. They wouldn't let me stop . . .'

It was as if he believed that by confessing his sins, he could achieve last-minute absolution. Each time he regained consciousness, more ghastly horrors spilled from his phlegmy lips.

Then came the worst revelation of all. 'Anna made me do it. She had hidden the jewels. They were yours, Adolf. I had no choice but to kill her. I wanted to take you with me then, but it was impossible . . .' His crabbed hand crept out from under the sheet and reached towards Dolfi.

As clearly as if it were yesterday, Dolfi saw his mother's corpse lying on her bedroom floor, a stocking knotted round her neck, her face purple and bloated. He felt a sense of revulsion so great that he feared he might vomit. 'You killed my mother?' he asked, shakily.

'She would have told the police about me . . .'

Another convulsion of such intensity overtook Otto that it seemed he must choke himself to death. Dolfi hoped that he would, except that even death seemed too kind a fate for him.

Outside, the first blush of dawn was creeping into the sky. A blackbird sang. The sound of a cuckoo echoed across the valley. For a long time, Dolfi sat immobile. Then he stood up and crossed the room.

'Adolf, don't leave me,' Otto pleaded, his tongue thick, his lips swollen and saliva slobbering from his jowls. 'Adolf, have pity on me . . .'

Dolfi ignored him. With bitter hatred burning in his heart, he went downstairs to the garage to call the emergency services.

At Freiburg hospital, Otto was placed in an isolation ward and given an intravenous injection to tranquillize him, while tests were carried out to try and identify his illness. A physical examination revealed an old scar on his forehead, the remains of a scar in the place where the SS tattoo used to be under his armpit, and a recent scar on his arm.

In a small office nearby, a police inspector listened rather incredulously to Dolfi's incoherent story, while his constable took down his statement in shorthand. 'Why in God's name didn't you tell someone earlier?' he asked, when Dolfi had finished.

'Despite everything he'd done, he was still my father. I couldn't betray him. But when he said he'd killed my mother . . .'

The inspector pursed his lips, picked up the telephone and made a series of short, incisive calls. The station officer at Bergtal was ordered to go to Dolfi's home, search for papers belonging to Rudolf Tatschek and bring them to the hospital immediately. An officer at Freiburg police headquarters was instructed to look out the murder file for Anna Feldmann, formerly Tobisch. A colleague in Ludwigsburg was asked to search the archives for all records relating to Otto Tobisch.

By ten o'clock, the effects of the sedative were beginning to wear off. Otto opened his eyes and found himself in a white, clinical, hospital ward. Beside his bed were two policemen.

'Who are you?' one of them asked.

He was too sick, weak and exhausted even to attempt to deny his true identity. '*Ich bin Otto Tobisch*,' he whispered.

They were the last words he ever spoke. At midnight, Otto Tobisch died.

Dolfi remained in hospital for a month. The classic symptoms of hydrophobia exhibited by his father led the doctors to suspect that he had been suffering from rabies, a diagnosis which was supported by his description of Prinz's sudden illness. A veterinary surgeon went to Bergtal, exhumed the dog's body, and, in the police laboratory, carefully removed its brain and undertook prescribed tests in a post mortem examination. Prinz was discovered to have been rabid.

The immediate fear was that Dolfi, too, might have contracted the disease. Although, unlike Otto, he had not been bitten, he could be infected if the dog's saliva had entered any kind of open wound, even a small scratch or a cut. He was given a series of rabies vaccine injections, but the doctor had to admit that there was no sure means of immunization, nor any certain cure if Dolfi should turn out to be infected. The usual incubation period for the disease in man was between six and eight weeks, but it could be as short as ten days or as long as two years, depending upon the distance of the bite or the wound from the central nervous system.

To the consternation of the police and the government, there was a spurt of neo-Nazi rallies in several cities, with demonstrators wearing black armbands. These were swiftly quashed, but there was nothing anyone could do to stop the bouquets of flowers and cards which arrived at the hospital for Otto Tobisch and his son, many bearing the sign of the swastika.

With Dolfi's consent, the date and location of his father's funeral was not made public. Only Dolfi, the Albers and Gabi were present at the brief service. Otto's body was cremated and his ashes buried in an unmarked plot.

It was thanks uniquely to Gabi that Dolfi survived the period following his father's death. She sat at his bedside and persuaded him to talk through the fears which haunted him. She convinced him that he was not infected with rabies. She made him go through Prinz's last days and finally got him to recall that Prinz had been acting so strangely, that he could not get close enough even to stroke him. The nearest they had been was when Prinz had snapped at him, before Otto had knocked him out of the way and plunged the bread knife into him. Gabi also convinced him that, by killing Prinz and thus saving Dolfi's life while sacrificing his own, Otto had proved himself to be not wholly bad.

What she could not do was persuade him that his mother and the Albers had not purposely deceived him about his father. 'Why didn't they tell me?' he asked, time and time again. 'Why did they let me think he was a great man?'

'They probably thought they were being kind,' Gabi replied.

'If only they'd told me the truth . . .'

Dolfi never returned to Bergtal. After his release from hospital, with the help of Gabi's parents, he and Gabi moved to Frankfurt, where they found a small workshop for sale. Gabi's father bought the lease for their wedding present in September. A new sign went up over the doorway, reading: A. FELDMANN – AUTO REPAIRS. Feldmann was a common name and none of their neighbours or customers even thought of connecting the owner with the notorious Otto Tobisch.

At Christmas, Gabi announced she was pregnant and in the summer of 1964, she presented her husband with a son, the first of three children she would eventually bear him. She knew no better way of proving that she did not believe bad blood to be hereditary.

They never spoke about Otto and Gabi hoped that Dolfi had forgotten about him. But the days he and his father had spent together and his father's fearful revelations were etched forever on Dolfi's mind, gnawing into him like a canker.

Chapter 16

In the early summer of 1963, a tour of the Federal Republic by President Kennedy was announced, including visits to Frankfurt and Berlin. Both Jochum hotels were inundated with requests for rooms from business notables, politicians and the world press, including Mortimer Allen, whom Viktoria had not seen since a brief visit in 1961 when the Berlin Wall had gone up.

After galvanizing her staff in Berlin into a frenzy of preparation, Viktoria flew to Frankfurt. It was soon apparent that she need have no worries about the Jochum-Frankfurt being in readiness for the influx of important guests staying there during the presidential visit. As Eduard said, 'We never know when you may turn up unannounced, Frau Viktoria. Therefore, we are always at our best.'

'And the personnel situation?' Viktoria asked.

At the time that the Berlin Wall had gone up, West Germany had already been suffering from an acute labour shortage and, when the Wall had stopped the flood of refugees from the Soviet zone, workers had urgently had to be recruited from elsewhere. A lot of the staff at Jochum hotels now, cleaners, chambermaids and kitchen menials, were 'guest workers', mainly Italians, but also Turks and Greeks, who were pouring into Germany to earn more money than they could ever hope for in their own impoverished homelands.

They brought with them problems the West Germans had not encountered with German refugees, the obvious one being that of language, but also, especially in the case of the Turks, a totally different religion and alien traditions. Integration into the West German way of life was not easy for the foreigners and often extremely frustrating for their employers and fellow workers.

The guest workers were given equal employment rights, but

363

no rights to citizenship or participation in local or national government. If, after ten years, they wished to apply for German citizenship, they would be allowed to, but West Germany was very reluctant to grant dual nationality.

Not that this appeared to pose any immediate problem. Most guest workers were single people, interested in earning as much money as possible as quickly as possible, so that they could return home as soon as possible.

'We're making slow progress,' Eduard replied. 'The Italians aren't bad, but the Turks are a real problem. What with praying to Mecca and religious taboos about washing – I could tell you stories which would make your hair stand on end. And some come from such primitive backgrounds, they have absolutely no idea how to behave in civilized surroundings . . .'

Viktoria sighed. It was the same problem everywhere.

Next day, Mortimer arrived. It had been Viktoria's sixty-ninth birthday a few days earlier and he brought with him a big bouquet of red roses. 'As a token of my undying love and admiration,' he said, presenting them to her.

She returned his kiss with very real affection. She might not see him for years, but their friendship was immutable. No matter what tests it was put to, it remained as strong as ever.

That evening, over dinner, he remarked, 'Well, I see your old friend Tobisch has at long last shuffled off this mortal coil in a satisfyingly unpleasant manner.'

'Yes, and there's something very strange about him, that I must tell you. One of the newspapers showed a snapshot of him taken some time ago in Syria. For days after I saw it, I racked my brains to try and recall where I'd seen it before. Then, suddenly, it came to me. I hadn't seen the picture. I'd seen the man himself. Only he didn't call himself Tobisch, but Tobler. He was the building foreman at the Jochum-Hamburg. Can you credit it, Mortimer? He was working on my hotel! I remember him well, because he dropped a scaffolding pole just where I'd been standing a few moments earlier. If I hadn't moved, it could well have killed me.'

'If it was Tobisch, that was probably his intention.'

'I think it was. He disappeared the next day and nobody ever saw him again.' She paused. 'I remember Norbert telling me that

364

he originally arrived in Luebeck with some kind of introduction from Werner.'

'Werner ran the Kraus steel works next to Tobisch's camp. They were colleagues. After the war, men like that helped each other out. That's how so many Nazis escaped. However, if Werner did help Tobisch, he must have regretted it many times since, particularly with the growing support for the neo-Nazi cause.'

'I simply don't believe all this about neo-Nazism,' Viktoria objected. 'There will never be a Nazi revival in Germany.'

Mortimer gave a deep sigh. 'I'm not so sure. One hears distressing stories about refugees from the Soviet zone being treated as second-class citizens, and more recently about discrimination against guest workers. That's how Hitler started, Viktoria. Sometimes I fear that, thirty years on, history is already about to repeat itself . . .'

The following evening, Werner and Dr Schulte arrived at the hotel to join a party of bankers, businessmen and financial journalists who were attending a dinner hosted by Bruno von der Eschenbach in a private banqueting room. Forty-six now, Werner was rapidly balding and his figure had become almost gross, although his well-tailored clothes disguised much of his bulk. He greeted Viktoria condescendingly and Mortimer with frigid politeness. He had neither forgotten nor forgiven the fact that the American had witnessed his humiliating arrest at Castle Waldesruh, all those years ago.

However, when Bruno invited Mortimer and Viktoria to join them for aperitifs, Werner had no alternative but to adopt a more gracious attitude. Mortimer Allen's occasional and extremely perceptive articles in such papers as the London *Times* and the *New York News* were greatly respected in German business circles and it was generally considered unwise to offend him.

The conversation immediately turned to the subject of Kennedy's visit, with those present very divided in their opinions of the American President. 'What worries me is the growing American intervention in Vietnam,' Dr Schulte said. 'I have a feeling that the Americans hope to succeed where the French failed and, if they do, we'll find ourselves with an even more potentially explosive situation on our hands than we did during the Korean War or the Cuban missile crisis last autumn.'

'Decisions of this kind shouldn't be left in the hands of one as young as Kennedy,' another man opined.

'I disagree,' Werner said. 'Intelligence, diplomatic skill and political ability are not the sole prerogative of the old. There are too many old men in charge of the world, not least among them Khruschev, Adenauer and de Gaulle.'

Dr Schulte laughed. 'If I'm right, Kennedy's the same age as you, eh, Werner? Well, I'll have you know that there's not much difference between my age and Khruschev's and I certainly don't consider I'm past it.'

'Herr Kraus has a point, however,' Mortimer interjected unexpectedly. 'I'm seventy and I must confess to having moments when I feel my age. I'm not as tolerant or as flexible in my attitude as I used to be, and I'm sure my reactions aren't as quick.'

'Tolerant isn't a word I would ever have used to describe you, Herr Allen,' Bruno remarked, with a smile which took away the barb in his words.

Mortimer grinned appreciatively. 'But without old men like Adenauer and de Gaulle, who, whatever you may think of them, are not lacking in courage, not only Europe but the whole world would be a different and not necessarily better place,' he said, neatly bringing the conversation to an end, as the *maître d'hôtel* came to announce that dinner was ready.

European and trans-Atlantic unity were very much in President Kennedy's mind when he addressed the people of Frankfurt. He called for an Atlantic partnership, in which burdens and decisions could be shared. And he stressed the need for a united, democratic European community.

But the high point of Kennedy's tour took place on 26 June in Berlin. All schoolchildren were given the day off in honour of the occasion and many shops, offices and factories were closed. With Chancellor Adenauer and Mayor Brandt, Kennedy toured the streets in an open car, receiving the homage and gratitude of the hundreds of thousands of Berliners who turned out to greet him, many of them breaking through the police cordons and tossing flowers at him. At Checkpoint Charlie and at the Brandenburg Gate, the cavalcade stopped at the Berlin Wall, which was now starting to be daubed with murals and political graffiti. Then it made its way to the town hall at Schoeneberg where, Mortimer told Viktoria afterwards, over a million people were gathered, and Kennedy made the pronouncement which was to endear him for ever in the hearts of all Berliners: 'All free men, wherever they may live, are citizens of Berlin. And therefore as a free man I take pride in the words: "Ich bin ein Berliner".'

When, a scant five months later, on 22 November 1963, a special news bulletin announced Kennedy's assassination, Viktoria stood stock still in her bedroom, where she was changing for dinner, then she sank slowly down on a chair. Kennedy – the young man who had inspired them all with such hope – was dead . . .

The event cast into a shade all that had happened in the intervening months: the days Viktoria and Mortimer had spent together in Berlin after the Kennedy tour; Adenauer's eventual, reluctant retirement and Erhard's succession to the Chancellorship; and the resignation of the British Prime Minister, Harold Macmillan, his position deeply undermined by the 'Profumo Affair'. All these things, so important at the time, faded into insignificance with Kennedy's death.

Tens of thousands of students made their way that evening to the town hall, mourning the young man with whom they had so identified. In windows throughout the city, candles burned.

The square outside the Schoeneberg Town Hall was renamed the John F. Kennedy Platz.

In December, there was a sudden, apparent easing of the restrictions between East and West. For the first time since the Wall had gone up twenty-eight months earlier, West Berliners were allowed to visit relatives in East Berlin. Dr Vogel once again came to West Berlin and Holger Busko met him at Dr Stange's offices in the Bundesallee and pleaded on Stefan's behalf.

The East Berlin lawyer said that enquiries had revealed that Stefan was not only alive, but that the GDR government might be prepared to consider his release in return for a suitable ransom payment. Putting the tragedy of Kennedy's murder behind her, Viktoria prepared to celebrate Christmas with greater hope than she had known for a decade.

In the mean time, Senta had started work at the Jochum-Frankfurt. Although she had passed her degree with flying colours, Viktoria was determined not to make the same mistake with her grand-daughter as she had with Lili, and Eduard was given exact instructions concerning her. During her first year, Senta was to work in every department, so that she was familiar with all aspects of the hotel. Then, if she survived this probationary period, she could take her place as a management trainee, in whichever area she seemed most suited. She might be family, but she was to be given no preferential treatment.

So Senta cleaned rooms, made beds, peeled potatoes, learned silver service, trained to work the switchboard and was eventually allowed to assist the reception manager. She put on no airs and graces, but worked as hard as any of the other staff, and she was quickly accepted as an equal.

As she and Eduard got to know each other, they became good friends. Sometimes their mealtimes would coincide and they would eat together in the kitchen, after the rest of the staff had finished, and while the kitchen hands washed up and prepared for the next meal, they would talk shop.

By then Senta knew the story of Eduard's flight from East Prussia and the death of his parents. He had no family and seemed to have few friends. She could not imagine why, at the age of thirty-three, he was unmarried. By any standards, he was a good-looking man, with his broad, blond features, and he had a quiet, pleasant personality. 'I think he had an unhappy love affair,' one of the receptionists told her. 'He never dates anyone. In fact he hardly ever leaves the hotel.' If that was the case, Eduard never hinted at the identity of the girl who had broken his heart.

Senta was certain he was very lonely. As General Manager he could not become too intimate with his colleagues. But, because she was a Jochum, he felt able to confide in her to a certain extent.

When Senta had first arrived at the hotel, Eduard had been shocked by her likeness to Lili, but over the months he had

368

grown to realize their similarity was only skin-deep. She was far less volatile than Lili, far less prey to her emotions and, as a result, even if she did not exercise the same fascination over him, he somehow found her easier to be with. He could talk to Senta about subjects which Lili would have found boring. Already, Senta cared deeply about everything that went on in the hotel. Lili, he was forced to admit, would long since have tired of doing her work, but Senta never complained. On the contrary, she found every new experience interesting and rewarding. In his reports to Viktoria, he had only good to say about her.

Eduard was not the only man at the Jochum-Frankfurt to be attracted to Senta. Another of her conquests was Dino Cattani, a black-haired Neapolitan guest worker, with startling blue, long-lashed eyes and an irrepressible smile, who worked in the kitchens. Dino was attending a weekly German evening class and practised his developing language skills on anyone who would listen to him. He had no intention of returning to Naples, but informed Senta, 'I shall open an ice cream parlour in Frankfurt. When it is making much money, I shall rent *un appartamento bello* and my parents will come and live with me.'

Once, when they both had an evening off at the same time, Dino invited her to see *Tosca* and, to the embarrassment and amusement of the people in the neighbouring seats, wept unashamedly throughout most of the performance. 'That was marvellous,' he told Senta as they made their way out of the Opera House. 'It was like being in Italia again. Now I do not feel so homesick.'

When they arrived back outside the hotel staff entrance, Senta took his hand and thanked him for a lovely evening. He kept her hand in his and gazed deeply into her eyes. 'You are a very sensitive girl. I think I am in love with you.'

She thought he was going to kiss her and was half hoping he would, when voices sounded, the door opened and the moment was gone. And back in her room, she was glad that kiss had not taken place. She liked Dino Cattani, but she was still very conscious of the decision she had made while she was staying with Lili. She was not going to make Lili's mistake of wearing her heart on her sleeve.

Next time Dino invited her out, this time to a meal at an Italian

369

restaurant on his birthday, she thanked him, but refused. His hurt was very apparent. 'It's because I'm a guest worker, isn't it? I'm not good enough for you?'

'That's not true,' she assured him, appalled that he should think such a thing, although she understood why. Guest workers were treated very much as second-class citizens in the Federal Republic, just as she and her parents and other refugees from the Soviet zone had been in earlier years. Unable to tell him the real truth, however, she had to find another reason he would accept. 'It's just that I don't think it's very sensible to try to mix one's private and working lives. Friendship is one thing – but if we became too emotionally involved, it could lead to bad feeling . . . Our careers . . .'

She had hit absolutely the right note. Dino's career was more important to him than anything else, even love. His ego still intact, his expression brightened. 'Maybe several of us could go to the restaurant,' he suggested. 'Then there can be no gossip, no misunderstanding.'

And that was what happened. Six of them, Dino and another Italian, a German commis, Senta, a Hungarian chambermaid and a Greek barmaid, celebrated Dino's birthday together.

Senta's friendship with Dino Cattani aroused an unexpected feeling of jealousy in Eduard and he even toyed with the idea of inviting her out himself. But he could not forget Lili. Ever since he had learned that her marriage with Norbert had broken up, he had clutched at the hope that she would return and finally realize how much he loved her.

Then Lili herself forced the situation. She wrote to Senta that she was at a loose end for Christmas, and Senta suggested she came to the hotel.

After a year and a half of living in the Kleinwalsertal, the novelty of Lili's existence was wearing off. That summer she had become friends with a mountain guide, a strong, bronzed young man, who had shared her pleasure in walking and initiated her in the skills of rock-climbing. In due course, he had taken to coming back to her house with her and ended up spending the night with her. Then, when the summer season ended, he had departed.

Although Lili had entered into the affair with her eyes fully open and no thought of establishing a permanent relationship, she was shaken when he left. As, day after day, the mountains were shrouded in cloud and the first snows began to fall, she realized that Senta had been right. She would always love the mountains, but she no longer wanted to live in them. Even the coming winter sports season held little attraction. She was twenty-six, an age when most of her contemporaries were either well embarked upon fine careers or married with young families. But Lili had nothing. She was young, beautiful, very lonely and extremely bored.

She arrived at the Jochum-Frankfurt on Christmas Eve. From the window of his office, Eduard saw her drive up, took a deep breath and went to meet her. It was over seven years since they had last met, after her disastrous affair with Volker Busko had ended and Viktoria had sent her to Hamburg.

Lili saw him standing in the doorway, very formal in a dark grey, pin-striped suit, the smile on his face relieving the severity of his attire, and ran towards him, as he had, in the past, seen her run towards Norbert. Then she was in his arms and exclaiming, 'Eduard! It's been ages! I was trying to work out on the way here how long it's been. Five years . . . ?'

Before he could respond, Senta appeared and Lili let go of him to embrace her. 'Come inside,' Senta said. 'It's freezing out here. Did you have a good journey? Oh, it is good to see you again! You haven't been here before, have you? We've put you in Grandmama's room. I'll show you the way. One of the pages will bring your luggage.'

Eduard watched them go: Lili in a three-quarter length fur jacket with a big, fluffy collar, her hair piled high on her head in the latest bouffant style, emphasizing her heart-shaped face and huge, dark-lashed eyes; Senta, shorter, sturdier built, her features less fine-boned, her hair tied back in a ponytail, her clothes far less expensive and less fashionable.

Apart from her appearance, Lili had not really changed. She still retained a capacity for simple pleasure, and was thrilled when Eduard allowed her to decorate the trees in the restaurant and ballroom and arrange the table decorations, seeking his approval for her achievements. She had brought carefully wrapped gifts and watched impatiently while they undid them to make sure they liked the contents.

'She reminds me in a way of Peter Pan,' Senta remarked fondly afterwards. 'I don't believe she'll ever grow up.'

That observation, Eduard reflected, perhaps best summed up Lili. For all her glamorous life, she remained engagingly naive and unsophisticated.

Perhaps, he tried to convince himself, that was why she was unaware of the depth of his feelings towards her. She would tease him, take his arm and give him the occasional, affectionate little kiss, but all these things she did as she had always done, more as if he were her brother than a potential lover. To make matters worse, she told him quite a lot about her affair with Jeremy and her marriage to Norbert, apparently quite unconscious of how these details hurt him. When he hesitantly asked about her plans for the future, she merely shrugged. He longed to take her in his arms and declare his love, but something always stopped him.

On New Year's Eve, Monika and Hans, awkward in hired evening clothes, came from Worms for the ball. Because Senta was too busy to spare much time for them, Lili took them under her wing, sat with them at dinner and saw them settled in the ballroom. They were not the easiest people to get on with. Both had acquired a set, middle-aged attitude, and were still highly critical of life in the Federal Republic, comparing it unfavourably with their recollections of Fuerstenmark. After only a short while, Lili found their conversation extremely tedious.

The band started to play the Beatles' hit 'I Want to Hold Your Hand.' Lili stifled a yawn. She knew she looked beautiful that evening, in a simple cream dress which flared from the hips, with matching gloves and shoes, and a pearl choker round her throat. Surely someone among the mass of other guests must ask her to dance?

At that moment, she sensed a figure standing beside her. She looked up to see a distinguished, immaculately dressed man, with lightly tanned skin and dark hair silver at the temples. It was a face she knew she ought to recognize, but could not place. 'You don't remember me, Lili?'

372

She shook her head. 'I'm sorry.'

'Bruno von der Eschenbach,' he said and lifted her fingers to his lips.

Of course . . . 'I do beg your pardon.'

'It doesn't matter. It's a long while since we met.' He smiled and the skin around his eyes crinkled most attractively. 'I admit to being unaccomplished in modern steps, but would you like to dance?'

She could have wished salvation to come in a rather different form from Aunt Vicki's business partner, but escape of any kind was welcome from Senta's parents. She took his hand and allowed him to lead her onto the floor, where he belied his words by proving himself a surprisingly expert jiver, although not indulging in the acrobatics of some of the other dancers.

After three numbers, she was slightly out of breath, but their exertions appeared not to have affected Bruno von der Eschenbach. Although considerably older than herself, he apparently possessed a young man's stamina.

'Some refreshment, perhaps?' he suggested and, placing his hand lightly in the small of her back, he guided her towards a table at the opposite end of the room from where Hans and Monika were sitting.

When they had both been served with champagne, he admitted, 'I was watching you for quite a while before I felt I had to come to your rescue. I can't remember ever seeing anyone quite so beautiful looking quite so bored.'

As Lili had instinctively liked him the first time they met, so now she felt drawn towards him again, but in a rather different way. On the occasion of their last meeting, however, she had been a 19-year-old student and had categorized Bruno as a contemporary of her aunt. Now she was a woman.

Again, he gave that disarming, crinkling smile. 'Are you still living in Munich?'

'Hasn't Aunt Vicki told you?'

He shook his head. 'The relationship between your aunt and myself is strictly business. We seldom discuss personal matters. I know you are no longer married to Norbert Kraus, but only because I saw your divorce mentioned in the paper.'

'I've been living in the Kleinwalsertal. Do you know it . . . ?'

Eduard stood at the entrance to the ballroom, apparently making sure that his guests were enjoying themselves and that the staff were carrying out their duties efficiently. But all he saw was Lili gazing into the eyes of Bruno von der Eschenbach. Heavy-hearted, he turned and walked away.

The following evening, Bruno took Lili out to dinner in the country. His chauffeur drove them in the Eschenbach Bentley. 'I did wonder whether, after your divorce, you might become involved in the hotels,' Bruno commented, as they glided through the wintry countryside. 'If I remember correctly, you worked at the Hamburg hotel after you left college.'

Lili still found it difficult to believe that Aunt Vicki had not discussed her with him. 'That didn't work out very well. After a few months I went to England.'

'Really? I didn't know that. What were you doing there?'

It appeared he had been telling the truth when he had said that he and Viktoria seldom discussed personal matters. He knew nothing about her experiences in London or about her brief fame as a fashion model. 'I'm sure you were extremely successful,' he said. 'You have the face and figure. Why did you stop modelling?'

There was something about Bruno which invited confidences. To Lili's own amazement, she found herself telling him about Jeremy and Major Harrison-Browne. They had reached the restaurant by then and ordered their meal from an obsequious head waiter, who insisted on addressing Bruno as *Herr Graf* at every opportunity.

When Lili had finished describing her reception at Tillbridge Manor and her shock at Joyce Allen's revelations, particularly her father's involvement in Luftwaffe bombing raids, Bruno was silent for a long time. Then he said, 'I was in the Luftwaffe, too. I knew your father. Of course, I was considerably younger than him, but at the time of the Battle for Britain we were both stationed in France. He was a man I admired tremendously and I was deeply upset when he died. The Air Ministry said it was an accident, but we were all sure it was suicide. Goering drove him to it. Your father and Goering had both flown in the Richthofen Wing during the First War, but Goering ignored old friendships when he achieved power.' He looked at her quizzically. 'You hardly remember your father, I imagine?'

Lili shook her head. 'I was four when he died . . .'

'He was a hero, a very brave man, who preferred death to dishonour.'

'Yet he took part in the destruction of Warsaw, Rotterdam, London . . .'

'He was bitterly opposed to bombing raids on civilian targets. That was one of the main reasons he and Goering fell out. Sepp Nowak was a fighter pilot. Above all, he was a flier.' For the next hour, Eschenbach told her what he knew about her father and gradually Lili began to form a picture of him: a slight man, with tilted, laughing eyes, who had devoted his life to flying, and had died under mysterious circumstances on the Russian front.

'I think it was his death as much as anything which opened my eyes to the disastrous path down which Hitler was leading us,' Bruno said. 'Until then, I, like so many others, had blindly obeyed orders. Suddenly, I realized that someone had to act, to stop him. Unfortunately, we did not succeed . . .'

'You were part of the 20th July plot to kill Hitler?'

'I played a very minor role,' he said, dismissively.

By the time they arrived back at the Jochum, Lili felt as if the door to the past, which Viktoria had kept so resolutely shut against her, had finally been opened. For the first time, her father had started to become real and a man whose memory she could respect and love.

Bruno remained ten days at the Jochum-Frankfurt. During the daytime, he attended meetings in the city. In the evening, he took Lili out to dinner and, during their conversations, other aspects of the past also began to come clear. Of course, there were many details of her family's life with which he was unacquainted, but he had known the people and could describe them in the context of their time. In a way, it was like opening a photograph album which had, until then, been filled with images of people who had only shadowy personalities. Suddenly, they became living entities.

Above all, Lili started to understand the background to her own upbringing. 'Put yourself in Viktoria's position,' Bruno

375

said. 'Wouldn't you have put your little niece's safety and health first?'

'But I didn't see it that way,' Lili sighed. 'Why didn't she explain things to me?'

'You were only a child. Even if she had been able to explain, you wouldn't have understood.'

'I wasn't a child when she sent me to Hamburg.'

'You must admit now that she was right about Volker Busko?'

Lili frowned. 'How did you know . . . ?'

'If you remember, you persuaded me to buy one of his paintings.' Bruno smiled. 'Incidentally, I don't know if you've followed Volker's career, but he went to America, where he's making quite a name for himself. That picture could turn out to be an investment.'

'You still have it?'

'Of course. I bought it because I liked it. It's hanging in my study at the Alte Hofburg. When you come, you'll see it.'

Lili did not question his assumption that she would one day go to the Alte Hofburg. Already she knew theirs was destined to be more than a fleeting friendship.

On his final evening, they dined at an hotel in Koenigstein in the Taunus hills and, after their meal, they wandered, arm in arm, through the hotel park. Around them, the night was very still. Their breath steamed in the wintry air. 'If anyone had asked me, a couple of weeks ago, whether I would ever fall in love again, I should have laughed outright,' Bruno said. 'I would have said that I am fifty-seven, far too old, experienced and disillusioned. Yet I would have been wrong.' He stopped and turned to Lili, placing his hands on her shoulders. 'During the last few days, you have captured my heart.'

And you mine, Lili wanted to reply, but he did not give her time to respond. Instead, he kissed her very gently on the lips. Then he took her hand and said, 'Let's go back to the car. I don't want you to catch a chill.'

During the journey back to the hotel, they did not speak. Out of the chauffeur's view, their hands remained entwined. From time to time Lili felt Bruno glance at her and the pressure from his hand increased.

376

She knew what was going to happen when they returned to the Jochum. He would take her up to his room and they would make love. Briefly, she considered the idea of saying no, but she knew she would not.

How many other women, she wondered, had he seduced with the same sweet words? And what had happened to them afterwards? Did he see her as a swift conquest, a one-night stand, an interlude in his hectic life? And yet, she was already certain something far deeper existed between them. In a strange way, she felt as if she had known him for years. Despite the difference in their ages, they had so much in common. They shared the same tastes, they liked the same books, art and music, they found the same things amusing. The attraction between them was not just physical, but spiritual.

Outside the hotel, the chauffeur opened the car door and let her out, then hurried round to Eschenbach's side of the car. Bruno put his hand under her elbow, gave a swift, questioning smile, then nodded.

In his bedroom, a chambermaid had turned on the bedside light and turned back the bedclothes. Eschenbach gently helped Lili out of her coat. Then, his voice husky, he said, 'I love you, Lili Nowak.'

And suddenly she was sure that he meant what he said, that they were not empty words, that he did love her. His arms folded around her, holding her tightly to him and she pressed herself against him, letting her body tell him that she loved and desired him every bit as much as he wanted her.

He was different from any of her previous lovers. Perhaps because he was older, he found no need to assert or prove himself, but took his pleasure in giving pleasure to her, playing her body with a virtuoso skill, bringing her to such a shattering climax that she felt she was flying through the sky, laughing and crying from the sheer, utter glory of it.

When she awoke in the morning, it was to the music of Mozart. Bruno had already completed his toilette and was sitting on the edge of the bed, wearing a burgundy coloured, silk dressing gown. 'You are even more beautiful asleep than awake,' he said, reaching to the bedside table and handing her a glass of champagne. 'Today I am going to Hamburg. I shall

377

be away for a week. While I am gone, I want you to think about your feelings towards me. If you decide that you love me, then I would like to ask you to marry me.'

Before she could say anything, he continued, 'I am deliberately giving you time, because I don't want you to make a decision you might later regret. As you know, there is no guarantee of happiness in any marriage, and certainly not where one partner is thirty years older than the other. You must consider what you will feel like in ten, twenty years' time, when I am in my dotage and you are in the prime of life. But I hope there will be compensations. As my sons Konstantin and Leonhard take over more of the business, I'll be able to spend more time with you. I can offer you a lifestyle which I think you will enjoy, a beautiful home, travel, arts – and love . . .'

Lili opened her mouth to speak, but he held his finger to her lips. 'No, don't say anything now, my dear. Just do as I ask and think my proposal over while I am away and give me your reply when I return.'

There was nothing to think over, no decision to make except the obvious one. When she was with Bruno she felt happy and complete, in a way she had never felt with anyone before, not even with Norbert in the early days of their marriage. Yet, as the week went by and she heard nothing from him, she began to wonder if their time together had been a dream. She longed for some sign from him, a telephone call, a letter, a telegram, a bouquet, something to reassure her that the events of the last few days had really happened. But Bruno kept his word and made no attempt to influence her.

In the end, unable to contain her secret any longer, Lili took Senta and Eduard into her confidence, one evening over supper. Eduard went very pale as she made her announcement, while Senta asked incredulously, 'He wants to marry you?' Then she said, 'I understand how you feel. It's all happened so suddenly. It seems too good to be true, doesn't it?'

'Yes,' Lili admitted. 'I suppose that's it. It's the sort of unlikely thing that happens in films, not in real life.'

'But that's the kind of person you are, Lili. You attract unusual situations. I can't imagine you living in a flat, doing the shopping, washing and housework, with two-point-four children and a husband who goes out to work every morning at exactly the same time.'

'Neither can I. But in a way, that's what I'd like. I'd like to be married to someone ordinary like Eduard, someone utterly safe and reliable.' She turned to him and gave a rueful smile. 'But I know that would never work. I love you dearly, Eduard, but we'd drive each other crazy within a couple of weeks. You'd get fed up with my restlessness – I should get annoyed with your predictability. After a while I'd be having an affair with someone like Bruno – and you'd be wanting a divorce.'

What little colour was left in Eduard's face drained completely from it, but Lili did not notice. 'I don't think it matters that Bruno is so much older than me. He doesn't look his age and he certainly doesn't act it.'

'All that really matters is whether you love each other,' Senta said.

'Yes,' Lili said softly. 'I love Bruno. And he loves me . . .'

In an unusually harsh voice, Eduard said, 'Then you'd better marry him.'

Startled, Senta glanced at him and, suddenly, everything fell into place. The fact that he had never married. The feeling of heightened excitement she had sensed in him since Lili's arrival. There was a sudden, sharp pain in her heart. Then, almost immediately, she felt a deep pity. How Eduard must have suffered all these years being in love with Lili, and how he must be suffering now, knowing – once and for all – that his feelings would never be reciprocated.

Lili and Bruno were married in April 1964 in the private chapel at the Alte Hofburg. Lili had fallen in love with the Alte Hofburg the moment she set eyes on it. A beautiful Gothic building, with high, steep roofs and half-timbered walls built around a central courtyard massed with flowers, its ancient, mellow rooms, with their warm, worn furniture, it emanated a sense of tradition and tranquillity. Unlike many ancestral homes, the Alte Hofburg was not a museum, but a real home. It seemed to welcome and respond to her.

So, too, did Bruno's two sons who, despite Bruno's assurances to the contrary, Lili had feared might disapprove of the marriage.

Not that, as Bruno pointed out, it really concerned them. Both were married now, with children of their own. Konstantin lived near Frankfurt and Leonhard in Munich. As for any fears that their inheritance might be threatened, Bruno's lawyer had drawn up a marriage contract, in which Lili was well provided for in the event of Bruno's death through Ricarda's legacy and Bruno's own interest in the Jochum hotels, but which ensured that the Eschenbach estate passed to his children.

The other person from whom Lili had expected opposition, although Bruno was again convinced otherwise, was Viktoria. If she had objected to her other romances and her marriage to Norbert, Lili was certain her aunt would not like the idea of her marrying a widower over twice her own age, even if the marriage did mean a closer union of their business interests.

In this, however, she misjudged her. Viktoria, although she admitted misgivings at the disparity in their ages, liked Bruno immensely. She replied immediately to the letter Lili wrote announcing her engagement, wishing them both every happiness.

After the wedding, attended by Viktoria and Senta, Bruno's sons and their families, the couple spent their wedding night at the Alte Hofburg. Bruno woke Lili early the following morning, pulled the curtains wide and looked out at the clear blue sky with an expression of satisfaction.

When they had breakfasted, the chauffeur drove his Ferrari into the courtyard, leaving the engine running while a housemaid handed him two overnight bags, which he placed in the small boot. Bruno took Lili's hand. 'Ready?' he asked, and she sensed an air of boyish excitement about him.

'Driving a fast sports car is the next best thing to flying,' he said, as he expertly negotiated the winding hill roads.

Then they turned off the road and onto a small airfield and ahead of her she saw an old bi-plane. Bruno drew to a halt and on the side, in large letters, Lili saw painted her own name.

'It's my wedding gift to you,' Bruno said. 'I hope that, in flying, you will discover the spirit of your father . . .'

He could have given her no more wonderful present. Since her first flight from Berlin to Hamburg during the Blockade, Lili had flown many times, but her lasting impression remained that of the uncomfortable transport plane. It was during that journey that she had first begun to wonder what kind of man her father had been. Now, the final piece of the puzzle slotted into place.

Not only did she understand the love of flying which had dominated her father's life, but she discovered the sensations which Sepp had known, the wind streaming through the open cockpit, the smell of the exhaust, the rattle of the struts, the sheer freedom of the open sky, the utter exhilaration of being suspended between heaven and earth in a fragile aircraft. Nothing in the world Lili had ever experienced could compare to it, except being made love to by Bruno.

Lili's words, so bluntly honest, so candidly dismissive – *someone ordinary, someone utterly safe and reliable* – had cut Eduard to the quick. Yet at least he finally knew the truth. And he had the slight consolation of knowing he had not made a fool of himself in the process. Nobody, not even Lili, was aware how much she had hurt him.

The next few days had been hard. Bruno had returned from Hamburg. Lili had proudly displayed an engagement ring. Then they had both departed – where, Eduard did not want to know – and he had been left alone to come to terms with his fate. Lili loved him dearly, but . . . But she was going to marry Bruno von der Eschenbach.

Of course, it was possible that Bruno would die and leave Lili a widow and, within a few years, she would be free to marry again. She might then decide that dear, ordinary, predictable Eduard was the man with whom she wanted to spend the rest of her life.

She might. But, already, Eduard was not sure if he would want her. He loved her. That was something which would never change. But he did not want to be anyone's second – or, in Lili's case, sixth – choice. He still possessed more than a vestige of self-pride.

Senta watched as, with quiet dignity, he concealed his pain and disappointment. On Eduard's recommendation, her grandmother had decided to give her more responsibility and she was now working in the general office as his assistant, which

381

made things easier in some ways, but more difficult in others. She wished she could tell him that she had guessed his secret, but she knew this would be wrong. Like herself, Eduard was a very private person: he needed time to recover from the harsh blow Lili had dealt him. But when he did get over it, she would still be there.

She was wise enough, however, not to allow her life to centre totally around Eduard and the hotel. She worked long hours and had limited free time, but she used this to the best advantage, going for long walks in the forest or taking the hotel minibus into town, usually just to look at the shops, on other occasions to go to the cinema, the theatre or view an art exhibition. Often she went with a female colleague, sometimes with Dino Cattani.

Dino's command of German improved by the day and Senta had used her influence to get him promoted from the kitchen to the restaurant, where the head waiter spoke very highly of him. Now, Dino no longer dreamed of running an ice cream parlour, but of becoming restaurant manager at a Jochum Hotel. Although she knew he had a tough struggle ahead of him, Senta said nothing to dash his aspirations. On the contrary, she encouraged him.

One crisp, sunny afternoon, after it had been snowing for several days, she found Dino building a snowman on the lawn. 'It's wonderful,' he exclaimed. 'We don't have snow in Napoli!' Infected by his pleasure, she helped him, finding him a carrot for a nose, coal for the eyes and winding her scarf round the snowman's neck as a final touch.

When she came in, Eduard said, 'I'd rather you didn't become too friendly with guest workers. Management should keep their distance from the staff.'

Senta opened her mouth to object, then shut it again. At least he had noticed. After that, he started to pay her several little attentions, lending her books to read, joining her sometimes on her forest walks and even coming with her into town.

Then Lili's marriage took place, after which she became a frequent visitor to the hotel. Until then, when Bruno made his weekly visits to Frankfurt, he had come alone. Now, Lili accompanied him and, being Lili, did not contain herself to her suite or keep her happiness to herself. Within half an hour of

Bruno's departure for his office, she would arrive in the general office, where she would perch on the desk, swinging her long legs, telling Eduard, Senta and anyone else who might be in the vicinity all about herself, Bruno, the Alte Hofburg and the exciting things which had been happening to her.

The situation could not be allowed to continue. Eduard had already become tense and irritable, snapping uncharacteristically at the staff and being short-tempered even with Senta. Senta herself was feeling the strain. She knew Lili did not mean any harm, that she was probably lonely while Bruno was away and came in search of company, but Lili had already done damage enough and Senta was not going to allow her to do any more.

Meeting Lili in the foyer, she took her arm and steered her into the grounds. 'Lili, dearest, please don't misunderstand me, but although we love to see you, Eduard and I haven't time to chat. You know what it's like in an hotel. There's always one crisis or another needing to be dealt with. And when you're there, we simply can't get on with our work.'

Lili looked at her aghast. 'I'm sorry. I should have realized. I suppose that's the danger when you don't have a job yourself.'

They walked on a few paces, then Senta said, 'I know you and Bruno are very happy, but if you're not careful you're going to become very bored. Isn't there some way you can work with him? That way you could share his life in every sense.'

To her surprise, Lili did not laugh the idea off. Instead, she nodded thoughtfully. 'That might be the answer . . .'

The truth was, that although Bruno tried to balance business with pleasure and keep his promise to spend as much time as possible with her, it was easier said than done. Konstantin and Leonhard had taken over the day-to-day management of Eschenbach Estates, but Bruno still kept his hands tightly on the reins, as well as continuing his involvement with the many charities he supported. On average, he spent three days a week in Frankfurt. Once a month he went to Munich, where Leonhard was managing the brewery, and on other days, there were meetings to attend, functions to address and institutions to visit in different parts of the country. Lili was left with a lot of loose time on her hands.

Sooner than Senta had dared hope, her suggestion bore fruit.

The very next week, instead of remaining at the hotel, Lili drove into town with Bruno, spending the day at his office. In the evening, they attended a charity concert together.

Bruno was delighted when Lili asked if she could work with him, something he had hoped for but had not liked to suggest. Not only did she prove a very good social secretary, but an excellent hostess. Even more importantly, sharing his activities made her feel part of his life. With great satisfaction, he watched her develop and grow in self-confidence, finding untold pleasure and pride in helping her become a full person, and above all, giving her that vital sense of security she had always lacked. He was not just a husband and a lover, but a father figure, a role he had quite deliberately fostered, someone upon whom she could rely absolutely.

Lili, herself, had only one regret. She longed to bear Bruno a child.

But as one month after another passed, she was forced to accept the bitter truth that she would never become pregnant. Yet she had so much to fill her mind and her time, and she loved Bruno so much, that her childlessness began to matter less and less.

When Norbert's marriage to Lili had broken up, Reinhild had said, 'I knew it would never last. She was much too young for him.' Apart from Reinhild's insatiable appetite for all scandal attaching to her ex-husband and disapproval of everything he did, Norbert's remarriage and subsequent divorce meant little to his children. They had never visited his home in Munich. Sometimes, he came to Hamburg on business and took them out for the afternoon, but Lili had never been with him.

When Lili married Bruno von der Eschenbach, Reinhild had the additional satisfaction of saying, 'She's a little money-grubber. First she took in Norbert and got a large divorce settlement from him. Now she's married one of the richest men in Germany. Probably she's hoping he'll die and leave her his entire fortune. To think I felt sorry for her once! It just shows how mistaken you can be.'

However, no sooner had the excitement surrounding Lili and Bruno died down, than Norbert's name again hit the headlines with news of his third marriage, not to the raven-haired British beauty, Jill Grenville, for whom he had left Lili, but to a 20-year-old French film starlet called Désirée Daudet, who had sultry eyes, pouting lips and a phenomenal figure.

'I don't know what they have in common. They can't even speak each other's language,' Reinhild said in disgust, staring at a photograph in the *Bild Zeitung* of Désirée clad in a skimpy bikini which left little to the imagination. 'What can he see in a woman like that?'

Kris, who was eighteen and, unknown to his mother, had long since lost his virginity, whistled appreciatively. 'I'd have thought that was obvious.'

'Tristan!' Reinhild always called him that when he annoyed her. 'Don't be crude.'

Kleo frowned. Like Kris, she too was no longer a virgin. Last time Dieter had come to stay, they had found themselves unexpectedly alone in the house and seized the opportunity to go beyond petting and go to bed together. Nevertheless, the idea of her father and Désirée Daudet doing the same things as she and Dieter had done was somehow repugnant. But she was nothing if not fair. 'You know what the papers are like, especially the *Bild*. They probably picked that picture because it's sensational and she's really a very nice, decent young woman. I hope so, anyway.' But the fact remained that her father's third wife was only three years older than herself.

'I can't see what you're all making such a fuss about,' Helena commented. 'Father couldn't care less about us. Why should we care about him?'

'Of course he cares,' Kleo said. Reinhild always said, and Kleo believed she was right, that Norbert's desertion had hit Helena hardest.

The situation was exacerbated when, on the rare occasions that they saw their father, he clearly showed that he preferred Kris and Kleo to Helena. Unfortunately, Helena did not help herself. Whereas Kris had inherited his father's height and lopsided grin, and Kleo was very pretty, with her dark, springy curls and vivacious smile, Helena was not an attractive-looking girl. Her mid-brown hair was straight and lank, her eyebrows were unusually heavy and her nose was too long for her rather

385

angular face. Naturally serious and intense, she always seemed to be frowning, although, when she smiled, her features took on a certain, unusual charm.

At fifteen, she had reached what Reinhild called 'that difficult age'. She had her own very fixed ideas on virtually every subject, ideas which were inevitably diametrically opposed to her mother's. She was a member of Amnesty International and had become a vegetarian, causing a dreadful scene whenever her mother wore her prized mink coat; and, needless to say, she was a supporter of nuclear disarmament.

Whereas Kris would talk about cars and Kleo would find some general topics to tell her father about during their reunions, Helena usually managed to introduce some contentious social issue. Her pet belief at that time was that capitalist greed in the developed world was causing deprivation and starvation in the Third World and made no attempt to conceal the fact that she held her father personally responsible.

When Norbert laughed off her accusations and chided her for being too serious, the corners of her mouth would turn down sullenly and she would refuse to contribute any more to the conversation.

Perhaps if Norbert had been in more frequent contact with her, he would have understood her better. As it was, he simply said, 'I can't make head nor tail of the girl.'

On Kris's eighteenth birthday, Norbert had paid for him to take driving lessons and bought him a sports Mercedes. The very day he took possession of it, Kris crashed it into a traffic island. The car was a write-off, but Kris emerged uninjured except for the odd bruise, his confidence totally unimpaired. Asking him to be more careful in the future, Norbert gave him another one.

Reinhild was horrified. 'He could have killed himself,' she screamed at Norbert down the phone.

'He won't make the same mistake again,' Norbert assured her.

Kris himself was unrepentant. 'I took the bend too quickly, that's all. You'll have to get used to accidents, Mother. When I'm a racing driver, I'll probably spend more time in plaster than out of it.'

386

He was in his last year at school and could not wait to leave. Norbert had promised to send him to England on a racing driving course as a nineteenth birthday present and, if he did well enough, to buy him his own racing car. Reinhild dreaded the idea, but there was nothing she could do, except blame Norbert for encouraging him.

Kleo's ambitions were very different. For as long as she could remember, she had wanted to be a doctor. Kris's childhood illnesses had influenced her a lot and a stay in hospital to have her own tonsils removed, when she was ten, had given her an insight into hospital life which, far from lessening her ambition, had increased it.

Her mother tried to dissuade her. 'When I was young, attractive girls didn't think about careers,' she complained. 'We just wanted to get married.' She could not understand any girl putting a career before love and marriage. She certainly did not understand why her daughter should choose to enter a predominantly male profession, like medicine. But Kleo knew instinctively that this was her vocation.

Marriage, however, still played a part in her plans, but she had listened to enough accounts of her mother's own life to decide that marriage and pregnancy were not something to be rushed into willy-nilly. She and Dieter were both determined to be established in their chosen careers before they even thought about marrying and having a family, which meant at least another seven years to wait, by the time Kleo had left school and completed her six-year degree course.

Dieter did everything to encourage her. So, too, did her father, promising her moral and financial support when she commenced her studies and, in the mean time, sending her expensive tomes on medicine, which few other students of her age could afford.

But for Helena, Norbert could do little. If he offered her clothes or jewellery, she turned up her nose. If he gave her books, they were of the wrong kind. So, on her birthday and at Christmas, he sent her cheques, which Reinhild put into a savings account.

Gradually, once Eduard realized he had been relieved of

387

the intolerable emotional pressure of Lili's almost constant presence, he started to relax. One afternoon, he asked Senta, with studied casualness, 'Since we both have this evening off, would you like to have dinner with me?'

They went to a restaurant in Sachsenhausen and, afterwards, strolled arm in arm along the Main embankment. It was a mellow May evening and the chestnuts were in full bloom. 'Have you ever been to Paris?' Eduard asked.

Senta shook her head.

'It's a city I've always wanted to visit.'

'Me, too.'

They leaned against the railings and looked across the river to the cathedral and the Roemer on the opposite bank. At last, Eduard broke the silence. 'I don't quite know how to say this, so be patient with me, Senta. For a long time, I thought I was in love with someone, but now I've realized she wasn't really the person I believed her to be.'

Senta held her breath.

'I was a fool in more ways than one. Not only was I deluding myself about this other girl, but I was running the risk of losing the one person who could bring me happiness, who was so close to me that I simply took her for granted.' He turned and looked at her. 'Do you know what I'm trying to say?'

'Yes,' she said softly, 'I know.'

His hand reached out tentatively for hers and she clasped it. For a long moment, they gazed into each other's eyes, then he took her in his arms and kissed her. 'Senta, I love you.'

'And I love you, too, Eduard.'

They drove back in silence to the hotel, a silence filled with excited anticipation, with unspoken words of passion. After he had parked the car, he asked, 'Will you come to my room?'

She nodded, not trusting herself to speak.

During their long night of love, Eduard eventually brought himself to confess that it was Lili with whom he had been in love. Senta did not tell him that she already knew. It was better that the truth was out in the open. All she did permit herself to say was, 'She would never have made you happy.'

'Yes,' Eduard admitted. 'I know that now.'

The change in Eduard after he and Senta became lovers was

388

remarkable. He seemed to shed years overnight and completely lost his rather careworn expression. He ran upstairs two at a time and hummed when he made his rounds of the hotel. Staff morale, which had reached a low ebb with his dark moods, improved noticeably, although he and Senta were so discreet that nobody knew the reason for his sudden good humour.

Only Dino commented to Senta, 'I think Herr Eduard is in love.' And looked at her in such a fashion that she blushed.

Eduard soon discovered that Lili had lost her power over him. He could watch with equanimity as she went up to her suite with Bruno, secure in the knowledge that, when night came, he would have Senta in his arms. This final proof that the spell which had held him bound for so long was broken, gave him the confidence to ask Senta to marry him.

They announced their engagement on Viktoria's seventieth birthday in June. No news, except that of Stefan's release, could have given her greater pleasure. There had been many occasions when she had worried as to who would take over the hotels when she was no longer able to run them. Now her mind was set at rest.

Their marriage took place on Senta's twenty-fourth birthday on 10 September 1964. For their honeymoon, they went to Paris.

Chapter 17

Gradually, the conditions of Stefan's imprisonment had improved. The first two years had been spent in solitary confinement, although their torture had been mitigated, unknown to his captors, by the presence of the man in the next cell, whose messages in Morse had kept Stefan from insanity. But one day the taps on the wall had ceased. His fellow prisoner was gone. Had he been released? Had he been moved to another cell? Had he gone to his execution? Stefan had no way of knowing. He could only pray it was the former.

However, just when the loneliness again threatened to overwhelm him, Stefan was himself moved, to a cell which he shared with a succession of different inmates, mostly petty criminals, with none of whom had he anything in common. Yet even their company was preferable to solitude. His interrogations became self-criticism sessions, where he was fed propaganda and asked to review his past actions in the light of socialist thinking. But even these provided an intellectual stimulus and challenge.

Then, suddenly, in the autumn of 1964, his conditions changed dramatically. He was transferred to an upstairs cell, with a small window looking out onto the prison courtyard, permitted access to the prison library, given two hours' exercise a day and the quality of his meals improved beyond recognition. After his body had adjusted to the shock of fresh air and proper food, his gaunt frame gradually began to fill out. No longer was his head shaved, but his hair was left to grow. His warders became less bullying and he was given a small packet of mail, the first he had received since his imprisonment: letters from his mother, Udo Fabian, Mortimer Allen and other friends, the dates illegible and the contents heavily censored, but real communications from the outside world.

Finally, one day, he was taken up to the room, where he had

spent so many hours in interrogation. The same light shone in his eyes, disguising the identity of the SSD officer sitting opposite him, but, on this occasion, there were no questions and no self-criticism. Only the bland announcement that the GDR government had reviewed his twenty-five-year sentence and decided to free him early. Then he was handed two photographs.

The first showed a man and a woman, arm in arm, outside a building. The man wore a carnation in his buttonhole and the woman was carrying a small bouquet of flowers. She was Erika. A little older and plumper than Stefan remembered her, but still very recognizably Erika. Stefan stared mutely at the photograph. Their love affair seemed to have taken place in another life and he had long ago forgiven her for deceiving him.

The other was a family group. The same man was again present, standing, his hand resting on Erika's shoulder, and next to him was a younger man, with a marked family resemblance. Erika herself was seated and holding a baby. Her face wore a tender expression.

'Your friend married her next-door neighbour two years ago,' the voice said. 'He was a widow. That is his son. The baby girl was born just four months ago. As you can see, they are a happy family. However, if after your release you write anything detrimental about the GDR or reveal any of the circumstances of your time here, their happiness could find itself severely threatened.'

Then the photographs were taken away again and, in their place, Stefan was handed the clothes he had been wearing in November 1953, at the time of his kidnap.

It was dark outside when he was taken from the prison and put in a car. A blindfold was tied round his eyes. They drove for what seemed like hours. Finally, the car stopped and the blindfold was removed. The car drove onto a bridge and stopped again in the glare of spotlights. Armed soldiers converged around them. Another car came from the opposite direction and a man got out, carrying a small attaché case. Stefan's guard opened the car door. 'Out you get,' he said gruffly. The attaché case changed hands. Arms grabbed hold of Stefan and propelled him swiftly into the back of the other car. Then they sped away, towards the bright lights of West Berlin. A man leaned over from the front passenger seat, his hand outstretched. 'Congratulations, Herr Jochum. You're free.'

For a few days after Stefan's release, he was kept at the American Military HQ in Dahlem for de-briefing, during which Viktoria was able to visit him. Then he was allowed to go, free to start his life again.

He was thinner than he had been, but, according to the American army medical officer, in remarkably good health. Even his teeth had been well cared for. He was very pale, of course, and his hair was more silver than brown. But apart from such obvious symptoms of long-term captivity and the fact that time had taken more than its fair toll on him, his incarceration appeared to have told upon him less than Viktoria had feared.

'Everyone reacts differently when they come out,' the American medical officer advised her. 'Some want peace and quiet in order to adjust. Others are hyper-active. My guess is that your son is one of the latter. He was thirty-nine when the East Germans grabbed him. Now he's fifty. He's lost eleven vital years of his life.'

He was right. Stefan was desperately aware of those lost years. When Viktoria proposed they spend some time in the country for him to recuperate, he rejected her suggestion impatiently. 'I've just spent eleven years doing nothing. I want to get back to work again.'

Neither would he leave West Berlin, although he was advised to do so, in case he was taken hostage again. After spending one night at the Jochum-Berlin, he returned to his apartment in Wilmersdorf. It was exactly as he had left it, his books and papers just as he had last seen them. Viktoria had made sure of that, paying the rent and employing a cleaner to air the place and keep it clean.

Viktoria was naturally concerned about what had happened to him while he was in prison, but he refused to talk about it. She had assumed that he would welcome being reunited with his family and friends and particularly with his mother, as much as she had been looking forward to seeing him again, But he showed little interest in them or their lives during his absence.

392

The following weekend, Mortimer flew over from London. By then, Stefan had discovered the truth behind his sudden release. He knew the contents of that attaché case which had changed hands on the Glienicke Bridge. Instead of being grateful that the government had paid a ransom for him, he was extremely bitter. 'They shouldn't have paid to get me out,' he stated angrily. 'If I'd known, I would have refused to leave. I'd rather have served my full sentence.'

'Remember that nobody knew how you were,' Mortimer said. 'Until quite recently, nobody was even sure you were still alive.'

'But to pay for my release! That's simply playing into the Communists' hands. And, in the mean time, hundreds of thousands remain imprisoned who have no commercial value . . . This government is not only corrupt, but weak! I had hoped that, in my absence, something would have changed, but nothing has . . .'

And, to Viktoria's dismay, he repeated this line in press conferences and in his articles for *Aktuell*.

'I don't understand,' she told Mortimer, unhappily. 'Why is he so bitter against us, and not the East Germans?'

Mortimer sighed. 'My guess is that this is his way of asserting himself again as a person, and of hitting back against the horrors he has undergone.'

'But it's so hard, Mortimer. I love him so much, but he doesn't seem to need me at all . . .'

'You always hurt the one you love,' Mortimer quoted. 'Of course he needs you, Vicki. He needs all of us. But most of all, he needs time to adjust. For eleven years, he's been totally cut off from the rest of the world. Consider how our lives have changed during that time. In many ways, we must seem like strangers to him . . .'

'Perhaps I was expecting too much of him . . .' Viktoria conceded slowly. 'The main thing is that he is home, safe and well . . .' She felt angry with herself then for being unreasonably demanding. Love should not be conditional upon need. Love could not be bartered. You either loved somebody or you didn't. It was as simple as that.

*   *   *

393

Had it not been for Wolfram, it was unlikely that Erika would have known that Stefan had been freed, for the news was not reported in the GDR, and the Schwidinskis did not own a television, so they were unable to watch forbidden West German programmes. They were on the waiting list for a set and hoped that, by the time Karsten retired on his sixty-fifth birthday in 1969, their turn might have arrived.

But Wolfram's father-in-law was an electrical engineer and had been able to buy a set, under the counter, from a colleague. It was a simple matter for him to twist the aerial to receive West German programmes, a risk well worth taking to obtain an unbiased account of what was happening in the world.

Wolfram and Ilona had married in February that year and were living on the sixth floor of the same apartment block as Ilona's parents. Both had graduated successfully, Wolfram had completed his military service, and they now had good, if poorly paid jobs, Wolfram as a junior lawyer, and Ilona as a technician at a chemical plant on the outskirts of Leipzig, combining a full-time career with looking after a husband and running a home.

Fond though Erika was of Wolfram, she was not insensible to his defects. Although he possessed the same kindly, gentle nature as his father, he was not as considerate. Whereas Karsten helped with the housework, even doing the shopping on occasions, Wolfram left all domestic matters to Ilona. Ilona excused her husband by saying his work was very demanding, which was doubtless true, but so was hers. And during such free time as remained to her, she had to do her housework, washing, ironing, mending and join interminable queues to shop. Erika did what she could to help her, as did Ilona's own mother, but there was only so much they could do without interfering.

Most Sundays, Wolfram and Ilona came to see Erika and Karsten, and sometimes, when the weather was fine, they would go into the country, away from the grime and smog of Leipzig, but latterly, Erika's pregnancy and the birth of her daughter had curtailed these expeditions and they had stayed at home.

This particular autumn Sunday, however, was unseasonally warm, the sun bright in an unusually clear blue sky, and they went to the park, Karsten and Wolfram walking ahead, deep in low-voiced conversation, while Ilona and Erika, pushing Paula in her perambulator, strolled leisurely behind.

Apart from her everyday worries, Erika was happier than she had ever imagined herself being. Karsten was a gentle and considerate husband. Wolfram had grown to become more like her own son than her stepson, and Ilona more like a daughter than a stepdaughter-in-law. Paula – named, at Karsten's suggestion, in memory of Erika's father – was the crowning jewel in Erika's marriage. To find herself pregnant with her first child at the age of thirty-nine had come as something of a shock, but her pregnancy, although tiring, had gone smoothly, with fewer problems than those experienced by far younger women. And Paula, with her fair hair and blue eyes, just like Erika's, was a sweet-natured and undemanding baby, adored by her middle-aged mother, elderly father, grown-up half-brother and his wife.

In fact, it appeared that it would not be long before Ilona and Wolfram had a child, too, for, as they walked through the park that afternoon, Ilona confided that she was pregnant.

Erika expressed her delight at this news, but could not help feeling misgivings. For one thing, Ilona, always delicate, had looked ill ever since she had started work and developed a harsh cough, caused, Erika was sure, by the fumes she breathed in at the chemical works. She was also convinced Ilona did not eat enough, but tried to save money by scrimping on her meals.

But Ilona was thinking further ahead and was more concerned that after her baby's birth she would be able to continue her career. One great advantage of the GDR system was the provision of State crèches, enabling mothers to resume work very soon after their children were born, although the reason for the crèches was not altogether altruistic. As a result of the millions who had fled to the West, the GDR was still suffering a great shortage of manpower.

Karsten and Wolfram, however, had been discussing quite different subjects, as Erika realized that evening, after Wolfram and Ilona had returned to their own home. She and Karsten were sitting beside the stove, having their routine cup of coffee before going to bed, when Karsten said, 'I thought you would want to know that Stefan Jochum is free. Wolfram told me this afternoon.

He was watching a West German news programme at Ilona's parents the other night and saw him giving a press conference.'

Erika's sense of relief at Stefan's release was short-lived. 'I didn't think Wolfram knew about Stefan and me . . .'

Karsten frowned. 'No, I don't think he does. Certainly he's never said anything. I didn't realize until today, but he was involved with a group of students at university who were very concerned about human rights. Stefan Jochum became a symbol to them. Somehow or other, they used to obtain copies of his magazine. They identified with his ideas on militarism and peace and German unity. And Wolfram still belongs to an underground opposition movement . . .'

'Oh, I am sorry,' Erika sighed.

Karsten shook his head. 'It's not your fault, my dear. But it's still very worrying. If Wolfram is discovered . . .'

Erika tried to find a ray of comfort. 'Does Ilona know?'

'I don't believe so. Certainly, Wolfram didn't mention her in connection with his activities.'

'She's expecting a child. Perhaps, when the baby is born, Wolfram will come to his senses and realize he is wrong to endanger his family.'

Karsten brightened at this news. 'I hope so.'

'Why did Wolfram suddenly confide in you?' Erika asked curiously.

'I've been wondering that, too, and can only decide that he needed someone to talk to. He was very disappointed about what Stefan Jochum said on television. Apparently, he didn't once criticize our government, but kept blaming the West Germans for everything . . .'

Erika tried to imagine Stefan as he was now and how he must be feeling after eleven years in prison, but she could only remember how she had felt on her release: shaky, disorientated, above all, frightened of the damage she could do to other people. Stefan did not have quite the same problems: he was safely back in the West. Unless his sister and her family were still in Fuerstenmark . . . That was the only reason Erika could think of, which would explain Stefan's attitude – that he was trying to protect them . . .

* * *

396

The same inner core of strength which had fortified Stefan throughout his long incarceration sustained him during the months after his release. Whilst he was in prison, hope, above all, had kept him alive. Hope that in his absence, a new, gentler, more caring society would have evolved. Instead, he found his family more concerned than ever with materialistic objectives. The Cold War had accelerated, Germany had been divided by a Wall, and a new trade in human beings had developed, a trade in which Stefan himself had, albeit unknowingly, been a commodity. It was a bitter pill to swallow.

There were, however, some rays of comfort. Udo Fabian had retained the original integrity of *Aktuell*, and the publication's readership had expanded considerably, despite – or perhaps because of – the meteoric rise in popularity of right-wing newspapers, such as the *Bild Zeitung* and others owned by Axel Springer. There were still a large number of Germans who had learned the hard way that newspapers were more than capable of distorting the truth and wanted a publication in which they could trust.

Stefan's greatest source of consolation was Holger Busko, whom he discovered had campaigned untiringly for his release. He liked Holger from the moment they met, recognizing in him a kindred spirit, who had taken it upon himself to continue many of Stefan's causes, not only in the press, but among students and in the government.

It was Holger who said, 'Why don't you put behind you the circumstances of your liberation and concentrate on the future?'

It was Holger who brought Stefan up to date with events which had happened while he was away and explained the background to things which were taking place now. Viktoria told Stefan about Otto Tobisch's death, but it was Holger who told him about Heinrich Luebke being re-elected as President, despite allegations that he had been involved in building concentration camps during the war. 'You see, it still goes on,' Holger said, angrily. 'As you feared, the country is still run by ex-Nazis . . .'

From Holger, Stefan learned about the running battle between Khruschev and Kennedy, about Kennedy's death and his succession as President by Lyndon Johnson, and Khruschev's own recent demise from power and his succession by Alexei Nikolayevich Kosygin, after Khruschev's deteriorating relations with Mao Tse-Tung had threatened a Sino–Soviet War.

And, most frightening of all, Holger told him about the Vietnam War. Holger was vehemently against American intervention in the poor, trouble-ridden, partitioned Republic and deplored the manner in which Bonn was supporting the United States.

Often, the two men met at Stefan's flat, talking long into the night, and frequently they were joined by Holger's student friends from the Free University, including two whom Stefan had known when they were children – Dieter Duschek and Matthias Scheer. The growing student protest movement, he soon realized, was one of the most optimistic signs for the future. The students were strongly influenced by the American 'free speech' movement which had begun in the late fifties at Berkeley University in California and by Martin Luther King's civil rights movement.

'We believe in racial and social equality and we want peace,' Dieter Duschek informed Stefan earnestly. 'We're determined not to repeat the mistakes of our parents.'

'We'll fight with every means at our disposal for a new Germany – and a new world,' Matthias insisted. 'This war in Vietnam should be abhorrent to every right-thinking person. Germany should not be supporting it.'

As well as an escalation of the war in Vietnam, with horrific reports and pictures from the battlefields, civil war flared up in April 1965 in the Dominican Republic, in which the United States also intervened.

The students of Berlin again took to their streets and Stefan not only supported them in their denunciation of America and Bonn in *Aktuell*, but marched with them.

On the international arena, there seemed to Stefan, in those months immediately following his release, to be only one cheering event. That May, Queen Elizabeth II and Prince Philip came to Germany, the first visit of a British monarch for fifty-six years, since Edward VII had come to see his nephew, Kaiser Wilhelm II in 1909. Exactly twenty years after the end of

398

the Second World War, it was final evidence that Great Britain had forgiven Germany for two world wars.

Despite Ilona being considerably younger than Erika, her pregnancy was very much harder, partly due to her fragile build, but also because of the external pressures exerted upon her.

Six weeks before her baby was due, she was still getting up at five to do the washing or ironing before going to work, then queuing at the shops for items which would inevitably run out just when she reached the counter. Upon returning home, she had to contend with the household chores and prepare Wolfram's supper, although he kept unpredictable hours, often not leaving his office until ten.

That was what happened on the evening Ilona collapsed. She had carried the dustbin down to the courtyard and was returning up the dimly lit staircase, where half the light bulbs were missing and could not be replaced because there were none in the shops, when she suddenly came over faint. She reached out to grasp the banister, missed, swayed dizzily, then fell, jolting back down the stairs, until her inert body reached the landing. She was still lying there when Wolfram came home an hour later.

It was another half-hour before the ambulance arrived and, when they reached hospital, it was two hours before the overworked casualty staff could attend to her. By then, her labour pains had commenced.

For twelve hours, Ilona remained in labour, fluctuating between consciousness and unconsciousness. Rudimentary tests revealed that she was severely undernourished and suffering from a lung infection. Eventually, a surgeon, who had already been on duty all night, decided that, although the hospital possessed no premature baby unit, there was no alternative but to perform a Caesarian section.

Wolfram never saw his son, who was stillborn. But Ilona miraculously survived the operation, although she was extremely weak and haemorrhaging so badly that the surgeon held out little chance for her survival. 'If we possessed the necessary equipment and drugs, we might be able to save her,' he sighed wearily. 'But, as it is, Herr Schwidinski . . .'

The following day, septicaemia set in. Two days later, Ilona died.

The tragedy of Ilona's death affected Wolfram in many ways. He held himself greatly to blame for having ignored her state of health and having allowed her to work so hard. He could better have excused his inattention if it had been office work which had kept him away from home so much, for although he had told Ilona he was working late, he had been lying. Those hours had been spent at meetings of the underground '17th June Movement', the existence of which he had once hinted to his father, but kept secret from Ilona, not wanting to implicate her in his dangerous activities.

The irony was that, on the evening Ilona fell, the movement was in the throes of breaking up. It had been formed in August 1961, in angry reaction to the Berlin Wall, while Wolfram and his friends were still students. But although they had drawn up manifestos and held endless discussions, they were impotent to effect any of the changes they desired within the GDR, and the Wall prevented them from being able to contact any outside power, that might support their demands for political democracy and personal freedom.

Yet although Wolfram's membership of the '17th June Movement' had not only proved futile, but been indirectly to blame for Ilona's death, he could not regret the motives which had caused him to help found it. On the contrary, he was grief-stricken at Ilona's loss, but his overwhelming emotion was anger: anger at a so-called socialist system, which was so contemptuous of the welfare of its citizens, that a young woman of twenty-five could work and starve herself to the bone, and then not receive the vital medical treatment necessary to save the lives of herself and her unborn baby.

As he took part in Ilona's funeral, a bald ceremony at Leipzig crematorium, utterly devoid of religious or human sentiment, Wolfram made to himself a solemn vow that he would dedicate the rest of his life to seeing basic human rights restored in the GDR.

Major Rudolf Sommer of the Leipzig State Security Police watched Ilona Schwidinski's coffin disappear behind the shabby red velveteen curtains and tiptoed out of the crematorium into the hazy sunlight, leaving her family alone with their grief. Outside, he lit a cigarette and inhaled deeply, then got into his car. But instead of immediately driving back to *Stasi* headquarters, he sat for a few moments, trying to come to terms with his tangled thoughts.

Ilona Schwidinski had meant nothing to him as a person. His attendance at her funeral was simply part of the routine surveillance which he was employed to keep over the Schwidinskis, ever since he had been transferred to Leipzig just before Erika's release from prison, although his professional connection with them dated back to when, at Basilius's instigation, he had conducted his first interview with Erika in 1951.

Yet the circumstances of Ilona's death affected him deeply. He could not help feeling that it was a grave indictment against the State that she should have died as she had.

Not that he could communicate his feelings with anyone. He had no wife or children, no family, in fact, except for Basilius, and his relationship with his cousin had become less strong, since he had come to Leipzig. But even if they had remained closer, Rudi would have found it hard to confide his thoughts to him for, over the years, he had come to realize that he and Basilius represented two very different kinds of socialist. Both came from impoverished backgrounds in working-class districts of Berlin, but whereas Basilius had long left Wedding behind him, Rudi could never forget the dingy tenements in the Prenzlauer Berg when he had grown up, even though while he had lived there he could not wait to get away.

Now he had escaped, however, now he lived in a comfortable apartment and was provided with his own car, he felt guilty about those he had left behind. Although his mother was dead, whenever he went to Berlin, he made a point of visiting her old neighbours and his childhood friends, and never ceased to be dismayed at the conditions in which they still lived, conditions which he saw mirrored every day in Leipzig.

Nor had Rudi forgotten the true socialist principles on which he had been brought up, and there were many occasions when he felt these to be sorely lacking in this postwar German so-called Democratic Republic, to the extent that he privately sympathized with young people, like Wolfram Schwidinski, who rebelled against the Wall which separated them from their fellow Germans and denied them the basic freedoms, which had earlier been denied Rudi and his generation under the Nazis. The GDR was as much a totalitarian state as Germany was during the Third Reich, and Ulbricht as great a tyrant as Hitler.

That was why, despite being aware of the 17th June Movement since its formation, Rudi had hesitated to do anything about it, although if it had not broken up, he would soon have had no alternative but to order the arrest of its members.

Yet for all that, he continued to serve in that most feared of organizations: the State Security Police. For one thing, it was easier said than done to give up a position towards which one had worked hard and long, for the sake of one's conscience. But there was another reason, which sounded pretentious, even to his own ears. He had joined the SSD because of Basilius. He remained because he had seen how power could pervert. If such a thing were possible, he wanted to ensure that, within his small sphere of influence, justice was carried out.

The mourners began to leave the crematorium chapel. Rudi stubbed out his cigarette and turned the ignition key in his Trabant. Then, amidst a cloud of blue smoke from his exhaust, he chugged through the grounds to the exit.

Who, he suddenly found himself wondering as he drove away, would attend his own funeral and mourn his passing?

That summer of 1965, Kris Kraus embarked upon his career as a racing driver. His medical history, particularly the collapsed lung and his childhood stay in the Swiss sanatorium, ensured that the medical board turned him down for military service. He had left school with poor examination results and, failing to find what his mother called a 'proper job', appealed to his father to keep his promise to send him to Jim Russell's Racing Drivers' School in England. There, he demonstrated a natural talent for driving, quick reflexes and a complete lack of fear. 'If the kid doesn't kill himself, he could be a champion,' was the verdict of his instructor, when Kris left.

Of his three children, Norbert identified with Kris the most. His son had inherited his own disregard for convention, he was

402

popular with the opposite sex and had a devil-may-care attitude to life. When Kris returned from England, Norbert gave him a flat of his own on one of the Landgut estates in Hamburg, where he swiftly established a very satisfactory bachelor existence. He also bought him a silver-grey, single-seater Cooper from John Cooper's factory in Surbiton, which was shipped to Hamburg. Furthermore, he agreed to pay for the Cooper's transport to race meetings, his son's entry fees and two mechanics.

One of the mechanics Norbert had known for a long time: Egon Weber, a service manager at Daimler-Benz in Stuttgart, a man in his mid-fifties, who had himself raced in his youth, driving a Mercedes on the legendary Avus and Nuerburg circuits in the 1930s, until a serious accident, when his car had overturned and he had broken both legs, which had put an end to his racing career. Despite repeated applications to join Alfred Neubauer and Rudi Uhlenhaut in the company's postwar racing programmes, he had been consistently passed over in favour of somebody younger. Then fortune intervened and Norbert asked if he would like to manage Kris's future. Egon leaped at the chance.

At Kris's first race, the long Eifel hill climb, he made fastest time in his class, beating the existing record by a handsome margin. It was a glorious sunny day and Norbert and Désirée were there to witness his triumph. Norbert shook his hand and congratulated him, while Désirée, in a tight-fitting ribbed sweater and a skirt which was at least six inches above the knee, embraced him in a far from stepmotherly fashion.

They had rooms at a nearby hotel and celebrated Kris's victory at a dinner during which the champagne flowed copiously and Désirée flirted with her stepson. Egon drank sparingly, but the rest of them indulged themselves to the full. When they went up to their rooms, Norbert's face was florid and he was staggering slightly.

Kris was woken during the night by a knock at his door. He pulled on his dressing gown and opened the door to find Désirée, clad in a lacy négligé, standing in the corridor. Waving her hands expressively, she pouted, 'I cannot sleep.'

Letting his dressing gown fall away to show his erection, Kris demonstrated to his father's wife that, although her husband

403

might fail her, his son was more than capable of rising to the occasion.

Kris's next race was a minor event in France at Clermont-Ferrand, which business commitments in Germany prevented his father and Désirée from attending. Instead of racing the clock, Kris was racing other drivers. Over-confident of his success, he ignored Egon's orders to go to bed early and did a round of the town's nightspots, arriving back at his hotel as dawn was breaking. Instead of the first place he had hoped for, he came fifth.

He found solace that night in the arms of an extremely well-endowed French girl. When he eventually got up the next morning, he was exhausted, but his self-esteem had been restored.

Egon looked at him disparagingly as he entered the restaurant and handed him a cup of sweet black coffee. 'It's a pity,' he said. 'You're a good driver, but you're never going to make it to the top if you continue like this. You can be Caracciola or Casanova. But you can't be both. You've got to make up your mind. Which is it going to be?'

Kris sipped the coffee and grinned. 'How about a compromise, Egon? We'll do it your way before the race. But, once the race is over, I'll decide how I spend the night.'

'And one other bit of unsolicited advice. Don't crap on your own doorstep, Kris. For reasons best known to himself, your father is a generous man, but he's no saint. If he ever discovers what happened that night at Nuerburg, you'll find yourself homeless, carless, jobless and moneyless.'

Kris stared at him open-mouthed. 'How do you know ... ?'

'I'm no fool, lad. No matter how much they try to disguise it, when a man and a woman have had sex together, they give off a certain aura. When you and Frau Kraus came down to breakfast that morning, I knew what had happened. Don't try it again. Leave other men's wives alone, especially your father's.'

When Kris left home, he left a big hole in the lives of his mother and sisters. For all his laziness and general inconsiderateness, he had been a man about the place. After he was gone, the all-female household soon began to get on each other's nerves. Reinhild was in her early forties and approaching the menopause. The departure of her son from the maternal nest and Norbert's third marriage to a girl little older than his own children, had convinced her that her life was now on a downhill path. She took less care with her appearance, developed a host of imaginary ailments and found constant fault with her daughters, especially Helena.

Helena's attention that summer was riveted on the so-called 'Auschwitz Trial' which had been taking place in Frankfurt and ended that August.

Reinhild refused to read about it. She was sick and tired of these recurring reminders of the past.

Helena absorbed every detail in the papers. 'How could you have let these things happen?' she asked her mother accusingly. 'Why didn't you do something?'

Reinhild tried to explain that she had known nothing about concentration camps, let alone the atrocities which had been committed in them.

But Helena did not believe her. And at that point she found a reason for the antagonism she had so long felt towards her parents, her teachers and, for that matter, all members of their generation. They had made the horrors of Auschwitz possible. They were the enemy. Such people were capable of anything. They had sent Jews and Slavs to the gas chambers and felt nothing. No wonder they did not care about the hurts they inflicted upon her.

She began to identify with the victims of the Holocaust. Deserted by her father, unloved by her mother and misunderstood by her teachers, she saw herself as a social outcast.

Kleo did not allow the constant bickering between Helena and her mother to upset her. Instead, she quietly resolved upon the way she wanted her life to develop and set about achieving her own ends which were, quite simply, to study to become a doctor and live very much nearer to Dieter.

Dieter was now in his final year at the Free University in Berlin and determined to get a job in Holger Busko's practice when he graduated.

Holger had become a dominating influence in Dieter's life. Although his busy political life meant he could only give occasional lectures at the Free University, he still involved himself in student protest movements. It was due in great part to him that Dieter was a leading member of the SDS, the Socialist Student Union.

Reinhild's daily paper was Axel Springer's *Bild Zeitung*, Germany's most popular tabloid newspaper, and she had absolute faith in the right-wing views it expressed. As a result, she believed that the students were Communist agitators, and that the United States were right to intervene in the Dominican Republic and Vietnam, in order to stop the spread of Communism.

Helena despised the Springer press. Whenever Reinhild quoted the *Bild Zeitung*, she opposed its views, ranting against Springer, his publishing empire, his immense wealth and the media power he wielded, dismissing everything written in his newspapers as perfidious lies. To make matters worse, she annoyed her mother even further by persistently playing, at very high volume, the Rolling Stones' hit record, 'I Can't Get No Satisfaction.'

The Rolling Stones were the musical phenomenon of the decade, so far as Helena was concerned, expressing feelings of which she had long been aware but had never been able to convey. Kleo preferred groups like the Beatles, but Helena could see nothing special about dirges like 'She Loves Me, Yeah, Yeah, Yeah' or 'I Want to Hold Your Hand.' The Beatles were soft, nice young boys, of whom even her mother almost approved. But the Rolling Stones were altogether different, with their wild appearance, their long hair and tight jeans, and the savage, insistent rhythm of their music, which seemed to strike some deep primeval chord within her. The anarchic lyrics and the music of 'No satisfaction' expressed everything Helena felt about herself and the world she inhabited.

That winter, in cities throughout the world, there were demonstrations against the Vietnam War. In Berlin, students stuck posters on the walls of America House by the Zoo Station bearing the slogan AMIS GET OUT OF VIETNAM, tore down the Stars and Stripes and staged a sit-down, singing the 'Internationale' and chanting the name of the Vietcong leader, Ho Chi Minh. Helena endorsed the anti-Vietnam War protests wholeheartedly, going around the house chanting, 'Ho-Ho-Ho Chi Minh' and wearing 'Ban the Bomb' and 'Mao Tse-Tung' badges.

At Christmas, Dieter told Kleo, 'I know you were thinking of going to Hamburg University, but if you want to be with me, you'll have to come to Berlin. For one thing, I'm not leaving Berlin just to be conscripted. And for another, Holger Busko's promised me a job.'

Reinhild put her foot down, when Kleo told her this. 'I forbid you to go to Berlin. I'm not having you mixed up with all that student riff-raff.'

However, Kleo, for all her warm-hearted, easy-going manner, possessed an underlying streak of rebellion, in its way every bit as strong as Helena's. Kris had left home at eighteen, without any parental opposition, and she did not see why she should not do the same. When her mother continued to insist that she remained in Hamburg, Kleo appealed to her father, who responded by telephoning his ex-wife and saying, 'For God's sake, Reinhild, you can't tie the girl to your apron strings for ever.'

A fortnight of stormy exchanges followed, at the end of which Reinhild, outnumbered by her ex-husband and both her daughters, eventually gave in, although not without tears and recriminations, and, in the early spring of 1966, Kleo went to Berlin to enrol at the Free University.

Afterwards, Dieter took her for lunch. Then they strolled, hand in hand, through the Tiergarten, up the Street of the 17th June, to the Brandenburg Gate, partially concealed behind the Wall. On its Western side, the Wall was no longer drab concrete, but decorated with graffiti and murals in a courageous attempt to make an attraction out of an obscenity. From its Eastern side, armed border guards looked down on them, stony-faced.

Kleo could not help but feel rather afraid and clutched Dieter's hand tightly. The Soviet presence was very near and very real, bearing in oppressively on her. But Dieter presumably now took the Wall for granted. Certainly he seemed more concerned about student problems.

'Students should have much more say in the administration of the University,' he was saying. 'Only two students sitting on

407

the Council is iniquitous! And the professor–student ratio is far too high! You'll see for yourself. There are often as many as eighty students to a professor . . .'

He continued to grumble as they walked along under the shadow of the Wall to what had once been Berlin's city centre, the Potsdamer Platz, little changed from how it had been at the end of the war, a desolate, derelict area of ruined buildings and makeshift shacks. They came to the fragmented façade of all that remained of the old Anhalter Bahnhof, once Berlin's main railway station. They passed Checkpoint Charlie and had a glimpse of East Berlin. Finally, in the Kochstrasse, Dieter pointed to a nineteen-storey building towering over the Wall. 'That's the Springer building.'

'Whatever one thinks of Springer's politics, his building seems a rather brave, defiant gesture,' Kleo commented. 'It must have an amazing view over East Berlin.'

Dieter stared at her in surprise, then stood for a few moments in silent contemplation of the Wall. 'What you've just said is very interesting. I've never thought about it before. All of us who have been in West Berlin for any time have got used to the Wall. We don't think much now about what goes on on the other side. I wonder if one of the worst things the Wall has done is to cut off our view . . . ?'

He put his arm round her. 'Darling, I'm sorry. I seem to have been getting very heavy. This is supposed to be a celebration. Can you forgive me?'

She nestled her head against his shoulder. 'There's nothing to forgive. It's all very interesting. This is new to me, remember. And it's about to become my life . . .'

Upon receiving the news that Kleo would be starting at the Free University in May, Norbert sent her a large cheque and suggested she live at the Heiligensee cottage. But Kleo did not want to live in remote splendour, she wanted to be part of University life. So she thanked her father, put the cheque into a savings account and moved into hostel accommodation, where she was fortunate enough to be given a study-bedroom of her own.

Not long after she had commenced at the University, Norbert

came to Berlin. They sat on the verandah of the cottage at Heiligensee, looking out across the gardens to the lake, sipping lemon tea and talking generally about their own lives. After a while, Norbert asked, 'Are you still seeing young Duschek?'

'Yes, of course. But he's in Frankfurt at the moment, taking part in a Vietnam Congress organized by the SDS, the Socialist Student Union.'

'I thought he had a job now, working for that Busko fellow?'

'He's still very involved in the student movement.'

Norbert sighed. 'When I was a young man I was more interested in having a good time than in politics. Does he often do this sort of thing? Go off to Frankfurt and leave you here alone?'

'I can't help noticing that you haven't brought Désirée with you to Berlin,' Kleo pointed out.

'Yes, er ... To tell the truth, things aren't going all that well between myself and Désirée. In fact, we've split up. She met some young up-and-coming French film director who offered her a part in a film and so she went back to France.'

Kleo looked at him and suddenly saw him as he really was: an expensively dressed, middle-aged man with a receding hairline and a paunch. Poor Father, she thought, all his life he's been a playboy, but now he's starting to grow old. He has three marriages behind him, but still he hasn't found happiness. I wonder if he ever will?

'Do you know what Désirée told me before she departed?' he continued. 'After Kris's first race at Nuerburg, she and Kris slept together. To be honest, that shook me more than the news that she was leaving me.'

'Kris did what?' Kleo was outraged. 'After all you've done for him, he went to bed with Désirée?'

'Yes, that was what hurt me most. I may have been an absentee father, but I've tried to do my best for Kris, as I have for all of you. But, not content with taking my money, he had to have my wife too.' He gave a deep sigh, then forced a smile. 'Now, what would you say to a spot of dinner?'

They ate at an old, traditional, village inn: fresh asparagus swimming in brown butter, followed by green eels with dill sauce and potato purée, and washed down with beer. Kleo told her father about her course, her fellow students and the lecturers, trying to make her descriptions light and amusing, to relieve his heavy mood.

They talked about Reinhild and Helena. They discussed the Vietnam War, China, Russia, Cuba and America, and Kleo admitted to certain misgivings about Dieter's part in the student protest movement. 'As a result of the Vietnam demonstrations, the University Senate has forbidden any political organizations or events to take place within the University. That's certainly wrong. It makes a mockery of the whole concept of the origins of the Free University. But I must admit that sometimes I wonder if Dieter isn't in danger of neglecting his career for the sake of his principles.'

Norbert was impressed. It seemed that his elder daughter had more than her share of common sense. 'I gather Stefan has also become involved with the student movement, since his release from prison. Do you see him at all?'

'I don't, but Dieter does. He admires him tremendously. Above all, I believe he sees Stefan and *Aktuell* as bulwarks against the Springer Press.' She paused. 'I feel sorry for Aunt Viktoria. She's never actually said so, but I think she's very disappointed in Stefan. He virtually ignores her now. And Monika seldom comes to see her. It's rather sad. But at least she has Senta. Have you met her? She is Monika's daughter. She and her husband, Eduard, run the Jochum-Frankfurt. They've just had a baby girl. Aunt Viktoria's thrilled. It's her first great-grandchild.' She paused, then said, 'But you must know all this . . .'

Rather shame-faced, Norbert admitted that he had not seen Viktoria for a long time. 'She was very upset when Lili and I got divorced. Somehow, I . . .'

'Father! If Aunt Vicki was upset with you, I'm sure she's forgiven you now.'

Later, they wandered back to the cottage, arm in arm. 'I'll go and see Aunt Vicki tomorrow,' Norbert promised.

Kleo reached up and kissed him. 'Thank you. And thank you for coming to see me. It's funny, but for the first time in my life, I feel as if I've started to get to know you.'

* * *

410

After Kleo left home, the relationship between Reinhild and Helena worsened rapidly. Reinhild tried not to antagonize her daughter, she tried not to say things which would annoy her, she tried to take an interest in her activities and understand her point of view, but it seemed that, no matter how careful she was, Helena was always spoiling for a fight.

'Children go through these difficult stages. Don't worry, she'll get over it,' her sister-in-law, Else, said soothingly, when, in desperation, Reinhild poured out her troubles to her on the telephone.

'She's been going through this difficult stage for as long as I can remember,' Reinhild stated, exasperatedly. 'And far from getting over it, she's getting worse. Else, I'm at my wit's ends. I don't know what to do with her. She shuts herself up in her room for hours at a time, listening to those dreadful records of hers.' From Helena's room came the sound of the Rolling Stones' latest hit, 'Paint it Black.' 'She smokes. She drinks. And she won't work. I've had terrible complaints from her school . . .'

Else murmured words of sympathy.

'And you should see her clothes! I don't know when I last saw her in a dress. All she wears are blue jeans, which she shrinks in the bath. And sloppy pullovers down to her thighs. And her hair! Her fringe almost covers her eyes. It looks really ugly.' Reinhild lowered her voice slightly. Not that she was really afraid that Helena would hear her above the din the Rolling Stones were making, but the girl had a talent for making an unexpected appearance at the most inconvenient moment. 'Then there are her friends. They come to see her and walk past me to her room as if I don't exist. I don't know where she meets them, but they're most uncouth. Scruffy, dirty, with long hair . . .'

From Else's end of the telephone came the clamour of girlish voices. 'Excuse me a moment,' she said. Reinhild could hear her asking, 'Yes, Margarete, what is it? Goodness! Is that the time?' She came back on the line. 'Reinhild, I'm sorry, but I have to take the twins to their ballet class. Brigitta, where are your shoes? Oh, that's all right. Reinhild, dear, I do hope you sort out your problems soon. I hope my two turn out better, but, of course, you never can tell . . .'

No, Reinhild thought bitterly, as she said a quicker goodbye

411

than she had intended, and put down the phone. Else's twins would not turn out like Helena. They were far too good-natured. She had seen them earlier that year, at Norbert's mother's seventieth birthday party. Helena had refused to go with her, Kleo had been in the middle of exams, and Norbert had apparently forgotten all about the event. But Werner, Else and the nine-year-old twins had been there. The two little girls had sat to either side of their grandmother, identically dressed, their round faces beaming angelically under haloes of blonde curls.

It was so unfair, Reinhild reflected. Why should Werner and Else be blessed with such sweet children, when she had such difficult ones?

She made her way across to the sideboard, where she poured herself a brandy. It was a habit she had got into, since Kleo left home. She had never been a great drinker, but now she found that a couple of drinks during the evening and another just before she went to bed helped keep her nerves steady and ensured a night's sound sleep.

From Helena's room, came the strident, rasping voices of the Rolling Stones insisting, 'Get Off, Get Off, Get Off of My Cloud'.

Reinhild didn't know the half of it. She certainly didn't know about Hartmut Senger. Helena had made sure of that. She couldn't bear the idea of Reinhild criticizing Hartmut. And she couldn't stand the thought of Hartmut seeing the bourgeois home in which she lived.

Helena had met Hartmut Senger at the traditional Easter peace rally. She had been striding along through the centre of Hamburg, carrying her placard and shouting, 'Amis out of Vietnam!', 'Mao Tse-Tung!' and 'Ho Chi Minh!', when the figure in front of her had unexpectedly stopped and she had careered into him, sending him flying to the ground and giving him a rather nasty bang on the head. She had dropped her placard and fallen to her knees, to see if he was all right, causing the marchers behind her to pile into each other. The police lining the route, waiting for the slightest hint of trouble as an excuse to break up

412

the rally, had surged forwards. 'Fascist pigs!' Helena muttered.

Her victim had staggered to his feet. 'Don't antagonize them,' he said.

'Why not? They provoke us.'

He gingerly touched the back of his head, picked up her placard and started to walk on. 'Because it's a waste of energy.'

'I didn't mean to bump into you. I hope I didn't hurt you.'

'It was my fault. I wasn't concentrating.'

'Shall I take my placard back?'

'No, I'll keep it. I don't fancy being whacked round the head a second time.'

If anyone else had said that, Helena would probably have snatched the placard angrily and stormed away. She hated criticism, even if only implied. But there was something about this young man, with his long, dark hair, parted in the middle, his pale, aesthetic face, and his widely-spaced, hazel eyes, which prevented her. For a few moments, she joined the other demonstrators chanting loudly, 'Amis out of Vietnam!' 'Amis out of Vietnam!' Then, swallowing her pride, she said, 'My name is Helena Kraus.'

'I'm Hartmut Senger.'

After that, he seemed to become immersed again in his own thoughts. Unlike Helena, he did not shout slogans, but loped along in silence. Once or twice, Helena tried asking him something, but he did not hear her. Even during the speeches at the end of the rally, he paid little notice, apparently oblivious to the speakers' stirring words. Then, just as the meeting broke up and everyone started to disperse, he asked Helena, 'Would you like a coffee?'

'Why did you bother to attend, if you were so disinterested?' Helena demanded, as they settled down on a café terrace.

'Because I support the cause. But I can't help feeling that words alone aren't sufficient to bring about change. They have to be accompanied or followed by action.'

'What kind of action?'

'That's what I've been thinking about. It has to be something that makes people realize what it's like in Vietnam, having

413

American bombs raining down upon them, something more effective than words and photographs.'

'The Germans, of all people, should know what it's like to be bombed.'

'They should, but they choose to forget. Do your parents ever talk about the war?'

'No,' Helena replied. 'If I ever mention the war to my mother, she immediately changes the subject. I don't know about my father. I hardly ever see him. My parents are divorced, you see.'

'I never knew my father. He was killed at the very end of the war, just before I was born.'

So they were both fatherless. Helena warmed towards him. She also saw that he had a very personal reason for detesting war. 'I'm sorry,' she said.

He shrugged. 'Don't be. I'm not. He only had himself to blame. He was a soldier. He helped make the war.' He reached in his pocket, took out a tin of tobacco, some cigarette papers and a roller and rolled a cigarette. 'Do you smoke?' he asked.

'Is that an ordinary cigarette?'

He glanced around, saw they weren't being observed and said, 'It's hashish.'

'I've never smoked hashish.'

'Then better not start now. It sometimes has a strange effect the first time.' He lit his cigarette, inhaled deeply on it, keeping the smoke down for a long time, then, very slowly exhaled, his eyes semi-closed.

Helena lit one of her own Marlboros and, for a few moments, they talked about their families. Her mother's relations were all dead, Helena explained, but her father was Norbert Kraus, head of Landgut AG and a grandson of the notorious Baron von Kraus. She detested the Kraus family from the bottom of her heart. When she was younger, her mother had made her go to family parties, but now she refused to have anything to do with them. 'All they can think about is money!' she said bitterly.

'You mustn't be so angry,' Hartmut said. 'Anger is a waste of emotion. And it makes you look ugly, quite different from how you looked after you hit me with your placard. Then

414

your eyes were full of compassion and you looked quite beautiful.'

Nobody had ever before told Helena she looked beautiful. The experience completely took away her breath.

Hartmut gave a dreamy smile. 'My mother lives in Hamburg,' he said. 'Unlike your mother, she's married again. Her husband is Erwin Senger. You've probably heard of him, he owns Senger Electrics. My two older brothers work there. The family wanted me to join the company when I left school, but I have no intention of spending the rest of my life assembling radio and television sets, washing machines and hair driers. I went to University instead. I'm at the FU, the Free University, in Berlin.'

Helena had succeeded in composing herself. 'My sister's at the FU. Do you know her? Kleo Kraus? She's studying medicine. Her boyfriend's Dieter Duschek. He was a law student.'

'Rather serious guy, dark-haired, with spectacles? Yes, I know him. He's a big noise in the Students Union. I joined the SDS when I first started at the FU, but I don't have much to do with it now. I don't like unions. As soon as people are organized, they lose their identity, as well as any individual thought process. I believe in spontaneity.'

'What are you studying?' Helena asked.

'Sociology and social psychology. But I may give it up. It's a waste of time. Nobody understands the need for social change. So long as we continue to follow established, traditional, capitalist social orders, society will continue to deteriorate.'

'What do you mean?'

'Capitalist society is based on possession. *My* money, *my* home, *my* car, *my* husband, *my* wife, *my* children. From the moment we are born, we belong to someone, we are prisoners. I disagree with the whole bourgeois concept of marriage. Take your family as an example. Because your mother married a Kraus, you are tied to people with whom you feel nothing in common. You are filled with guilt, tensions and anxieties not of your own making. You are caught in a trap from which you cannot escape, simply because your father once coupled with your mother. Men and women aren't by nature monogamous,

415

but Western law decrees that they should be. Your father is certainly not monogamous. But he's rich. He can afford to get divorced. Most men and women can't. They can't pay the legal fees and the alimony. They have to suffer – and their children have to suffer – for the rest of their lives.'

'What alternative is there?' Helena asked.

'To live as I and my friends do, in a commune, where everything is shared, possessions and responsibilities, where nothing belongs to any one person, including children. That is the true meaning of Communism.'

It was as if Hartmut had opened Helena's eyes to the possibility of a whole new way of existence. 'I've never thought of that before. I've always thought of Communism as being just political.'

'That's the fate of many ideologies. Their origins are forgotten as a result of the manipulations of devious, power-seeking men. People are often shocked when I describe myself as a Communist, especially since my father was killed by the Russians, but I don't want the sort of Communism they have in the Soviet Union. I want to help create the kind of society Marx and Christ originally conceived, the kind of Communism which is practised in China.'

Helena met Hartmut several times before he returned to Berlin, but she never visited his home or he hers. At their last meeting, he took her in his arms and pulled her close to him. 'You're free to join us at the Commune, if you want to. Just turn up.'

That summer, Helena's school work suffered even more, as she devoted herself to the study of the social and political problems threatening to engulf Germany. On an old typewriter she discovered in the attic, she wrote a series of articles which she submitted to one newspaper and magazine after another, one or two of which were accepted by extreme left-wing publications, but most of which were rejected, including those she sent to Udo Fabian at *Aktuell*, who replied, saying, 'If you want to be published by *Aktuell*, you must concentrate more on facts and less on propaganda.'

Helena was not discouraged by the rejections. On the contrary, she dismissed Udo Fabian and his fellow editors as old fogies, who were not prepared even to consider the opinions of the young.

One day, in mid-June, Reinhild discovered a half-finished article in Helena's typewriter, next to a book by Herbert Marcuse called *One-Dimensional Man*. Helena had forbidden her to enter her room, but Reinhild could not abide the dirt and disorder and seized every opportunity when Helena was out to go round it with a duster and carpet sweeper.

Helena was so secretive that it was the first time Reinhild had seen any of her essays into journalism. 'It is youth's mission to lead the workers of Germany, our country's most exploited force, in revolutionary uprising,' she had written. 'The workers are so ignorant and so indoctrinated that they believe themselves to be free. But they are not, any more than youth is. Although we have material comforts that those who live in totalitarian states do not enjoy, we are every bit as subjugated, politically and spiritually, as our counterparts in the Soviet zone. Factory bosses think they can buy off the workers with money. Parents believe that by giving their children all the luxuries they did not have themselves, they can assuage their guilt for the past . . .'

Reinhild pulled the sheet of paper out of the typewriter and took it across to the window to read it again, trying to understand what it meant, not realizing that the ideas had been taken from Marcuse's book. That was how Helena found her, when she burst into the room. Her grey eyes glittering with rage, she demanded, 'How dare you intrude in my room? How dare you pry into my private affairs?'

For once, Reinhild was too perplexed and troubled by what she had read to be intimidated by her daughter. 'What's all this about a revolutionary uprising?' she asked. 'And what do you mean about parents?'

At that moment, the resentment against her mother which had long simmered in Helena turned into a seething hatred. 'It means just what it says,' she replied contemptuously. 'You believe that provided you give us everything we need, you can buy our love and forgiveness.'

Reinhild shook her head. 'I've never tried to "buy" your love and certainly not your forgiveness, whatever you mean by that. I've only ever wanted the best for you, for all of you.'

'The best!' Helena spat out, derisively. 'The best would have been to tell me the truth about yourself and Father and the past. The best would have been to try to right the wrongs of the past, instead of pretending they never happened. The best would have been to give us love, instead of worrying about what the neighbours would think . . .'

'Helena, what do you mean?'

'Even if I explained, you wouldn't understand. God, how I hate you . . .'

Reinhild felt tears welling to her eyes, tears of hurt, incomprehension and self-pity. Rather than let Helena see them, she left the room. Helena slammed the door behind her.

When Reinhild got up in the morning, Helena's bedroom door stood open. Upon closer inspection, she found some of Helena's clothes gone from her wardrobe, books from the bookshelf, her toothbrush and flannel gone from the bathroom and the typewriter gone from her desk. Where it had stood was a note reading, 'I've gone to Berlin. Don't expect me back – ever.'

Chapter 18

Reinhild assumed that Helena had gone to Kleo, but when she finally got through on the telephone to her elder daughter that evening, Kleo said she hadn't seen or heard from Helena for weeks. Reinhild started to panic. She rang Norbert and demanded that he went to Berlin to look for Helena, but after Reinhild had been forced to admit that she and Helena had quarrelled, he said that Helena was old enough to look after herself and would probably come back after a few days. In desperation, Reinhild rang Viktoria, asking for her help. Ever practical, Viktoria suggested she reported Helena's disappearance to the police.

The last thing Reinhild wanted to do, however, was involve the police and have to divulge all sorts of personal details to officious strangers, as well as having to admit that she did not have control over her own daughter. She consoled herself with the thought that Helena had not simply vanished. There was the note. Her disappearance had been, apparently, premeditated.

On 22 June, there was a meeting of the Free University Senate. While the Rector and professors met inside the Senate Room, some 3,000 students gathered outside the windows to debate the same contentious problems as were being discussed inside – increased student participation in the running of the University, a reduction in the professor–student ratio, the introduction of seminars, as well as lectures . . .

For the most part, the students were in good humour. They considered their demands legitimate and hoped for a conciliatory attitude from the Senate. However, they had put up for long enough with being ignored and repressed and, when the Rector and his colleagues refused to enter into their open discussion, they moved into the University building and staged a sit-in strike. As night drew in, various professors and outsiders,

419

including Holger Busko and Stefan Jochum, who were on the side of the students, arrived at the University and the sit-in turned into a teach-in.

It was while Stefan Jochum was talking that Dieter, seated at the front of the hall, with an overview of the students, noticed Helena. She was sitting, cross-legged on the floor, her chin propped on her hands, next to a second-year sociology student whom Dieter recognized as Hartmut Senger. They were with a group of a dozen young people – most of them students, one or two of them unemployed – who had recently set up a self-styled commune in a large house on the Kaiser Friedrich Strasse in the smart, fashionable district of Charlottenburg, much to the disgust of the other residents, who had been making vociferous protests in the local press and to the City government.

When, at about midnight, the teach-in ended and the main body of students prepared to go home, Dieter found Kleo. 'Helena's over there,' he said grimly. Together they pushed their way through the crowd.

Grabbing hold of Helena's arm, he demanded, 'What the hell do you think you're doing, you silly little cow? Couldn't you have let someone know where you were? Your family's worried sick.'

Helena was not at all abashed. 'Hello, Dieter. Hello, Kleo. How gratifying to know I've been missed so much.'

Dieter drew in his breath. 'Would you mind getting in touch with your mother and father and telling them you're all right?'

'Hi.' Hartmut Senger put his arm round Helena's shoulders.

Helena gave Kleo and Dieter a defiant look. 'Well, now you've seen me, you can tell them I'm fine.'

'Come on, Helena,' Hartmut Senger said.

'Where are you living?' Kleo asked.

'With Hartmut,' Helena replied. 'Come and visit me some time. You'll find the address in any newspaper.' Before Kleo could say any more, she turned and walked away.

Kleo went to see Helena first thing the following morning. A rather grubby little girl opened the door, dressed in dungarees, with food stains down the bib. When Kleo asked to see Helena, she said, 'They're in there.'

There were a dozen or so people sitting round a large table, littered with the debris of breakfast and scattered with newspapers. 'Here's a good one,' Helena was exclaiming excitedly. 'It says the commune indulges in wild sexual orgies every night – with the lights on and the curtains open!'

'Helena,' Kleo said quietly, 'is it possible to talk to you, alone?'

Helena looked up. 'Oh, it's you, Kleo. You can talk to me here. We don't have any secrets from each other. We share everything.'

Hartmut Senger said, 'We don't mind. Take your sister into the bedroom and talk to her there.'

With bad grace, Helena sighed and stood up. She led Kleo into a big room, smelling of stale tobacco smoke, a sweetish scent which Kleo recognized as cannabis, body odour and unwashed clothes. It was dominated by two double beds, both covered by off-white quilts. Propped up against a wall, which was decorated with posters of Stalin, Ho Chi Minh, Che Guevara and Mao Tse-Tung, was a guitar. On the floor were overflowing ashtrays, an untidy pile of books and several opened cans of beer. Helena went across to the record player in the corner of the room. Bob Dylan's tuneless voice began to drone: 'The Times They are a-Changing . . .'

While Kleo perched primly on the edge of one of the beds, Helena sprawled on the other. 'If you've come to tell me to go home, don't waste your breath,' she said. 'I'm never going back.'

'Don't you care that you've worried and upset lots of people?'

'Nobody's ever cared about my feelings before. Why should I worry about theirs now?'

'You're not intending to stay here?'

'Why not? What's wrong with it?'

In Kleo's opinion, everything was wrong with it, not least the fact that a number of unmarried people of both sexes were living together. But all she said was, 'It's not very clean.'

Helena lit a cigarette, blew out the match and threw it onto the carpet. 'I'm sick and tired of living in a rarified atmosphere, where every little speck of dust is cleaned away before it even has time to settle, where everything belongs in its proper place. That sort of bourgeois existence may suit you, Kleo, but I can't stand it any longer.' She blew a smoke ring towards the ceiling, then said, 'Come on, Kleo, admit it. It isn't so much the dirt that worries you, but what we get up to. You're no different from anybody else. You want to know how we live!'

'Well . . .'

'Well, I'll tell you. Hartmut and I sleep in this bed and Astrid and Thomas sleep in that one. At least, that's the arrangement at the moment. But, as I said, we share everything. If someone wants to sleep with someone else, they just do it.'

Kleo knew Helena was hoping to shock her and had no intention of letting her know she was succeeding. 'I hope you take some kind of birth control precautions,' she observed drily.

'We believe in letting nature take its course,' Helena replied loftily. 'Having children is easy here. Everyone looks after them. They're a communal responsibility.'

Kleo reflected that, judging by the appearance of the little girl who opened the door, the commune didn't seem to be doing a very impressive job.

She pursed her lips. 'I suppose it's inevitable that as well as sleeping with Hartmut, drinking and smoking, you're also on drugs?'

Helena shrugged. 'Occasionally I share a joint.'

Kleo let that one go. 'But what are you planning to do? You won't get into University unless you pass your *Abitur.*'

'I don't intend to go to University.'

'You're not yet seventeen. You're still your parents' responsibility.'

'Then they can look after me,' Helena retorted with inexorable logic.

'Why should they, in view of the way you're treating them?'

'Hartmut's mother gives him an allowance. I'll ask Father to give me one, too. After all, he's supporting Kris and you. It's only fair that he should look after me, as well.'

'Father helped Kris get started in his career and he's helping me while I'm a student. Why should he pay you to lie around and do nothing? I think he'll insist that you go back to Hamburg and finish your schooling.'

'Who said I was going to do nothing? I'm going to be a journalist. I've already written several articles.'

'I didn't know that.'

'There's a lot you don't know.'

For another half-hour, Kleo remained, trying to persuade her sister to see reason, but she might as well as have been talking to a brick wall. Helena had made up her mind. Nothing was going to change it. When Kleo left, Bob Dylan's rasping voice was declaring, 'It's All Over Now, Baby Blue'.

That evening, the telephone wires hummed between Berlin, Hamburg and Munich. Dieter had shrugged when Kleo had described the commune. 'The novelty will soon wear off,' he said. 'My advice is to leave her alone and let her come to her senses in her own time.'

'Mother's going to want to know details.'

'Tell her that Hartmut's mother is Senger Electrics. Suggest your mother goes to see her. They can thrash the problem of their delinquent children out between them.'

In the end, Kleo told her mother that Helena seemed well and that, in her view, there was no point in forcing her to come home, as she would probably just run away again. She carefully avoided mentioning the commune but did tell her about Hartmut. Immediately, Reinhild's attitude changed. 'His mother is Helga Senger! Why on earth didn't Helena mention him? The Sengers are most respectable and very rich . . .'

Having dealt with her mother, Kleo rang her father.

Norbert gave a sigh of relief when he heard Helena had been found. Kleo's call meant that he did not have to make the trip to Berlin which Reinhild had been insisting he make. There was nothing he could not do from Munich. 'You warned me that Helena was going through a difficult stage,' he said. 'Leaving home is probably the best thing she could do. Give me her address. I'll put a cheque in the post to her tomorrow.'

Finally, Kleo rang Viktoria to tell her that Helena was all right. 'Thank you so much for letting me know, my dear,' Viktoria said. 'I was beginning to get worried. As I well know, dreadful things can happen in Berlin, and Helena is so young and inexperienced. She's had a very sheltered life. But now you know where she is, you can keep an eye on her.'

423

What she would most like to do, Kleo thought with uncustomary savageness, as she put down the telephone receiver, after promising to visit the old lady soon, was to wring her sister's neck. But upon deeper reflection, she decided that her parents did not emerge very much better from the whole affair. For all that they professed to care, neither of them could be bothered to come to Berlin and see Helena themselves. Her mother was more interested in a connection with the Sengers, while her father believed that money was the solution to every problem.

Helena did not bother to thank her father for the very large cheque which arrived in the post two days after Kleo's visit, but took it immediately to the bank and cashed it. Half the proceeds went into her purse. Some of it she would give to the commune, to pay for her keep. Some she intended to spend on herself. But with the other half of her father's cheque, she opened a new bank account in her own name. Helena had a suspicion that when the commune spoke about sharing everything, that included money.

Then she went on a shopping spree. In a department store on the Ku'damm, she bought several pairs of jeans, some cotton polo-neck sweaters, a black leather jacket and a wide leather belt. Her wardrobe replenished, she went into a hairdresser. While she was waiting for her hair to dry, she amused herself with changing her make-up. When she emerged again onto the Ku'damm, her eyes were lined with black kohl and her hair was jet black. From time to time, she glanced at her own reflection in shop windows.

When she returned to the house on the Kaiser Friedrich Strasse, Hartmut looked at her admiringly, then asked, 'Have you had your bush done as well?' He took her into the bedroom and, without bothering to shut the door, unzipped her jeans and pulled them down. 'You should match, you know. I'll have to get some dye and do it for you. In the mean time, I'll do something else.'

His voice was husky with desire and Helena felt a by now familiar tingling in her body. She had discovered in herself a voracious appetite for sex. She simply could not get enough of this new experience. Having sex was considered at the commune as natural as any other bodily function. Nobody so much as raised an eyebrow when a couple went off to the bedroom. But it heightened Helena's excitement: she liked the thought of others knowing what she and Hartmut were doing, just as she enjoyed the knowledge that Thomas and Astrid were listening from the other bed at night.

During Helena's first few weeks at the commune, time passed quickly and easily. The communards ate breakfast together, then they combed the newspapers for items of interest, about the commune, students or world events, which were discussed at length, as a result of which Helena's previously rather sketchy knowledge of politics improved considerably. Although she was not old enough to vote, she was already a staunch socialist supporter.

Household duties were supposed to be equally shared but, in fact, it was Katharina, a big, mother-earth young woman, with long corn-blonde hair and gentle brown eyes; who wore flowing dresses, open sandals and strands of beads; who was the mother of the commune's two children, although nobody knew who their natural father was: it was Katharina, who did most of the chores. When Hartmut went to university, Helena tended to go out too: she hadn't left home in order to clean, wash clothes and cook for other people. She considered that, by paying into the communal kitty, she was doing her share.

The evenings were the time Helena enjoyed most. Then the living room would fill with visitors. The air would cloud with smoke. Katharina would cook a cauldron of soup. Cans of beer would be consumed. Hashish joints would be passed around. And deep into the night they would sit talking about their revolutionary aims.

Among their visitors were larger-than-life characters, already becoming legendary heroes of their time, like Fritz Teufel, bearded, shaggy-haired, bespectacled, the originator of self-styled 'satirical happenings', which would have been treated as good-tempered student rags in other countries but which earned Teufel the wrath of the University Senate and the disapprobation of the press; Rainer Langhans, with a wild mop of hair like Struwelpeter; Rudi Dutschke, with his black hair, piercing eyes and distinctively striped jerseys, a colleague of

425

Dieter Duschek in the SDS; Matthias Scheer, the grandson of Pastor Scheer, who delighted in announcing himself an atheist and adopted the most outlandish fashions; and Dieter himself, outwardly conventional in his appearance, inwardly, as Helena soon came to realize, far from conformist. Kleo accompanied him once, neat and prim, but, when Helena ignored her, she never returned.

After the first sit-in at the Free University, there were a number of other such demonstrations, but although Hartmut participated in them all, they quickly palled on Helena. Not being a student herself, she found the students' causes trivial, compared to the far greater issues at stake in the outside world. She also found their methods of dealing with the University authorities very tame. Sit-ins, teach-ins and distributing flysheets did not seem a very promising means of achieving the revolutionary objectives they all discussed deep into the night.

Patience was not Helena's strong point. Wars of wills had little to commend themselves to her. What she wanted was action. But when she mentioned this to Hartmut, he merely gave his dreamy smile and said, 'All in due course. Revolutions have to evolve slowly. We have taken a major step in setting up the commune.'

A sociological step, maybe, but not revolutionary enough for Helena. Indeed, she could imagine a time not too far distant, when the novelty of her new lifestyle would wear off. Her dramatic step had not had the effect she had anticipated. Her parents had not rushed to Berlin to take her away. Kris had not been sent to persuade her to leave. Kleo had been the only person to visit her – and she had quickly given up.

'When I first met you, Hartmut, you said that action was needed to make the German people realize what it is like for the people of Vietnam.'

'Yes, I remember. We talked about bombs. But what do you want, Helena – that we should bomb Berlin?'

'Everyone just seems to me to be being so damned ineffective. Everyone talks so much – and does nothing.'

He laughed. 'My little firebrand.' Then he unbuttoned her shirt and cupped her breast in his hand. 'Come to bed and I'll give you some action.'

426

As always, Helena could not resist him. He had an unbreakable physical hold over her. But already her mind was beginning to slip away from him. Mentally and spiritually, she craved more than he could give her. She had the sense of life going on, somewhere else, without her, a whole big world of which she desperately wanted to be a part.

The summer vacation came and went. Although Hartmut spoke again of dropping out of university, he recommenced lectures in the autumn and Helena discovered that his mother had threatened to cut off his allowance if he did not complete his course. Conveniently ignoring the fact that she was being subsidized by her father, she felt Hartmut fall in her estimation.

In the General Election in October, the Social Democrats failed to win the victory everyone at the commune had been confidently predicting and, instead, formed a coalition government with the Christian Democrats. Dr Erhard resigned in November and was succeeded as Chancellor by another CDU politician, Kurt-Georg Kiesinger, a former Nazi. Franz-Joseph Strauss, the erstwhile Defence Minister, one of the main protagonists of rearmament and a nuclear deterrent, whose career all socialists hoped had been halted by the so-called *Spiegel Affair* in 1962, was reappointed to the cabinet as Finance Minister. And Berlin's former Mayor, Willy Brandt, the Social Democratic leader, became Foreign Minister.

Helena who had set herself up in her own eyes as being an expert on political affairs, needed no greater proof of the perfidy of all politicians. She refused to take into account such basic matters as expediency and cooperation. Her own politics were those of high ideals. Above all, she was upset by what she saw as Willy Brandt's defection to the Right. That was a betrayal of the basest kind.

Her personal disappointment in Hartmut, coupled with her political disillusionment, sent her into a state of deep depression. She lost her appetite and mooched unkempt around the house, refusing Hartmut's attentions and turning her back on him in bed.

Subconsciously, of course, she was hoping to attract attention and sympathy. But her timing was unfortunate. Thomas and

Astrid had just split up and Thomas was now sleeping with Eva, a newcomer to the commune. Instead of trying to coax Helena out of her black mood, Hartmut simply got into bed with Astrid. Night after night, Helena cried herself to sleep, putting the pillow over her ears to shut out the sounds of copulation from the other bed. Astrid, meaning to be kind, said, 'Why don't you join us, Helena?' But Helena didn't particularly want Hartmut any more and she certainly didn't want to share him with another woman. She became ever more deeply immersed in self-pity and suddenly aware of her surroundings, seeing them as they really were: rather squalid and lacking in essential home comforts.

What to do now? It had never occurred to her that the idyll would end. She could not bear the thought of going to live with Kleo, even if Kleo would have her, and she was certainly not going back to Hamburg . . .

Then, like a bolt from the blue, Marko burst into her life. He just turned up at the house one evening and stood surveying the room, crowded as always with people, drinking, smoking, talking, arguing, drafting pamphlets, organizing demonstrations, discussing sit-ins and strikes, deploring the latest news from Vietnam or just hurling abuse at the Americans, the government and the world in general. Or in the case of Hartmut and Astrid, huddled together, Hartmut's hand inside Astrid's pullover, playing with her breast, and hers on his crotch.

Marko stepped through them to where Helena was sitting alone in a corner, dressed entirely in black. 'Hello,' he said, 'I'm Maximilian Markovic. People call me Marko. I've just arrived from Nuremberg.' He was tall and very slim, with the longest legs Helena had ever seen, a straw-coloured thatch of hair, a wide mouth, and deep, forget-me-not blue eyes, framed with curly, enviably long lashes. He took a tobacco tin from his pocket and let himself down onto the floor beside Helena. 'Fancy a joint?' he asked.

'Thanks,' she replied.

He reached across and gave her a light. 'Don't look so tragic,' he said. 'Things can't be that bad.'

Katharina put on Procul Harem's record 'A Whiter Shade of Pale', and, as the hashish started to take effect, suddenly things didn't look so bad.

428

'Do you live here?' Marko asked.

'Yes, I've been here for about six months. But I'm thinking of moving out. I – I don't really fit in very well.'

'I can see that. What are you going to do?'

'I'm not sure.'

'I'm staying at a friend's studio, while I look for a place of my own. Why don't you move in with me?'

The question did not take her by surprise. She already felt there was something preordained about their meeting. He had walked straight across to her, ignoring everyone else in the room, as if drawn towards her by a magnetic force. She found herself extremely attracted to him. He looked so vital, so alive. 'Wouldn't your friend mind?' she asked.

'She's in Paris at the moment.'

'She?'

His blue eyes gazed into hers, full of laughter. 'She's in her forties, too old for me, but she's a real Bohemian. She's an artist. You'll like her. Well, what do you say?'

Helena couldn't think of anything else to say but, 'Yes.'

Marko had been born in April 1945, four months after his father, who had been a manager at a ballbearing factory in Nuremberg, was killed in a thousand-bomber raid. His mother, Johanna Markovic, had been staying on her sister's farm at the time, at a small village outside the city. After her husband's death, she remained there and Maximilian, whom she had named after his father, grew up in the country until he was seven. Then, as the housing situation eased and jobs increased, mother and son moved back to the city. Johanna obtained a job as a secretary. Maximilian went to school.

An only child, he was outrageously spoiled by his mother, his aunts and his grandparents. His was a butterfly nature and he was not very good at school. He grew quickly bored with any subject that required any degree of effort, but, although his teachers complained about his lack of concentration, his family excused him. He was such a sunny little chap, with such an engaging smile, that it was impossible to scold him.

Sporty and agile, he could run like a gazelle, jump and hurdle. Fear seemed an emotion utterly foreign to him. While other

429

children hid their faces in their mothers' skirts when confronted with strangers, Maximilian looked them straight in the eye, even frightening-looking officials like policemen, and gave them his disarming smile.

Although the Markovic family was not well off, there was always money enough to buy Maximilian whatever he needed, as a result of which he had an enviable collection of toys. He liked to share his belongings. In fact, as Johanna had frequent occasion to realize, he did not seem to have any real sense of possession at all. All too often, she would discover that the latest plaything she had bought him had been given away to some other child. What she did not realize was that it had been swopped for something more desirable and usually more expensive.

Although he continued to obtain poor marks at school, Maximilian showed considerable talent – at least in his family's eyes – for literature, the theatre and art. He loved reading adventure stories and would entertain his family with amusing sketches, in which he dressed up as a pirate, a cowboy or a spaceman. For a while, Johanna entertained hopes that he might become an actor. He was certainly good-looking enough. But he failed to get into any school dramatic productions, because he would not learn his lines. Drawing and painting required no feats of memory and when he began producing colourful sketches of the city and the surrounding countryside, his mother fondly imagined him becoming an exponent of what she vaguely described as 'modern art' and decided he should go to art school.

In fact, he did have sufficient ability, although he failed to pass his *Abitur*, to be accepted by Nuremberg Art College, where, unknown to Johanna, he spent less time studying art than studying girls, particularly those from rich homes.

Maximilian had recognized at a very early age that he could achieve with a flirtatious flutter of his thick eyelashes or a winning smile, what others, less endowed with charm, never even dared to aim for. Why work for a living, he asked himself, unless it was really necessary?

Then one of his girlfriends became pregnant. Unfortunately, although she looked older, she was only fifteen. Her father gave Maximilian an ultimatum. Either Maximilian left college and registered for military service or he would tell the police and Maximilian could go to prison. Maximilian chose the army.

There followed the most disagreeable period of his life, when he had to endure training exercises so strenuous that he sank exhausted into bed every evening, discipline stricter than he had ever encountered and constant humiliation from his superiors. At the end of six months he went AWOL and fled to West Berlin. He took with him the knowledge of how to use a bayonet, handle firearms and throw a grenade. Whether the army had profited at all from his service was extremely doubtful.

He went immediately to the address of Sabine Frank, a visiting lecturer at the Nuremberg Art School, who had always assured her students that her studio in Berlin was open house to them. True to her word, Sabine took him in, commiserated with his recent experiences, gave him some more money, and flew to Paris to open her latest exhibition.

Within a fortnight, Maximilian – now calling himself Marko – obtained a job in a cafeteria which enabled him to remain in Berlin, investigated most of the dives around the Ku'damm, attended several parties, acquired a supply of hashish, and discovered where the student action was taking place. When he heard about the commune on the Kaiser Friedrich Strasse, he decided to give it a try.

The moment he saw Helena, his instincts told him it was his lucky night. Her clothes were regulation student gear, but of a more than usually expensive label. Her earrings were gold. Her watch was a genuine stainless steel Rolex. The sullen pout to her lips told of sexual frustration. She was not beautiful, but she was strangely attractive with her pale, gaunt face and black hair, and the thrust of her breasts in her tight, ribbed sweater and the smouldering light in her black-lined, grey eyes gave promise of a sensual and passionate personality. Poor little rich girl, Marko thought to himself, she deserves some happiness in her life.

Marko was everything Helena had subconsciously been searching for all her life. He was charming, handsome, feckless and very good in bed. He was what she had imagined Hartmut to be and had failed miserably to be. Only Marko did not

431

have any pretentious ideas about changing the world, which he would never carry out. Marko was content to leave the ideas to Helena.

In bed, Helena was everything that Marko had anticipated, and more, making his previous girlfriends seem very tame in comparison. What he had not foreseen, however, when he had spied her sitting alone in that crowded room in the Kaiser Friedrich Strasse, was that she was also filled with wild ideas to overthrow the world.

Those had come as a surprise. But so passionate and persuasive was Helena in her arguments that Marko discovered in himself a latent idealism of which he had until then been unaware. Or possibly it was that he had always been a bit of a rebel, with a desire to shock and pit his wits against authority. When he was a child, he had enjoyed dressing up and enacting swashbuckling roles. Now he saw an opportunity to do the same in real life.

'The difference between our revolution and all previous ones is that, among other things, our process of revolution will be very long, a very long march,' Helena told him earnestly, quoting what she had heard Rudi Dutschke say, 'like Mao Tse-Tung's continually evolving state of revolution in China.'

The idea of being a revolutionary amused Marko.

From the very beginning, Helena was determined not to make the same mistakes with Marko as she had made with Hartmut. She was not going to risk sharing him with any other woman. As soon as Sabine Frank returned from Paris, Helena rang her father and asked if she could move into the cottage at Heiligensee.

Since Norbert seldom visited Berlin and Viktoria made little use of the cottage, he thought it was an excellent idea that his daughter should live there. Furthermore, he sent a large cheque, to cover any repairs which might need doing.

His experience in Nuremberg still uncomfortably clear in his mind, Marko felt slight reservations about living off his girlfriend's father, fearing unpleasant repercussions in the not-too-distant future when Norbert Kraus discovered that his daughter was keeping an unemployed art student on his money, but Helena had no such misgivings. 'My father's money was immorally earned,' she stated angrily. 'It is only right that it should now be returned to the people. He and his generation are the pigs who made Auschwitz. He and his generation are the pigs who have elected Kiesinger and Strauss. Now they must pay.'

Marko doubted very much that any Kraus would agree with any of those sentiments, but decided not to argue. On consideration, it promised to be rather fun helping Helena return Kraus money to 'the people', particularly since it looked as they were going to live not altogether uncomfortably in the process.

Heiligensee was, it was true, an inconveniently long way from the city centre, meaning that friends were, at first, rather reluctant to visit them, but once they discovered the luxury of the establishment, distance ceased to be important. Norbert might not have spent much time at the cottage, but he had thrown money at it during the twenty years since he had bought it. And, in the garage, was an almost new Volkswagen.

Soon, there was a constant procession of visitors to the cottage, some of whom came merely for the evening, for a drink, a joint and conversation; others, like Matthias Scheer and Heinz-Georg Lindner, who simply moved in to the spare bedrooms. Heinz-Georg was a chemistry student, who had recently provided the special effects for a student drama production of Shakespeare's *Henry V*, wonderful pyrotechnics which had seemed like real cannon fire, and had impressed Marko particularly.

Just before Christmas, they all participated in 'Vietnam Week' demonstrations organized by the SDS. It was the first protest march Marko had taken part in and he quite enjoyed the sensation of marching to America House, carrying a placard and chanting, 'Ho-ho-ho Chi Minh!' 'Amis out of Vietnam!' and 'John-son Mur-der-er!' Even when the police moved in and the mood of the demonstration turned ugly, with angry scuffles and a lot of arrests, students being dragged shouting into waiting police vans, Marko still found the event rather entertaining.

The evening promised to be even better. They gathered on the Ku'damm, near the Hotel Jochum, and erected a Christmas tree, which they covered with the *Stars and Stripes*, and flanked

433

on each side with papier-maché heads of Lyndon Johnson and Walter Ulbricht. There were several journalists present.

Marko, who had had a joint before they left home, had a feeling of carnival. Sure, Helena and the others were taking the whole thing very seriously, chanting, 'Bourgeois of the world unite!' and trying to get passers-by to understand the gravity of the demonstration and join them, but Marko could not believe that this was how revolutions were staged. Most by-standers looked rather shocked, particularly when the students tried to set fire to the tree and the heads. Not that they caught fire – that, to Marko, was the funniest thing of all. The tree was too newly cut. Its needles sizzled and failed to catch light. Even the papier-maché heads were too damp. Only Johnson's hat burned. The reporters' cameras flashed. There were titters, boos and jeers from on-lookers. What should have been high drama had become a farce.

Until the police arrived. There were no smiles on their faces as they marched menacingly forward, truncheons at the ready, beating out the tentative flames licking round Johnson's head with their truncheons, hauling the tree to the ground and carrying it away, and indiscriminately seizing anyone who looked like a student.

Marko had instinctively withdrawn into a shop doorway as he saw the police approach, huddling into the collar of his sheepskin coat. Helena, however, was still belting out invectives against the government and the Americans, about the murder of innocents in Vietnam, and she was still yelling when the policemen yanked hold of her arms and dragged her across the pavement, arms and legs flailing, to one of the ever-waiting police vans. The cameras flashed again.

Helena was one of over a hundred demonstrators – and some totally innocent onlookers – who spent that night in a police cell.

'I think I must be starting to feel my age,' Viktoria told Stefan. 'I can't cope with these things any more. They leave me feeling tired – and rather depressed. I saw them putting that Christmas tree up. They weren't doing any harm. It was just a student prank. Rather tasteless, in my opinion – I do so dislike the way everyone blames the Americans for everything! – but still only a prank. Then the police marched in and everything suddenly became extremely serious.' She sank back in her armchair and sipped her whisky soda. The wings of the chair seemed to enfold her and she suddenly seemed to Stefan small and frail, looking indeed her seventy-three years.

'None of these Vietnam demonstrations has been violent,' he agreed. 'All the students have done is walk around, carrying banners and chanting slogans. A "stroll-in", they have called it. But their right of way has been stopped, there have been hundreds of arrests . . . I was nearly arrested myself today, on my way to see you. Simply because I stopped to take a pamphlet. Before I knew what was happening, a policeman had grabbed hold of my collar! And a young man beside me was arrested, just because – I would swear – he was wearing jeans and a leather jacket and his hair was rather long. So much for the rights of free speech and public protest!'

'I saw Helena being arrested,' Viktoria said. 'I didn't recognize her, at the time. She looks so different with all that black hair. I only realized it was her when I saw her name in the paper. The press would have to pick on her, wouldn't they? Anything to do with the Krauses is guaranteed to make the headlines. Reinhild's in a dreadful state. She was on the phone to me for ages, asking what she should do. Apparently, Helena refuses to speak to her. She's living at Heiligensee now with a young man called Marko something. Norbert, of course, is subsidizing them.'

She drew in a sharp breath. 'The trouble is, Norbert runs away from his responsibilities. The only one of those children who's turned out all right is Kleo. In the end, I suggested Reinhild came here for Christmas. Hans and Monika will be here, so will Senta, Eduard and little Gisela. I've invited Kleo and Dieter, too, and told them to tell Kris he's welcome as well, but I gather he'll be winter-sporting in Switzerland.'

Stefan sighed. 'Mama, you don't have to get involved. What Norbert's family gets up to doesn't really concern you.'

He was right, of course, except for one thing: she wanted to be involved. Reinhild had once been her employee and she still felt a certain responsibility towards her. She also felt a sympathy for her plight which Stefan could not be expected to understand.

435

From personal experience, she knew how it felt to lose touch with one's children.

In fact, that Christmas reunion turned out very well. Reinhild had always stood rather in awe of Viktoria and, as a result, tried to put on airs and graces, but when she realized Viktoria was genuinely concerned about Helena, she ceased trying to impress and unburdened her heart, revealing a simple but well-meaning nature.

Matters were considerably helped by the presence of Gisela, a chubby, red-haired one-year-old, who gurgled her way happily through the Christmas proceedings and endeared herself greatly to Reinhild, who loved babies and was constantly vying with Monika for the little girl's attention.

Neither Viktoria nor Stefan could find anything at all in common with Monika now. She had grown staid, middle-aged and interested in very little outside her own domestic world, and revelled in her new role as a grandmother.

Older than Monika, Stefan felt younger at heart and spent most of his time in the company of Kleo and Dieter. On Christmas night, after the rest of the family had gone to bed, he and Dieter had a long conversation. 'A number of issues emerge from this business, which trouble me,' Dieter confided, as they had a final brandy and smoked a last cigar. 'The Christmas happening and the stroll-in were not against the law and Holger Busko is considering demanding that the State Prosecutor takes an action against the policemen who arrested Helena and the others. The police have over-stepped their duty.

'Secondly, if the police and the press continue like this, they are going to force the more militant students into much more violent forms of protest. When I saw Helena after her release she was vowing to "return violence with violence". Even Matthias is talking about "permanent revolt". Now, if that happens, we shall lose all the advantages we have gained. Nobody will bother to differentiate between those hotheads who are in favour of violence and those – truly pacifist – students, who aren't.

'Thirdly,' Dieter ticked his points off on his fingers as he spoke, 'the attitude of the press, Springer in particular, is detracting from the very valid points we are trying to make in our protests. By trying to ridicule the students, Springer is blinding the eyes of the public to the facts that there is a very real need for University reform – and that, however much we Germans should be grateful to the Americans for what they have done for us, they are still doing wrong in Vietnam.'

'*Aktuell* does what it can,' Stefan pointed out.

'I appreciate that. But I'd like to ask you to do more. For instance, would you interview, say, Rudi Dutschke?'

'I'd be delighted.' Stefan paused thoughtfully. 'We could probably get some coverage in the international press, as well. It's the kind of story Mortimer Allen would like. In fact, last time I spoke to Mortimer, he said the BBC was giving him his own current affairs television show.'

Stefan's interview with Rudi Dutschke, which was published in January 1967 in *Aktuell*, was not read by nearly as many people as read Springer newspapers, but it did reach a small, thinking section of the population who, as a result, had a very much clearer idea than before of the aims of the SDS: the purpose of its so-called extra-parliamentary opposition and the urgent need it saw to change the parliamentary system, so that the interests of all citizens were represented, especially on questions such as reunification, NATO, security of employment, State finances and the economy, all the more important at the present time, when Germany was in recession.

As a result of Stefan's interview and others Dutschke gave, the SDS leader started to become quite a media personality. The Springer press continued to mock and ridicule his ideas, but young people in particular, not just in the Federal Republic but throughout Europe, came to see Rudi Dutschke as their hero and their champion.

On Easter Monday 1967, Helena and Marko took part in the Easter peace march. Armed with plastic bags filled with paint, they marched down the Ku'damm, then on to America House and threw their 'Easter eggs' at the building's facade and, when the police moved in with truncheons, at the police.

Ten days later, the American Vice-President, Hubert Humphrey, visited Berlin and was accorded a very different reception from that which had welcomed Kennedy four years before. He was

437

greeted by a placard-waving, slogan-shouting crowd, who pelted his car with eggs and bags of flour.

On the evening of 22 May, people throughout the world were shocked to learn of a massive fire which had that day swept through a crowded department store in Brussels and in which hundreds were feared to have died.

A couple of days later, a pamphlet circulated in Berlin, explaining that the store had at the time been promoting American merchandise and announcing,

If there's a fire anywhere in the near future, if an army barracks goes up in the air, if a stadium or grandstand collapses, please don't be surprised. Just as little as when the Amis cross the demarcation line, bomb Hanoi city centre or send the Marines marching into China.

Brussels has given us the only answer: 'Burn, warehouse, burn!'

Whoever had written it was a person after Helena's own heart. Like herself, they could see that throwing eggs and flour was a waste of time. Direct action was needed.

The next visitors to Berlin, on 2 June, were the Shah of Iran and Empress Farah Diba. Their appetites whetted by descriptions in the popular press of the Shah's glamorous lifestyle, his palaces, yachts, cars and wives, most Berliners waited excitedly for their first royal visit since the Queen of England. Not so Berlin's young generation. Helena, Marko, Matthias, Dieter and Kleo were among the hundreds who, the day before the Shah's arrival, attended a teach-in at the Free University, at which Iranian exiles told of the other side to the Shah's rule: of the more than 20,000 political prisoners in Iranian gaols; of the hunger and poverty in which the Iranian people lived; of the fact that 90 per cent of the population was illiterate; of the vast sums the Shah spent on arms.

Although thousands of supporters and well-wishers turned out to greet the Shah and Farah Diba as they drove in a bulletproof car from Tempelhof Airport to the town hall at Schoeneberg, the protesters made certain that the royal visitors realized this was a far from unanimous and jubilant welcome.

438

Again, placards were waved, slogans shouted and eggs thrown, one of which broke over the shoe of one of the Shah's bodyguards. Fights broke out between the two factions. The police intervened. Several anti-Shah demonstrators, including Fritz Teufel and Rainer Langhans, were arrested.

In the evening, a command performance of *The Magic Flute* was being performed in the royal couple's honour at the Opera House in the Bismarck-strasse. Long before the motor cavalcade bearing the Shah and his Empress, President Luebke, Foreign Minister Brandt, their wives and other dignitaries arrived, fans and demonstrators had gathered, separated from each other by the police. The police were there in such numbers that, as Marko remarked, the street looked like a garrison. In order to control the crowd, a high wooden fence had been erected opposite the Opera House, behind which the protesters were barricaded.

Kleo felt a sense of panic as she and the others were rammed in behind the fence. A number of demonstrators, including – to Kleo's dismay – Helena, Marko and Matthias, suddenly showed themselves to have come armed with sticks, stones and bottles. Even before the motorcade arrived at the Opera House, missiles were being hurled over the barricade at the police, who retaliated by beating back indiscriminately with their truncheons.

After the royal party entered the Opera House, the demonstrators started to disband. Kleo was never sure exactly what happened then. Some students near her tried to clamber over the barricade. There was screaming and shouting as they were thrown bodily back. Then the police charged and pandemonium broke loose. 'Sit down!' someone yelled. But there was no room to sit. The police broke through the barricade, their truncheons flailing, hitting out to right and left. Kleo saw Helena turn on a policeman, thrashing out ineffectually at him with a broken bottle. Two of his colleagues pinned her arms behind her back. Marko and Matthias, too, were struggling with several uniformed assailants.

Dieter seized Kleo's hand. 'Come on!' he shouted, pulling her deeper into the jostling, shouting mass of people. She staggered after him and eventually, they reached the Krumme Strasse, where the crowd started to thin. 'Run!' Dieter ordered.

Kleo tried to run, but nerves had turned her legs to jelly and

439

she stumbled and fell. Heavy boots pounded on the roadway behind her and would have trampled over her had not Dieter dragged her into the shelter of a doorway. A water-tank lorry lumbered past them, its water cannon drenching the fleeing students. Then, from further down the street, above the din of panic-stricken demonstrators, came the sound of a gunshot.

Later that night, after he had taken Kleo home, Dieter went to the SDS office on the Ku'damm and it was there that he, Rudi and the few other Union leaders who had not been arrested, learned that a student called Benno Ohnesorg had been shot by a policeman in the Krumme Strasse, and died.

The following day, in a special broadcast on Radio Free Berlin, the Mayor announced, 'We shall no longer allow ourselves to be terrorized by a minority. What took place in the last twenty-four hours had absolutely nothing to do with the rights of free speech. The patience of Berliners has come to an end. Safety and order in this city must be guaranteed. For this reason, the City Senate has forbidden all open demonstrations until further notice . . .' In a press interview, he insisted that the policeman responsible for firing the shot which had killed Benno Ohnesorg had been acting in self-defence.

His statements were supported by the Springer newspapers, which twisted events to suit their own purposes, accusing the students of starting the violence by attacking the police with knives. Unfortunately, Stefan's reasoned account was relegated to an inside page of *Aktuell*. Unlike the Springer press, which concentrated its attention on sensational, domestic affairs, *Aktuell* prided itself on being an international publication, and, that week had not been uneventful in the world arena.

Throughout May, Arab troops had been massing on Israel's frontiers. On 5 June, Israel launched simultaneous, surprise attacks on airfields in Syria, Egypt, Jordan and Iraq, virtually destroying Arab air forces on the ground. Within two days, Israeli forces had destroyed Egyptian tanks in Sinai and the Suez Canal and overrun the West Bank of the Jordan. Compared to this inflammatory situation in the Middle East, another student demonstration in Berlin and even the death of a student was relatively unimportant.

*   *   *

440

Marko seemed to find his brief spell in police detention rather amusing and gloried in the notion of having a criminal record. Helena and Matthias, however, both emerged determined to meet violence with violence after Benno Ohnesorg's death. Dismayed, Kleo, Dieter and Holger used all their powers of persuasion to convince them they were wrong, but they would not listen. 'If the pigs are going to use guns on us, we'll use guns on them,' Helena stated, years of pent-up anger suddenly released. 'Like Malcolm X said in America, the days of non-violent resistance are over.'

Still badly shaken from her experiences on the Krumme Strasse, Kleo took hold of her sister's arm. 'Helena, please, don't talk like that. Everyone panicked that night, including the police.'

'Rubbish!' Helena retorted. 'There's a conspiracy to silence us and you know it.'

'Helena's right,' Matthias said. 'This country is turning into a police state. If the government is going to use violence against us, we must use violence in return.'

' . . . *thou shalt give life for life, eye for eye, tooth for tooth* . . .' Holger quoted. 'Is that what you're saying, Matthias? If so, your grandfather would not have agreed. He would have been of the opinion that you should offer the other cheek . . .'

Matthias turned on him in a white fury. 'All my life I've had the example of my grandfather thrust down my throat! Well, I tell you, many were the times when I went on peace demonstrations with him that I longed to have a gun in my hand and shoot it in the faces of all those people staring at me.'

Dieter gasped. 'Matthias, you don't mean that, surely!'

'I certainly do! We've offered the other cheek far too often. If we hadn't been so terrified of fighting back, the Nazis would never have got into power . . .'

'If people had stood up against the Nazis, millions of Jews would never have been slaughtered in the concentration camps,' Helena added, her face white and gaunt. 'We are fighting for the rights of all oppressed peoples . . .'

Kleo tried one last appeal. 'Helena, I know you're upset, but promise me that you'll think carefully before you do anything rash. You told me once that you wanted to be a writer. Why

441

don't you do what Stefan and Holger do - use words to achieve your end?'

Helena cast her a withering look. 'For a supposedly intelligent human being, you do talk crap. Who the hell is going to read anything I write? But my actions seem to get me noticed all right.'

There was no point in arguing. Kleo knew from experience that the more one opposed Helena, the more obstinate she became.

When they had gone, Dieter, still looking badly shocked, said, 'I've known Matthias for more than ten years, but I've never realized how he felt about Pastor Scheer.'

Holger sighed deeply. 'Possibly he hasn't realized it himself before. But when you think about it, it's understandable. He's rebelling, just as Helena is, just as – for that matter – you and I are, against our families and above all, against the past. That's why you embraced socialism, Dieter, in direct opposition to your father's right-wing, capitalist tenets. We are all reacting against examples we have had stuffed down our throats.'

'But we are not all advocating violence,' Dieter protested.

'No, thank goodness, we're not . . .'

After that, although they still lived in the same city and had many acquaintances in common, their ways parted. Holger, Dieter and Kleo remained close friends, but Helena, Marko and Matthias moved in different circles.

For the next few months, Berlin was reasonably quiet. Most action was on an intellectual level and took place at the University. Some students tried various unusual means to obtain Fritz Teufel's release from prison. In August, despite the ban on demonstrations, an American military parade was disrupted by students. In November, the police sergeant who had shot Benno Ohnesorg was found not guilty of manslaughter. When Teufel and Langhans finally appeared in court later that same month, a thousand students demonstrated outside the Moabit Prison and were dispersed by mounted police and water cannon. In December, Teufel and Langhans were released from gaol, but the charges against them were not dropped. Their trial continued.

On Christmas Eve, while students demonstrated outside the Kaiser Wilhelm Memorial Church, Rudi Dutschke interrupted the service with an impassioned intercession against the horrors of the Vietnam War, in which over half a million American soldiers were now deployed. To the delight of Springer reporters, one of the congregation knocked him to the ground when he tried to leave the building and other worshippers set upon the students outside.

Helena, Marko and Matthias spent Christmas together at Heiligensee, in as defiantly an un-Christian, unfestive manner as they could devise. 'Words, words, words,' Helena exclaimed in exasperation, when Dutschke's escapade was reported on the radio. 'I'm fed up with this place and these people. When is anyone ever going to do anything?'

'I'm afraid that's it, Mortimer. We could try and operate, but, unlike other brain tumours, the complete removal of a glioma is seldom possible.' Dr David Roper-Wilkinson's deep-set eyes peered sympathetically over the top of his half-spectacles at his patient, sitting the other side of the antique mahogany desk. 'I wish it could be better news, particularly at Christmas . . .'

Mortimer Allen brushed his hand through his hair, then reached in his pocket for his cigarettes. 'From what you've told me, one more of these isn't going to make any difference.'

'It would be a waste of my breath telling you to give up now. How long have you been smoking?'

'I started when I was about fifteen. Sixty years ago . . . So, if I'm lucky, I've got another six months? And, if I'm less fortunate, I could be dead tomorrow?'

'Putting it crudely, yes.'

'But I can continue to work?'

'So long as you feel up to it, but you shouldn't drive. The symptoms you've already been experiencing – the headaches and disturbed vision – will increase, but your intellectual faculties shouldn't be affected, at least, not immediately . . .'

Mortimer gave a thin smile. 'Thank you for being honest with me, David. I appreciate that. However, I hope I can depend on your Hippocratic oath not to tell anyone else? Not even Joyce and Libby.'

'Of course I shall respect your wishes, Mortimer. But are you sure that's wise? Joyce has a right to . . .'

'If she knew I was ill, she'd flap around me like an old mother hen. I've no desire to spend the last months of my life as a cosseted invalid. In any case, we all risk death every day. I could leave here and get run over by a bus.'

The consultant made a weak attempt at humour. 'There are no buses in Harley Street.'

'A taxi then, you old pedant.'

David Roper-Wilkinson was silent for a moment, then he asked, 'So what do you intend to do, Mortimer?'

'Go on living, of course. What else do you expect?'

As the winter continued, the war between the Springer publishing company and the students intensified. In the middle of February, the International Vietnam Congress took place at the Berlin Technical University. In a sudden change of heart, the City Senate gave permission for a demonstration, and some 12,000 anti-Vietnam War protesters, including many from abroad, marched through the city, singing the 'Internationale', chanting, 'Ho-ho-ho Chi Minh', 'Amis out of Vietnam!' and waving the Red Flag, banners, and posters of the Vietcong leader, Rosa Luxemburg and Che Guevara. As Stefan wrote in *Aktuell*,

Who says this is a small, radical minority? If 12,000 adults marched through Berlin, the government would have to take notice. Just because the students are young, does this mean they should not be listened to? Or have we, the older generation grown so complacent . . .?

The answer came fast and furious. Five days later, the Berlin Senate, the Federation of German Trade Unions and the Springer press organized their own counter-demonstration, in which over 60,000 people participated, many carrying banners reading: 'Dutschke out of Berlin' and 'Dutschke public enemy number one'.

Throughout March, the attacks became more vicious and the students more angry. The trial of Fritz Teufel and Rainer Langhans finally ended and they were acquitted of all charges. But the mere fact of the false charges levied against them

444

inflamed the mood of the students. They were, they felt, being victimized and persecuted. Their indignation spread to other countries.

In Oxford, Mortimer scoured British, German and other foreign papers for every scrap of information he could glean on what he was increasingly sure was a growing, international student revolt. There was little enough to find. When Stefan rang him, distraught and embittered, Mortimer assured him, 'It's not just in Germany. The same thing is happening in Paris, Milan, London, the United States, and even Japan. But the strange thing is, nobody seems to be aware of it, even the media . . .'

'They are,' Stefan replied bitterly. 'But they're not listening . . .'

Mortimer was supposed to be working on the script for a television programme he was presenting on Czechoslovakia, where Alexander Dubcek seemed to be in favour of reforms which would introduce new measures of political and personal democracy and freedom. 'Springtime in Prague?' the producer had entitled the programme.

What was taking place in Prague was vitally important, but what was happening in Germany, and particularly Berlin, meant far more to him personally. He gazed out of the window across the garden. Buds were bursting on the trees. Crocuses and early daffodils were dancing in the grass. Joyce and Julie turned the corner of the house, Joyce pushing a wheelbarrow, Julie big with child. His grand-daughter was twenty-three now and married. Would he live to see his great-grandchild? Six months, David Roper-Wilkinson had said. Four were already nearly gone.

And suddenly Mortimer knew that, before he died, he had to return to Berlin.

Mortimer arrived back in Berlin on Saturday 6 April 1968, the weekend before Easter. The Tuesday before, fire bombs had exploded in two Frankfurt department stores, causing extensive damage. Within a couple of days, four students had been arrested. On the Thursday, the black American Civil Rights campaigner, Martin Luther King, had been assassinated in Memphis, USA.

But Berlin, when he arrived, was tranquil, his friends there remarkably composed. He, Viktoria and Stefan had a leisurely luncheon in the 'glass-house', on the fourteenth floor of the Jochum-Berlin.

'It doesn't seem possible that we've known each other for thirty-five years,' Viktoria said. 'The most remarkable thing about our friendship is that we always seem able to pick up again where we left off. Do you realize that it's four years since you were last here? But, now you're back, it's as if we've never been apart.' Then she looked at him critically, 'Except that you look different, somehow, Mortimer.'

'Probably because I'm tired,' Mortimer replied. 'I was up early this morning to catch the plane.'

'Then you must take a siesta. I often take a little nap after lunch. Even I have had to admit that I can't do as much as I used to.'

The next few days passed quickly. Mortimer spent a lot of time with Stefan, mixing with the student community and trying to gauge their mood. In the early evenings, he joined Viktoria for an aperitif in the bar and they reminisced about the past and caught up on the present. Yet all the time, he was haunted by a sense of impending doom, as if a volcano was simmering . . .

Then, on Maundy Thursday, it erupted. As Rudi Dutschke was riding along the Ku'damm on his bicycle outside the SDS offices, a young man fired three shots at him. Nobody at the Jochum-Berlin saw it happen, but word reached them quickly and in no time at all Mortimer was out on the street with crowds of other spectators, staring at Dutschke's fallen bicycle and his boots lying in the roadway.

Dutschke had been rushed to the West End Hospital, where, his life hanging in the balance, he underwent emergency treatment. Josef Bachmann, the young man who had shot him, was arrested, interrogated and said that he had shot Dutschke because he hated Communists and had been inspired by the assassination of Martin Luther King. There was little doubt that he had also been inspired by the systematic campaign waged against Dutschke by the Springer press.

That night, several thousand students marched through the

streets of Berlin towards the Springer building in the Koch-strasse, chanting, 'Ru-di Dutsch-ke', 'Spring-er murd-er-er', 'Burn, Spring-er, burn!' When they reached the Springer building, they found it surrounded by armed Springer security guards, police cordons and water cannon.

They surged forward, stones, bricks, sticks and bottles in hand, regardless of the water pelting down upon them, throwing themselves against the police barricade, hurling their missiles towards the building, cheering at the sound of shattering glass; kicking, pummelling, striking out at the police and security guards, lashing them with heavy stakes, lunging at them with broken bottles. Some cars and delivery vans were standing unattended. Students forced open the doors, unloaded bales of newspapers waiting ready to be delivered, cut the strings binding them, scattered the sheets of paper and set fire to them. Others began rocking the vans, trying to overturn them.

Helena, Marko, Matthias and Heinz-Georg drove to the scene in Norbert's Volkswagen. Parking as near to the Springer building as possible, they joined the fringe of the demonstrators. 'We'll never get near enough,' Helena muttered.

'Not to the building,' Matthias agreed. 'But we shall to the vans.'

They made their way back to the car, opened the boot and took one each of the Molotov cocktails Heinz-Georg had prepared. With the petrol bombs carefully concealed in the deep pockets of their duffel coats, they returned to the Springer building. A couple of vehicles had been overturned. 'Stand clear!' Heinz-Georg yelled, lighting the petrol-soaked rag wick to his 'molli' and pitching it towards a Springer van. It exploded, setting fire to the petrol flooding from the petrol tank.

Matthias, Marko and Helena followed suit. Mesmerized, Helena stood listening to the ear-rending explosions, watching the flames leaping high into the sky, and knew a supreme sense of satisfaction. All around her was the dense, heaving, angry, tumultuous crowd, prepared to fight to the death for freedom, justice and peace. No eggs, no flour, no satirical happenings. This was real. And in that instant, she knew that mass terror and violence were the only ways for revolution to be achieved.

She had a sudden memory of accounts she had read at the

447

time of the Auschwitz Trial of *Kristallnacht*, of that night on 9 November 1938, when stormtroopers had set fire to Jewish synagogues, shops and offices. The government believed it could treat the students in the same way as the Nazis had treated the Jews. Now, thirty years later, the same thing was happening again. We are the Jews of today, Helena thought. We are on our way to our Auschwitz.

'Burn, Springer, burn!' she screamed, and the flames from the blazing vehicles reflected golden and red in her dark eyes.

But later, when the police had dispersed the students, making countless arrests, the flames had died down and the action was over, Helena was left with a feeling of anti-climax. By some extraordinary fluke, she and her friends had not been apprehended. The four of them drove aimlessly round Berlin, the remainder of their 'mollies' still in the boot. 'Let's chuck them at Springer's villa,' Heinz-Georg suggested. But no one knew exactly where Springer lived.

Eventually, as dawn started to break, they drove back to Heiligensee. Marko was still on a high from the night's events. Immediately inside their room, he tugged open the zip of his jeans and guided Helena's hand inside his underpants,

She slid to her knees and took him in her mouth. Gradually, excitement mounted in her. She wriggled out of her own jeans and soon they were locked together on the carpet, rolling over and over, trying to recapture in their own bodies the exhilaration and frenzy of the night.

The Springer building in Berlin was not the only one to be attacked that night. Throughout Germany, students marched in their thousands on Springer offices, smashing windows, setting fire to vehicles, fighting pitched battles with the police.

On Good Friday, the demonstrations and the violence continued, not just against Springer, but in front of America House, outside American military bases and at the Greek Embassy, in protest at the right-wing military junta which had seized control in Greece. The Kurfuerstendamm turned into a veritable battlefield, as hundreds, if not thousands, of young men and girls engaged in furious combat with the police.

From a window on the first floor of the Hotel Jochum,

448

Mortimer had watched the students march, almost at a run, down the wide, police-lined street towards the deep ranks of police barricading the roadway.

For a long while, he looked on. Although Stefan had joined the students the evening before, Viktoria had persuaded Mortimer to stay away. 'What will you achieve by being part of it,' she had asked Mortimer, 'other than to get hurt?' Yet it went against the grain to be a passive onlooker. He had always been in the thick of the fray. Everything he had reported had been from first-hand experience.

On the street outside, policemen were trying to push back a group of students armed with stakes tied together in the form of a cross, which they were handling like a battering ram. In the middle of the roadway, a young man wearing a guerilla-type beret was advancing on another police contingent. More skirmishes were taking place on the far pavement. A water cannon was shooting out a great spout of water, drenching everyone in sight and setting the road awash. The double-glazed window cushioned the noise, but the sheer, implacable hatred blazing in all their eyes was clearly visible.

Ignoring Viktoria's protests, Mortimer went down to the foyer, pushed his way past the security guard and out into the street. For a few minutes he stood, adjusting to the wet, the shouting, jeering, screaming, the anger and the violence, and the sheer, physical buffeting and pummelling of bodies.

From a side road, a gang of boys and a few girls arrived, dressed in duffle coats and donkey jackets, marching abreast, carrying banners and chanting the student battle-cry of 'Ho-ho-ho Chi Minh!' At the centre of the front row was a raven-haired girl and a tall, young man, with blond, shoulder-length hair.

They had scarcely entered the Ku'damm before a number of policemen turned their attack on them, striking out with their truncheons. Mortimer watched, aghast, as the black-haired girl received a vicious, totally unprovoked blow across the face, knocking her to the ground.

And, at that moment, something snapped in Mortimer. Totally uncaring of his own safety, he charged through the police, yelling at the top of his voice, 'What do you think you're doing, you bastards? She hasn't done anything wrong! Leave her alone!'

With a strength he had not known he possessed, he lifted the girl by the shoulders and tried to drag her towards the pavement. As he did so, her friends launched themselves at the police, revealing themselves to be armed with a lethal assortment of weapons. In the ensuing turmoil, Mortimer felt a swingeing clout on the back of his head and he collapsed, unconscious, into the gutter. Around him, the battle continued to rage.

By the time an ambulance was able to reach the scene and take him to hospital, Mortimer Sydney Allen was dead.

After a post-mortem examination, Mortimer's body was flown back to Oxford for burial. Two other people had been killed and hundreds more injured during the Easter demonstrations, but the death of an American, particularly one who enjoyed such international respect as Mortimer Allen, could not be hushed up or ignored, and the Justice Minister, Dr Gustav Heinemann, announced an inquiry into the manner of his death.

The press had already revealed the basic details. Helena Kraus had been identified as the girl student to whose defence Mortimer had gone. Pictures of her being dragged away by police after the 'Christmas happening' in 1966 were taken out of the files and reprinted. Statements she had made about meeting violence with violence were repeated. Above photographs of the brawls on the Ku'damm were headlines such as, 'Sign of Peaceful Protest?'

No tribute and no inquiry would help so far as Viktoria and Stefan's feelings were concerned. To Stefan, Mortimer had been like a second father, and he went to Oxford for the memorial service being held at Mortimer's former University College chapel.

But Viktoria remained in Berlin. At the time that the service was taking place, she had the hotel chauffeur drive her to Heiligensee, to the place, where, over thirty years ago, Mortimer had said, 'I wanted to show you that love between a man and a woman is a beautiful experience, that loss of control is not loss of soul . . .'

Her love affair with Mortimer had never happened. She had no doubt now, although she had suffered untold anguish at the time, that it was better so. There are some things which are meant to be and others not. Yet that did not change the very simple fact that she had loved him, had gone on loving him, would always love him. And, now he was dead, it was as if a part of herself had died too.

A tear trickled down her cheek and she made no attempt to wipe it away. Alone at the lakeside, she mourned the passing of the man who had meant more to her than anyone else in her life except her son, and whose death was going to leave the world an immeasurably emptier place.

Chapter 19

As Mortimer had foretold, the student discontent crossed international borders. By summer 1968, there were uprisings, demonstrations and strikes in countries throughout the world. In Paris, where the French university system was as archaic as that in Germany, students occupied the Sorbonne and a large part of the Quartier Latin. Unlike in Germany, the French workforce came out on strike in sympathy and for weeks, street battles raged, during which thousands were injured. Only last-minute promises of educational and social reform saved De Gaulle from having to resign – and, indeed, ironically, won him an overwhelming majority in the next election.

But in the Federal Republic of Germany, although later generations would see 1968 as a watershed, the government made no concessions and there were no immediate changes to the educational system. Yet the student rebellion had reached its peak. The violence had shocked and frightened people, including many of the participants. Parents threatened to withdraw allowances and many employers refused to consider students known to have taken part in the troubles. The assassination attempt on Rudi Dutschke, who was still suffering from his head injuries, had left the movement without a strong leader. And perhaps the most shattering blow was caused by the end of the 'Prague Spring': the invasion of Czechoslovakia in August 1968 by troops from all Warsaw Pact countries, including the GDR.

As always when something uncomfortable occurred, Helena conveniently ignored the massacre which took place in Prague. In the same way, she refused to accept any responsibility for Mortimer Allen's death. After all, she hadn't asked for or even needed his help. It was his fault that he had got in the way of a police truncheon and in any case, he had turned out to be a sick old man, who was going to die soon anyway.

In October, Klara Scheer died. Matthias had recently become involved in a passionate, and so far as his friends were concerned tedious, love affair with a girl called Angelika. Marko said, 'Love should be spread around, man.' But Matthias did not agree and the couple spent most of their time locked in a bedroom. When they decided to move out of Heiligensee into the Scheer apartment in Schmargendorf, nobody was really sorry. 'One day, my parents may come back from deepest Africa and want the flat,' Matthias said, 'but in the mean time, I may as well take advantage of it.' Heinz-Georg also drifted away. Winter was coming. He was bored with Berlin. He thought maybe he'd go to Spain or Marrakesh.

That same month, the trial commenced of the arsonists responsible for the Frankfurt department store fires in the spring – Gudrun Ensslin, Andreas Baader, Thorwald Proll and Horst Soehnlein. The trial created a lot of attention in the media, not least because of the unconventional behaviour and appearance of the accused, their lawyers and their witnesses. At the end of it they were given a three-year sentence.

In an address to the Frankfurt SDS and much repeated in the press, Fritz Teufel said, 'Well, it's better to burn a store than to run one.'

'Let's get out of Berlin,' Helena said to Marko. 'I'm bored with it, too. Let's go to Frankfurt.'

Marko visualized himself being recognized and returned to complete his military service, but Helena shrugged away his misgivings. 'Nobody need know where we are. My father will give me a flat.'

It was as easy as that. Judging by the hum of conversation and music in the background, Norbert was entertaining guests when Helena rang. He sighed rather impatiently, as Helena gave some spun out reasons for wanting to leave Berlin and said, yes, Landgut did have an empty flat in the Beethovenstrasse to which she was welcome. Helena withdrew all her money from the bank, she and Marko packed a large suitcase each, and they departed from Berlin.

* * *

453

It did not take Helena and Marko long to discover kindred spirits in Frankfurt. By way of the SDS, they were introduced to the Club Voltaire near the Opera House, a rendezvous for student anarchists and revolutionaries from all over the world. Shortly after their arrival, they took part in a demonstration led by Dany Cohn-Bendit against the award of the German Book Trade's Peace Prize to Leopold Senghor, President of Senegal, creating massive disturbances at the Frankfurt Book Fair and in the city centre, pelting Senghor and his host, Willy Brandt, with stones and other missiles.

They also discovered the Mephisto bar, off the Kaiserstrasse, from where 'The Doctor' controlled the city's best-earning prostitutes and conducted a thriving drug-dealing business. The Doctor also possessed an excellent underground communications network and knew who Helena and Marko were the moment they entered the Mephisto. Not long after he met them, he said, 'Anything you need, drugs, an abortion, guns, travel visas – you name it, I can get it – for a price, of course.'

Helena and Marko's circle of acquaintances in Frankfurt grew quickly to include not only students and former acquaintances from Berlin but people from many other walks of life, including left-wing journalists, broadcasters, film directors, advertising agency executives, lawyers and other professionals, who were attracted by the young couple's bohemian lifestyle, the liberal flow of drugs and drink at the Beethovenstrasse flat, the beat of the music and the glamour of being associated with anarchists.

Helena did not attempt to deny her family connections. On the contrary, she took a perverse pride in villifying them. What with her father's Landgut estates, Werner Kraus KG's headquarters on the Boersenstrasse, Bruno von der Eschenbach's offices on the Zeil, and the Hotel Jochum, her family seemed to control a large part of the city. Her friends admired the fact that she had sacrificed the comforts of her wealthy background to embrace socialist principles and promote the causes of the downtrodden and oppressed. They applauded the way in which she declared, 'I have rejected my family.'

Not long after arriving in Frankfurt, Helena realized she was pregnant. She did not seek The Doctor's services: she and Marko were both delighted with the novel idea of having a baby. For hours on end, they would lie in bed, smoking hashish, often with Marko's ear to her stomach in the hope of feeling the baby move, discussing what they would call it. Of one thing they were certain. It would be a true child of the revolution.

Norbert might have given a little more thought to Helena and the problems she always seemed to leave in her wake, had his mind not been totally absorbed by the new love in his life, Ursula Metzner. Norbert had met Ursula at a party during a weekend visit to friends in Zurich and the following evening had taken her out to dinner. At eleven o'clock, she had said, 'I have to go now. I make it a rule never to go to bed after midnight. I start work at eight. If I haven't had enough sleep, I don't function at my best.'

When Norbert offered to drive her home, she said, 'Thank you, but I have my own car.' It was a silver-grey Porsche.

Ursula was forty-six, just three years younger than himself, a little over five feet tall, with a slim, neat figure and gleaming, shoulder-length blonde hair, which was possibly but not obviously dyed. Her husband had been the founder of Leo Metzner Advertising and, when he had tragically died in a motor accident ten years earlier, Ursula had taken over the running of the agency.

'I trained as a graphic designer, which was how I met Leo,' she explained. 'I applied for a job and married the boss. That was twenty years ago. When Leo died, I was faced with the choice of selling the agency or running it myself. There wasn't really any decision to make, was there?'

Most of the women to whom Norbert had been close during his life would have considered there was. But Ursula was different from any of them. She and Leo had never had children and she did not regret her childlessness. 'I'd have made a dreadful mother,' she said once, when they were talking about families and Norbert had described some of the difficulties he had with his. 'I can cope much better with the cut and thrust of business than the tangled web of human relationships.'

455

Her apartment was open plan, painted white throughout and furnished deceptively simply in Scandinavian style, with splashes of colour created by rugs, cushions, pictures, flowers and plants. Everything, including books and newspapers, had its ordained place.

Even her cat seemed designed to match its surroundings. A seal-point Siamese called Chang, it had its own chair, from which it watched Norbert disdainfully. When Norbert made friendly overtures to it, it growled and scratched him. Like the rest of the apartment, and for that matter, its owner, Chang seemed to be saying, *Noli me tangere*, do not touch me.

By Christmas, Norbert had not even attempted to make his usual advances towards Ursula, although she had obtained a firm hold not just on his emotions but his business activities. Landgut fascinated her and she expressed great admiration for Norbert's dedication during the harsh, postwar years. His neglect of the business during recent years, when he had been content to let the company run itself under the supervision of his general manager, Oskar Stallkamp, and his accountant, Erwin Hoffmann, impressed her far less. 'I can't imagine your brother being so lax,' she commented drily.

Norbert couldn't imagine Werner discussing business matters with a woman.

'You're rather lazy, aren't you?' She tempered the sharpness of her words with a little smile.

'I'd prefer to say that I'm not greedy.'

'But you could be taking advantage of the recent upward revaluation of the Mark by expanding into foreign markets. Holiday homes in Spain and Italy, for instance.'

'I could. But I don't need to. I don't really need any more money.'

'Then you're either very unusual or you're deceiving yourself.'

Ruefully, Norbert thought of the demands Reinhild, Helena and Kris made on his bank balance, and wondered whether she might not be right.

In February, when Norbert suggested Ursula came to Munich for *Fasching*, she wrinkled her nose with distaste and proposed that they left the city to its carnival celebrations and visited

456

Landgut properties throughout the Federal Republic. But if he had hoped that romance would burgeon during the trip, he was mistaken. Ursula insisted on single rooms at their hotels and in one town and city after another, they had breakfasted by eight and were inspecting Landgut properties by half past. To Norbert's chagrin, he found many of his buildings, especially those housing estates built with sub-standard materials immediately after the war, in a sad state of disrepair.

At Ursula's instigation, while they were in Frankfurt, they tried to see Helena, but nobody answered the door and, despite the note they left, Helena did not contact them at the Jochum, where they were staying.

After their arrival in Hamburg a few days later, they also made an effort to contact Kris, but again with no success. Kris, Egon Weber informed them dourly, was skiing in Lech.

Kris's career was going from strength to strength. Not that Norbert ever watched him race: the way his son had deceived him with Désirée still rankled. But he could not resist reading the reports in the papers, from which it seemed that Kris was making his mark in Formula Three racing. Sometimes there would be a photograph of him in the pits at the end of a race, surrounded by admiring, long-legged girls in miniskirts, and Norbert would have to give a wry smile. Whatever Kris's failings, at least he understood him, which was more than he did Helena.

The Cooper had been replaced by a Lotus, upon which Egon and Rolf Meier, Kris's mechanic, were working when Norbert and Ursula arrived at Kris Kraus Cars, the new and secondhand sports car dealership and engineering workshops on the outskirts of Hamburg, for which Norbert had supplied the capital, and the profits from which were supposed to make Kris's racing self-financing. However, Kris took little interest in the day-to-day running of the garage and it was left to Egon Weber to manage Kris Kraus Cars, just as he managed most other aspects of Kris's life.

'Like father, like son,' Ursula remarked, as they drove back to the city centre. Norbert grinned sheepishly.

At the long meeting he had with Oskar Stallkamp, his manager blustered excuses for neglecting his duties, blaming

457

Norbert for failing to take a responsible interest in Landgut. Erwin Hoffmann, however, the company's financial controller, had positive recommendations to put forward.

'Since you already have a house in Berlin, it might be worthwhile considering moving Landgut's head office there and, indeed, expanding your interests in the city,' he said.

'Surely so long as the political situation remains as it is, there's no future in Berlin?' Norbert objected.

'You're quite right, but any losses you make can be offset against the profits you make in the Federal Republic. The Berlin Senate encourages investment in the city with very generous allowances for depreciation and extremely favourable tax incentives. For example, income tax is thirty per cent lower and corporation tax twenty-six per cent lower than here.'

As a result of this meeting, their tour ended in Berlin, where Ursula finally met two members of Norbert's family, Kleo and Viktoria. She felt an immediate liking for them both: steady, studious Kleo, now in her sixth semester at university; and Viktoria, an elegant *grande dame*, whom she hoped she might herself resemble when she was old.

'Why else do you think Jochum Hotels are run from Berlin?' Viktoria asked, when Norbert explained what he had learned from Erwin Hoffmann. 'The Jochum-Berlin is still running at a loss, but thanks to Berlin's taxation system, at least I can afford to keep it going. And should the Wall ever come down and Germany be reunited . . .'

'Aunt Vicki, the Wall will never come down.'

'What goes up can come down . . .'

Norbert smiled at her, affectionately and disbelievingly.

He and Ursula went to look at the old Kraus Village site in Wedding now housing various small factory units, a car park and a street market, still overlooked by dark, nineteenth-century tenement blocks. Ursula shuddered. 'If you built new flats here, those hideous buildings could be demolished. There could be a proper village here . . .'

Viktoria was enthusiastic about the idea. 'Berlin is becoming a city of old people and guest workers,' she sighed. 'Everything which brings work is welcome. And cheap, modern housing will

458

hopefully attract younger people. You could include a shopping parade, car parks and a playground.'

Before they left Berlin, Viktoria asked Ursula if she had ever thought of remarrying. 'To begin with, after Leo's death, I couldn't imagine it,' Ursula replied slowly. 'But life can be very lonely when you're on your own. You find you have a lot of acquaintances, but very few friends.'

Viktoria nodded. 'I know . . .'

'Sometimes, I do think that it would be nice to have someone in whom to confide at the end of a long, hard day, or even to share a joke with,' Ursula continued. 'Chang, my cat, isn't a very good conversationalist. But, on the other hand, I've grown selfish over the years. I've come to enjoy my privacy. I don't know how I'd cope with having someone else's belongings about the place, with having to share my bathroom – or, for that matter, my bed.'

She offered a sterile view of marriage. 'But if you love someone, you want to share things with them,' Norbert commented, rather hesitantly.

'I don't know that I believe in love any more, certainly not the romantic image of it portrayed in poetry and films, and certainly not for a woman of my age. Oh, I loved Leo dearly and I still miss him dreadfully, but our marriage wasn't a bed of roses. Most of the time it was sheer hard work.'

That evening, after Ursula had retired to her room, Viktoria said to Norbert, 'I approve of her. She's attractive and she's got a good head on her shoulders. She's exactly what you need. I hope you're not going to do anything stupid and blow your chances, Norbert.'

Helena's son was born on 21 July 1969, in Frankfurt Hospital. In everyone's life but her own, the event was overshadowed by the Apollo 11 Mission. While Helena was in labour, Marko was in a nearby waiting room, glued – like most of the rest of the world – to the television screen, watching Neil Armstrong step out of the lunar module *Eagle* in his cumbersome astronaut's outfit on to the surface of the moon and say: 'That's one small step for man, one giant leap for mankind.'

The baby's name was registered as Ho Che Markovic Kraus,

but Marko called him Moon Child. For a while, Helena persisted in referring to him as Ho Che, but soon she simply gave in – and Moon Child he was.

Being a mother was very different from what she had anticipated. The baby demanded constant attention. There were times, when he was feeding or sleeping after he had been fed, that she would feel a gush of tenderness, a burst of what she supposed people meant by maternal love, but for the most part she felt endlessly tired and drained, as if she were no longer in control of her own life.

When she got up in the morning, after yet another interrupted night, she needed a joint to give her the energy to face the day, and she took to drinking before she went to bed in the hope that she would not hear Moon Child crying.

To give Marko his due, he tried to help, but his hamfisted efforts only served to increase Helena's irritability and provoke their first real arguments. Never one to invite trouble, Marko found excuses to get out of the flat and meet his friends elsewhere in the city. Their sex life became almost non-existent. Helena, whose greatest fear was that she might lose him, became convinced that he was seeing another girl.

She knew only one way to keep him. She had been out when her father had called at her flat during the winter and had not been bothered to reply to his note. Now she telephoned him and confessed her secret, pretending a guilt at having an illegitimate child which she did not feel. True to form, Norbert increased her allowance and sent her a large cheque in addition, which she used to buy Marko the silver Audi in a nearby car showroom, after which he had long been lusting.

The bribe worked. If there had been another woman in Marko's life, she was immediately replaced by the car. Mechanically, Marko was hopeless and he never did any more than fill it with petrol, but driving it was another matter. Hurtling at full speed down the autobahn was his idea of heaven.

Helena's telephone call to her father had another, less expected result. A week later, her mother rang. 'I've just been talking to your father. He tells me you've had a baby. Why didn't you let me know?'

Under different circumstances, since Helena knew there was

460

little likelihood of getting money out of her mother, she might well have informed her that it was none of her damned business. But she was suffering from a severe period, while Moon Child had suddenly developed a rash which was making him very irritable.

'Are you all right?' Reinhild asked. 'How is the baby?'

'We're dreadful,' Helena told her, truthfully.

Two days later, Reinhild was in Frankfurt. She booked in at the Jochum, then took a taxi to the Beethovenstrasse. A long-haired youth, wearing tight jeans and a T-shirt and smoking a strange-smelling cigarette, opened the door to her. 'I'm Helena's mother,' she explained. 'Is Helena in?'

He took a drag on his cigarette and exhaled the smoke slowly, looking somewhere above her head from eyes which seemed not to focus properly. From the depths of the flat came the sound of voices rising and falling against the persistent beat of pop music. 'Sure,' he said. 'She's in bed.'

Another fair-haired young man appeared in the hall, holding a screaming, naked baby. Seeing Reinhild, he said, 'Hi, I'm Marko. Do you know how to fix a nappy?'

Sucking in her breath, Reinhild rescued her grandson from his arms and followed him into the kitchen, strewn with unwashed crockery, where he handed her a damp, off-white nappy. As Helena had mentioned, the baby had a bad rash and his private parts were very sore. 'Do you have any baby powder?' she asked.

'Try looking in the bathroom,' Marko suggested and disappeared.

Reinhild found the bathroom, but no baby powder. Lying casually on the washbasin surround, however, she did find a syringe.

Having made the baby as comfortable as possible, she cuddled him close to her for warmth and went in search of clothing and bedding for him. In the first room she entered, she discovered Helena lying in bed, her breasts shamelessly exposed, a book in one hand, a glass in the other and an overflowing ashtray balanced on the rumpled eiderdown. 'I wasn't expecting to see you,' she said.

Reinhild had come prepared to feel sorry for her daughter,

461

to forgive and forget, let bygones be bygones, to suggest that she came back to Hamburg to live with her and that they brought up her baby together. Instead, she demanded, 'Where are his clothes and his cot? And when was he last fed? Is he due for his bottle?'

'Probably. All he ever seems to do is cry, crap and guzzle.'

Reinhild was already dismayed with what she had found in Frankfurt. By the end of the day, she was utterly disgusted. Ignoring the living room, where various uncouth, unwashed young people seemed to be holding some kind of party, judging by the incessant, strident music emanating from it, she set to to tidy up the flat. In the hall, she unearthed a grubby carrycot, which she wiped down and fitted with a blanket, in which she put the baby.

Then she started on the kitchen, doing the washing-up, cleaning the work surfaces and floors. When Helena eventually emerged from the bedroom, she vacuumed the carpets, stripped off the bedclothes and put several loads of dirty linen, including a pile of soiled nappies and grubby baby clothes, through the washing machine.

'What are you doing?' Helena asked, leaning against the doorframe, bare-footed, in a pair of faded jeans and a grubby sweatshirt with a Ban-the-Bomb logo.

Tight-lipped, Reinhild replied, 'Trying to make this place fit for a small baby.'

Helena shrugged. 'Why bother? Moon Child's used to it.'

When she returned to the Jochum that evening, Reinhild was exhausted but, tired though she was, sleep did not come easily to her. She was angry with her daughter, but even more worried about the conditions in which Moon Child was living. Not that she called him Moon Child. She did not like that name, any more than she liked Ho Che. Her romantic soul yearned for a more classical, dignified name for her grandson and she decided upon Alexander.

The following morning she arrived at the flat armed with disinfectant, baby powder and lotion, packs of disposable nappies, bottles and tins of powdered milk and food, new baby clothes, rattles, toys, a pram and a cot.

A bleary-eyed Marko eventually answered her ring on the

462

doorbell and let her and her packages in. 'Hey, man,' he said, 'make yourself at home. I'm going back to bed.' Reinhild followed him into the bedroom, where Helena was sleeping and little Alexander was howling in his carrycot.

Soon he was bathed, clothed, fed and lying in his new cot, a contented smile on his chubby little face. 'Poor little diddums,' Reinhild crooned.

To begin with, Helena was resentful of her mother's intrusion into her life, but it did not take her long to recognize the advantages of having someone else to take care of Moon Child. If Reinhild wanted to take Moon Child for walks, feed him, wash him, buy him furry toys, sing him nursery songs and make baby talk, who was she to complain? So long as Reinhild did not interfere in the rest of her life, Helena did not care. It was like having a nanny, except that she didn't have to pay her.

So Reinhild continued to stay at the Jochum, arriving early every morning to take charge of her grandson, and Helena resumed her old way of living. Gradually, she recovered from her tiredness and her relationship with Marko regained its original fervour.

That year had seen changes more far-reaching than those in Helena and Marko's domestic life. In March, Dr Gustav Heinemann had been elected Federal President. After a hard-fought election that September, Kiesinger's CDU failed to win its expected majority, the 'Grand Coalition' ended, and Willy Brandt became Germany's first socialist Chancellor since 1930, heading a new SPD/FDP coalition government.

Helena was not so naive as to mistake this apparently radical swing in public opinion for an overnight conversion to socialist ideals or the final victory of the working classes. All over Europe, socialism was suddenly becoming fashionable among the affluent middle and upper classes, or the 'chic left', as Ulrike Meinhof scornfully described them.

Ulrike Meinhof was one of several new friends – or comrades, as they preferred to call themselves – Helena made that autumn, all older than herself and more experienced in revolution-ary action. Among them were the heroes of the department store fires, recently released from prison after serving fourteen months of their three-year sentences and awaiting the outcome

463

of an appeal to be heard in November. They had become involved in social work at homes for illegitimate, abandoned and delinquent boys, work with which Helena, as a mother, could identify, recognizing in these children the victims of society.

In Gudrun Ensslin, she found a kindred spirit, someone who, like herself, was tired of words and demanding action; while Marko, lazy, rebellious and hungry for adventure, was amused and inspired by Andreas Baader. 'He wants to liberate the inmates of every home in the country,' he told Helena. 'What an army that would be . . .'

Willy Brandt introduced a wide-reaching programme of social, legal and educational reforms, which seemed to go down well with the students and the chic left, although they did little to satisfy extremists like Gudrun, Ulrike and Helena, and infuriated the right-wing electorate who could see socialism costing them money.

Convinced that, despite the Soviet invasion of Czechoslovakia, *rapprochement* with the Soviet Union was better than the confrontation which had marked the last twenty years, Brandt pursued an independent policy of appeasement, which became known as *Ostpolitik*. While his Foreign Ministry colleagues had talks with their counterparts in Moscow and Warsaw, Brandt arranged a meeting in Erfurt with the GDR President, Willi Stoph. This historic encounter took place on 19 March 1970 and marked a new beginning in the relationship between the two Germanies. 'But it still doesn't recognize the GDR as a state in its own right,' Helena commented bitterly.

By that time, further dramatic changes had taken place in her life. The Supreme Court had rejected Gudrun and Andreas's appeal and, rather than complete their prison term, the couple had fled the country, going first to Paris, then to Switzerland. Helena was among those comrades who sent funds to help them survive their exile, from the monthly allowance which Norbert sent her, although, by then, Moon Child was no longer at the Beethovenstrasse.

When the baby caught a bad cold, Reinhild seized the opportunity to suggest that she took him back to Hamburg. Relieved at not having to nurse Moon Child through his illness, Helena agreed. Once, Reinhild brought him to Frankfurt to

464

see his parents, but the next time she came, although she had telephoned beforehand, nobody was in.

'They went away a couple of days ago,' a neighbour, with whom Reinhild had become quite friendly, informed her. 'They didn't say where they were going and I didn't ask. I'm just enjoying the peace and quiet while it lasts.'

The next time Reinhild saw Marko and Helena was at Christmas, when they visited her in Hamburg. For weeks before she had been preparing food, decorating her apartment and putting up a tree, surrounded with presents for Alexander, but Marko and Helena made little attempt to enter into the spirit of the festivities.

'I don't understand,' Reinhild complained, distressed. 'It's your baby's first Christmas. Don't you care?'

Her daughter shrugged. 'Why all the fuss? He's too young to understand what's going on.'

'I assume you'll be taking him back with you to Frankfurt?'

For the first few hours of her reunion with Moon Child, Helena had felt a surge of tenderness towards her son. Then he had become fretful and, with a sense of relief, she had handed him over to Reinhild. If he had responded to her as a person, she might have felt differently towards him. But he did not seem to feel any mother–baby bond. All he wanted was to be fed.

'It's up to you,' she said.

When Helena and Marko had gone, Reinhild cradled Alexander to her bosom, murmuring, 'You poor little darling. But don't you worry, sweetheart. Grandma loves you. Yes, *Oma* loves you.'

In March, Gudrun Ensslin and Andreas Baader came back to Germany. Alerted to their return by Ulrike Meinhof, Helena and Marko drove to West Berlin to see them. Kleo reluctantly agreed that they could sleep on her floor for a night. 'But if the house warden finds out you're here, I'll be in trouble. We're not allowed overnight guests. I don't understand why you can't stay at an hotel or at Heiligensee,' she commented tartly. 'Father's at the cottage. You could stay there too.'

Helena could not explain that she and Marko were in Berlin for the sole purpose of meeting up with two of the country's

465

most wanted fugitives, police photographs of whom adorned hoardings wherever one went.

'Mother says you've had a baby,' Kleo said.

Helena simply shrugged. She had more important matters on her mind.

After a night with Kleo, they moved in with Dieter, who was reluctantly persuaded by Kleo to let them stay at his flat. Dieter was scarcely recognizable as the rebel who had master-minded demonstrations, strikes and sit-ins a couple of years earlier. He had forsaken his jeans and donkey jacket for a pin-striped suit and given up his committee post on the SDS. 'Not that I've changed my mind on any of the major issues for which we campaigned,' he assured Helena, 'but I do believe we've entered a new era, when decisions can safely be left to the government. So does Holger.'

With the accession of the Social Democrats to power, Holger Busko's political career had finally taken off. In his mid-thirties, married, with a couple of children, Holger was gaining a reputation as an astute politician and it was widely predicted that he would soon be given a post in the Ministry of Justice. According to Dieter, he spent three days a week in Bonn, where he had an apartment, returning on Thursday evenings to attend his office on the Knesebeck-Strasse on Mondays and Fridays, and spending his weekends at his home in Charlottenburg. As a result, Dieter had profited from his prolonged absences and recently been made a junior partner at his practice.

Helena was disgusted with this portrait of middle-class respectability and hypocrisy, but fortunately they saw very little of Dieter. Their days and much of their nights were spent with Ulrike, Andreas, Gudrun, Astrid Proll, Horst Mahler and a small group of other loyal comrades, planning the next stage of the revolution. At Horst's suggestion, they called themselves the Red Army Faktion, after the newly formed Japanese 'Red Army', giving them the sense of belonging to an international organization. The weapon of their future campaigns was going to be terror, its instruments not words, but firearms.

For this, money was a prime requirement and, although they were all convinced they could count on a certain amount of support from the 'chic left', they agreed the best means of obtaining funds would be by bank robberies, an idea which appealed tremendously to Marko, who fancied himself as a gun-toting bandit.

Their plans were curtailed by an unfortunate incident. Driving Astrid Proll's car too quickly through the city, Andreas was stopped by a traffic policeman. The following day, he was arrested. 'Amazingly, the police didn't recognize him,' Dieter told Helena and Marko. 'The car had a Frankfurt numberplate and they thought it was stolen. Only after they'd detained him, did they realize who he was. Well, he's inside Tegel Prison now.'

'I don't expect he'll stay there for long,' Helena said quietly.

Dieter stared at her, then let out a long, slow breath. 'Don't tell me you're mixed up with that lot?'

Helena shrugged. Now the police had Andreas, there was no need to deny their association.

'You silly little idiot. Don't you realize the risk you're taking? And the danger in which you're putting others, including Kleo and myself? Well, you're not staying here any longer.'

Helena didn't care. Their visit to Berlin might not have turned out as expected, but it had performed one vital function. At last she had a plan of campaign in her mind. She was more than happy to leave Berlin and return to the Federal Republic.

In a daring operation which made headline news in papers throughout the world, Ulrike Meinhof, with the assistance of several comrades, helped Andreas Baader escape from gaol at the beginning of May. Although his liberators all carried guns and did not hesitate to use them, the Berlin police – the memory of Benno Ohnesorg still fresh in their memory – did not shoot back.

From a hurried telephone call with Gudrun after Andreas had been sprung, Helena learned that the East German government had promised to help them flee to Jordan, where they hoped to join forces with Yasser Arafat's Popular Front for the Liberation of Palestine. She and Marko could have accompanied them, but because they had not been involved in Andreas's escape, there was no need for them to run away. Better that they should remain in Germany, build up support for the Red Army Faktion and set the revolution in motion.

At the end of June 1970, Heinz-Georg suddenly turned up in Frankfurt, his skin tanned, his hair halfway down his back. He had, it transpired, spent the last two years in Marbella, then his money had run out. Helena and Marko let him have the spare room.

Shortly after that, Matthias appeared, driving a BMW motorbike. 'Angelika got God,' he explained. 'Must have been something to do with the surroundings. She wanted me to go back to university, study theology and become a pastor! So I split. Can I doss down here for a bit?'

The idea of robbing a bank could not have appealed more to either him or Heinz-Georg.

The first thing they did was to obtain firearms, small-bore sub-machine guns which The Doctor happily supplied, albeit at an extortionate price. At his suggestion, they took them out to the Stadtwald near the Jochum-Frankfurt, where the roar of aircraft landing and taking off from the airport effectively drowned the noise they made.

Marko, the only one who had done military service, was their teacher, although he proved himself a far from accurate shot, consistently firing high and missing the tin can targets he had set up. Heinz-Georg and Matthias soon proved themselves much better, while Helena, once she had got the hang of handling the weapon, was the best shot of them all.

Marko lay back on the grass, his legs outstretched, his head against a tree trunk, lit another joint and grinned lazily as Helena held the Landmann-Preetz against her hip. 'You look great. I want to fuck you.'

'Marko, give over, will you,' Matthias sighed. 'This is serious.'

'So is fucking . . .'

Helena glanced at him, saw the bulge in his trousers and felt herself grow moist. She aimed her gun at the row of cans and, in swift succession, knocked one after another from their stand. Firing a gun was orgasm of a different kind.

They decided upon a bank in Darmstadt, sufficiently far from

468

Frankfurt to make it unlikely that anyone would recognize them, and near enough for them to make several reconnaissance trips. The bank was all on the ground floor, with low counters, and appeared to have only one entrance. Late afternoon was clearly the best time for the raid to take place. Not only were the tills full, but the cashiers were concentrating more on reconciling the day's transactions than serving last-minute customers. And there was on-street parking nearby.

The get-away car was the only remaining problem. Using their own Audi or Matthias's motorbike was out of the question. Stealing a vehicle was the obvious solution, but although Marko bragged that any idiot could break into a car with a piece of bent wire, he failed miserably when he tried to show how it was done.

Then fate played into their hands. One afternoon on their way back from Darmstadt, the Audi broke down. While Marko lifted the bonnet and peered helplessly inside, Helena said impatiently, 'There's no point in looking at it. Go and find someone who can repair it.'

Marko trudged off up the road and returned ten minutes later in a van. The driver tinkered with the engine for a few moments, tried the ignition again, then grunted, 'We'll have to tow it back to the workshop.' His voice had a southern burr. Helena thought he came from Swabia or the Black Forest.

The workshop was set back from the road, up a pot-holed driveway, with high walls separating it from the houses on either side. Above it was a sign reading A. FELDMANN – AUTO REPAIRS. About twice the size of a domestic garage, it had a pit and ramps, and the floor was littered with engines, tools, rags and other paraphernalia. 'This your place?' Marko asked.

'Yes. I'm Dolfi Feldmann.' There was an almost defensive note in his voice as the mechanic introduced himself.

'I'm Marko. This is Helena.'

Feldmann nodded and turned his attention to the Audi. It took about ten minutes and various new plugs, leads and filters to get the car going. 'When did you last have it serviced?' he asked.

'Never,' Marko admitted.

'It's a beautiful car. You ought to look after it. You should think of having an alarm fitted, too. Easiest cars in the world to nick, these.'

Marko offered him a cigarette. 'You're a bit off the beaten track here. Do you keep busy?'

'I do all right, but I could do with a better class of trade, a few more Audis like yours. At least a lot of my business is in notes, so the taxman doesn't get much of it. With two young children and a new baby I can't afford to give him any more than I have too. I thought things would get better when we got a socialist government, but I was wrong. Everything's gone up.'

Marko took the hint and pulled his wallet from his trousers pocket. 'We'll pay you cash, of course, and we don't need a bill.'

Feldmann wiped his hands on his greasy overalls. 'Thanks a lot.'

Helena studied him thoughtfully. He was about thirty, with blond hair, light blue eyes and a rather dour expression, as if life had dealt him a raw hand. But from the way he had sorted out the Audi, he clearly knew his job and, by the sound of it, he also knew about stealing cars. 'We belong to a revolutionary group who feel very like you about the government,' she said, 'not just socialists, but all governments. We want to overthrow society and start again with a new system, where the rich give to the poor . . .'

Feldmann sucked in his breath. 'Are you fascists – neo-Nazis?'

The hatred which gleamed in Helena's eyes was unmistakable. 'Neo-Nazis?' she hissed. 'The Nazis are our greatest enemy. We want to rid the country of every last vestige of the Nazi past . . .'

For a long time Feldmann was silent. Then he asked, 'Why are you telling me?'

'We need someone who knows about cars.'

'I've been a mechanic for fifteen years. I've worked on nearly every kind of car.'

'Would you consider joining us?'

'What would it involve?' he asked cautiously.

'Before I tell you that, show us how you'd break into our car,' Helena said.

Dolfi Feldmann showed them. It took him thirty-five seconds.

If Marko and Helena had been ordinary car thieves, Dolfi would not have joined them, but they weren't. They didn't want to make a profit from the cars they stole: they needed them as a means of transport. 'Don't think about it as stealing at all,' Marko said. 'Consider it as a loan. When we've finished with the car, the owner can have it back. And you'll be well paid.'

Dolfi's financial situation was more desperate than he had let on. Gabi had been working part-time in a supermarket to help make ends meet, but her third pregnancy and the birth of Klaus a few months ago had meant she had had to give up her job. Dolfi was finding it an almost impossible task to look after his family, pay the rent on the flat and the workshop, insurance premiums, bank charges and the hire purchase repayments on his new van.

Even for money, however, he would not have turned to crime. But although Marko and Helena were planning to rob banks, they weren't doing it for personal gain. They wanted to finance their revolution.

'We represent the downtrodden, the persecuted, the oppressed,' Helena told him earnestly. 'You know what the Nazis did to the Jews during the war?'

Dolfi's hands trembled. 'Yes,' he said, in little more than a whisper.

'We are the Jews of today. But, unlike them, we are going to fight back with every means at our disposal . . .'

As she spoke, Dolfi finally saw a way of avenging the deaths of the hundreds of thousands of people his father had killed.

The bank raid proved ludicrously, almost disappointingly, easy. They drove in to Darmstadt just after lunchtime, Dolfi at the wheel of the dark blue Mercedes he had stolen the previous day from a car park in central Frankfurt. They were all disguised. Helena had dyed her hair red and was wearing a miniskirt and enormous sunglasses. Heinz-Georg had allowed her to cut his hair to shoulder length and grown a moustache. Matthias's distinctive white-blond hair had blackened with what Helena

471

assured him was a temporary wash and his eyebrows and lashes had also been darkened. Marko had shaved his head and was dressed in the style of Yul Brynner in *The Magnificent Seven*. Dolfi was wearing a cap and spectacles with plain lenses.

The car itself had spent the night at his workshop, during which its contents had been stripped and its numberplates changed. In the event that the police should stop them, it had been decided that they would drive like hell, dump the car as soon as possible, split up and make their way separately back to Frankfurt.

However, nothing went wrong. The car was not stopped. Dolfi found a parking space just round the corner from the bank. Nobody paid them any attention at all.

Carrying a rather battered briefcase, Marko led the others into the bank. There were two sets of swing doors, between which they pulled balaclavas from one pocket and guns from the other. 'This is a raid,' Marko shouted, waving his Landmann-Preetz threateningly. 'Hands up! Anyone who moves will be shot.'

There were just three customers, who raised their hands above their heads. None of the cashiers or clerks even reached for their alarm buttons. While Helena and Matthias held them at gunpoint and Heinz-Georg guarded the doorway, Marko agilely leaped over the counter and filled his case with the contents of the tills. Then he jumped back again to the public side and, unable to resist the flamboyant gesture, gave a sweeping bow and announced, 'Don't worry, it's all going to a deserving cause.'

After which they were on the street again, discarding their helmets, racing to the car, where Dolfi already had the engine running, driving out of Darmstadt, back to Dolfi's workshop.

There, the car safely out of sight, they counted their winnings. The haul was not as great as they had hoped, but it wasn't bad for a first go: just over fifty thousand Marks. They each took a thousand Marks and the rest went into the revolutionary fighting fund.

That night, Dolfi dumped the stolen car, wiped clean of finger-prints, its original numberplates restored, in a side street on the other side of the city.

That evening, Bruno von der Eschenbach left his office late.

He and Viktoria were in the throes of buying another hotel, the Prinz Luitpold, one of Munich's oldest hotels.

Munich was hosting the Olympic Games in 1972, when millions of visitors could be expected from all over the world. The first jumbo jet service was already operating across the North Atlantic and the new Intercity train service was due to start that year. In Munich itself, work had commenced on the Olympic Village, a complete underground railway system and a new motorway to Italy. It was set to be a boom city, which was, of course, why Bruno had suggested opening a fourth Jochum hotel there.

Viktoria had left the negotiations to him. Although she had turned seventy-six that June, she still possessed the energy of a woman twenty years her junior. Her hearing was perfect, she needed glasses only for reading, and her mind was as agile as ever. Apart from occasional twinges of rheumatism, the legacy of the immediate postwar years spent in Café Jochum's cellar, she was in amazingly good health. 'I haven't got time to be ill,' she would tell people sharply, who commented on her fitness.

But in certain things, her age showed. She no longer drove herself, but had her chauffeur take her wherever she needed to go. She had never been particularly fond of travelling. Now, she only left Berlin if absolutely necessary.

That evening, Bruno's solicitor had telephoned to say that his last offer for the Prinz Luitpold had been accepted, after which Bruno had rung Viktoria, then sat discussing details with Konstantin.

The street outside was dark as he entered the multi-storey car park behind the Eschenbach building on the Zeil. The night attendant was nodding over his newspaper and the car park itself was gloomily lit. Bruno's footsteps echoed hollowly as he made his way up the stairs to the fifth storey, then down the concrete-pillared gangway, past empty parking lots, to where his new Ferrari Daytona waited in its reserved double space, minimizing the danger of its being damaged by other cars.

He unlocked the door, got in, turned the key in the ignition switch and sat, letting the engine idle for a few moments, wishing Lili was there to share the journey home. Normally they would have spent the night at the Jochum, but Lili had a summer cold and had stayed at the Alte Hofburg.

The engine warmed up, he drove down the ramps, past the dozing attendant and into the road. There, the radio, left on the local news service since the morning, sprang into life. '. . . At 3 o'clock this afternoon, armed thieves stole an estimated fifty thousand Marks from a Darmstadt bank . . .' He turned the dial until he found some classical music, Bruch's Second Violin Concerto, one of his very favourite pieces.

There was a police road block on the Deutschherrnufer, presumably something to do with the Darmstadt bank robbery, but they waved Bruno through.

As he drove along, Bruno wondered if Lili would consider supervising the interior design of the Prinz Luitpold. She had recently organized the very tasteful redecoration of the Alte Hofburg and shown an unexpected feel for old buildings. And he might suggest to Viktoria putting Eduard and Senta in charge of the hotel when it was completed. He had a lot of time for that young couple and Lili was fond of them, too. Senta had recently given birth to a second child, a little boy named Karl after his great-grandfather. Lili adored the two children: four-year-old, red-haired Gisela, with green eyes so like her own, and little, blond Karl . . .

Although he would never have admitted it to anyone, he knew he had been taking a business gamble when he had offered his help to Viktoria and gambling with his emotional happiness when he had married Lili. But time was proving them to be the two best decisions he had ever made.

Lili was waiting for him when he reached the Alte Hofburg. 'You're late. I was beginning to worry,' she said, putting her arms around him and kissing him. And he knew himself to be the most fortunate man on earth.

Chapter 20

For over a year, Norbert had been dividing his time between Munich, Zurich and Berlin, as well as accompanying Oskar Stallkamp to his various sites throughout the Federal Republic, monitoring the vital repair work. It was a punishing routine and one which, as Norbert would have been the first to admit, he would not have even considered undertaking had it not been for Ursula's influence. She had driven him as she drove herself, expecting him to give the same commitment to Landgut as she gave to Leo Metzner Advertising.

Oskar had refused to move to Berlin and remained at the Landgut Hamburg office, but Erwin Hoffmann had leapt at the opportunity, master-minding the relocation of Landgut's new head office, dealing with all formalities with the Bonn and Berlin Finance Offices and setting up a new, small administration.

As a result, everything which Erwin and Ursula had planned was being achieved: the value of Landgut properties were rising; the company's tax liabilities had been reduced; and a brand-new estate was being erected on the Kraus Village site, two blocks of which had been completed and were already inhabited, while the third was making rapid progress.

To begin with, when Norbert was in Berlin, he had stayed at Heiligensee, but, as Ursula was quick to point out, it was a long and often tedious journey to and from Wedding. 'I don't know why you keep that place,' she said. 'Helena's the only person who's ever lived there for any length of time. In your position, I'd sell it.'

That was Ursula, practical as always. But in this one matter, Norbert did not give in. The only person to whom he would ever sell the Heiligensee cottage was Viktoria and, although she still went there occasionally at weekends, she claimed not to want it back.

So at Ursula's suggestion, a penthouse apartment, with a separate lift and its own entrance, was built on the top floor of the apartment block in Wedding which also housed Landgut's new office.

Ursula's opinion of Norbert was changing. What she had originally assumed to be laziness, she now recognized as a quality which had been lacking in herself. Norbert had a tremendous capacity for living. No matter how tight his schedule, he still found time to go to the theatre and the opera, see a new film, read a new book, visit an art exhibition and buy a new picture. When they were driving from one place to another, he would leave the autobahn to lunch at an inn or restaurant to which someone had recommended him in a village or town off the beaten track.

When Ursula complained that their diversion had made them late for an appointment, or that a show, followed by dinner, had led her to oversleep in the morning, Norbert would laugh at what he called her 'in-built Swiss cuckoo clock' and 'Swiss work ethic'.

Sometimes they would spend the weekend at her apartment in Zurich or at his home outside Munich and, although Ursula would never like the house – to her, it seemed haunted by the ghosts of the other women in his life – she now found herself comparing it with her own apartment, of which she had always been so proud, but which appeared suddenly sterile and lacking in character.

As the summer was reaching its end, they discovered an empty villa on a hillside overlooking Lugano, with a panoramic view over the lake. Enquiries revealed that it was for sale and the estate agent drove up to show them round. A small *palazzo*, its rooms were high-ceilinged with marble floors and tall, shuttered windows; it had a colonnaded terrace, statues in the gardens and an empty pool built in the style of a Roman bath.

While Norbert and the agent discussed practical details, Ursula wandered through the grounds until she found a sundrenched courtyard with a ramshackle greenhouse, stacks of terracotta pots, a headless cherub and a south-facing wall covered with an ancient vine. She sat down on a stone bench and lifted her face to the sun.

476

Never before had she seen a house in which she had instantly known that she could be truly happy, and certainly not in the company of the only man in the world with whom she wanted to spend the rest of her life. True, the place was badly in need of modernization and would cost a fortune to run. As for the grounds, she had never done more than tend her balcony and knew nothing about gardening. Yet she could see herself helping decorate and furnish the building, and getting up at dawn to supervise the gardeners . . .

Eventually, she heard a car door slam and Norbert's voice calling her. He entered the courtyard and sat down beside her, putting his arm round her shoulders. 'Why are you hiding here? Don't you like it?'

'On the contrary, I think it's absolutely beautiful.'

'Ursula, I love you – and I think you love me. Marry me and we can move in together, start a new life . . .'

For a long time, she sat gazing sightlessly at the headless cherub, trying to convince herself that the dream he offered could come true. But, deep in her heart, she knew it was an illusion. They had long ago become lovers: as their lives had become ever more closely interlinked, it had been impossible to maintain that cool distance between them. She had given him her body and, even though he might not realize it, she had given him her heart. But to marry him would be to give him all of herself.

Was he prepared to make the same commitment? She already knew the answer. After a year or two, he would grow bored with her as he had his other wives and girlfriends. He might let her keep the villa, but he would be gone. 'No,' she said, 'I prefer to remain friends with you than become the fourth ex-Frau Norbert Kraus.'

After the easy success of Darmstadt, Helena's group undertook several more bank raids, all more profitable than the first. Marko's favourite record became the Georgie Fame hit, 'The Ballad of Bonnie and Clyde'.

In the autumn, Ulrike Meinhof, Andreas Baader, Gudrun Ensslin, Horst Mahler and the others unexpectedly returned to Germany from the Middle East and, after a couple of months in

Berlin, during which time they carried out several bank raids and a number of their gang were arrested, turned up in Frankfurt.

Helena nursed great expectations of this reunion, but she was swiftly disillusioned. The Berlin factioneers talked a lot about the urban guerilla tactics they had learned in Jordan but did little to launch their vaunted revolution. Much of their time seemed to be spent arguing among themselves and sorting out their complicated personal relationships. Because they were still wanted by the police, they adopted pseudonyms, carried false papers and assumed various disguises, but from comments they let drop, it was clear they had been betrayed in Berlin, probably by one of their own members.

Helena was worried that they would soon all have the police on their trail. Matthias was openly scornful of them. 'They talk about revolution, but they don't do anything.'

Marko lit a joint and watched the smoke float up to the ceiling. 'What is there to do, man?'

'We should be doing more than just robbing banks. We should be attacking the system . . .'

'Bank raids attack the capitalist system,' Marko pointed out.

'I know what Matthias means,' Helena said. 'The bank raids are meant to finance the revolution, not to be an end in themselves.'

After that, they gradually broke away from the 'Baader-Meinhof gang' and formed their own splinter group, which they named the Black Kommando Movement, and which had its own uniform of black trousers, black boots and black leather jackets.

Long, spaced-out evenings were spent at the Beethoven-strasse discussing how to achieve Black Kommando's aims. Dolfi was seldom present on those occasions. Marko said, 'He's one of the oppressed workers we're going to liberate. He doesn't understand enough to help himself.' The truth was, none of them felt comfortable in Dolfi's presence. For one thing, he was still very countrified. He didn't smoke, drink or take drugs. He didn't like their music. All he was interested in was his family and cars. Yet, for some unfathomable reason, he identified with their cause.

More often than not, however, Helena, Marko, Matthias

478

and Heinz-Georg were joined by others among their Frankfurt acquaintances, people who knew nothing about the bank raids but who shared their political ideals, who, on a drug-induced high, would suggest the most fantastic operations, all of which at the time seemed perfectly feasible. During those trancelike evenings, they considered the assassination of Chancellor Brandt or President Heinemann; they discussed kidnapping a top politician like Franz-Joseph Strauss and holding him for ransom; they talked about setting fire to the Bundeshaus; and planned how to place a bomb in NATO or army headquarters.

Yet, in the cold light of day, they were forced to discard these ideas as wildly impracticable. Most public figures were surrounded by tight personal security. A kidnap victim had to be kept somewhere. It was no simple matter to walk into the Bundeshaus or a military headquarters and plant a bomb. Special passes would be required, uniforms, get-away vehicles, walkie-talkie sets, guns, ammunition, explosives, detonators . . . Above all, they required money and Black Kommando's funds were already diminishing. It was a Catch-22 situation. As Marko said, 'It's too much hassle, man.'

So, during the winter, they resumed their bank raids, in cities as far apart as Munich and Luebeck, Hanover and Stuttgart, Kiel and Cologne. They became rich, with suitcases overflowing with notes. Dolfi closed his repair business and devoted himself solely to stealing and doctoring cars. Marko created a range of ever more ingenious disguises. Matthias talked their friends into letting them have keys to their apartments and holiday homes, so Black Kommando had bases throughout the country.

Then, in the early summer of 1971, disaster struck. They robbed a bank in Essen, not only getting the money from the cashiers' tills, but the safe contents as well. Helena, Marko and Matthias, balaclavas over their heads, were out of the building with their haul and clambering into the stolen BMW which Dolfi, wearing a ginger wig and sunglasses, had waiting at the kerb, when Heinz-Georg, who had been holding staff and customers at gunpoint and was last out of the bank, stumbled and fell.

A passer-by leaped on him and pinned him to the ground. Matthias loosed off a wild round from his sub-machine gun.

From all directions, people appeared, screaming and shouting. A passing car tried to ram the BMW and Helena sprayed a burst of fire at its wheels, with the result that it lurched out of control and collided with another vehicle coming in the opposite direction. Dolfi put down his foot on the accelerator and, with screaming tyres, took off down the street, dodging in and out of the traffic, ignoring red traffic lights and pedestrian crossings.

From way behind them came the sound of sirens. 'We must switch cars,' Matthias said. 'Take the next turning to the left. Now the next one. Slow down.' They were in a residential area, near a school, from which parents were collecting their children. A Mercedes was parked on the other side of the road, its engine running, the driver's door slightly ajar, while a mother went to shepherd her offspring across the road. 'Stop!' Matthias shouted. 'I'll drive. Marko, Dolfi, bring the bags and the guns.'

Quick as a flash, Matthias was out of the Audi and into the Mercedes. Helena, Marko and Dolfi threw themselves into the back. Then they were off again, screeching past the Mercedes' astonished owner, heading towards the autobahn and safety.

They dumped the Mercedes near the main railway station in Cologne and, travelling in different compartments, caught a train back to Frankfurt.

On the television evening news, the announcer said, 'A man has been arrested, but four other thieves escaped in a stolen car after a raid on a bank in Essen this afternoon, during which shots were fired. The man, who has been named by police as Heinz-Georg Lindner from Berlin-West, was apprehended as a result of the courageous actions of a passer-by . . .'

Helena rolled herself a joint, lit it and inhaled deeply. 'This is the opportunity we've been waiting for,' she said slowly. 'Let's use Heinz-Georg to make the world aware of Black Kommando.'

Heinz-Georg knew sufficient of his legal rights to know he was entitled to a lawyer. The only one he knew of was Dieter Duschek.

Although Dieter was surprised to receive the telephone call

480

from Heinz-Georg Lindner at Essen police station, he was also rather flattered at being remembered, and agreed to visit him to discuss his case.

His immediate reaction upon meeting his client was to wish he had refused. Heinz-Georg's first request was for hashish and when Dieter explained that was impossible, he turned churlish and uncooperative, refusing absolutely to name his associates in the bank robbery; giving his address as an apartment block in West Berlin, which turned out to have been demolished; and his occupation as student, although records showed he had left university three years earlier. The police eventually traced his mother to a different address, but she said she had lost touch with him years ago.

Dieter was about to recommend that Lindner looked for another lawyer, when he was sent through the post a photocopied typed sheet calling itself *The Black Kommando Manifesto*. It was a list of political demands, with some of which Dieter totally agreed, such as the abolition of nuclear weapons and nuclear power stations, the withdrawal of American troops from Vietnam, the recognition of the GDR; and some of which were arrant nonsense, like replacing parliamentarianism in the Federal Republic with a proletarian system. But what particularly caught his attention was the message in large capital letters at the bottom of the page: HEINZ-GEORG LINDNER IS INNOCENT!

When he rang Stefan, he discovered *Aktuell* had also received one of these communications and, in the course of the next couple of days, it emerged that politicians, judges, newspapers, radio and television stations throughout the country all had copies, posted on different days from different towns.

Dieter returned to Essen, showed Lindner the so-called Manifesto and asked him about Black Kommando. Heinz-Georg shrugged. 'It's like it says, man. It's a revolutionary peace movement. We did the bank to raise funds.'

When Dieter asked why, if he was an advocate of peace, he had been armed with a sub-machine gun, Lindner replied that he and his comrades were prepared, if necessary, to kill for peace.

481

'And who are your comrades?' Dieter asked. 'Are you part of the Baader-Meinhof gang or the Red Army Faktion?'

'Shit, man, no. They're just amateurs.' But more than this, Lindner adamantly refused to say.

It was Holger Busko, who believed passionately that everyone was innocent until proved guilty and was therefore entitled to the best possible defence, who convinced Dieter that they should take on the case. 'Leave Black Kommando out of it for the moment,' he said, when he returned to the office in Berlin's Knesebeckstrasse on Friday, after his routine three days in Bonn. 'Consider the case on its own merits. Lindner took part in a bank robbery, but didn't actually steal anything. He was caught with a gun, but did not fire it.'

'We can't ignore Black Kommando,' Dieter argued. 'It would appear to be central to the whole issue.'

'No. Lindner has been charged with robbery, not with belonging to an organization. His reasons for committing the crime are only relevant if they can be used to show mitigating circumstances, such as diminished responsibility.'

'That postscript worries me. There's a threat inherent in it. We can do our best to ensure he is given a fair trial, but we cannot pervert the course of justice. Lindner is guilty, if not of armed robbery, certainly of being an accessory. And when the verdict is reached, what will Black Kommando do? My guess is, it intends to take the law into its own hands.'

Holger shook his head. 'Dieter, take my advice, concentrate on the actual case in hand.'

Yet after Dieter had left the room, Holger found himself pondering over their conversation and, suddenly, from the depths of his memory an image emerged of Matthias Scheer, standing in that very office, after being released from police custody following the disturbances at the time of the Shah of Iran's visit to Berlin in 1967, the day Benno Ohnesorg had been shot. He could still remember, almost word for word, Matthias's tirade against his grandfather and his admission, which had so shocked Dieter, that during the early peace demonstrations there had been occasions when he had longed to fire a gun wildly into the crowd.

He could still hear Helena Kraus saying, 'If the pigs are

482

going to use guns on us, we'll use guns on them. The days of non-violent resistance are over!'

And Lindner had told Dieter, 'We are prepared, if necessary, to kill for peace.'

It could be a coincidence. But the three of them had all been in Berlin at the same time. It was possible they had stayed in touch.

However, Holger said nothing to anyone about his suspicions. He had no proof to back them up. They were pure surmise.

That summer of 1971, Kris reached the pinnacle of his Formula Three racing career. It had been his season on the circuits, winning one race after another. Racing magazines throughout the world were prophesying he would soon be moving to Formula One. He drove down to Monaco in a new Lotus Elite with his latest girlfriend, Juliette Marvaux, the temperamental and sultry singer whose latest single 'Baise-Moi Ici' – Kiss Me Here – had been topping the charts ever since it had been banned by the BBC.

Practice day at Monaco, however, did not go according to plan. Kris could only get second fastest time against his great rival, Tomi Pedersen, who was driving a Cooper. When he returned to pits, he berated Egon and Rolf. 'The engine isn't giving full power. I'm going quicker than Tomi through the bends and corners, but I'm not going as fast down the straights. Get the damn thing sorted out.'

Egon watched him go off, arm around Juliette's waist. 'Maybe if you learned to bloody drive . . .' he muttered.

Grinning, Rolf gave an admiring glance at Juliette's legs under its micro-skirt, then took off the Lotus's bonnet. Egon Weber was the only person on the team allowed to criticize Kris. If any of the mechanics dared say so much as one word against the driver, their heads would be for the block. 'He has a point, though. Both cars have the same Coventry Climax power unit . . .'

Egon returned his attention to the Lotus. 'I don't want to alter the engine tune.' He sighed. 'I suppose we could try a new fuel pump, in case pressure is fractionally down.'

An hour later and a new fuel pump in place, he glanced at

483

his watch, then turned to Rolf. 'There's just time for a couple of circuits before the roads are cleared.' He told one of the younger mechanics, 'Go and find Kris. Try the bar first.'

Kris, however, was nowhere to be found. 'Getting shagged, I suppose,' Egon growled in exasperation. 'I'll kill him one of these days. Rolf, you'll have to take it round. Test it out at full revs.'

Rolf was no longer grinning. 'You know how I feel about driving fast . . .'

'Well, I can't drive the damned thing . . .'

'*Signori, Signori*, what is the problem?' An Italian voice interrupted their argument; the debonair figure of motoring correspondent and racing driver Piero Copproni intervened between them. 'You want someone to drive this Lotus?'

Egon sighed. 'Well, I guess you'll do as well as anyone . . .'

After a couple of laps, Piero returned. 'Is-a beautiful.' He kissed his fingertips. 'It goes like a dream. And I reach peak revs in top gear . . .'

Egon did not see Kris again until the following morning at breakfast. 'Where the hell have you been?' he snarled.

'Up in the mountains. Juliette . . .'

'Fuck Juliette. We changed the fuel pump after your practice run yesterday. As you weren't there, Piero Copproni took your place . . .'

'You let that wop drive *my* car?'

'What the hell else were we supposed to do?'

Kris knew Egon had right on his side but he wasn't going to admit it. After leaving the pits yesterday, Juliette had asked that they drive into the mountains, where she had informed him that she was pregnant, claimed he was the father and demanded that he marry her. When he had refused, she had taken his car and disappeared into the distance. He had had to walk for miles before a peasant had taken pity on him and given him a lift in his cart back to civilization.

The day got worse. Kris started second on the grid, made a poor start and was lying fifth by the end of the first lap.

In the pits, Egon's face was pale and drawn. 'What the devil's got into him?' he demanded.

As if Kris could hear him, he put his foot down on and,

within a few laps, had overtaken the three cars between himself and Tomi Pedersen and was sitting on the Swede's tail.

'He's over-revving. He'll blow up the bloody engine!' Egon fumed, signalling frantically. But if Kris saw him, he ignored him.

It was not often that Kris lost control of his temper, but the combination of Juliette's lies, her theft of his car, Egon's accusations, Piero Copproni driving the Lotus the previous day and now Pedersen, were simply too much for him. During the tenth lap he saw, and seized, the opportunity to overtake Pedersen. Their wheels brushed and only good fortune and great skill prevented Pedersen from crashing. Now in the lead, Kris used every trick in the book to stop Pedersen getting past him.

'What the hell's he think he's doing?' Egon muttered, as Kris's Lotus roared past, with Pedersen's Cooper so close on its tail that the two cars were almost touching. The slightest mistake and they would both be killed.

A steward hurried up to him. 'Monsieur Weber, you should know that the stewards are considering black-flagging your driver for dangerous driving.'

Egon took a deep breath. 'It's Pedersen who's driving dangerously. He's too close . . .'

'Your driver overtook . . .'

Anger meant that Kris was not concentrating on his driving. On the fast run to the slow gasworks hairpin, he made a poor gear change – and Pedersen sped past. Kris ground his teeth and put his right foot down, relegating Juliette and all his other problems to the back of his mind. Only one thing mattered right now: to win the race.

At a speed of 140 mph, over-revving drastically, he pulled alongside Pedersen. They were going neck and neck, neither driver prepared to give way. The bend approached. Brakes smoking, they slowed down, then just past the marker boards, Pedersen's common sense prevailed and he let the Lotus go. It was too late. He was going much too fast and, after spinning wildly several times, hit the straw bales.

God alone knew how, but Kris negotiated the bend. However, as his foot came off the brakes to put on power again, his overheated brakes stayed locked and the Lotus ran straight on, into the straw bales and the Armco barrier, then somersaulted twice, end over end, before landing, battered but right side up. As marshalls ran towards the car, a sheet of flame erupted from the ruptured fuel tank.

An ambulance rushed Kris to hospital, where his injuries proved extensive. He had suffered severe bruising and burns, both his legs were broken, his collarbone was cracked and he had two broken ribs. Kris himself, however, was unaware of anything: of the hours he spent in the operating theatre; of the press clamouring at the hospital doors; of the fact that Tomi Pedersen had limped home to finish the race; that he himself had been black-flagged; and the stewards were holding an enquiry with a view to banning him from racing. Although X-rays showed that, miraculously, his skull had not been fractured, he did not regain consciousness after the accident.

It was left to Egon to break the news to Kris's family. He telephoned Norbert first, but it took several calls to Munich, Hamburg, Berlin, Zurich and finally Lugano before he located him. Next, Egon rang Reinhild, who had hysterics and had to ring him back for more details, after she had called in a neighbour for support and been persuaded by her to have a medicinal brandy. Both parents contacted the hospital, where the consultant told them that possibly the familiar sound of their voices would arouse Kris from his coma.

Norbert arrived first, his natural bombast deserting him immediately he saw Kris lying in bed, his legs encased in plaster, his ribs strapped up, his face bandaged, tubes attached to various parts of his body. Concealing his shock as best he could, he sat down and tried to do as the doctor instructed, talk naturally to his son. But it was hard to know what to say to someone with whom he had virtually lost contact and who did not respond with even so much as a blink of the eyelid or the squeeze of a hand.

Then Reinhild entered the room, gazed at Kris, let out a scream and was hurriedly shepherded away by the nurse. When she returned, she told Norbert bitterly, 'You're hardly likely to do much good. It's all your fault he's in this state.

486

I tried to bring him up properly, but you went behind my back. You gave him his first car. You've always encouraged him in his mad ideas. If it wasn't for you, he wouldn't be here now.'

The consultant quickly realized that the presence of Kris's parents was going to hinder rather than help the patient's chances of recovery and recommended that they return to their respective homes, promising to contact them as soon as there was any change in their son's condition.

Week after week, Egon remained at Kris's bedside, only leaving the hospital at night to sleep in a nearby guesthouse. He remembered saying the day before the race, *I'll kill him one of these days*. He hadn't meant it. He had grown to love Kris, spoiled, cocky brat though he was. Over the years he had come to think of him almost as his own son. He was the only German racing driver around with a very real talent, the ability to be a Grand Prix winner, a champion. The last thing Egon wanted was for him to die.

The burns slowly healed. The breaks and fractures progressed as satisfactorily as they could without Kris being able to exercise his damaged limbs. Day after day, Egon talked aloud to him. 'Come on, lad,' he would urge. 'We've got to get your muscles working again. You won't be any good on the circuit if you can't use your legs and arms.'

Then, suddenly, one day, when Egon had almost given up hope that he would ever regain consciousness, Kris opened his eyes, turned his head and asked, 'Where am I?'

Tears prickled at the back of Egon's eyes and there was a lump in his throat, but he managed to reply, 'In hospital, you stupid bugger.'

Kris's accident, and the realization that Egon had succeeded where both his parents had failed, had a chastening effect on Norbert. He was fifty-one that year and, for the first time, he looked back on his life and instead of seeing it in terms of material and financial triumph, recognized it as one of personal and moral failure.

His children had slipped away from him. Even Kleo made it clear that she felt she owed her success far more to her own,

487

independent efforts and Dieter's unflagging support, than to Norbert's paternal influence.

He had been through three marriages and made none of his wives happy. For three years he had been courting Ursula and still there seemed little likelihood that she would marry him.

With an unfamiliar feeling of remorse, he wondered where his life had taken its wrong turning.

'Egon Weber has encouraged Kris in his career. For weeks on end, he sat next to his bed in that hospital,' he eventually told Ursula, one weekend, after dinner at her Zurich apartment. 'Time, that's what he's given Kris, while all I've given is money. I've always been so intent on living my own life, I couldn't be bothered to give my children my time. I've used money to try to secure their affections.

'Money has never been important to me, not in the way it is to Werner. If Werner had had to keep on meeting divorce settlements and footing the bill for his children's mistakes, he'd have done some careful self-analysis before now. But it was so easy to write out another cheque. That was the worst thing for me to do, though, wasn't it?'

He gave a deep sigh. 'I can't go back on the past. I can't undo all the mistakes I've made. But I can try not to make the same mistakes again.'

Ursula did not trust herself to speak.

'So, among other things, I've decided to sell Landgut.'

'You can't sell Landgut!' The words escaped her involuntarily.

'Why not? If I'm honest, it ceased to mean anything to me except as a source of income a long time ago. While I was building the business it was a challenge. But once I had achieved what I wanted, it bored me, which is why – if it hadn't been for you – it would probably have fallen into rack and ruin. Now, thanks to you and Erwin, I'm in a very good position to sell.'

'But what would you do?'

'Devote my energies to the Villa Salvatore, which is still on the market. And, I hope – spend much more time with you . . .'

Ursula looked down at her nails, then up at him. 'What makes you think I am any different from anything or anyone else in your past, that you won't get bored with me?'

A vestige of a smile flickered over Norbert's lips. 'Because you are the unachievable in my life. You have proved that I can't win or buy you. You are the one thing I most want and shall never own.'

Chang, who had been curled up asleep in his armchair, disinterested in the conversation, suddenly yawned, stood up, arched his back and stretched first his back legs, then the front. Then he jumped down and padded across the carpet. For a few moments, he sat at Norbert's feet, studying him. Then, claws in, he leaped onto Norbert's lap, turned a couple of times to make himself comfortable and settled himself down to sleep again.

As Norbert tentatively stroked the cat's silky fur, Ursula gave a jerky laugh. 'They say cats have a sixth sense. Chang obviously believes you . . .'

'I love you, Ursula. I want to make you happy.'

'I love you, too . . .'

'Will you marry me?'

After a long pause, she said, 'Yes, Norbert, I will marry you.'

On their next visit to Berlin, Norbert and Ursula invited Kleo and Dieter to join them and Viktoria for dinner at the Jochum. Kleo was in her final year at university, preparing for her finals.

'What about you, Dieter?' Norbert asked. 'The criminal classes keeping you busy?'

'Dieter's involved in the Lindner bank robbery case,' Kleo explained.

'Lindner? Well, we all know about him. Wherever you go, there seem to be slogans painted on walls saying "Heinz-Georg Lindner is innocent!" Is he?'

'Everyone is innocent until proved guilty,' Dieter replied.

'Funny business, though. If I remember rightly, he belongs to some organization which wants to abolish everything, but doesn't know what to replace it with, and was robbing a bank in Essen in order to get funds.'

Dieter laughed grimly. 'That's about right. But Black Kommando also has a more sinister side. It is, apparently, prepared to kill for peace.'

489

Waiters cleared their plates and served the next course and Norbert took advantage of the interval to change the subject. 'Now to the real purpose of this dinner. I'd like you all to be the first to know that Ursula and I are getting married – and that I'm selling Landgut.'

Ignoring the last part of the statement, Kleo leaped from her chair and rushed round the table to embrace and kiss them both. 'Oh, that's wonderful news! I am so pleased.'

A blush of pleasure coloured Ursula's cheeks. 'Thank you, Kleo. I would understand if you felt some antagonism towards me . . .'

'Towards you? It's not your fault that Father has been so foolish in the past! But I am glad that you've finally brought him to his senses.'

Viktoria laughed and Norbert cleared his throat sheepishly.

Dieter shook their hands and wished them happiness, then said, 'You're selling Landgut, Herr Kraus? May I ask why?'

Norbert explained his reasons, then went on, 'Furthermore I have a buyer. I'm selling the company to my brother.'

'To Werner Kraus KG?' A frown darkened Dieter's features.

Norbert gave a thin smile. 'There were other interested parties but, in the end, the best solution seemed to be to let Werner have it.' Briefly, he described the circumstances under which, in 1951, he had exchanged his shares in Kraus Industries for Werner's holding in Landgut.

'When I informed Werner, as a matter of courtesy, that I was selling Landgut, he immediately dispatched your father to see me. Joachim told me that I had no right to sell Landgut. He denied that any deal had taken place and claimed that Werner had a fifty per cent holding in Landgut.'

'Wouldn't that mean you are also entitled to half of Werner Kraus KG?'

'Difficult to prove. I wasn't a shareholder in Werner Kraus, but in Kraus Industries, which doesn't exist any more.'

Dieter glowered. 'If you'll excuse me saying so, my father and your brother are a couple of corrupt, immoral scoundrels! Werner Kraus spent five years in prison because he was a war criminal. Yet what is he now? One of the wealthiest men in Germany! And who helped him get there? My father!'

490

'I agree with you. However, Joachim also informed me that if I sold Landgut on the open market, my brother was prepared to contest my actions in court.'

'Fight him,' Dieter urged. 'We'll represent you. It's the kind of case Holger would really enjoy! So would I.'

'You might, but I wouldn't. I don't want my wedding to be haunted by the spectres of past Kraus scandals. If you want to expose the malpractices of Werner Kraus KG, you'll have to find another reason. I've lived extremely well from Landgut, and the price to which Werner has now agreed is more than sufficient to keep Ursula and myself in comfort for the rest of our lives, as well as providing a legacy, in due course, for Kleo, Kris and Helena. That's my main concern. However, I must admit that it would be satisfying to think that Werner will, one day, get his just retribution.'

Norbert and Ursula's wedding took place in November 1971. The sale of Landgut had not yet been completed, but lawyers on both sides were making steady progress in their negotiations. The purchase of the Villa Salvatore had proved a speedier matter and the couple were already in possession of their new home.

Following Norbert's dramatic decision to sever his ties with the past, Ursula had been forced to consider her own position with regard to Leo Metzner Advertising. She could not bear the idea of relinquishing all interest in the agency. Eventually, after much soul-searching and long discussions with her colleagues, she decided upon a compromise. Her top managers would, over a period of five years, buy her shares in the company, and she would remain president.

Strangely, once her decision was reached, instead of sadness, she felt a sense of relief, as if a burden had been lifted from her shoulders. Only then did she realize how heavily her responsibilities had weighed on her over the years since Leo's death. She followed Norbert's example in selling his Munich house, by putting her flat up for rent.

The wedding took place in Lugano and was attended by Viktoria, Kleo, Dieter and Kris, who, outwardly at least, seemed recovered from his accident.

Norbert was not the only one upon whom the crash had

491

had a chastening effect. Kris himself admitted that he had been a fool to drive so dangerously and had apologized to Egon Weber and Tomi Pedersen for his behaviour. Under the circumstances, the stewards had decided to give him another chance. With surprising humility, Kris said, 'I've realized that it's not just winning, but how you win that's important.'

Reformed character though he might be, Kris had not lost the impudent sense of humour he had inherited from his father. When, the wedding ceremony over, they were seated for lunch at a lakeside restaurant, he said, 'I've been to all the other weddings, including the one which took place before I was born, so I thought I might as well come to this one as well.'

Norbert laughed. 'Well, make the most of it. There won't be any more.'

'I should hope not. You've got to leave some women for the rest of us.'

Ursula took his jests in good part and countered with a parry of her own. 'Are you thinking of getting married then, Kris?'

'Not after the example Father has set!'

'I can't imagine many girls would want him,' Norbert commented. 'He rather belies the glamorous image of the racing driver, doesn't he?'

'Don't worry, I'll be racing again next season.'

'I look forward to watching you,' Ursula assured him.

'However, unlike Kris, Dieter and I have decided to take a leaf out of your book,' Kleo said, proudly displaying an engagement ring.

More kisses were exchanged, more toasts drunk, and Kleo went on, 'We've decided to get married in spring, when I graduate. We're having a church wedding and we'd like to hold the reception at the Jochum.'

Viktoria beamed and Norbert said, 'I congratulate you both. You deserve every happiness.'

Kleo took his hand. 'You will give me away, won't you?'

'Is that what you want?'

'Yes, Father,' Kleo said softly, 'that's what I would like.'

Viktoria spent a long weekend in Lugano, then took advantage of her visit south to stop off at Munich on her way home and

492

inspect progress at the Jochum-Prinz Luitpold. The transformation Lili had achieved far exceeded all her expectations. More than any of her other hotels, it was acquiring an essence of the old Quadriga, so that when Viktoria walked round it, she felt as if she had stepped back into the past. Eduard and Senta, who, at Bruno's suggestion, Viktoria was transferring to manage the hotel, agreed that it was the jewel in the Jochum crown.

Lili, too, had changed during the last year. It was strange, Viktoria reflected, the effect an inanimate building could have upon a person. Throughout her own life, she had identified with and placed her faith far more in buildings than people. Or was the feeling of happiness which Lili radiated simply the combination of a happy marriage to an attractive, caring man, a sense of inner fulfilment at creating something of her own and seeing her ideas come to fruition?

Whatever the reason, Lili was very warm and loving that day, and the feeling of harmony and contentment which Viktoria had brought with her from Zurich continued throughout her brief stay.

While Lili was working on the hotel, she divided her time between the Alte Hofburg and Munich, staying at a flat in a nearby apartment block owned by the Eschenbachs, where, as often as possible, Bruno joined her.

That Tuesday evening, Bruno arrived from Frankfurt in time for supper, a simple meal of smoked salmon, with brown bread, salad and a bottle of hock.

Afterwards, they moved to the sitting room and Lili lay on the settee, her head on Bruno's lap, his arm casually around her shoulder, while Viktoria told them about the wedding. 'I like the sound of Ursula,' Lili laughed. 'She won't put up with any nonsense from Norbert. I'm glad he's found happiness at last. It's good when things work out right in the end.'

'You romantic,' Bruno chided fondly. 'I suppose you liked fairy stories when you were a little girl, because everyone lived happily ever after.'

'I still like them now I'm a big girl.' She lifted her face to him and he leaned over and kissed her. 'We're like a fairy story, aren't we, Bruno. I was the poor little servant girl and you were Prince Charming.'

'Well, I suppose I did meet you at a ball.'

'Do you realize we've been married over seven years now, Aunt Vicki? It doesn't seem possible, does it?'

It was an evening which would remain in Viktoria's memory for the rest of her life, one of those rare, supremely happy occasions, when it seemed that everything was right in the world.

Chapter 21

Despite Dieter Duschek's eloquent plea to the court for leniency, Heinz-Georg Lindner was found guilty of armed robbery and sentenced to six years' imprisonment.

In Frankfurt, Black Kommando prepared to take its revenge.

For months, they had been arguing about what to do in such an eventuality. Helena had wanted to keep to their original plan and kidnap a top politician, only now, instead of holding him for a ransom, offer to exchange him for Heinz-Georg. But the idea was fraught with too many difficulties.

'Does it have to be a politician?' Marko asked.

'Who else do you suggest?'

Marko was sprawled over the settee, a joint in one hand, the newspaper dangling from the other. 'What about your dear Uncle Werner? Everyone's heard of him.'

'You must be kidding,' Matthias said. 'It would be easier to get to Brandt than to him. I went past the Kraus villa the other day. It's like Fort Knox. Security men everywhere. The same at his office.'

'Well, what about Bruno, Graf von der Eschenbach? There's a bit on him, here. "... is throwing a party in December to celebrate the opening of the Jochum-Prinz Luitpold Hotel in Munich." Rhubarb, rhubarb. "The refurbishment is believed to have cost several million Marks, but for someone in the position of Bruno von der Eschenbach, a Deutschmark billionaire, photographed below with his ..." Jee-sus! Look at that Ferrari! You have to give the guy his due. At least he has style.'

Dolfi went to look over Marko's shoulder at the picture. 'So that's who it belongs to! I've often seen it driving up the Zeil.'

'Why not?' Helena said slowly. 'Eschenbach epitomizes the most despicable aspects of capitalist society. And he was a general, or some kind of high-ranking officer during the war, in the SS, I think. His money probably came from Hitler.'

Dolfi's eyes narrowed.

'He'll do as well as anyone,' Matthias agreed. 'Do you know where he parks the car, Dolfi?'

'Should be easy enough to find out.'

'Then we'll plant a bomb in it. The Doctor can get us explosives and a detonator. Dolfi can fix it. When Eschenbach drives off – bang!'

'You're going to blow it up?' Marko asked, in genuine horror. 'Couldn't we just shoot Eschenbach and steal the Ferrari?'

It was a damp, foggy, Tuesday morning in mid-December and, as always when the weather was bad, the traffic was extremely heavy. Eventually, an hour later than usual, Bruno reached Frankfurt city centre, crawled up the Zeil and into the car park entrance. The attendant, a young Italian called Giuseppe, who eyed the Ferrari lustfully whenever he saw it, emerged from his little office, lifted the barrier and said smartly, 'Good morning, Herr Graf.'

'A pretty disgusting one, if you ask me,' Bruno replied, more cheerfully than he felt.

'Would the Herr Graf like me to wash the Ferrari when I come off duty this afternoon?'

There didn't really seem any point. It would get filthy again on the way to Munich that evening. But Giuseppe was a good, conscientious kid.

'If the Herr Graf will allow me to have the keys, I'll clean the interior as well,' Giuseppe said eagerly.

'All right. Come up later and collect them from Fräulein Hanstein.' Then Bruno raised a warning finger. 'But no driving the car. *Capito?*'

The young Italian looked shocked. 'Of course not, Herr Graf.'

Giuseppe watched the Ferrari disappear up the ramp towards the fifth floor and went back into his little office to dream of the day when the Count would say, 'My chauffeur is leaving. Would you like his job, Giuseppe?'

He was still dreaming when the telephone rang and a female

voice said, 'This is the office of Bruno Graf von der Eschenbach. Fräulein Hanstein speaking . . .'

Fräulein Hanstein was the Count's personal secretary, a very efficient middle-aged lady, of whom Giuseppe was secretly rather afraid.

'At eleven o'clock a mechanic will be coming to deal with an electrical fault on the Herr Graf's car. His name is Johann Schmidt. All you need do is tell him where the car is. Understood?'

'Yes, Fräulein Hanstein, I understand.'

Triumphantly, Helena put down the phone in the grubby little office at Dolfi Feldmann's workshop. It had been easy enough to obtain Fräulein Hanstein's name from the Eschenbach switchboard, but less certain that she could pass herself off as the Count's secretary to the car park attendant. 'I think he's foreign. In any case, he believed I was her.'

'So long as he doesn't come up with me to the car,' Dolfi muttered.

'He won't,' Matthias reassured him.

'Maybe he'll ring up Eschenbach's office to tell him I've arrived.'

'Oh, stop worrying and get dressed,' Helena said impatiently.

With trembling fingers, Dolfi lit a cigarette and left the office to go and change.

'He's shit-scared,' Marko observed.

'Once he's on the job, he'll be OK,' Matthias stated confidently. He reached into his duffel bag, pulled out what looked like a lump of grey plasticine, threw it into the air, caught it and grinned.

'That isn't the bomb?' Marko asked, apprehensively.

'Sure is. But don't worry, kiddo. It can't explode on its own.'

'You're certain Dolfi knows how to fix it?' Helena demanded.

'Sure. There's nothing to it.' Considering the fortune The Doctor had charged them for the explosive and the detonator, the bloody thing had better be foolproof.

When Dolfi returned, he looked very different. They had all had a hand in his disguise. Since Ferrari overalls were

497

impossible to obtain, Matthias had suggested he get some new flared jeans and smear them with a little grease. Marko had acquired Ferrari badges which Helena had laboriously stitched on to an anorak and a baseball cap, as well as stickers to plaster all over Dolfi's new toolbox. Dolfi himself had been growing a moustache and Helena had bought him a shoulder-length wig and a pair of heavy, chrome-framed sunglasses.

Dolfi seemed a little more confident. 'Even the wife wouldn't recognize me now,' he said. But he was still frightened. Stealing cars, driving the gang around the country and robbing banks was one thing. Blowing people up was quite another. If they hadn't told him that Bruno von der Eschenbach was a former Nazi, in cohorts in the SS, possibly even a colleague of his father, he would have refused . . .

In fact, everything went like clockwork. Dolfi arrived at the car park in the white van he had stolen a week earlier and spent the intervening days in cleaning, changing the chassis and registration numbers, and laboriously stencilling on the coachwork: Johann Schmidt, approved repairs, Ferrari, Maserati, Alfa Romeo.

Trying to control the trembling in his hands, he showed the car park attendant his identity card and drove, as directed, to the fifth storey, where he found the Ferrari parked well away from all the other vehicles. He reversed his van into the space next to the Ferrari, leaving the driver's door ajar and his keys in the ignition, in case he had to make a quick get-away. Then he opened the Daytona's doors, bonnet and boot, and studied the wiring for a few moments, as if trying to identify a genuine electrical fault. The car park was very quiet. Not a footstep sounded.

After moving aside the boot carpeting, he pressed the ball of plastic explosive against the Ferrari's petrol tank, then, with his index finger, poked a hole in it. Unwrapping the high velocity detonator from its foam plastic wrapper, he put it into the hole he had made and carefully tamped the plastic explosive around the detonator leaving its terminals exposed. Next, he took out the panel covering the brake and tail light bulbs, and replaced the stop light bulb with one that he had modified back at the garage. Two short lengths of wire to the detonator completed his task. The first time the brakes were applied, the bomb would go off.

Finally, he put back the carpet, so that, when Eschenbach put his briefcase in the boot that evening, he would see no evidence of his work. Then, he shut the boot lid, packed his tools back into the van and got the hell out of the car park.

The attendant saluted him as he left, but Dolfi did not respond. His stomach was churning and his legs felt as if they had turned to jelly. Out in the road, he glanced at his watch. The complete operation had taken exactly twenty-five minutes.

Early that afternoon, a motorcyclist dressed in black leathers, a helmet concealing his features, delivered two envelopes, one to the *Frankfurter Allgemeine*, the other to the *Frankfurter Rundschau*. Typed in capital letters, they read: 'Today's bomb is a warning from Black Kommando. If Heinz-Georg Lindner is not freed, more members of the exploiter class will die. More Nazis will be killed.'

At three o'clock, Giuseppe came off duty. 'I'm coming back soon to clean Graf von der Eschenbach's Ferrari,' he told his replacement, Hermann, an elderly man, who did not share his passion for cars.

'Hope he gives you a decent tip,' Hermann grunted, opening his newspaper to the crossword puzzle.

Fräulein Hanstein was pounding on her typewriter when Giuseppe entered her office. 'The keys are there,' she said, indicating the corner of her desk. 'Don't forget to bring them back.'

'No, Fräulein Hanstein.' Giuseppe wondered if he should mention the mechanic's visit, but at that moment the telephone rang.

He made a beautiful job of cleaning the Daytona, polishing it until its red bodywork gleamed like new and its chrome shone like a mirror, blacking its tyres and trim, and vacuum-cleaning dust and dirt from its interior. When he had finished, he could not resist sitting in the driver's seat.

What must it be like to drive such a car? He imagined himself

499

speeding down the autostrada towards his parents' home in Bari, the envious glances he would get from other motorists, the way the girls would flock to him.

He put the key in the ignition and turned it. The engine emitted a potent, throaty purr.

Giuseppe's hand hovered over the gear lever. He knew he had promised the Count, but what harm could it do just to reverse out of the space and drive back in again? He took off the handbrake and edged backwards. After a few yards, he put his foot on the brake.

That was the last Giuseppe ever knew.

From the boot came a deafening blast as the plastic explosive detonated, followed by another massive bang as the petrol tank caught light and twenty gallons of petrol ignited in a whoosh of flame. So violent was the explosion that the whole building seemed to shake. The car flew apart, doors, bits of engine, seats, pieces of metal and shards of glass hurtling through the air. Giuseppe's body disintegrated, too. Within minutes, all that remained of him and the Ferrari was a smouldering, blackened, molten shell, surrounded by a confusion of debris.

Bruno looked again at the scene of devastation, at the police photographers and forensic scientists working on the carnage, then turned away, his eyes watering, his lungs choked with acrid smoke and fumes.

'I shouldn't have let him have the keys,' he said. 'I should have realized. He was crazy about the car . . .'

The police inspector shook his head. 'You mustn't blame yourself, sir. The bomb wasn't intended for him. There's no doubt it was you they were after.'

'But why? What did they hope to achieve? How does blowing up my Ferrari - how would killing me – help free this bank robber? I know nothing of him. I have nothing to do with him. Why me?'

'No good reason, I suspect, sir, except that you are a public figure.'

'Have you any idea who they are, this Black Kommando movement?'

'I'm afraid not, sir. But we'll find them.'

500

'Lindner won't be freed, will he?'

'No, he'll serve his full sentence.' The police officer paused. 'I think you would agree, that if there is one lesson we Germans should have learned from our past, it is that we must never again submit to terror.'

Heavy-hearted, Bruno went back to his office and telephoned Lili in Munich. He wanted to be the first to tell her the news, before she heard rumours from anyone else. Then, having spoken to her, he asked Fräulein Hanstein to tell his chauffeur to drive the Bentley up immediately from the Alte Hofburg and take him to Munich.

By the time he joined Lili that evening, the assassination attempt was making headlines on the radio and television and was plastered over the front page of every evening paper. Lili was waiting for him at the front door of the apartment block and threw herself into his arms when he got out of the car. Her face was drained of colour and she was trembling.

He put his arm round her shoulders and led her upstairs. 'I'm perfectly all right,' he assured her.

But it was a long time before Lili calmed down. Bruno's near escape from death had revived in her terrifying memories of the war and all the people she had lost then. She had believed that she was at last safe from bombs and death and destruction, but in one afternoon her illusions had been shattered. She clung to Bruno that night and cried as if her heart would break, terrified that the happiness and security she had begun to take for granted was about to be snatched from her.

At the flat on the Beethovenstrasse, Helena, Marko, Matthias and Dolfi stared disbelievingly at the television screen, where a police officer was saying, 'It is believed that a bomb exploded when the car park attendant moved the vehicle. Forensic experts are searching the wreckage. A note claiming responsibility for the incident was received earlier today by two Frankfurt newspapers from an organization calling itself the Black Kommando Movement.'

A few moments later, the cameras moved to the front of the Eschenbach building, where Bruno von der Eschenbach was pushing his way through a crowd of excited reporters and cameramen. His face was grave, but he appeared unshaken. 'My thoughts are for the innocent victim of this tragedy,' he said.

'Will you still be attending the opening party for the new Jochum-Prinz Luitpold Hotel in Munich on Saturday?' a journalist called.

'Of course. Now, if you will excuse me . . .' Eschenbach strode towards a chauffeur-driven car waiting for him at the kerbside.

'We could put a bomb in the hotel,' Marko suggested.

Matthias shook his head. 'We'd never get near. The whole bloody place will be swarming with police.'

Later that same evening, Holger Busko appeared on television to make an impassioned attack against the terrorists. 'I grew up under the terror of Nazi rule and fled from the terror of a Stalinist dictatorship,' he said. 'I hold the possibly naive yet nevertheless strong belief that it is possible for the nations of the world to live together in peace and unity. I have campaigned, and continue to campaign for multilateral disarmament. But peace can only be achieved by peaceful means. Violence will beget only violence.

'In a warning note released prior to the explosion, the killers stated that if one of their members was not released from prison, more of the "exploiter class" and more "Nazis" would die. These references to Herr Graf von der Eschenbach would be laughable if the consequences of Black Kommando's action had been less tragic. Bruno von der Eschenbach has contributed greatly to the prosperity and freedom of this country. Far from being a Nazi, he was a member of the resistance, who tried to save Germany from Nazi terror and, as a result, spent months in a concentration camp. Now, once again, Nazi-style terrorism has been practised against him . . .

'. . . One of the people who influenced me most in my life was Pastor Bernhard Scheer, another courageous man who suffered terribly at the hands of the Nazis. He once told me that no matter what decisions I made, I should think not of myself, but of the generations ahead. "Think of my grandson Matthias and the thousands of children like him," he would say.

'No holds must be barred to stop this new terror before it

502

spreads any further, not only for our own sakes, but for the sake of generations to come.'

'He knows!' Matthias growled.

'No, come off it, man,' Marko said. 'It's a coincidence. He's yammering on about peace, so he mentions your grandfather.'

Helena was sitting on the floor, her knees hunched between her arms. 'This is propaganda, the sort of crap Dr Goebbels used to put out. And Holger accuses us of using Nazi tactics. He accuses us of betraying our cause, but he's a far worse traitor. By defending Eschenbach, he's betrayed the socialist cause. He's defected to the Right. What a shit!'

'So what do you want to do?' Marko asked. 'Eliminate him?'

Dolfi stood up, his face white. 'No! No more bombs! No more killing!'

'Hey, man, what's up with you?'

'Is that true what he's been saying – that Eschenbach was never a Nazi? That he was in a concentration camp?'

Marko shrugged. 'I don't know. Who cares?'

Dolfi cared. He cared very much indeed. 'It is true, isn't it? You all lied to me. You told me he was in the SS . . .'

'What the hell does it matter?'

'It matters to me,' Dolfi muttered. For a few moments he stood, staring at them, hurt and perplexed, then he said, 'I don't want anything more to do with you. I want out.'

'Helena, did you hear that? Dolfi wants to split.'

'Yes, I heard.' Helena's entire body felt like a tensed-up spring, ready to burst with impotent, frustrated anger. She jumped to her feet and confronted Dolfi. 'It's your fault!' she screamed. 'You got the wrong fucking person! You're no use to us! Get out!' She pushed him to the door and on to the landing. He stumbled down the stairs and still her voice echoed shrilly after him, 'You fucked it up . . .'

Dolfi did not return home that evening. For a long time, he wandered aimlessly through the streets, trying to understand how he could have been so deceived by Black Kommando, that he had been brought to the pitch of murder. But none of it made any sense. All he knew was that he could not bear to go on living with himself after what had happened.

503

Eventually, he went to his workshop, inside which the white van was concealed. After locking the workshop doors behind him, he got into the van, opened its windows and doors and switched on the engine.

Gabi had grown used to the erratic hours Dolfi worked, but he never stayed out all night without warning her beforehand. When morning came and he had still not returned home, she left the children with a neighbour and went to his workshop. The van had run out of petrol by the time she arrived, but the carbon monoxide fumes from the exhaust had done their job. Dolfi was slumped back in the driver's seat – dead.

They drove in convoy to Berlin, Matthias on his BMW motorbike, Marko and Helena in the silver Audi. For once, Marko kept strictly within the speed limit and they attracted no attention as they headed up the autobahn to the Herleshausen-Wartha border transit point. Before they crossed into the GDR, they filled up with petrol, then continued their journey, two vehicles inconspicuous amidst the many others in the long convoy making the tedious trek across the flat, snowbound countryside that Sunday.

It was evening when they reached Berlin. They drove straight to Schmargendorf and, while Matthias let himself into the Scheer apartment, Marko and Helena unloaded the luggage from the boot. The first two cases they carried up to the flat were the most important: one contained large-denomination bank notes; the other was apparently filled with clothes but, concealed under a false bottom, lay two sub-machine guns, a couple of revolvers, ammunition, and a copious supply of marijuana and LSD.

In the church nearby, where Pastor Scheer had once valiantly preached in defiance of the Nazis, the faithful were celebrating evensong.

The following Sunday, Holger took his children, Franz and Petra, to visit his wife's parents in Grunewald. Normally, Erna would have come with them, but she had a bad cold and remained at home. As always, the old couple made a great fuss of their grandchildren. Grandma baked their favourite apple pudding, served with lashings of whipped cream, and Grandad allowed them to play with his old wind-up gramophone. When they left, 7-year-old Franz was given a racing Mercedes for his slot racer track and 5-year-old Petra a teddy bear which growled when its tummy was pressed.

Throughout the journey home, Holger was distracted by noises from the back seat of Franz imitating the roar of a racing car and Petra's bear being pummelled into non-stop vocal action. It was dark and sleety, and he was unaware of the van which followed him from the Pohls' home, and took no notice of the motorbike which sped past him as he turned off to Charlottenburg. Then, suddenly, the van overtook him, turned into the dimly lit residential road in which the Buskos lived, lined on either side with parked cars, and slewed to an abrupt halt, blocking the road. Holger slammed on his brakes.

A motorcycle pulled out from the shelter of a parked car, drew up alongside him, and the biker, who was wearing a visored crash helmet, a black leather bomber-style jacket, black leggings and black boots, gesticulated towards the van. Holger wound down his window.

Even as he did so, instinct told him something was wrong, but it was too late to do anything. The motorbike immediately edged forwards a couple of feet and Holger found himself confronted by a similarly visored pillion passenger who pulled out a sub-machine gun from inside his jacket, and sprayed a deafening, deadly salvo of bullets into the car.

One of the first shots killed Holger on impact, smashing his forehead and penetrating deep into his brain. Another hit Franz in the chest and another Petra in the shoulder. They screamed in terror, but the barrel of the gun continued to sweep relentlessly backwards and forwards across the car, its bullets shattering the windows, tearing into the upholstery, striking Holger and his children again and again, until the magazine ran out. Then the motorcyclist revved his engine, the van driver pulled away, and both vehicles disappeared into the night.

Helena returned to Schmargendorf on a tremendous high. This time, there had been no mistake. The right person had been killed.

After the tense preparations of the previous week, during which they had taken it in turns to tail Holger round the city, hired a van and had false numberplates made up for Matthias's bike, their efforts had been rewarded. Furthermore, nobody could have any clue as to their identity. Marko had been dressed very respectably in an overcoat, hat and leather shoes, and was wearing glasses, when he hired the van and while he was driving it. He had left a cash deposit and given their former Frankfurt address. He alone had followed Holger to Grunewald, telephoning Matthias and Helena to let them know where he was. Disguised in their motorcycling gear, they had both been unrecognizable. Helena had certainly not been identifiable as female.

After the shoot-out, Marko had dumped the van outside the hire office, gone into a gents lavatory and changed into jeans and anorak, and caught the U-Bahn back to Schmargendorf, while Matthias and Helena had driven to a quiet spot on the edge of the Tiergarten, removed the false plates from the bike, thrown them into the Spree and replaced them with the original ones.

Back at the Scheer apartment, Marko dialled the numbers of the *Tagesspiegel* and *Die Welt*'s Berlin offices. Holding a handkerchief over the mouthpiece, he read from the short statement they had prepared beforehand: '*Black Kommando* has struck again. If our claims are not met, more traitors will die. Heinz-Georg Lindner is innocent and must be freed!'

The central heating was turned up to full. The lights were low. In a highly charged mood, the three of them popped some LSD. During the trip which followed, the feeling of power Helena had experienced when she had loosed her sub-machine gun into the pale oval of Holger Busko's face and the dim interior of his car intensified.

She had the sensation of being outside herself, yet being acutely conscious of her own body. This person who was called Helena, she suddenly saw, was not only strong and utterly fearless, but beautiful and highly desirable. She took off her sweater and cupped her breasts in either hand. Marko moved across to her and tried to nuzzle his face between them, but she pushed him away and thrust herself towards Matthias.

Throughout their long friendship, he had always recognized her as Marko's property, but she was suddenly sure that he desired her.

She played with her nipples and saw him get a hard on. The tip of her tongue protruded moist and pink between her lips. She unzipped her jeans and slipped out of them.

Marko was throwing off his clothes but she continued to ignore him. Instead, she undid Matthias's trousers, released his tumescent penis and, kneeling in front of him, lowered her mouth on to it. Marko thrust himself into her from behind and, within moments, the three of them reached a simultaneous climax.

The hours which followed were awesomely beautiful, as they discovered a new dimension to life, one in which the last of their inhibitions were abandoned. Every aspect of each other's bodies was explored and each physical sense stimulated to a pitch of intensity almost beyond endurance. Yet the experience seemed spiritual rather than sensuous. Their bodies seemed to follow a choreographed sequence, floating, converging, melting in together, shifting away, regrouping and merging again, withdrawing and re-engaging, in ever-changing shapes and patterns until, at last, spent and exhausted, they drifted into sleep.

Helena awoke to find herself in bed, her head resting on Matthias's hairy chest, her legs entwined with Marko's. She felt languid and lazily content. That pent-up feeling of frustration which had plagued her since the failed car bomb attempt on Bruno von der Eschenbach had completely disappeared. Marko stirred, muttered, 'I need a pee,' disentangled himself, stood up, looked down at Helena and Matthias's naked bodies, rubbed his eyes, grinned and wandered off to the lavatory.

Helena changed her position, so that her head was cradled on Matthias's shoulder, her body pressed tightly against his. The movement disturbed Matthias, who also woke, but, instead of responding, rolled away, dislodging her, and lay on his side, staring at the bedroom wall. Then, abruptly, he got up and stomped out of the room. Suddenly that warm, voluptuous feeling to which she had awakened, had gone. She felt heavy and depressed, as if she was about to burst into tears.

Across the corridor, Matthias's bedroom door shut and a few minutes later opened again. Then the front door slammed. Helena turned over and buried her face in the pillow.

After she eventually got up, showered, dressed and went into the kitchen, she found Marko making instant coffee and Matthias with newspapers spread over the table. She felt a rekindling of the previous evening's excitement. 'What do they say?' she asked.

Instead of replying, Matthias pushed a paper towards her. BLACK KOMMANDO MURDERS ON, it announced on the front page, and underneath, 'Terrorist gang guns down Berlin MP and his two children'. A photograph showed the ambushed car and, lying pathetically in a puddle beside it, a bedraggled teddy bear.

'We've hit the headlines!' Helena breathed triumphantly.

His face very pale, Matthias asked Marko, 'Did you know the kids were in the car?'

'I was parked twenty metres down the street, man. It was dark.'

'It wasn't dark when they set off in the morning. You must have seen them get into the car. You could have told us when you rang. We could have put off the operation for another day.'

Marko shrugged, unable to understand what Matthias was making a fuss about.

Matthias turned to Helena. 'You must have seen them before you fired. For God's sake, why did you shoot? Two little kids, playing with their new toys . . .'

She hadn't seen them. She had seen nothing except the white, muzzy shape of Holger's face staring at her through the window. The gun had already been at her hip, her hand already on the trigger. But even if she had been aware of them, she could not have stopped.

'Cool it, man,' Marko said. 'They didn't suffer. The paper says they died instantly. They had no idea what was happening. Anyway, what do a couple of kids more or less matter? The world's over-populated. The Chinese are only allowed to have one child . . .'

Before Marko knew what was happening, Matthias had jumped to his feet and in one stride was across the kitchen, his hands round Marko's throat. 'Shut up. Shut up or I'll kill you, you stinking, unfeeling son-of-a-bitch.'

For an instant, Helena was too surprised to react. Then she threw herself onto Matthias and tried to drag him away. 'For God's sake, Matthias, don't be crazy. Let him go.'

But Matthias did not release Marko. His eyes staring, his knuckles white, he continued to grasp him in a stranglehold.

Helena realized the situation was deadly serious. Since the previous evening, Matthias had changed. Something had snapped in him. Possibly it was the kids but maybe they were just an excuse. 'Marko's sorry about the kids. Just like I am. But we got Holger. That's what really matters . . .'

For a long time, Matthias remained immobile, then he let his hands fall. Marko moved hurriedly out of reach and massaged his throat.

Helena took Matthias's arm and drew him back to the table, hoping to re-establish their intimacy of the night. 'You know what it was like. It was dark. And it was a big car. The children were on the back seat. You didn't see them either . . .'

Slowly, as if speaking to himself, Matthias said, 'What a mug I've been, what a crass, stupid idiot. But you seemed so plausible. Violence must be met with violence, you said. And I was sick to the teeth with people preaching about peaceful demonstrations, while the authorities used fascist police brutality against us. But we were wrong and Holger was right. Killing innocent kids was just the sort of thing the Nazis did . . .'

'Matthias, for fuck's sake, don't be melodramatic! It was an accident.'

'It wouldn't have made any difference to you if you had known they were in the car, would it? You've never cared about anybody other than yourself. You don't give a damn about those children, any more than you care about your own child. In your eyes, everyone is expendable, including your own flesh and blood. You just use people. Life is just a game for you. You'll do anything for kicks.'

Helena ignored his reference to Moon Child and latched onto the last part of his statement. 'You're one to talk about kicks. You were quick enough to join in our games last night. I know what's really the matter with you. You're jealous of Marko. It isn't Holger's kids who concern you, but the fact that you can't have me all to yourself.'

What little colour remained drained from Matthias's face. 'You slut! You depraved, perverted whore. You're rotten to the core.' He hit her, hard, across the face.

She flinched but did not move, or even cry out, as his hand cut across her cheek, just stared back at him with withering contempt. Then, when she knew he would not hit her again, she turned her back on him and said to Marko, 'Let's get the hell out of here.'

Marko shuffled towards the door, taking care to keep out of range of Matthias. 'I agree. This place stinks.'

While they were packing, he asked, 'What are we going to do about him?'

Helena's cheek was burning red and stung badly. She reached into the secret compartment in the suitcase and took out the revolver.

While Marko carried their cases down to the car and locked them in the boot, she went back to the kitchen. The newspapers had all been swept onto the floor. Matthias was sitting at the table, his face buried in his hands. She released the safety catch on the revolver. 'Don't even think of squealing to the pigs,' she said.

He did not look up. 'Go on, shoot me. You'll be safe then and I'll be out of my misery.'

She did not intend to shoot him, merely to frighten him. Vicious though she felt towards him, her common sense had not deserted her. Killing Holger in a dark, deserted street, where their getaway was assured, had been one thing. Shooting Matthias in a flat, with neighbours all around, was quite another. 'No, I'd rather you suffered. But if you rat on us, you won't have a second chance.'

Then she put the gun in her shoulder bag, left the apartment and went down to Marko waiting in the car with the engine running.

'I didn't hear a shot,' Marko said.

'It would have been a waste of a bullet. Now, get moving.'

A feeling of relief surged through Marko. For all his faults,

510

Matthias was a mate. He didn't like the idea of him dying. 'So where are we going?'

'Stop asking damnfool questions,' Helena snapped. 'Drive.'

The Breschinskis were not pleased when Helena appeared unannounced on their doorstep and asked for the key to the Heiligensee cottage. 'Why didn't your father telephone and warn us you were coming?' Waltraud complained. 'The place must be freezing. There's no food. The beds aren't aired . . .'

'It doesn't matter,' Helena told her impatiently. 'We can sort all that out. Just give me the key.'

'Well, if you're sure,' Waltraud said. 'Alfons can come down with you and put the heating on.'

'We'll be quite all right,' Helena assured her irritably.

'I wonder if Herr Norbert even knows she's here,' Alfons said grimly, as they watched her get back into the car.

However, Helena anticipated the Breschinskis. Angry though she was with the world, she was still clear-sighted enough to cover herself. That evening, she rang her father in Lugano and in a wheedling, little girl tone, which Norbert scarcely recognized, said, 'I hope you don't mind, but I'm at Heiligensee. Something happened in Frankfurt – I don't really want to go into it now – but I had some kind of breakdown. Is it all right if I stay here for a while?'

'I suppose so . . .' Norbert began.

'I'm all right for money,' she went on. 'I don't need anything, except time alone to think things out.'

She could imagine his surprised expression. 'Well, of course. Umm, would you like Kleo to come and see you?'

'No, Father. I'd rather you didn't tell anyone where I am . . .'

Helena and Marko kept themselves very much to themselves. Unlike the previous occasion, Heiligensee was not plagued by an influx of young people in cars and on motorbikes at all hours of the day and night, there were no riotous parties, no loud music. Had it not been for the couple's occasional visits to the shops or their Audi driving up the main street on its way to the city centre, the village would scarcely have been aware of their existence.

* * *

511

Willy Brandt was among the Berliners who attended the funeral of Holger, Franz and Petra Busko that early winter of 1972. So many were the mourners that there was not room for them all in the church and the service was relayed through loudspeakers to the thousands who assembled in the churchyard and the neighbouring streets.

Security was extremely tight. Police surrounded the church and plainclothes men mingled with the crowd. Erna Busko, her parents and Holger's brother, the famous artist Volker Busko, who had flown over from New York, were driven to the church in separate police cars. Chancellor Brandt arrived in a bulletproof car, accompanied by personal bodyguards and a police escort. Other politicians and public figures, even Dieter, Stefan and Viktoria, were afforded a police guard.

'I still remember the first time I met Holger,' Viktoria murmured, as they were driven to Charlottenburg. 'He was so young and unkempt and full of wild ideas, but there was something compulsive about him even then. If he had lived, I think he might well, in due course, have become Chancellor.'

Stefan nodded, knowing no words to express his grief. He personally owed Holger an unending debt of gratitude for the untiring campaign he had conducted to secure his release from East German imprisonment. Holger and Mortimer. Were it not for those two men, he might himself be dead. Now both had themselves met a violent and tragic end.

'And those two children,' Viktoria continued, echoing words which had been said and would be repeated hundreds of thousands of times by others, 'no punishment is bad enough for the monsters who killed them . . .'

Only members of the family and close friends attended the actual burial and it was as they were making their way through the police cordons to the grave that Stefan recognized Matthias among the crowd. The young man's face was very pale and drawn. Of course, Stefan thought, suddenly remembering Holger's television broadcast, Holger had met the Scheers when Matthias was still a little boy . . .

More to take his mind off Holger's death than anything else, when he returned home that evening, Stefan looked in Mortimer's book *Return to Berlin* for his account of his reunion

512

with Pastor Scheer in 1945. 'What will these children think when they are old enough to realize the stupidity and blindness of their parents and grandparents?' the Pastor had asked. 'Will we ever be able to explain convincingly the reasons why we permitted such evils to take place? We are leaving them a fearful legacy, for they must bear the brunt of our shame. We all bear a terrible burden, a guilt that will take generations to absolve.' And later, the words which Holger had repeated, 'Whatever you do from now on, ask yourself only if it is right for Matthias and the thousands of children like him.'

Stefan shut the book, pulled the blinds and poured himself a stiff drink. The police were understandably reluctant to hypothesize about the identity of Black Kommando, but believed they could be former students, contemporaries of Heinz-Georg Lindner. In which case, Stefan reflected, they would be about the same age as Matthias, the very generation of which Pastor Scheer had been speaking. *We are leaving them a fearful legacy*, the Pastor had said. He of all people, however, would not have envisaged them trying to exorcize the evils of the past by inflicting a new terror of their own . . .

At Heiligensee, Helena was in the tense, restless mood she had been in ever since they had left Schmargendorf, striding up and down the living room. 'All they care about is the bloody kids!' she muttered angrily, for the umpteenth time since she had switched off the television news. 'A brief mention of Black Kommando, but nothing about our aims and demands, and nothing about Heinz-Georg.'

Marko lay stretched out on the couch, watching the smoke from his reefer curl up towards the ceiling. Their manifesto had been drawn up so long ago, he could no longer remember what it contained. As for Heinz-Georg, he had long since dwindled into a shadowy figure belonging to the past.

'Next time, there will be no mistakes,' Helena went on. 'Next time, they're going to have to pay attention to us.'

In the middle of February 1972, the sale of Landgut to Werner Kraus KG was completed and thousands of tenants throughout the Federal Republic found themselves with a new landlord.

513

So far as Werner was concerned, the acquisition meant little except in terms of a personal triumph against his brother. Joachim Duschek was despatched to Berlin to carry through an assessment of the company. He stayed in the penthouse apartment in Wedding.

On his last evening in Berlin, Dieter and Kleo came to supper with him. Joachim himself had no great desire to see Dieter. He and his son had ceased to see eye to eye a long time ago, when Dieter had gone to the Free University and become involved in student politics. However, he knew that if he returned to Frankfurt without seeing Dieter, Annelie would create a dreadful fuss.

But the evening began better than he had anticipated, mainly thanks to Kleo, who diplomatically steered the conversation clear of topics like Holger Busko's death and the manner of Werner Kraus's acquisition of Landgut, which were likely to upset both her fiancé and his father. For the most part, she chattered on about the wedding. 'I'm sending out invitations this weekend,' she said. 'I do so hope Uncle Werner, Aunt Else and the twins will come. It's such a long time since I've seen Brigitta and Margarete. In fact, it's been a long while since we've had any kind of real family reunion . . .'

The maid had brought in beer to accompany the casserole she had left simmering in the oven and Dieter had come armed with a bottle of schnaps. From time to time, Kleo discreetly refilled Joachim's glass and when, their meal over, they moved into the sitting room, she placed the now half-empty bottle on the side table beside his chair before going into the kitchen to make coffee.

Joachim was by now feeling pleasantly relaxed. Knowing his son as he did, he had feared a tedious lecture on Holger Busko's attributes and a storm of abuse on the way Werner Kraus KG had acquired Landgut. Instead, Dieter had let Kleo do most of the talking. Now he was sitting on the settee, absorbed in an old magazine.

Kleo returned with a tray. 'Will you be spending a lot of time in Berlin from now on?' she asked, pouring the coffee and handing Joachim his cup. She sat down opposite him, one knee decorously crossed over the other in a skirt which

514

displayed a modest amount of thigh, but was nowhere near as revealing as the pelmet-like minis Annelie so deplored. 'I wondered if Uncle Werner was thinking of moving his head office here, like Father did.'

'Such a move has to be considered in the context of all the company's other activities,' he replied.

Kleo gazed at him from under long dark lashes. 'You must lead a very interesting life. Uncle Werner appears to be involved in so many different things. He must rely on you tremendously.'

He helped himself to another measure of Steinhaeger. 'I suppose you could say he does. Landgut is just one of many projects I've been working on during the last year or so. Before I go home, I have to stop off at Mainz in connection with another matter which has been occupying a lot of my time.'

Kleo solicitously refilled his coffee cup and his glass. 'Something to do with property?'

Joachim was filled with a sudden, uncontrollable need to impress. 'No, this is in connection with a new electricity power plant being developed by Krafterzeugung, one of many companies your uncle controls. Electricity supply is an area in which Kraus Industries has a lot of expertise. You may not realize it, but back in the 1890s, Baron von Kraus was granted a contract by the Kaiser to provide the first electricity supply to Berlin.'

'I didn't know that,' Kleo murmured. 'How interesting.'

There was a rustle from the direction of the settee. Joachim glanced across and saw Dieter's head nodding over his magazine. How different his life would have been had he been blessed with a daughter like Kleo, he thought, instead of a son like Dieter. But when she and Dieter were married, she would become his daughter. As it was, she was Werner's niece. She was almost family already.

'Of course, things have advanced a lot since then,' he said. His voice sounded rather thick and his eyes were misty, as if they were not focusing properly. He knew he had had slightly too much to drink. Normally he drank very little alcohol, but normally he was not talking to a pretty girl with dancing curls and big, brown, admiring eyes. Usually he was in the domineering

515

presence of Werner Kraus or the company of unresponsive executives like Erwin Hoffmann. Seldom did anyone show him the respect he deserved. Most people, including Annelie, took him for granted.

'Now, we're talking about nuclear power.' What the hell. The project would be public knowledge soon enough, when the Rheinland-Palatinate government announced its support for Krafterzeugung GmbH's plans.

Kleo's eyes opened very wide.

'Now, I know what you're thinking, my dear,' Joachim said, reassuringly. 'You're making the same mistake a lot of other people make. You're remembering Hiroshima and Nagasaki and Bikini Atoll. But nuclear power stations are very safe. There's no danger of them exploding like an atomic bomb.' Under the influence of Werner and the scientists who were developing the plans for the proposed new plant in the countryside outside Mainz, Joachim had become a strong supporter of nuclear energy. For a quarter of an hour or so, he expounded his recently acquired knowledge of nuclear reactors. From time to time, he refilled his glass from the rapidly emptying bottle.

Kleo seemed fascinated, asking intelligent questions about safety, radiation and waste, all of which Joachim was able to answer.

Then Dieter stirred, dislodging the magazine which had fallen onto his chest, and she gave a tinkling laugh. 'Dieter's obviously had too much to drink. I think we'd better be getting home.'

Dieter yawned and glanced at his watch. 'Sorry about that. I didn't intend to drop off. Any chance of another coffee before we leave?'

'Of course, darling. I'll make a fresh pot.'

She went out to the kitchen and Joachim said, 'Your mother and I have always approved of Kleo, but tonight's the first opportunity I've had for a long time to talk to her. I've always known she was an attractive young woman, but she's intelligent as well, Dieter, very intelligent.'

Half an hour later, Kleo and Dieter took their farewell. When they were safely in the car, Dieter said, 'When I asked you to try and get him talking, the most I was hoping for was an indication of what was going to happen to Landgut. Good God, a nuclear

516

power station . . .' He shook his head disbelievingly. 'Wait till Stefan hears about that . . .'

Kleo turned to him pleadingly. 'Do you have to tell Stefan now? Couldn't it wait until after our wedding?'

'By then it could be too late,' Dieter replied grimly. 'I'm sorry, but we can't keep something as important as this to ourselves.'

In the next edition of *Aktuell*, Stefan described Werner Kraus KG's involvement in a hitherto unknown plan to build a nuclear power station outside Mainz in the Rheinland-Palatinate, the region in which Helmut Kohl, a young CDU politician and protégé of former Defence Minister Franz-Joseph Strauss, had recently been elected Minister-President.

'. . . From producing nuclear power, it is a short step to producing nuclear weapons,' Stefan wrote. 'Such a capability should not be allowed to rest in the hands of a former war criminal . . . The Steel King's grandson is set to become the Nuclear King.'

Werner's fury knew no bounds when he saw Stefan's article. The number of people who knew that it was an atomic power station and not a conventional one which Krafterzeugung was proposing to erect outside Mainz could be counted on one hand. Summoning Eckhardt Jurisch and Joachim Duschek to his office, he demanded, 'How the hell did that information get out?'

'Of course I shall conduct an investigation, but I'm positive there's been no leak at this end,' Eckhardt said.

Joachim, white-faced, merely shook his head blankly.

'Issue a writ for libel!' Werner spluttered. 'Slap an injunction on them and stop them publishing any more of these damned articles.'

'We are in a rather difficult position,' Eckhardt said quietly. 'The story happens to be true.'

Werner's day went from bad to worse. Helmut Kohl telephoned, objecting to his implied involvement in the proposed power station. Impromptu protest marches were staged in Mainz and Frankfurt, which rapidly spread to other towns and cities. Demonstrators converged on town halls and military bases, waving placards, shouting slogans, throwing stones and bottles, and causing traffic chaos. The rowdiest crowd gathered outside Werner Kraus KG's offices, where occupants of the building were incarcerated inside, while police sealed off the surrounding streets and brought in water cannon to disperse the mob.

The officer in charge of the operation offered Werner police protection for the next couple of days, but suggested that, in view of the attempt on Bruno von der Eschenbach's life right there in Frankfurt and Holger Busko's murder in Berlin, he should increase his personal security arrangements.

When Werner arrived home that evening at his villa on the outskirts of Frankfurt, Else and the twins were waiting for him in the drawing room, in that close female formation which Werner knew heralded the delivery of an ultimatum. Else always gathered her forces around her when she needed support against her husband. There were pink patches of excitement on her cheeks and Brigitta and Margarete's eyes were tense with expectation in their silly, simpering, plump faces.

'We've received an invitation to Kleo's wedding,' Else informed him, as he marched towards the bar. 'The entire family will be there. We can't let them down.'

Werner's hands trembled with impotent rage as he poured his whisky. Colour suffused the back of his neck, where his collar cut into the thick flesh, and flooded into his cheeks. A sudden, familiar, intense stab of pain constricted his chest. He gulped half his drink, then turned to confront her. 'Haven't you listened to the news? Don't you know what's happened? Rabble-raisers stormed my office. My life was in danger. And all you can talk about is some bloody wedding!'

The twins drew closer to their mother. Nearly sixteen, they were about the same height as her. 'No,' Else said, 'we haven't listened to the radio all day. But whatever has happened, I'm sure you deserved it.'

Werner held his glass so tightly to prevent himself from throwing it at her that he nearly crushed it. Then he turned on his heel and left the room, slamming the door behind him.

'Well, girls,' Else said, 'he didn't say no. I'll write to Kleo tomorrow and tell her we'll be coming. Then we'll go shopping. I'm not having you going to Berlin looking like paupers . . .'

In the sanctuary of his study, Werner slipped a nitro-glycerine

518

tablet under his tongue. Nobody except his doctor knew about his high blood pressure and his attacks of angina pectoris. His doctor said his symptoms were common in men of his age, in their early fifties, who led stressful lives, but to Werner they were a sign of weakness. He carried his pills with him everywhere, but never took them in the presence of anyone else.

When the pain had eased, he forced himself to concentrate on the real issue at stake. The Mainz power plant project was out in the open. Nothing could be done about that. However, the problem of his own safety remained. The first thing, of course, was to take every possible precaution to protect his life. But just as important was the protection of his company. As things currently stood, his whole estate, including Werner Kraus KG, went to Else in the event of his death. That must change.

For a long time, he was lost in silent contemplation. Then, he picked up the telephone and rang Eckhardt Jurisch. 'Come over here immediately. I want to make a new will.'

Marko brought a copy of *Aktuell* back with him from a trip into Tegel to buy cigarettes and beer. 'Your uncle's a real sweetie, isn't he?' he commented to Helena, opening a bottle and drinking straight from it.

Helena sat down at the kitchen table and read through the article with an intense, excited expression.

The following morning, the postman delivered an invitation to Dieter and Kleo's wedding. On a separate note, Kleo had written, 'Dearest Helena, Father told me you were here, but I have deliberately not intruded on your privacy. However, it would be wonderful if you would come to the wedding. Whatever our differences in the past, I am still your loving sister, Kleo.'

For the rest of the day, Helena went around with a preoccupied air. Marko knew better than to disturb her. He found a football match on the television and watched that.

The Saturday of the wedding was April at its brightest and best. Small, puffy, white clouds scudded across an azure blue

519

sky. Trees were bursting into leaf. Gardens and window-boxes were golden with forsythia and daffodils.

Despite past differences and the recent furore created by Stefan's article, family and friends turned up in Berlin to celebrate the event. Reinhild brought Alexander with her, a charming, chubby little boy, now nearly three years old.

Reinhild had invented her own story regarding Alexander, namely that Helena had been unfortunate enough to find herself in the family way and her boyfriend had left her on discovering she was pregnant. Pretending a closeness with Helena which did not exist, she put herself across as an understanding mother and doting grandmother. Viktoria was one of the very few people outside Reinhild's most intimate circle, who knew not only that Helena and Marko were still together, but that Reinhild had not seen Helena since she had taken over custody of Alexander. But Viktoria was one of those rare old ladies to whom one could say almost anything and who was never shocked and who never betrayed a confidence.

Fortunately, most of the other guests were too preoccupied with their own affairs to probe too deeply into Reinhild's explanations. Norbert was reluctant to provoke any argument with his ex-wife and Ursula was certainly not going to reveal any family secrets. Kris, who could have inadvertently blurted out the truth, was obsessed with his latest girlfriend, a stunningly beautiful Italian, with waist-length black hair, incredibly long false eyelashes and wearing a scarlet maxi-coat draped over a black lace mini-dress.

Joachim Duschek was still smarting about the manner in which Dieter and Kleo had abused his hospitality and was terrified in case Werner discovered his part in the *Aktuell* exposé, while Werner and his family, to the surprise of everyone, were attending the wedding, although they were not staying at the Jochum, but at the Landgut penthouse apartment.

Stefan was keeping a diplomatically low profile, having been warned by Viktoria not to spoil Kleo's special day.

Werner's car, in fact, drew up just in front of the one in which Viktoria and Stefan had driven to the church. 'Who on earth's in that?' Stefan asked, staring at the Mercedes limousine, with dark-tinted windows.

A broad, hulking man emerged from the front passenger door and, with his hand held at the opening of his jacket, scanned his surroundings, then nodded to the chauffeur, who walked round to the rear door, opened it and stood back to allow his passenger to get out.

Seconds later, another car pulled up, from which Else and the twins appeared. There were no bodyguards for them. 'So much for the women and children,' Stefan remarked.

After the service when everyone gathered for photographs to be taken, Werner waited in his car. 'Perhaps he thinks the camera is a gun,' Stefan muttered. Viktoria, intent on producing a lovely smile for the photographer, ignored him.

There were over a hundred guests at the reception, including a large number of university and professional friends of Kleo and Dieter. Champagne flowed, inroads were made into the appetizing buffet, and the 'glass-house' hummed with conversation. Norbert was an urbane and genial host, apparently oblivious to the undercurrents of tension. With Ursula on his arm, he mingled with the guests, radiating bonhomie, even towards his brother and Reinhild. Kleo and Dieter flitted from one table to another, greeting distant relatives, chatting with close friends.

It was just after the speeches had been made and toasts drunk, that Helena made her appearance.

She stepped into the room, looking very different from how they all last remembered seeing her. Gone was the long, black hair and heavy fringe, the extreme make-up, the blue jeans and leather jacket. Instead, her hair was back to its original colour and hung in a neat plait over one shoulder. She still wore trousers, but they were stylishly cut and made of maroon, crushed velvet, belted at the waist beneath a cream, puff-sleeved, satin blouse.

'I'm sorry I'm late,' she said, in a little voice, unrecognizable as that which had once screamed, 'Burn, Springer, burn!'

'Helena!' Kleo hurried across the room as quickly as her long dress would allow. 'How lovely to see you! Oh, thank you for coming.'

'I've been standing outside, trying to summon up the courage to come in.'

521

Kleo took her in her arms. 'You've no idea how happy you've made me!'

Norbert hurried across the room and Helena put her arms round his neck. In a voice choked with emotion, she murmured, 'I'm sorry. I've been such a fool ...' Then Reinhild and Alexander joined them. Helena picked up her little son and covered him with kisses. 'Oh, Moon Child, darling ...'

After that, holding Alexander by the hand, with her mother and Kleo in eager attendance, Helena circulated among the wedding guests, disarmingly sweet and anxious to please. She was especially nice to Else and the twins. Seating Alexander on her knee, cradling him in her arms, she complimented them on their clothes, and told them that she had lived in Frankfurt for a while and was sorry she had not been to see them. 'But perhaps if you're staying in Berlin for a while, we can make up for lost time,' she suggested.

It was a new phenomenon for the twins to have a grown-up girl cousin to take an interest in them. They looked appealingly at their mother.

Else tried to make a quick evaluation of the situation. On the one hand, she wasn't sure that she wanted her daughters consorting with the mother of an illegitimate child. On the other hand, Helena did not seem like a scarlet woman and she was their cousin. 'Well, maybe,' she said. 'If your father agrees ...'

Helena turned to Werner, ignoring the hard-faced bodyguards standing sentinel behind him. 'Uncle Werner, you must have business to occupy you in Berlin. I should so like to see more of Margarete and Brigitta. Kleo will be away on her honeymoon, of course, but I could show them round. They could come out to Heiligensee. It's so pretty there.'

She could sense the argument raging inside him. She knew he wanted to say no, but like herself, he was aware of the sea of faces gazing expectantly at him. To say no would be to prove himself, not only to his wife and daughters, but to the rest of his family and all the other curious onlookers, not just the tyrant the press reported him to be, but a heavy father as well. 'All right,' he said grudgingly, 'we'll stay on for a few days.'

*   *   *

522

Never had Reinhild felt herself emotionally pulled in so many different directions as she did that day. There was the excitement and sadness of Kleo getting married, the realization that her elder daughter was now a woman. There was the strangeness of being in the same room again with Norbert, of posing beside him for photographs, of being Kleo's mother, yet not being Norbert's wife. There was the shock of seeing Helena again and believing, for a while, that she was a reformed character. And there was the fear that Helena might want Alexander back, that she might lose her darling grandson.

Then, at the end of the day, after Kleo and Dieter had left for the airport to fly to Tenerife for their honeymoon, had come the greatest shock of all. When Reinhild had asked whether she would like to bath Alexander and put him to bed, she had said, 'No, thank you. I've better things to do with my time.' When Reinhild had hesitantly suggested that she might like to return with her and Alexander to Hamburg, she had retorted disdainfully, 'Why the hell should I do that?'

'I don't understand,' Reinhild told Viktoria later. 'One moment, she was being so affectionate towards little Axel, and the next moment it was as if she couldn't care less about him.' She sighed. 'Well, at least, he has a good home with me. That's the most important thing.'

Chapter 22

Over the next few days, Wilfried Thomas, the security guard at the car park under the apartment block housing the Kraus penthouse grew used to seeing Helena. The first time she appeared he made her wait while he telephoned up to the penthouse, but after that he just lifted the barrier and waved her through. She parked her car, then chatted with him for a few moments before taking the private lift up to the penthouse. She and her young cousins were a sweet sight, he thought, when they went off on their sightseeing and shopping expeditions, a twin to either side of Helena, their arms linked, the three of them chatting and laughing.

One evening, however, Helena arrived just after Frau Kraus and the twins had gone out. The Landgut office had shut for the day and all the staff cars had left. Only Werner's Mercedes stood in its reserved bay. Thomas leaned out of his booth. 'They went out about ten minutes ago, Fräulein Kraus.'

'But we're going to the theatre. I arranged to meet them here.' Helena paused, then sighed. 'They must have misunderstood and thought we were meeting at the theatre.' On the passenger seat lay a bunch of flowers. 'Oh, what a pity. My flowers will wilt if I take them with me.' She glanced towards Werner's Mercedes. 'Is my uncle upstairs?'

'Yes, he went up to the apartment just after Frau Kraus and the young ladies departed.'

'Then I'll leave the flowers with him.' She parked her car in the nearest bay and, leaving the engine still running, got out, looking unusually elegant in a silver lurex catsuit and matching elbow-length gloves, with a mohair shawl round her shoulders. 'Herr Thomas,' she called. 'My car sounded really strange on the way here. It was making a kind of knocking noise.'

He unlocked the door to his booth and came across to her.

'It sounds all right to me, but if you release the bonnet catch, I'll take a quick look.'

So intent was he on the engine that he was quite unaware of Marko sprinting down the ramp. The first he knew of his presence was when an arm encircled his neck and a hand clamped a cheesecloth pad stinking of chloroform over his mouth and nostrils. For a few seconds, he felt a burning sensation, then he sagged to his knees and fell unconscious to the ground.

Marko opened the car boot and extracted some cord which he bound firmly round the man's wrists and ankles, then gagged him with a piece of rag. While he lifted Thomas's shoulders, Helena took his feet and they bundled him into the boot. Panting slightly, Marko locked the boot, Helena took her handbag and the flowers and they made their way over to the lift. During their uninterrupted journey up to the twentieth floor, Helena reached into her handbag and withdrew a revolver.

The lift did not open directly into the apartment but onto a small L-shaped landing outside, from which an emergency exit led to the fire escape. Marko went round the corner and flattened himself against the wall, while Helena pressed the bell. After a few moments, Werner's voice came testily through the intercom. 'Who's there?'

'It's Helena.'

'I thought you were at the theatre.'

'Can I leave something here first?'

A deep, impatient sigh from inside the apartment. The sound of footsteps as Werner came down the hall. She sensed him looking through the spy-hole. Then, 'All right. Come in.' The door opened and she walked in.

She thrust the bouquet into his hands, revealing her Beretta. 'Put your hands above your head. Stand against the wall.' Gone was the affectionate smile. Her mouth formed a thin, hard line; her eyes were steely cold.

Werner was taken by surprise but was not actually surprised. It was the attack he had known had to come some time, except that he had not imagined it would take place in his own home or that it would be Helena who made it. 'Young women like you shouldn't play with guns,' he said, moving the cumbersome bouquet to his left hand and trying, unobtrusively, to edge

525

his right hand towards the Colt he wore in a holster under his jacket.

A tall, blond-haired young man appeared behind Helena in the doorway. He, too, carried a gun. 'Don't do that, sunshine,' he said. There was a click, as he released his safety catch. 'We're Black Kommando. We don't mess about. We kill people.'

The two guns pointed directly at his heart and Werner knew a very real frisson of fear. 'Hands up,' Helena repeated. 'Against the wall.'

This time, he did as he was told. 'Marko, search him!' The young man unfastened his holster and threw it to Helena, then frisked him in time-honoured gangster tradition. In the breast pocket of Werner's jacket, he found two small bottles of pills. 'Hey, man, what are these? Purple hearts?'

'They're prescription drugs,' Werner said. 'They're no use to you.'

Marko slipped them into his pocket.

Then Helena said, 'Turn round. Now come with us.'

'Don't be ridiculous,' Werner blustered. 'What do you want? Is it money? If so, I'll have to get my briefcase . . .'

'Don't try playing games with us, Kraus,' Marko said. 'Just do what she says. If not, we'll kill you.'

Although Werner was considerably bigger than either of them, while they were armed and he wasn't, he stood no chance of overpowering them. If he wanted to stay alive, it seemed wisest to do what they said.

Helena picked up the decoy flowers and they took him at gunpoint down in the lift to the car park, where they ushered him into the back of their car. She drove and Marko sat beside him, his revolver poking into Werner's ribcage. 'Where are you taking me?' Werner demanded. Marko simply gave an inane grin. It was almost night, but Werner had sufficient knowledge of Berlin to know they were heading towards Tegel. Then they went through the forest, into the old village of Heiligensee and down the drive to Norbert's cottage, where Helena slewed to a halt on the gravelled courtyard.

She unlocked the door to the house and, still at gunpoint, he was conducted along the hallway to an open door. Marko kicked him hard on the rump and Werner stumbled down steep stone

526

stairs into yawning darkness. Behind him, the door slammed shut, a bolt slid home and a key turned.

Somehow, he managed to stop himself from falling and stood for a few moments, leaning against the cellar wall. The angina pain clawed at his heart and he reached for his pills. But the two bottles were gone.

With Werner safely in the cellar, Helena and Marko returned to the car. Helena unlocked the boot. Fully conscious again, wild-eyed and struggling to release himself from his bonds, the security guard was revealed.

'What do we do with him now?' Marko asked.

Until that moment, all Helena's thoughts had been concentrated on kidnapping Werner and she hadn't actually considered what they should do with Thomas, other than that he must not be left in Wedding to blab to the police about their visit. But now she was faced with the predicament, the solution was startlingly simple. 'Give him another dose of chloroform. Then get the wheelbarrow from the shed.'

A wind had sprung up. Heavy clouds scudded across the sky, intermittently obscuring the moon. With more difficulty than they had had putting him in, they dragged Thomas's body out of the boot, loaded it into the wheelbarrow and trundled it down to the jetty. Helena went to the boathouse to fetch the anchor from the old sailing boat.

When the anchor was securely tied round Thomas's legs, they tipped the barrow on its side and the body slid into the water with a splash. A cloud of silt rose from the river bed. Marko consoled himself with the thought that, like a hospital patient dying under an anaesthetic, Thomas knew nothing about his death. On a sudden impulse, he ran back to the car, grabbed the bouquet and returned to the jetty. Ripping off the paper wrapping, he tossed the flowers onto the watery grave.

Else and the twins were surprised when Helena did not turn up at the theatre, where they had agreed to meet, and when she had still not arrived at the first interval, Else telephoned Heiligensee from the public phone in the foyer. In a strange, rather guarded voice, Helena said she had had a puncture. Else attributed her tone to understandable annoyance, said, 'Never mind, hopefully you can get it mended tomorrow and we'll see you later,' then went back to enjoy the second act of the show.

Their driver was waiting outside the theatre when they emerged and took them back to Wedding. 'That's funny,' he murmured, when they entered the basement car park and found the barrier up and the attendant's booth empty. 'Not like Thomas to leave his post.'

He parked the car next to Werner's and accompanied his ladies up in the lift to the penthouse. There the mystery deepened. The door to the apartment stood wide open and of Werner there was no sign.

'He's probably been called away suddenly,' Else said, but even as she spoke, she knew a niggling doubt. Werner had become so neurotic about security, he was most unlikely to go out leaving the door open. Furthermore, his briefcase, which he took everywhere with him, was lying on the desk in his study, his keys beside it.

Else stood, the twins close beside her, uncertain what to do. 'I'll go down to the office,' the driver said, taking Werner's key ring, but returned to say the offices were totally unoccupied. Next, he rang Werner's bodyguard, who lived in a flat in a neighbouring block, but he reported that Werner and Dr Joachim Duschek had been in conference together until seven-thirty, at which time Dr Duschek had returned to the Jochum-Berlin and he had accompanied his employer up to the penthouse. As usual, he had searched the apartment before Werner entered. 'I think you should inform the police,' the driver told Else.

Two policemen duly arrived, who suggested that husbands were known to go off to a bar when their wives went to the theatre. But, on hearing who Werner was and after obtaining statements from his bodyguard and chauffeur, the senior of them radioed a message back to headquarters. Not long afterwards, a Superintendent Schneider from the Anti-Terrorist Squad arrived, who took the matter very seriously indeed.

Descriptions of the two missing men were radioed to all West Berlin police stations and patrol cars were ordered to be exceptionally vigilant for them. A telephone call was put through to the Jochum-Berlin, asking Joachim Duschek to come to Wedding immediately.

Then, while his colleagues went to interview other occupants of the building, the Superintendent asked them all to go back over everything they had done since arriving in Berlin and to try, especially, to remember anything that struck them as unusual or suspicious.

But their excursions with Helena had meant Else and the twins had seen little of Werner, except in the evenings, and even then he had usually shut himself away in his study while they watched television. Apart from attending Kleo and Dieter's wedding, Werner himself had scarcely left Landgut's office.

Eventually, after insisting that a policeman remain with them in the apartment for the night, Superintendent Schneider took his departure. 'What do you think has happened to my husband?' Else asked.

'I don't know,' Schneider replied. 'But I very much hope that before the night is over, he'll turn up safe and sound.'

Joachim, uncomfortably reminded of his last visit to the penthouse and his fateful dinner with Dieter and Kleo, remained for a short while with Else, but he felt rather relieved when she said, 'You don't need to stay. The girls and I will be quite all right.'

When he had gone, she sent the twins to bed with a hot milk drink, then, leaving the policeman to his vigil, she retired to her own room. But, although she undressed and got into bed, she was too plagued by a host of conflicting emotions to be able to sleep.

The truth was that she did not care if she never saw Werner again. If he had left a note saying he had decided to leave her, she would have felt nothing but an overwhelming sense of relief. If he had committed suicide or been murdered, she could have pretended grief, but known that all her troubles were over. As it was, she did not know what had happened to him and that uncertainty was worse than any kind of loss. Added to which was the knowledge that, by thinking in this way, she was guilty of a great sin which, next time she went to confession, she would have to admit.

Towards dawn, she fell into a fitful sleep, but her dreams were haunted and she was glad when Margarete and Brigitta came into the room and sat themselves on either side of her bed, with

529

haggard expressions which mirrored her own. 'Has there been any news of Father?' Brigitta asked.

When her mother shook her head, Margarete said, 'I don't feel like going out with Helena today.'

Else didn't want to see Helena either. She didn't want to see anyone. 'I'll ring and put her off,' she said. 'I'm sure she'll understand.'

As soon as Helena put the phone down, she forgot about Else and the twins. She had found their outings boring and their company tedious to an extreme, but they had served their purpose, by gaining her access to Werner. To the anxiety they must be feeling she gave not a thought.

Ever since she had received the invitation to Kleo's wedding, she had been planning Werner's kidnap, determined that, on this occasion, nothing would go wrong. The cellar, in which little had changed since the war, when it had been used as an air-raid shelter, was ideally suited for a prison.

For the first day of Werner's captivity, he was left completely alone. A strip of light under the cellar door showed that he had found the light switch and occasionally he banged on the door and shouted. Helena ignored him and ordered Marko to do the same.

She spent the day preparing the ransom note, which claimed that Werner Kraus had built up his empire by illegal means and demanded that all the companies he controlled should be given over to worker management. All companies involved in arms manufacture should be forced to stop. The proposed nuclear power plant at Mainz must be forbidden. All houses belonging to Landgut should be given to their tenants.

Last, but not least, was money. Without a demand for money, no ransom note would be complete. A million Marks? It seemed a paltry sum for someone in Werner's position. Five million seemed reasonable.

Finally, she wrote that if an advertisement did not appear within three days in the personal column of the *Die Welt* agreeing to Black Kommando's demands, Werner would be tortured and starved, exactly as he had treated Jews during the war. After making a long-hand copy, she painstakingly cut words and letters out of newspapers and stuck them on a sheet of paper, addressing the envelope to Else in the same way.

Before she sent Marko to post it from a central post office, she let Werner see the handwritten version. While Marko, sub-machine gun at the ready, stood guard at the top of the cellar steps, Helena confronted her uncle. Aiming her revolver at his head, she made him sit on the floor, then thrust the sheet of paper at him. 'If you sign your agreement, you could be free within days,' she said. 'If not, you'll remain here until someone else agrees on your behalf.'

Choking back his fury, Werner read slowly through the note. 'I shall never agree and nobody else has the power to agree on my behalf.'

'We mean what we say.'

'So do I.'

For several minutes, their eyes remained locked, then Helena shrugged. 'You've had your chance.'

'On the assumption that you want to keep me as a living hostage, you must give me food and water,' Werner said. 'And my pills . . .'

'Sign this paper and you can have everything you want.'

But about an hour after they had gone, the cellar door opened again and a plate of stale bread and a bucket of water was placed at the top of the stairs. Werner's pills, however, were not there.

In Landgut's boardroom, Superintendent Schneider and his assistant sat in conference with Else Kraus, Joachim Duschek and Eckhardt Jurisch, who had travelled to Berlin immediately upon learning about Werner's disappearance. In front of each of them was a photocopy of the ransom demand. The original was being examined at police headquarters.

'So now we know,' Schneider said. 'He's been kidnapped. That explains the disappearance of the car park attendant. The kidnappers couldn't risk being identified, so they took him along as well. But they still had to get Herr Kraus to open the door to the apartment. They must have been known to him, otherwise he wouldn't have let them in.'

'The obvious person to spring to mind is Helena Kraus,'

Eckhardt Jurisch said. 'That girl's always been trouble. Back in the '68 student riots, she was constantly in the headlines.'

'So were thousands of other young people,' Schneider commented mildly, 'including Dr Duschek's son. Most of them are perfectly respectable pillars of society now. According to Frau Kraus, so is Helena. I'll interview her, but I think it's unlikely that she's involved. It's quite possible that she may agree with Black Kommando's views on Werner Kraus KG's activities, but, if so, she wouldn't be alone in that. Many other Germans seem to feel the same, probably even many Kraus employees.' His tone implied that he did, too.

Eckhardt Jurisch glared at him across the table. 'You people don't suggest that we give in to the kidnappers' demands?'

'Certainly not. Unfortunately, we have a vast experience of kidnapping, mainly in connection with our friends across the Wall. Only in the very last resort would we consider submitting to threats and blackmail.'

'Could Black Kommando be a GDR organization?' Joachim asked.

'Unlikely. You have to remember the bank raids, the Frankfurt bombing and the murder of Holger Busko. No, we're dealing with West Germans, although not necessarily West Berliners.'

For the first time, Else spoke. 'What about the announcement in *Die Welt*? What do we say?' She was pale and drawn, but remarkably composed.

'I can only recommend what you should do, Frau Kraus, the final decision must be yours. But, in your position, I would not offer them anything, even money, although five million Marks might be sufficient for them to forget their other demands. What we would most like is to get into dialogue with them and draw them out into the open. To date, we have kept the news of the kidnap away from the press. Now, we should like to make it public. But while that may help your husband, it will also mean rather unpleasant publicity for you and your daughters.'

Else nodded. 'I will do whatever you suggest, Superintendent.'

The four men each heaved a mental sigh of relief. Else Kraus was made of stronger stuff than they had dared hope.

After the first day of his captivity, Werner recognized the futility

532

of trying to attract attention by shouting and banging. All he had done was exhaust himself. The cottage was too isolated for any of the neighbours to hear him and it was unlikely that Helena and Marko would receive visitors, except – hopefully – the police.

He reasoned to himself that by now a police hunt would have commenced for him and that Helena would be among their list of suspects, for Else must have realized that there had been an ulterior motive behind her sudden friendship. When the cottage was searched, he would be found.

Yet, when he thought back over the extraordinary chain of events which had brought him here, he was forced to admit that Else might well not recognize Helena's duplicity. She had seemed so plausible, even Werner had been taken in by her. There had certainly been no grounds for suspecting her as a potential kidnapper. In which case, it could be days, if not weeks, before the police came to Heiligensee. By which time, he could be dead.

As the pain in his chest grew steadily worse, Werner grew increasingly frightened. He had assumed that, if his life was threatened, the attack would be in the same manner as those on Bruno von der Eschenbach and Holger Busko. He had never imagined it would be because his life-preserving pills had been taken from him.

To conserve his energy and avoid putting unnecessary strain on his heart, he spent most of his time on the camp bed, covered with a blanket. Each time his captors appeared, he asked for his pills, not attempting to conceal the fact that if he did not take them he would die, gambling on the assumption that they realized a dead hostage was no use to them, that, if he died, they would lose their bargaining power.

To his surprise, he found Marko more sympathetic than Helena to his plight. 'I know how you feel, man,' he said, on one occasion, when Werner was finding the pain almost unbearable. 'You need a fix.'

'All he has to do is sign,' Helena said coldly.

Marko stayed on in the cellar after she had gone, sitting on the steps, his sub-machine gun on his knees, gazing curiously at Werner as if he were a rare species of animal. 'Why don't you give in, man? You'd not only be doing yourself, but the whole

533

world a good turn. If you stopped trying to nuke the planet, you could go home – and you'd be able to sleep easy at night.'

Werner recognized the possible advantages of getting into dialogue with him. 'If my company ceased its activities another would start.'

'Maybe. But wouldn't you feel better . . . ?'

'What about you?' Werner asked. 'You're a freedom-loving man. How do you justify to yourself keeping me prisoner?'

'Like Helena says, if you signed, you could be free.'

'Do you always do what Helena says?'

'It's not like that. We're partners.'

'Have you thought about what will happen to you afterwards? You'll be a marked man, always on the run . . .'

Marko narrowed his eyes. 'Why are you concerned about me? It's you who've got the problems.'

One day, the cellar door burst open and Marko appeared alone. He bound a gag round Werner's mouth and stuck his gun against his ribs, exactly where the pain was worst. 'One squeak out of you and you're dead.'

Above them, Werner could hear footsteps, the scraping of chairs and a faint murmur of voices. If he shouted, would Marko really shoot? Werner stirred and the gun barrel dug into his chest. 'For fuck's sake, man, didn't you hear what I said?' Marko muttered. There was a wild, almost frightened look in his eyes and Werner knew that he dared not take the risk. Marko might not want to kill him, but he was capable of it.

After what seemed an interminable period, chairs scraped again in the room above and footsteps moved away. In due course, Helena entered the cellar. She stared mockingly at Werner. 'That was the police. They wanted to know if I had any idea who might have kidnapped my dear uncle . . .'

The following day, when they gave him his ration of bread and water, they also brought a copy of *Die Welt*. 'You've made the headlines again, man,' Marko said. 'So has Black Kommando. Isn't that great?'

'They want a signed, handwritten note to prove you're still alive,' Helena said. 'Here's a piece of paper and a pen. Sit up. Write something.'

534

Werner did not move from his recumbent position. 'Give me my pills.'

Her eyes narrowed and she pointed her gun at his forehead. 'Sit up!'

Still Werner did not move.

She slashed him across the face with her revolver. 'So you'd rather die. Well, I'm sorry, Uncle Werner, but death is too good a fate for you. We meant what we said in that note. First, you're going to have done unto you what you did unto others. Marko, tie him up.'

The effect of the violent blow caused such an excruciating surge of pain in Werner's chest, all down his left arm and up into his neck, that he could only lie, his eyes closed, a soundless scream on his lips.

Marko pulled the blanket off him, took a ball of nylon twine from his pocket and tied his legs to the bed. Then he bound more cord round his chest and arms. 'Take off his shoes and socks,' Helena ordered, lighting a cigarette. After puffing at it for a few seconds until its tip glowed red, she applied it to the sole of Werner's right foot.

That final shock was too much for Werner's heart. For a few moments, it struggled to continue beating. Then it stopped.

A wet stain appeared on Werner's trousers and a foul smell mingled with the pungent odour of burning flesh. Marko wrinkled his nose in disgust.

Werner did not move. He just lay on the camp bed, his mouth slightly open, his eyes shut. Helena touched the sole of his other foot. It did not even twitch. She took his wrist and searched for his pulse. Nothing. She undid his bonds, seized him by the shoulders and tried to shake him. She slapped him round the face. She splashed water over him. To no avail.

For a long time, she just stood, staring down at him in utter disbelief. Then she cried, 'No, it isn't possible! It can't be true! He can't be dead!'

Marko stood transfixed. He had never seen anyone actually die before. Even Thomas, when they had thrown him into the lake, had still been alive, if unconscious.

Helena turned and made her way across the cellar, stumbling up the stairs, down the hall and into the fresh air and the spring

535

sunshine. She sank down on the verandah steps and gazed out, blindly, across the garden. Months of preparation had gone into this operation. Nothing had been left to chance, like it had in the Eschenbach fiasco. Everything had been planned.

And still it had gone wrong. The one thing she had not anticipated had happened. Werner had died. And she knew she had only herself to blame. She let out a little, keening cry and tears trickled down her cheeks. 'I should have let him have his pills . . .'

Marko sat down beside her and shrugged sympathetically. 'What the hell. You weren't to know.'

She leaned her head against his shoulder, the tears streaming faster down her face.

Marko reached in his pocket, pulled out his tobacco tin, rolled a joint and held it to her lips. 'Here, have a drag.'

The marijuana calmed her a little, took away the immediate sense of panic, but did nothing to abate her feeling of desolation, despair, and, above all, failure. 'I meant so well,' she gulped. 'I wanted to stop all the senseless horrors. But I can't. It will all go on just the same. All the wars, all the killing, all the bombs. Nothing will change . . .'

All afternoon and well into the evening, Helena remained on the verandah step. Marko tried to get her to drink and eat, but she refused. Worst of all, she did not know what they should do next. Always before, it had been she who had decided upon their next course of action. Now, for the first time in their relationship, she seemed to expect him to give the orders.

With a sense of rising panic, Marko remembered what Werner had said about him being no use to them if he died and about the police coming after them. Helena was convinced nobody suspected her, but Marko was less sure. When they drew a blank with all other leads, they'd come back to Heiligensee.

If they were found with Werner's corpse in the cellar, they would be charged not only with kidnap, but murder. Then there was Matthias. It only needed him to blab and the whole story of Eschenbach and Holger would come out, and he and Helena would be spending the rest of their lives in prison.

The first thing to do, Marko decided, was to get rid of Werner and the easiest way to do that was to dump him in the lake like

536

they had Thomas. But moving Werner proved no simple task. Not only did he stink, he was sixteen stone of dead weight. They managed to drag him to the bottom of the cellar stairs, but getting him up the steps was impossible. With another man to help him, Marko might have succeeded, but not with Helena.

'I say we leave him where he is and go back to the Federal Republic,' he said finally, prodding Werner's corpse with his shoe. 'Even if they find him, they won't find us. Come on, let's get the hell out of here.'

Fear led speed to Marko's actions and in an hour, they were on their way, the false-bottomed suitcase with their weapons and the other, with the remains of their cash and drugs, their contents concealed with clothes, stowed in the boot of the car, the rest of their belongings hastily piled on top of them. Marko drove, Helena, silent and chain-smoking beside him. At the last gas station before the border, he filled up the tank. At the checkpoint, their car, like every other, was given a cursory search, their papers were examined, their transit visa was issued and, for the last time, they left Berlin.

It was well past midnight when they crossed the Helmstedt-Marienborn border crossing-point safely into the Federal Republic. Helena was asleep by then, her head lolling uncomfortably against the back of her seat. As soon as he could, Marko left the autobahn and looked for somewhere to stop. Not that he was sleepy: his nerves were too taut for that. But he needed time to think and decide what to do next.

He found a layby and parked inconspicuously between a couple of lorries. Always before in the past, things had sorted themselves out and turned out right in the end. But, always before, there had been someone else to take the initiative and make the major decisions. Now, suddenly, responsibility had been thrust onto his shoulders.

They had to get rid of the car. That was essential. But even with a different vehicle, they couldn't spend the rest of their lives driving and sleeping in laybys. They couldn't go back to Frankfurt: that was the first place people would look for them. Sure, they could go to friends, but how many friends could be relied on to conceal a couple of wanted criminals for weeks, months or even years? Perhaps they should go abroad, to Spain

537

or Marrakesh or Turkey or India, but to do that, they would have to cross international frontiers. They would need false papers . . . Eventually, his troubles still unresolved, Marko fell into an uneasy sleep.

In the morning, when he woke, the lorries had gone and the Audi was fully exposed to the passing traffic. Heading south, he pulled out on the road and switched on the radio. A few minutes later came the hourly news summary. To his immense relief, there was only a brief mention of Werner and no reason to believe his remains had been found. 'The hunt for kidnap victim, fifty-five-year-old businessman Werner Kraus, continues in Berlin today. Police do not believe Herr Kraus has been taken from the city. Now, the weather forecast. Today will be sunny and dry . . .' Helena sat motionless, staring straight ahead through the windscreen, her hands clenched in her lap.

Instinct told Marko that they would be wise to avoid motorways and keep to minor roads. After Fulda, they began to climb up through the gently rolling landscape of the Rhön mountains, with their thick woods and ancient volcanic peaks. Something in the lonely countryside appealed to both of them. Helena saw in it a reflection of her own dark mood; Marko the possibility of finding somewhere to hide, at least for the night.

It was a weekday and too early in the year for there to be many tourists about. Marko was able to drive slowly, looking for an opportunity to leave the road. Soon, a rutted track branched off into pine woods and he went up it. After about half a mile, he came to a clearing where foresters had been at work, but which had obviously been unused for some while. He had hoped there might be shelter of some kind, but there was none.

He parked the car under a tree, got out, stretched and wandered across to a tall pile of felled trees, where he sat down, leaning back against the logs, the afternoon sun shining warmly on him. After a while, Helena joined him. Still she said nothing, just sat, her knees hunched up, staring desultorily into the forest.

'You must have thought about what we were going to do after we let Werner go,' he said. 'You must have had some kind of plan.'

She shook her head. Their own escape was something which

538

had scarcely crossed her mind. She had been so obsessed with the idea of the kidnap, she had simply assumed that, as part of the ransom deal, they would be able to set their own terms for their safe passage to freedom.

She leaned back and closed her eyes in the hope of shutting out a reality she could not bear to contemplate. For months she had been keyed up, tensed, brittle as a tightly coiled spring. Now, she was utterly drained and exhausted, totally incapable of thought or action. After a few moments, she was asleep.

Marko, too, must have dozed, for he awoke with a start to the sound of a van trundling into the clearing, of doors slamming and a man's voice saying in English with a strange accent, 'Right, let's get a fire going, Jude. I'll collect some brushwood.'

Marko shook Helena awake.

A bronzed, fair-haired young man in shorts and T-shirt emerged from the undergrowth. 'Hey, I'm sorry. Saw a car, but didn't realize you were here. Hope we didn't disturb you.'

Cautiously, Marko replied, also in English, 'It doesn't matter.'

'You speak English? Great. We're just putting the billy on. Fancy a cup of tea?' He held out his hand. 'I'm Sam McKuen. My girlfriend's Judy Flanders. We're Australians.'

Marko thought very quickly while he was getting to his feet. 'I am Max. This is Else. She was not feeling very well, so we stopped for a rest.'

'Sorry to hear that. Hope it's nothing serious.'

'No, just car sickness.'

Sam strode back across the clearing, calling, 'Jude, we got guests!'

'Are you crazy?' Helena asked. 'We don't want to get involved with them!'

Marko stared towards the Australians' van. 'You haven't seen what they're driving,' he replied, with a sense of mounting excitement. 'They've got a VW camper – with Australian numberplates.' Suddenly, he could see a beautifully simple way out of their predicament.

The two Australians could not have been more hospitable. Not only did they provide tea, they gave their new-found German friends supper, sausages and baked beans cooked

539

over the campfire, washed down with several pints of lager. Proudly, they showed off their van, which seemed to contain most necessary comforts. Helena said little, but Marko excused her, explaining that she didn't speak much English. When night drew in, and Marko admitted they weren't in any hurry to go anywhere, Sam suggested they slept in the camper while he and Judy dossed down outside in a tent.

'Why did you say yes?' Helena asked, as they went back to the car to get their night things.

Marko lifted the boot lid. 'Surely that's obvious? We get rid of them and have ourselves new identities. Don't worry. You haven't got to do anything. Just leave this to me.' Within the space of twenty-four hours their roles had completely reversed. He was now firmly in control.

The first hint of dawn flushed the sky, when Marko slipped out of the camper and padded across to the car to get his gun. Sam and Judy were lying cuddled together in their sleeping bag when he opened the flap of their tent and let loose a burst of sub-machine gun fire, which killed them before they had any inkling of what was happening.

Next, he drove the Audi across the clearing and emptied its contents into the camper. Then, after removing the small rucksack which contained Sam and Judy's passports, traveller's cheques and other papers, he dismantled the tent and dragged it and the bodies – both considerably lighter than Werner's – to the car, putting Sam in the driver's seat and Judy in the passenger's seat. Finally, after driving the camper to the top of the track, he went back to the Audi, chucked petrol from the spare can over its interior and pushed it forward so that it was positioned over the burning embers of the campfire. Then, he lit a thick spill of newspaper and threw it in.

When they reached the road, he stopped and looked back. There was a muffled explosion, muted by the forest, then a column of black smoke rose into the sky.

The following Saturday afternoon, when Alfons came to mow the cottage lawn, he found the garage doors open and no car in the courtyard. He rang the front door bell and received no response. He went to the shed to get the mower and wheelbarrow, but although the mower was where it should be, he did not find the barrow until he reached the boathouse at the bottom of the garden. 'Who put it here?' he muttered. 'One thing's certain, it didn't walk by itself. Now if they ever did any gardening, I'd understand it, but they don't do a bloody thing. Look at those weeds . . .'

By the time he had finished the lawn he had worked himself up into a fine old temper. After putting mower and barrow back in the shed, he stared balefully at the house. What sort of state was the place in? A right mess, he'd no doubt. Last time, it had taken him and Waltraud weeks to clean it up. Well, there was one way to find out and that was to go in and have a look. He'd got the spare key with him. If they came back and found him there, he'd tell them . . .

The moment he opened the door the stench assailed his nostrils and it grew more powerful the further down the hall he went. When he finally opened the cellar door, it was so strong that it sent him reeling backwards. Holding his handkerchief to his face, he turned on the light and peered down the stairs. The sight he saw there sent him running, gagging, to the phone.

On hoardings, across the front pages of newspapers, on radio and television, the news of Werner's death was blazoned and, with it, photographs of the couple wanted for his murder and suspected also of murdering Holger Busko and an Italian car park attendant in Frankfurt. The search was still continuing, according to a police statement, for a garage attendant missing in Berlin.

The press had to make do with old pictures of Helena with dyed black hair and Marko with a shoulder-length thatch, and descriptions from people who had seen them recently.

After a post-mortem examination and an inquest at which the coroner returned a verdict of death caused by a heart attack under suspicious circumstances, Werner's remains were flown to Frankfurt, where his funeral took place at the Roman Catholic church where he and Else had been married, a ceremony attended by government ministers, heads of finance and industry, and many other public figures. Dressed entirely in black, Else and her two young daughters presented a tragic spectacle. Photographers succeeded in taking some touching pictures of the three of them with Werner's brother Norbert, the man whose daughter was suspected of being responsible for his death.

By then, Helena and Marko had reached the Fichtel Mountains, just north-east of Bayreuth, and spent the night in a secluded field beside a rushing stream, just outside a small village. 'I'm tired of travelling. I want to stay here for a few days,' Helena announced, as they ate their breakfast of fresh bread, butter and eggs, given to them by the farmer on whose land they were camping, who had delighted in practising his few words of English.

'You're mad!' Marko retorted. 'We're Australians, remember. Australians don't stay anywhere. They travel. Helena, we've got Australian passports and visas, an Australian van, with Australian registration and insurance documents and a green card. We're free to go almost anywhere in the world.'

'You go if you want to, Marko. I'm staying here.'

Marko sighed. He could not imagine what attracted her to this godforsaken spot, but he couldn't be bothered to argue. 'OK. But we ought to tell the farm people something.'

'Tell them I'm writing a book.'

Perhaps she should, Helena thought, perhaps if she put down on paper the confusion raging inside her, she would begin to understand herself and know what to do next with her life. Until Werner's death, everything had seemed so clear-cut. Even when things had gone wrong, some new idea had always occurred to her, some new challenge inspired her. Now, suddenly, there was nothing. She didn't believe in anything any more. Not even Marko.

It was almost as if, from having been at the centre of everything, she was on the outside looking in. That was how it had been when Marko had killed the Australians and set fire to the car. She had just sat in the camper, watching, feeling nothing, no pity, no remorse, no fear. All the other times, there had been something – disappointment, excitement, satisfaction, even anger, and, in the case of Thomas, regret. But for the Australians, nothing. Nothing had the power to move her any more, not even death . . .

*   *   *

542

On the evening of Werner's funeral, after the rest of the family and close business acquaintances whom Else had invited back to the Frankfurt villa had departed, Eckhardt Jurisch asked Else, Joachim Duschek and Hannelore Hahn to come to the study. There, seated at his late employer's desk, from which, a scant four months earlier, Werner had dictated to him the terms of this same document, Eckhardt apprised them of the contents of Werner's will, of which he and Joachim were appointed executors and trustees.

There were two specific legacies. One was of the villa and its contents, and Werner's personal goods and chattels, which he left to Else. The second was of fifty-one preferential voting shares in Werner Kraus KG, which he bequeathed to 'my loyal secretary, Hannelore Hahn'.

'To sum up the rest of the will, which I recommend you all read in detail,' Eckhardt said, 'Herr Kraus devises Dr Duschek and myself to sell all his remaining property, including all shares in Werner Kraus KG, except those bequeathed to Fräulein Hahn. In other words, Herr Kraus wants the company to be floated on the Stock Exchange. Of the proceeds, twenty million Marks are to be held upon trust for Frau Kraus and her daughters, the capital and the income deriving therefrom to be given to the beneficiaries at the discretion of the trustees. The rest is to be used to found an institute for nuclear research and development, bearing Herr Kraus's name.'

For a long time, the room was silent. Then Else asked, 'Do you have any idea of the total potential value of Werner Kraus KG shares?'

'Not at the moment. However, as an indication, I can tell you that, in the last accounts, Werner Kraus KG was valued at just over three thousand billion marks.'

'Of which I receive only twenty million?'

Eckhardt Jurisch sucked in his breath. 'That sum will not be freely available to you, Frau Kraus. It is to be held in trust on your behalf. Needless to say, Dr Duschek and I will ensure that you, Margarete and Brigitta suffer no hardship. Let me assure you now that you will be able to live extremely comfortably on the income.'

'And Hannelore's shares? What are they worth – approximately?'

Before Eckhardt could reply, Hannelore said, 'I promise you, Frau Kraus, I shall not be selling my shares. What they represent is worth far more to me than any money they might realize.'

Ever since she had left school in 1927, forty-five years ago, Hannelore Hahn had worked for Kraus companies, first for Kraus Industries, then for Landgut and finally for Werner Kraus KG. From her humble beginning as a typist to her present position as private secretary to the Chairman, hers had been a lifetime devoted to the Kraus family, and she had given her employers, especially Werner, to whom she had been closest, what few women gave their husbands, despite their marriage vows: obedience, service, honour, possibly, in a strange way, even love.

Now she knew that her loyalty and dedication had been recognized. When Werner had made his decision not to leave his empire to his wife but to let it go public, he had needed someone upon whom he could rely to ensure that the company continued in the direction upon which he had set it. There was only one person in whom he could place such absolute faith: herself.

She might never be a director of any company belonging to the Werner Kraus Group, let alone a director of the holding company. But, because of those fifty-one precious shares – fifty-one out of a total of one hundred – she would always possess the controlling vote. Werner Kraus himself might be dead, but in Hannelore Hahn his spirit lived on.

At Heiligensee, a corpse was found in the lake, who was identified as the missing security guard, Wilfried Thomas. In the Rhon mountains, a burnt-out car containing two bodies was discovered. Forensic examination proved the car to have been that belonging to Helena and Marko, and for a brief moment the press speculated that the two terrorists had committed suicide. Then a pathologist's report revealed the dead couple to have been foreigners: their dentistry was not German.

When Marko heard these items on the news, he grew twitchy again, his condition made all the worse by the fact that he had run

544

out of marijuana. Isolated though their camping spot was, he felt dreadfully vulnerable and would have been much happier if he and Helena were hiding out in a city. Helena, however, refused to budge.

Then, one glorious mid-May morning, when the meadow was golden with buttercups, the woods were loud with cuckoos and larks were singing jubilantly in the sky, in a sudden, illuminating flash of insight, Helena knew where her life had taken its wrong turning. It had been nothing to do with Werner's death. That had merely been a sign that she reached the end of one particular road, that the revolution in which she had so deeply believed was not going to be achieved by death and destruction.

No, her mistake had been made a long time before then. It had been when she had given birth to her son, when she had been given the chance to mould a new life and help create a new world, and thrown that opportunity away. Her mistake had been to let Moon Child go.

She thought of Moon Child as she had last seen him at Kleo's wedding, his round, innocent, little face gazing up at her, his hand grasped trustingly in hers. A child of the revolution, she and Marko had described him before he was born. She remembered Matthias accusing her of not caring about anyone, even her own child. 'In your eyes,' he had said, 'everyone is expendable, including your own flesh and blood.' He had been right. She had concentrated on death, when she should have been thinking about life. She had destroyed, when she should have been creating. She had been so intent on influencing the world, that she had ignored the single most important person in it . . .

'You want what?' Marko asked incredulously.

'I want Moon Child back.'

'You're crazy! What are we going to do with a bloody baby?'

'He isn't a baby any more. He's three years old.'

Marko took a deep breath. 'The police could have your mother's house under surveillance.'

'I doubt it. I haven't been to see her since I left home. That's the last place anyone would expect to find me.'

'What if she tells the police?'

'She won't. She won't betray her own daughter.' Now Helena

had analysed her problem and found the solution to it, she was suddenly very sure of herself again.

'And if she refuses to let you take Moon Child away?'

'She won't have any choice,' Helena stated darkly. 'Marko, she stole my baby from me. If necessary, I'll use force to get him back.'

Reinhild had just put a batch of cakes into the oven that Wednesday morning when the telephone rang. Leaving Alexander in the kitchen busily engaged in scraping out the remains of the cake mixture with a wooden spoon, she went into the hall to answer the call. She was totally unprepared for the voice which came down the line.

'Mother, it's me, Helena. I have to see you. I need help.'

Reinhild tried to gather her scattered wits. 'Where are you?'

'In a phone booth. Listen, we're coming to see you tonight. And, for God's sake, don't tell anyone.'

'Helena, did you kidnap Werner? Did you kill those other people?'

'Of course not. It's all lies.'

'Then why don't you go to the police and tell them?'

'It's too complicated to explain now.'

Axel appeared in the hall, clutching the mixing bowl against his chest, cake mixture smeared over his chubby cheeks. 'Oma, who's that?'

If he had not been there, Reinhild might have demanded that Helena explain herself more fully there and then, but she did not want to risk upsetting Axel.

'Is that Moon Child?' Helena asked and, even down the phone, there was an unexpected note of tenderness in her voice.

'Yes,' Reinhild replied feebly. 'We're making cakes.'

Axel had reached the age when he liked talking to people on the phone. He held out sticky fingers towards the handpiece.

'I've run out of change,' Helena said. 'I'll see you later. Remember, don't tell anyone we're coming.'

The receiver went dead. With trembling fingers, Reinhild put down the phone. Axel dropped the wooden spoon on the carpet and wiped his fingers round the bowl, glancing mischievously at

546

her, waiting for her to scold him. But, for once, his grandmother seemed oblivious to him.

She returned to the kitchen and, while she filled the kettle to make a much needed coffee, asked herself the same question she had been asking ever since Werner's death had been discovered and the police had come to interview her. Helena had always been a rebel, but was she really a murderer? The proof seemed incontrovertible, yet still she could not believe her daughter was guilty of the atrocious crimes of which she was accused.

However, now there was another, even more immediate question. Why did Helena suddenly want to see her? She had said she needed help. Was she hoping her mother would put her and Marko up for a while, conceal them while the police hunt continued? If that was the case, what should she do? However much Helena had hurt her in the past, she could not turn away her own daughter in her hour of need. But if she and Marko were guilty? If they were responsible for the deaths of at least eight people, including two small children . . . ?

The kettle boiled. From the oven came the warm, comforting smell of baking cakes. Axel tugged at her apron. 'Oma, look how clean this basin is. You won't have to wash it up.'

Reinhild gazed down into his smiling, trusting little face, surrounded by flaxen curls, and was overcome by a feeling of love for him far more intense than anything she felt for Helena. And then she knew that, whatever the truth, she must do nothing which might put her grandson's life at risk. Nothing, not even to protect her own daughter.

On the kitchen clock, the minutes were ticking inexorably away. Already it was nearly noon. Before she could change her mind, Reinhild went back to the telephone.

Half an hour later, she and Axel were driving in an unmarked police car to the airport. A plainclothes police woman accompanied them on their flight to Berlin. And at Tempelhof another police car was waiting to take them to the Jochum.

It was a long evening of waiting, of listening to every news bulletin on the radio, of watching every news programme on the television, of hearing Reinhild repeat over and over again

547

her telephone conversation with Helena and wondering whether she had made the right decision in calling the police.

'You did absolutely the right thing in putting your own and Axel's safety first,' Viktoria told her for the umpteenth time. 'And you were very sensible to come to Berlin. Whether or not Helena and Marko are guilty, this is the one place they won't dare follow you.'

'I wish I knew why she wanted to see me. I should have let her explain, but Axel came out of the kitchen and I didn't want him to hear anything which might upset him.'

Axel had long since been put to bed in a cot in a corner of the room near the window. Tired after the unexpected adventure of flying to Berlin, he was sleeping soundly.

'He's too young to understand what's happening,' Kleo assured her mother.

'One day he'll find out,' Reinhild sighed. 'The more I think about it, the more sure I am that I should have stayed. I can't believe that Helena is a terrorist . . .'

'All the evidence points towards it,' Dieter said quietly.

'Perhaps she won't turn up,' Reinhild said. 'Perhaps she'll have changed her mind . . .'

Marko drove past the imposing houses on the Alsterufer and turned into a quiet residential side road. 'It's there,' Helena said. He slowed down. There was a cluster of lock-up garages, overshadowed by a large tree, then some bushes, between which a path led to the entrance to the apartment block. A man was walking his dog. A couple strolled, arm in arm. None of them so much as glanced towards the camper.

Still Marko was uneasy, probably because he did not want to be here at all. He did not want the responsibility of Moon Child. What he wanted was to be out of Germany, travelling south, *en route* to some new, carefree existence. Being a revolutionary had been amusing to begin with, but, since he and Helena had been on the run, it had lost its appeal. Not that Marko regretted any of the things they had done. He just had an instinctive sense of self-preservation, which had served him very well thus far in his life, and, at that moment, he was aware of pushing his luck.

He knew he should have been firm with Helena and refused

to embark upon this crazy scheme, but once she set her ideas on something it was impossible to make her change her mind. Of course, he could have walked out on her, but that was something he had scarcely even considered. Life with Helena might be difficult – life without Helena was inconceivable.

He continued up the road, turned right, then right again on to the waterfront, then returned back up the road where Reinhild lived and parked the camper in front of the block of flats before hers. The couple and the man with the dog had disappeared. The area seemed deserted.

He took his revolver from the map compartment, released the safety catch, put the gun in the waistband of his jeans and got out of the van. From the passenger side, Helena also emerged, her weapon in her pocket. Along the pavement they went, past the garages and up the path between the bushes, their rubber-soled shoes making no sound on the concrete. It was a still night, with a new moon and not even a breeze to stir the leaves.

They had almost reached the entrance to the flats, when the entire area was suddenly flooded with light. A voice shouted through a loudhailer: 'This is the police. You are surrounded. Drop your weapons. Put your hands above your heads.' There was an onrush of shadowy figures among the shrubs. Marko glanced behind him. Silhouetted at the end of the path were policemen, their guns sharply defined in the light of a street-lamp.

For a few seconds, there was a tense silence, while the police waited for the couple to recognize the hopelessness of their situation and surrender. Then, Helena took a small step forwards and carried on the clear night air came a rapid series of distinct clicks. The policemen moved in nearer.

Helena's voice rang out, high-pitched and defiantly taunting. 'Go on! Shoot to kill! That's your policy! That's the way the Nazis did it! That's the way the German police still do it! That's the only way you can be sure we shan't be brought to trial and be found innocent. Go on! Shoot a mother on her way to see her baby son! Rob an innocent child of his parents!'

Perhaps if they had brought sub-machine guns with them, they might have been able to shoot their way out of the ambush, Marko reflected desperately. In a blast of bullets, they might have been able to blaze their way back to the camper and freedom. But revolvers were of no use against the arsenal ranged against them.

Through the loudhailer, the voice boomed, 'Nothing will happen to you if you give yourselves up. Put your hands above your heads.'

At the main door to the flats there was a slight movement. Light glinted momentarily on the barrel of a shotgun being aimed directly at Helena. Quick as a flash, she whipped her revolver from her pocket and fired.

Almost instantaneously came a burst of retaliatory fire and her pistol was knocked from her hand. Another bullet hit her in the leg and she fell, screaming, to the ground.

Panic-stricken, Marko pulled his gun from his waistband and let fly a wild volley. If he had stayed where he was, the returning police fire would have hit him, as it had Helena, in a limb, wounding him, but not fatally. As it was, he turned to run and the shot caught him between the shoulder blades. The impact flung his arms upwards and his revolver was jerked out of his hand. He staggered forward a few paces, then his legs crumpled under him. For a moment, he knelt, his arms lifted almost in an attitude of supplication, then he slumped onto the pathway.

The police surged in. Helena tried to struggle to her feet, but the pain in her leg prevented her. Firm hands grasped her by the shoulders. She twisted and wriggled, biting and lashing out at her captors, but they were too strong for her. Handcuffs were clamped firmly about her wrists. 'You have no right to do this!' she spat. 'All I wanted was my son. I just wanted my baby back. What's wrong with that? He's mine! He was stolen from me!'

From the distance came the wail of sirens and ambulances appeared on the scene. Attendants with stretchers hurried towards them. A police doctor knelt beside Marko, felt his pulse, lifted his eyelids, listened to his heart, then grunted to his colleagues, who placed him on a stretcher and covered him with a blanket.

In the glare of lights, Helena could see what they were doing, and to the injustice of her arrest and the pain in her leg was added a new and even more terrible anguish. 'You've killed

550

him!' she shrieked. 'You've killed Marko!' Her agonized cries rent the night.

She was still screaming hysterically as they strapped her onto a stretcher and carried her down to the ambulance which was to take her, under police escort, to the nearest hospital.

It was midnight when the telephone rang in Viktoria's suite and the reception clerk announced the arrival of Superintendent Schneider.

Dieter let the Special Branch officer in. 'We've just heard from Hamburg,' he said. 'It's a good job you weren't there, Frau Kraus. They turned up all right. And they were both armed.' He paused for a moment, then went on, 'Apparently, once your daughter realized the police were there, she fired at them. Our men had no alternative but to shoot back.'

'You mean Helena's . . . ?'

'She was only slightly injured. However, her boyfriend tried to run away and was hit in the back. He would appear to have died instantly.'

Reinhild shook her head uncomprehendingly. Kleo moved to her mother's side and put her arm round her shoulders.

'Has Helena admitted to belonging to Black Kommando?' Dieter asked.

The Superintendent grimaced. 'She has apparently made no attempt at all to deny it. On the contrary, she claims that Black Kommando will take revenge on the police for murdering her lover and on society for stealing her child. However, as you'll understand, according to standard police procedure she has been cautioned not to make any statements without first consulting a lawyer.'

Kleo looked anxiously at her husband and Dieter knew she was hoping that he would volunteer to act for Helena, but he avoided her gaze, staring at a mid-point in the room, trying to absorb the irony of his situation. Through his own actions he had attempted always to atone for the mistakes of his father's generation and to rectify the heinous crimes committed by the Nazis. In this, as in so many other matters, he had agreed with Helena. Yet she, who had so vilified the Nazis, had practised the same terrorism to which she was opposed. She and Marko

551

were to blame for the deaths of at least eight people, including his friend and mentor, Holger Busko. Could he bring himself to defend her, even if she was his sister-in-law?

He seemed to be caught up in a tangled web of circumstances, which had started when he had defended Heinz-Georg Lindner. Yet if he had not taken on that case, would events have been any different? Black Kommando would still have continued their terrorist activities. At some point or another, whether through Holger's death or Werner's, he must have become involved. Indeed, when he thought about it, he wondered if he might not be indirectly responsible for at least one of the incidents. It was he who had persuaded Kleo to pump his father for information, which had led to Stefan publishing that article on Werner in *Aktuell*.

He sighed and turned to the police officer. 'Thank you for giving us the news in person, Superintendent. Perhaps you would let your colleagues in Hamburg know that I shall arrive on the first plane in the morning.'

'Does that mean you will be there in a professional capacity, Dr Duschek?'

'Yes,' Dieter replied, heavily. 'I will act in Helena's defence.'

PART FOUR

1985–1989

Those who close their eyes to the past become blind to the present.

Richard von Weizsäcker
(German President)
during a speech made in May 1985 marking the
40th anniversary of the end of the Second World War

Chapter 23

Gabi Feldmann had never discovered why Dolfi had taken his own life. Because the children were so young, she had told them that their father had died in a motor accident and, gradually, over the years, she had come to believe this herself. Of more immediate urgency had been how to survive.

It had not been easy, but she had scraped by. After Dolfi's death, the family had moved to a council flat on a large housing estate in an industrial suburb of Frankfurt, and Gabi had returned to her former job at the supermarket. A kind neighbour, with a young child of her own, had minded Klaus and taken care of Erich and Inge when they came home from school and during the holidays. By the time Klaus went to school, Erich was old enough to look after his younger sister and brother until their mother returned from work.

All three children took after their father in looks, but in Klaus the similarity was most apparent, although his features were coarser than Dolfi's and his hair, eyebrows and lashes were so fair as to appear almost white, while his eyes were a curiously light grey-blue.

Klaus's personality, however, bore little relationship to Dolfi's. He had a quick temper, followed by sullen behaviour and, as a young child, threw violent tantrums for no apparent reason. Throughout his school life he was in trouble, and Gabi was constantly having to take time off to see his teachers and hear their complaints about his behaviour.

When he began secondary school, he and some other boys formed a gang. They had their hair cropped very short in the skinhead fashion and always seemed to be getting into fights. When he was just thirteen, Klaus was arrested for hitting a policeman with a broken bottle and sent for three months to a reform school.

555

For a short time after he returned home, he appeared a reformed character. Then, one day, while cleaning his room, Gabi came across some pornographic videos concealed at the bottom of his wardrobe, a knife in his desk drawer and some tubes of glue in his anorak pocket. When she confronted him with her finds, he let loose a foul stream of abuse and stormed out of the flat.

Unfortunately, Erich, whom Klaus used to look up to when he was younger, was away from home. Erich had inherited Dolfi's enthusiasm for cars and worked for a vehicle transport company, travelling all over Europe and sometimes as far afield as the Middle East, so that days, sometimes weeks, passed and his family did not see him.

When he came back, Gabi asked him to have a word with his young brother, but Klaus paid no more heed to Erich than he did to his mother and after that he became a complete law unto himself, playing truant from school, staying out late at night and sometimes not coming home at all. He smoked and was often drunk, though where he got the money from, Gabi did not know. Without Erich to give her support, she dared not tell him off. His behaviour could be so threatening she was frightened for her own safety.

As for Inge, it was useless to expect her to have any influence on Klaus. At fifteen, she had met Rod Miller, a long-haired, twenty-year-old rock musician, the illegitimate son of a German girl and an American GI, who had himself just completed his military service. After meeting Rod, Inge had dyed her hair shocking pink, had a stud put in her nose and wore punk make-up. On leaving school, she had got a job in a record store and at sixteen, become pregnant. To give Rod his due, he had not deserted her and they had moved in to a flat on the same estate as her mother. Now their little boy was four.

Rod's band was not successful: its latest record release had not even made the German Top Fifty. Occasionally the boys were asked to do a local gig, but, apart from that, Rod did not work. To Gabi's disgust, he was quite content for the State to subsidize him and his family. 'The army had eighteen months of my life,' he said, 'now I want something back.'

Unfortunately, Klaus hero-worshipped Rod and saw no reason why he should work either. He left school at the age of fifteen in the summer of 1985, without any scholastic qualifications, although with an abundance of the street wisdom native to many city kids.

By that time, the boom years of the 1950s, 60s and early 70s were over, and West Germany was suffering from rising unemployment. Such jobs as Klaus went after – these were mainly on building sites and in factories – he was refused. Gabi was despairing. He was not eligible for unemployment benefit and she could not afford to support him much longer.

Then, just when she was giving up hope of him ever getting work, the miracle occurred. Suddenly he smartened up his appearance, grew his hair and took out his earring. Not only was he offered a job, but it was an extremely good one – as a page boy at the Hotel Jochum-Frankfurt. Gabi heaved a mental sigh of relief. She had done her best for all her children under difficult circumstances. Now it was up to them to do their best for themselves.

What Gabi did not realize was that Rod had seen the vacancy advertised and talked Klaus into applying for it. 'Anyone who can afford to stay at the Jochum has to be a millionaire,' he said. 'You get in there, kid.'

'I'm not going to dress up in no poncy uniform and lug suitcases around,' Klaus told him aggressively.

'Sometimes I think you haven't got the brains you were born with. A room there costs more than you'll ever make in a month. The guests all drive flash cars, and wear expensive clothes, watches and jewellery. All you got to do is get into their rooms. I'll give you a good deal on everything you nick.'

Rod was already giving Klaus quite a few good deals, the best being on drugs. Klaus wasn't a junkie, not like some kids on the estate. He had sniffed glue when he was at reform school, graduated to smoking pot at fourteen and amphetamines when he was flush. But he preferred beer to coke. It was cheaper and you didn't get hooked. Getting hooked was stupid. Better to be like Rod and push the stuff.

Rod also gave Klaus and his mates a good deal on handbags, wallets and briefcases they stole – less the cash, of course, which they kept for themselves. And on car radios. They all prided themselves on being able to break into a car and take out the radio in under five minutes.

Now Rod gave Klaus the benefit of his experience in the army to tell him how to behave in hotel service. 'Suck up to the bastards,' he said. 'Call them sir and madam. Look as if you're doing everything at the double. And don't give them no lip . . .'

However, when Klaus started at the Jochum, he encountered several problems. The first was that he was expected to work – hard – for his living. And, secondly, most of the cleaners, kitchen hands, washers-up and chambermaids were Turks.

If there was one thing Klaus hated above all else, it was Turks.

When the first guest workers had arrived in West Germany in the early 1960s, there had been more Italians in Frankfurt than any other nationality. Some, like Dino Cattani, the General Manager of the Jochum-Frankfurt, had remained and, in due course, become a German citizen. Dino had even married a German girl and now spoke German so fluently that few people realized he was an original guest worker. But many Italians, deterred by the strict conditions imposed by the German government before it would grant citizenship, had been encouraged by the gradual improvement in the Italian economy to return home.

The Turkish economy, however, had seen no improvement and, instead of the Turks returning home, the reverse had happened and their families had joined them in West Germany. In Frankfurt, as in other large cities, they had settled in the cheapest housing in the poorest districts, which had become virtual ghettoes, with their own shops, cafés and mosques.

Despite having lived in Germany for a quarter of a century, many Turks were still illiterate and did not speak more than a few words of German. They tended to do the menial jobs nobody else wanted, like collecting refuse, sweeping streets, cleaning hospitals and working on public transport.

Their children's command of the language was better, because they attended German schools, but they still spoke only Turkish at home. Out of school hours, there was little social intermixing.

Turkish fathers were ambitious for their children, particularly their sons, and were strict disciplinarians, distrustful of the liberal attitude of German parents. And German parents did not encourage their offspring to become too friendly with Turks, who lived in squalid surroundings, ate strange food, followed an alien religion, and made no apparent attempt to integrate with the rest of the community.

So far as Klaus Feldmann was concerned, he cared nothing for the economic and sociological reasons behind the large Turkish presence in Frankfurt. He just hated Turks. As his mate Johann said, they were foreign, there were too many of them, they were dirty and they stank.

Johann knew what he was talking about. There were enough Turks round where the Feldmanns lived, but Johann's family were almost the only Germans on their estate. Johann had introduced the gang to Turk-bashing. They used to wait for Turkish kids after school, beating them up, messing up their exercise books and taking any money they had on them, in the certain knowledge that their fathers would give them another hiding when they got home. They also amused themselves by spraying *TUERKEN 'RAUS!* Turks out! on walls round the estate, with aerosols they stole from do-it-yourself stores.

Now Klaus was at work, his contempt for the Turks knew no bounds. One, in particular, got up his nose from the moment they met. He was the hotel odd-job man, a shortish guy of about twenty, with liquid brown eyes and gleaming white teeth under a drooping black moustache. The first time he saw Klaus, he beamed and said, '*Ich* Mustafa. *Du* . . . ?'

It was quite usual for young people to call each other by the familiar form of 'you', but Klaus wasn't having any of that from a Turk. 'I am *Herr* Feldmann,' he snarled, 'and use "Sie" when you talk to me.'

But whether because he simply didn't understand much German, or because the nuances of 'du' and 'Sie' were beyond him, Mustafa just grinned and, whenever he saw Klaus, addressed him as, 'Herr Feldmann, *du* . . .'

When Klaus arrived at the hotel in the morning, Mustafa would already be emptying dustbins, raking the gravel drive or unloading beer barrels and wine crates into the cellar, and when

Klaus left in the evening, Mustafa would still be sweeping up litter, mopping floors or cleaning the lavatories.

'I'll make that Turkish bastard sorry that he was ever born,' Klaus bragged, one Saturday evening a couple of weeks after he had started his new job. He was at Harry's, a seedy bar near the main railway station, with Johann and Heinz, another of the gang, who hadn't got jobs yet.

His opportunity arose shortly before Christmas. A stockbroker, a frequent visitor to the Jochum, who had been staying in the Forest Suite, was taking his departure. Klaus had carried his luggage out to his red Porsche 944 and was waiting while the man reached in his pocket for some change, when he noticed his room key lying on the bonnet. It was a simple matter to slip it up his sleeve, then take it to his locker and put it in his coat pocket.

The stockbroker was in a hurry. When he settled his bill at reception, he could not remember where he had left his key. Klaus was despatched upstairs to look for it and by the time he returned, empty-handed, to reception, the stockbroker had departed. 'He's probably packed it!' the reception clerk exclaimed in exasperation. 'Always in a rush, that's his trouble.'

New Year's Eve was hectic. Every member of staff was on duty and extra personnel had been brought in from outside to help. Every bed in the hotel was occupied and about a thousand guests were attending the gala banquet and ball. The occupants of the Forest Suite were a middle-aged man and a considerably younger woman.

As midnight approached, a lull descended, as the guests congregated in the ballroom. The Hall Porter gave Klaus permission to take a short break and get himself a cold drink.

Nobody saw him go to his locker and take the key to the Forest Suite from his coat pocket, neither did anyone see him walk up the service stairs to the first floor and, if they had, they would have assumed he was on a legitimate errand. Quick as a flash, he turned the key, entered the room, shut the door behind him and turned on the light.

His luck was in. Lying on the dressing table, amidst a mess of face powder, hair pins and cotton wool balls, were a watch, a ring and a pair of matching earrings, set with glittering stones, and a wallet. Klaus slipped them all into his pocket.

Back at the staff lockers, he wrapped the watch, ring and earrings in a handkerchief and stowed them in his coat pocket. Then, with a quick twist of a piece of bent wire, he opened Mustafa's locker door and dropped the wallet on the floor and put the key to the Forest Suite on the shelf.

Klaus was sent off duty at one o'clock and given New Year's Day off, so it was not until he returned to work on 2 January that he learned about the commotion which had taken place in his absence: the young woman's hysteria upon finding her jewellery missing; the consternation of her companion, who was supposed to be in New York on business, and did not want the police involved in case his wife discovered his true whereabouts; the search of the hotel; and the eventual discovery of the wallet and key in Mustafa's locker. Mustafa, of course, had denied all knowledge of the crime, but the evidence was so overwhelmingly against him that he had been immediately dismissed.

'That showed him,' Klaus bragged at Harry's Bar that evening. But Rod's reaction was not what he expected. 'You stupid little git!' he exclaimed. 'You left a wallet full of credit cards and kept the bleeding jewels?'

'Well, I thought . . . They're diamonds, aren't they?'

'Sure, they're diamonds. But they'll take weeks to shift, whereas credit cards, they're like cash . . .' In the end, Rod gave him seven hundred Marks, not as much as he had hoped but enough for Klaus and the gang to get very drunk. Parked near Harry's Bar, they found a brand-new Audi. Klaus smashed the driver's window with a brick, they all piled in and Klaus drove them home, speeding through red traffic lights, bumping off parked cars, lurching over pavements and traffic islands, followed by the blaring of horns and flashing of lights from other motorists. He stopped in a dark side street beside a block of flats occupied mainly by Turks.

'Do you see what I see?' Klaus asked. Approaching them was a young Turkish couple.

They were out of the car before the Turks knew what was happening. A slug with the brick on the back of his head knocked the young man unconscious and the girl was dragged, a hand

561

round her mouth to stop her screaming, into the car. Klaus had her first, while the others watched. Then they each took her. When they had finished, they left her in the car, and took off down the street, to be swallowed up by the night.

After the theft from the Forest Suite, however, security was considerably tightened up at the Jochum, and Klaus found it impossible to get hold of any more keys. With no incentive left to work, he took to arriving late or simply not turning up at all. When he was warned by the Hall Porter about his time-keeping, he said, 'Stuff your fucking job.'

'Bleeding wonderful!' Rod said in disgust. 'You've just blown the best bloody opportunity you're ever likely to have.'

But Klaus didn't care. Breaking into cars was easier than breaking into hotel rooms and Rod would still act as a fence. He told his mother he had been made redundant and didn't bother to look for another job, but lay in bed till lunchtime or later, watched a video or two, then met up with Heinz, Johann and the others at Harry's Bar. He shaved off his hair again, had his left ear pierced for five earrings, and, on the knuckles of both hands, had tattooed the words LOVE and HATE.

Over the years, Basilius Meyer had risen to become one of the most important men in the GDR. At sixty-six, he was a Member of the all-powerful Politburo and held the position of Secretary for Cultural Liaison on the SED Central Committee, a position which afforded him wide-reaching involvement in all aspects of the internal and external affairs of the State.

His wife, Irina, was SED Central Committee Deputy Secretary for Youth, responsible directly to Margot Honecker. Their son, Reinhardt, who was thirty-three, married and with a young son of his own, was in the diplomatic service. His first posting abroad had been to Warsaw and now he was in Chile.

Due to the prominence of his position, Basilius's face and name were well-known to the general populace, but beyond that people knew little about him, for the GDR leadership did not cultivate personal publicity. This was not America, which even had a former Hollywood movie star as President. The GDR government, including First Party Secretary Erich Honecker, who had succeeded Walter Ulbricht in 1971, was comprised of

562

grey, elderly men, wearing apparently identical spectacles, blue suits and raincoats, who were to be seen at May Day parades and on national anniversaries, standing on a podium, flanked by top military brass, inspecting the troops.

The Meyers now lived in a fine house in Wandlitz, a very pleasant settlement in the countryside forty kilometres north of Berlin, alongside other prominent SED members, including Erich Honecker himself. Chauffeur-driven Volvos conveyed them every day to and from the SED Central Committee Building on the Werdeschen Markt.

The change in their circumstances had taken place so gradually that Basilius had scarcely noticed it. Not that he had forgotten his impoverished childhood in Wedding, although he did not harp back to it constantly, like his cousin, Rudolf Sommer, who still revisited his childhood haunts in the Prenzlauer Berg district whenever he came to Berlin.

However, Basilius did refer to Wedding occasionally during Central Committee debates on welfare and housing. That those tenements still existed in West Berlin, even if modern apartment blocks had been erected alongside them, proved as much as anything else the inequalities of the capitalist system, where the rich grew richer as the poor became poorer.

Since the erection of the Berlin Wall twenty-five years earlier in 1961 had stopped the flood of emigrants to the West, the economy had picked up to such an extent that outsiders marvelled at East Germany's 'economic miracle'. The Berlin Wall had also led to social and political stability, as new generations had grown up who had only known two separate Germanies. Over the years, trade links between the two Germanies had strengthened, to the extent that the Federal Republic had become the GDR's second most important trading partner after the Soviet Union.

There had also been a relaxation of certain restrictions affecting people's private lives. GDR citizens were now allowed to watch West German television; there was greater religious tolerance; and travel regulations had also been eased.

Most people now were allowed to take vacations in other Soviet bloc countries, although only on special occasions, like family weddings and funerals, could they visit the Federal

Republic. As a safeguard, married couples were not permitted to travel together to West Germany and very few young people under twenty-six were allowed to go at all, especially if they were single.

Pensioners, however, could leave the GDR for up to sixty days a year, including as many visits as they liked to the Federal Republic, and it was generally understood that if they decided to remain, the State would not object. The brutal fact was that the young were vital to the economy and the military, while the old were a burden, costing the State money.

However, there were occasions – as in the case of extreme political dissidents and penniless foreign refugees – when the GDR government deemed it expedient to take advantage of the Federal Republic's liberal asylum laws and ship these 'undesirables' quietly across the border.

This traffic was not entirely one-way. At times, the GDR was also prepared to give asylum. One particular instance of this had been the case of Helena Kraus and Heinz-Georg Lindner.

Basilius had watched with considerable interest the activities of Black Kommando, the Baader-Meinhof gang and the Red Army Faction: these terrorist gangs could hardly have done better at destabilizing West German society if they had been working under direct orders from the *Stasi*, the State Security Police.

Dieter Duschek had put up a stalwart defence for Helena Kraus at her trial, pleading that her relationship with her boyfriend had placed her under such extreme emotional pressure that she had become mentally unbalanced. The court had eventually found her guilty of manslaughter, but not murder, and committed her for ten years' detention in a West Berlin high security mental hospital.

In 1977, Heinz-Georg Lindner, sentenced in 1971 on bank robbery charges, had been released from prison. Acting on Basilius's instructions, *Stasi* agents in the Federal Republic kept Lindner under surveillance for a while, then approached him with a proposition he could not refuse. Three months later, newspaper headlines and television news programmes throughout the world had announced Helena's escape.

For months the search for Helena had continued, until all leads eventually ran out. Investigations were carried out into

564

the prison's security and eventually a warder, whose suddenly and dramatically improved lifestyle had attracted attention to him, admitted to having been handsomely bribed by a certain Herr Schmidt to change places with him for a few hours. But who was behind Helena's escape and where she was now he had no idea.

In the mean time, Helena Kraus and Heinz-Georg Lindner were safely inside the GDR. Basilius undertook part of their interrogation and they gave him a fascinating insight into the lives and minds of West German young people. Helena was particularly interesting, expressing very lucidly her bitter disillusionment with the capitalist, militarist society she had inherited.

They had settled down well. Lindner had a laboratory job at Pharmazeuta in Leipzig, and Kraus, who had started working as a hospital orderly, had gone on to train to become a qualified children's nurse. They had been given pseudonyms: Lindner was Peter Mueller; Kraus was Sylvia Kunert.

By effecting their 'disappearance', Basilius had added yet further to the West's sense of insecurity. With this and other similar coups under his belt, he looked forward with assurance to the future. He had even heard rumours tipping him as a possible eventual successor to Honecker.

Then, in April 1986, the new Soviet leader, Mikhail Sergeyevich Gorbachev, came to East Berlin for the Eleventh Party Congress and Basilius's confidence faltered. It was a year since Gorbachev, a short, balding, youthful-looking 55-year-old, had been elected Secretary General of the Soviet Communist Party, and immediately launched a programme of economic reform and openness, *perestroika* and *glasnost*, upon the Soviet Union.

First, Gorbachev and his wife, Raisa, went to the Berlin Wall and were filmed and photographed by the Brandenburg Gate. Then he launched an unprecedented Soviet peace initiative.

With Congress deputies and representatives of the world press as his witnesses, he pleaded for a reduction of conventional troops in Europe from 'the Atlantic to the Urals'. The USSR, he stated, wanted to see stockpiles of weapons, including nuclear weapons, destroyed or at least stored within national boundaries. 'Never will our country begin military actions against Western

Europe,' he stated, 'unless we and our allies become the targets of an attack from NATO.'

When, in 1983, the United States had installed its first Pershing-2 and Cruise missiles in West Germany, there had been outrage. Whilst Soviet missiles based on East German soil were necessary to defend the peace, the introduction of American nuclear weapons onto West German soil was a clearly hostile move.

But now Gorbachev was showing the Soviet Union's peaceful intentions by offering to withdraw its nuclear weapons from the GDR if the United States would do the same, and hinting that it would be prepared to consider multi-lateral disarmament. This example of *glasnost* brought long, loud and very genuine applause from the delegates.

The leadership applauded, too. Yet Basilius's thoughts belied his apparent enthusiasm and probably typified those of his colleagues. Gorbachev had made his announcement without consulting them. Were they in danger of losing their autonomy?

In the twenty-one years which had passed since the tragic death of his wife, Ilona, Wolfram Schwidinski had devoted all his energies to human rights causes, campaigning – so far as this was permitted – on behalf of civil liberties, especially those of speech and movement; for nuclear disarmament; and, above all, on environmental issues.

He now lived and practised as a lawyer in Liebenroda, an industrial town of about 60,000 inhabitants in Saxony, not far from Leipzig. His father, Karsten Schwidinski, had died a couple of years earlier, but Erika, his stepmother, and his half-sister Paula and her husband, Manfred Bauer, still lived in Leipzig. Childhood sweethearts, Paula and Manfred had married immediately upon leaving university the previous year, and Paula was expecting their first child at the end of October. Having lost his own wife and baby because of the dreadful conditions under which they were expected to live, Wolfram was determined to do all he could to protect the future of this next generation.

The principal source of employment in Liebenroda was Auto-Roda, a vast, antiquated factory, which had been part of Kraus Industries until the end of the war, when it had been taken over by the State and, instead of building tanks, had started manufacturing automobile parts.

In June 1983, Wolfram had organized a march from Liebenroda town centre along the bank of the misnamed Weisse Elster, the White Elster river – whose waters, far from being white, were so dark as to be almost black – to the Auto-Roda works, in protest at the sodium cyanide, used in chrome-plating, being pumped into the river. This had led to his first confrontation with the Liebenroda police. Five hundred people, mostly Auto-Roda employees, had joined in the demonstration, fifty of whom, including himself, had been arrested and spent the next few weeks inside the State Security Police prison, deep underneath *Stasi* headquarters on the Marx-Engels-Platz.

Later that same year, Wolfram had been in prison again, this time for organizing a peace demonstration. He and Christoph Margraf, the Pastor of St Thomas's, had led a candlelit procession of some 300 supporters from the church into the Marx-Engels-Platz, where they had sat in silent protest against the nuclear missiles now ranged each side of the border.

The GDR leadership had a characteristically hypocritical attitude towards peace. Official State peace rallies were one thing. Spontaneous, people-led demonstrations were quite another. For a short while the police had tolerated the protesters' presence in the square, then they had moved in and arrested them.

Although the burgeoning peace movement was immediately banned, the Church had stood its ground, claiming that peace was not a political, but a moral issue. Following his release, Pastor Margraf had instituted peace services at St Thomas's every Monday evening, after which the small congregation would remain to hold discussions on peace and other related topics. Because the Church had the right of free assembly, there was nothing the *Stasi* could do, although Wolfram and Christoph were sure Police Chief Sommer had informers planted to report back on their meetings.

Gorbachev's peace initiative gave rise to cautious optimism in Liebenroda, as elsewhere in the GDR, particularly when the American President, Ronald Reagan, responded positively to it. But this satisfaction was short-lived. On 28 April, a scant week after Gorbachev's visit to East Berlin, news emerged of a terrifying catastrophe in the Soviet Union. At the Chernobyl nuclear power complex in the Ukraine, a reactor had blown up. The Soviet Union first denied, then tried to play down the accident, saying everything was under control, denying the dangers from radioactive fall-out. But two weeks later, the reactor was still burning and a nuclear cloud had fanned out over Europe.

So far as the people of Liebenroda and Leipzig were concerned, Chernobyl was the latest crisis in an ecological disaster which had long been overtaking them.

Never were the skies clear above Leipzig. Even in summer a haze shielded the sun. Most days, the city was shrouded in smog, a yellowish pall of smoke, soot and sulphurous fumes, emitted from a hundred thousand household chimneys, mingled with the dense, black, mushroom clouds of smoke belched out from the giant petro-chemical combines at nearby Bitterfeld, and the hydrogen sulphide and nitric acid fumes blasted out by the power generating station at Espenhain.

Nowhere could one escape the pollution. The countryside was barren, ruined by the sulphurous sludge which drained out of the brown coal slag heaps into the marshy ground, by deadly chemicals released into rivers and sulphuric acid hanging in the atmosphere. Houses were being eaten away. Forests were being killed. Lakes and rivers were biologically dead.

People wrapped scarves round their mouths to avoid breathing in the air, but even indoors they were not safe. The smog crept through gaps in ill-fitting windows and doors, holes in roofs and cracks in walls, clinging to curtains, carpets and clothing, befouling and poisoning everything with which it came in contact. They boiled their drinking water, but still the sweet, deathly smell of almonds clung to it.

Not surprisingly, doctors' waiting rooms were crammed with people suffering from eczema, asthma and chest infections, and hospitals were full of patients ill with bronchial complaints, tuberculosis and cancer. That Karsten Schwidinski had attained the age of seventy-eight when he died was little short of a miracle. The wonder was that any babies survived infancy and anyone at

568

all reached old age, particularly since there was an even more chronic shortage of drugs and medical facilities than there had been in 1965, at the time of Ilona's death.

And Leipzig and Liebenroda were far from unique. Throughout the GDR, the same problems existed. There were laws defining the State and society's responsibilities to protect the environment, but the government did nothing to enforce them. It would, of course, be horrendously – if not prohibitively – expensive to do so. The country's whole industrial base was hopelessly outmoded, inherited from the nineteenth century and unchanged since, its factories decrepit, its equipment and technology obsolete.

Just as the Soviet government had tried to conceal the disaster at Chernobyl, so the GDR government kept to itself its environmental plight. As Wolfram knew from Western television, West Germans were unaware of the dire ecological condition of their neighbouring country. And there was no way of informing them.

The mood at the Liebenroda sports stadium, where the junior football championship final had just ended, was ecstatic. Throughout the second half the score had stood at two-all, then, in the very last minutes of the match, Gert Koenig had shot the winning goal. The spectators stamped, shouted and cheered as the team filed off the pitch. In his seat in the front row of the main grandstand, Gert's father, Lieutenant Colonel Heinrich Koenig, could scarcely contain his pride.

The man next to him clapped him on the shoulder. 'What a match! What a goal! You should feel proud of that son of yours, Heini.'

Heinrich beamed, revelling in Gert's reflected glory, the moment all the more satisfying because Rudi was beside him to witness his triumph. His voice was choked with emotion, as he replied, 'I do, Rudi.'

In an orderly manner, the spectators began to leave the stands. Hooliganism, such as they knew from the television was rampant in Western European countries, was unknown in the GDR. A few hotheads existed, of course, some punks, skinheads and other rowdies, but their activities were carefully monitored by

569

the police and a few months in jail usually tended to cure them of their antisocial behaviour.

Heinrich and Rudi left the stadium together and, when they reached the main exit, people recognized them and moved deferentially aside to let them pass: Police Chief Colonel Rudolf Sommer and Lieutenant Colonel Heinrich Koenig were the two most feared men in Liebenroda.

To complete his satisfaction, Heinrich was travelling home the same way as he had come, in the police chief's chauffeur-driven Mercedes, which was waiting outside the stadium. The driver saluted and opened the rear doors, and the two men settled themselves inside. The car glided past long bus queues, cyclists and pedestrians making their way home. Although the town's principal industry was the manufacture of automotive parts for Trabants and Wartburgs, this did not give the workers any precedence in buying cars of their own.

'Gert's got great talent,' Sommer commented. 'He could make a career in football.'

'That's what he wants – and won't have,' Heinrich stated. 'Sport is too insecure a profession. An injured ligament, a broken limb, and one's career is over. He will follow my example and become a regular soldier. That way, his sporting accomplishments will be encouraged and his future secure. In November, he's due for military service. After eighteen months in the army, he'll do as I say and sign on for a further term.'

Gert had all the makings of an excellent soldier. Discipline was inbred in him, at home, at school and through the Free German Youth, which he had joined at the age of six. He had been taking defence education classes since he was eleven. At fifteen, he had begun para-military training and was familiar with all kinds of weapons. He was a skilled marksman and already knew how to strip, load and fire many guns.

His son's future was far more assured than his own had been at that age, Heinrich reflected, as Sommer offered him a cigarette. Gert wasn't starting with all his disadvantages. Even now, Heinrich shuddered when he remembered his uncle, Stefan Jochum, being arrested as a spy, and, above all, he tried to forget that dreadful day in 1959, when his mother and grandmother had come to East Berlin and announced that

570

they were escaping to the West, that his father and sister had already left, and that his grandfather was following them.

When Heinrich thought back, he was embarrassed by the brief moment of sentimental weakness, which had made him delay reporting his mother and grandmother. Certainly the same weakness had not applied to his feelings towards his grandfather. The pastor, he knew, had been arrested. And so had his grandmother, who had stupidly come back to East Berlin to meet him. Since Heinrich had never heard from his family, nor made any attempt to contact them, he had put all thoughts of them to the back of his mind.

By 1968, he had risen to the rank of major and in August of that year he had been among the National People's Army troops sent to Czechoslovakia, with troops from other Warsaw Pact countries, to give socialist fraternal assistance during the counter-revolution that August. That had been a major turning-point in his life. A staunch Party member, a fervent believer in law and order, and an unwavering patriot, he had been disgusted by the rebellious rabble he had encountered on the streets of Prague.

He had been married a couple of years by then and Gert was just two months old. His wife, Eva, who was a schoolteacher, was hinting that she would like him to leave the army and settle down to a more domestic existence. His father-in-law was a prison officer at Marzahn in East Berlin and, on his recommendation, Heinrich applied for a transfer from the National People's Army to the prison service. Now, at the age of forty-seven, he was a Lieutenant Colonel in the State Security Police, in charge of the prison at Liebenroda.

The family had a comfortable existence. Not for them a drab flat on the vast, soulless Karl Liebknecht housing estate – which the car was just passing – but an apartment in a pleasant land-scaped compound, with other Party officials, including Police Chief Sommer, who had been posted to Liebenroda about the same time as himself. Their status entitled them to cars, servants, and to buy luxury Western goods at Party stores.

As the car rattled over the town's cobbled streets, past timbered houses and quaint shops, Sommer lit yet another cigarette. When they crossed the Weisse Elster river bridge, he exhaled and broke the silence. 'Schwidinski's up to his tricks again.'

Startled, Heinrich looked towards him. 'What is it this time?'

'He and Margraf are planning a so-called pilgrimage to Espenhain. They think they can overcome the ban on demonstrations that way.'

Encouraged by the unusual feeling of camaraderie between them, Heinrich commented, 'I don't understand why you permit Schwidinski to continue practising. In your position, I'd have locked him up for good years ago.'

'I'd rather he continue to operate in the open,' Sommer replied. 'That way I know what he's up to. There's something to be said for *glasnost*.'

He stubbed out his half-finished cigarette and immediately lit another one. Then he went on, 'To tell you the truth, I'm more worried by Gorbachev than Schwidinski. Schwidinski can be dealt with easily enough. But if Gorbachev continues making himself into a kind of cult figure, and doesn't just talk about *glasnost* and *perestroika*, but actually tries to implement his policies, there will be chaos. I have a feeling that we are standing on the brink of a new and potentially very dangerous era . . .'

Heinrich felt as if the breath had been knocked out of him. If it had ever occurred to him to criticize the Soviet leader, he would never have dared do so, certainly not to anyone outside his immediate family and, even then, he would have been very cautious, for the same system of informers applied now as when he had been young. He believed he could trust Eva and Gert, but he couldn't be absolutely certain.

He glanced at the window dividing them from the driver and noted thankfully that it was closed. Sommer gave a thin smile. 'Basically, I suppose I don't trust the Russians. Never have.'

Heinrich could scarcely believe his ears. This was Police Chief Sommer, who was responsible for the district's political security, who reported directly to State Security Minister Erich Mielke and was related to Politburo Member Basilius Meyer. This was Sommer, who commanded a vast network of secret policemen, agents and informers; in whose offices were dossiers on every single inhabitant of Liebenroda; who had the final say in everything, right down to authorizing travel permits, monitoring job applications and allocating student places at the town's various schools and colleges.

The sense of well-being Heinrich had experienced at the end of the match was all gone and he suddenly wished he were not travelling in Sommer's car. He did not want to be party to such treasonable and subversive confidences.

'But I'm ten years older than you,' Sommer continued. 'I can remember the war clearly. And I was in Berlin when it ended. I saw Red Army soldiers rape my mother . . .'

'I didn't know that,' Heinrich mumbled. In fact, he was suddenly realizing that, although he had known Sommer for some sixteen years, he didn't really know him at all.

The car entered the Marx-Engels-Platz and Sommer leaned forward and rapped on the glass. The driver drew up in front of the *Stasi* building. 'My driver will take you home,' he told Heinrich. 'I have work to do.' As the driver hurried to open the door, he added, 'Pass on my congratulations to Gert. I hope you're going to celebrate tonight.'

'We'll probably have a beer or two,' Heinrich acknowledged. 'You're welcome to join us.' Earlier, he would have meant it. Now he hoped Sommer would be too busy.

Sommer ignored the invitation. After instructing the driver to deliver Heinrich home, he walked purposefully past the armed sentries into the gloomy, cavernous interior of the security police headquarters, a short man, with grey hair and triangular eyes under dark, bushy eyebrows, his head sunk between his shoulders. Once inside the empty expanse of his first floor office, he went over to the window, where he stood looking down through the security bars onto the wide square, across flower beds and a fountain, to the town hall and beyond that, the church.

His mind was no longer on Schwidinski and Gorbachev, but the Koenigs. Heinrich Koenig and his son Gert, he reflected, not for the first time, were perfect examples of what someone had once called 'planned German men after the Soviet pattern'. They looked typically Germanic, with their blond hair, blue eyes, broad features and athletic build. But they had been programmed from birth and were now little more than human robots.

Why, then, knowing that, had he submitted to that sudden

573

moment of indiscretion and admitted his fears to Koenig? Such behaviour was not only unprofessional but quite untypical. I must be getting old, he thought wrily.

It did not occur to him that, a bachelor, with no near family except for Basilius Meyer, he was probably the loneliest person in Liebenroda.

Chapter 24

Viktoria lay listening drowsily to the muted early morning sounds of the city beyond her bedroom window – a dustcart, a tram, a police siren, some drunks wending their rowdy way along the Kurfuerstendamm. Nothing unusual there, so why had she woken so suddenly and with a sense of excitement, as if something special were happening today?

It wasn't her birthday. That had been in June and she had been ninety-two. The years became vitally important when one was very old, just like they were when one was very young. Each day was precious, when one did not know whether it might be one's last.

No, it wasn't her birthday, and it wasn't Christmas. That still lay ahead. Oh, it was ridiculous, this habit her memory had of playing tricks on her! And the stupidest thing was, the most recent events were the first she forgot, no matter how important they were to her, while things which had happened years ago remained vividly clear.

If she was asked, for instance, when Senta and Eduard had moved to Berlin and taken over the general management of the Jochum Hotels chain, she could never remember. Although when she thought about it very hard, she knew they had come after that dreadful business with Helena and Moon Child – or Axel as everyone called him now – so it must have been about the time of her eightieth birthday.

Occasionally, particularly after she had been dozing, she even needed to be reminded who Senta was, confusing her with Luise and Lili. 'It's the red hair and green eyes,' her grand-daughter would laugh. 'Although there will soon be more grey than red . . . !'

Yes, incredibly, Senta and Lili were both approaching fifty, while Eduard would soon be sixty and Bruno eighty. Even her great-grandchildren were children no longer. Gisela was twenty and Karli eighteen. The passage of time was perhaps the strangest aspect of being very old. It was as though the younger generations were moving swiftly towards her, while she remained static.

Although nobody mentioned Heini nowadays, she sometimes thought about him and wondered whether she had more great-grandchildren in the GDR. How difficult to imagine Heini, just a teenager when she had last seen him, as a middle-aged man. How tragic the way families had been divided and completely lost touch with each other because of the Wall . . .

Families . . . Yes, what was happening today was connected with the family. But with whom? With Gisela, perhaps – or Karli?

At the mere thought of them, a fond smile etched itself on Viktoria's lips and she nestled her head more comfortably into the pillow. Fate might have dealt her many cruel blows, but it had been very kind to her when it came to giving her two such wonderful great-grandchildren.

Gisela was another redhead, clever and artistic, passing through school with outstanding marks in languages, literature, music and art. Eduard had hoped she would go to university, but Gisela had been impatient to start work and, in the end, they had agreed upon a compromise, so she now spent three and a half days a week at the Jochum and one and a half days at college, studying for a diploma in hotel management. Already she was showing a flair for organization and Eduard was able to delegate quite a lot of his workload into her capable hands.

Karli reminded Viktoria very much of her own father. Not only did he bear the same name, he even looked like him, tall and broad, with high colouring and the beginnings of a fair moustache. He had left school at sixteen, with disappointingly low grades in the subjects Gisela excelled in but good marks in maths, economics and science. He, too, had immediately entered the family business, although not in Berlin, but at the Jochum-Stuttgart, the newest acquisition.

That was typical of Karli. He hated doing things the easy way. In temperament, he was a true Jochum, dogged and determined, often to the point of obstinacy, or – as Stefan had unkindly

576

remarked, when Karli had insisted on doing military service, even though as a Berlin resident he could have been exempted – to the point of stupidity. For Karli was in Stuttgart that autumn when his call-up papers came through and, disgusted by his friends running away to Berlin to avoid conscription, had enlisted. To Stefan's further dismay, he seemed to be enjoying his time in the army. But as Viktoria reminded Stefan, 'So did my father. It was his ambition to be a Guards officer, but his parents couldn't afford it . . .'

Stefan . . . Whatever was happening today had to do with Stefan. She glanced at the luminous hands on the old-fashioned alarm clock beside her bed. Half-past seven already. She must have fallen asleep again . . .

The door opened and Senta came in, carrying her breakfast tray, which she put down on the bedside table. That proved it was a special occasion. Normally a maid brought her breakfast.

Senta kissed her and asked, 'Did you have a good night?' After pulling the curtains, so that the light streamed in, she helped Viktoria sit up in bed, put her bed jacket round her shoulders and placed the tray on her lap. Viktoria looked at its contents approvingly: coffee, orange juice, toast and a boiled egg. 'My favourite,' she announced.

'It's going to be a busy day. You have to keep up your strength.'

Of course! Stefan's book was being published today. A special lunch was being held in the restaurant and, in the evening, Stefan was going to be on television. How *could* she have forgotten something as important as that?

After breakfast, the hotel nurse helped her into the bath, then to dress in her favourite clothes: black, tailored slacks; black, patent leather court shoes; an ivory-coloured blouse, with lace frills at the wrists and neck; and a royal blue velvet jacket. Around her neck hung a silver pendant of the Quadriga, which Benno had given her for her twenty-fifth birthday, the only item she had kept when selling her other jewellery after the war.

Then the hairdresser arrived and waved her white hair softly around her face. She was still sitting at the dressing table when

577

Gisela came in to wish her good morning and said, 'You do look lovely, Oma.'

'Thank you, dear. Now, if you'll hand me my cane . . .' Because of her arthritis, she needed a stick to get about now, but it was a very smart ebony cane with a gold knob, which Norbert had given her.

Slowly, they made their way into Viktoria's living room, where the old lady settled herself, surprisingly upright, into her chair by the window overlooking the Kurfuerstendamm. Gisela placed her handbag on the little bookcase beside her and her cane near at hand. 'Is there anything else you need?'

'You can tell your father that I'm ready to see him now.'

'But it's only ten o'clock,' Gisela protested.

Every morning, at eleven o'clock, Eduard came to see Viktoria, bringing with him guest lists, menus, and reports from the other Jochum hotels in Hamburg, Frankfurt, Munich, Cologne, Nuremberg, Dusseldorf and Stuttgart.

It was a source of unceasing amazement to her family that Viktoria's mind, while vague on many subjects, remained absolutely lucid when it came to the hotels. Eduard and Senta might be responsible for their everyday management, but she still kept a very close eye on everything that went on, even to the point of going through the financial reports sent off monthly to Eschenbach Estates.

'I want our meeting finished well before Stefan arrives,' Viktoria told Gisela tartly.

'Oh, yes, of course.' Gisela smiled indulgently. Nothing was allowed to come between Viktoria and her son, not even the hotels.

Shortly after that, Eduard arrived and, putting on her spectacles, Viktoria looked quickly through the papers he brought with him, but of greatest concern to her that day was Stefan's luncheon. She cast a critical eye over the menu and wine list for the buffet, then nodded approvingly. 'When are the guests due to arrive?'

'At noon, Frau Viktoria.'

For another half-hour or so, they discussed the arrangements, then Eduard hurried away to catch up with his disrupted schedule. Other men in his position might have resented the tenacious hold Viktoria still kept on the business, but he felt it extremely important that she should. Without the hotels, her main purpose for living would be gone.

Semra, one of the Turkish maids, came in to clean her suite and, as always, Viktoria enquired after her family. Semra chattered away in Turkish-German about her parents, ten brothers and sisters, cousins, nieces and nephews, as she dusted and polished, but Viktoria only half-listened that morning and was rather thankful when the vacuum cleaner brought a halt to all conversation and, after that, Semra left her alone to her thoughts.

She picked up the pre-publication copy of Stefan's book, which she had already read from cover to cover and leafed through many times since. *Crusade*, he called it, this story of his life. How differently he told it than she would have done, with far more emphasis on the moral and political implications of events than on the events themselves and the personalities of those who had brought them about. Often, she had felt as if she were reading the words of a stranger, someone she was getting to know for the first time.

She gazed out of the window, but she did not see the flashing neon signs or hear the roar of the traffic. To her, the family had always been so important. A book about her own life would be quite incomplete without descriptions of her parents, sister and children, without Lili and Bruno, Norbert, his wives and children, Reinhild and Axel, or, going back into the past, Sepp, the Baron – and even Olga and Reinhardt.

However, as Stefan said, he had not set out to write a family history, but an account of the times through which he had lived. Where members of his family had played a relevant part in his professional life, they were mentioned, otherwise they didn't appear.

Hence, there was a lot on Werner, but very little on Norbert, except that, after Helena's arrest, he had given the cottage at Heiligensee to a children's charity and provided the funds for it to be turned into a home for handicapped children. Kleo, who had become a respected paediatrician, was mentioned in the context of her work at the home. Dieter, however, featured prominently, not only because he had conducted Helena's

579

defence, but because of his career as a founder member of the Green Party and Reichstag Deputy. Helena, of course, kept cropping up, but Stefan ignored Kris, who had gone on to become World Sports Car champion, and said nothing at all about Axel and very little about Matthias Scheer, although several pages were devoted to Pastor Scheer.

How different would his book have been, Viktoria wondered, if Stefan had married and had a family of his own? For that matter, how very different his whole life would have been. What had gone wrong? There had been Christa – but he had got over her – and there had been that girl from East Berlin – then, of course, he had been kidnapped, and when he was released from prison he had been fifty . . . No, perhaps it was not surprising that he had not married.

Still, it was rather sad. Her own children, including Stefan, might have caused her heartache on occasions, but they had brought her a lot of joy. If it weren't for Monika, she wouldn't now have Senta, Gisela and Karli. At his age Stefan, too, should be experiencing the pleasure of grandchildren . . .

There was a knock on the door and she started. Her spectacles had slipped down her nose, but she was still clutching the book firmly.

Stefan entered the room, casually dressed in slacks and a blazer, a cravat knotted at his neck, his silvery hair combed back from his face. 'Good morning, Mama.' He kissed her, then laughed. 'Good heavens, you're not reading it again?'

She laid the book carefully aside and took his hands in hers. 'Stefan, it's a wonderful book. I'm so proud of you . . .'

In a West Berlin television studio, the cameras zoomed in on Rainer Rahne, whose chat show, 'All Men's Lives,' was compulsive viewing for millions on both sides of the border.

Dapper in the sombre pin-striped suit and bow-tie which were his hallmark, Rahne said, 'Good evening. As you know, the name of our series derives from a Shakespeare quotation: "There is a history in all men's lives." Of few people is this more true than my guest this evening – Stefan Jochum.'

The camera panned to the entrance and, to loud studio applause, Stefan walked on to the stage and took a seat. Rahne neither stood nor shook hands with him, but swivelled in his chair to face him and launched straight into his attack. 'Your autobiography, *Crusade*, came out today, to coincide with the fortieth anniversary of *Aktuell*, first published in September 1946.'

Stefan forced himself to remember his publisher's advice. 'I know you wrote *Crusade* because you have a message to put across,' Anton had said, 'and not because you want to become a best-selling author. But I'm in publishing – it's my business to sell books. And Rahne, obnoxious man though he may be, has a tremendous following.'

Reminding himself that, whatever Rahne said, he must not show his annoyance, Stefan pointed out, 'I'd like to stress that *Crusade* is less an autobiography, than a reflection of the times through which I have lived.'

'Nevertheless, there must have been many occasions when it was difficult for you to draw a dividing line between the private and public aspects of people's lives, especially your own family. Take your cousin, Werner Kraus, as an example. There can be few readers of *Aktuell* who are not aware of the contempt in which you hold the Kraus family. Many people would say that this is a personal vendetta. Even after your cousin's death, you continued your attacks on him.'

'On his business,' corrected Stefan. 'If Werner Kraus had not been my cousin, I would still have sought every means to bring his company's unscrupulous activities to the public notice. I have always considered it immoral that the Krauses should have been permitted to rebuild their empire.'

'The Kraus Group is a public company now.'

Stefan shook his head. 'When Werner died, he left the controlling votes in the concern to his secretary who, on her own death, left them to Werner's twin daughters. The Kraus Group is still controlled by Krauses.'

Rahne did not pursue this aspect of the Kraus Group's affairs. Instead, he said, 'You were vehemently opposed to the first nuclear power station built by the Kraus Group near Mainz back in the mid-1970s. What is your objection to nuclear power?'

'A naive question, surely, in view of the disaster at Chernobyl in April?'

'I don't think so. Our safety standards are far higher than those of the Soviet Union.'

'According to Chancellor Kohl . . .' Stefan shrugged expressively, implying without actually saying so that Kohl had a vested interest in the success of nuclear power plants. 'Above all, I deplore the fact that the proceeds of Werner's estate were used to found an institute for nuclear research and development, particularly since it has transpired that one of the Kraus Group companies mines uranium.'

Rahne narrowed his eyes. 'Are you suggesting that Kraus uranium is being used in the production of nuclear weapons?'

'No. But I am saying that the capability exists.'

'However, since the Federal Republic is forbidden to possess nuclear weapons under the terms of the Potsdam Treaty, that is not likely.'

'That hasn't stopped us providing bases for American Pershing and Cruise missiles. Our Constitution states that the *Bundeswehr* is to be a purely defensive force, but by permitting nuclear missiles to be stationed on our soil, I contend that it has become an offensive force and is breaking the terms of our Constitution. As you know, this is something I feel so strongly about that I was among the demonstrators who blocked the road at Mutlangen, near Stuttgart, when the first American missiles arrived.'

'For which you were arrested, as I recall,' Rahne commented drily. 'However, one could argue that Soviet nuclear missiles, stationed in the GDR, present a far greater threat to peace and that, if it weren't for them, there would be no need for American missiles.'

'Gorbachev has clearly demonstrated the Soviet willingness to withdraw their weapons, but however much multilateral disarmament is to be welcomed, it must necessarily be a slow process. Even I am not so naive as to believe that the Cold War can end overnight.'

'If Gorbachev were genuine in his desire for peace, he could order the Berlin Wall to be pulled down.'

'I believe that by inspecting the Wall during his visit to East Berlin in April before announcing the Soviet peace initiative, he was implying that such a possibility might exist.'

Rahne raised a sceptical eyebrow, then changed his line of

questioning. 'Your feelings about Chancellor Kohl are well known, so you are obviously not a CDU supporter. Where do your political loyalties lie?'

'I have never belonged to any political party.'

'Dieter Duschek is a close friend of yours, isn't he?'

'Yes, and someone for whom I have a lot of personal respect,' Stefan said. 'However, I am not a member of the Green Party.'

'Duschek defended Helena Kraus in the Black Kommando case. Bearing in mind your opinion of Werner Kraus, you must have found yourself in a difficult situation when she was found responsible for his death. She, too, was against nuclear power and weapons. You must have sympathized with her aims.'

That was an old line. Dieter, too, had been accused of sympathizing with the terrorists because he had conducted Helena's defence. 'I have never condoned murder,' Stefan said, stiffly.

Rahne returned to his original question. 'The Social Democrats, then? You are known to be a great admirer of Willy Brandt.'

'In my opinion, Herr Brandt is a very great man. As a result of his *Ostpolitik* in the early 1970s, relations with the GDR have been considerably improved, as have the living conditions of our fellow Germans across the border.'

'Your own life has been closely interlinked with the GDR. Your sister and her family used to live there. In fact, your nephew is still over there. And you have another relation, Basilius Meyer, who is a Politburo member . . .'

This was getting to feel rather like a *Stasi* interrogation. Stefan thought he could see the way the interviewer's mind was moving and cut him off in mid-flow, reminding him sharply, 'I was also kidnapped in 1953 and spent eleven years in prison in the GDR.'

Rahne was not to be deflected. 'Yes, I know. And I find it strange that, considering the effect your kidnap and imprisonment must have had on your life, you describe the circumstances so superficially in *Crusade*. Most people would be extremely angry and bitter, but you have never said a word in criticism of the GDR regime. Even when you were released, I remember your being more critical of the West German government who paid your ransom, than the East Germans who took you hostage.'

Stefan was right. By showing him up to be anti-capitalist and pacifist, and now by introducing his family contacts in the GDR, Rahne was trying to imply that he was a closet Communist.

He forced himself to remain calm and said, 'You commented earlier on the difficulty I must have encountered in writing *Crusade* of drawing a dividing line between the private and public aspects of people's lives. The same applies to myself. You may recall that, at the time I was kidnapped, I was in love with a girl from East Berlin. For her sake, in order to protect her, I have drawn something of a veil over my experiences in prison and refrained from any comments since about the GDR.'

He could sense Rahne probing for a name, but Stefan had deliberately not identified Erika in *Crusade*. Since his release in 1964, when he had been shown the photographs of her with her new family, he had received no further news of her. 'My friend was also imprisoned because of her relationship with me,' he continued. 'She has already suffered enough without me inflicting any further hurt on her.'

'Are you telling me that, for this reason alone, you have kept virtual silence regarding what happened to you in prison, even to the point of appearing to condone the Communist system?'

'Putting it simply – yes.'

Realizing that he had failed to cast aspersions on Stefan's political integrity, Rahne tried to retrieve the situation by continuing the romantic aspect of his story. 'It is presumably over thirty years since you last saw this woman and you have never married. Are you still in love with her?'

Stefan had had enough. Rumours were circulating in the newspaper world that Rahne's wife – his third – had recently found him in bed with the sixteen-year-old daughter of one of the directors of this television channel and was threatening to sell her story if Rahne did not grant her a divorce on her own, very expensive terms. 'I think your love life might provide a more interesting topic of conversation than mine,' he said drily.

The audience tittered and Rahne recognized the wisdom of changing the subject. 'Udo Fabian, who co-founded *Aktuell* with you, has already retired. With your family money, surely you don't need to go on working?'

'I shall never retire,' Stefan responded, 'certainly not until I am forced to do so by ill-health. There will always be some cause to fight, some wrong to be righted, some crusade . . .'

Rahne cut him off in mid-sentence. 'I'm sorry to say that we've run out of time.' He swung back in his seat so that he was facing into camera. 'Thank you, and until next week, when my guest will be . . .'

At Erika Schwidinski's flat, the curtains were drawn to shut out the foggy, autumn, Saturday night. The stove gave out a tepid heat, sufficient to make the living room bearable to sit in, but not enough to dry out the damp walls. The old black and white television cast a bluish glow over the faces of the four occupants, gazing raptly at the screen. It had become a ritual for Wolfram, Paula and her husband, Manfred, to keep Erika company on a Saturday evening.

'All Men's Lives' finished and a comedy programme began. 'You don't want to watch this, do you?' Paula asked, switching off the set. She and Manfred made a fine couple in every respect. At twenty-two, she had turned into a lovely girl, with Erika's blonde hair and blue eyes and Karsten's high cheekbones. And Manfred was a good-looking young man, tall, well-built, with dark brown hair and eyes.

Manfred shrugged indifferently, his mind elsewhere, wondering – as he so often did – about life in the Federal Republic. None of them in that room had ever crossed the Wall. West Germany was a foreign country, known only by what they saw on the television.

Wolfram shook his head and stroked his reddish-grey beard in a preoccupied manner. Erika did not respond at all, just sat gazing, trancelike, at the blank television screen.

'Mum, are you all right?'

'Er, yes, I'm fine . . .'

Paula looked at her doubtfully. Bulky from her pregnancy, her baby due in two months, she said, 'I'll make some coffee.'

Still staring at the television set, Erika nodded. This was not the first time she had seen Stefan on television since

585

she and Karsten had obtained a set in the early 1970s, for he appeared fairly often on news programmes, usually in connection with peace issues – and every time she saw him her heart gave a queer lurch, as the memories of their long-ago love affair came flooding back. Of course, he was older now, and more distinguished-looking, but apart from that, he had changed little.

But never before had she heard him talk about his captivity – and certainly never mention herself. She had assumed that, after all these years, he would have forgotten her. It had certainly never occurred to her that he was protecting her. She was deeply touched.

Paula returned from the kitchen, bearing four cups of coffee and a plate of biscuits. 'Mum, what's the matter?'

Erika took a deep breath. When Karsten had died, she had decided the moment had finally come to tell Wolfram and Paula about her early life. Karsten himself could no longer be hurt and the children – though they were hardly children now! – were old enough to cope with the truth. But Paula had been so upset about her father's death, even though he had been ill for some time, that Erika had felt unable to deal her a further shock. And since then, the opportunity had simply not arisen.

Now, however, it was imperative that they be told. If anyone should now dig further into Stefan's past, discover her name and broadcast it over the television, they would find out – and possibly never forgive her for having deceived them. 'There's something I think you should know,' she said.

Paula looked slightly wary and Erika gave what she hoped was a reassuring smile. 'It's rather a long story. It started, I suppose, during the war, when I married a young soldier called Kurt Quanz . . .'

Paula stared at her, flabbergasted. 'I didn't know you'd been married before you met Father.'

What followed was even more astounding.

'. . . My father was released from concentration camp and we lived in what was then the Soviet sector of Berlin . . . In 1951, we met Stefan Jochum . . .'

Manfred was suddenly very alert, Paula gasped, and Wolfram leaned forward slightly in his chair.

586

' . . . Stefan and I fell in love . . .'

Erika described the tragic consequences of their love affair, a story all the more incredible, because she appeared such an unlikely subject of such a drama, with her neat features, grey hair and plumpish figure, a typical elderly Leipzig housewife. She told them how she had been emotionally blackmailed by the *Stasi* into informing on Stefan; how his family's security had been threatened; how she and her father had been arrested on false charges of espionage and anti-State propaganda; how Paul had died in jail, and how, when she was released, it was to learn that Stefan, too, was in prison.

'Did Father know all this?' Paula asked.

'Of course. I never concealed anything from him. It was he who insisted, when you were born, that you be named in memory of my father.'

'I never realized . . .' Paula shook her head wonderingly.

Wolfram took off his spectacles and cleaned them, a habit he always adopted when greatly moved.

'Why didn't you tell us before?' Paula asked.

'Your father and I agreed never to refer to my past, so there should be no possibility of either of you inadvertently letting slip something which might count against you. The less you knew, the less danger you were in.'

'So you are the girl Stefan Jochum referred to in the programme . . .'

Wolfram huffed on his glasses. 'I actually knew. I used to read *Aktuell*. Of course, I hadn't met you then, but I remember Stefan Jochum's article at the time you and your father were arrested. But, until today, I never understood why he didn't hit back at our government for what it did to him. Now I do . . .'

For a few moments, the room was silent as they came to terms in their different ways with the startling effect of 'All Men's Lives' on their own lives. Then Paula asked, 'Do you still love him?'

For a moment, Erika wondered whether Paula would understand if she said there were many different kinds of love: the passion she had felt for Stefan; the very deep affection she had felt for Karsten; the tenderness she felt for her daughter and stepson. But, rather as Stefan had, when Rahne asked him

587

the same question, she gave an indirect response. 'How can you ask such a thing? I was married to your father for twenty-three years . . .'

Paula's relief was evident. She went over to her mother and kissed her. 'Thank you for telling us . . .'

Wolfram replaced his glasses on his nose, cleared his throat and finished his coffee.

A little later, he asked, 'Would you be prepared to go to West Berlin and meet him again?'

Erika's immediate reaction was panic. 'Go to West Berlin? Meet Stefan again?' she echoed faintly.

'You should have no problem in getting a travel permit now you're retired. You'd just take the train to Berlin and the Underground into the West. Hundreds of people, particularly pensioners, do it every day . . .'

Maybe, but Erika had not left Leipzig once in the last twenty-six years, not since she had been released from prison.

'You said yourself that Jochum means nothing to you any more,' Wolfram urged. 'Erika, he's exactly the person we need. He has contacts in the press, on television, in the government. But while he thinks you're at risk, he won't do anything, he said so himself. If you were to see him, you could assure him there is no danger any longer to you or to us.'

She shook her head. 'I'm not so sure. You heard Rahne mention Basilius Meyer. Stefan believed that Meyer was directly responsible for all that happened to us, that he was carrying out some kind of personal vendetta . . .'

'That could have been the case,' Wolfram said doubtfully, 'but it can't be true any longer. A man in Basilius Meyer's position isn't going to bother with the likes of us.'

'No, I suppose not . . .'

'In any case, I wouldn't expect you to do anything dangerous. All I'd like is for you to take him information about our lives, photographs of our factories and our countryside. Nothing that could possibly be construed as espionage . . .'

'Wolfram, no. I'm sorry, I can't . . .'

To Erika's relief, Paula came to her rescue. 'Wolfram, don't push her. Surely you understand that she's frightened? After all she went through, I'm not surprised. I would be, too . . .'

588

'I'm sorry. Of course I understand. It just seemed such a wonderful opportunity . . .'

'But if it were possible, I'd go,' Paula announced with sudden vehemence. 'And I certainly wouldn't come back.'

'Do you mean that?' Wolfram asked.

'Yes, I do.' She looked around her despairingly. 'I hate it here. I want to live in a flat where the wallpaper isn't peeling because of damp seeping up from the cellar and rain leaking in through the roof; where the paintwork isn't flaking and worn through to the wood, and the wood itself isn't decayed and rotten; where there isn't mould growing everywhere and all the pipes aren't rusted; where there aren't cracks and holes in the walls . . .'

'Paula,' Erika cut in, distressed, 'your father did what he could while he was alive – and I've tried to keep the flat nice . . .'

'I'm not blaming you, Mum. It's not your fault. Everywhere's the same. Our flat's even worse. I dread the thought of trying to bring up my baby in such conditions . . .'

Erika sighed, understanding very well what Paula meant. The greatest irony was that from the outside the decay was scarcely apparent, certainly not to the visitors who attended the twice-yearly Leipzig Trade Fair and stayed at the Hotel Merkur. They saw only what the authorities wanted them to see: quaint old houses and shopping arcades, traditional bars, cabarets and pavement cafés, piazzas and parks, the Gewandhaus Concert Hall, the University, impressive government buildings, churches, museums and art galleries. For these showplaces there was money available for restoration and maintenance, but not for the rest of the city. In the suburbs, walls in danger of collapse were shored up with scaffolding and holes in roofs covered with tarpaulins, temporary measures which had become permanent.

When the Trade Fair opened, there would be a sudden influx of goods into the shops. Fresh fruit and vegetables, meat, soap and clothing would become plentiful and astoundingly cheap, and customers would be served promptly, without standing for hours in queues. The smog would mysteriously become less dense, and visitors would comment on Leipzig's prosperous, if drab appearance; and give their opinion that socialism seemed to be working better in East Germany than elsewhere in the Soviet bloc.

589

They saw only the façade. They did not realize that once the Fair was over, the smog would again descend and the shop shelves be empty. They did not recognize the cost to the people of the GDR of the 'economic miracle'. Above all, they did not see the unfairness and corruption in a system where all were supposed to be equal, but the Party hierarchy enjoyed privileges to which the ordinary citizen could not hope to attain.

'It isn't just the housing,' Manfred added. 'We want to live in a free society, where we can express our ideas without fear of being overheard by some *Stasi* informer, where we have a proper vote and a say in the way the country is run. Paula should be allowed to choose whether or not she returns to work after the baby's born, not have to put it in a crèche and go back to teaching, which she doesn't enjoy anyway. For that matter, we should all be able to choose our own jobs, not just do what the authorities tell us . . .'

'In other words, you want to live in a democracy,' Wolfram stated.

'Yes, we do. Don't you?'

'Of course. But I don't believe you have to leave the GDR in order to attain it. We have the basic framework within our Constitution for democratic government – a multi-party parliament elected by universal suffrage . . .'

Manfred cut him off before he could go any further. 'Wolfram, you know the *Volkskammer* is a farce! Every election is rigged, so the SED gets a majority. And the *Volkskammer* has no powers at all. All policy decisions are made by the SED Central Committee and the Politburo, about whose membership we have no say at all.'

'I'm well aware of that,' Wolfram replied patiently. 'What I'm saying is that the mechanism exists and what we should be doing is agitating for change.'

'Perhaps,' Erika said hesitantly, 'Gorbachev will do something . . .'

Paula jutted her chin obstinately. 'No, things will never improve. We have only one life – and I don't want to spend the rest of mine here.'

January 1987 was bitterly cold, with driving snow. Gabi struggled

590

to work every day, but Klaus didn't go out, except to Harry's Bar. One evening he reached the bar early and was waiting for the rest of the gang to turn up, when an old man came in and took the stool next to him. Klaus didn't remember seeing him before, but Harry obviously recognized him, for he gave him a slightly wary glance before asking, 'Double Steinhaeger, Colonel?'

The colonel downed his schnaps in one gulp, ordered another, then announced, 'There's only one of these parties got the right idea and that's the Republicans.'

West Germany was in the grip of general election fever. Day after day, there were meetings and rallies. Wherever one went, posters displayed the faces of earnest politicians and exhorted people to vote for Helmut Kohl and the CDU, Franz-Josef Strauss and the CSU, Johannes Rau and the SPD, Hans Dietrich Genscher and the FDP, Petra Kelly and Dieter Duschek of the Greens, Franz Schoenhuber and his new, right-wing party, the Republicans.

Klaus didn't give a shit about politics. Even if he were old enough to vote, he wouldn't bother. So far as he was concerned, all politicians were pompous pricks and election hoardings merely surfaces to deface with aerosols.

'Get rid of the Turks, the Reps are saying,' the colonel went on. 'Get rid of all these refugees and asylum seekers. Give Germany back to the Germans. Hitler would have approved of them.'

Klaus wasn't sure who Hitler was. He had a vague idea that he had been a Communist who had put his opponents, who had been Nazis, in concentration camps, where they had been gassed and burned to death.

'We had the same problem in the nineteen-thirties. Only then it wasn't Turks, it was Jews. Bleeding the country dry, they were. But we put paid to them, the bastards.' The colonel turned to Klaus. 'You ever met a Jew?'

Klaus shrugged.

'I'll never forget the night we burned down their synagogues and smashed up their shops.' The old man gave an evil cackle. 'That's what we should do now with the Turks. Burn them out! If we'd won the war and Hitler had stayed in power, we wouldn't have all the problems we have now. There wouldn't

591

be any unemployment. There wouldn't be any Turks. What this country needs is another Hitler.'

'Colonel, you want to be careful . . .' Harry warned.

'And so should you be careful,' the colonel retorted. 'I know all about your pimping and drugs pushing and dealing in stolen goods. We had people like you, too, back in the thirties. Like the Jews, they didn't last long after Hitler came to power.'

He drained his glass and rose, rather unsteadily, to his feet. Swaying slightly, he crossed the bar to the door and there he suddenly stopped, raised his hand in a salute and shouted, '*Sieg Heil!*'

Harry raised his eyes to heaven and tapped his forehead. 'Loco.'

'What was all that about?' Klaus asked.

'He was an officer in the SS,' Harry replied. 'He's still hoping for a Nazi revival.'

By sheer coincidence, a few afternoons later, Johann and Heinz came round to Klaus's place with a couple of videos. Armed with cigarettes and cans of lager, they all made themselves comfortable in Gabi's living room.

One of the videos was called *Schutzstaffel*, which Klaus soon realized was what SS stood for, although the black-uniformed heroes did not in the slightest resemble the colonel, but were all young men looking very like Klaus himself. He also soon realized that it hadn't been Nazis who were put in concentration camps, but that they ran the places, while all kinds of foreigners, but mostly Jews, met their just deserts there.

The Jews wore strange clothes, talked a strange language and indulged in all sorts of weird practices. One scene in the video showed a girl slitting a cow's throat and sucking its blood, while another showed an old man in a black coat and hat, with outlandish side curls, putting the evil eye on a German baby, so that it died a dreadful death. Yet another showed young Jewish men raping German women and cutting off their breasts. When the SS eventually managed to catch them, the Jews were made to undergo similar tortures once they were safely inside the concentration camp.

Klaus had watched a lot of videos in his time, but never one with such brutal violence and explicit sex. 'Fucking hell,' he breathed. 'Where did you get that?'

Johann shrugged with assumed casualness. 'Tilo lent it me.'

Klaus was even more impressed. Tilo was three or four years older than them and ran the Werewolves, a skinhead gang operating on the other side of town. They all wore studded, black leather gear and most of them had high-powered motorbikes. 'How come you know Tilo?'

'He's a mate of me brother. They're neo-Nazis. Videos like that are banned, but Tilo's on a mailing list.'

The other video was called *Hitler Lives*. The principal character was Adolf Hitler, wearing a brown uniform with a swastika armband, who, with two other men called Hess and Bormann, one of whom had apparently just escaped from prison in Berlin and the other returned to Germany from South America, led a gang of similarly dressed young men through the Turkish district of a city on a journey of destruction, looting and rape, to the background of a marching song. It ended with them all raising their arms in the salute the colonel had made and shouting, *'Sieg Heil!'*

'You know it's forbidden to make that salute and say *Sieg Heil?*' Johann giggled. 'You know what the Werewolves do? They say *Heil Sieg* and use a three-fingered W salute.'

The next time Klaus saw the colonel the election was over, with Kohl in for another term. The colonel was sitting at a corner table in Harry's Bar, gazing morosely into an empty glass. Klaus sauntered over to him and asked, 'Want a refill?'

The old man looked up at him from bleary eyes and, in a slurred voice, said, 'Don't mind if I do.'

'Give us some dosh then.' With the money the colonel handed him, Klaus bought him another Steinhaeger and himself a Pils, then took the chair opposite him. 'Were you really in the SS?'

The colonel straightened himself. 'Not were – am. Because the SS is banned, doesn't mean it doesn't still exist. We have members throughout the world, not just in Germany and Europe, but in Africa, America and Australia. One day, we shall again rule the world.'

'Did you know Hitler and these geezers Bormann and Hess?'

'I had the honour to meet the *Fuehrer* and most of his colleagues.' However, to Klaus's disappointment, instead of talking about concentration camps, the colonel rambled on about Rudolf Hess. 'He's over ninety-two. He's been in solitary confinement in Spandau for forty-six years. Why don't they release him and let him end his life in peace?'

Shocked to discover that one of the heroes of *Hitler Lives* was a boring old fart of over ninety, Klaus finished his drink and left the colonel to talk to himself.

In the months which followed, he watched a lot more videos and also met Tilo, who turned out to be better educated and considerably more intellectual than himself, with a load of political crap which Klaus couldn't be bothered with, about social revolt and racial struggle. It was unlikely that his interest and involvement with the neo-Nazis would have gone beyond drinking, fighting and watching videos if Rudolf Hess had not died that August under rather mysterious circumstances.

According to a joint statement issued by the four Occupying Powers in Berlin, Hess had died from choking. The following day, another Allied announcement, denied by the Russians, hinted that he had taken his own life. The colonel told everyone who would listen to him, 'Such a man as Hess would not kill himself. He was murdered by the Russians or the Jews.' Tilo and the Werewolves blamed the Americans.

Whoever was responsible, Tilo said the event called for revenge. About fifty skinheads rode in convoy to a neo-Nazi rally at Wunsiedel in Bavaria where Hess was being buried, but before they reached the cemetery they were turned back by the police. So they decided to cause some disruption in Frankfurt instead.

Not owning a motorbike, Klaus had been unable to go to Wunsiedel, but he took part in the rally Tilo organized in the city centre, not from any sympathy for Hess or from any political or moral conviction, but because he enjoyed a bit of aggro.

That Saturday, skinheads, rockers and Hell's Angels converged onto the Hauptwache. A few carried banners with slogans reading: HESS IS FREE or the old Nazi rallying cry: *DEUTSCHLAND ERWACHE!* – Germany awake! – and flags bearing a three-legged swastika. They marched into the large square, shoving aside any other pedestrians stupid enough not to get out of their way, their arms raised in the W-salute and shouting, '*Heil Sieg! Heil Sieg!*' 'Americans out!' 'Turks out!' Most, like Klaus, were drunk. All were armed with weapons of some kind: knives, broken bottles or stones.

Within minutes, the police turned up and were greeted with a shower of verbal abuse and a hail of missiles. After ordering the neo-Nazis through loudhailers to disperse and clearing the area of shoppers, they formed ranks and, armed with riot shields and truncheons, advanced purposefully towards the demonstrators.

This was Klaus's first experience of being part of an angry crowd in confrontation with the police and it gave him a kick. '*Heil Sieg! Heil Sieg!*' he yelled. '*Tuerken 'raus!*' 'Foreigners out!'

Then the police were upon them and the rally turned into a free-for-all, as the neo-Nazis pulled their knives and the police mercilessly brandished truncheons. Klaus forgot all about the ostensible purpose for their presence in the Hauptwache and gave himself over to the brawl. He had the satisfaction of slashing one policeman in the face and kneeing another in the groin before he was knocked to the ground and dragged away, kicking and swearing, into a waiting police van.

A press photograph immortalized the image of Klaus, hand raised, lips curled back, eyes shining in an apparently fanatical gleam. The picture of the unnamed young thug was syndicated among several newspapers, but in *Aktuell* it appeared under the headline: THE GROTESQUE AND UGLY FACE OF NEO-FASCISM.

Friedland had been established by the British in 1945, just a few kilometres from the border with the Soviet zone, as a transit camp for returning German prisoners of war. It was from here that Hans Koenig had made his escape across the 'green border' into the Soviet zone and home to Fuerstenmark in 1946. By 1987, the 'green border' had become highly fortified, and the camp was still there, although the accommodation was considerably improved, the Nissen huts replaced by modern houses and bungalows. In the intervening forty years, it had accommodated some three million refugees and asylum-seekers, and, more recently, ethnic Germans from the Soviet Union and Central Europe, who had, as a result of *glasnost*, finally been permitted to return to their homeland.

Organized to receive a hundred and fifty arrivals a day and sleep a thousand, Friedland in the summer of 1987 was bursting at the seams, housing a record 3,000 refugees.

To 18-year-old Axel Kraus, who came to the centre as a volunteer worker that summer, Friedland was a revelation. 'What will happen to all these people?' he asked Matthias Scheer, who had been two years at the camp, working for the Red Cross.

'Every new arrival is given two hundred Marks welcome money,' Matthias explained, 'then after a few days here, while their papers are sorted out, they are sent on to relatives – if they have any – or to secondary camps in other provinces, until they can obtain work and homes of their own.'

Axel had an endless stream of questions about the refugees, which Matthias answered gladly, pleased beyond all measure that the young man had come to Friedland.

Who would have thought that Helena's son would turn out as he had? He carried the mark of Cain. He should have inherited the worst characteristics of his Kraus forebears. But he hadn't. On the contrary, he had a strong social consciousness and a very real determination to bring love and peace to the world, instead of hatred, war and bloodshed.

And Matthias knew that the way Axel had evolved was due in no small way to himself, which was in itself ironic, since he had played so large a part in the violence which had marked the 1960s and 1970s.

But he was convinced that this – his friendship with Axel and his work with refugees, above all the children – was why his life had been spared, why he was not now in a prison cell or dead, like Marko, because of a policeman's bullet.

He had never understood why Helena had not shopped him after she was arrested. In a way, he had hoped she would, and there were many times when he considered giving himself up. It would have been easier to cope with a prison sentence than live in freedom with the enormity of his guilt. But it was perhaps typical of Helena that she had not informed on him. As she had said, that morning in Schmargendorf, 'I'd rather you suffered.'

And he had suffered as Black Kommando had continued to murder its way through Germany, and gone on suffering after Marko's death and Helena's arrest and throughout her trial. Then his parents had returned to Berlin and, shocked by his appearance, had tried to get him to admit what was the matter.

He could not tell them. But, by describing their mission work in South-West Africa, they had given him a sign of the direction his life should take. He knew he had no vocation for the Church. But there were other ways to help the underprivileged, particularly children.

His parents' reputation and especially his grandfather's name ensured that he had no problem in enrolling for a course in social work, and he duly obtained his first job at a home for physically handicapped children in Heiligensee, although when he discovered where he was to be working, he could imagine no crueller twist of fate. For the home was that same house on the lake shore, where Helena and Marko had set up their commune in the mid-1960s and later held Werner Kraus hostage.

The place looked very different now. The original part of the cottage still stood, but the building had been considerably extended, to provide rooms for some thirty children. There were swings, seesaws and a sandpit on the lawn and a fence to prevent the children accidentally straying into the lake. The cottage, Matthias discovered, had been donated by Helena's father, Norbert Kraus, who had also paid for all the building work, furniture and fittings, medical and sports facilities, and continued to be a generous sponsor of the home.

It was there Matthias had met Kleo again, who held a weekly clinic at the home and who, unsuspecting of his involvement in Black Kommando, had invited him back to her and Dieter's flat in Dahlem. Quite unwitting of the torment they were inflicting upon him, they talked to him about Helena and Axel. With absolute trust, they allowed him to babysit their own small son, whom they had named Oskar after Dieter's grandfather.

Not until Axel's ninth birthday in 1978, the year after Helena

597

escaped from prison, did Matthias eventually find the courage to contact the boy. Then he wrote a letter to Reinhild, explaining that he was a friend of Dieter and Kleo's, and enclosing a small birthday gift. When Reinhild replied kindly, he summoned up the nerve to go to Hamburg.

It was the beginning of a friendship, which became stronger after Reinhild died and Axel moved to live with Kleo and Dieter in Berlin. Matthias, in his mid-thirties, unmarried and childless, became a father figure to Axel, and took the responsibility extremely seriously. But the real test had come when Axel was fifteen and had asked, 'Matthias, will you tell me about my parents?'

Matthias would remember that moment until the end of his life. It was evening and they were walking up the drive to where he had parked his car at Heiligensee, where Axel had taken to coming with him at weekends, washing up and doing other odd jobs at the home. He was popular with the children, who called him Struwelpeter on account of his unruly thatch of hair. He had inherited Marko's hair, just as he had his father's height and loping gait, and Helena's angular features, but he was far more intelligent and, despite the strangeness of his upbringing, had a remarkably sunny disposition and an adult attitude to life.

'At school they say my parents were terrorists and murderers, while Uncle Dieter and Aunt Kleo say they were just misguided,' Axel said. 'But nobody will explain to me why they did what they did.'

Matthias opened the car door and they got in, but instead of heading for home, he went down the Faehrstrasse and parked where the ferry had once crossed to Nieder-Neuendorf on the opposite shore of the Havel, and now the mined and barbed wire barricade of the Iron Curtain divided the river and West Berlin from the GDR. He knew he could have opted out like Dieter and Kleo had done, or given Axel newspaper reports of Helena's trial. But to do this would have been not only to betray the boy's trust but his own innermost self. He said, 'I'll tell you my story, and perhaps that will help you understand a bit about your parents.'

598

Night had fallen by the time he finished. For a very long time, Axel remained motionless, gazing out across the dark river. Then he said, 'You've never told anyone all that before, have you?'

Matthias shook his head.

'But that's why you're doing the work you're doing now. Because of those children who died, who my mother shot.'

'I was driving the motorbike. I was as guilty as her.'

'Do you think she ever regretted what she did?' But, before Matthias had time to reply, Axel answered his own question. 'No, if she had, she wouldn't have escaped from prison and run away.' Again he was silent. Then he said, 'Why do you think she came back to Hamburg for me that night?'

'At her trial, she said it was because your father had made her give you up, but she had come to realize her mistake.'

Matthias turned to glance at the boy. He was still staring ahead through the windscreen. His eyes were glittering, but whether it was from tears or from lights reflecting in them from the spotlights on the water, it was impossible to tell. Gruffly, he said, 'I'll take you home.'

After this, they had had many long conversations about the past, about Pastor Scheer, the Krauses, Reinhild, Dieter and Kleo, and the events which had shaped them into the people they were. When Matthias did not know the answers to Axel's questions, they would invite themselves to Stefan's flat or sit on the terrace of Café Jochum, listening to his explanations about the rise of Hitler, the war and the division of Germany. Despite being a very busy man, Stefan always had time for them and what he had to say was always thought-provoking. 'When I was a student, my eyes were opened by the American journalist, Mortimer Allen, and a Jewish professor,' he once explained. 'What I learned from them made me the person I am today.'

Above all, what Stefan had to say about freedom influenced Matthias to work with refugees. His first job was at the Red Cross reception centre in Spandau for foreign refugees sent across by the GDR authorities from East Berlin, and, a year later, he had come to Friedland. He was deeply touched, but not altogether surprised when Axel had announced that he was going to follow his example and train in social work when he left school. In a letter, Axel had written: 'You have chosen your life path to atone for your guilt. In my case, I must expiate my parents' sins.'

Chapter 25

It was three in the morning and, other than the sleety rain hammering against the window, the city of Leipzig was deathly quiet. Inside the flat, the only sound was the steady plop-plop-plop of water trickling down the cable, which suspended the bare electric light bulb from the middle of the ceiling, and dripping into the bucket below. On the living room table, a candle flickered. Apart from the danger, Paula Bauer knew there was little point in switching on the light. Whenever it rained, the mains power seemed to fail.

She had been wakened half an hour earlier by the sound of Heike coughing, the harsh, metallic cough which signalled an attack of false croup, from which her daughter had been suffering for the past year, since she was just four months old.

False croup was a common disease among young children in Leipzig and the doctor had assured Paula that although debilitating, it wasn't dangerous, and in due course Heike should grow out of it. But that didn't stop Paula being terrified that, in the mean time, she would choke so badly she might suffocate.

Every night, she and Manfred went to bed tensed and waiting for an attack to happen, but on this occasion Manfred had been so soundly asleep that he had not stirred when Heike began coughing and, not wanting to wake him, Paula had lifted Heike out of her cot and carried her into the living room.

Manfred himself had a bad chest cold. The factory where he worked as an engineer made glass-fibre car parts and it was doing his health no good at all to breathe in glass-fibre dust all day long. Wolfram's concern about the environment had a very real meaning to Paula now.

Eventually Heike's choking fit passed and, breathing wheezily, the little girl drifted into an exhausted sleep, dark shadows under

601

her eyes, her face pale and damp with sweat. Paula wrapped the worn blanket more tightly around the thin little body, and held her closer to her chest. Although she herself was exhausted and shivering in her threadbare dressing gown, she dared not move for fear of disturbing her.

A few days ago, they had celebrated the beginning of a new year with Erika, Wolfram, Manfred's parents and his brother, and a few friends. Now that year seemed to stretch bleakly ahead, empty of hope.

Not a day passed when Paula did not dream of getting away from Leipzig, but that possibility was more remote now than ever. Certainly, there was no chance at all of emigrating to the Federal Republic. In the past year, so many people had taken advantage of visits to West Germany and not returned, that the authorities were clamping down on all travel visas, including those for holiday trips to other Soviet bloc countries.

Heike whimpered in her sleep and from the bedroom came the sound of Manfred coughing. Outside, the sleet turned to snow. A distant clock chimed four. In two hours, the alarm would go off and it would be time to start another day: making breakfast; seeing Manfred off to work; queuing at the shops before they ran out of stock; taking Heike to the crèche; then going to work herself, to a job she did not want to do.

She knew that when she reached school and was standing in front of her class, things would seem better. She was fond of her pupils and they responded well to her. But she had never wanted to be a teacher. She had hoped to be a translator or, most of all, a writer, but when she had graduated there had only been teaching posts available.

When she came home, there would be homework to mark, household chores to do, the evening meal to prepare – and probably the power would fail again, the toilet would not flush and there would be no hot water . . .

Tears welled in Paula's eyes and she brushed her lips across Heike's fine, golden hair. God only knew, there had to be a better way to live than this.

It was Sunday 15 January 1988. Throughout the GDR, the anniversary was being commemorated of the assassination in

602

1919 of the Communist revolutionary leaders, Karl Liebknecht, Rosa Luxemburg and Reinhardt Meyer. In Berlin, an official rally was being held in honour of the day, with a special address given by Basilius Meyer.

At Liebenroda's Church of St Thomas, Pastor Christoph Margraf had his own message to put across to his congregation. 'The Spartacists were protagonists of freedom,' he told the rapt faces gazing up at him, 'fighting to liberate the German people from the despotic, militarist rule of the Kaiser. The significance of their ideals and achievements has been twisted to suit the purposes of our present rulers. If Liebknecht and Luxemburg were alive today, they would be fighting to liberate the people of the GDR from the Communists.'

It was the most defiantly outspoken speech against the government Christoph had ever made and Wolfram Schwidinski, sitting towards the front of the church, knew that Police Chief Sommer would be unable to allow it to pass unnoticed.

He was right. After the service, he stayed behind until Christoph was ready to leave. Outside the church, the police were waiting. Rough hands seized them by the shoulders the moment they left the building and propelled them swiftly into a police van. At the Marx-Engels Platz, they were separated. Wolfram was charged with aiding and abetting a priest in anti-State activities, by using a religious service as a cover for a subversive meeting and a church building as a political forum.

He was then handed over into the custody of Chief Prison Officer Heinrich Koenig, who plainly showed his malicious pleasure at having him in his control again. With obvious satisfaction, he looked on as, with unnecessary brutality, his subordinates searched and stripped Wolfram, then kicked him into a cell.

Gert Koenig was on border guard duty at the Wall, near the Bornholmer Strasse checkpoint in Prenzlauer Berg. A crowd surged towards him, waving banners and shouting. Suddenly, a girl broke away from them, scrambled up the fence and down the other side, then hared off across no-man's-land towards the Wall. She had brown hair and was slightly built, wearing blue jeans, trainers and an anorak. The crowd fell silent. Gert did

603

not hesitate. Unslinging his sub-machine gun, he aimed at the girl's back and let loose a round of ammunition. Her screams rent the air. Her blood splattered the smooth white concrete of the Wall. Colleagues lifted her bullet-ridden body from the ground and carried her away. As they passed him, he saw her face. It was Jana . . .

He awoke, bathed in sweat, his heart pounding, his head throbbing, his throat dry. Then he heard the regular snoring of the eleven other occupants in his army billet and realized that it wasn't true, he hadn't killed Jana – it had only been a dream . . .

He glanced at the luminous dial of his watch. Half-past five. Half an hour to reveille. Turning onto his back, he lay, with his hands under his head, staring into the darkness.

Yesterday evening, after the military parade in honour of the Spartacist leaders, he had telephoned Jana at Zum Kastanien, the bar where she worked in Prenzlauer Berg to tell her that, because all leave had been temporarily cancelled, he would be unable to meet her.

'You wouldn't be able to see her anyway,' the manager informed him. 'She's been arrested, along with a couple of hundred other people, so far as we can make out, for taking part in a demonstration.'

'A demonstration . . . ?'

'A counter-demonstration to the official rally. It started off at the church. They want the right to visit West Berlin and the Federal Republic. They want to be free to cross that Wall you guard, lad . . .'

Jana, arrested, possibly already in prison, being interrogated by someone like his father . . . For the first time, Gert found himself wondering what methods the *Stasi* used to obtain information, but he was sure they were far from gentle. He was well aware that his father was a bully. Many times he had driven his mother to tears and never hesitated to beat him for even a minor misdemeanour.

In the end, Gert had drowned his confusion and sorrow in schnapps. Now, he wondered how Jana was, how long she would be in prison and whether, when she was released, she would want to see him again. He had only met her a month

604

ago, just before Christmas. He had taken her to the cinema once, when they had held hands during the film and she had allowed him to kiss her afterwards. He hardly knew her. They had talked a little, generally, about themselves, but he hadn't told her that his father worked for the *Stasi* and she certainly hadn't told him she felt so strongly about the Wall ...

He was awoken from his reverie by the whistle, a hefty banging on the door and the light going on. His fellow soldiers grunted and moaned, wiping the sleep out of their eyes. Another new day was beginning.

The morning ran its usual course: sport, bath-house, parade, roll-call, breakfast, fatigues, instruction, lunch. Then, at one o'clock, Gert's company marched in pairs out of the barracks to the trucks which would take them to the Brandenburg Gate, where they were on duty.

The lorry stopped at the end of Unter den Linden on the edge of the Pariser Platz, a military zone, where the public were not permitted. The soldiers got out of the truck, stood in formation, then goosestepped across the square, past the towering columns of the Gate to the Wall itself.

Their duty was uneventful. No demonstrators besieged the Gate. Nobody tried to escape. Yet as Gert stared, westwards across the Wall, along the Street of 17 June to the Victory Column, he became increasingly aware of the impact upon him of Jana's arrest.

Until then, he had simply never questioned the necessity for the Wall. It was a border, like that which separated the GDR from Czechoslovakia and Poland to the east. He knew he had relatives in the Federal Republic: his mother had told him once that his father's parents, Hans and Monika, and his sister, Senta, had moved there before the Wall was erected, but since his father never mentioned them, Gert had never given them much thought.

His grandmother's people owned several hotels over there, according to his mother, including one in West Berlin. Once, they had seen Monika's brother, Stefan Jochum, on Western television. Not that, as a soldier, Gert was allowed to watch West German television. That was forbidden, as so many things were forbidden to the military. But at home, he and

605

his mother sometimes watched it, when his father was not there.

Suddenly, those relations acquired a great importance in Gert's mind. He gazed along the length of the Wall, overlooked by watchtowers, with its wide strip of mined no-man's-land. Why should it be such a crime for East Berliners to visit the Western half of their city? Why shouldn't those West Berliners, staring up at him with such loathing in their eyes, be able to come over into East Berlin? Perhaps they, like him, had family on the other side, whom they had never met . . .

In March, shortly after Honecker had made a most unexpected public pledge that the State would never interfere with the right of individuals to practise their religion, Rudolf Sommer reported to Berlin for a routine meeting at the Ministry of State Security.

During his visit he saw Basilius who, in an unusual burst of frankness, accused Honecker of trying to curry favour with Gorbachev by showing himself an advocate of reform. 'If Honecker persists in following a moderate path,' he threatened, 'we shall have no alternative but to force his resignation before his five-year term in office expires.'

Sommer absorbed this information without comment.

Whilst in Berlin, he also went to Prenzlauer Berg, something he tried to do whenever he was in the capital. Unlike Basilius, he believed in keeping in touch with the people, and did not forget that it was in working-class areas like Prenzlauer Berg that the 1953 uprising had started. Sommer had no family there any more, but there were still some who remembered young Rudi from his childhood and, even if they did not trust him now he had reached the high ranks of the *Stasi*, were prepared, albeit cautiously, to confide in him.

One such was the manager at Zum Kastanien, a middle-aged man, whose mother had been a neighbour of Sommer's mother. Sommer went to see him in the mid-afternoon, when the bar was quiet. 'A lot of my customers see it like this,' he explained. 'Gorbachev is releasing more and more political prisoners and even allowing them to emigrate – like Sakharov and Shcharansky. But here, travel rights are being cracked down

606

on. It's television that's making people discontent. They can see for themselves what's going on in the rest of the world. And young people, in particular, are politically very aware. They want freedom of movement and expression, free elections. Not that these things worry me, you understand.'

'No, of course not . . .'

'Incidentally, we've been seeing quite a lot recently of a young conscript who comes from Liebenroda – think he's interested in a local girl. His name's Gert Koenig. Mean anything to you?'

It meant a lot, but Sommer merely shrugged expressionlessly. 'Koenig's a common enough name. I'd have to look him up in the files.'

Someone else told him that Koenig was keen on the barmaid from Zum Kastanien and that she was currently in gaol for taking part in the protest on 15 January. That was the way intelligence worked. One snippet of information in exchange for another – and every one had its importance.

Not long after Sommer returned to Liebenroda, orders came through from Berlin to release certain categories of political prisoners, which included Wolfram Schwidinski and Pastor Margraf.

Heinrich Koenig made no attempt to disguise his disgust, when Sommer gave him his orders. 'If I had my way, they wouldn't go free,' he asserted. 'I'd shoot the bastards – or send them to Siberia.'

Sommer wondered if Koenig knew that Gert had fallen for one of the demonstrators arrested in Berlin on the same day as Schwidinski and Margraf. But he doubted it. Koenig was the type who would inform on his own son in order to keep his own record clean. He eyed him coldly. 'Are you questioning my orders, Comrade Koenig?'

'No, of course not. But I do think we're getting too damn lenient.'

Once, Sommer would have agreed. Following his visit to Berlin, he was less sure. Freedom of movement – as Schwidinski had seized the opportunity several times during interrogation to point out – was acknowledged within the Constitution. However, the Constitution had to be read in conjunction with the Penal

607

Code, which forbade demonstrations. But, at the same time, there was *glasnost* . . .

In his off-duty hours, Gert had been going to the Zum Kastanien bar, in the hope of discovering news of Jana. Finally, at the beginning of April, he found her back at work. She was very pale and her attitude towards him decidedly cool. 'It was not particularly enjoyable,' was all she would say about her imprisonment. Then, in a defiant undertone, she added, 'But I still don't regret anything. We should be free to go where we want . . .'

Gert glanced around him cautiously, also wary of listening ears. 'Jana, you may not believe me, but I do actually agree with you.'

She looked at him sceptically. 'Then why are you on border guard duty?'

'You know I have no choice. I have to obey orders. But when I leave the army at the end of May . . .'

'I thought your father wanted you to become a regular . . .'

'I've been doing a lot of thinking during the last ten weeks . . .'

Yes, he'd done a lot of very deep thinking, in the course of which he had found himself rejecting almost everything he had accepted as gospel from birth, everything he had been taught by his parents, at school, in the Free German Youth and in the army. He had listened with a far more attentive ear than before to what people were saying and heard an undercurrent of discontent, even among his fellow conscripts, of which he had previously been unaware. One word kept recurring: freedom.

'So what are you going to do?'

'Play football, go to college, train to be a sports instructor . . .' He paused, then gave a little smile. 'And, one day, I'm going to watch Hertha play in West Berlin.'

'Jana!' the manager called.

'Will you come out with me again next time I'm off duty?' Gert pleaded.

Jana shrugged. 'Maybe.' But they both knew she meant yes.

His father was predictably furious when Gert announced his future plans during his next home leave. But apart from uttering empty threats, there was nothing he could do. His son was too big now to beat. Gert had a nasty feeling his wrath would be taken out on his mother and was sorry. But you only had one life – and he intended to live his his way.

That summer, Klaus Feldmann was eighteen, but although young men in the Federal Republic were given the choice between military and community service, Klaus preferred to do neither. He went to Berlin, where Tilo had some draft-dodger friends with a squat in Kreuzberg.

He didn't tell his mother what he had in mind, but when Gabi found his room empty and her purse, credit cards and cheque book gone from her handbag, it wasn't hard for her to guess what had happened. Her overwhelming reaction was one of relief. Klaus might be her son, but she had never been able to control him and, recently, since he had become mixed up with the neo-Nazis, she had gone in virtual terror of him.

She reported the thefts to the police and her bank. She had the apartment locks changed. And, for the first time in years, she felt able to relax in her own home.

Kreuzberg came as a shock to Klaus. Situated in the shadow of the Wall, it was very much a working-class area, run down and rather seedy, which was why so much property had been left to go to rack and ruin and taken over by squatters. There were six guys and four girls in the squat Tilo had recommended, all neo-Nazis, but Klaus soon realized that people just came and went. The facilities were extremely primitive. There was cold running water and a stove fuelled by brown coal briquettes. Basically nobody bothered to wash very often and certainly nobody cooked.

Every kind of weirdo and drop-out seemed to come to roost in Kreuzberg: homosexuals, Greens, commies, hippies and druggies. But essentially, it was the home of the Turkish community. Never in his life before had Klaus seen so many Turks, most of whom seemed to be unemployed. Kiddy, who was a contemporary of Tilo and the oldest member of the squat, claimed there were over a hundred thousand and, as they produced more and more kids, their numbers were

609

growing. Shops were called souks in Kreuzberg. The street signs were in Turkish. Every bar and refreshment stall sold skewers of shish kebab.

'The trendies try to be friends with the Turks,' Kiddy said disparagingly. 'I assume you're not like them.'

Klaus raised a clenched fist on which the word HATE was tattooed.

A few months after his arrival, elections took place in West Berlin. During the very early days of the election campaign, a couple of strangers appeared in the Red Bear, the neo-Nazis' local bar, and took the table next to them. One, quite smartly dressed in a suit, was probably in his late twenties. The other, slightly older and wearing a thick, polo-necked sweater and jeans, possessed the physique and battered features of a heavyweight boxer.

For a while they sat quietly, then the younger man edged his chair towards them and said, 'Excuse me for intruding, but I take it that you live locally?'

'What's it to do with you?' Klaus demanded.

'I was just thinking that it can't be very pleasant having Turks as neighbours. If I lived here, I know I'd want to do something about it . . .'

'Like what?'

The boxer-type leered maliciously, displaying a set of broken, blackened and missing teeth.

His colleague glanced at their empty glasses and, reaching into his breast pocket for his wallet, called to the barmaid, 'We'll have another round.'

'Here, what's your game?' Kiddy asked, suspiciously.

The man in the suit shrugged. 'Let's just say I like making new friends.' He opened his wallet and quite deliberately displayed a thick wad of notes, from which he took a hundred-Mark note, which he handed to the barmaid and said, 'Keep the change, love.'

He turned back to Klaus and Kiddy. 'Let me introduce myself. My name is Siegfried – and this is Erik. Now, I've got a little business proposition to put to you . . .'

Franz Schoenhuber's Republican Party emerged from the West Berlin local election in the January of 1989 with a staggering 7.5 per cent of the vote. Kiddy, Klaus and the rest of Kreuzberg's neo-Nazis did more than a bit to assist them. While Schoenhuber preached a xenophobic hymn of hate against the immigrants who were being subsidized by the State for doing nothing except producing children, the neo-Nazis wreaked havoc in Kreuzberg, beating up Turks, plundering their shops, overturning and setting fire to their cars.

And Siegfried paid them very handsomely for their unofficial support.

That winter, Heike caught pneumonia. At first Paula thought she had a particularly bad cold, but when Heike began having convulsions, she called the doctor, who immediately ordered her into hospital.

That Heike not only survived the illness but recovered as swiftly as she did was due in very large part to Nurse Sylvia Kunert. Despite the urgency of the situation, Paula was not allowed time off to be with her daughter, although when school ended for the day, she would hurry to the hospital, and Manfred would join her as soon as he left work. There they found Erika, often with Nurse Kunert, sitting at Heike's bedside, sponging her face with warm water or inducing her to sip bouillon to keep up her strength.

Nurse Kunert was an angular, plain-featured woman of about forty, considerably older than her colleagues, and who should have been holding the position of Sister or at least Staff Nurse. But if she was bitter at her lack of promotion she gave no indication of it. In any case, she was a taciturn person. During the long hours they spent in vigil together, Erika found herself wondering about her background, but even if the nurse had been more communicative, it was not done to pry into other people's personal lives.

When, on the sixth day, the fever reached its height, the nurse stayed on after duty to see Heike through the crisis. When the fever broke, the tears in Nurse Kunert's eyes were as real as those of Erika, Paula and Manfred.

'I had a little boy of my own,' she explained, once Heike had fallen into an exhausted slumber. 'I lost him when he was very young.'

611

They were in no state to ask her to go into any detail, and later there was no opportunity. But, because she had helped save Heike's life, Nurse Kunert would remain someone whom they would remember with gratitude and affection for the rest of their days.

Helena had no clear memory any more of her trial and her time in prison, except that her overriding emotions had been hatred and frustration. They had been years spent in a vacuum, with nothing to mark the passage of time except the infuriatingly well-meaning visits of Kleo and Dieter. Then, suddenly, Heinz-Georg had returned and she had found someone who, because of his own experiences in prison, understood how she was feeling.

Not that there had been anything sentimental about their conversations. On the contrary, they had been philosophical, mainly about the kind of society they had wanted to bring about. It was Heinz-Georg who had said, 'That society exists in the GDR.'

Helena had never met anyone who had fled from the East and imagined the GDR as a kind of socialist utopia, where everyone had equal rights to education and work, where capitalism had been overthrown and the people were dedicated to peace. 'When I'm released,' she said, 'that's where I'll go.'

She did not have to wait that long. One night, Heinz-Georg, dressed as a warder, had come to fetch her. Outside the prison, a car had been waiting to speed them through the streets to one of the checkpoints. Then she had found herself in East Berlin, inside the Ministry for State Security.

She had no idea that she and Heinz-Georg were part of a complex political deal, but believed they had been rescued as an act of solidarity. Even when her interrogators denigrated Black Kommando, saying that it was not a revolutionary, Marxist movement and accusing them of enjoying violence for its own sake, she had assumed that they were only doing their duty and that this was their way of ascertaining that her and Heinz-Georg's motives had been genuine. She found their attitude intimidating and humiliating, but tried not to be offended by it.

612

Finally, she was brought before an older man, a civilian, whom his colleagues addressed, very respectfully, as Comrade Meyer. Again, she had had to tell her story. Meyer heard her through expressionlessly, then said, 'Socialism is not achieved by destruction, but construction. Our youth movement has a song which goes: "Build up! Build up! German Youth . . ." The government is prepared to let you stay, provided you are willing to accept that you must contribute positively to the building up of socialism. It won't be easy, but as you know from your studies of Mao Tse-Tung, the process of revolution is a very long march . . .'

Since then, Helena had known many moments of disillusionment with the reality of living in a socialist state, the shortages, the drabness, the bureaucracy and the curbs on personal freedom. Yet she saw these things as an unfortunate necessity rather than an evil and found a strange comfort in the knowledge that everyone she encountered was in a similar situation to herself. Best of all, she knew moments of great satisfaction, once she had trained as a nurse, in saving lives, like that of little Heike Bauer.

So far as her personal life was concerned, she and Heinz-Georg got on remarkably well. Their relationship contained none of the passion, drama and danger which had epitomized her affair with Marko. Sometimes they went to bed together, but, for the most part they led virtually separate existences. Helena had only one real regret and that was Moon Child. As the years passed, she imagined him growing up and going to school, and had to face the heart-breakingly incontrovertible fact that she would probably never see him again.

As the winter of 1989 turned to spring, Wolfram Schwidinski experienced a great surge of hope. Unprecedented changes were taking place throughout the Communist world. In January, the Soviet Foreign Minister, Eduard Schevardnadze, had apparently told his West German counterpart, Hans-Dietrich Genscher, that the Berlin Wall had been 'built under particular circumstances' and they must look to see whether those circumstances still applied, although Honecker retorted that the Wall would still be standing in a hundred years. Schevardnadze

613

also asserted that Soviet short-range missiles were being with-drawn from Eastern Europe.

In Poland, Lech Walesa's Solidarity movement looked set to form a democratically elected government. In Afghanistan, the Red Army was being withdrawn after eight years of occupation. In Armenia and Azerbaijan, nationalists were staging massive demonstrations. The Baltic States of Latvia, Lithuania and Estonia were demanding independence. Even in China there was unrest, as students demonstrated for democracy and reform.

Most encouraging of all was what was occurring in Hungary, where political and economic change was being implemented with Gorbachev's apparent approval: where the parliament had voted to allow the formation of independent political parties and free elections were scheduled to be held within a year; where a free market economy was being introduced; where Soviet occupying troops had already begun withdrawing.

On Tuesday 2 May, amidst a blaze of publicity in the Western media, Hungarian border guards began to dismantle the fences and fortifications between Hungary and Austria. The first of the Soviet satellites was breaking away from its orbit. The Iron Curtain had been breached!

The following Sunday, municipal elections took place in the GDR. In church that morning, Pastor Margraf took his text from the third chapter of the Book of Ecclesiastes: *To every thing there is a season, and a time to every purpose under the heaven . . . a time to keep silence, and a time to speak . . .*

Wolfram was not alone in believing that the time had finally come to speak. Several hundred people joined him after the service in a demonstration in the Marx-Engels Platz, chanting: 'We are the people!' and carrying banners reading: 'Bring the election tricksters to court!' 'Freedom, equality, honesty!' 'Socialism, yes – SED, no!'

Only after much argument had he persuaded Christoph not to join in the demonstration. If, as he expected, the People's Police were waiting to break it up, no good would be served by them both being arrested.

He was right to be cautious. Over a hundred people were detained that day in Leipzig and Liebenroda and many more in the rest of the country. Wolfram was among those destined

614

to find himself again in the custody of Prison Chief Heinrich Koenig under *Stasi* headquarters.

In the middle of May, Gorbachev visited China and in the capital, Beijing, an estimated million people crowded onto the streets to give him an ecstatic welcome. The morale of the Chinese students was given a tremendous boost: their numbers swelled and their demands became more clamorous. Two weeks later, on the evening of Saturday 3 June, in a horrifying massacre seen on televisions throughout the world, tanks of the Chinese People's Army moved into Tiananmen Square and crushed the student rebellion. The GDR leadership gave its formal approval of the Chinese government's action.

That Monday evening, the Church of St Thomas was full long before the peace service was due to begin. Apart from the occasional cough, shuffling of feet and murmurs, the building was very quiet. Candles flickered beside the altar and in niches in the walls, illuminating pictures of political prisoners, prominent among them a photograph of Wolfram Schwidinski.

Nervously, Paula Bauer slipped into a pew at the back of the church, merging in inconspicuously with her neighbours in her sweatshirt, jeans and trainers. Under perfectly normal circumstances, which this was not, she would have felt uneasy, for it was the first time she had ever been inside a church.

Then Manfred arrived and she relaxed a little. *Vopos*, the People's Police, were stopping people in the streets and turning them back if the church was not in the district where they lived. For this reason, she and Manfred had travelled on separate trains to Liebenroda.

For his text, Pastor Margraf chose a passage from the Book of Isaiah: *The Lord hath anointed me to preach good tidings unto the meek; he hath sent me to bind up the brokenhearted, to proclaim liberty to the captives, and the opening of the prison to them that are bound ...*

He closed the Bible. 'Brethren, let these words give you hope and inspire you with courage. All over the world, innocent people are being persecuted and even killed in their search for freedom. Many of our own friends and relations are in prison for staging a peaceful demonstration. Yet they are not the only prisoners of the State. We are every one of us prisoners, confined behind concrete walls and barbed wire fences . . .'

Not since 1953 had the leadership found itself in such an invidious position. Then it had been Stalin's death which had sparked the people into the 17th June uprising. Now the reformist policies of a new Soviet leader were inspiring them with the desire for freedom and spurring them into potential rebellion.

Opinion was deeply divided within the Politburo as to what action should be taken. Hardliners, including Basilius, were in favour of harsh measures against all rebels, even if this meant conflict with the Kremlin. Gorbachev was already making himself extremely unpopular in the Soviet Union, not least with the KGB and the military, who were rapidly being deprived of their powers. If their patience snapped and they should decide upon a military coup, another leader would replace Gorbachev. By having opposed Gorbachev, the GDR leadership would have proved its loyalty to the Party and emerge with its reputation unscathed.

Other more liberal members, however, were in favour of backing Gorbachev and implementing his reforms. It was obvious how their minds were working. They were counting on Gorbachev remaining at the Kremlin, while the old guard was ousted from power in the GDR, in which case one of them would be in line to succeed Honecker.

Eventually, as a sop to international opinion and in the hope of appeasing the population, a compromise was reached. Orders were again given for some political detainees to be released. Travel and emigration restrictions were slightly relaxed. But it was still not enough. The fortunate few permitted to emigrate intensified the anger of those forbidden to leave.

Hungary had become the most popular holiday destination for East Germans, with thousands applying for travel permits to visit it and many of those who succeeded then trying to cross the border illegally into Austria, although those who were caught were sent home again by the Hungarians, where they were charged with *Republikflucht* – fleeing the Republic – and gaoled.

616

As the holiday season reached its peak in August, there were an estimated 200,000 East Germans on holiday in Hungary, with another 100,000 passing through in transit to and from Romania and Bulgaria. So many East Germans sought asylum in the West German diplomatic mission in East Berlin that it was forced to close, and the West German embassies in Budapest and Prague were said to be full to overflowing with asylum-seekers.

Several older Politburo members suffered from ill-health that summer. Honecker had a gall-bladder complaint and was awaiting an operation. His Deputy, Egon Krenz, had diabetes. Others had heart trouble, kidney and liver conditions. Basilius, himself, who was seventy that July, was afflicted by stomach cramps and attacks of nausea. He was admitted for tests to the Berlin-Buch Clinic, where the medical needs of all the leadership were attended to, but, to Basilius's relief, Dr Vith could only identify a slight inflammation of the stomach lining and prescribed special medication.

In Liebenroda, Police Chief Rudolf Sommer asked for Schwidinski's file to be brought to him. For a long time, he leafed through the reports, photographs and tapes it contained, then scribbled a memorandum ordering the lawyer's release.

Shortly after that, Schwidinski received a visit from a well-known East Berlin peace and human rights campaigner, an artist called Bärbel Bohley, who had herself been in prison several times. They met, not at Schwidinski's office, but at the art gallery. Sommer's adjutant brought him the report of their meeting that same evening.

A couple of weeks later, Schwidinski went to East Berlin. Sommer's agents, who followed him there, reported that he and Bohley again met in cultural surroundings – viewing the Collection of Modern Art at the National Gallery. Unfortunately, it was not possible to monitor their discussion.

When Schwidinski next met Pastor Margraf, the hidden microphones in the Pastor's home clearly relayed Schwidinski's enthusiastic description of the paintings he had seen in Berlin, then someone turned on the radio very loudly for a few moments and the vital part of their conversation was lost.

* * *

617

At the end of July, Heike fell ill again. Terrified that she had again caught pneumonia, Paula took her to the doctor. But he diagnosed her complaint as asthma. 'It's the air here,' he sighed. 'She really needs to get away from Leipzig. Do you and your husband still have holiday due?'

She nodded. 'School's just broken up. And my husband hasn't taken any leave yet this year.'

'It would do him good to get away, too. I don't like that cough of his.'

Paula summoned up all her courage. 'Our neighbours are going camping in Hungary – by the Danube. They've asked us to join them.'

If the doctor suspected any ulterior motive in their choice of destination he gave no sign. 'I've heard the climate there is very good. Well, I'll certainly recommend you for travel permits.'

Karen and Ingo had moved into the next flat to Paula and Manfred a year earlier and the two couples had immediately formed a rapport. Karen was a machinist in a textile works, while her boyfriend, Ingo, was an electrical engineer, who supplemented his state-regulated wage by doing private, cash jobs, with the result that they could afford a car – an old, not very reliable Trabant, it was true, but still a car. In their early thirties, they had no children and made a great fuss of Heike.

When asking Paula and Manfred if they would like to come with them to Hungary, they had admitted that they hoped to escape. Ingo had an uncle and aunt in Darmstadt, who had fled in 1958. Last September, his uncle had revisited Leipzig for the first time to attend the trade fair and told Ingo that, if he could get out, he would help him on his arrival over there. That evening, the four of them pored over a map of Hungary, trying to visualize conditions at the border.

'You're serious about this, aren't you?' Manfred said. 'You really mean to escape if you have the opportunity?'

Ingo sucked in his breath. 'I'm thirty-three years old and I've been being slowly stifled to death by the Communist system since the day I was born. I want to get out. We all do. So, let's agree, we're going to try.'

'What about our families?' Paula asked.

'We mustn't tell anyone what we're planning. The risk for them is too great. So far as our families, friends and neighbours are concerned, we're going on a fortnight's holiday and we'll see them when we return.'

Their arrangements went without a hitch; they obtained their visas without any untoward questions being asked. As much as possible was loaded into the Trabant's boot and onto the roofrack. In her rucksack, Paula packed a framed photograph of her parents and a watch which had belonged to Manfred's father – two items to remind them of home should they make it to the West. For Heike, they took the teddy bear Erika had given her for Christmas.

On the evening of their departure, they went to supper with Erika and Wolfram at Erika's flat, as they usually did on a Saturday. They tried to behave normally, talking about the things they planned to do on this, their first holiday in a foreign country. But despite all their efforts, there was an undercurrent of fear and sadness, an unspoken awareness of the real purpose of this holiday. When they came to leave, tears welled in Erika's eyes as she kissed them goodbye and Wolfram's voice was unusually gruff as he wished them a good journey.

Throughout their preparations, Paula had tried to ignore this moment of farewell. Now it was upon her, she very nearly broke down. And, in the privacy of their bedroom that night, she came very close to saying to Manfred, 'Let's change our minds and stay here.' Then, in the cot beside them, Heike coughed in her sleep.

Early the following morning, the old, overloaded Trabant set off for Hungary. It was Sunday 13 August 1989. On that same day, exactly twenty-eight years earlier, the Berlin Wall had gone up.

When they reached Hungary and set up tent on a camp site not far from Budapest, where the skies were clear and the air pure, Heike's asthma immediately stopped. Once they became acquainted with people in the other tents, they realized that many of them had come here with the same underlying intention as themselves. If the opportunity arose, they would get out.

619

They heard stories of the desperate lengths would-be fugitives had gone to: crawling through barbed wire fences, hiding in lorries, swimming across Lake Neusiedl, even trying to cross the Danube on air mattresses. Some of these attempts had apparently succeeded. Most had failed.

And even in Hungary, there was the *Stasi* to beware of, agents and informers disguised as holiday-makers, ready to pounce and arrest anyone who incautiously admitted they were considering *Republikflucht*.

Since the Austro-Hungarian border had first opened in May, however, there had been one vital change in the Hungarian government's attitude towards would-be East German escapees. Realizing that it was committing them to certain imprisonment at home, it was giving them sanctuary, claiming that, having recently signed the United Nations Convention on Refugees, it did not have to return people to their own countries against their will. But, by adopting this stance, it was risking badly upsetting not only the GDR, but its other Communist bloc partners, with possibly dire political repercussions. Furthermore, as ethnic Hungarians poured over the border to escape repression in Romania, Hungary had a growing refugee problem of its own.

On the Thursday after their arrival, rumours spread like wildfire through the camp and copies circulated of Austrian newspapers announcing a 'Pan-European Picnic' and freedom march being held on Saturday at the Hungarian border town of Sopron. From mouth to mouth, word spread, 'Austrians are going to be there. They've got to get back again. If you mix in with them, you might not be noticed.' But others warned, 'Be careful, it's a *Stasi* trick.'

There was no doubt in Ingo's mind what they should do. 'We can't lose,' he said. 'At worst, it's a trick. At best, we get out.'

So, on Saturday morning, they packed their belongings, dismantled their tents and set off towards Sopron. But the little Trabant, which had so staunchly made the long trek from Leipzig to Budapest, baulked at covering another hundred and fifty miles. Just outside Györ, it broke down. The weather was cold and rain was threatening to set in. By the time Ingo and

Manfred had identified the fault, hitched a lift into the town to buy a replacement part and fitted it, it was gone five in the afternoon and they were all chilled to the marrow.

They continued their journey, but when they reached Sopron, the narrow wooded road to the border was blocked by a jeep manned by armed border guards. 'Passport,' one demanded. Nervously, they showed their papers. The guard shook his head. 'Austria?' They nodded. Again he shook his head. 'Nix Austria.' There was nothing for it but to turn back.

When they reached the nearest camping site, they discovered, to their intense disappointment, that the border had indeed been opened that afternoon and remained open for three hours, and from the radio, they learned that over 600 East Germans had passed on foot into Austria. Because of the sheer volume of people pushing against the narrow gate, the guards – rather than let them be crushed – had unofficially let them through.

Paula could have wept from sheer frustration. 'We should have left the car and caught a train,' she wailed.

Manfred put his arm round her shoulder. 'We weren't to know. If the border hadn't opened, we could have been stranded here without anything.'

Yet, in a way, that day was the turning-point. They might not have got away, but they had made the final decision to leave.

The days of uncertainty which followed were the longest Paula had ever known. It was soon obvious that they could not cross the border by car: if they escaped, it would have to be on foot. With Heike in her pushchair or carried on Manfred's shoulders, they tried every possible path through the woods and across the fields, but wherever they went, armed guards were waiting for them. 'Nix Austria. No more try to escape.'

The weather grew worse and Heike caught a bad cold. One night, Karen and Ingo tried to make it on their own. Paula and Manfred lay awake, tense with worry. In the distance, dogs barked. Once they thought they heard shots. In the morning the couple returned to the camp site, wet to the skin and shivering with cold. 'We were caught,' Ingo said. 'They shot at our feet. Then they locked us up for three hours.'

'Perhaps we should go back home,' Paula said. Dreaming of getting away had been one thing. Doing it was quite another. She

621

had become dreadfully aware of the futility of their enterprise. Even if they did escape, where were they going to go? Ingo and Karen would be all right, but she and Manfred had no relations or even friends over there.

But when their travel permits expired, they – and hundreds of others – were still camped outside Sopron.

A few days later, new rumours started. Some kind of political agreement had been reached between the Federal Republic and the Hungarian governments. The border was going to be officially opened. Coaches and trains were waiting to take those without cars to special reception centres in Bavaria. Suddenly it didn't matter any more that they all had colds, that their rations and their money had all but run out.

Yet they had to wait another week before the rumours were confirmed, until, at seven o'clock on the evening of Sunday, 10 September, the Hungarian Foreign Minister, Gyula Horn, announced, on television, that from midnight that night, the border would be open. The impossible had happened: one Communist state was helping the inhabitants of another Communist regime to leave.

All over the camp site, tumultuous cheers broke out. Ingo opened their last beers, saved for just this occasion. They dismantled their tents for the last time. Well before midnight, theirs was one of the seemingly endless queue of Trabants and Wartburgs waiting to cross into Austria.

Those final hours were the longest of all, sitting in the dark, the engine switched off, as the seconds and the minutes ticked by. At last, the cars ahead began to edge forward. Eventually the crossing point came into sight. Then they were there and, in stark contrast to the anguish of the weeks before, the guards merely glanced at their passports and waved them on. Then they were in no-man's-land, in another long queue. All around them, horns were hooting, people were singing, cheering, shouting.

Finally, they drew up at the Austrian border control. Here, their passes were examined and stamped. Then they were waved on again to be confronted by a bewildering mass of people. Photographers rushed up to them. Television cameras whirred. The air was loud with the popping of champagne corks. Glasses were handed to them through the open car window. A girl thrust a microphone into Ingo's face and asked, 'How does it feel to be free?'

Ingo replied, 'Bloody wonderful!' He was grinning broadly, and at the same time, tears were streaming down his cheeks.

'Such a day as wonderful as this one, Such a day should never ever end . . .' It was Manfred who burst into song, as they drove through the night, through Austria towards the Federal Republic, and soon they had all joined in, except Heike, who had fallen into a deep, exhausted sleep.

The reception centre at Vilshofen in Bavaria, where they were directed, was rather spartan and, because of the enormous influx of refugees, they had to sleep in tents again, but this did not matter, compared to the sheer excitement of finally finding themselves in the Federal Republic.

First they had to complete the registration formalities, answer questions about their contacts in the Federal Republic and other matters relating to state security. Then they were given 200 Deutschmarks each, including Heike, and finally, after snatching a few hours' sleep, they were free to explore their new surroundings.

Heike slept in her pushchair, but the others looked around them wide-eyed as they walked through the town. The shops, above all the supermarket, held them mesmerized. Never in their lives before had they seen such an abundance of merchandise. Following the example of other shoppers, they took one of the massive trolleys and entered through the electronic doors. The greengrocery stand was stocked with every conceivable kind of fruit and vegetable, many of which they had never seen before – bananas, grapes, pineapples, mangoes, kiwi fruit . . . Pasta – not just spaghetti and macaroni, but green, yellow, brown and coloured pastas, in every imaginable shape. Cheese – not just Edam or Gouda. Salami, perhaps a hundred different varieties. Coffee, tea, meat, fish, cereals, frozen foods, bread, soft drinks, wine, beer – the choice was so bewilderingly great, it was terrifying. They all bought some little luxury – an ice cream for Heike, Paula biscuits, Karen chocolate, Ingo some cans of beer, Manfred a bottle of wine. Out of habit, they all chose the cheapest brand.

623

From the Post Office, Paula telephoned Wolfram. 'We're here,' she said, 'and it's wonderful. Are you all right? Give Mum our love . . .'

Then Ingo rang his uncle in Darmstadt. His expression, as he put down the phone, gave a hint of the bad news he was about to impart. 'He says their flat is very small. Karen and I can sleep in his living room for a while, until we find a place of our own. But I'm sorry, there's no room for you . . .'

Manfred smiled bravely. 'We weren't expecting him to take us in as well. Don't worry, we'll be all right.'

Back at the reception centre, they were told they had to be moved on as quickly as possible to make room for other new arrivals. Although they asked if they could go to Darmstadt with Ingo and Karen, this was apparently not possible, and arrangements were made for Manfred, Paula and Heike to be accommodated in an asylum home in Hamburg.

'You can come with us as far as Darmstadt,' Ingo said, 'and catch a train from there.'

The following day they were *en route* again. As they drove along, other drivers waved and flashed their headlights, when they saw the Trabant with its GDR numberplate. Strangers guided them through towns and cities. Some even offered them food and pressed money upon them. To the excitement of being free was added the elation of being treated like heroes.

But after they parted from Ingo and Karen at Darmstadt, that initial euphoria quickly subsided. The asylum home in Hamburg was the first major disappointment. It was situated beside a railway line in the industrial area of Rothenburgsort, which was so drab and depressing it could almost have been a suburb of Leipzig. Instead of having a room to themselves, they were expected to share a sixteen-bed dormitory with three other families.

Then they discovered that bureaucracy was the same in whichever Germany one found oneself. They had to register with the police, register to obtain new identity cards, register at the refugee office, the social security office and the housing office. Every government department was in a different building. Everywhere there were queues and endless forms to be completed.

The worst shock came at the employment office. There were no vacancies for schoolteachers and very few for engineers. 'In any case,' the interviewer told Paula and Manfred, pursing her lips, 'your diplomas aren't valid here. If you want to continue with your chosen professions, you'll have to re-train.'

For a few hours, they had been heroes. Now, their clothes, their accents, above all, their poverty, differentiated them very clearly from their new neighbours in affluent Hamburg. After just a few days, they realized that many local people simply thought of them as *Zonies* or *Ostis*, derogatory names for refugees from the East. Some magazine articles asked: What do we do with them? Others felt it necessary to point out: They are welcome – they belong to us.

Scrawled on the wall of their home they saw OSTIS RAUS! with a crude swastika beneath it. Once, when they were out, a gang of skinheads crowded in on them threateningly and shouted obscenities.

Their only consolation during those dark days was the kindness of a young social worker called Axel Kraus. When, after just a week in Hamburg, Heike's asthma returned, Axel arranged for her to see a doctor and ensured that she obtained the necessary medicaments free of charge.

Ingo wrote from Darmstadt that he and Karen had both found jobs and his uncle was hopeful of obtaining them a small apartment. For Paula and Manfred, there were merely the ghastly spectres of homelessness and unemployment.

At the peace service on Monday 11 September, the same day that Hungary opened its border with Austria, Pastor Margraf first prayed for the emigrants, then begged his congregation to think carefully before following their example. 'They are fleeing out of desperation,' he said, 'because they have lost faith in their homeland. But every one who goes leaves the rest of us personally more alone, and weaker as a people.'

He stepped back and Wolfram took his place. 'Today the formation has been publicly announced of New Forum, a nationwide opposition group, an alliance of individuals from widely different walks of life and political beliefs, united by a common cause – that of reform. Its founders are Bärbel

Bohley and Jens Reich, two names with which most of you will already be familiar, as a result of their courageous campaigns for civil and moral rights. I have volunteered to coordinate New Forum's activities here.

'Our first purpose is to compile a list of reforms, which we intend to put to the leadership – among them the introduction of democratic elections and economic reforms. For this, we need all the support we can get – signatures on our petition, and help from people with specialist knowledge, who can provide positive suggestions as to how our proposed reforms can be implemented.'

He scanned the faces gazing up at him in rapt attention. 'This is our country. We are the people. We must overcome our fear, for our own sakes – and for the children of tomorrow. I ask you to join me in the fight for the moral and civil rights which have so long been denied us. Show your support by joining New Forum. As you know, we meet here every Monday. Next week, bring another with you . . .'

After the service, every member of the congregation took a candle, waiting in readiness at the back of the church, and lit it. There was a shortage of electric light bulbs in the GDR, but candles, made from crude oil imported from Romania and the Soviet Union, were nearly always available.

With Wolfram and Christoph at their head, they filed along the Lenin-Strasse, across the bridge over the Weisse Elster and into the Marx-Engels Platz. When they reached *Stasi* headquarters, they did not stop but walked round the block. Three times they did this, once for freedom, once for democracy, once for unity. The armed sentries guarding the *Stasi* building watched them coldly, but, to everyone's amazement and relief, made no move against them.

Despite the uncertainty of their situation – or maybe even because of it – the mood of people in Liebenroda and Leipzig became increasingly determined. Erika was an example of how they felt when she said, upon being one of the first to join New Forum, 'Now I know Paula is safe, I'm not worried about myself. But if we don't show the courage of our own convictions, nobody will ever take us seriously.'

Some hospital staff and several workers from Auto-Roda

626

were among those who also joined New Forum and quite a few of them were threatening to strike if the authorities cracked down on the protest movement, as well as leaving the factory combat groups, which formed a vital, auxiliary part of the country's military. A works foreman and a captain in the factory militia told Wolfram entirely seriously, 'If they try and stop us now, it means war.'

Government reaction to New Forum was surprisingly mild. An Interior Ministry official had said there was no social need for the New Forum's existence and the State press denounced it, accusing it of being a subversive platform and its members of being fifth columnists. However, the movement was not banned.

Police Chief Rudolf Sommer looked down from his office window onto the Marx-Engels-Platz as the flickering lights circled the *Stasi* building, for the third Monday running.

He could read the words on the banners: 'Travel freedom – not mass flight.' 'Democracy – not SED!' 'Socialism, yes! – SED, no!' 'New Forum!' And hear the voices chanting: *'Wir sind das Volk!'* 'We are the people!'

Each week, the number of protesters increased. To begin with, there had been about 300 people. Now, there were two, maybe three thousand.

Liebenroda was not the only place in which such a scene was being enacted. Every Monday, Sommer knew, there were similar demonstrations in Leipzig, Dresden, Karl-Marx-Stadt, Plauen and other towns and cities.

He lit a new cigarette from the butt of the last one. His cigarette consumption had gone up considerably in recent weeks. If he were in charge of the country, what would he do?

There was a knock on the door and Heinrich Koenig strode across the room and stood beside him. 'We should do what the Chinese did and send in the tanks,' he muttered. That solution was typical of Koenig, who had helped suppress the Prague Spring in 1968.

But Sommer was not Koenig.

He gazed down on the shadowy figures and flickering lights

and, as the candles circled the *Stasi* building for the third time, words from the Bible, which he had not heard since childhood, came unbidden to his mind: *The light shineth in the darkness; and the darkness comprehended it not.*

Chapter 26

Despite New Forum and the fledgling opposition groups being formed under its umbrella, the exodus of East Germans continued. Thousands continued to flee via Hungary. Three and a half thousand were occupying the West German embassy in Prague. Western television showed incredible pictures of people clambering over the railings to get in, the squalid conditions inside the building and the tent village which had been set up in its grounds. The Bonn embassy in Warsaw was also full to overflowing and duly forced to close its doors.

Then, on Saturday 30 September, the West German Foreign Minister, Hans-Dietrich Genscher, appeared on the balcony of the Prague embassy and announced: 'Dear fellow countrymen, we have come to you to tell you, that this evening, your departure . . .'

As they had been in Budapest, twenty days earlier, television and press cameras were waiting to record the historic moment and the jubilant reactions of the East Germans who had finally been granted their liberty.

Wolfram was at Erika's, as he was every Saturday evening, for although she never complained, he knew she felt very lonely since the departure of Paula, Manfred and Heike.

'Have you noticed how young they all are?' she murmured. 'Wolfram, what happens when a country loses its youth?'

He shook his head gloomily. The international media was not helping the situation by exaggerating the drama and introducing a quite unreal sense of urgency, as if every refugee had a death threat hanging over them.

Yet possibly they had. The following weekend was the fortieth anniversary of the GDR and Gorbachev was due to attend the celebrations being held in Berlin. Who knew but that, after Gorbachev departed, the loopholes in the Iron Curtain would

629

not again be sealed and the government would not follow the example of the Chinese?

'I met Nurse Kunert the other day,' Erika went on, 'that nurse who was so wonderful to little Heike when she was so ill last winter. She was telling me about the problems at the hospital. Apparently so many doctors and nurses have fled they're having to cancel operations and shut down wards. I told her I used to work at the hospital and she said if I wanted to come back I'd be very useful. I'm starting tomorrow – on a purely voluntary basis, of course.'

'Please don't overtire yourself . . .'

'I'm glad of something to take my mind off other things . . .' Erika sighed. 'I do wish I knew how Paula is getting on. Apparently Nurse Kunert lived over there once. When I told her that Paula had escaped through Hungary, she grew very bitter. "They'll soon discover the reality is very different from what they imagine," she said. "They'll find out they've just joined a capitalist rat-race." When I pointed out that they'd gone for the sake of Heike's health, she said, "Unless they've paid into the health insurance, they won't receive treatment. In fact, they'll be lucky to get anything, including work." '

'That's nonsense. I saw a news item the other evening, showing how companies over there are welcoming our people with open arms. They'd much rather employ their fellow Germans than foreigners, like Turks.'

'I saw that programme, too. But did you notice, the jobs they were talking about were nearly all unskilled? There was no mention of teachers and engineers being in demand.'

'Don't worry about them. If you remember, Paula said it was wonderful when she rang. I'm sure they're fine. But the point is, they shouldn't have to leave.'

Erika started at the hospital next morning, making beds, sweeping wards and helping prepare patients' meals. When the opportunity arose, she asked Nurse Kunert more about life over there. But perhaps because she feared she had already said too much, the nurse was reluctant to discuss the subject.

Special West German trains evacuated the Prague embassy and more were sent to Poland to evacuate the Bonn embassy in Warsaw. On 3 October, the Prague embassy had to be closed again after another 4,500 East Germans had crammed themselves inside and, in the afternoon, it was literally besieged by East Germans unable to get in through the doors. Yet more West German trains were laid on to take them to freedom. The trains had to pass through the GDR to reach the Federal Republic and at stations along their route, angry demonstrations took place.

A GDR government spokesman said the emigrants were being allowed to go 'for humanitarian reasons'. Honecker stated, 'We do not mourn their leaving.' But, as from that day, severe new travel restrictions were introduced. Those left behind in the GDR were again cut off from the outside world.

Like everyone else in West Germany, the Bauers had been following the plight of their fellow countrymen in Prague on the television in the communal lounge at the asylum home and watched their dramatic rescue and ecstatic welcome at Hof in Northern Bavaria. But they could not share their rejoicing. After a month in the Federal Republic, they were all too aware of the fate which awaited most of them, except those fortunate enough to have relations over here, like Ingo and Karen, who could help them make a new start.

Their own circumstances had, in fact, improved a little, for Manfred had obtained a job through the Employment Office, although it could scarcely have been more back-breaking or depressing. He worked at a car-breakers' yard, destroying cars which anyone in Leipzig would have been proud to own. His wages were abysmal: just 200 Marks a week; and the cheapest flat they had found cost 700 Marks a month, which, compared to the 60 Marks rent a month they had been paying in Leipzig, seemed exorbitant, but was apparently very reasonable by Hamburg standards. On Manfred's wage they could live or eat, but not both.

And, as thousands more East Germans arrived, the employment and housing situation could only get worse. Manfred put a brave face on things, but there were moments when Paula felt very near to despair. Least of all did she feel up to writing to her mother and Wolfram.

Rather than stay in all day at the home, which would have

631

been utterly soul-destroying, she took Heike out every day, pushing the little girl in her buggy when her legs grew too tired to walk. They covered miles around the Alster lakes, among the wharves beside the Elbe and through the parks.

Then, one morning – it was the day after Honecker had reintroduced travel restrictions – they were wandering through the arcaded Gaensemarkt shopping precinct and Paula was gazing despondently at the displays of exquisite clothes she could never hope to afford in the beautifully dressed boutique windows, when a voice said, 'Hello, Paula. Hello, Heike.'

She turned, astonished that anyone should recognize and know her, to see Axel, the young Red Cross aid worker. 'You remember me?'

'Your family was among the very first I met from the GDR,' Axel explained. 'Would you like a coffee?'

Paula bit her lip. Café prices were well beyond her purse.

'I'm sure Heike would like an ice cream,' Axel said. 'And I'm starving. I missed breakfast this morning.'

Before Paula could demur, they were seated at a table outside a café and Axel was ordering coffee, rolls, cheese, salami, and a strawberry ice cream for Heike. 'What do you think will happen in the GDR?' he asked. 'Go on, dig in, I can't eat all that by myself. Do you think Honecker will send in the troops like Deng Xiao Ping, or will Gorby intervene this weekend and tell him he has to agree to reforms?'

It was the first time anyone had asked her opinion on a political matter. Paula sipped her coffee, then said cautiously, 'I hope he will introduce reforms, but I don't believe he will.'

'I suppose if you had thought he would, you wouldn't have fled.' Axel wrapped a slice of salami round a gherkin and popped it into his mouth.

'I don't know. We left mainly because of Heike. At least she seems much better here than at home.'

Axel smiled. 'The bracing North Sea air! It either kills or cures.' Then he became more serious. 'Tell me about Leipzig and what your lives were like over there.'

Hesitantly at first, then with growing confidence, Paula described her old life. When she felt she had talked quite

632

long enough, she paused to finish her coffee. Axel frowned thoughtfully. 'Can you write as well as you speak?'

Paula shrugged diffidently. 'I'm not sure.'

'I know Stefan Jochum, the owner of the magazine *Aktuell*. If you could write an article along the lines of what you've been telling me, I think he might publish it. It's the sort of environmental issue he's keen on. I have a typewriter you can borrow.'

In a sudden flash of memory, Paula was transported back to that evening, three years earlier, when her mother had made her extraordinary confession about her love affair with Stefan Jochum. She heard Wolfram saying, 'I'd like you to take him information about our lives, photographs of our factories and our countryside.'

'*Aktuell?*' she stammered. 'Stefan Jochum . . . ?'

'You've heard of him? I guess most people have. He lives in Berlin, but *Aktuell*'s head office is here in Hamburg. I've met the editor, Christian Horst, a couple of times. So, what do you say?'

'Thank you,' Paula said, dazedly. 'You don't realize how much this means to me. I've been feeling rather down . . .'

'I'm not surprised. The trouble is, a lot of people here don't understand why you're all running away. They assume it's because you want the material benefits we enjoy – all of this . . .' Axel flung out his arm to indicate the Gaensemarkt. 'They have no idea that life over there is how you've just described it.'

She looked at him puzzledly. He seemed so young, yet he spoke so maturely. 'What makes you so understanding?'

He waved to the waitress to bring the bill. 'Maybe one day I'll tell you the story of *my* life,' he laughed.

That same morning, in Liebenroda, a plainclothes policeman arrived at Wolfram's office, with orders to escort him to *Stasi* headquarters. But to Wolfram's amazement, instead of being handcuffed and delivered into Prison Officer Koenig's tender care, he was taken into the *Stasi* building by a back entrance and led up to Police Chief Sommer's office, where, to his further astonishment, Sommer shook his hand and offered him a cigarette.

When they were alone, Sommer said, 'Your half-sister and her family have emigrated to the West, but you have remained. Why did you not go?'

'Because, like most other people, I want to live in my own country.'

Sommer nodded. 'Let me offer you a hypothetical situation. If you were given the political freedoms you are asking, what would you do with them?'

Extremely wary of a trap, Wolfram replied, 'The first step would be to hold free elections and form a democratic parliament.'

'The sentiment is noble. But you and your colleagues have no experience of organizing elections. Where are you going to find your candidates? How do you intend to vet them to make sure they have – umm – political integrity?'

'I'm sure we'll quickly find a way,' Wolfram replied. If Sommer was hoping for him to reveal New Forum's membership and plans, he was mistaken.

'And our current leadership? What would be your attitude towards them?'

'I hope they would endorse the democratic process and also put themselves forward for election.' He said that, but doubted very much that the SED would receive many votes. Certainly the Politburo and SED Central Committee would not survive. As for the *Stasi* . . .

Sommer blew a smoke ring and watched as it circled up to the ceiling. 'You are in touch with the people. Travel restrictions have already been reintroduced. If the ban on demonstrations were also enforced, what do you think would happen?'

Wolfram hesitated. So far he had said nothing which was not generally known or could potentially incriminate anyone other than himself.

Sommer leaned forward in his chair, his expression suddenly very earnest. 'Comrade Schwidinski, I have to know. Trust me. Please.'

For a long time, the two men stared silently across the table into each other's eyes. Then Wolfram took a deep breath. 'At our meetings, workers are threatening strikes and mass walk-outs from factory militias.'

634

'They remember what happened in 1953?'

'Yes, and they know that our leadership endorsed the Chinese government's recent action in Tiananmen Square. But they believe Gorbachev will be on their side, as he has supported the Hungarians and Poles. And they are hopeful of gaining the support of the Federal Republic, since Genscher negotiated the release of the emigrants from Prague.'

Sommer stubbed out his cigarette into a brimming ashtray and lit another. 'As a result of our emigrants, the Czech people are now demanding reforms and freedom of movement. Genscher has not made himself popular with the Czech government – or with those of other Soviet bloc countries. He could well be extremely wary of intervening again in another country's affairs.'

'So far as the Federal Republic is concerned, we are not another country. Genscher called us his fellow countrymen,' Wolfram reminded him.

'So, despite the danger to themselves, the people would go on strike?'

'I am not saying they would, but I believe they could, if their demands are not met. Tens – if not hundreds – of thousands have fled the country, leaving everything behind them. To do that takes enormous courage. Those of us who have stayed are not lacking in courage either.' He paused. 'We have all of us been pushed too far . . .'

Sommer rubbed his hand across his distinctive, triangular eyes. Then he said, 'Thank you, Comrade Schwidinski. Thank you for being honest with me.'

Wolfram eventually left the building by the same back exit. Although Sommer's office had not been excessively warm, his palms were sweaty and his shirt clung clammily to his body.

Much of what Wolfram Schwidinski had told Sommer confirmed what he had already heard from Party colleagues in Liebenroda and Leipzig and from his agents, with their networks of informers in factories, offices, schools, shops and hospitals. Unless reforms were forthcoming, workers were prepared to take desperate action and, to a very great extent, they had the unofficial backing of their superiors and local Party bosses.

635

On Friday, when Rudolf Sommer stepped into his chauffeur-driven Mercedes to set off for the fortieth anniversary celebrations in Berlin, he had in his inside pocket a report, which he had typed himself, that concisely analysed the situation – and contained his recommendations for dealing with it.

Through the streets of East Berlin they marched, rank upon serried rank of Young Pioneers and Free German Youth, carrying flaming torches, bearing standards with portraits of their leaders and banners proclaiming Party slogans; phalanx upon phalanx of People's Police; group upon group of factory militia; regiment after regiment of the National People's Army in field grey uniforms, flared helmets and white gloves, their rifles held cross arms style, their eyes turned right in salute as they goosestepped past the leadership. Flags waved. Drums rolled. Military bands played stirring marches. The streets echoed to the rhythmic tread of boots.

From time to time, from his position in the front row on the podium, Basilius Meyer glanced at Honecker, his arm held in a shaky salute. There was little doubt in the minds of anyone on the Politburo that Honecker's days were numbered. Just over a month ago, he had undergone a gall-bladder operation which, although apparently successful, had left him very frail. There were rumours that he was, in fact, suffering from cancer. It was not just his health, however, which was casting doubt upon his ability to remain in power, but the inept manner in which he was handling the crisis besetting the country.

Basilius pursed his lips. If it were not for himself and other so-called hardliners on the Politburo, Honecker would have continued to waver, people would go on fleeing and the opposition movement growing, resulting in the inevitable breakdown of the entire State. Old age and illness had robbed Honecker of his political deviousness. He was confused by the muddled signals and lack of clear directions being sent to him from Moscow.

Basilius and his supporters had been able to convince Honecker that action must be taken the moment Gorbachev flew back to Moscow. The regional Security Police chiefs were to be briefed on the operation first thing tomorrow morning

636

and the necessary People's Police and army units given their orders immediately after that meeting. Once order was again restored in the country, Basilius's next move would be to persuade Honecker to resign, at which point he would achieve his lifelong ambition and be appointed Head of State.

Basilius looked past Honecker, to his possible rivals for that coveted post, Egon Krenz, Werner Jarowinski, Guenter Schabowski . . . No, they stood no chance. He alone had the backing of a majority in the Politburo.

Then his glance fell on Gorbachev, staring impassively at the troops. How different the Russian's expression had been during his walk-about, when he had smiled and shaken hands with people in the crowds who had turned out to greet him, ecstatically cheering and shouting, 'Gorby! Gorby!'

The man was an upstart, a traitor to Communism. It was due to him that East Germans were fleeing their country in their thousands and the GDR leadership was being made a laughing stock. Well, Gorbachev might be prepared to allow the Soviet Union to slide into anarchy and chaos, but the German Democratic Republic was not going to follow his example. Very soon, Gorbachev would realize that the GDR leadership controlled its own destiny and these troops were not just for show.

In previous decades, Rudolf Sommer had taken pride in his country's anniversary celebrations. This year, he knew them to be a hollow front. Since his arrival in Berlin the previous afternoon, he had found plentiful opportunity for discreet discussion with old colleagues, who, despite his connection with Basilius, trusted him with their confidences. From them he had gained the impression that many shared his own misgivings about the leadership's intransigent attitude towards reform.

There was considerable speculation about who would succeed Honecker, who was apparently far more ill than he would admit, and from the innuendoes let drop, Rudolf could imagine the clandestine plotting and counter-plotting which had been taking place in anticipation of his retirement.

Basilius seemed to be considered Honecker's most likely successor, although Rudolf received the impression that his

637

cousin was not a favourite choice. As well as his uncompromising conservatism, his age counted against him, and so did his health. During the summer, he was known to have been treated for a stomach complaint.

Most of the contenders, in fact, seemed to be suffering from ill health. Honecker's deputy, Egon Krenz, who, despite being twenty-five years Honecker's junior, was another unswerving hardliner – just the previous week during an official visit to China, he had commended the action in Tiananmen Square – was a diabetic, although his enemies claimed he was an alcoholic.

Werner Jarowinski, Secretary of the Central Committee for Trade, had gout. And Guenter Schabowski, the East Berlin SED chief, who was reputed to be in favour of a more liberal course, was having treatment for a kidney disorder.

The only fit one among them seemed to be Hans Modrow, who was undoubtedly also the most popular. Modrow's chances, however, were not rated highly. The head of the Party in Dresden, he had recently fallen out with Honecker when he had declared, 'I am not here for the Party, but for the people.' While Krenz was in Beijing, Modrow had been in Stuttgart, meeting members of the West German Social Democratic Party and telling them that Gorbachev's ideas must be implemented in the GDR.

That Saturday evening, as Rudolf's Mercedes turned off Unter den Linden towards the main entrance to the Palace of the Republic, where the culminating reception was being held, Rudolf could not help but notice the police barricade across the bridge over the Spree and the crowds gathered on the river bank. He wound down the window and their voices reached him: 'Gorby! Gorby!' 'We're staying here!' 'We are the people!'

Their words were no empty gesture of defiance. As Schwidinski had said, they had been pushed too far . . .

He did not enjoy the reception, with its predictably sententious speeches. His fingers kept moving to the inside pocket of his jacket and his glance kept travelling to the high table where Basilius was seated with Gorbachev, Honecker and visiting foreign heads of state. So far, there had been scant opportunity for conversation with his cousin, but he had already obtained an invitation to go to Wandlitz the following afternoon. And greatly to his surprise, overhearing Basilius and Rudolf make their arrangements, Egon Krenz had suggested genially that he might also like to pop in for a quick drink at his house.

Rudolf knew Krenz from his Berlin days, since Krenz had started his ascent in the Party hierarchy a quarter of a century ago as head of the Free German Youth. Although Basilius had frowned, Rudolf had said he would be delighted.

Before his visit to Wandlitz, however, he had a meeting to attend at the Ministry for State Security, where the police chiefs were addressed by the Deputy Minister for Internal Security, who informed them that he was acting on Honecker's direct orders.

'Anti-socialist elements, skinheads, punks and other rowdies, led by counter-revolutionaries controlled from the Federal Republic, have become a danger to our socialist Fatherland,' he read from a prepared memorandum. 'A combined police and army operation is being launched to bring the situation under control. Preliminary action is being taken today against demonstrators in Berlin. The main operation will be launched tomorrow evening. Special units are being posted to provincial cities and towns to supplement existing troops and defend State property against the counter-revolutionary movement. The operation will be coordinated by the State Security Police.'

Honecker's timing was perfect, Rudolf thought grimly. Gorbachev was back in Moscow. The need for an outward show of reconciliation towards the Kremlin was over. Troops had been massing in Berlin to participate in the military parades. Nobody would see anything untoward in their dispersal to new bases.

He glanced at his colleagues, but it was impossible to tell from their expressions what they were thinking.

When at last the meeting ended, he went to where his car was waiting outside. 'Take me to Prenzlauer Berg,' he told his driver.

The car was stopped soon after it entered the Schoenhauser Allee. A *Vopo* scrutinized their identity cards, advised them to turn back, but when Rudolf insisted that they continue, reluctantly signalled them on. Soon, however, they could go no further, for their road was barred by police lorries.

Telling the driver to remain where he was, Rudolf got out and continued on foot. Several more times he had to show his identity card, before he had a clear view of what was taking place.

Here in Prenzlauer Berg, where little had changed since the tenement houses had been built in the nineteenth century, where the inhabitants had fought the Free Corps during the Spartacist Revolution, battled against Hitler's stormtroopers, defended themselves fiercely against the Red Army in the final Battle for Berlin in 1945, marched for their rights during the 1953 Workers' Rising and demonstrated for freedom in January 1988, another unequal battle was being fought out.

Line upon line of *Vopos* in visored helmets, carrying anti-riot shields and lethally thin truncheons, backed up by water cannon and dogs, were advancing upon civilians armed only with banners and candles.

Among the protesters, Rudolf saw several whom he recognized. But two figures above all held his attention riveted. A young man and a girl, they were chanting slogans and holding aloft a placard. The youth was Gert Koenig. The girl was the barmaid from Zum Kastanien, Jana Seifert.

As Rudolf watched, the *Vopos* charged the demonstrators. Gert and Jana's placard was wrenched from them and trampled underfoot. Rough hands seized Jana by the shoulders. A truncheon sliced through the air and descended across Gert's shoulders.

Hardened though he was to violence, Rudolf felt sickened. This was his birthplace. These were his people. He turned away and made his way back to his car.

As Rudolf Sommer's car drove towards Wandlitz that afternoon, his driver tuned the car radio to Radio Free Berlin. The news reader announced: 'In East Berlin, police have moved in against demonstrators demanding democratic reforms. Hundreds of arrests are believed to have been made. Demonstrations have also been taking place in Leipzig, Dresden and Karl-Marx-Stadt. At the Bonn Embassy in Warsaw, more GDR citizens are applying for asylum . . .'

640

The settlement at Wandlitz, with its luxurious villas and spacious gardens, provided a stark contrast with the tall, grey, sunless tenements of Prenzlauer Berg. Possibly because he was a bachelor, perhaps because he could never rid himself of the memory of his impoverished childhood, Rudolf had taken no advantage of the perquisites of power, beyond those necessary to his position, like the Mercedes and driver. Indeed, people like the Koenigs had often criticized his spartan apartment, his sparse wardrobe and his preference for spending his leave walking in the Harz Mountains rather than at a Black Sea resort. Basilius had once even accused Rudolf of setting a bad example by living so ascetically: those in power, he said, had a duty to inspire confidence in the people.

After passing through several security checks, they reached Basilius's house, with its own security fence and guards. Again Rudolf showed his pass, the gates opened and the car was waved through.

Basilius had never been one for social chit-chat. For a quarter of an hour or so, while they drank coffee in the beautifully appointed living room, Irina sat with them and they talked about the anniversary celebrations, Reinhardt in Chile and Basilius's health. Then Irina excused herself and the two men were left alone.

Rudolf made no attempt to beat about the bush. 'Basilius, in my belief, we stand before a catastrophe of the direst kind . . .'

Basilius's expression hardened. 'You're right. Never before has the country been in greater danger. The Federal Republic is enticing away our workers and they are being encouraged into subversion by the Soviet Union.'

'I was at a meeting this morning at the Ministry for State Security. After that, I went to the Prenzlauer Berg . . .'

'I understand the operation there was very successful.'

'You support Honecker's decision to use force against the demonstrators?'

'Honecker didn't take the decision alone. At all costs, our State must be protected.'

'Even at the cost of the lives of our own people?'

'Of traitors. That is what they are. My parents both died in

641

the revolutionary cause, died so that the hammer and sickle would fly over Germany. Do you expect me to reject all that that they sacrificed their lives for?'

'No, that is not what they died for. They died because they believed in freedom, equality, democracy ... Basilius, Honecker's decision to use force against the protesters is morally and politically wrong.'

Basilius stared at him in disbelief, then the colour drained from his face. 'So they have contaminated even you with their treasonous ideas.' There was a bitter edge of disappointment in his voice. 'Get out of here. Go, before I have time to change my mind and order your arrest.'

Rudolf would have liked to say that what he was advocating was not treason but common sense; that most of the rest of the world could see that the GDR was hovering on the brink of either collapse or revolution; but that timely intervention could still save the country – and those in authority – from a debacle. But Basilius was the wrong man. It was a waste of time to continue the discussion. There was no point in handing over to him his painstakingly prepared report. Rudolf stood up, took his coat and left his cousin's house for the last time.

Yet he could not leave the matter there. Not just for the sake of his own conscience or even his office – it had not escaped his notice that the State Security Police would be held responsible for whatever happened – but for the people of Prenzlauer Berg and Liebenroda, for the GDR as a country – who knew, maybe even for world peace? – he must try every means at his disposal to get tomorrow evening's action stopped.

He told his driver to take him a short way up the road until they reached house number 4, Egon Krenz's residence. He had little expectation that a personal appeal of the kind that he had hoped would work on Basilius would have any effect at all on Krenz, for theirs was a purely professional relationship, with no blood ties to bind them. But there was one other possibility ...

He found Krenz in ebullient mood, radiating bonhomie and gushing with hospitality. 'My dear Rudi, how kind of you to take up my invitation.' He led Rudolf into his study. 'May I offer you a drink? Whisky? Cognac?'

642

When they were comfortably seated, drinks in hand, he said, 'In view of everything that's going on, I expected you to go straight back to Liebenroda.'

'That's why I'm here,' Rudolf said heavily. He decided on a different approach with Krenz and pulled out his report. 'I would be grateful if you would read this . . .'

Krenz cast his eye swiftly over the first page, which summarized Sommer's conclusions. Then he looked up. 'You prepared this before you knew about tomorrow evening's operation?'

'In anticipation of it . . . Comrade Krenz, I am a patriot. I love my country above all else. If blood is shed tomorrow, if shots are fired against the people, the consequences will be incalculable . . .'

'The State cannot be dictated to. It has to keep its authority. You know what would happen if we let the demonstrations continue unchecked.'

'If you read my report you will see what will happen if the government doesn't agree to consider reforms.'

Krenz flicked through the sheets of the report. 'This is true? There will be strikes, mass walk-outs from factory militias, resignations from the Party . . . ?'

'I, for one, would hand in my Party card . . .'

Krenz stared at him searchingly, then he stood up and began pacing the room. 'You have discussed this with Basilius?'

'Basilius would not discuss the matter. He said that the decision to use force came from Honecker and that he fully supported it.'

Krenz nodded. 'Confrontation is unavoidable now. The Politburo has made a unanimous decision.'

'Which is most important?' Rudolf pleaded. 'The unity of Politburo or the welfare of the people?'

Krenz paused in his pacing. He knew as well as Rudolf that the Politburo was far from united. Rudolf pushed home his advantage. 'The people have lost all faith in the Party and the leadership. That faith will not be restored by military confrontation, by a massacre . . .'

'What is the alternative?'

Rudolf took a deep breath. 'In my opinion, Comrade Honecker should retire at the earliest opportunity. I am of the firm belief

643

that his resignation would be welcomed by the majority of the Party membership. What we need is a different kind of Party leader, a younger man, a man of courage and vision, with leadership qualities which can hold the Party together during these difficult times, while at the same time conciliating the people . . .'

For a long time, Krenz was silent. Then slowly, a smile formed itself upon his features. His expression reminded Rudolf of the wolf in *Little Red Riding Hood*.

In Liebenroda, the first auxiliary troops moved in at the dead of night and tanks rumbled over the cobbled Marx-Engels- Platz into the central courtyard of *Stasi* headquarters. But it was impossible to keep military activity on such a massive scale secret. News of it reached Pastor Margraf by telephone before dawn broke, Wolfram arrived on his doorstep at first light and after that the telephone did not stop ringing.

The tanks were being fitted out like giant cow-catchers, with massive shields made out of wire-netting, with which it was intended to herd the demonstrators along the streets into lorries waiting to take them to prison. Chief Prison Officer Koenig was supervising the erection of special secure cages in hangars at the military airfield to create extra cells. Police reservists were being armed. Water cannon were being prepared. Emergency beds were being set up in the hospital. Extra blood supplies had been brought in.

Every time the door bell rang, Christoph and Wolfram expected to find the *Stasi* come to arrest them.

In the dining room at the SED Central Committee building on Berlin's Werdeschen Markt, the Politburo gathered punctually at one o'clock for lunch. Over the past weeks, the atmosphere at these communal mealtimes had been steadily deteriorating. Each knew that the others were planning against Honecker's retirement, but no one dared openly to show his hand. Nobody trusted anybody else. To back the wrong man might be to herald one's own political demise.

Never had the atmosphere been more icy than at lunch on Monday 9 October. All attempts at small talk were met by a

644

frosty silence. When the meal ended, Honecker stood up and asked Krenz to come to his office.

As he made to leave the room, Krenz turned and his eyes met Basilius's. His teeth were bared in a lupine smile.

Upon his return from Berlin the previous evening, Rudolf Sommer had gone straight to his office and remained there all night. Now that he was back in Liebenroda, he was assailed by doubts about the success of his mission. The more he thought about it, the less likely did it seem that the man who had so recently justified the massacre in Tiananmen Square would suddenly change his mind and stick his neck out in favour of reform. He had certainly not promised to halt the military operation. That wolfish smile might not have meant that he would intervene with Honecker. On the contrary, it could have been a presage of Rudolf's own imminent downfall. Yet to whom else could he have gone? Jarowinski was a nonentity. Schabowski and Modrow were in favour of reform and did not therefore enjoy Honecker's trust. Basilius and Krenz were the only ones who had influence over the leader.

It was a very long night and an even longer day.

Then, as whistles and bells sounded in factories and offices to mark the end of the working day, the telex arrived. The moment it was decoded, Sommer's adjutant brought it to him and stood, hovering curiously, while the Police Chief digested its contents.

Sommer's expression revealed no hint of his relief as he read Krenz's message. 'Thank you, Comrade Eppel. All senior officers are to report to me immediately.'

Cautiously, the first people headed towards Liebenroda's Church of St Thomas, prepared to find their way barricaded by troops and tanks, unsure what they would do if it was. But although there were more *Vopos* and police trucks about than normal on a Monday evening and *Stasi* agents were, as usual, lurking in doorways, no attempt was made to stop them.

The church gradually filled, until people were standing in the aisles and sitting on the floor. Late-comers were crammed into the doorway and overflowed into the churchyard.

At the end of the service, Christoph prayed: 'Defend us thy humble servants in all assaults of our enemies; that we, surely trusting in thy defence, may not fear the power of any adversaries . . .'

The congregation murmured, 'Amen.' Then they made their way out of the church again. In the roadway, they unfurled their home-made banners and set off towards the Marx-Engels-Platz.

What happened after that took even Christoph and Wolfram by surprise. They had counted on two or three thousand people at most attending the demonstration, possibly even fewer than normal because of the massive police and army presence. Instead, from every street, people were converging onto the square, young and old, students, families with young children, and the more who came, the more who seemed to follow them, until the Marx-Engels-Platz was a vast, jostling sea of humanity, rippling with banners and the shouting of impatient voices. 'Forty years are long enough!' 'We want free elections!' *'Wir sind das Volk!'* 'We are the people!'

For two, three hours, the protesters remained in the square, their numbers growing by the minute, until there must be 10,000 at least. Wolfram felt a great surge of triumph. Despite the danger, despite the fear, the people of Liebenroda were showing that they were not to be intimidated.

The mood of the security police watching from the windows of *Stasi* headquarters, grew increasingly angry. They held sub-machines at the ready to fire on the crowd, but unless Sommer gave the order they were impotent to act.

Sommer himself was host to a gamut of mixed emotions. He had helped avert one terror – but what would follow? He watched as Wolfram Schwidinski impaled his candle on a spike of the metal railings surrounding the *Stasi* building. Others followed his example, until the railings were full and the pavement, too, was covered with flickering candles, twinkling like a galaxy of stars. *A light shineth in the darkness . . .*

Then, as they had arrived, the people gradually dispersed.

The tanks had not moved from the *Stasi* courtyard. The soldiers were still in their barracks. Koenig's makeshift prison at the airfield was unoccupied and there were no new prisoners in the dungeons under the *Stasi* building. Not a shot had been fired. Not a drop of blood had been shed.

Christian Horst looked up from the neatly typewritten pages of the article entitled *Our Dying City* to its author. Paula Bauer had conveyed very vividly the atmosphere of Leipzig and the mood of its people. It was a damning indictment of life in a German industrial city in 1989. 'I suppose you don't have any photographs?'

'You mean – you like it?' Paula stammered. After leaving Axel Kraus that morning in the Gaensemarkt, she had remembered the rest of that television programme, including Stefan's explanation of why he did not publish anything derogatory about the GDR.

'It's concise, factual and your descriptions are very graphic.'

'But I thought *Aktuell* didn't publish articles on the GDR . . .'

'What gave you that impression? This is a news magazine.'

'I once saw Herr Jochum on television. He said . . .' Paula had thought very hard about mentioning her mother's one-time relationship with Stefan and finally decided against it.

Horst smiled. 'Our proprietor used to be rather nervous about upsetting the GDR authorities, but since you people have taken up cudgels on your own behalf, he's fully prepared to weigh in on your side, certainly on a topic like this, which is very near to his heart. So – pictures?'

'No, I'm sorry. My half-brother has some, but he's in Liebenroda.'

'Liebenroda?' Horst's eyebrows shot up. Forgetting about photographs, he rummaged through the pile of faxes and telexes on his desk until he found the paper he was looking for. 'I thought so. That's one of the towns where it looked as if the army was going to move in yesterday evening.'

The blood drained from Paula's cheeks. 'The army . . . ?'

'So far as we can gather, nothing happened, though it's difficult to get any clear idea of what's going on over there right now. Of course, we have a correspondent in East Berlin and stringers in most big cities, but all their reports are censored. Telephone lines, of course, are bugged. If the *Stasi* hear someone saying something they don't like, they just pull

647

the plug. So, at the moment, we're pretty well reliant on official news agency statements.' He paused. 'Your half-brother isn't on the phone?'

'At his office . . .'

Horst grimaced. 'It's not fair to involve him . . .'

'I think he'd be happy to give you any information you need, regardless of the danger. He's one of the leaders of the protest movement.'

'What's his name?'

Paula hesitated, then said, 'It's Schwidinski – Wolfram Schwidinski.'

'Schwidinski? That's familiar.' Again he rifled through his papers. 'Yes, I thought so. He appears to have been a founder member of New Forum. Good God! And he's your half-brother . . . ?'

As a result of the ensuing telephone conversation, *Aktuell* published not only Paula's article on Leipzig, but Wolfram's first-hand account of events in Liebenroda leading up to 9 October. Paula, in her first contact with home since August, was able to bring Wolfram up to date about herself and her family.

She received a 600 Mark fee for her article and Christian Horst also commissioned her to write another on the problems encountered by refugees on their arrival in the Federal Republic. 'You'll soon be able to afford a flat of your own,' the editor promised her.

In Liebenroda, Rudolf Sommer read through the transcript of Schwidinski's telephone conversation with the West German journalist and reflected wrily that he had portrayed the GDR authorities in an almost benevolent light. He gave orders that the lawyer's line continue to be tapped, but that his reports be allowed to go through unhindered.

Eight days later, on 18 October, at an extraordinary meeting of the Politburo, Honecker was removed from power and replaced as Head of Party by Egon Krenz, who publicly admitted that the Party had made mistakes and pledged himself to reform. Two other Politburo members, both notorious hardliners and supporters of Honecker, resigned.

The following Monday, 300,000 people took part in demonstrations in Leipzig, 20,000 in Liebenroda and tens of thousands in other towns and cities. The slogans grew bolder and more defiant: '*We* are the people: *you* should be going!' 'Privileges for all!' 'Get off your arses!' 'Demo – cracy!' 'Anti-SED – Pro-New Forum!' 'We're staying here!'

On Thursday, there came the first official recognition of New Forum in the form of a visit to Leipzig by Guenter Schabowski. But, although he repeated Krenz's vague assurances of travel and emigration concessions, he would make no firm commitment to a free press or a multi-party electoral system.

Wolfram, who was at that meeting, stopped by to see Erika before returning home to Liebenroda. He had already let her know that he had talked to Paula and was pleased to find his stepmother looking brighter than when he had last seen her. 'It's Heike's third birthday today,' she mused. 'Little did any of us think, this time last year, that she'd be celebrating it in Hamburg.'

Then she asked, 'Do you believe Krenz is genuine? Or did he change sides because he was frightened of going down with Honecker?'

Wolfram shrugged. 'He's certainly cunning, but the mere fact that he changed sides so quickly proves to me that he can't be trusted.'

'He can't continue making promises he doesn't keep,' Erika observed. 'Since I've been working at the hospital, I've met a lot of people and I can't get over how determined they all are. It's as if they've gone beyond the point of fear – nothing now is going to stop them . . .'

The Monday after that, Erika went to the demonstration with Nurse Kunert. As always, they went first to the Nikolai Church, then they all made their way to the Karl-Marx-Platz in Leipzig's city centre, where tens of thousands of demonstrators arrived from other parts of the city. Then, five, ten, twenty abreast, they set off to march round the city ring road, so many of them that they formed a dense, continuous circle. Despite the rain, the atmosphere was good humoured, with people applauding new banners as they were unfurled, which proclaimed: 'Egon Krenz

– incompetence.' 'Egon – who elected you?' 'Deeds first, Egon, then smile.'

But Nurse Kunert seemed unimpressed. 'Words, words, words,' she muttered, impatiently, as they walked along.

The nurse had brought a friend with her, a man called Peter Mueller, who now glanced at her mockingly. 'You never change, do you? What would you like to do – throw eggs at the police, set fire to the *Stasi* building? End up in prison again?'

Erika could not help but overhear this exchange, although she knew better than to comment upon it. For what reason, she wondered, could such a committed socialist as Sylvia Kunert have been sent to gaol?

Afterwards, it was reported that 500,000 people had taken to the streets in Leipzig, 80,000 in Schwerin, nearly 60,000 in Liebenroda – almost the entire populations.

On Wednesday, Krenz flew to Moscow for talks with Gorbachev and, on Friday, he called another extraordinary meeting of the Politburo, the outcome of which was in itself quite extraordinary. The border with Czechoslovakia was being reopened and yet more resignations were announced. The heads of the Confederation of Free German Trade Unions and the Metal Workers' Union had left after allegations of corruption. The leaders of the National Democratic and Christian Democratic Parties, token positions to give an illusion of democracy, had both been dismissed from office. Five Politburo members, all aged between seventy-three and eighty-one, had gone, including Erich Mielke, the head of the *Stasi*. Of the old guard, only Basilius Meyer remained.

In his telephone conversation with Christian Horst, Wolfram announced triumphantly, 'The balance of power is shifting. The Politburo is finally having to bow to popular and political pressure.'

On Saturday 4 November 1989, a million people took to the streets of East Berlin. There were babies and great-grandfathers, housewives and students, skinheads and graveyard hippies, teachers, nurses, miners, chimney sweeps, plumbers,

650

lawyers, factory workers, athletes and priests. They reached from the edge of the cordoned-off Pariser Platz in front of the Brandenburg Gate, up the wide avenue of Unter den Linden and into the adjoining streets, past the University, the Opera House and the statue of Frederick the Great, the Neue Wache – the memorial to the victims of fascism and militarism, the Arsenal – now the Museum of German History, across the Marx-Engels Bridge to the Marx-Engels-Platz, across the Liebknecht Bridge into the Alexanderplatz; a milling, chanting sea of humanity, almost hidden beneath their swirling banners, all bearing different slogans, all with the same message: reform.

Two of them were Gert Koenig and Jana Seifert. Far from deterred by the three weeks they had spent in prison after their arrests on 8 October, they were more determined than ever to continue the campaign for freedom.

East Germans were fleeing at a rate of 10,000 a day. Over a 100,000 were estimated to have left since Hungary opened its borders in September. The situation could not be allowed to continue. The GDR could not afford to lose so many workers and the Federal Republic was encountering problems in accommodating them and finding them jobs. Even West German politicians were pleading to them to stay at home and not bleed their country dry.

The Politburo met in session after session, trying to agree the legislation needed to bring about the new direction. Never before had events dictated to them. Never before had the members been so sharply divided among themselves. Never before had each member been as greatly aware of another waiting behind him ready to stab a knife into his back. Unanimity had become a thing of the past. Now each was looking to his own survival.

On the Monday after the massive demonstration in East Berlin, a compromise was reached and the Politburo agreed a new travel law, which allowed GDR citizens the right to visit the West for thirty days every year – although it did not lift the visa requirement and retained the right of the authorities to refuse a visa. Unappeased, thousands more left through Czechoslovakia

651

and an estimated three-quarters of a million took to the streets throughout the GDR.

The following day, when, under normal circumstances, they would have been celebrating the anniversary of the 1917 Bolshevik Revolution, the unthinkable happened. The parliamentary Justice Committee turned down the new law on the grounds that it was inadequate. For the first time in the Republic's history, the *Volkskammer* – the parliament – resigned. Constitutionally responsible to the *Volkskammer*, the Politburo had no alternative but also to resign.

When the new Politburo convened, with eleven instead of the previous twenty-five members, Krenz, Schabowski and the reformist Hans Modrow were among them, but Basilius Meyer was no longer of their number.

Right up to the end, Basilius had believed that Krenz would fall and that he would then be nominated to take over the leadership. But when it came to the vote, his colleagues unanimously heeded Krenz's recommendation that 'younger blood' was needed to steer the GDR on its new course.

The stomach cramps and nausea, which had plagued Basilius in the summer, but almost disappeared when he had believed himself to be within grasp of the leadership, had returned with a vengeance since Honecker's dismissal and Krenz's appointment as Head of Party and Head of State. And with every traumatic event which had occurred since then, his symptoms had worsened.

That night, he was gripped by pains more intense than he had ever experienced. His chest was so constricted that he could hardly breathe. His stomach hurt intolerably and his intestines felt as if they had become rigidly knotted up inside him. He lay flat on his back, his teeth clenched, his eyes shut, waiting for the agony to pass.

Irina turned on her bedside light, came across the room and sat down on the edge of his bed. Taking his hand, she said, 'I understand, Vasili. I know how it feels, the pain of betrayal. I, too, was dismissed today.' She spoke in Russian, as they had done during their courtship, all those long years ago, when the Republic was in its infancy.

652

How long since she had held his hand? How long since she had called him Vasili? Certainly not since they had moved into twin beds, thirty-five years ago, shortly after Reinhardt's birth. They had not been given to shows of affection and tenderness. Theirs had not been a romantic relationship, but a marriage of true minds. Their lives, unlike those of ordinary couples, had not been devoted to each other, but to the Party and the revolutionary cause.

Yet, at the end, they had only each other left.

At his office in Wilmersdorf, Stefan was watching the press conference being held by the new Minister of Information, Guenter Schabowski, at the International Press Centre on the Mohrenstrasse in East Berlin, broadcast live on both East and West German television. It was nearly seven o'clock on the evening of Thursday 9 November 1989.

For nearly an hour, Schabowski had been sitting behind a barrage of microphones, eloquently and relaxedly answering one question after another. The new citizens' movement, he said, had contributed decisively to the recent changes in Party policy and would soon be given official recognition. The Party was suggesting that consultation groups from both states should meet to discuss the question of travel and tourism in both directions. The SED was in favour of free, democratic elections . . .

Suddenly, an agitated-looking official appeared on the podium and handed him a note. Schabowski glanced at it then, almost casually, read its contents aloud. 'I have just been informed that the Council of Ministers of the GDR has decided . . . Private journeys abroad can now be undertaken without the conditions previously pertaining . . . In order to ease the burden on allied states, it has been further decided to open the border crossings between the GDR and the Federal Republic and West Berlin.'

For a moment, absolute silence reigned. Then pandemonium broke loose. 'Is that for emigration or for simple visits?' one reporter managed to make his voice heard.

Schabowski consulted his piece of paper. 'For both.'

'From when?'

'If I am correctly informed,' Schabowski said slowly, as if the implications of his incredible announcement were only now becoming clear to himself, and studying the piece of paper again to make sure that he had read its contents correctly, 'this regulation is valid immediately . . .'

Chapter 27

The Zum Kastanien bar in Prenzlauer Berg could have been any one of thousands of similar establishments throughout the GDR. It served weak local beer, Eastern bloc wines and spirits, and at eight o'clock on a Thursday evening, it was empty except for a few regulars playing cards, reading *Neues Deutschland* or cracking wary anti-government jokes with the landlord.

Jana yawned, not so much from tiredness as from boredom. What would it be like, she wondered for the umpteenth time, to work in a bar in West Berlin, in the Europa Centre or on the Kurfuerstendamm? West Berlin, it was said over here, never slept. In East Berlin there was nothing to keep people awake.

She thought about the demonstration the previous Saturday. Things seemed to have moved a bit since then. But there had been changes in the leadership before and they had not affected the ordinary people, except for the worst . . .

At that moment, the door burst open and Gert rushed in, his cheeks flushed, his eyes glowing with excitement. 'They're going to open the Bornholmer Strasse crossing point!' he yelled.

For a few seconds, there was a stupefied silence. Then came the sound of beer spilling on to the floor. Somebody laughed. 'Look what you've done! You've given Fritz such a shock he's forgotten where his mouth is!'

'It's true,' Gert said. 'Schabowski announced it on the radio. They're opening the border crossing to West Berlin.'

Within minutes, the bar had emptied. Jana looked hopefully at the landlord, who nodded understandingly, then she and Gert were heading up the dimly lit Schoenhauser Allee. People were leaning out of open windows, screaming excitedly across to their neighbours and down to others in the street, pouring out of doorways, many pulling on coats over their nightclothes and bundling their children into pushchairs as they went. Well before Jana and Gert reached the Bornholmer Strasse, the traffic jam began. There was a clamour of car horns, shouting and singing.

Hundreds of other pedestrians were waiting ahead of them at the checkpoint. Then, at quarter past nine, a mighty cheer arose. 'At last!' voices roared out. The crowd slowly began to edge forward. Other, anxious voices muttered, 'I haven't got a passport, only an identity card.' Word came back: 'An identity card will do – the guards are stamping special visas.'

The excited throng formed itself into an impatient but orderly queue. Jana's heart was thumping. 'I don't believe it! I don't believe it's really happening!' she kept repeating.

Then they reached border control, where their identity cards were stamped by a bewildered-looking guard. 'I can imagine how he must feel,' Gert murmured, recollecting his own border guard duties and more thankful than ever that his military service was behind him.

They crossed no-man's-land and approached the sign that announced: You are now entering the Allied Zone. Then, finally, they were through the Wall and hands were reaching out, dragging them into the ecstatically waving, laughing, cheering crowd on the other side. One person after another embraced and kissed them. 'Welcome to West Berlin!' 'Welcome!' 'Welcome!' Champagne corks were exploding like machine gun bullets. A young man thrust a glass into Jana's hand. 'Cheers, darling! Here's to freedom!' A little girl handed Gert a red rose.

'Have you ever been to West Berlin before?' someone asked them.

Gert shook his head dazedly. A lump in his throat prevented him from answering.

'Are you going to stay here?' somebody else asked.

'No,' Jana replied. 'I just want to see it with my own eyes.' But suddenly she couldn't see anything, for torrents of tears were streaming uncontrollably down her face. 'It's crazy,' she gulped. 'Oh, I'm so happy . . .'

Gisela had raced out of the Jochum as soon as she had heard the news. Warmly wrapped against the cold night in her skiing anorak, black ski pants and fleecy lined ankle boots, she had

656

joined the crowd bearing down the Street of 17th June towards the Brandenburg Gate, shouting, 'Down with the Wall!' 'Let them out!' 'The Wall must go!'

Not long after she reached the Wall, the crowd's anger turned to triumph. Cheers broke out. Hands were raised in the victory sign. Word passed from mouth to mouth: 'Bornholmer Strasse has been opened.'

A taunting voice yelled up to the border guards, 'You're about to become obsolete!' People broke into song, chanting, 'We shall overcome' and 'We shall tear down the Wall', putting new words to the tune of an old folksong.

Then, some time later: 'They've opened Checkpoint Charlie. They're letting people through on the Underground from Friedrich Strasse . . .'

Further cheers broke out as a young man actually clambered up on to the top of the Wall itself. After grinning defiantly at the guards, he drew himself upright and stood with his back to them, his arms outstretched, his fingers splayed in the victory sign. An East Berlin water cannon drenched him. Cameras flashed and the moment was recorded for posterity: the first time any civilian had ever stood on the Wall and not been shot.

Undeterred by the water, another youth joined him. Then another and another, until along the length of the Wall, West Berliners – including Gisela – were clambering up, hoisted onto the shoulders of others below and pulled upright by willing hands waiting above. Soon, there were hundreds of them, waving, singing and cheering, and the water cannon ceased.

The crowd continued to swell and the atmosphere grew ever more jubilant. To all the other sounds was added that of hammering, as people began attacking the Wall with sledge-hammers and crowbars. 'Hey, look!' someone called, pointing over the heads of the border guards across the Pariser Platz. Shadowy figures could be seen dodging the guards – who were amazingly doing nothing to stop them – sprinting across the square, running between the columns of the Brandenburg Gate. 'Come on, Zonies! Come up and join us!'

Some West Berliners even jumped down from the Wall onto the Eastern side and still the guards did not react. As from

657

nowhere, more and more East Berliners appeared under the Gate and raced past the guards.

Gisela felt tipsy, but it was as much from the excitement as the champagne she had drunk, bottles of which seemed to be appearing out of nowhere. Everyone was singing: 'Such a day, as wonderful as this one, Such a day should never end . . .'

By the early hours of the morning, West Berlin had turned into one huge impromptu street party, which stretched from the Street of 17th June, renamed with a makeshift sign Street of 9th November, past the vast Europa Centre shopping precinct and the Kaiser Wilhelm Memorial Church, way down the Ku'damm, which was ablaze with light, and where, although shops and department stores were closed, bars, pubs, cafés and discos were still very much open.

The traffic was jammed solid, the progress of the stinking, spluttering Trabbis and Wartburgs constantly hindered by hands beating on their roofs and bonnets, by people insisting on shaking hands with and kissing all the occupants, and showering them with confetti, flowers and sweets. Added to the volume of voices and blaring music, was the triumphant honking of car horns.

Gert and Jana had reached the Ku'damm and were gazing wonderingly at the displays in shop windows. 'Everything's so expensive,' Jana murmured. 'A hundred and fifty Marks for a pair of jeans! Who can afford that?'

'Not us, that's certain,' Gert commented wryly. He pointed to a sign put out by an enterprising nightclub owner, offering to exchange fourteen East Marks for one Deutschmark. 'That's about two thousand East Marks! You could buy forty pairs for that at home and still have change.'

'Look at that fruit!' Jana exclaimed, as they passed a pavement barrow doing a roaring trade. 'I'd love to take some bananas home for my Mum.'

'Here you are, love.' The costermonger overheard her. 'Have these with my compliments. Bring your Mum with you next time. If you take after her, she must be a good-looking woman . . .'

Jana took her gift disbelievingly. 'Thank you . . .'

Gert was staring, wide-eyed, at the photographs displayed outside a Sex Club. 'Come on in,' the doorman invited. 'The show is free of charge tonight for Zonies.' Gert clutched Jana's hand more firmly and they moved on.

Suddenly, he stopped dead on the pavement. 'Good God! Café Jochum ... The Hotel Jochum ...' He gazed in awe at the canopied entrance, flanked by two splendidly uniformed commissionnaires, past whom a stream of people were flowing in and out.

An attractive, auburn-haired young woman, who was about to enter the hotel, overheard his words and turned to smile at them. 'Come and look round if you want,' she said.

Gert looked at her doubtfully and she laughed infectiously. 'Tonight is open night in West Berlin, including the Hotel Jochum!' As Gert still hesitated, she asked, 'Where do you come from?'

Since Gert seemed lost for words, Jana replied, 'Prenzlauer Berg. I work in a bar there. I've never been in a hotel like this in my life. Would it really be all right for us to come in?'

Again the young woman laughed. 'Of course.'

Finally Gert found his tongue. 'Do you know anything about the owners – about the Jochums?'

'Quite a lot – why?'

'Well, er, I know it sounds crazy, but I think I may be related to them. My father's parents and sister came over here just before the Wall went up. My grandmother's name is Koenig, but her maiden name was Jochum – Monika Jochum ...'

The young woman gazed at him, open-mouthed. 'Your – your grandmother is called Monika Koenig?' she finally managed to stutter. The throng of pedestrians pushed their way past them, as they stood, blocking the pavement. 'But that's incredible ... That means ... Yes, that means you're – *my* cousin!'

'*Your* cousin?' Gert gasped.

'I'm Gisela Wild. My mother is Senta, your father's sister ...'

She was amazing, this elegant old lady, who was Gert's great-grandmother, of whose existence he had never been aware. There she sat in her high-backed chair by the window,

659

as if it were the most natural thing in the world to be awake at three o'clock in the morning, drinking champagne. From time to time, she glanced down onto the Ku'damm where, judging by the noise, the revelries were reaching their peak, and murmured, 'What a wonderful night. But I always said the Wall could not last for ever. It was such an unnatural boundary.'

'It was put up to stop the people from getting out,' Jana laughed. 'Now it's been opened to stop people from running away. If that isn't logic!'

Viktoria smiled. She liked her new-found great-grandson and his little girlfriend. They made a good pair. Gert reminded her of Karli, rather serious, unsure in his new surroundings, but determined not to let on that he was at all intimidated. 'It wouldn't have happened if it weren't for the courage of people like yourselves,' she said. 'As my son, Stefan, remarked recently, you have all voted with your feet . . .'

Gisela plied them with questions about their lives, how they lived, where they had gone to school, where they worked, how much they earned, explaining, 'I've met so few people from the GDR until tonight.'

When Jana said she earned 800 East Marks a month, she was horrified. 'But how can you live on that?'

Jana shrugged. 'Rents and food are cheap. And most of the things you would like to buy aren't available. For instance, a Trabant costs fourteen thousand Marks, but since there's at least a ten-year waiting list for a car, you have plenty of time to save up.'

As for entertainment, when Jana said she and Gert sometimes went to a cabaret or the pictures, but mostly their free time was spent talking to friends, Gisela exclaimed that she could not imagine an existence where she could not go to the theatre, opera or a nightclub whenever she chose.

'We enjoy a lot of sport and outdoor activities,' Gert said defensively. He was starting to feel rather oppressed by the conversation. Gisela was extremely friendly and undoubtedly kind, but she was cross-questioning them as if they were some kind of freaks and judging them by Western criteria of affluence and sophistication. When the novelty wears off, she'll despise

660

us, he thought. 'We go walking, whenever we can, out of Berlin. And swimming.'

'Gert's at college, training to be a football instructor,' Jana cut in. 'His team won the Junior First Division championship three years ago.'

'My daughter Monika – your grandmother – used to be very sporty,' Viktoria said. 'She and her husband lived in Fuerstenmark. Is that where your parents live, Gert?'

'No, they're in a town called Liebenroda.'

He did not want to talk about his parents. For a short while they had been joined by Gisela's mother, one of whose first questions had been about her brother. 'Heini was in the army when I last saw him,' she had said. 'What's he doing now?' Senta's tone of voice clearly conveyed the fact that she had little love lost for him. If Gert had known her better, he might have told her the truth, but he simply could not bear the idea of admitting that his father worked for the hated *Stasi*. Instead, he had replied vaguely, 'He's a government official.'

'First thing in the morning,' Viktoria went on, 'I'll telephone Monika and tell her we've met you. She'll be so thrilled. She was so fond of your father. She and Hans live in Worms – that's near Frankfurt. Hans was a schoolteacher, before he retired. They could fly here tomorrow afternoon and we could meet up again in the evening. Perhaps your parents could come as well . . .'

The mere idea of meeting a grandmother who still dreamed of dear little Heini filled Gert with dread, while the thought of a family reunion of the kind Viktoria was suggesting was beyond the scope of his imagination. He said, 'I'm afraid I'm busy tomorrow evening.'

Viktoria studied him from shrewd, hooded eyes, as he perched uneasily on the edge of his chair, tightly clutching the stem of his champagne flute, and wondered why he was so nervous. 'What a pity,' she said evenly. 'Well, hopefully another time. You will always be welcome here, both of you.'

The sheer raw emotion of that night of 9 November 1989, the night the Wall was opened, was something no one would ever forget. All night long, thousands upon thousands upon

661

thousands of East Berliners streamed into the West on foot, by Underground and in cars. When an icy dawn broke on Friday morning, it was to reveal them contentedly, if wearily, returning to their homes and jobs, and long queues of cars still waiting to enter West Berlin for the first time.

At the Bornholmer Strasse checkpoint, a taxi drew to a halt. Gert shook Gisela's hand. 'Thank you for your hospitality.'

'Yes,' Jana said, clutching her bananas, 'thank you for everything.'

They waved Gisela goodbye, then, before they crossed the border, Gert turned round to look at Wedding. 'It's just as sad and grey as Prenzlauer Berg,' he commented. 'Even in the West, there are poor people and rich people. They can't all afford to stay at the Hotel Jochum.'

'Gert, what's wrong? They were so kind, especially the old lady. Why don't you want to see them again?'

He sighed. 'It's too complicated to explain. I guess everything just happened too quickly . . .'

'It's your father, isn't it? Every time they mentioned him, you went all strange.'

Gert's mouth tightened grimly. He had still not been able to bring himself to admit to Jana what his father did. He reached in his anorak pocket for his cigarettes. 'My father runs the *Stasi* prison in Liebenroda,' he said.

For a long time she was silent. Then she took his hand. 'Now I start to understand. Come on. It's freezing. Let's go back to my place and have some breakfast.'

'I thought, if you knew, you might not want to see me again . . .'

'Then you obviously still have a lot to learn about me,' Jana said.

The guards waved them through without so much as a glance at their papers.

At the Brandenburg Gate, drunken youths from both sides of the city were hurling obscenities at the border guards, together with beer cans, empty bottles and chunks of Wall. Army lorries drove into the Pariser Platz, from which armed troops in combat gear jumped down. A voice blared through loudspeakers, 'I ask

662

you, please, in your own interests, to leave the Wall. I cannot guarantee your safety if order is not restored at the State border of the German Democratic Republic . . .'

'No China!' somebody shouted. 'Not the 17th June again!' came from another. Klaus Feldmann staggered to his feet and raised his hand in the Nazi salute. '*Heil Scheiss!*' he shouted in a slurred voice. 'Fuck the *Stasi!*'

Until that evening, when he had met up with East Berliners for the first time, he had scarcely been aware of the existence of the *Stasi*, any more than the Zonies had known about neo-Nazis. Now they had all joined up, with one very definite object of hatred. 'Fuck the *Stasi!*' Klaus yelled again.

The voice behind the megaphone ordered: 'Turn the hoses on them!'

Not only did the checkpoints remain open and other transit points between the GDR and the Federal Republic open that weekend, allowing through streams of cars which, at times, formed queues sixty kilometres long, but the Berlin Wall began to come down.

On Friday night, bulldozers arrived at Eberswalder Strasse, just a few hundred metres from Zum Kastanien, and in the early hours of the morning a crane lifted away a large slab of the Wall. Although Gert was reluctant to go near the Hotel Jochum, he and Jana could not resist joining the crowd which poured through this first real breach in the Berlin Wall.

By Sunday night, there were ten gaps, including one at the Potsdamer Platz, the heart of Berlin at the time when Karl Jochum had opened the first Café Jochum in 1883 and a derelict wasteland since the end of the war when it became part of the Soviet Sector.

Souvenir-hunters vied for bits of the Wall to take home with them. A Californian multi-millionaire publicly offered Egon Krenz 50 million dollars for the right to break up the Wall and sell it at three dollars a piece.

The Federal government gave one hundred Deutschmarks 'greetings money' to every one of the millions of East Germans who swarmed across the border that weekend and, all day long, there were long queues outside banks. But, thanks to

663

the generosity of West Berliners, most East Germans were able to save their hundred Marks for their next visit, for most entertainment was free to them.

Café Jochum was one of many establishments on the Ku'damm serving free coffee to visitors from the GDR, but it also did a thriving general trade, as West Berliners urged their hospitality upon East Berliners, plying them with food and drink. A Stuttgart businessman, a guest at the hotel, instructed the staff in Hasso's Bar to serve the Zonies beers on his account up to a value of 10,000 Marks.

Gert was at last able to fulfil his ambition to see Hertha play live in a match for which all East Berliners were given free tickets. At Checkpoint Charlie, against the colourful graffiti background of the Wall, the cellist, Mstislav Rostropovich, gave a solo recital of the music of Bach in memory of the seventy-eight people who had lost their lives trying to escape over the Wall and the hundred and eleven who had been killed along the rest of the border between Germany and Germany. The Berlin Philharmonic put on a free concert and there was a free rock concert at the Deutschlandhalle, which lasted twelve hours and where the audience was so huge that many fans never saw their idols but only heard them through loudspeakers.

Whilst the celebrations continued, politicians were determining Germany's destiny. From East Berlin came the news that four members of Egon Krenz's new Politburo had been sacked and Krenz himself assured a rally that free elections would be forthcoming, although he set no date. 'Reforms will not be turned back,' he promised. 'They will lead to a new revolution on German soil with a socialism that is morally pure and politically democratic.'

Cutting short an official visit to Poland, Chancellor Helmut Kohl arrived on Friday evening to address a massive freedom rally in front of the City Hall in Schoeneberg, where once President Kennedy had uttered those famous words: '*Ich bin ein Berliner.*' What Kohl said was to have an even more dramatic impact upon his audience. Flanked by his Foreign Minister, Hans-Dietrich Genscher, the Mayor of Berlin, Walter Momper, and Willy Brandt, who had been Mayor of Berlin at the time the Wall went up, Kohl announced, 'Long live a free German fatherland, a free united Europe!' He waited for the cheers – and the boos, inevitable in this traditionally most socialist of all German cities – to die down, then went on: 'We are and will remain one nation and we belong together. Step by step, we must find the way to our common future.'

As the headline 'WE ARE ONE NATION' was splashed across newspapers across the world and interpreted as an announcement of German reunification, others tried to defuse the situation. On Saturday, Mayor Momper impressed upon a press conference that the Chancellor was 'out of touch with the current feelings of the people in this historic time' and had not understood what was happening in the GDR.

Needless to say, there was one television programme after another on the weekend's events and that evening, Stefan took part in a live debate on their long-term outcome. When the chairman asked the CDU panellist why Kohl had made his statement, he replied, 'I believe the Chancellor was carried away by the euphoria of the moment. The atmosphere here has been emotionally very highly charged, as we all know. When he said, "We are one nation," he was meaning we are all Germans. It was intended as a expression of solidarity towards our brothers in the GDR.'

'It's a pity he didn't choose his words more carefully,' Stefan observed drily. 'Reunification has come onto the agenda very much sooner than it should, if, in fact, it should have appeared at all. As Mayor Momper has pointed out, the Chancellor should heed more carefully what our fellow Germans in the GDR are saying. Their words are, "We are the people" not "We are one people". That's why they have been saying, "We're staying here!" They want the GDR to remain an independent – but a united – state. They want freedom to cross the border: they do not want the border taken away.'

'Our Constitution still contains the reunification clause,' the CDU man reminded him. 'However, I agree that there is no hurry to implement it.'

Dieter Duschek was also on the panel, his concern very much the dire environmental state of the GDR, which *Actuell* had done a lot to expose in recent weeks, since Paula Bauer's first article. 'In my opinion, as well as actively encouraging the democracy movement, we should be seeking to improve living conditions in the GDR, perhaps by means of financial aid.'

'Why should our taxpayers finance another state's inefficiency?' demanded the fourth member of the panel, a member of the Bavarian CSU.

The following morning, Stefan spoke to Wolfram Schwidinski on the telephone, who said, 'We saw you on television yesterday evening. It was interesting to note that all four panellists were against reunification. What do you think caused Kohl to make such an ill-considered statement?'

'He's an opportunist. He'd like to be King Kohl of Germany.'

'Which would be the very worst thing that could happen. We are happy being a socialist state. We do not want to be run from capitalist Bonn.' Schwidinski paused. 'Has it occurred to you that the Federal Republic seems to be deciding our future for us? What would happen, I wonder, if unification did take place?'

'Come to Berlin,' Stefan urged. 'I'd like to meet you and I'll ensure your voice is heard.'

Schwidinski hesitated for a moment, then promised, 'I will come. But not yet. There's still too much to be done here.'

'What's the next stage in your campaign?'

'Today the *Volkskammer* is meeting in a session which is being televised live. But until New Forum and other political parties are legalized and we have the guarantee of free elections, we shall continue to hold our usual Monday evening demonstrations . . .'

'You did *what?*' Heinrich Koenig demanded, the blood rushing to his face.

'I went to West Berlin. I went to the Hotel Jochum. I met your sister, Senta, my cousin, Gisela, and my great-grandmother,' Gert repeated defiantly down the telephone. 'I've been invited to meet your parents . . .'

'And they turned your head,' Heinrich said scathingly. 'They welcomed you to the bosom of the family. And told you all sorts of lies about me.'

'No,' Gert replied, 'you were hardly mentioned. There were other far more important things to talk about.'

666

'So what is the object of this telephone call?'

'I thought you might be interested to know how your family is, and that you, too, might like to see them again.' It had taken Gert several days to get clear in his mind what he wanted to say to his father, but now he was absolutely sure of his words.

'They aren't my family. They ceased to be my family when they defected to the West. They're traitors to the socialist cause.'

'No,' Gert said, calmly, 'it is you who are the traitor. Did you see the television yesterday? Members of the *Volkskammer* accused Party big-wigs of abusing their office – and those men apologized. Will you also admit that you have made mistakes?'

Heinrich had seen the programme on the television at *Stasi* headquarters, or rather as much of it as he could bear to watch: the first ever secret ballot to elect a speaker, the election by the *Volkskammer* of Hans Modrow as the new Prime Minister, the humiliating self-criticisms and apologies by ex-Ministers and, finally, the expulsion of many former Politburo members, including Erich Honecker and Basilius Meyer, from the Party. The manner in which this latter had been carried out had particularly appalled Heinrich. Honecker had been too ill to attend the *Volkskammer* and speak out in his own defence. He was said to have cancer and to have suffered a recent heart attack. Meyer had been there, but clearly crippled with pain.

Even while the proceedings had been going on, Schwidinski's demonstrators had arrived in the Marx-Engels-Platz with their flickering candles and their slogans. 'We are the people!' 'Reform not cosmetics!' 'Egon has made mistakes – he's still making them!'

'The only mistake I have made,' Heinrich informed his son coldly, 'is not to have shot anarchists like Schwidinski while I had the chance. If you believe that what is happening now is going to lead to democracy, you're a fool, Gert. You're being misled, like all the others. This is a fascist, counter-revolutionary conspiracy, master-minded by Kohl, to gain control of our beloved fatherland ...'

Gert put the receiver back on its cradle and turned to Jana. 'I wonder what will happen to him ... Poor Mother ...'

667

'Now you've made the final break with him, will you go back and see your people in West Berlin?' Jana asked.

He shook his head in indecision. 'I don't know. I'd have to tell them about my father. I'm still afraid that they'll assume I'm tarred with the same brush . . .'

Jana gave a sigh of exasperation. 'I think you're being over-sensitive. It's not your fault he's in the *Stasi*. You haven't anything to feel guilty about.' Then, as Gert continued to prevaricate, she said, 'Well then, I'll go on my own. The old lady invited us both. I want to see her again. I thought she was wonderful . . .'

In the face of her determination, Gert had no alternative but to give in.

Viktoria lifted her sherry glass to the young couple. 'How lovely that you have come back again so soon to see us. Monika was very excited, when I told her about you. Then I realized we didn't know where either of you live.'

'I knew that Jana worked in a bar in Prenzlauer Berg,' Gisela laughed, 'and that Gert was at a sports college.'

'And she was fully prepared to go looking for you,' Senta added.

Very conscious of Jana's fixed meaningful gaze, Gert looked from one to the other of the three women. Then, summoning up his courage, he said, 'There's something I think you should know. You see, I wasn't entirely honest with you last time. I told you my father was a government official. In fact, he works for the *Stasi*. He's senior prison officer at the *Stasi* prison . . .'

But his announcement did not cause the shock waves he had feared. Senta nodded calmly. 'That doesn't surprise me in the slightest. Even when he was a little boy, Heini used to inform on the rest of us . . .'

'I think you were the unusual one, Senta, dear,' Viktoria said. 'Under the Nazis everyone informed on everyone else and the Communists continued the same system. Heini was simply a child of his time . . .'

'That doesn't excuse him!' Gert exclaimed hotly. 'He enjoys the power he holds over people and the fear he inspires in them.'

668

Senta nodded. 'I can imagine that. He was always a bully.'

Gert took a gulp of sherry.

'Surely you didn't think we would hold your father's job against you?' Gisela asked.

'You could well have assumed that like father, like son.'

Viktoria laid a wrinkled hand on his. 'When you get to know us better, Gert, you'll realize that we would never have done that. But I can understand your trepidation. I experienced a similar sort of thing at the end of the war. Then, the rest of the world assumed that all Germans were Nazis. Since then, I have believed more firmly than ever that everyone should be judged as an individual . . .'

'You see!' Jana told Gert triumphantly. 'I said you were over-reacting!' She turned to the others. 'He's daft. If it doesn't bother me that his father is in the *Stasi*, I couldn't see why it should worry you. I've never met his father, but I know Gert doesn't take after him. He's a rebel, for a start. His father wanted him to stay in the military, but Gert refused – and since then, he's opposed his father all the way . . .'

Gert stared at her. He had never thought of himself as a rebel before, let alone heard himself described as one. And in a sudden flash, it occurred to him that he had Jana to thank for the course his life had taken. If he had not met her, he would probably have remained a soldier and never taken part in any demonstrations, in which case he would certainly not be sitting in this room today . . .

All night long Basilius had been raving deliriously. 'All I ever wanted was the good of the people,' he kept repeating, as he had stated in front of the *Volkskammer*, 'Irina, you know that. I've never abused my power. They accused me of corruption. They've expelled me from the Party . . . No, they can't . . . They can't expel me from the Party . . .'

Irina sat by his bedside, hoping that he would fall asleep from sheer nervous exhaustion, but at the same time trying to decide what to do if his condition did not improve. In the past, their status had entitled them to priority medical treatment, but now everything had changed. Would Dr Vith refuse to treat him?

Would he say that Basilius had to report to a general hospital like anyone else?

Surely not? Surely Dr Vith would realize that to put Basilius in a general ward would be to kill him? But there was no certainty about that any more than there was about anything else. There was no certainty that they could remain in their house, that they would not suddenly find themselves homeless – or even in prison. The hostile demonstrators outside the *Volkskammer* yesterday evening had been baying for blood, demanding that the former leadership be brought to court and tried. She would not put it past Krenz and Modrow to give in to the rabble, if only in a last-ditch attempt to save their own skins.

Basilius burst into an uncontrollable flood of tears and Irina knew she had no choice but to call the doctor. However, when she got through to his office, she did not say that her husband appeared to be having some kind of mental breakdown, but that he was suffering from a severe worsening of his stomach condition.

Dr Vith arrived surprisingly quickly, felt Basilius's pulse, took his temperature and blood pressure, listened to his heart, and administered a sedative. Then he asked Irina if he could have a few words with her alone.

Standing in their lounge, looking out through the picture window on to the garden, he said, 'I think the best thing would be to take him into the Buch Clinic. He'll be safe there.'

'You're on our side?' The words burst out before Irina could stop them.

Still with his back to her, he said, 'This new regime will not last long. After that, who knows what will happen? My job is secure at the moment – but in a month, two months' time . . .' He reached into his breast pocket and withdrew a cigar. 'A change of climate would do Comrade Meyer good. Your son is in Chile, if I recall? Then why not combine convalescence with a vacation . . .?'

An hour later, an ambulance arrived to take Basilius to hospital. Irina watched it drive off, then sat down to begin a letter to her son.

*   *   *

670

Although most of the estimated three and a half million East Germans who had visited West Berlin and the Federal Republic that weekend returned home, there were many who ignored the pleas of politicians on both sides to stay in the GDR. According to official figures issued by Bonn, a quarter of a million East Germans had already fled to the West that year, as well as another 300,000 ethnic Germans, mainly from Poland and the Soviet Union.

Bremen had announced that it could not cope with any more refugees, while the Mayor of Stuttgart had described the situation as a 'state of national emergency.' Although the flood of refugees via Hungary and Czechoslovakia had dried up to a trickle, the number arriving in West Berlin was increasing and the camp at Berlin-Marienfelde was filled to overflowing.

For much the same reasons as he had been sent to Hamburg – because he knew the city and could easily obtain accommodation – Axel Kraus was one of several social workers relocated to Berlin to help cope with the influx.

Shortly after his arrival, he was interviewed briefly during a television report on the refugee crisis. In a deliberately provocative statement, the interviewer pointed out that the constitutional right to asylum was meant to ensure that anybody persecuted elsewhere should be able to find sanctuary in the Federal Republic, and asked, 'Since most emigrants from the GDR are leaving for economic reasons, not as a result of political and religious persecution, wouldn't you agree that they should be refused asylum?'

Axel had his answer ready. 'No, I would not. I have met many East Germans who have been imprisoned because of their beliefs – or whose families have been. What we need most at the moment, in my opinion, is charity. When a similar situation occurred in the 1950s, we welcomed our fellow Germans from the Soviet zone with open arms, because we were in desperate need of workers and, indeed, when the Berlin Wall went up, we had to import guest workers. Now, we are faced with rising unemployment. The rules can't be changed just to suit our personal economic circumstances.'

He was home at Dieter and Kleo's when the programme was broadcast. 'Well said,' Dieter congratulated him. The television

671

cameras moved to East Berlin to show a drunken gang of skinheads causing a disturbance near the Alexanderplatz, then panned in on an overturned police car and a swastika painted on a wall. Dieter sucked in his breath. 'And there's another part of the equation . . .'

As Erika and Nurse Kunert went about their increasingly arduous duties at the hospital, hampered by the lack of clean bedlinen, dressings, toilet paper and medicaments, the nurse asked, 'Have you been across to the West since the border opened?'

Erika shook her head. She found the sheer speed at which everything was changing not only staggering, but bewildering and rather frightening. It was only three months since Paula had gone on holiday to Hungary and already she was embarked upon a new career in Hamburg. Just two months had passed since the formation of New Forum and now Wolfram was not only speaking on the telephone to Stefan, but talking about meeting him. A mere month ago, it had looked as if Basilius Meyer might take over the leadership from Honecker, yet now he had been sacked from the Party.

In theory, there was nothing to fear any more. But although the physical borders were open, there was still a barricade in Erika's mind. Everyone else seemed so overjoyed at the Wall coming down, but for her it had provided a strange sense of security. She had felt safe with her memories. 'Everything's happened so quickly,' she replied hesitantly. 'I can't adjust as swiftly as young people.'

'Aren't you going to visit your daughter?'

'Maybe,' Erika prevaricated. She did not know Nurse Kunert nearly well enough to admit that, much though she would love to see Paula again, she was afraid she would feel very out of place in the sophisticated new life Paula was creating for herself, and she certainly could not tell her how nervous she felt at the possibility of seeing Stefan again.

Paula had not met Stefan yet, for he apparently lived in West Berlin and only occasionally went to Hamburg, but she mentioned him during her telephone calls home, just as Wolfram did during their everyday conversations. From

672

having been a distant figure, Stefan had suddenly become almost frighteningly close.

He still meant so much to her. But when she tried to visualize a reunion, her imagination failed her, so unlikely did it seem that the distinguished figure she watched on television would want to have anything again to do with her . . .

'My son was on television last night,' Nurse Kunert said suddenly.

Sure she had once told her that her son was dead, Erika stared at her in astonishment, but the nurse was too engrossed in her own thoughts to notice. Then she went on, 'I have to see him again. I have to.' Erika was shocked out of her own reflections by the very real and deep anguish in her voice.

Axel did not take any particular notice of the woman waiting outside the refugee centre gates when he came off-duty that evening. Another refugee, he assumed and, pulling the collar of his sheepskin jacket up around his ears, hurried towards his car. Only as he unlocked the door, did he realize she had followed him. Then she said, 'Moon Child . . .'

For a moment, his heart seemed to stop beating. Slowly, he straightened himself and turned to face her.

'Moon Child,' she said again, coming towards him, her hands outstretched. 'I'm your mother.'

She looked different from what he had imagined, taller and more angular, her face more lined, her hair a nondescript shade of mid-brown, flecked with grey.

He wanted to get into the car and drive away to the security of Kleo and Dieter's home in Dahlem, where Kleo would be getting supper and Oskar doing his homework. But it was as if he were cemented to the spot and could not move. And all he could think to say was, 'My name is Alexander.' His voice sounded curiously high-pitched and defiant, like a boy's. He cleared his throat.

'They called you Axel on the television programme. But it doesn't matter. To me you will always be Moon Child.'

'What do you want?'

'To talk to you. Is that so strange?'

673

'I don't want to hear. Please go away – back to wherever you came from.'

An expression of very real pain distorted her features. 'I knew they would have poisoned your mind against me. It was inevitable. But I've changed, Moon Child. I'm no longer the same person. I realize now that I made some terrible mistakes.'

He hesitated and she seized her advantage. 'I heard you say on the television, "What we need most at the moment is charity." Do those refugees, those strangers, mean more to you than your own mother? You're helping them, Moon Child – help me, too. At least listen to what I have to say . . .'

It was very cold. She shivered and huddled her arms around her poor-quality windcheater. He noticed she was wearing no gloves. 'All right,' he said, gruffly, 'get into the car.'

Automatically, he set off in the direction of Dahlem and while he drove, she talked. 'They told you that I murdered innocent children, didn't they? They told you I killed my own uncle? I promise you, I didn't mean to kill them.'

Axel gazed stonily through the windscreen, trying to ignore the passion in her voice, reminding himself of what Matthias had told him, all those years ago at Heiligensee. 'I was driving the motorbike,' Matthias had said. 'Helena was riding pillion with the gun.'

'They still died,' he said. 'Eight people died because of you. Nine, if you include my father.'

She grasped his arm. 'No, I didn't kill Marko. The police killed Marko. I loved him. I loved him more than anyone in the world, apart from you.'

'At the trial, Marko was portrayed as the master-mind behind Black Kommando,' Axel heard Matthias's voice saying, 'but he wasn't. Marko was weak. He did what Helena ordered. To Helena, everyone was expendable, including her own flesh and blood . . .'

'You had a funny way of showing your love,' he said. 'You abandoned me when I was only a few months old.'

'No, that's not true! My mother stole you from me, like she took everything else.' In an emotional, almost incoherent, outburst, she described her sense of alienation as a child, how

674

she had been discarded by her father, hated by her mother, ignored by her brother and pitied by her sister. She told how she had identified with the Jews and felt herself to be persecuted as they had been, and how she had turned against an immoral society from which she felt herself excluded and to which she did not want to belong.

Her voice rose to an ever higher pitch. 'That's why I formed Black Kommando. I wanted to destroy the State, I wanted to destroy the structure of fascist, imperialist, capitalist society. But I was wrong. Instead of destroying, I should have been creating. That's why I came back for you in Hamburg. And that's why I've come back now. I want you to return with me to the GDR. We have to save socialism from defeat . . .'

Axel drew up at a red traffic light. 'You've been living in the GDR?'

'It's where I should always have lived, in a country which practises social equality, solidarity, internationalism, pacifism. It frightens me that all this may be lost.'

He glanced at her. A fanatical light glittered in her eyes. 'If life is so wonderful in the GDR, why are so many people leaving?'

'They're money-grubbers, traitors to the socialist cause . . . But there are many wonderful people over there, too. I know. I work with them.'

'What work do you do?'

'I'm a children's nurse at a Leipzig hospital. I told you, I've changed. I've tried to rectify the mistakes I made . . .'

She's mad, Axel thought. So is whoever allowed her to work anywhere near children. And when she realizes that her utopian socialist state will never exist, she'll start the killing all over again . . .

The traffic moved on. They were approaching Dahlem now. He glanced at his watch, then, as casually as he could, said, 'I was supposed to be meeting someone. I'd like to call them and tell them I can't make our appointment.'

'Oh, yes, of course . . .'

He stopped at a telephone box and took the keys from the ignition. When he had finished his call, he got back in the car. 'You phoned the police, didn't you?' Helena asked tonelessly.

675

He did not answer.

She laid her head against his shoulder and began to cry – strange, soundless tears, which streamed down her cheeks and splashed on to her hands. Her hands were rough and worn, he noticed, the nails cut short and square. For some reason, they filled him with pity. Impulsively, he laid his own protectively over them.

There was a wailing of sirens and blue lights flashing through the night, a screeching of tyres, as the police cars slewed to a halt, then a slamming of doors and pounding of feet.

In a voice little more than a whisper, Helena said, 'I still love you, Moon Child. I always shall . . .'

'Former member of the Black Kommando terrorist gang, Helena Kraus, was apprehended in West Berlin yesterday evening,' the news reader announced. 'Kraus and her lover, Maximilian Markovic, were responsible for a series of bank raids, a car bomb attack and several murders in the early 1970s . . .'

Erika stared, aghast, as a police photograph of Nurse Kunert was flashed up on the television screen. 'Kraus's son, a social worker in West Berlin, was unavailable for comment, but her lawyer, Dr Dieter Duschek, stated at a press conference this afternoon that, since her escape from West Berlin in 1977, Kraus has been living in Leipzig. A Bonn spokesman says that the matter of her escape and entry into the GDR will be raised with the GDR government. With another five years of her original sentence to complete, Kraus is now being held in a high security prison . . .'

Everything fell into place. '*I had a little boy of my own. I lost him when I was very young.' 'You never change, do you? What would you like to do – throw eggs at the police, set fire to the Stasi building? End up in prison again?' 'I have to see him. I have to.*'

'In the GDR, there have been further revelations of corruption. Members of Erich Honecker's Politburo ran expensive Western cars, went on luxury cruises and owned private hunting lodges, all paid for from State funds. It is reported that some even amassed fortunes in Swiss bank accounts . . .'

Erika switched off the television and thought about Nurse Kunert. Surely she had already suffered enough? Whatever crimes she had committed in the past, she had made up for them since . . .

Police Chief Rudolf Sommer looked down on the chanting crowd, swirling banners and flickering candles in the freezing, foggy Marx-Engels-Platz. It was 27 November – only twelve weeks since the demonstrators, led by Schwidinski and Margraf, had staged their first protest march, that evening the formation of New Forum had been announced; eight weeks since the fortieth anniversary celebrations, when he had made those desperate pleas to Basilius and Egon Krenz to stop the massacre on 9 October; not yet a month since the Berlin Wall had been opened.

Since then, every day, more of the Wall and the rest of the border between the two Germanies had been dismantled. Press and television censorship had been stopped. Token ministers from other political parties had been introduced into Modrow's Cabinet. There had been more Politburo resignations and, in their wake, revelations of corruption among the leadership, which had fuelled the resentment of an angry population thirsting for revenge.

The people had achieved the apparently impossible so quickly, that they believed all the other changes and reforms to which they aspired could take place with equal speed and ease. They were like children, to whom, after years of saying, 'I want', had suddenly been given, and now they wanted more. Seeing no further than their immediate horizon, they were heedless of the consequences upon their own long-term future or the reactions of the wider world beyond.

Sommer's glance travelled over the square, taking in the messages on the placards. 'Travel freedom isn't everything!' 'Ecology not economy!' 'Freedom - equality – honesty!' 'Modrow and Kohl make Germany whole!'

Kohl's words had struck a disturbingly responsive chord in some minds. Although Sommer knew most people did not want reunification, he could hear a group chanting the first line of the West German national anthem, 'Unity and law and freedom' and see other slogans reading, 'If the DM comes, we'll stay – if it doesn't come, we'll go to it!' and 'For hard work – hard currency!'

677

The lure of the Deutschmark . . . Even before the opening of the Wall, everyone had known its buying power. Now many had seen with their own eyes the affluence of the West. They had witnessed the West German Treasury handing out millions as 'greetings money', while the GDR allowed its people to exchange just fifteen East Marks a year for Deutschmarks. Sommer was convinced that the banners reading 'We are one people!' were less a demand for reunification than for financial parity.

'We are the people!' was still the all-important message. That and 'Free elections for new directions!' Krenz and Modrow had agreed to round-table talks with other political parties to discuss changes to the Constitution, electoral law and preparations for free elections. As an interim measure, the SED Party conference, due to take place from 15 to 17 December, was being upgraded to a Party Congress, at which a new leadership was to be elected.

New Forum, Democratic Breakthrough and other embryo parties, including revitalized Social Democratic and Christian Democratic parties funded by their counterparts in West Germany, were planning their own launch for the same date. Schwidinski looked set to be chosen as the New Forum Member for Liebenroda.

Sommer found himself remembering his interview with Schwidinski at the beginning of October, when he had asked how new parties would cope with organizing elections and vetting potential candidates. The question had been hypothetical then. Now, it had very real implications.

In that crowd of forty, fifty thousand, how many were without political and moral blemish? Ten thousand at least were Party members, even if some had recently handed in their Party cards. Some five thousand were paid police informers. Nearly all had, at some time or other, spied on their families, neighbours and friends, and passed that information, directly or indirectly, to the *Stasi*.

The evidence was contained in the files, secured in the vaults of the *Stasi* building, which documented the lives of every single inhabitant, from the Liebenroda Party Head to the humblest of workers – files which now, probably more than at any other time, could make or break a person's life.

678

And the only person with control over all those vital files was himself.

No longer could Sommer avert his eyes from the warning being sent to him by the demonstrators. 'De-Stalinization – De-Stasinization!' 'Legalize New Forum – Criminalize the *Stasi*!' 'To gaol with the *Stasi*!' '*Stasi* out! – People in!' 'Sommer and *Stasi – raus! raus!*'

He turned away from the window and began to pace up and down the office, his hands clasped behind his back, his head sunk deep between his shoulders, dark shadows under his eyes and the stale aftertaste of nicotine in his mouth. Outside, in the Marx-Engels-Platz, the demonstrators chanted rhythmically: '*Stasi raus!*' '*Stasi raus!*' '*Stasi raus!*'

The following Saturday, it was reported on the news that legal proceedings might be taken against Honecker. In the same bulletin, it was announced that former Politburo Member, Basilius Meyer, who had been in hospital, apparently being treated for stomach cancer, had been taken by ambulance to Schoenefeld airport, where, with his wife and doctor, he had boarded a plane for Santiago.

The public reaction was fury. Honecker was so ill, he was unlikely to live long enough to stand trial. In the mean time, one of the perpetrators of the terror under which they had lived for so long had already skipped the country. The television that evening showed Egon Krenz being booed off stage by an angry and impatient audience. Next day, hundreds of thousands of people formed a human chain across the entire country.

Recognizing that they had lost all last remaining shreds of public credibility, the Politburo and SED Central Committee resigned, including Krenz. A caretaker committee was appointed to run the country in tandem with Modrow's *Volkskammer* until the Party Congress in twelve days' time.

Captain Eppel brought Sommer the decoded telex from Berlin first thing Monday morning. Short and to the point, it ordered him to 'destroy all records which could be mistakenly construed as evidence of corruption and malpractice'.

'The engineer is stoking the boilers,' Captain Eppel said. The *Stasi* might possess sophisticated surveillance equipment but it had no such thing as a shredder. The only way to destroy papers

679

was to burn them in the brown coal furnaces which fuelled the building's antiquated central heating system.

Sommer lit his tenth cigarette that morning. Everything in him rebelled against the order, although it did not surprise him. Those files had been meticulously built up and maintained over the years. To burn them would be to burn his life's work. Then there was the sheer physical impossibility of doing what Berlin wanted. To sift through 60,000 files, many extremely bulky, and remove offending documents, would take months, if not years. But what dismayed him most was the implication of the order. Destroy all evidence of corruption – that was, in itself, the final admission of corruption and the ultimate act of corruption.

He found himself thinking back over the long years of his career to those days of his youth, when he and Basilius had believed that out of the ruins of the Third Reich they could help create the consummate socialist state. Yet their dreams had been doomed from the outset: whether under Ulbricht or Honecker, German socialism had always been Stalinist totalitarianism. The GDR had always been fettered by the yoke of Russian domination. Or was that merely an excuse? As a result of their service to the State, he and Basilius had both risen to positions of high power. It had not been in their own interests to oppose the regime . . .

Captain Eppel shifted from one foot to another and Sommer started. He had forgotten his aide's presence. 'The files, Comrade Sommer?' Eppel's voice betrayed his nervousness.

Of course, Eppel's file was in the vaults, as were those of every other *Stasi* employee. Not that he had ever been allowed access to it, any more than Sommer had ever had sight of his own dossier, kept at the Ministry building in Berlin. But Eppel was aware that it must contain details which he would prefer not to become common knowledge, like the fact that he had informed on his own brother when he had been planning to escape through Czechoslovakia that summer.

Yes, Eppel would like his file to be destroyed. So, undoubtedly, would Koenig, whose file showed that he had sent his grandparents to their death in 1958. So, too, would all the others . . .

Sommer took the telex between finger and thumb and read its

message again. Not only was it proof in itself of the Party's guilt, but the order it contained condemned to perdition everything that might follow in the future – for any new regime would be founded on a deception.

Destroy all evidence . . .

He held his lighter to the telex. Flames crept up it and he dropped it into his ashtray. The colour drained from Eppel's face. Sommer told him, 'You may go.'

By burning that telex, he knew he was sealing his own fate.

Like every other town in the GDR where Klaus Feldmann had been since the Wall had opened, Liebenroda was a dump. Apart from the sports stadium and a couple of bars, which served beer that tasted like piss and didn't even have fruit machines, there was nowhere to go and nothing to do. No wonder people couldn't wait to get away from the place.

But Klaus wasn't going to be in Liebenroda long enough for the lack of social amenities to bother him: after two or three days he'd be on his way to another town. He was now an important member of a new political party, the German League, his job to recruit new members, as Siegfried had once recruited himself and Kiddy in the Red Bear in Kreuzberg.

He and his team's expenses were paid for out of party funds and he was paid commission for every new member. It was easy money. All they had to do was find out where the kids gathered, buy them a beer, rant on against the Communists, and then put the fear of God into them about their country being taken over by Turks and refugees from neighbouring Eastern bloc countries.

The kids were already so full of hatred against the Communists that they needed little encouragement to throw a few bricks at the *Stasi* headquarters.

Wolfram sensed the change in the mood of the crowd the moment he entered the Marx-Engels-Platz that Monday evening. Until then, the demonstrators had been resolute but largely good-humoured. Tonight, there was an undercurrent of scarcely subdued fury. Word had got round that the *Stasi* were intending to burn all incriminating files.

People power had removed Honecker, knocked down the

681

Wall, overthrown the Politburo and the SED Central Committee, and brought the promise of free elections. Now the people were determined to prevent the evidence being destroyed which would prove the guilt of the SED and the *Stasi*.

Few now came to church before the demonstration. There was no more need for subterfuge. The Church had outworn its usefulness. The pacifying words of Pastor Margraf had little effect upon them. Neither did they pay much heed to Wolfram, speaking from a makeshift platform, begging them to remember that far more serious issues were at stake than the desire for revenge and retribution and urging them not to ruin all they had achieved by violence.

Wolfram was still talking when the first cobblestones were hurled against the *Stasi* building and a group of demonstrators charged the steel gates. It was then he realized that there were a number of people in the crowd whom he could not recall seeing before, particularly some gangs of skinheads and punks, dressed in Western denims and combat jackets. With a sinking heart, he knew what they were. Already pamphlets published by the West German Republicans and the new German League were circulating in Liebenroda. Now, the influx of so-called neo-Nazi rabble-raisers had also begun.

Five evenings running, protesters charged the gates of the *Stasi* building, hurled missiles at the sentries and attempted to climb over the railings, but the guards, and particularly their dogs, deterred them from trying too hard.

Inside the building, tension mounted. Sommer had issued instructions that on no account were shots to be fired or the dogs unleashed. It would not be long before the crowd realized that the defence of *Stasi* headquarters was no more than a false front.

Mutiny was threatening. Eppel had spread the word that Sommer was ignoring the order from Berlin to destroy the files. Other incidences of erratic, reactionary and possibly treasonable behaviour on Sommer's part were remembered from the past. Heinrich Koenig, in particular, recalled disturbing events, like the time Sommer had criticized Gorbachev shortly after he had come to power, a number of occasions when he had shown undue

682

leniency towards Schwidinski and Margraf, and his persistent reluctance to use force against the demonstrators.

The obvious conclusion was that Sommer had secretly been conspiring with the protest leaders. 'Next thing is, he'll give the order to open the gates and let that mob in,' Heinrich prophesied. In some other towns, demonstrators were actually succeeding in entering and occupying *Stasi* buildings.

Under normal circumstances, they could have sought help from the Ministry for State Security in Berlin, but the Ministry had apparently suddenly become an Office for National Security: there was no Minister any more and the staff were reluctant to make decisions of any kind.

Second in seniority to Sommer, Heinrich was chosen to lead a deputation to the Police Chief's office on the Saturday morning to tell him that either the files must be destroyed or he must resign.

Sommer listened expressionlessly as Koenig, flanked by half a dozen previously loyal officers, levelled their accusations against him and presented their ultimatum. He was saddened but not surprised at the confrontation. 'And if I refuse to do either?' he asked.

'I shall have no alternative but to place you under arrest.'

'I see.' Sommer nodded. 'Then I should like to be alone for a while to consider my decision.' But he already knew what that would be. There was only one honourable course.

They left the room, but from the mumbled words in the corridor, he knew they had placed a guard outside his door.

He had just one cigarette left. He lit it and went across to the window, where he stared down through the security bars on to the Marx-Engels-Platz. Demonstrators were already gathering in small groups, carrying their placards and banners, mostly students and young couples with children, for it was too early in the day for skinheads and punks. The chant had already begun: '*Stasi raus!*' '*Sommer and Stasi – raus! raus!*'

If he were able to go out there among them, they would lynch him. None of them, not even Schwidinski or Margraf, would believe that he had tried to help them, and, if they did, they would not understand why. There was no future for him within the *Stasi* and no future for him without it. Perhaps he should

683

have seized the opportunity, like Basilius had, of escaping. But the idea of living in exile held no appeal. Like Schwidinski, he loved his own country. At the final count, he was a staunchly patriotic German ...

His cigarette had burned down to the butt. With one last look at the square outside, he returned to his desk and stubbed it out. Then he reached into his desk drawer and pulled out his revolver.

When they heard the gun shot, the guards burst open the office door. But Sommer's hand had been firm and his aim sure. One bullet had been sufficient to end his life.

Chapter 28

Sommer's suicide proved a hollow victory for Heinrich Koenig. The arguments with his colleagues began when they started on the files Sommer had refused to allow them to destroy. Each out to protect themselves, they could not agree on what evidence to keep and what to burn. And when they did find themselves in agreement, it was to discover that the boilers simply could not cope with huge amounts of paper. By the time the Party Congress took place ten days later, pitifully small inroads had been made into the vast archives.

After that, events moved at a terrifying speed. The date of 18 March 1990 was set for a general election – an election in the Western style, with different political parties freely competing for seats. In the interim, the SED was to run the country in conjunction with a round table of opposition groups; the same system applying to local government.

Far, far worse, however, was the announcement that the *Stasi* was to be disbanded. On 15 December, a directive came from Berlin ordering Heinrich to hand over control of the Security Police headquarters and prison to delegates of the Liebenroda Round Table, including his arch-enemies Wolfram Schwidinski and Pastor Margraf.

So large and rancorous was the crowd waiting on the Marx-Engels-Platz, that an armed unit of *Vopos* was detailed to protect him as he left the *Stasi* building and escort him home. Furthermore, a police guard was left outside his house, where Schwidinski told him that he was to remain a prisoner until his eventual fate was decided. Heinrich found it almost impossible to take in that his colleagues in the People's Police should thus turn against him.

But the ultimate humiliation was inflicted by Eva, who informed him coolly that she was leaving him and going to

685

live with her sister in Dresden. Once she was settled she would be commencing divorce proceedings.

Within two weeks of Police Chief Sommer's death, Heinrich's known world had entirely disintegrated.

As he did just before Christmas every year, Stefan went to Hamburg to attend the *Aktuell* Christmas lunch. He caught the early morning flight from Berlin, where he was met at the airport by the deputy editor. Before lunch, the quarterly editorial policy review meeting was held in Christian Horst's office.

The first item on the agenda concerned the magazine's environment campaign. 'As you know, Bonn has announced a billion-Deutschmark package to help the GDR fight water and air pollution,' Stefan told his colleagues. 'Dieter Duschek is going to the GDR in early January as part of a fact-finding mission, but he is already confident – as I am – that the Bonn subsidy will prove a mere drop in the ocean. While he's there, Dieter is going to Liebenroda to meet Schwidinski, Pastor Margraf and various factory managers. Auto-Roda is a typical example of the problems we have to contend with . . .'

'A quick question regarding Dieter Duschek and the Helena Kraus affair,' the deputy editor interrupted. 'Paula Bauer's little girl was apparently looked after by Kraus in Leipzig. She says Kraus helped save the kid's life. And Paula's mother was working with Kraus at the hospital. She feels so strongly that Kraus has turned over a new leaf that she has sent quite a glowing character testimonial to Paula, which she has asked her to pass on to Duschek. What line do you think *Aktuell* should take?'

Christian shrugged. 'Kraus served five years of her sentence here. She's been in the GDR for twelve years, which must have been tantamount to prison.'

'I'd like to meet Paula Bauer before making any decision,' Stefan stated.

'That's easily rectified. She'll be at the lunch later on . . . And while we're talking about Krauses, when I was in Frankfurt earlier in the week, I picked up a fascinating little rumour. The Kraus Group is apparently putting in claims to the GDR government for the assets it confiscated after the war. My source reckoned these were then valued at about a quarter of a billion,

686

but could now be worth some six billion Deutschmarks. If they can't get the properties back, Kraus are going to claim compensation.'

Stefan narrowed his eyes. 'If they do, I hope Israel puts in a corresponding claim for compensation and reparations against Kraus! That's certainly a story we must keep very close tabs on.'

The meeting continued for another hour, then Christian's secretary rang through to say that, with the exception of a telephonist, the other employees had set off for the Jochum, where the Christmas lunch was taking place, and the car was waiting outside to take them to the hotel.

Aktuell's full-time staff still only numbered ten, but with printers, distributors and freelance contributors, there were some sixty people in the festively decorated, private reception room at the Jochum when Stefan and his colleagues entered it.

A waiter handed them glasses of champagne and Christian clinked his glass against Stefan's. 'Who would have dreamed this time last year that we'd now be celebrating the end of the GDR?'

Stefan sighed. 'I'm delighted, of course. But I can't help thinking some of the celebrations are premature. Once the initial euphoria dies down, people are going to realize the sheer immensity of the problems needing to be tackled – and the cost. The GDR is going to have to introduce modern manufacturing methods and a lot of factories will have to close down completely, which will lead to unemployment. It's going to cost hundreds, if not thousands, of billions to bring the GDR up to our . . .' He broke off abruptly. 'Christian, who's that?'

The young woman was deep in conversation with another journalist. She was in her mid-twenties, tallish, slim, with blonde hair and clear blue eyes.

The editor followed Stefan's gaze. 'Ah, that's Paula Bauer. Come, I'll introduce you.'

But Stefan stood rooted to the spot, transported back in his mind to a day nearly forty years ago in East Berlin, when Paul Drescher had said, 'This is my daughter, Erika.' He saw a photograph and heard a voice saying, 'Your friend married her next-door neighbour two years ago. He was a

687

widower. That is his son. The baby girl is four months old . . .'

At that moment, Paula Bauer glanced across the room. Her eyes met Stefan's and, in her look of instant, if slightly apprehensive, recognition, Stefan knew he was right. Seized by a wild, uncontrollable feeling of joy, he strode past Christian and seized Paula's hands in his. 'You are, aren't you?' he asked. 'You are Erika's daughter?'

On 22 December 1989, the Wall was opened by the Brandenburg Gate. The hotel chauffeur drove Viktoria and Gisela as near to the Gate as the crowds would allow, then they wandered past the massive Christmas tree which had been erected nearby, through the Gate, across the Pariser Platz and on to Unter den Linden.

Gisela shivered in the icy wind gusting down the wide avenue with its central tree-lined promenade, but Viktoria, normally susceptible to the weather, was so lost in her memories that she was scarcely aware of the cold. Pointing with her cane at one of the forbidding-looking East German Ministry buildings, she said, 'That's where the Hotel Quadriga used to be.'

Gisela took her arm to steady her. 'We may be able to build another Quadriga now, Oma, perhaps even here on Unter den Linden.'

Viktoria's eyes glazed over. 'I doubt that I shall be around to see it.'

'I'm not so sure!' Gisela laughed. 'I bet you live to be a hundred at least. That's still five years away. The new Quadriga could open on your hundredth birthday. Karli could run it . . .'

'Another Quadriga a century after the first one, run by another Karl,' Viktoria breathed. 'What a lovely idea . . .'

Christmas was, as always, a quiet occasion. Karli was still in Stuttgart. He had completed his military service, but the hotel was too busy for him to get away. So there were just Viktoria herself, Senta, Eduard, Gisela and Stefan present. Not that Stefan contributed much to the proceedings. Viktoria had never known him to be so abstracted, although when she asked him if he was worried about something, he vigorously denied that anything was the matter.

688

New Year's Eve, however, was very different from Christmas. From having been an isolated, rather tawdry backwater, Berlin had suddenly become the most popular and fashionable city in the world. Every room in the Hotel Jochum was booked for the New Year celebrations.

Eduard, Senta and Gisela were up at the crack of dawn, organizing the staff, checking through guest lists, making sure rooms were ready, supervising preparations for the New Year's Eve dinner and ball.

Viktoria spent the morning in bed, so that she should not be too tired to see the new year in. She visualized the familiar frenzied activity taking place elsewhere in the hotel: the hum of vacuum cleaners, the whirring of washing machines, the steaming of cauldrons and roasting dishes in the kitchens; bottles of wine and champagne being brought up from the cellars; garlands and balloons being hung in the ballroom; limousines and taxis constantly drawing up at the doors; the reception clerks handing over keys to new arrivals; page boys carrying luggage up to rooms and suites; everywhere a fever of cheerful excitement.

In the mean time, there was the surprise to look forward to which they had planned for Monika and Hans. What a wonderful idea that had been of Gisela's not to tell them that Gert and Jana would be here today. She could scarcely wait to see their reaction . . .

At noon, the nurse helped her bathe and dress and settled her comfortably in her chair by the window. Then Hans and Monika arrived, and scarcely had the waiter poured them sherries, than Gert and Jana turned up. It was every bit as emotional a meeting as Viktoria had hoped for and Monika, the doting grandmother, could not hear enough about Gert's sporting successes and aspirations, while Hans was clearly deeply moved by the reunion.

Furthermore, over lunch, Gert and Jana took advantage of the occasion to announce their engagement, which was a cause for renewed celebration. Eduard, Senta and Gisela were duly summoned from their duties to drink the young couple's health.

In the afternoon, they were joined by other members of the

689

family. First came Norbert and Ursula, Norbert still with that old roguish twinkle in his eye, and Ursula, cool and sophisticated – just the right wife for Norbert, as Viktoria had always known. Shortly after them Bruno and Lili arrived, Bruno, very frail, but wonderfully elegant and gallant, leaning over Viktoria's hand to kiss it, while Lili, slender and beautiful as ever, held his arm. Finally, Kleo, Dieter, Axel and young Oskar turned up, with Kris – on crutches, of course! Apparently he had broken a leg water-skiing in the Caribbean. Norbert teased him mercilessly, while Gert gazed at him in awe-struck admiration.

Everyone talked nineteen to the dozen, so that Viktoria could hardly keep up with the conversation. But it didn't matter. For once, she felt right in the centre of things. It was one of her good days. Her memory was pin sharp. She was not having any difficulty in remembering who anybody was.

When Axel told her that Matthias Scheer had gone with the Red Cross to Romania, she knew exactly who he was talking about; and when Norbert and Bruno discussed Margarete and Brigitta, she knew they were Werner's twins, and was not at all surprised to learn that their husbands were involved in some typically dubious Kraus business in the GDR.

Time passed so quickly that it hardly seemed possible that it was already five o'clock when Senta appeared again, announcing that it was time for her to rest. Maids cleared the room, her guests obediently departed and Senta helped her over to the sofa, took off her shoes and covered her with a blanket.

'Senta, where is Stefan? I haven't seen him all day.'

'I expect he's been busy, dearest.'

'Everyone else was here, but not Stefan . . .'

'I'm sure he'll arrive soon. Now, try and sleep a little,' Senta said, turning off the main light, so that the room was illuminated only by a standard lamp.

Viktoria closed her eyes and, rather than worry about Stefan, allowed her mind to travel back to another New Year's Eve, exactly ninety years ago. She saw her beloved Papa, tall and broad, his fair hair combed across his forehead, his moustache impeccably curled and waxed, and her Mama, auburn curls piled into an elegant chignon, wearing an emerald green gown,

690

welcoming guests to the Quadriga at the gala ball to usher in a new century.

She herself had been just five: it had been the first time she had been allowed to stay up and see in a new year. She had met Benno for the first time and they had danced together. How sweet they must have looked, two children imitating the adults, trying to waltz ... How innocent they had been, how blissfully ignorant of the horrors which lay ahead, the wars and carnage which would scar the twentieth century ...

She shook her head to clear away the shadows of the past. This New Year's Eve was different. This was truly a new beginning.

No, never had there been a New Year's Eve to compare with this one. It made everything which had happened since the war finally worthwhile – all those years of hardship and uncertainty – the cellar café, the black market, the Blockade, the Cold War, the partition of Berlin, the division of Germany, Stefan's doomed love affair and his kidnap, Hasso's death, the Wall ...

Do the dead know what happens after they have departed, she wondered. Is Papa aware that we are thinking of building another Quadriga? Does Hasso know that Stefan was released? Does Mortimer realize the Wall has come down? Is there rejoicing in heaven tonight? Were all her relations and friends up there sitting round a vast celestial table, raising glasses of nectar, celebrating a new era of freedom and hope?

She smiled at the whimsical image and at that instant there was a gentle knock on the door. The maid, she assumed, come to help her change for dinner.

Footsteps padded across the carpet. Someone leaned over her. Lips brushed her cheek. 'Mama, are you awake?'

Stefan ... At last ...

She opened her eyes, but already he was walking back towards the doorway, in which another person was silhouetted. He reached out his hand and the shadowy figure moved hesitantly forward into the pool of light shed by the standard lamp.

Viktoria's first, fleeting, impression was of a rather elderly, pleasant-featured woman, dressed in a neat, if somewhat old-fashioned style. But her attention was held by the woman's eyes – eyes that were of a startling, forget-me-not blue and

691

were shining with the same radiance as she saw reflected in Stefan's own expression.

'You remember Erika, don't you?' Stefan asked.

THE END

Little, Brown now offers an exciting range of quality titles by both established and new authors. All of the books in this series are available by faxing, or posting your order to:

Little, Brown and Company (UK) Limited,
Mail order,
P.O. Box 11,
Falmouth,
Cornwall,
TR1O 9EN
Fax: 0326-376423

Payments can be made as follows: Cheque, postal order (payable to Little, Brown Cash Sales) or by credit cards, Visa/Access/Mastercard. Do not send cash or currency. U.K. customers and B.F.P.O.; Allow £1.00 for postage and packing for the first book, plus 50p for the second book, plus 30p for each additional book up to a maximum charge of £3.00 (7 books plus). U.K. orders over £75 free postage and packing.

Overseas customers including Ireland, please allow £2.00 for postage and packing for the first book, plus £1.00 for the second book, plus 50p for each additional book.

NAME (Block Letters) ....

ADDRESS ....

....

....

☐ I enclose my remittance for ....

☐ I wish to pay by Visa/Access/Mastercard

Number ☐☐☐☐☐☐☐☐☐☐☐☐☐☐☐☐

Card Expiry Date ☐☐☐☐